CONTEMPORARY CHINESE SHORT-SHORT STORIES

当代中文小小说

CONTEMPORARY CHINESE SHORT-SHORT STORIES

A PARALLEL TEXT

当代中文小小说汉英对照读本

AILI MU

WITH MIKE SMITH

COLUMBIA UNIVERSITY PRESS

NEW YORK

Columbia University Press gratefully acknowledges the generous support
for this book provided by a Publisher's Circle member.

Columbia University Press wishes to express
its appreciation for assistance given by the Pushkin Fund
in the publication of this book.

Columbia University Press
Publishers Since 1893
New York Chichester, West Sussex
cup.columbia.edu
Copyright © 2017 Columbia University Press
All rights reserved

Library of Congress Cataloging-in-Publication Data
Names: Mu, Aili, editor, translator. | Smith, Mike, 1973- editor.
Title: Contemporary Chinese short-short stories : a parallel text /
Aili Mu with Mike Smith.
Description: New York : Columbia University Press, 2017. |
Includes bibliographical references and index.
Identifiers: LCCN 2016050352 (print) | LCCN 2017010214 (ebook) |
ISBN 9780231181525 (cloth : acid-free paper) | ISBN 9780231181532 (pbk.) |
ISBN 9780231543637 (electronic)
Subjects: LCSH: Short stories, Chinese.
Classification: LCC PL2653 .C85 2017 (print) | LCC PL2653 (ebook) |
DDC 895.13/5208—dc23
LC record available at https://lccn.loc.gov/2016050352

Columbia University Press books are printed on permanent
and durable acid-free paper.

Printed in the United States of America

Cover design: Lisa Hamm
Cover image: plainpicture/Hexx

目录
CONTENTS

自序 Preface ix
绪论 Introduction xiii

1. 礼和仁 LI AND REN 1

1. 剃脑袋／赵新 Skull Shave / Zhao Xin 5
2. "明星"外祖母／刘震云 "Star" Grandma / Liu Zhengyun 15
3. 洗礼／聂鑫森 Catharsis / Nie Xinsen 23

2. 孝 XIAO 35

1. 灯祭／迟子建 Father Makes the Lantern / Chi Zijian 41
2. 秀鸭婆／韩少功 Little She / Han Shaogong 53
3. 寄钱／白旭初 Money Order / Bai Xuchu 69
4. 过完夏天再去天堂／墨中白 Heaven-Bound, but After Summer / Mo Zhongbai 77

3. 阴阳 YIN-YANG 89

1. 心事／王琼华 Two Minds / Wang Qionghua 93
2. 翠兰的爱情／李伶伶 Cuilan's Love / Li Lingling 105
3. 糟糠／伍中正 Forever by Your Side / Wu Zhongzheng 115

4. (统)治 GOVERNANCE 123

1. 铺石板／周波 The Stone-Paving Project / Zhou Bo 129

2. 清潭／蔡楠 The Clear Pond / *Cai Nan* 141
3. 大红苕／曾平 Big Sweet Potatoes / *Zeng Ping* 157

5. 自我（特征、身份、认同）IDENTITY 165

1. 舅母／俞胜利 Auntie / *Yu Shengli* 171
2. 兄弟们长大／周涛 Brothers / *Zhou Tao* 191
3. 恋人／史铁生 The Love of Her Life / *Shi Tiesheng* 203
4. 并不自知水多少／高怀昌 Water in the Well / *Gao Huaichang* 213

6. 脸面 FACE 223

1. 重逢／吴念真 A Golden Rain / *Wu Nianzhen* 229
2. 脸面／魏永贵 Face / *Wei Yonggui* 239
3. 茶楼／陈勇 At the Teahouse / *Chen Yong* 251
4. 鸡怕鸽破脸／刘心武 Chickens Hate Pecked Faces / *Liu Xinwu* 259

7. 情爱 (ROMANTIC) LOVE 271

1. 小忧伤／赵瑜 Little Heartaches / *Zhao Yu* 275
2. 伪造的情书／邹静之 Fake Love Letter / *Zou Jingzhi* 283
3. 古典爱情／王奎山 A Gentleman's Love / *Wang Kuishan* 293
4. 如果你爱他，就让他心静／安石榴 Give Him Peace / *An Shiliu* 303

8. 婚姻 MARRIAGE 315

1. 张玛丽／兴华 Mary Zhang / *Xing Hua* 319
2. 结婚成本／赵瑜 The Cost of Marriage / *Zhao Yu* 327
3. 怀念张美丽／叶仲健 Missing Zhang Meili / *Ye Zhongjian* 337
4. 薄荷的邀请／田双伶 The Mint's Invitation / *Tian Shuangling* 349

9. 易 CHANGES 363

1. 未来／王蒙 Future / *Wang Meng* 369
2. 不可知的偶然／格非 Unknowable Possibilities / *Ge Fei* 377

拼音索引 *Pinyin Vocabulary Index* 387

英文索引 *English Vocabulary Index* 429

原文出处 *Bibliography* 471

语言文化的互动与融通——如何使用这本汉英对照教材
How to Use This Parallel Text to Teach Chinese Language and Culture 473

自序

中文小小说是我自2002年以来学术研究的重点。2004－2005年间，在美国国家人文基金会研究奖的资助下，我与葛浩文、赵茱莉合作完成了《喧嚣的麻雀：当代中文小小说》一书。该书于2006年由哥伦比亚大学出版社出版。2007－2008年间，在富布赖特研究基金的资助下，我有机会去中国从事实地调查、资料收集和作者采访等工作，完成了这部中英对照读本大部分的准备工作。我在爱荷华州立大学的本职工作是教授高年级语言、文化和翻译等课程，同时研究当代中国日常生活的审美向度。过去的几年中，工作和研究的结合为我提供了开发整合语言文化教学结构的机会。这本书也算是这些年努力尝试和建构的起始成果吧。

本书双语平行的形式要求我的翻译必须尽可能地贴近原文，最大限度地忠于原文。这样做的结果是英译文虽然更多地捕捉到了中文的"原汁原味"，但它需要加工雕琢才能使所译故事更契合英文读者的情感和文化。2015年夏天，我参加了美国国家人文基金会在肯特大学举办的题为《翻译赐予我们什么？》的暑期班。在那里，我十分有幸地遇到了我的合作者，诗人作家迈克·史密斯。翻译的实践激发出我们乐观的精神，志同道合的我们携手踏上了征程。

我们一起花了很多时间审慎讨论、斟字酌句。希望我们的努力使本书达到了如下的设计目标：(1) 充分地利用了我们各自母语文化、语言、教育背景的长处，及时为读者提供了一本具有智能挑战，文学高度和深度，以及学术价值的双语读本；(2) 我们的翻译既能紧贴中国文化和社会，又能让英文读者从陌生中感受到亲近，产生共鸣；(3) 在试图重现原文多元意

PREFACE

Chinese short-short stories have been the focus of my research since 2002. A National Endowment for the Humanities research grant (2004–2005) led to my collaboration with Howard Goldblatt and Julie Chiu and to the publication of *Loud Sparrows: Contemporary Chinese Short-Shorts* by Columbia University Press (2006). Most of the site visits, collection of material, and author interviews for the current project were done in 2007 and 2008 with the support of a Fulbright research grant. My remit with Iowa State University, to teach and research the aesthetic in everyday China while instructing advanced Chinese and translation in the past few years, has enabled me to develop a curricular structure that integrates language and culture learning. This volume is one of the first products of this emerging structure.

The nature of the parallel format dictates that I must translate the texts more literally than literarily, staying as faithful to the original as possible. Although the translation captures the Chinese "accent," it needed help to bring these stories to closer emotional and cultural resonance with readers of English. I am most fortunate to have met my collaborator, the poet and essayist Mike Smith, at the NEH Summer Institute "What Is Gained in Translation?" at Kent State University, Ohio, in the summer of 2015. Filled with the unique optimism the act of translation engenders in its practitioners, we embarked on a journey of collaboration to address these issues.

After many hours of discussion and deliberation, we hope that we have reached our goals for this project: (1) to take advantage of our different cultural, linguistic, and educational backgrounds to produce a timely reader of academic challenge, literary sophistication, and scholarly stature; (2) to ensure that the translated texts stay in cultural and social contexts and resonate in English with both intimacy and alterity; and (3) to honor the

义的同时，我们也预见到了读者的困难，并为他们提供了必要的方便学习（自学）的工具。

书中我还选用了四位学生的优秀翻译习作。刘馥华和孟江南都是有中文母语背景的美国学生；张姝涵和陈桥则是来自中国的国际学生。我希望他们的范文能激励更多学生投入到严肃认真的翻译实践中来。这里，还要特别感谢克里斯托伯·马迪拜格，贾斯汀·王，尼克·科皮和蕾雅·约翰森，他们在本书的不同阶段给了我启示和帮助。我还要感谢甘丽阳和徐逸然两位同学为课后生词表所做的工作，以及甘丽阳为拼音和英文索引的合成所提供的技术帮助。

我很幸运在爱荷华州立大学的中文部有李同路和蔡玲两位同事。李同路的中文写作绝妙超群；蔡玲对中文的驾驭精准无误。正是因为有了他们仔细认真的校对、纠错，以及他们弥足珍贵的润色改进，我才能有信心地把本卷里的中文写作和中文翻译呈现给大家。在此谨向他们致以真诚谢意。

最后，我要向爱荷华州立大学那些热爱这些故事的学生们致以诚挚的谢意。感谢他们提出的问题和他们为理解做出的努力。他们是此书灵感的来源。

穆爱莉
爱荷华州立大学
二零一六年秋于阿姆斯

plurality of the original works while anticipating difficulties and providing necessary tools to enable and aid (self)learning.

Excellent work from four students from the past few years has also been included in this reader. Cara Liu and Meng Jiangnan are heritage learners of Chinese, while Zhang Shuhan and Chen Qiao are international students from China. I hope their exemplary work will encourage more engagement with critical translation from students. Special thanks also go to Cristóbal Matibag, Justin Wang, Nick Korpi, and Lea Johannsen, who have worked with me at the various stages of translation. I am also grateful to Liyang Gan and Yiran Xu for their help in creating the vocabulary lists and for Liyang's technical assistance in putting the Pinyin and the English appendixes together.

I am very lucky to have Tonglu Li, an excellent writer of Chinese, and Ling Cai, an expert teacher of Chinese, as my colleagues at the Chinese Studies Program at Iowa State University. My confidence in the Chinese writing I have done in this volume came about only after they carefully checked everything, correcting misuses and improving my rendition of Chinese with many helpful recommendations.

I also give my sincere thanks to all students at Iowa State University who have been fascinated by these stories, raised questions, and struggled to understand them. They are the inspiration for this book.

Aili Mu, Iowa State University
Ames, Iowa
Fall 2016

绪论

全球化进程压缩了我们籍以生存的时空，也加速了不同国家、文化与人民之间的交流。然而毋庸置疑，我们需要花费较以往更大的气力来增进相互之间的了解。随着中国在国际事务中的作用日益吃重，我们可以看到，西方学习中国语言的兴趣也大大增强，了解中国文化的热情也空前高涨。但与此同时，依然还有很多人坚持认为中文异常难学；对他们来说，中国也依旧神秘莫测。

目前，在美国校园读书的中国学生已超过304000人[1]。相比之下，美国学生中有能力运用中文在中国学习的人却寥寥无几。此种状况让我们不得不产生一种紧迫感。早在1976年，诺曼·丹尼森了就提请我们注意，在世界许多地方，"成人具有多种语言能力是普遍的现象，而非例外"。（Delabatista and Grutman 第12页）虽然大多数国家只有一种官方语言，但在这一表象下，多种语言的交叉使用在我们生活中早已是不争的事实。将语言与文化结合起来，用创新的教学方式去面对这一现实，才是对学生负责的做法。

迈克尔·克罗宁将对创新教学的思考置入了更大的背景之中。他认为，从翻译角度看，英语是一个少数人群的语言。原因在于："英语不是翻译**的**语言，而是为翻译所**用**的语言"。（Cronin 160）克罗宁的视角，无疑是在召唤一个的新模式，以便能够积极参与到"处于持续关系调整中的世界"："力量对比的不断变化"要求我们"不断校正"应对的策略。（161）本书

---

1. 请访问http://www.iie.org/Research-and-Publications/Open-Doors/Data/Fact-Sheets-by-Country/2015#.V2xQFVf93dk 查看美国国际教育协会（IIE）2015年《门户开放报告》公布的数据。

INTRODUCTION

Globalization compresses the time and space in which we live and accelerates exchanges among nations, cultures, and peoples. It goes without saying that we need even greater effort to understand one another. As China's role has grown in world affairs, we have seen a surge of interest in Chinese language in the West and an unprecedented enthusiasm to learn about Chinese culture, yet the myth of the Chinese language as exceptionally difficult to learn and of China as enigmatic remains a truism for many.

We feel a sense of urgency when more than 304,000 students from China are currently studying on U.S. campuses,[1] while few American students have the language competence to study in Chinese in China. Norman Denison had, as early as 1976, called attention to the fact that there were places in the world where "adult multilingual competence is the rule, not the exception" (Delabatista and Grutman 2005, 12). Beneath the surface of official monolingualism of most nation-states, multilingualism has become a fact of life. It is in our students' best interest to embrace this phenomenon with innovative approaches to language and culture education.

Michael Cronin contextualizes the problem thus: English is a minority language in translation terms because "it is not a language *of* translation but a language *for* translation" (1998, 160). His perspective is a call for a new model of proactive participation in "a world of continuous relational adjustments." The "constantly shifting power nexus" requires "endless calibration" of our strategy of engagements (161). This book takes a first

---

1. Please see the Institute of International Education's "Open Doors Data: Fact Sheet: China," last accessed June 23, 2016, www.iie.org/Research-and-Publications/Open-Doors/Data/Fact-Sheets-by-Country/2015#.V2xQFVf93dk.

所追求的目标，或者说是为实现鸿鹄之志而迈出的第一步，便是为培养未来的世界公民而对当下汉语语言文化教学的策略与方法进行调整。

* * *

这本汉英对照双语读本将汉语语言学习与中国文学、文化的学习融为一体；它的结构框架能够帮助学习语言的高年级学生克服学习瓶颈。在这一双语框架中，英文翻译帮助理解中文原文，而理解又有助于发展批判性思辨能力。两者都是学生与当今中国进行深入互动所必需的。

　　小小说[2]的文体特征，以及它在中国的广泛普及，使这一文体成为实现整合式语言与文化教学的关键。这一读本所选的作品，长度一般在1,500字左右，尤其适合课堂教学。中文高年级的学生亟需扩大词汇量和用法积累；双语平行的格式为他们主动参与，拓展、积累这两方面知识提供了平台。学生积极地在中英文之间做交叉参考，也能加快他们在语境中学会遣词造句的速度。书中每章的每个故事后，都附有一个综合的词汇用法表。表中所给出的定义，都是基于该特定故事的上下文情境，而非这些字词、成语、俗语或口语表达的终极解释。字、词、语、用法等的入选与它们出现的频率关系不大，表中的词语或表达往往用法特殊，发音有难度，或意思可能容易造成误解。有关如何在教学中使用本书，请参照本书卷尾的《语言文化的互动融通——如何使用这本汉英对照教材》。无论计划将此书用于普通课程、专题研讨课、或是一对一的研读课，阅读这篇文章可能都会有所裨益。

　　本书的基本理念简单明了：意欲熟练掌握语言，必须认真学习文化。书中的故事都是当代中国作者的原创作品。它们既是当今中国社会的写照，也反映了中国人民共同关心的问题。在为了解中国人日常生活带来方

---

2. 对中国小小说文体更详细的介绍，特别是它在过去30年中的发展和普及，请参考哥伦比亚大学出版社2006年出版的《喧嚣的麻雀：当代中国小小说》一书中的引言，以及穆爱莉在列克星敦出版社2012所出的《中国和新左派愿景：政治和文化的参与》一书中题为"小小说文体的崛起"一文。

step toward an ambitious goal—adjusting current Chinese language and cultural learning strategies for the education of future global citizens who will embrace this new model.

...

This parallel textbook integrates the learning of Chinese language with the learning of Chinese literature and culture for advanced students. The format helps overcome the plateau in language and culture learning by facilitating reading original Chinese texts with English translation and by developing critical skills necessary for in-depth interactions with China today.

Because of the genre's formal properties and its popularity in China, the short-short story[2] is key to achieving the goal of integrated learning. Averaging fifteen hundred characters in length, the selected stories have proven particularly effective for classroom study. The parallel format allows students to participate in the construction of a necessarily large repertoire of vocabulary and usages. The active cross-references between Chinese and English also accelerate the learning of how to use terms properly in context. A combined glossary and usage guide is also provided for each story, to define in context verbal, idiomatic, and local or colloquial expressions that resist interpretative mastery. The selection of words and expressions is based on their uniqueness of usage and pronunciation and the possibility for ambiguity rather than on the frequency of their appearance. For detailed suggestions on how to use this book for a course, seminar, or independent study, please look at the short essay "How to Use This Parallel Text to Teach Chinese Language and Culture" at the end of this volume.

This volume is based upon the conviction that the learning of culture complements mastery of language. The selected stories are all original works by contemporary Chinese writers. They offer authentic glimpses of Chinese society and address issues of common concern. However, these stories provide more than convenient access to everyday life in China.

---

2. For a detailed introduction of the genre in China, especially its development and popularity in the past thirty years, please see the introduction to *Loud Sparrows: Contemporary Chinese Short-Shorts* (New York: Columbia University Press, 2006) and Aili Mu's article "The Rise of the Short-Short Genre" in *China and New Left Visions: Political and Cultural Interventions* (Lanham, MD: Lexington, 2012).

便的同时，这些作品更为我们提供了进入传统中国的途径。因为，中国人每日每时的生活，便是中国五千年文化和传统积淀的最佳呈现。书中的三十一个故事按照不同的主题分为九章，每章的故事都围绕着一个传统观念。这些至今仍然渗透在中国人生活的方方面面的观念是：礼和仁、孝、阴阳、（统）治、自我（特性、身份和认同）、脸面、（浪漫）情爱、婚姻以及易。

书中每章都以一篇短文开篇。虽然并非试图为读者的阅读体验划定藩篱，但它的确具有引导读者理解文化传统观念意涵的功能。短文所起的作用，是扩大而非限制读者对每一章主题观念的理解；它能够帮助读者拓宽解读故事的视野。这些短文往往会谈及中国历史、文化中特有的习俗或经验。其目的，是使读者对于故事的理解根植于其特定的文化语境之中。每个故事之后都附有一系列开放式讨论话题，以便启发进一步的阅读思考。话题源自穆爱莉在美国教授这些故事时的经验，其设计对学生可能会遇到的困难都有所针对。

本书所选的三十位作家，属于三个不同群体。其中三分之一是知名作家，如韩少功、王蒙、格非、迟子建、刘心武、史铁生、刘震云、聂鑫森、吴念真和邹静之等。他们代表了小小说文体最文艺的一面。第二类由当代中国特有的一类文学艺术专业人员组成。他们或是在国家或集体的文学艺术机构里担任职务，或是组成这些机构的作家和编辑。最后一类，虽然在中国也都是全国知名的小小说作家，却也同时是来自各行各业的普通百姓。你会在他们当中发现村支书、政府官员、民工、退休公务员、项目经理、保安、农民、乡下残疾女青年、创业者、教师、会计等等。这些人，虽然与那些努力为自己的生活而奋斗的当代中国人没有什么不同，却代表着那些珍视写作、将文学与审美当作生存中不可或缺的组成部分的草根群体。每篇故事后都附有作者简介，向读者提供了作者现状，写作背景，以及他们在中国所受欢迎程度等信息。希望这些信息能够帮助读者积极主动进入故事当中，并从中获得对故事原产地文化新颖独特的看法。

They are also pathways to China's past and traditions, in that China's five thousand years of culture and tradition are best conveyed by the lives of its people. The thirty-one stories are grouped by theme into nine chapters, each of which centers on a traditional concept that still permeates those lives. These nine themes are: *li* (礼 ritual or propriety) and *ren* (仁 humanity or benevolence); the concept of being filial (孝 *xiao*); the working of yin-yang (阴阳); approaches to governance ([统]治); the sense of identity (自我[特性、身份、认同]); the importance of face (脸面); (romantic) love (情爱); the issue of marriage (婚姻); and the meaning of *yi* (易 change).

Each of the nine chapters is prefaced with a short essay. Though it does not mean to chart the course of the reading experience, the essay does function as a guide to the meanings of the concept in Chinese cultural tradition. The essay should open up rather than limit the reader's understanding of each chapter's theme, broadening the interpretative horizons of the stories. When a chapter preface invokes particular Chinese cultural or historical practices or experiences, it anchors particular understandings in their specific contexts. Reading and reflection are further guided by a series of open-ended discussion questions at the end of each story. Generated from Aili Mu's experience of teaching these stories in the United States, these questions anticipate and target problem areas of understanding.

The thirty authors selected belong to three different groups of writers. One third of them are celebrity writers such as Han Shaogong, Wang Meng, Ge Fei, Chi Zijian, Liu Xinwu, Shi Tiesheng, Liu Zhenyun, Nie Xinsen, Wu Nianzhen, and Zou Jingzhi. They represent the genre at its most literary. The second group is composed of literary professionals unique to contemporary China. They either hold offices in state institutions for art and literature or work as writers and editors for these institutions. The last third, though nationally known as short-short writers, are ordinary people from all walks of life. Among them you will find a village leader, some government officials, a migrant worker, a retired civil servant, a project manager, a security guard, a handicapped daughter of a farmer, a business owner, a teacher, and an accountant. They, like many others trying to live a successful life in contemporary China, represent those at the grass-roots level who value writing as an essential part of life. A brief biography of the author follows each story. The additional information on authorship, background, and reception encourages readers to approach each story proactively to gain nuanced perspectives on each story's culture of origin.

促进中国语言文化学习的目的贯穿了本书的整个翻译过程。在这一过程中，我们既努力做到忠实于原文，也充分利用了我们的英语语言文学知识和对中国文化的了解，尽力设法将学生的学习收益最大化。英文的自然晓畅是我们始终如一的准则；我们对每个故事审美意味的再现一丝不苟。这样做的目的，是期望读者的理解能由表及里，达到对文本深层内涵的把握。为此，我们还尽力保持作品的"原汁原味"，尽可能多地留住作品的陌生感。这样做的目的，是希望激活读者的好奇心、审视反思的能动性、以及创新发现的动力。

此双语读本主要面向学习中国语言文化的中、高年级学生。当然，它也适用于那些对当代中国小说和文学有兴趣的一般读者。本书的设计，让它既可以用作一门课的主要精读教材，也可以用作多类课程的补充阅读文本，或用作自学读本。学习语言的高年级学生还将受益于本书所提供的丰富的辅助学习资源。这些资源有助于他们温故知新，提高汉语水平，拓展新的文化视角。当然，本书与任何其它文学翻译的主要目的并无二致，它也为读者提供学习语言文化新内容的体验。在说中文的地区，这本书或许可以帮助以中文为母语的读者学习英语。

在本书的自序中，我们已详述了来自不同语言和文化的两个学者之间的合作，也交代了本书诞生的经过。接下来，本文将重点阐述本书的独特形式所具有的优势，尤其是汉英对照的文本和翻译实践本身如何推进语言学习的自我指导、以及如何启发批判性反思和文化探索。在保持原文的复杂性和追求英文的完美性两者之间走钢丝，一直是我们编写这本书时最大的愉悦。因此，使用这本书必要且关键的一步，就是要对我们的工作做审慎的分析和推敲。希望我们的译文会让读者"有所触动并感到不安"；而那"坐不住"的感觉会激励他们对翻译作为多义阐释活动的认真思考。

The goal of facilitating Chinese language and culture learning has compelled the translation process. The texts in English attempt to remain faithful in lexical meaning to their Chinese originals but are also informed by our knowledge of both English language literature and Chinese culture to maximize learning efficiency. That the English must be natural and read well has been a driving principle. We paid close attention to the reproduction of the aesthetics of each story to make sure that connotative meaning might be grasped in addition to denotative understanding. To achieve this, we strove to preserve the "accents" of the original works and as much of their "defamiliarizing" effects as possible. The intention is to activate the readers' agency of inquiry, reflection, and discovery.

The primary audience for this text is intermediate and advanced learners of Chinese language and culture, but our translations are also aimed at the general reader interested in contemporary Chinese fiction and literary translation. The book is designed to serve as both an intensive primary text or supplemental reading text and a text for self-study. Advanced learners of Chinese will also profit from the wealth of resources included, which will aid in maintaining and improving their Chinese proficiency or help to develop new cultural perspectives. Of course, the main goal of any literary translation is to allow new readers the experience of learning new aspects of culture and language. In the Chinese-speaking parts of the world, this volume may also benefit native Chinese speakers learning English.

In the preface we have elaborated on how the collaboration between two faculty members from two different languages and cultures resulted in this volume. The following pages describe the benefits of the particular format of the book, especially how the parallel arrangement and translation practice encourage self-directed language learning, critical reflection, and cultural discovery. Walking the fine line of preserving the complexity of the original and maintaining the integrity of the English language has been a most exciting part of this project. Analytical scrutiny of what we have done is a necessary part of the critical composition of using this book. We hope that our translation "disturbs" and that the feeling of "unsettledness" motivates students to consider the interpretive act of translation.

语言文化学习的整合

目前有一个现象，就是学中文的学生很多，而能学到具有专业水平的却很少。如何将一个在飞机场能用简单中文与中国同僚打打招呼的学生，培养成一个懂得中国文化，能与中方发展与维持协作关系的人才？这是汉语语言文化教学亟待解决的问题。

正如张霓所著《表达、描述、比较、介绍》(Cengage Heinle 2010) 一书的标题所揭示，务实的应用是目前中、高年级中文教学的策略导向，而文化教学不过是"搂草打兔子"时的捎带。《变化中的中国》(Cheng & Tsui 2009) 所侧重的是阅读方法；而《体演中文》(Cheng & Tsui 2011) 则将重点放在了演示语言的能力和技巧。五卷本的《中国文化阅读系列》(Cheng & Tsui 2007 - 2014) 虽然强调文化学习的重要性，但其目标是为AP以及标准化考试做准备。四卷本的《故事和传统：中国文化阅读系列》(Cheng & Tsui 2009 - 2010) 也存在同样的问题。这些教材，还有《超越》(哥伦比亚大学出版社 2010) 等，都为培养学生的实用中文技能做了很好的工作。比如为了帮助学生记忆，《变化中的中国》和《中国面面谈》(MyChineseClass LLC 2008) 都有意识地增加了词汇使用频率等。但从整体上看，现存教材缺乏当代文化含量，也缺少对文化行为深入系统的关注。

假设现存于爱荷华州立大学的现象具有普遍性，那么我们可以推断，目前美国大学里学习中文的学生，来自其它学科和专业的人已经大大超过文科和传统人文专业的学生。在爱荷华州立大学，《今日中国》和《中国文化传统》两门课的学生大多数来自设计学院，工程学院，农学院，商学院以及教育学院，只有少数是历史、政治、语言学以及人类学等的学生。非文科、非人文专业的学生主动来上这类课，是因为他们相信，在其未来的职业生涯中，他们与中国社会和文化的互动，至少不会少于那些想进入学术界当中国问题专家的学生。如今的汉语教学，必须考虑到这些非中文和非中国研究专业学生的一般需求。为了让他们未来更好地与中国打交道，我们必须为他们提供中国语言和文化两方面的系统知识。

INTEGRATION OF LANGUAGE AND CULTURE LEARNING

Learners of Chinese are many; graduates with professional proficiency are few. How do we train a student who can greet a Chinese associate at the airport into someone who also understands Chinese culture well enough to develop and sustain collaborative relationships? This is an urgent issue for Chinese language and culture education.

As the title of *Developing Chinese Fluency* by Phyllis Zhang (Cengage Heinle 2010) suggests, the current pedagogical strategies at the intermediate and advanced levels of Chinese instruction are pragmatically oriented and only peripherally concerned with culture. *Reading Into a New China* (Cheng & Tsui 2009) places the emphasis on reading strategies and *Chinese in Motion* (Cheng & Tsui 2011) on performance-based language competency and skills. The five-volume *Readings in Chinese Culture Series* (Cheng & Tsui 2007–2014) stresses the importance of culture learning but the goal is for Advanced Placement and standardized test preparation. The same is true of the four-volume series *Tales and Traditions* (Cheng & Tsui 2009–2010). These textbooks and *Chaoyue: Advancing in Chinese* (Columbia University Press 2010) do a fine job of building practical skills, just as *Reading Into a New China* (Cheng & Tsui 2009) and *Discussing Everything Chinese* (MyChineseClass LLC 2008) help improve retention with increased word frequency, but they generally lack contemporary cultural components and are less concerned with in-depth systematic understanding of cultural behavior.

If what happens at Iowa State University (ISU) indicates a national phenomenon, we have far more students from disciplines other than the liberal arts and traditional humanities learning Chinese. Besides a few students from history, political science, linguistics, and anthropology, students from the schools of design, engineering, agriculture, business, and education are the ones most often taking courses on China today and Chinese cultural traditions at ISU. These students are motivated to learn because they are likely to have at least as much real-life interaction with Chinese society and culture in their future professions as those who wish to become China specialists in academia. We must take these nonspecialist students' general needs into consideration and afford them systematic knowledge in both Chinese language and culture to facilitate their future engagements.

将语言和文化学习结合起来，就要使学习语言的过程同时也成为学习中国不同的价值体系、思辨方法、修辞倾向、政治制度和生活方式等的过程。2015年夏天，翻译家、理论家弗朗索瓦·玛萨迪尔·肯尼教授在美国国家人文基金会《翻译赐予我们什么？》的暑期研讨班上，开门见山地陈述了一个事实：如今大家都知道跨文化交流的重要性。她还引用了达姆罗施的话为佐证："在今天，很少有哪位世界文学的教师会希望........将学生限制在英语体系的范围内"。（Damrosch 第4页）话虽如此，现状却难改变。肯尼教授对跨文化交流也远非乐观，原因之一是："这些教师缺少适用于教授跨文化交流的教材"。

近年来，已经有几个中文小小说的英文译本面市。 哈里·J·黄的《中国小小说选集》（外文出版社2005年）全面选取了自古至今的故事；而《喧嚣的麻雀：中国当代小小说》（哥伦比亚大学出版社2006年）则更为照顾英语读者的品味和价值。此外，还有《珍珠夹克和其他故事：当代中国闪小说》（石桥出版社2008年）。《个体人物：劳马闪小说》的平装本也于2013年出版(Make-Do Publishing 2013)；它所侧重的是当代中国生活中荒诞滑稽的一面。然而，这些书都不涉及语言学习，也不以综合系统地学习文化为目的。

我们这本书，将小小说文体的优势与汉英对照的形式结合起来，为学生搭建了一座通向中国文化精髓、同时跨越中级到高级专业语言能力的桥梁。小小说所提供的是有着文化复杂性的必要内容；而中英对照的形式则是激活学生学习积极性的教学设置。

本书是第一本以课堂教学为目的的小小说汉英双语读本，它的孕育成形受到了如下汉英对照读物的启发：约翰·巴尔科姆的《中文短篇小说：新企鹅双语平行文本》（2013），《现代中国文学双语系列》（中文大学出版社2003－）和《最佳中国闪小说文选》（上海外语教育出版社2007）。这些书都为读者提供了读书认字的方便，使其在阅读中不再需要不停地去查阅字典。

Language and culture learning must be integrated in such a way that the understanding of China's diverse values, reasoning methods, rhetorical tendencies, systems of government, and ways of life occur in the process of language acquisition. In her opening remarks at the 2015 NEH Summer Institute "What Is Gained in Translation?," translator and theorist Françoise Massardier-Kenney called attention to the fact that everybody knows the importance of cross-cultural communication: "Few teachers of world literature today have any wish to . . . confine students within the imperial boundaries of English" (Damrosch 2009, 4). Yet she is far from optimistic that cross-cultural communication can be facilitated: "That being said, they lack the materials to do so."

There have been a few collections of Chinese short-shorts published in recent years. Harry J. Huang's *An Anthology of Chinese Short-Short Stories* (Foreign Language Press 2005) is a comprehensive volume with stories from ancient times to the present, while *Loud Sparrows: Contemporary Chinese Short-Shorts* (Columbia University Press 2006) pays more attention to English readers' tastes and values. There is also *The Pearl Jacket and Other Stories: Flash Fiction from Contemporary China* (Stone Bridge Press 2008). *Individuals: Flash Fiction* by Lao Ma in paperback (Make-Do Publishing 2013) focuses on the absurd and the hilarious in contemporary Chinese life. None of these are concerned with language learning or intended for comprehensive culture study.

In the combined short-short genre and the parallel text format we find a bridge for students to reach the essentials of Chinese culture while crossing over from the intermediate to the advanced/professional level of language proficiency. The former supplies the necessary content of cultural complexity and the latter the pedagogical setup to activate student agency in gaining language fluency.

This volume is the first short-short bilingual reader in English and Chinese for classroom teaching. It is inspired by such bilingual texts as John Balcom's *Short Stories in Chinese: New Penguin Parallel Text* (2013), the *Bilingual Series on Modern Chinese Literature* (Chinese University Press 2003–), and *Best Chinese Flash Fiction: An Anthology* (Shanghai Foreign Language Education Press 2007). They all provide convenient access to meanings of words and expressions without the need to constantly check a separate Chinese-English dictionary.

在这些双语读本中，新企鹅和中文大学出版的两本选用了诸如老舍，茅盾，鲁迅，萧红，沈从文，以及一些更近期的如马原、李锐等著名作家的经典作品。尽管这些作家在中国文学史上占有重要地位，但其入选的作品篇幅过长，给课堂教学带来了不便。而且全面介绍当代中国社会也不是这些读本关注的焦点。由于没有提供任何辅助教学的工具，上海出版的闪小说集也难达到整合语言和文化学习的目的。为了弥补上述读本的缺憾，这一读本精心挑选了具有广泛代表性的当代小小说精品；它将作品按照中国文化概念分组的做法，可谓独具一格。此读本还为这些作品安排了各种辅助学习工具。所选的三十一个故事都短小可控，适合传统课堂的时限；而九个章节的结构也方便一个正规学期的使用。

教学策略

语言学习

本书使用双语参照的形式改进教学，并不意味着对交际教学法或沉浸式教学法的否定。相反，它不过是对已有教学方法的一个补充，不过是用新策略应对不断变化的教学环境带来的新挑战的一个尝试。如果沟通与互动是语言和文化学习的目标，那么沉浸于两种语言文化之中，通过沟通与互动来实现这一目标，则应是最合乎逻辑的选择了。

本书采用的方法，只是"在用中学"这一理念的一个新版本。这里，两种语言和文化的交流已然嵌入并行对照的文本形式当中，由此达到学用合一。虽然学生可以去中国或中国朋友处寻找口头沟通互动的机会，但这样一本书却可以让更多的人，在自己房间的静谧氛围中，感受、体味两种语言文化间深邃的思想交流。阅读本书，就如同踏上了思想的交流发现之旅。

The first two of these bilingual readers select canonical works from such famous writers as Lao She, Lu Xun, and Xiao Hong, or more contemporary ones like Ma Yuan and Liu Rui. As important as these authors are, the length of selected works presents pedagogical challenges for today's classroom. An eclectic coverage of contemporary Chinese society does not seem to be a focus of these bilingual readers. The flash fiction collection from Shanghai, with no instructional tools to facilitate learning, falls short of the goal of integrated language and culture learning. Making up for what these texts do not have, this parallel reader carefully selects contemporary short-short works of broad representation and uniquely groups them with key cultural concepts and accompanies them with various learning tools. Divided into nine chapters for a regular semester course, all thirty-one stories are in manageable sizes for traditional class meetings.

PEDAGOGICAL STRATEGIES

LANGUAGE LEARNING

Making adjustments to current pedagogies with parallel format does not negate the communicative approach or immersion methodology. Rather, this volume complements previous approaches with new strategies to meet the challenges of changing instructional environments. If communication and interaction are among the goals of language and culture learning, it is only logical that we also try to reach these goals by way of immersion in the communication and interaction between the two languages and cultures.

The methodology of this volume is but an additional way of learning through using, since communication between the two languages and cultures are embedded in the parallel format. Although some students are able to go to China or to their Chinese friends for oral communication opportunities and interactions, volumes like this one will allow many more to experience profound intellectual exchanges in the quiet of their rooms. To use this book is to begin a dialogue of discovery.

这样的交流发现，或称交流教学法，最具价值的方面就是其自我指导的能动性。自学的能动性需要在学习的过程中得到不断的肯定与鼓励；而双语平行的文本，恰巧能在汉英对照的阅读过程中将肯定与鼓励及时传递给学生。这本书的空间里，不存在令读者尴尬难堪之处，因为对与错并非评价的标准。当故事本身以及故事的翻译引起学生思考时，他们很可能会提出问题，并产生对文本／译文进行创造性改写的意愿。他们可能会追问接下来会发生什么，可能会为故事编写一个新结局，为一个单词、一组短语、一个段落、乃至全文想出新的译法；学生与文本的沟通交流，两种语言文化间的互动，便在这样自觉的自我指导中延续。

使学生沉浸于完全的中文环境是一个越来越难以实现的梦想。即便我们把学生送到中国，他们的中国室友，那些对于NBA球星和美国流行艺术了解得比美国学生还多的中国孩子，往往更有兴趣与他们的异国朋友练习英语。中国的接待机构也常常为吸引更多留学生而提供英文授课服务。要对中、高年级的学生进行更为有效的专业训练，必须在每星期三到五小时的课堂教学之外做文章。

观念／文本学习

普鲁弗雷德曾经说过，在现代世界，一个真正受过教育的人必须有过"反思式地"从一个社会迁移到另一个社会的经历。（Cook-Sather 第40页）艾莉森·库克－萨泽应和普鲁弗雷德的观点，并补充道，教育的内容应包括"对不同社会的价值体系进行比较"和"对世界的去中心化"。（第41页）她甚至认为，教育即是翻译。因为在一定意义上，教育也是从所获信息中推陈出新，同时，两者也均以带来转化为己任。所以，她认为课堂经验应是这样一个平台：学生在学习中走向自知，并在反思中使自身发生转化。（第36页）翻译即是教育这样的理念要求建构性教学，即教师为学生创造条件、提供环境，而由学生自己成就各自的学习和成长。

The most valuable aspect of this methodology of communication is its self-directedness. Self-directed learners need affirmation and encouragement. The parallel texts communicate these messages right back to them. In the space of parallel text, there is no room for embarrassment, because right or wrong are not evaluative norms. When students reflect on the stories and the translations, it is very likely that the process will provoke questions and desires for creative changes. The communication between students and the text and the interaction between the two languages and cultures thus continue as students think about what happens next or write a new ending to a story or come up with different translations for words, phrases, paragraphs, even entire texts incorporated here.

To immerse students in a Chinese environment has become a more and more difficult dream to pursue. Even when we send students to China, their Chinese roommates, better groomed with knowledge of NBA stars and American pop artists, are oftentimes more interested in practicing their English. Host institutions often offer courses in English to draw bigger enrollments. Effective training for professional proficiency at the intermediate and the advanced levels has to go beyond the three to five hours of immersion in class each week.

CONCEPTUAL/TEXTUAL LEARNING

In the modern world, Proefriedt has argued, to be truly educated a person must have undergone the experience of moving from one society to another "in the reflective fashion" (Cook-Sather 2006, 40). Alison Cook-Sather echoes Proefriedt's view and adds that education should involve "comparing values of societies" and "decentering of the world" (41). She actually defines education as translation in the sense that it is also about restructuring knowledge in light of newly acquired information. Education and translation share in the phenomenon of transformation. The classroom experience should be the platform for students to make themselves comprehensible and to allow transformation to take place through reflection (36). The concept of translation as education calls for a constructivist pedagogy wherein teachers create and present contexts for students to effect their own learning.

当今世界的现实证明全球化不会，也不可能烙平民族和文化之间的基本差异。作为语言文化教师，我们还是经常会陷入"交流不通的僵局"。博尔赫斯举过这样一个例子：同样一段话，"母语读者欣赏到的是，鲸鱼听到男人的哭声时死了；而译文读者的反映则是，竟有人相信存在这样致命的哭声"。（Borges第40页）虽然译文读者的反应无可厚非，但他们没有"反思式地"进行不同价值体系间的比较。因此，他们的阅读无助于对第一读者母语文化的理解，也难以促进第一和第二读者之间的沟通交流。

当美国学生所感兴趣的问题与母语读者所关心的问题大相径庭时，我们应该怎么办？皮埃尔·布迪厄认为，生存于"不同的[文化]生产场域"中，"外国读者一定会以不同的方式阅读文本"。他们所创造的"相似事物之间的虚假对立"或是"根本不同的事物之间的错误比附"，都不过是跨文化阅读实践中的普遍现象。（Bourdieu第225页）当阅读其它文学文化的个体无法摆脱自己特定的[文化]生产场域的限制时，作为教育工作者，反而去告诉学生，可以对一个文本随心所欲，可以将目标受众的喜好当作第一优先，可以一味地深化他们已知和乐于接受的东西，这是负责任的做法吗？在与中国打交道时，西方对持不同政见者的关注和对中国之路的质疑，并没有在中国公众当中引起多少共鸣。过去的三十多年中，西方沉迷于用自己熟悉的所谓"科学"方法和手段来解析中国的今天、预测中国的未来，但好像也一直不是特别有效。

卡罗尔·迈尔将用自己的观念／范畴去认识和鉴赏外国文化产品的做法称之为"拿差异当儿戏"。其后果，是把读者从跨文化阅读理解的责任中开脱出来。（Dingwaney and Maier 第312页）对弗朗索瓦·玛萨迪尔·肯尼和她的同事布赖恩·詹姆斯·贝尔来说，这样的开脱意味着一个性质严重的双重剥夺：学生被剥夺了设身处地"用他人的尺度审视他人言行、个性"的机会；而教师则失掉了"一个培养跨文化交流之伦理道德的关键环节"。（2015年美国国家人文基金会暑期班的报告）因此，作为教育工作者，让学生熟悉当地人民关心的问题，了解他们的思维与行为方式、价值体系和社会制度等，是我们义不容辞的责任。

The reality of the world today has shown us that globalization cannot and will not iron out the fundamental differences between peoples and cultures. As teachers of languages and culture, we often face "impasses of non-communication." Borges makes this point: "The first audience appreciated the fact that the whale died when it heard the man's cry; the second, that there had ever been men who lent credence to any fatal capacity of such a cry" (Borges 2000, 40). Valid as the second audience's response is, no comparison of values "in reflective fashion" happens, which does little to help us understand the first audience (i.e., the audience of cultural origin) or to facilitate communication between the first and the second audiences.

What do we do when issues of interest to American students are at odds with the concerns of readers of cultural origin? In Pierre Bourdieu's opinion, "foreign readers are bound to perceive the text in different ways" due to their presence in "different field(s) of production"; the creations of "fictitious oppositions between similar things" or "false parallels between things that are fundamentally different" are but a common phenomenon in reading (Bourdieu 1999, 225). If, as a human being, one cannot avoid being limited by one's particular "field of production," is it responsible to tell students to do what they want with a text, to make acceptability by the target audience the priority, and to continue internalization of the familiar? When dealing with China, the critical focus of the West on political dissent and contestation has not resonated much with the Chinese public. Familiar and "scientific" methods and applications used to analyze China's present, to predict its future, have not been particularly effective over the past thirty-some years.

Carol Maier regards the practice of applying our own categories of perception and appreciation to a foreign cultural product as "an uncritical assumption of difference" that exonerates readers from the task of ever reading cross-cultural texts (Dingwaney and Maier 1995, 312). For Françoise Massardier-Kenney and her colleague Brian James Baer, this means a double deprivation of a serious nature: students lose an opportunity to "see the behaviors and dispositions of others in their own terms," and educators miss "a crucial step in developing an ethics of cross-cultural communication" (presentation at the 2015 NEH Summer Institute). It is therefore incumbent on us to familiarize students with local concerns, practices, values, and systems.

诚然，按西方读者口味将中文作品"自然化"的做法也不无道理。但如果这样做会造成读者对于此种"自然化"的依赖，我们的策略就需要做出调整了。一部作品的母语语言文化与目的语语言文化有着何种关系，人们的看法迥异。韦努蒂的观点似乎接近偏激。他认为，保持原文的不透明度，让译文读者感受到它的阻力，也应该是翻译的一个目的。他甚至争辩说，翻译中使用"流行用法"，追求"译文语言的一惯性"和"对话般的节奏"等，虽能使阅读过程流畅，但这些做法带来的便利却会损害原文内在的"文本效应"。（May 第6页）本书的编写，将学生与语言的自发互动，以及他们在学习中对不同文化的切身感受置于中心地位。这样做既能帮助译文读者，又对韦努蒂的担心有所关照。

2015年暑期，在美国国家人文基金会于肯特大学举办的翻译研讨班上，我们学到了一个平衡协调法——让学生对陌生文本的体味，和与新奇文化的互动体验既愉悦又震撼。一个有责任感的教育工作者，应该努力去引发让学生感到不自在的思想挑战。2015年五月，托德·吉特林在《高等教育报》上发表了题为《不为受到震撼，你为何来上大学？》的文章。文中，他为阅读中产生的不自在，及这种感觉匪夷所思的伙伴——理性，进行争辩，将两者同样视为教育的动力。在本书编写的过程中，我们有意选择了突出不同历史感受和文化情怀——那些很难在西方经验中找到的感受和情怀——的故事。我们的汉英对照文本对最大限度地再现原文整体效果以及英文质量的关注，超过了对译文读者阅读舒适度的关注。我们遵循审稿人的宝贵建议，将那些在中国文化和中国人的宇宙观中并不存在、来自英文的说法从译文中删除了。我们将故事按主题分章并为每章写短文做序，目的是为了减少已知和所熟悉的东西对阅读的干扰，并削弱随心所欲选择解读和佐证自己"先见之明"的倾向。我们从理论的高度，依托对翻译的思考建构起了语言文化学习的框架，从而能够将他者性（otherness）问题置于认同与区隔，亲密与变异，共鸣与惊奇的动态关系中进行探讨。

Naturalizing Chinese works for Western audiences can be helpful, but we need to adjust our strategies of engagement if we develop a dependence on naturalization. Among views of the relationship between the target language culture and that of the source, Lawrence Venuti's seems extreme. In his opinion, keeping the opacity and the experience of resistance of the original for English readers should be a goal of translation. He goes as far as arguing that fluency in the target language, especially the convenience of "current usage," "linguistic consistency," "conversational rhythms," and so on, could be detrimental to the "textual effect" of the original (May 1994, 6). This volume takes into consideration both what helps target readers and what Venuti worries about by putting students' spontaneous interactions with the languages and their felt experiences of the culture at the center of learning.

The 2015 NEH Summer Institute at Kent University prepared us for a balanced approach—to make student interactions and experiences with unfamiliar texts and cultures pleasant and disturbing at the same time. Ethically responsible educators should work to cause intellectual discomfort. "You Are Here to Be Disturbed" is the title of Todd Gitlin's article in the *Chronicle of Higher Education* in May 2015. He argues for discomfort and its odd-duck partner, reason, and sees them as driving forces of education. So when structuring this book, we selected stories that highlight differences of historical and cultural sensibilities for which equivalents are hard to find in the West. When setting up the parallel format, we were more concerned with closer approximation of the macrostructural impact of the original and the quality of signification in English than the levels of comfort for English readers. We followed the reviewers' advice and eliminated the use of terms nonexistent in Chinese culture and cosmology. We theme-grouped the stories with a preface not to reinforce the known or the familiar, but to work against the tendency to cherry-pick elements as support for preexisting views. By theoretically framing the learning of language and culture with the problematics of translation, we anchor the issue of otherness in the dynamics of identification and difference, intimacy and alterity, and resonance and surprise.

英汉对照的形式与思辨能力

思辨

理论家皮埃尔·布迪厄认为，外国文学的引进常常是处于被支配地位的语言追求合法性的表现。(Bourdieu第222－225页) 然而，从中国引入这些小小说作品，我们关心的不是其政治功能，而是其内在的审美思辨潜能。当今的政治经济气候确实可能对中国语言文化兴趣的发展有利，但仅仅将学习和受教育当作服务于政治经济目的的权宜之计令人担忧。作为校园和学问的守门人，我们只想为学生把守住积极审视反思的机会和场地，以让其在对自身有限环境和经历"棱镜效应"的思辨过程中，完成重要的自我成长。

现在的学生懂得，不同的观点、价值观、思想和话语等都有自身的历史和文化成因，它们的形成和变化也都与意识形态密切相关。学生也明白，在与其它文化打交道时，有必要收起批评和指责的态度，悉心投入差异当中。本书意欲带他们再向前走一步——培养他们对"不同民族国家运行方式的认知"，让他们了解是什么成就了与自己生活方式不同的生活模式。(Bourdieu第226页) 这一步的必要性在于，它会激发学生对不同体系"存在缘由"的兴趣，并引起对"差异体系"的思考。(Antoine Berman第31页) 也正是这样的兴趣和思考，使得收起批评指责、认真投入差异有了成功实施的可能。正如《再探沉默的芬兰人》的两位作者所指出，偏见不是简单的"认知问题"，而是在"话语中进行的社会行为"。(Sajavaara and Lehtonen第269页) 在芬兰，与在中国一样，"积极的沉默"是一种颇为流行的行为方式。只有当学生在话语层次上对这一行为方式的德行功效有所理解，真正的基于尊重的沟通才有可能发生。

希望学生探讨不同体系并钻研其存在理由的愿望，也影响了本书作品的翻译。比如，译文没有为减少阅读难度而将学生不熟悉的表达"自然化"。这些表达包括古典、经典引文，历史典故，特殊文化现象，成语，习俗，特殊体制的构成和运作，对艺术品，故事和神话的援引等。这些陌生所在，正是学生有效学习不同价值、制度体系和思维范畴之处。因此，我们

INTRODUCTION xxxiii

THE PARALLEL FORMAT AND CRITICAL COMPETENCE

CRITICAL THINKING

According to theorist Pierre Bourdieu, literary imports are often dominated languages seeking legitimacy (1999, 222–225). We are more concerned, however, with the critical and aesthetic potential of these Chinese works than their political agency. The political and economic climate may have created the conditions for interest in Chinese language and culture to develop, but education and learning for political and economic expediency is bothersome. In our role as academic gatekeepers, we have no ulterior motive in offering students opportunities to take proactive account of the "prism effect" of limited fields of experience and to be able to think reflectively as part of critical self-development.

Students today know that views and values, ideas, and discourses are constituted historically and culturally and are shaped by ideology. They understand that it is necessary to suspend judgment and to engage differences when encountering another culture. This volume takes them further. It allows them to reach an "awareness and knowledge of the ways in which different national fields function" in sustaining different modes of life than their own (Bourdieu 1999, 226). This is necessary, because it leads to considerations of "the system of these differences" and "the reasons for this system" (Berman 2009, 31). Both considerations are crucial for successful suspension of judgment and the engagement of differences. As the authors of "The Silent Finn Revisited" have pointed out, perceptual biases are not simply "an issue of cognitions"; they are "social acts performed in discourse" (Sajavaara and Lehtonen 1997, 269). Only when students understand, at the discursive level, the virtue of "active silence" popular in China and Finland, for example, does true communication based on respect become possible.

The desire to allow students to search for systems of differences and to study reasons for different systems also influenced the translation of this volume. For example, instead of naturalizing expressions of estrangement for students, we translated them literally and footnoted them or listed them as new expressions where necessary. Such words and expressions include citations from the classics and canonical works, historical allusions, cultural specificities, idioms, local customs, institutional structures

的翻译尊重原文,也在必要时利用脚注或生词解释等工具为学生提供理解上的帮助。

然而,我们绝无意自诩权威,更不敢妄称这里的翻译恰到好处。我们的原则和实践都基于这样一个悖论:我们给出的不过是一个读者译本。我们的目的,是将学生调动起来做自己的翻译,激励他们投入到探寻文字至关重要、永无休止的变动之中,有所作为。这也是我们选择英汉对照形式的原因。我们希望双语平行状态中"悬而未决的知识"能使学生悟出些许"那知识的本真"。(Maier第163页)

汉英对照的形式

汉英平行对照的形式似乎是个冒险的选择,尤其是雅克·德里达早有著名论断在先:"翻译就是'不可能'的另一个说法"。(Derrida 第57页)然而,另一个同样著名的观点则认为,风险与机遇共存。我们不该,也不能将翻译看作是把作品从一种语言文化搬运到另一种语言文化;在微观层面对译文吹毛求疵实属下策。安托万·伯曼告诫我们远离评判,将精力集中到翻译活动本身所具有的潜力上。他借用阿布戴尔科比尔·喀梯比的一个似非而是的表达——"圣经经文般的自治"——来形容一部作品和它潜在的可能性之间的关系。(Berman 第73页)林恩·何吉年则认为,不同语言之间存在着"柔韧而不可摧毁的互惠";正是这一互惠关系使得会意成为可能。(Hejinian第297页)确如德里达的另一个著名论断所言,如果"没有什么是可译的;……那一切都是可译的"。(Derrida 第57页)翻译活动中到处都是对缜密理性挑战的空间:它既充满了意义磋商的机会和超越原文进行创意表达的可能,又是对原文和译本不可预知的多元潜能的不断呈现。

伊娃·霍夫曼在思考话语权、意识形态和翻译之间的关系时表达了这样的想法,"想要毫不失真地移植一个字,我们需要把环绕在这个字周围的整个语言都搬过来。"(Jaffe 第47页)二十年前,伊恩·梅森对这一想法有进一步的阐述:每个字、词都有多重含义,这是因为,每个字、词都可用于多种情境,同时每位读者的阅读目的也大相径庭。(Mason 第23-34页)

and practices, and references to artwork, myth, and mythologies. It is precisely at these unfamiliar places that effective learning of different values, systems, and categories happens.

Yet we do not assume a position of authority or claim absolute sufficiency of our translations. The paradox of our principle and practice—to present a reader's version in order for students to engage themselves in the act of translation—encourages students to immerse themselves in critical unsettledness and asks them to take action. The parallel format was chosen exactly for this reason. We hope the "unsettling knowledge" that the parallel texts embody enlightens students about "the nature of that knowledge itself" (Maier 2006, 163).

THE PARALLEL FORMAT

The parallel format may seem a risky choice, especially in the light of Jacques Derrida's famous statement—"translation is another name for impossible" (1998, 57). There is, however, an equally well-known view that regards risks and opportunities as two sides of the same coin. Translation should not and cannot be viewed as transference of a work from one language culture to another; to decry its defects at the micro level is not a productive endeavor. Antoine Berman advises us to move away from judgment and to focus instead on the potentialities of translation. He borrows Abdelkebir Khatibi's paradoxical term "scriptural autonomy" to describe the relationship between a text and its potential (Berman 2009, 73). Lyn Hejinian believes that there is a "resilient reciprocity" between one language and another that makes knowing possible (2000, 297). Indeed, as another famous line of Derrida's goes, when "nothing is untranslatable; . . . everything is translatable" (1998, 57). There is space in translation for rigorous intellectual challenge, full of opportunities to negotiate meaning, to create free expressions from the constraints of the original, and to render the unpredictable plurality of both the original and translated texts.

When contemplating the relationships between discourse, ideology, and translation, Eva Hoffman expressed the idea that "in order to transpose a single word without distortion, one would have to transport the entire language around it" (Jaffe 1999, 47). Two decades ago, Ian Mason further elaborated on this idea. Words are invested with multiple meanings by virtue of the various contexts in which they are used and by different readers for distinct goals (1994, 23–34). Both Hoffman and Mason make

霍夫曼和梅森所言清楚地表明，无论是在字词、句子还是全文的层次上，原文和译文都不会有意义上的完全重合。那么，这个结论对语言文化学习意味着什么呢？

也就是说，当学生意识到，这里译文的一字一句都出自见解必然有限的译者的个人喜好，会有什么结果？我们希望学生会用不同的方式来学习这些译作；其中之一是带着强烈的好奇心琢磨译者的抉择。每个认真学习中文的学生读了第一个故事后都会问，为什么用"Skull Shave"做英文标题。这种想要挑战译者的渴望，不仅会让他们自学"脑袋"一词的多重意思，还会带他们走入一个胆小的八岁孩子的心灵深处。学生们在悟出翻译中所有的选择都是可以批评的这一道理之后，他们的反应说明，从译文中学习与在翻译过程中学习非常相似。从根本上说，两者都是"一个认知过程"，都在"研究、审视认知／知识的本质，以及一切特定'认知／知识'以何种方式深植于具体情形之中"。（Hejinian 第296页）

以汉英对照文本这一形式将知识"深植"，或许最能解放思想、激发自学热情。一位学生曾经被故事《洗礼》中"慌忙"一词的第二次使用所困惑。于师傅像侍奉君王一般伺候一个被社会唾弃的人，他为什么要"慌忙"？这个问题促使这位学生对文本做了进一步发掘。她查阅了文化大革命的历史，探究了"天地君亲师"的文化传统。开始她以为，不是作者错用了"慌忙"，就是译者错译了原文；结果，对这一疑问的探索成了她解锁全篇的钥匙。在这里，汉英对照的形式既是建构两种语言能力的工具，又是促进两种文化互动的手段。为什么对在特定的文化时空中的特定人群来说，这样或那样的说法和做法就是规矩呢？学生的语言、词汇和理解能力的提高，通过对这一问题更深刻的理解得以实现。

充分发挥学生的能动性也是编写本书的指南。经过反复思考，我们最终还是将"省农展会"译成了"State Fair"。我们期待好奇的学生会因此去查看，这两个具有可比性的活动在参与者、参与兴趣、组织机构和活动目的等方面有何异同。第一个故事结尾处的设问句，"孩子怎么能不疼呢？"，我们的翻译有意识地与原文拉开了距离。这篇小说的读者常常忽略故事中二小"做戏"的成分。为了把注意力朝"做戏"上引，我们将这句话翻译成了

it clear that there can be no lexical equivalence between the source and target languages at the level of word, sentence, or entire work. What is the implication of this for language and culture learners?

And what will be the impact on students when they realize that every word we put down here results from the personal decisions of translators of necessarily limited perspectives? Among the many different ways students may reflect on the works translated here, one, we hope, will be a stronger curiosity concerning the translators' decisions. Every serious student of Chinese language who has read the first story will probably question our choice of "Skull Shave" as its title. In their desire to challenge the translators' intervention, they not only (self)learn the multiple implications of "脑袋," they may also find a way into the psyche of a scared eight-year-old child. Student reaction to the realization that all choices are open to criticism has proven to us that learning through translation is much like learning in translation; it is "fundamentally an epistemological project" that "studies—scrutinizes—the nature of knowing and the way in which any particular 'knowing' is circumstantially embedded" (Hejinian 2000, 296).

To be "circumstantially embedded" within the presence of a parallel format can be especially liberating. A student was once confused by the second use of "慌忙" in the story "Catharsis." Why should the person giving an outcast the royal treatment be "慌忙"? She further engaged the text by looking into the history of the Cultural Revolution and by delving into the cultural tradition of "天地君亲师." In the end, what she thought was a misuse or a mistranslation became key to unlocking the meaning of the entire text. In instances like this, the parallel format is at once a tool to build bilingual competence and an instrument to generate bicultural interactions. Linguistic, lexical, and semantic proficiency is achieved through a deeper understanding of why certain ways of saying and doing things are imperative for a particular people at a particular cultural moment.

This project is built with students' active agency in mind. We debated and translated "省农展会" into "state fair" because we hope curious students will look into the similarities and differences in the constituencies, interests, organizers, and agendas of two comparable events. The translation of the rhetorical question "孩子怎么能不疼呢?" at the end of the first story departs from the literal on purpose. Readers have tended to miss the "acting out" parts of the story. By rendering the sentence "We can't blame the kid for acting out" we call attention to them. But more importantly, the change of subject from "孩子" in the original to "we" in

"We can't blame the kid for acting out?". 还有更重要的一层原因是，原文的主语"孩子"在译文中变成了"we"，这样就又给学生创造了一个发掘文化习惯和语言模式差异的机会[3]。

同时，汉英对照形式的至关重要之处还在于，它使得想利用遗漏、添加、点缀等手段将自己的观点和审美趣味强加给文本的做法难上加难。但这还不是我们选择这一形式的全部理由。汉英对照的形式还将批评的注意力聚焦在翻译的主观性上。我们的英语版本与原文比肩而立，等待每位读者的审视和批评。"翻译部个作品就是将其置入过渡之中，使其处于悬而未决的状态"；（Hejinian 第297页）当理解发生分歧时，认真思考和学习的机会也就来了。（Berman 第73页） 因此，学生开始欣赏评鉴之时，也就是他们进入文字之丰富多义和文本之开放多元之时。只要他们不迷信我们或是任何其他人的翻译，而是将其当作引领自己发现新意的机会，那么诗意的创造便已开始了。

...

总之，这是一个为中文高年级学生设计、有大量辅助学习的内容、方便使用的汉英对照读本。它同时也是一个将当代中国文学某些重要声音带入英语世界的读本。这些声音，其形成受到了中国独特的审美品格影响，同时也浸润着中国独特的宏观与微观文化理念。面对书中的课文，每一个真心学习的读者，只要保持开放心态而不去纠结终极理解，他与文本的互益沟通就开始了。也许，学习语言、文学和翻译的方式与我们待人处事的方式并无不同：以尊重的态度进行必要交往时，需要敬畏他人的神秘难解。这样的敬畏，或许会成为我们共同感受与分享语言文化之美的希望，并使我们能够在感受和分享之中超越当今那些在人群地域中划界、制造各种区隔的执念。

爱荷华州立大学 穆爱莉
三角洲州立大学 迈克·史密斯

---

3. 王珩在2014年题为"中文二外语言教师跨文化能力发展的思考"一文中讨论了为什么"I like your shoes"应该译成"你的鞋子真好看"而不是"我喜欢你的鞋子"。他认为是两个文化对自我不同的看法和定位决定了这样的翻译。（130-131）

translation creates another occasion for students to dig into differences in cultural habits and speech patterns.³

The parallel format, as a critical mechanism, makes it difficult for us to impose our own perspectives or poetics through omission, addition, and embellishments. We chose it, however, for yet another important reason. The parallel format brings critical attention to the subjective nature of any translation. Our English versions are there beside the originals for every reader's critical scrutiny. "To place a work in translation is to place it in transition and to leave it there unsettled" (Hejinian 2000, 297). When differences in understanding occur, opportunities of critical contemplation and learning occur too (Berman 2009, 73). When students start to evaluate, they enter the rich polysemy and indeterminacy of words and meaning; when they do not treat our translation, or anybody's translation, as absolutely authoritative, but rather as a guide and opportunity to create their own meaning, poetry is probably in the making.

...

This volume, designed for advanced students of Chinese with sufficient paratextual elements to that end, also facilitates the bringing over into English of important voices in contemporary Chinese literature; voices shaped by particular aesthetics and informed by distinct micro as well as macro cultures. When readers come to the texts in this volume, all that is required to start a beneficial communication with them is an earnest desire to learn and a willingness to allow whatever understanding to remain, at times, elusive. Perhaps we should encounter languages, texts, and translation much the way we engage people with whom we are committed to interact with respect while allowing them to remain enigmatic. Perhaps we, in so doing, can transcend the current obsession with borders and separateness by way of the felt and shared beauty of languages and cultures.

Aili Mu, Iowa State University   Mike Smith, Delta State University

All translations are by Aili Mu unless otherwise indicated.

---

3. In his article "Reflection on the Development of Cross-Culture Competence in CSL Teacher Education" (*Chinese Language Teaching and Research* [华语文教学研究] 11, no. 1 [2014]: 127–49), Heng Wang discusses why "I like your shoes" should be translated as "你的鞋子真好看" instead of "我喜欢你的鞋子." He argues that the two cultures' different perceptions of the self dictate the translation (130–31).

REFERENCES

Berman, Antoine. 2009. *Toward a Criticism of Translation*. Translated by F. Massardier-Kenney. Kent, Ohio: Kent State University Press.

Borges, Jorge Luis. 2000. "The Translators of the Thousand and One Nights." In *The Translation Studies Reader*, edited by L. Venuti, 34–49. London: Routledge.

Bourdieu, Pierre. 1999. "The Social Conditions of the International Circulation of Ideas." In *Bourdieu, A Critical Reader*, edited by R. Shusterman, 220–28. Oxford: Blackwell.

Cook-Sather, Alison. 2006. *Education Is Translation: A Metaphor for Change in Learning and Teaching*. Philadelphia: University of Pennsylvania Press.

Cronin, Michael. 1998. "The Cracked Looking Glass of Servants: Translation and Minority Languages in a Global Age." *Translator* 4 (no. 2):145–62.

Damrosch, David. 2009. *Teaching World Literature (Options for Teaching)*. New York: Modern Language Association of America.

Delabatista, Dirk, and Ranier Grutman. 2005. "Introduction." *Linguistica Antverpiensia* 4:11–34.

Derrida, Jacques. 1998. *Monolingualism of the Other; or, The Prosthesis of Origin*. Translated by Patrick Mensah. Stanford, Calif.: Stanford University Press.

Dingwaney, Anuradha, and Carol Maier. 1995. "Translation as a Method for Cross-Cultural Teaching." In *Between Languages and Cultures: Translation and Cross-Cultural Texts*, edited by Anuradha Dingwaney and Carol Maier, 303–24. Pittsburgh: University of Pittsburgh Press.

Gitlin, Todd. "You Are Here to Be Disturbed." *Chronicle of Higher Education*. May 11, 2015. http://chronicle.com/article/A-Plague-of-Hypersensitivity/229963.

Hejinian, Lyn. 2000. "Forms in Alterity: On Translation." In *The Language of Inquiry*, 296–318. Berkeley: University of California Press.

Jaffe, Alexandra. 1999. "Locating Power: Corsican Translators and Their Critics." In *Language Ideological Debates*, edited by Jan Blommaert, 39–67. Berlin: De Gruyter Mouton.

Maier, Carol. 2006. "The Translator as Theoros: Thoughts on Cogitation, Figuration and Current Creative Writing." In *Translating Others*, edited by Theo Hermans, 1:163–80. Manchester, UK: St. Jerome.

Mason, Ian. 1994. "Discourse, Ideology and Translation." In *Language, Discourse and Translation in the West and Middle East*, edited by Robert de Beaugrande, Abdullah Shunnaq, and Mohamed Helmy Heliel, 23–34. Amsterdam: John Benjamins.

Massardier-Kenney, Françoise, and Brian Baer. 2015. Opening Day Presentation for NEH Summer Institute "What Is Gained in Translation." Kent, Ohio: Kent State University.

May, Rachel. 1994. *The Translator in the Text*. Evanston: Northwestern University Press.

Sajavaara, Kari, and Jaakko Lehtonen. 1997. "The Silent Finn Revisited." In *Silence: Interdisciplinary Perspectives*, edited by Adam Jaworski, 263–84. Berlin: De Gruyter Mouton.

CONTEMPORARY CHINESE SHORT-SHORT STORIES

当代中文小小说

第一章

礼和仁[1]

  用"礼"和"仁"开篇意在以儒家文化的传统透视当代中国。儒家伦理的中心是"礼"。在此，我们可以将"礼"理解为在日常生活中以"礼"的行为培育"仁"的品格；而"仁"即为仁人和爱心。"礼"常常被理解为"礼仪"或"规范的行为方式"，用来指在特定的情境中得体礼貌的言行。而"仁"则含义极广，它泛指儒家道德标准、原则和境界。

  《斯坦福哲学百科》中"儒学"条目中对如上所述"礼"与"仁"的关系有这样的阐释：

> 孔子教导说，利他的德行，即保持社会亲和力所必不可少的德行，只有那些已经学会了自律的人才会有。学会自我克制就意味着要学习和掌握"礼"，也就是说礼仪的形式和得体的规范。一个人通过这些礼仪和规范表达对上级／长者的尊敬，行使自己的社会职责，并在表达和行使的过程中赢得对自己的尊敬和钦佩。一个人在说每一句话、办每一件事儿时都要考虑是否妥当："非礼勿视，非礼勿听，非礼勿言，非礼勿动"。（《论语》12.1）

---

[1] 这篇短文源于多年来阅读中文版以及不同英文版本的《论语》。本文的写作尤其得益于《斯坦福哲学百科全书》。所参照网站的网址为：http://plato.stanford.edu/entries/confucius/。《斯坦福哲学百科全书》使用了对西方读者来说通俗易懂的概念和语言。书中关于孔子和儒家文化的条目既系统又简洁。

CHAPTER 1

LI AND *REN*[1]

To start the volume with *li* (礼 *lǐ*) and *ren* (仁 *rén*) is to see contemporary China through the lens of its Confucian tradition. Confucian ethics is anchored by the centrality of *li*, understood as the performance of rituals that cultivate *ren*, the ethical character of benevolence or love. Often translated as "ritual" or "right behavior," *li* denotes respectful conduct appropriate to a particular context; *ren* is understood more broadly, signifying Confucian virtues and general excellence.

The entry on Confucianism in the *Stanford Encyclopedia of Philosophy* has a paragraph on *li* and *ren* that speaks to these distinctions:

> Confucius taught that the practice of altruism he thought necessary for social cohesion could be mastered only by those who have learned self-discipline. Learning self-restraint involves studying and mastering *li*, the ritual forms and rules of propriety through which one expresses respect for superiors and enacts his role in society in such a way that he himself is worthy of respect and admiration. A concern for propriety should inform everything that one says and does: "Look at nothing in defiance of ritual, listen to nothing in defiance of ritual, speak of nothing in defiance or ritual, never stir hand or foot in defiance of ritual" (*Lunyu* 12.1).

---

1. This short essay comes from years of reading *The Analects* (论语 *Lunyu*) in Chinese and different versions of translations in English. The *Stanford Encyclopedia of Philosophy* (online at http://plato.stanford.edu/entries/confucius) especially benefited the writing of this essay. Its entry on Confucius and Confucianism, which uses concepts and language that are easy for Western audiences to understand, is among the most systematic and concise introductions to these subjects.

2　礼和仁

"礼"虽然有着构成和表达"仁"的中心地位,这个地位并不意味着要让个体／个性屈从于一成不变的行为模式;也不是说有"礼"就是达到了所谓静止、终极的道德常态。"礼"和"仁"来自于一个社会特定的习俗和实践,是灵活运用的累积,却又能超越任何特定的习俗和规范。在中国文化传统中,大家公认和遵循的伦理规范引导着品德的培养和监护;同时,这些规范也随时间的更替和社会环境的变换有所调整。这些规范运用的复杂性,相信你在阅读本章的故事时会有所体验。

在儒家伦理观中,道德和审美不可分割。与他人同心同德、和谐相处是美好的。那些想活得既有道德又有美感的人,遵循"礼"而达到"仁"是他们的必由之路。下面所选的每一个故事里,那些简单的善举和它们带来的愉悦都会加深我们对生活之美的感受。

《剃脑袋》讲的是怎样引领一个小男孩进入现存的、令他十分困惑的社会礼仪规范的故事。《"明星"外祖母》里,来自不同文化的外国人迁就一位中国老人的价值观、习惯,乃至荒诞的言行。他们以礼相待,呈现仁德。《洗礼》中那生死攸关的时刻展示了传统伦理价值如何在乱世中经受考验并得以延续。

这些故事里的人物之间没有敌对关系。即使是那些红卫兵,在齐校长眼里,也不过是些不知自己在做什么的孩子。请看你是否能从下面的故事中感受到"礼"和"仁"在这四个方面的体现:1)非对抗性的生活态度;2)对加强关系保持和谐的注重;3)对人类正能量的凭信;以及4)对德中之美的赞赏。

The centrality of *li* in constituting and expressing *ren* does not mean subjugating one's individuality to set patterns of behavior; nor does it mean achieving a static, final state of virtue. Flexible and cumulative, *li* and *ren* come from a society's specific customs and practices, while still transcending any particular set of norms. In Chinese cultural tradition, shared norms of ethical behavior guide the development of and instruction in morals; at the same time, they change with time and adjust to various social contexts. You will experience their complexity when reading the stories in this chapter.

In Confucian ethics, the moral and the aesthetic are two sides of the same coin. It is beautiful to be in sync with others and live harmoniously with them. Following *li* to achieve *ren* is the path of those who want to live both beautifully and morally. In all of the following stories, simple acts of kindness and joy deepen the beauty of life.

"Skull Shave" tells how a little boy is initiated into the established yet confusing norms of the community. In " 'Star' Grandma" the people from a different culture accommodate Chinese values, habits, and the quiddity of life with *li* and, in so doing, exemplify *ren*. The pivotal moment in "Catharsis" shows how these traditional ethical values endure even in times of chaos.

There is no antagonistic relationship in these stories. Even the Red Guards are, for the school principal Qi, simply kids who do not know what they are doing. See if you can find the following aspects of *li* and *ren* in all three stories: (1) a nonconfrontational attitude, (2) emphasis on strengthening relationships and preserving harmony, (3) trust in the positive potential of humankind, and (4) appreciation of the beautiful in the ethical.

1
剃脑袋

赵新

我 小时候理发不叫理发，叫剃脑袋;村子里不管谁的头发长长了(当然他得是个男人或者男孩)，一律要拿刀子剃,一律要把脑袋剃得精光精光。剃的过程很简单：在锅里烧上两瓢水，水热了，舀到脸盆里，把头发来来回回洗一洗，然后往墙根儿一坐，给你剃脑袋的人就下了刀子。他们手里的刀子都是铁刀子笨刀子，刀背厚，刀刃又钝，那不是剃而是刮，咯吱吱，咯吱吱，一刀一刀挖下去疼得入骨，疼得钻心!

我是村里最怕剃脑袋的人。看见有人剃脑袋，我就想到了杀猪，猪被杀死之后要用开水烫，然后把毛刮下来，露出白嫩的肚皮和脊梁，和人剃脑袋有些相仿。可是害怕剃也得剃呀，想躲也躲不过去呀!

1947年我长到了八岁。那年夏天我该上学了。

爹知道我害怕剃脑袋。爹和我商量说：二小，眼看你要上学了，把你的脑袋剃剃吧!

我说不剃，剃脑袋和上学有什么关系呀!

爹说：剃剃看着清秀啊! 你三个多月没剃脑袋，看着像个闺女啦!

我说闺女就闺女，闺女人家也让上学!

1
SKULL SHAVE

Zhao Xin

Translated by Cara Liu

When I was little, we didn't call what you get from a barber a "haircut," we called it a "skull shave." In the village, it didn't matter who you were when your hair grew long (so long as you were a man or boy, that is); all had to have their whole skull shaved clean by a blade. The process of shaving was fairly simple: you first put two dipperfuls of water in a large pot and, after heating it, poured the water into a basin, where your hair would be washed thoroughly. Then the person giving you a shave would seat you at the foot of a wall and start his work. He always used wide blades of iron; so thick and dull was the edge of the blade that it scraped the skull more than it shaved it. *Shhk, shhk!* With every rasping stroke came a pain that seeped into your bones, into your very core!

Of all the villagers, I dreaded getting my skull shaved the most. Whenever I saw someone getting shaved, I thought of the way pigs were slaughtered. After a pig was killed, its body was put into boiling water before the hair was shorn, revealing its tender white belly and the ridges of its spine. To my mind, skull shaving was a similar process. But as frightened as I was, I had to do it. There was no way around it.

In 1947, I turned eight years old. I was about to start school that summer.

Papa knew I was terrified of having my head shaved, so he talked it over with me beforehand. "Little man, you're going to start school, why not have your head shaved?"

I said no. What did skull shaving have to do with going to school?

Papa said, "After you shave, you'll look handsome! You haven't shaved your head for three whole months. You look like a girl!"

"So what?" I said. "They would still let a girl go to school!"

6　剃脑袋

爹说：二小，是学校的老师让你剃脑袋的，老师说给我好几回了。你剃不剃?

我含着满眼的泪水和爹达成了协议：第一，剃。第二，要请村里的赵清水大叔剃。清水大叔是剃头高手，赫赫有名，全村子人都说他的刀子快，刀法好，下手轻，剃脑袋一点儿都不疼，还很舒服。

第三，剃的时候爹要在旁边守着我，给我壮胆，因为四十岁左右的清水大叔身材魁梧，方脸大眼，威风凛凛，嗓门洪亮，往他跟前一站，我有些胆小！

爹一言未了，清水大叔来了。

那是中午，庄稼人歇响的时候。听说清水大叔要给我这个孩子剃脑袋，院子里围了不少人。我们院里有棵伞一样的老槐树，树凉儿很大，树荫很浓。

我在板凳上坐着，清水大叔在我眼前立着。他围着我转了一圈，然后用手拍拍我的后背说：挺直了，把腰挺直了！男子汉，你怕什么?

我十分紧张。我说：大叔，我胆小……

他哈哈大笑，把刀子一晃：胆小什么? 我剃脑袋不疼！

他一刀下来，我的脑袋上"沙"的一声，一把头发落在了我的衣襟上。我又毫无缘由地想起了杀猪刮毛的场景，身子就抖了一下。

清水大叔不高兴了：你抖什么? 你抖什么?

我怯怯地说：疼！

清水大叔更不高兴了，连着给我刮了几刀：你大声说，是真疼还是假疼?

我说：真疼。哎呀，越来越疼！

清水大叔恼怒了，收起刀子对我爹说：赵清和，你看见了吧? 当着这么多乡亲的面，你儿子砸我的牌子，坏我的名声，臭我的手艺，这脑袋我不剃了！我剃过的脑袋比地里的西瓜都多，谁说过疼?

Papa said, "Little man, it's your teacher who wanted you to get a shave. She's already told me several times. So are you going to do it or not?"

Holding back tears, I offered my father a compromise with three conditions: First, I would do it, of course. Second, I wanted to be shaved only by Uncle Qingshui Zhao, a master shaver, who was renowned for his quick blades, skilled work, and gentle technique. When he shaved your skull, it didn't hurt a bit; it might even feel pretty good.

Third, when I got my skull shaved, Papa must stand at my side to give me courage. The forty-something Uncle Qingshui was a burly man with a square face and big eyes. He had the air of a drill sergeant about him and a voice to match. When I came face-to-face with him, I would cower in fear!

Before Papa could agree, Uncle Qingshui showed up.

It was around twelve o'clock, and the villagers were taking their midday break. When they heard that Uncle Qingshui was going to give me a shave, many of them gathered around my courtyard. There was an old locust tree there with an umbrella-like crown that cast a broad, dense ring of cool shade.

As I sat on the stool, Uncle Qingshui towered over me. He circled me once, then patted me on the back. "Straighten up, young man. Up! What are you afraid of?"

I was extremely nervous. I said, "Uncle, I am scared..."

He roared with laughter, and with a swish of his blade, he added: "What's there to be scared about? When I shave a head, it doesn't hurt at all!"

With a downward arc of his blade, I heard a *sha!* and a handful of hair fell onto the flaps of my clothes. Irrationally, I remembered the slaughtered pigs and how their body hair had been shaved. My body trembled.

Uncle Qingshui was unhappy. "Why are you trembling? Why?"

I squeaked: "It hurts!"

Uncle Qingshui grew more upset. He gave me a few strokes of the blade and demanded, "Speak up! Is it really hurting or are you just scared?"

I cried, "It really hurts. Ouch! It's hurting more and more!"

Uncle Qingshui was furious. He put away his blade and turned to my father: "Qinghe Zhao, did you see? Your son is ruining my reputation in front of so many village folks! He's tarnished my name and sullied my craft. I will not shave his head any more! I have shaved more heads than there are watermelons in the fields, and who has ever said it hurts?"

8　剃脑袋

爹赶紧伸手拉他：兄弟，你别和我家二小一般见识，他还是个孩子……

清水大叔扬长而去，我的脑袋刚刚剃了一半。

院子里的人嘻嘻哈哈地走了，留下一只母鸡在那里悠闲地转悠。

摸着我的"阴阳头"，那天下午我没敢出门。爹下地之前给我说，别哭别闹别上火，晚上他一定想办法，把我那半个脑袋上的头发剃干净。

那天晚上月亮很大很圆。我们刚放下饭碗，清水大叔就气喘吁吁地跑到我们家里来了。他给爹深深地施了一个礼说：哥啊，对不起，难怪孩子说疼呢，原来是我拿错了剃脑袋的刀子———这把旧刀子我好几年不使了，孩子能不疼吗？

于是我又坐在了板凳上，清水大叔又拿起了一把剃头刀。

明亮的月辉里，大叔问我：二小，疼吗？

爹在旁边咳嗽一声，我赶紧说：不疼，不疼，挺舒服！

清水大叔说：疼就忍着点儿，剃脑袋哪有不疼的？他们说不疼那是糊弄我，抬举我，他们有他们的用心；不过就是疼，你也不能当着大伙儿面说，你懂这个道理吗？

(2012)

Papa quickly reached out his hand to grab him. "Brother, please, there's no need to mind my son. He is but a child."

Uncle Qingshui simply walked off, and I was left with a half-shaven head.

The people in my courtyard chuckled and walked away, leaving nothing behind but a hen wandering carefree.

I felt my "yin-yang head" with my hand and didn't dare to go out that afternoon. Before Papa left to work in the fields, he asked me to not worry or throw a fit. He assured me he would find a way to get the other half of my head shaved that evening.

That night, the moon was full and immense. We had just finished eating when an out-of-breath Uncle Qingshui sprinted up to our house. He gave my dad a deep, solemn bow and said, "Elder brother, I am truly sorry. It's no wonder the kid was in pain. It just so happened that I grabbed the wrong blade—I have not used this old blade for many years. We can't blame the kid for acting out."

Thus, I was soon back on a stool, and Uncle Qingshui once again took up his shaving blade.

In the luminous moonlight, Uncle Qingshui asked me, "Little man, does it hurt?"

Papa, who was standing beside me, gave a cough. I quickly responded: "No, it doesn't. Actually, it feels quite nice!"

Uncle Qingshui added, "If it hurts, just endure the pain for a bit. Since when was shaving your head entirely painless? Those who told me it didn't hurt were trying to get it over with or do me a favor, and they had their reasons. But as painful as the whole process may be, you can't say it aloud in public. Do you understand the sense in that?"

(2012)

VOCABULARY AND USAGE

脑袋	nǎodai	head; skull; brain	石块砸碎了他的脑袋。
一律	yílǜ	all; without exception	男女老少，一律平等。
精光	jīngguāng	with nothing left	他把家业输得精光。
瓢	piáo	gourd ladle; wooden dipper	爷爷把葫芦切开做了两个瓢，用瓢喝水方便多了。
舀	yǎo	scoop up/out	我从锅里舀出几勺菜。
刀刃	dāorèn	blade	好钢要用在刀刃上。
刮	guā	scrape	铁门刮了我的车。
钻心	zuānxīn	pierce to the heart	这天儿冷得钻心。
清秀	qīngxiù	handsome; pretty	这小姑娘多清秀啊！
下手	xiàshǒu	put one's hand to; start	现在下手还不晚。
壮胆	zhuàngdǎn	embolden	我喝酒是为了给自己壮胆。
魁梧	kuíwú	big and tall; burly	他肌肉发达，很魁梧。
威风凛凛	wēifēnglǐnlǐn	with great dignity	他穿上军服威风凛凛。
往	wǎng	go (in a direction)	你往这边来，这儿人少。
跟前	gēnqián	in front of; close to	她很快跑到妈妈跟前。
庄稼人	zhuāngjiarén	peasant; farmer	庄稼人靠种地生活。
歇晌	xiēshǎng	take a noon break	她有歇晌睡午觉的习惯。
槐树	huáishù	locust tree	槐树开花时香气芬芳。
缘由	yuányóu	reason	这场事故是有缘由的。
怯	qiè	timid; cowardly	面对强敌他毫无怯意。
砸	zá	smash; mess up; ruin	我的生意让他搞砸了。
牌子	páizi	brand	别砸了新产品的牌子！
一般见识	yībānjiànshi	lower oneself to the same level as someone	您知书达理，别跟不懂事的小孩子一般见识。
扬长而去	yángcháng érqù	swagger off	他把孩子一丢，扬长而去。
上火	shànghuǒ	get angry	这话会让老人上火的。
气喘吁吁	qìchuǎnxūxū	gasp; be out of breath	他爬山的时候气喘吁吁。
施礼	shīlǐ	salute; show courtesy	学生向老师施礼。

使	shǐ	use	这电脑旧了，不好使了。
糊弄	hùnong	fool; deceive; tongue in cheek	你是在说好听的糊弄我，我不会上当的。
抬举	táijü	show favor/respect	你叫他老师是抬举他。
用心	yòngxīn	motive; intention	你给老师送礼是什么用心？

QUESTIONS FOR DISCUSSION

1. Why does the story need the metaphor of the slaughtered pigs?
2. Did Uncle Qingshui really use the wrong blade? What might Papa have done that afternoon?
3. How is everyone, especially the child, granted maximum "face" in the story?
4. What brings about the reconciliation in the final scene?
5. Confucius says, "Restraining yourself and reenacting *li* constitute *ren* [克己复礼为仁 *kè jǐ fù lǐ wé rén*]."[2] How does the story illustrate this Confucian teaching?
6. If *li* may take a lifetime to learn, would you say that the boy is off to a good start?
7. Should absolute honesty be secondary to a sympathetic understanding of fellow human beings, mutual respect, and making people happy? Why?

1. 为什么这个故事的叙述中需要有杀猪的那一段话？
2. 我们确切知道清水大叔真的用错剃刀了吗？那天下午爸爸可能会有过什么动作？
3. 人们的面子，尤其是那孩子的面子，在故事中都是怎样受到精心关照的？
4. 是什么带来了这篇小小说最后一幕的和解／和谐？
5. 子曰，"克己复礼为仁。"这个故事怎样体现了孔子的教导？
6. 如果学习"礼"是一生的课程，我们可以不可以说这个孩子有了个良好的开端呢？
7. 对同胞悲悯的情怀，人与人之间的相互尊重，以及他人的快乐等，这些应该比绝对的诚实来得更重要吗？为什么？

---

2. This Confucian saying from *The Analects* (论语 *Lunyu*) has become part of everyday language in China.

AUTHOR BIO

Between the 1960s and the 1980s, Zhao Xin (1939–) followed a path typical of an underprivileged "literary youth" (*wénxúe qīngnián* 文学青年) of the time. After getting a college degree in Chinese in 1963, Zhao Xin taught at a middle school. He started to write creatively in the 1970s when he went to work at the county cultural center. He subsequently became a communications officer for the county publicity department, then an editor for the Baoding prefectural government and Baoding Federation of Literary and Art Circles. In 1994, when Baoding became a municipality, he presided over the local China Writers Association. Among his representative works are the full-length novels *Hunyin Xiaoshi* (婚姻小事) and *Zhang Wang Li Zhao* (张王李赵); the novellas *Zhuangjia Guandian* (庄稼观点), *He Dong He Xi* (河东河西), and *Er Yue Ba, Luan Chuan Yi* (二月八, 乱穿衣); and the short stories *Yi Ri San Can* (一日三餐) and *Shuidaoqucheng* (水到渠成). Although he began his career publishing longer forms of fiction, Zhao Xin has focused increasingly on short-shorts and has championed the genre for several years. His works, including the story here, earned him the Lifetime Achievement Award from *Selected Short-Shorts* (小小说选刊), a leading journal of the genre, in 2013.

2
"明星"外祖母

刘震云

我外祖母在她年轻的时候,在我们那儿方圆——我从小是在农村长大的——几十里是个"明星",有点像现在的张曼玉。无非张曼玉是一个演电影的,我外祖母是一个扛长活的。她扛长活在方圆几十里特别出众。她身高一米五几,但是她晚年告诉我,三里路那么长的麦趟子,她从这头割到那头不直腰。她给我留下的遗产就是这么一句话,她说,割麦子的时候可不敢直腰。如果你直第一次腰,接着想直第二次腰,第三次的时候你就不想再弯下腰割麦子了。

当时我外祖母因为是一个"明星",所以我们周围所有的地主,对她都非常尊重。听说我外祖母要跟谁签约,那家地主就非常高兴。她到哪个地主家,地主都要把他家的儿子认到我外祖母跟前。我小的时候,发现我外祖母有一群干儿子全是地主,到哪儿都有人喊她娘。所以最后斗地主我外祖母是特别的不同意。她说地主特别好。地主的儿子见我就喊娘,还能不好吗?"文化大革命"那时候放《白毛女》,她问这个事发生在哪里。当时我也不知道,我说可能是河北吧。她说河北的地主不好不证明河南的地主不好。

2
"STAR" GRANDMA

Liu Zhengyun

When she was young, my maternal grandma was a "star" in our local area—I grew up in the countryside—whose radiance spread for dozens of miles around. She was somewhat like Maggie Cheung is today. The only difference is that Maggie Cheung acts in movies and my grandma worked in the fields as a hired hand. My grandma's exceptional farmwork was well known throughout our region. She stood only about five feet tall, yet she told me once that she could cut a whole row of wheat, one and a half kilometers from end to end, without straightening her back. Her legacy to me is this simple piece of advice: When harvesting wheat with a sickle, don't even think of straightening up. If you do it once, you'll soon want to do it a second time. If you do it three times, you'll never want to bend down and get to work again.

Because of my grandma's "star" status, all the landowners in our region respected her greatly. Every landlord was thrilled when he knew my grandma intended to sign a work contract with him. No matter who he was, he would bring his sons to be "adopted" by her. When I was little, I found that my grandma had a bunch of foster sons, all offspring of landlords. Wherever she went, there would be someone there calling her "Mom." Naturally, later on, she was especially abhorred by those who fought against the landowners. She said the landlords were very nice people. "How could they be bad when their sons all call me 'Mom' when they see me?"

The White-Haired Girl, a movie about how peasants suffered at the hands of a landlord, was shown during the Cultural Revolution. She asked where it took place. I didn't know, so I made a guess: probably Hebei. "Just because landlords in Hebei are bad," she said, "doesn't mean the ones in Henan are bad too."

16 "明星"外祖母

1992年的时候有两个德国人到我外祖母家去看了一看。我跟他们一块儿去,他们跟我外祖母谈了一阵话,觉得特别好。

这两个德国人一个个子长得非常高,会汉语;一个长得很矮,不会汉语。

我外祖母问大个子:"你家住在哪里?"

他说:"我住在德国的北边。"

她又问小个子:"那你呢?"

"我住在德国的南边。"

我外祖母问:"那你们俩怎么认识的呢?"

把这两个德国人问愣了:是呀,我们俩怎么认识的?我觉着这也是一个世界上很根本的问题呀。

想了半天,这个大个子的德国人很幽默,说:"赶集。"

我外祖母理解了——啊,赶集认识的。

她说:"德国搞'文化大革命'了吗?"

又把这德国人问愣了。"搞了没搞啊?"

"没搞。"

我外祖母马上就急了:"毛主席让搞'文化大革命',你们为什么不搞?"

大个子想了半天,又回答得很圆满,说德国人很笨,大部分不懂中国话,所以毛主席说的话他们没听懂。

外祖母又问:"那你们德国每人划多少地啊?"

大个子虽然通汉语但是细节上搞得不是特别精确,亩和分搞不清,他说:"八分。"

我外祖母一听八分,从椅子上噌一下站起来了,拄着拐杖,

围着大个子转了一圈,说:"你这么高的个子怕吃不饱。"

德国人想也能吃饱啊,突然说:"姥姥,不对,八亩。"

我外祖母又着急了,又拄着拐杖转了一圈,说:"那你媳妇儿受累了。"

(2011)

One day in 1992, two German men visited my grandma. I went with them. They chatted with her for a while, and it all felt very pleasant.

One of the Germans was extremely tall and could speak Chinese. The other was extremely short and didn't speak Chinese.

My grandma asked the tall German, "Where do you live?"

He answered, "I live in north Germany."

She then asked the short German, "And you?"

"I live in south Germany."

"Then, how did you get to know each other?" my grandma asked them.

The two Germans seemed stunned: "That's right, how did we come to know one another?"

I thought this was really a fundamental question.

After thinking for a long while, the tall German said, good-humoredly, "At the country fair."

My grandma got it! "Oh, you met at the country fair."

She asked, "Did you have 'the Great Cultural Revolution' in Germany?"

The two Germans were again stunned by her question: "Did we have it or not?"

"No. We didn't."

Hearing that, my grandma became upset, "Chairman Mao said we should have 'the Great Cultural Revolution.' How could you not to do it in Germany?"

The tall German thought for a long time, and then gave her another perfect answer. "We Germans are dumb. Since most of us didn't speak Chinese, we missed what Chairman Mao said."

My grandma persisted, "How much land does each German get?"

Although the tall German knew Chinese, he wasn't particularly clear on the details of measurements, the difference between *mu* and *fen*, for instance. "Eight *fen*," he responded.

My grandma sprang to her feet upon hearing this. Leaning on her cane, she circled around the tall German and said, "A big guy like you will go hungry."

The German thought it over—he actually had plenty to eat. It suddenly came to him: "Grandma, I was wrong. It was eight *mu*."

My grandma got worked up again. Circling around the tall German once more, she leaned on her cane and said, "Your wife must have her hands full!"

(2011)

VOCABULARY AND USAGE

方圆	fāngyuán	surrounding area; radius	这儿方圆十里无人居住。
无非	wúfēi	simply; only	乘这班车无非是快一点儿。
扛长活	káng chánghuó	work as a farm laborer on yearly basis	他不过是个扛长活的，却因为活干得好很受尊敬。
出众	chūzhòng	outstanding	他才华出众，品学兼优。
麦趟子	mài tàngzi	rows of wheat	这里田小，麦趟子也不长。
遗产	yíchǎn	legacy	外祖母的遗产就是这句话。
签约	qiānyuē	sign a contract	她做事儿讲诚信不用签约。
认	rèn	enter into a certain relationship; adopt	她今天认两了个干儿子。
干儿子	gān érzi	godson; honorary son	
喊	hǎn	call; address a person as	他猜我年纪大些就喊我姐。
放	fàng	project on the screen	那时，放电影是个技术活。
矮	ǎi	short	两个德国人，一高一矮。
愣	lèng	be taken aback	没想到外祖母会这样问，他俩一时愣住了。
幽默	yōumò	humorous	我喜欢丈夫很有幽默感。
赶集	gǎnjí	go to a market/fair	今天我们去县城赶大集。
搞(革命)	gǎo (gémìng)	start; make; carry on	他说搞革命是为了帮穷人。
圆满	yuánmǎn	perfect; satisfactory	孩子让她感到日子圆满。
笨	bèn	slow-witted	这德国人可一点儿都不笨。
划	huà	assign; allot	村里重新划了地，把去世了的人的地划给了新生儿。
通	tōng	know well	他通六国语言。
细节	xìjié	detail	事情的具体细节我不清楚。
精确	jīngquè	precise; accurate	科学的方法一定精确吗？
亩	mǔ	a unit of area (= 0.0667 hectares)	外祖母觉得，一户人家八亩地太多，八分又太少。
分	fēn	a fen (1/10 of a mu)	
噌	cēng	whoosh!	我一推门，小鸟噌地飞了。

拄	zhǔ	lean on; support oneself with a stick	他老了，腿脚不灵了，走路要拄拐杖。
拐杖	guǎizhàng	walking stick	
怕(是)	pà (shi)	I'm afraid; perhaps	你的梦怕是难以实现了。
受累	shòulèi	be put to much trouble	我来晚了，让您受累了。

QUESTIONS FOR DISCUSSION

1. What's your impression of the grandmother?
2. How is the story structured? How do different parts of the story relate to one another?
3. Do we need to know the reason for the Germans' visit? Why or why not?
4. If "information" is not accurately communicated through their conversation, what is?
5. Why does the tall German go out of his way to humor the grandmother?
6. Why is it important that the story ends in a humorous "miscommunication"?
7. How does the story suggest that *li* and *ren* are not exclusively Confucian ideals?

1. 请说说你对外祖母的印象。
2. 故事的框架结构是怎样的？不同的部分之间靠什么连接？
3. 我们有必要知道德国人去那儿的公干吗？说说为什么。
4. 如果德国人和外祖母的交谈没有准确地交流信息，那他们的对话准确地交流了什么？
5. 为什么那位高个子的德国客人想方设法要让外祖母高兴？
6. 故事在幽默的"错误理解"中结束。为什么这样的结尾很重要？
7. 这个故事怎样表明"礼"和"仁"不仅仅是儒家的文化理想？

AUTHOR BIO

The author Liu Zhenyun is a well-known writer in China. Born in Henan in 1958, he developed a great attachment to the land and its people. He served in the military (1973–1978) before studying literature at Beijing University. Having received degrees from Beijing Normal University and Lu Xun Institute of Literature, he is now a professor of literature at Renmin University of China. His published works include eight full-length novels, four novellas, four collections of essays, and five screenplays. Four of his works have won major national awards, and his novel *Cellphone* (手机) was made into a film, a TV series, and a stage play. He adapted his 2009 novel *Back to 1942* (温故1942) into a screenplay; the film, released in 2012, featured Tim Robbins and Adrien Brody. Liu Zhenyun received the highest cultural award from Egypt's Ministry of Culture in January 2016. The award honors his literary impact, especially that of *Ta Pu* (塔铺), *Cellphone*, and *A Word Is Worth a Thousand Words* (一句顶一万句), on Egypt and the Arabic world. A serious writer of popular appeal, Liu Zhenyun earns some of the highest royalties in China. This story may give you an idea why. Based on real life, the story is Liu's tribute to his grandmother, who features prominently in Liu's writing.

3
洗礼

聂鑫森

　　这是1966年深秋的一个夜晚,古城湘潭平政街"洗尘池"澡堂墙壁上的挂钟,洪亮地敲了九下。
　　按规定,澡堂营业到晚上八点就下班了。顾客早已走尽,工作人员也陆续回家了,只剩下浴池班班长于长生和小徒弟张庆在打扫卫生。几个大池子里的水都已放干,池底、池沿也都擦拭干净了。原本有几个雅间,现在紧紧地关着,里面放着木浴盆,小床,茶几,浴盆上安着冷热水龙头。舍得花钱的顾客可以自己调节水温,可以洗过澡后舒服地躺到小床上,可以请人推拿按摩,可以喝一壶泡好的茶。但这个项目在几天前已经取消了,上级说,只有剥削阶级才有这些臭讲究!
　　于长生望着那些雅间,惆怅地叹了口气。
　　"张庆,关门吧,我们爷儿俩也该歇口气喝口茶了,今晚轮到我们值班哩。"
　　"好咧——师傅。"

3
CATHARSIS[3]

Nie Xinsen

It was a late autumn night in 1966 in the ancient city of Xiangtan. The wall clock at the Cleansing Pool bathhouse on Tranquility Street struck nine loudly.

The bathhouse, in keeping with standard business hours, had closed at 8 p.m. With the customers all gone, the staff left for home, one after another. Only the head of the tub and pool section, Yu Changsheng, and his apprentice Zhang Qing stayed behind to clean up. They had drained the water from the large pools and finished cleaning the bottoms and edges. What used to be the private rooms were now tightly sealed. Inside each room, there was a small bed, a tea table, and a wooden tub with hot and cold taps. A customer willing to spend more money could adjust the water temperature himself. He could lie down comfortably on the small bed after his bath, request a massage, and enjoy a hot pot of tea. But this service had been terminated a few days ago. The higher authorities had decided that only exploitive classes were that particular about taking a bath!

Yu Changsheng looked at those rooms and sighed pensively.

"Zhang Qing, let's call it a day. It's time for the two of us[4] to take a break and have a sip of tea. Remember, it's our turn to be on duty tonight."

"No problem, Master," Zhang Qing replied.

---

3. "Catharsis" as the translation of the title takes into consideration the meanings of both 洗礼 and 洗尘. Besides baptism, 洗礼 is often used to describe a person who has been through the trials and tribulations of life and emerged stronger than before—他经受了战火的洗礼. 洗尘 has the implication of "purification" and "cleansing." Please also see the vocabulary and usage section for more information.
4. The Chinese original 爷儿俩 (yé'er liǎ) generally refers to two males of two generations. It is most often used to address father and son or grandfather and grandson. In traditional China, a master in a profession is expected to treat his apprentice as his own son; the apprentice is expected to respect his master as his own father.

两个人刚走进店堂，忽见从外面急匆匆走进一个人来。四十岁出头，面黄肌瘦，额头上还有血迹，目光散乱，步履踉踉跄跄，身上的衣服很破旧，特别是膝盖那个地方磨损得很厉害。

　　张庆吆喝一声："喂，下班了，明天再来！"

　　那人收住脚步，小声说："我好多日子没洗澡了，今夜好容易才抽身来，是否可以……"

　　于长生几步走上前，把来人上下打量一番，然后说："您来啦，请！"

　　张庆觉得很意外：不是下班了吗？

　　于长生对着张庆一扬手，吼道："关门！"

　　张庆忙答应："是，师傅。"

　　"开雅间，把锅炉烧起来，让客人好好洗个澡！"

　　来人说："师傅我……没带那么多钱。"

　　于长生说："放心，还是五角！请您先去雅间稍等一会儿，我去沏壶茶来。"

　　张庆关好门，又去打开一个雅间，再一溜烟儿去了锅炉房，不久便听见鼓风机呼呼吼叫的声音。

　　又过了一阵，于长生端着一壶热茶和一个有盖的茶杯，走进了雅间，并顺手带上了门。

　　来人慌忙站起来，说："师傅，叫我如何感谢您！"

　　"坐！快坐！我认识您，您是成龙中学的校长齐子耘先生，我的二儿子就在贵校读高中。我曾经在家长大会上见过您。我叫于长生，活到五十岁倒真的糊涂了，有文化的人忽然都有罪了，怪事！"

　　齐子耘没有搭话，眼睛里闪出了泪光。

　　"我二儿子昨天回家，说是参加了什么批斗会。被我用木棍子狠揍了一顿，打得他鬼哭狼嚎，保证再不去胡来了。"

　　齐子耘轻声说："也不能怪他们，他们太年轻……"

No sooner had they reached the entrance hall than they saw a man rush in from outside. He looked to be a little older than forty. There were bloodstains on his forehead and his steps were unsteady. He was thin and pale, and his eyes reflected his evident distress. His clothes were shabby-looking and worn, especially around his knees.

Zhang Qing shouted out, "Hey, we're closed. Come back tomorrow!"

The man halted. "I haven't had a bath for a long time. It wasn't easy for me to get away tonight. I wonder if you could . . ." he said quietly.

Yu Changsheng took a few steps forward. He eyed the man up and down. "It's an honor to have you. Please come in," he said.

Zhang Qing was surprised. "Aren't we closed?" he asked.

Yu Changsheng waved off Zhang Qing and barked, "Shut the gate!"

"Yes, Master," Zhang Qing answered, hurriedly.

"Open a private room. Start the boiler. Let our guest have a good bath!"

"Master," the man stammered, "I . . . I don't have that kind of money."

"No worries," Yu Changsheng assured him. "Fifty cents as usual. Please go wait for a moment in a private room. I'll be back with a pot of tea."

Zhang Qing closed the gate and opened a private room before speeding off to the boiler room. Soon a whirring roar issued from the blower.

Before long, Yu Changsheng came back with a hot pot of tea and a cup with a lid. He entered the private room and closed the door behind him.

The man rose up, hurriedly. "Master, how can I ever repay you?"

"Sit down! Please sit down! I know you. You are Mr. Qi Ziyun, the principal of Chenglong High School. My second son is a student there. I saw you at a parents' meeting. I'm Yu Changsheng and, much to my surprise, a really confused man at fifty.[5] How come educated people have all become criminals suddenly? It's absurd!"

Qi Ziyun remained silent, his eyes glistening with tears.

"My second son came back from school yesterday, mumbling about being a part of some denunciation session. I beat him with a wooden club. He wailed and howled and promised not to fool around with them again."

Qi Ziyun replied softly, "It is not really their fault. They are too young . . ."

---

5. This is an allusion to the popular Confucian saying: "At fifty, I knew the decrees of Heaven" (五十知天命 *wǔshí zhī tiānmìng*). *Confucian Analects*, translated by James Legge, accessed June 7, 2015, www.cnculture.net/ebook/jing/sishu/lunyu_en/02.html.

聊了一阵，张庆在雅间外高喊一声："火旺——水热咧——"

于长生忙站起来，走到浴盆前，先打开热水龙头放水，白色的雾气立刻升腾起来；而后，轻轻拧开冷水龙头。浴盆的水渐渐满了，他不停地用手去试水的温度。这时节洗澡，水要热，但不要烫。

于长生关了水龙头，说："齐先生，您先泡澡。半个小时后，我来给您推拿按摩。"

"不，不，我不配，也别连累了您。"

"我不过是个工人，还能把我怎么样？"

于长生走出雅间，顺手把门带拢了。

"张庆，过半小时，给我到隔壁的饮食店去买一碗馄饨来！"

张庆吃惊地望师傅，然后说道："好咧！"

于长生到池子边搬了条板凳来，静悄悄地坐在雅间的门边。

约摸半个小时，于长生听声音就知道齐子耘洗好了，便立即推门走了进去。灯光下，他看见穿上短裤的齐子耘的身上，手臂上，点缀着一些红红紫紫的伤痕，便慌忙走上前，说："您请伏在床上。这个项目早就取消了，但我要为您显一段手艺。"

齐子耘伏在床上，于长生弯腰立在旁边，双手握成空心拳，开始在他的脊背上，小心地绕开伤痕，紧敲轻捶。

"痛吗？齐先生。"

"不……痛。"

拳头忽然停住了。于长生说："齐先生，有句话不知当问不当问？"

"您问吧。"

"如果我猜得不错，您是从学校逃出来的？"

"是。"

"您受了许多罪，从您的目光里我看出您很绝望。"

"对。您说这日子怎么熬过去，罚跪、批斗、挨打、游街，没完没了的。"

The two men chatted for a while, until Zhang Qing shouted from outside the private room: "Fire is burning—water is boiling—"

Yu Changsheng got up quickly and walked to the tub. The steam rose up instantly when he turned on the hot-water tap. Carefully, he turned on the cold water. As water filled the tub, he felt its temperature with his hand—for a bath at this time of the year, the water must be hot, but not scalding hot.

Yu Changsheng turned off the taps and said, "Mr. Qi, please enjoy your bath. I will be back in half an hour to give you a massage."

"Please don't. I don't deserve this. And I don't want to get you into trouble."

"I'm already a workingman. What else can they do to me?"

Yu Changsheng left, closing the door tightly behind him.

"Zhang Qing, in half an hour, go get a bowl of wonton soup next door."

Surprised, Zhang Qing looked at his master, but said, "Of course!"

Yu Changsheng brought a bench back from the poolside and quietly sat down by the door to the private room.

About half an hour later, he could tell from the sound of the movement inside that Qi Ziyun was done bathing. Yu Changsheng quickly pushed open the door and walked in. Under the light, he could see Qi Ziyun in his underwear, his arms and body dotted with bruises. Yu Changsheng hurried forward. "Please lie down on your stomach. Although this service has already been terminated, I'd like to take this opportunity to show you my skills," he said.

Qi Ziyun fell on the bed; Yu Changsheng bent over him. With both his hands in loose fists, Yu started pounding Qi's back, quickly yet gently, careful to avoid the bruises.

"Does it hurt, Mr. Qi?"

"No . . . It does not."

Suddenly he stopped pounding. "Mr. Qi, I have a question, but I'm not sure if it's appropriate to ask," Yu Changsheng said.

"Please."

"Correct me if I am wrong, but you must have run away from your confinement in school?"

"Yes."

"You've suffered a lot. I saw the despair in your eyes."

"You're right. You tell me how to tough it out when it's endless forced kneeling and public shaming, when you're beaten and paraded through the streets."

"那么，我告诉您一句话，这个世界不可能总是这样，而且什么人都可以没有，独不能没有老师！您要咬紧牙挺住，为了许许多多的孩子，好好地话下去。'天地君亲师'，这个道理是铁定的。假如连老师都不要了，这个世界也就完了！让我冒昧地叫您一声兄弟，您说是不是？"

齐子耘的肩膀猛烈地抽搐起来，终于压抑不住，伤心地伏在枕上痛哭起来。

"齐先生，像我，还有和我一样的人，把孩子交给老师，心里感激得很哪。"

齐子耘挣扎着爬起来，揩干泪，说："于师傅，我原本想好好洗个澡，就……现在，我要骂自己是个胆小鬼，是个不负责任的人！这个澡，把我洗明白了。"

于长生抓过一块大浴巾，给齐子耘披上，然后，对他毕恭毕敬地鞠了一个躬。

门外，张庆一声高喊："大肉馄饨——趁热吃哩——"

第二天上午，"洗尘池"门外的大街上，传来一阵一阵的锣声和惊天动地的口号声。

于长生和张庆从澡堂里跑了出来。

张庆说："师傅，走在前面的是昨夜洗澡的那个人。"

于长生说："那是齐先生，齐子耘校长！"

他看见齐子耘挂着黑牌子，敲着一面锣，从容地走着，脸色很是平静。他的目光又扫视那些戴红袖章的红卫兵，里面没有他的二儿子！

于长生忽然响亮地喊道："'洗尘池'有客人哟，里面请——"

(2012)

"Well, let me tell you one thing: the world will not stay like this forever. Moreover, no one is more indispensable than teachers! You must clench your teeth and bear it. You must cherish your life for the sake of the kids. Teachers ought to be worshiped as much as heaven and earth, as much as sage rulers and ancestors.[6] This is truth set in stone. Humanity comes to an end when we mistreat our teachers! Don't you agree, brother? Please allow me the liberty to call you my brother."

Qi Ziyun's shoulders twitched violently. Unable to hold back any longer, he burst out crying, his face buried in the pillow.

"Mr. Qi, there are still people like me, who are full of gratitude for teachers like you, taking in and taking care of our kids."

Qi Ziyun struggled to his feet. He wiped off his tears and said, "Master Yu, my plan was to wash myself clean before I . . . Now I want to slam my body against the wall for being a coward, an irresponsible man! This bath has cleared my mind."

Yu Changsheng grabbed a big bath towel and put it around Qi Ziyun. Then he bowed reverently.

Outside, Zhang Qing cried loudly, "Here comes pork wonton—eat while it's hot—"

Next morning, the thunder of gongs being struck and slogans being shouted reverberated in the street outside the Cleansing Pool bathhouse.

Yu Changsheng and Zhang Qing ran out.

Zhang Qing cried out, "Master, it's the man from last night walking out in front."

"That man is Mr. Qi, Principal Qi Ziyun!" Yu Changsheng replied.

Yu saw Qi Ziyun ringing a gong, a black plaque hanging from his neck. He walked with ease, his demeanor tranquil. Yu's eyes then glanced at the Red Guards wearing red armbands. His second son was not among them!

Suddenly, Yu Changsheng let out a resounding cry: "Guests of Cleansing Pool! Right this way please!"

(2012)

---

6. In his 2006 article "The Worship of the Heaven, the Earth, the Sage Rulers, Ancestors and Teachers—A Study of the Origin" in the *Journal of Beijing Normal University* (北京师范大学学报 no.2 [2006]:99–106), Xu Zi (徐梓) investigated the origin of this popular expression. He attributed the formation of the concept to Xun Zi (313–238 B.C.E.). Accessed April 25, 2016, www.cnki.com.cn/Article/CJFD2006-BJSF200602014.htm.

VOCABULARY AND USAGE

洗礼	xǐlǐ	baptism; severe tests	岁月的洗礼使他更加自信。
洗尘	xǐchén	welcome (a traveler); help wash off the dust	他为从美国归来的女儿接风洗尘。
尽	jìn	finish; all gone	他一仰头饮尽了杯中酒。
雅	yǎ	elegant; stylish	这大红的房间看上去不太雅。
推拿按摩	tuīná ànmó	massage	推拿和按摩有什么不同？
臭	chòu	disgusting	这孩子被惯坏了，一身臭毛病！
讲究	jiǎngjiu	pay great attention to; be particular about	中国人对吃很讲究。
惆怅	chóuchàng	sad; melancholy	漆黑的雨夜让我感到惆怅。
出头	chūtóu	a little over	你刚五十出头，别总说自己老了。
面黄肌瘦	miànhuángjīshòu	emaciated	他迷路三天，饿得面黄肌瘦。
散乱	sǎnluàn	scattered	她不讲究吃穿打扮，头发一向散乱。
步履踉跄	bùlǚliàngqiàng	falter	他的腿受伤了，步履踉跄。
磨损	mósǔn	wear and tear	桌子的四个角都有些磨损。
收	shōu	bring to an end; stop	天不早了，今天到这儿就收了吧。
住	zhù	fixed; not moving	等船靠岸停住了你再下去！
好多	hǎoduō	a good many	我在院子里种了好多树。
好容易	hǎoróngyì	with great difficulty	我好容易才考及格。
抽身	chōushēn	get away	他太忙，无法抽身来看你。
打量	dǎliang	look up and down	她能感觉到打量她的眼光。
一番	yīfān	bout	他不过是来问候一番。
沏茶	qīchá	make tea	茶道可不是简单的沏茶倒水。
一溜烟	yīliùyān	(dash off) swiftly	我跳上车一溜烟开跑了。
顺手	shùnshǒu	do as a natural sequence	他洗完澡总是顺手把澡盆刷干净。
慌忙	huāngmáng	hurried	妈妈一进门他就慌忙地把手机藏起来。
(反)倒	(fǎn) dào	yet; on the contrary	雪停了，天反倒更冷了！

贵(校)	guì (xiào)	(respectfully) your (school)	贵国的风俗我不懂，就不发表意见了。
搭话	dāhuà	accost	他从来不跟陌生人搭话。
胡来	húlái	fool with something; make trouble	千万别跟警察胡来！
配/不配	pèi/búpèi	be worthy/unworthy of	你不配做我们的领导。
连累	liánlèi	implicate	他的错误连累了朋友。
带拢(门)	dài long (mén)	close (door)	妻子还在睡觉，他出卧室时带拢了门。
约摸	yuēmō	about; roughly	我睡了约莫两小时。
显(手艺)	xiǎn (shǒuyì)	display (skills)	他常去公园的水石上写大字，显他的手艺。
绕(开)	rào (kāi)	bypass; detour	我不想跟他说话，所以看到他就绕开走。
紧(敲轻捶)	jǐn (qiāo qīng chuí)	urgent(ly); tense(ly); quick(ly)	枪声越来越紧了，咱们赶紧离开吧。
当(问)	dāng	ought; should	理当如此。
熬(日子)	áo (rìzi)	get through; survive	你是怎么熬过这么寒冷的冬天的？
咬牙	yǎoyá	grit one's teeth	听了我的话，他恨得直咬牙。
(咬)紧	(yǎo) jǐn	tight(ly)	这瓶盖盖得太紧，我打不开。
挺(住)	tǐng (zhù)	hold out	救护车快到了，你可要挺住啊！
铁定	tiědìng	definite(ly)	你放心，这场比赛我们铁定赢。
冒昧	màomèi	make bold	我可以冒昧地向您请教一个问题吗？
抽搐	chōuchù	twitch	他激动得嘴唇抽搐起来。
压抑	yāyì	hold back; constrain	我压抑不住好奇心，走了过去。
挣扎	zhēngzhá	struggle	我挣扎着爬上了楼。
爬(起来)	pá (qǐlái)	get up; climb	
揩(干)	kǎi (gān)	wipe (clean)	他小心地揩干手，接过礼物。
披	pī	put on (over); cover	这是一只披着羊皮的狼。
毕恭毕敬	bìgōngbìjìng	extremely deferential	村里的学生对老师毕恭毕敬。
大肉	dàròu	pork	有些东北人把猪肉叫做大肉。

趁 (热)	chèn (rè)	take the chance; seize the advantage	他趁休息的十分钟给家里打了个电话。
惊天动地	jīngtiāndòngdì	shock heaven and shake earth	昨晚的爆炸声惊天动地。
从容	cōngróng	calm and unhurried	从容不迫是说一个人不慌不忙很镇定。
扫视	sǎoshì	glance; run down	他扫视了一眼房间，决定不在这儿住。

QUESTIONS FOR DISCUSSION

1. Who is Qi Ziyun? What was his plight at the beginning of the Cultural Revolution?
2. How do you characterize Yu Changsheng's attitude toward and relationship with Qi Ziyun?
3. Why does Yu Changsheng tell Qi about beating his son?
4. List three details that support Yu Changsheng's belief in Chinese cultural tradition.
5. What do you think of Yu's breaking of the rules for Qi?
6. What do you suppose would be Qi Ziyun's purpose of fleeing his confinement that night?
7. Where in the story do you see the working of *li* and *ren*? In what ways are *li* and *ren* more powerful than political or economic power?

1. 齐子耘是什么人？他在文化大革命初期有着什么样的困境？
2. 于长生对齐子耘的态度是怎样的？他们是什么关系？
3. 为什么于长生要告诉齐子耘他打了自己的儿子？
4. 请找出三个细节说明于长生对中国传统文化的信仰。
5. 你觉得于长生该不该不顾规定为齐子耘破例？
6. 你觉得齐子耘那晚从学校逃出来原本想做什么？
7. 这个故事是怎样表现"礼"和"仁"的？"礼"和"仁"在什么意义上比政治、经济力量更强大？

AUTHOR BIO

"Keeping a low profile" doesn't quite convey the meaning of 守静 (shǒujìng)—an expression Nie Xinsen (1948–) uses to describe himself. Born in the ancient city of Xiangtan in Hunan, Nie started to write in middle school. He worked for Zhuzhou Timber Company for thirteen years, pursuing his passion in literature all during that time. He managed to get four years of formal training at the Lu Xun Institute for Literature and Beijing University between 1984 and 1988. He has published more than fifty books. Among them are four full-length novels, including *Furen Dang* (夫人党) and *Langman Rensheng* (浪漫人生); sixteen collections of novellas; and the short stories *Taipingyang Yuedui de Zuihou Yi Ci Yanzou* (太平洋乐队的最后一次演奏), *Youhuo* (诱惑), and *Sheng Si Yi Ju* (生死一局). He has published two volumes of poetry, six volumes of essays, and studies of aspects of Chinese cultural heritage such as the Chinese New Year, Chinese last names, and local styles of architecture. His work has been translated into English, French, Japanese, and Russian. Although he used to write short-shorts only on the side, recently he has turned to them increasingly, noting that he finds "the challenges of a superb performance on a very small stage exciting." A former vice chairman of the Hunan Writers Association, Nie now serves as the association's emeritus honorary head. He also brush paints illustrations for his books. He is recognized in China as a leading figure of the short-short genre today.

第二章

孝

这篇短文为《孝经》¹所启发。重返这一古老经典也是因为当"孝"被翻译为"孩子对父母的虔诚"时,太过经常地被误解为是一种交易关系,一种会迫使儿女对父母产生亏欠感,因而不得不回报他们养育之恩的关系。在《孝经》成典的时代,人们对人际关系的诠释跟我们今天可能不太一样。今天,当我们以权力的大小或利益冲突的轻重为基准解读家庭关系时,家庭成员间的交往就有了契约／合同关系的负面属性,孝也因此被错误地赋予支配和征服的蕴含。虽然利用和滥用孝之本意的现象不可避免,但这撼动不了孝在中国两千多年传统美德中至高无上的地位。近年来在中国,孝也再一次地吸引越来越多的关注。

《孝经》的开篇一章写到:"子曰:夫孝,德之本也,教之所由生也"。²我们可以把对父母的侍奉视为孝的开始,但孔子在本章所说的话明确强

---

1. 《孝经》相传是一位弟子问孝时,孔子回答的纪录。《孝经》的原文很短,只有十八个短章,却是中国从汉代(公元前206年 - 公元220年)以来启蒙教育的必读书。这个传统一直延续到20世纪。在中国历史上,打好道德言行的基础一直是教育孩子不可或缺的一部分,它比学会读书写字或许来的更重要。
2. 请去 http://ctext.org/xiao-jing 查阅《孝经》的中英文对照版。开篇的这句话引入了《孝经》的主题和目的。杰出的汉学家詹姆斯．理雅各(1815 - 1897)是这个版本的翻译。

CHAPTER 2

XIAO

The *Classic of Filial Piety*[1] was the inspiration for this introduction. We went back to the ancient text because *xiao*, translated as "filial piety," has too often been understood in the sense of business transactions that oblige sons and daughters to feel indebted and to repay their parents for raising them. Human relationships in China at the time of *The Classic of Filial Piety* were differently imagined than in our time. When family relationships today are represented as power based or framed by conflicts of interest, they take on the negative attributes of contractual relationships, and *xiao* thus inappropriately connotes dominance or subjugation. Manipulation and abuses do happen, but *xiao* has been a supreme virtue in Chinese tradition for more than two millennia and recently has been attracting renewed interest in China.

In the introductory paragraph of *The Classic of Filial Piety*, Confucius speaks of *xiao* as "the root of (all) virtue, and the (stem) out of which grows (all moral) teaching."[2] To attend to the needs of one's parents may be the start of *xiao*, but this passage clearly emphasizes that the goal of *xiao* is to establish one's character. The paragraph ends by quoting a line from the

---

1. Purporting to be the record of Confucius's answer to a disciple's question about *xiao*, *The Classic of Filial Piety*, a brief text of eighteen chapters, was a primer in schools from the Han (206 BCE–220 CE) until it disappeared in the twentieth century. Learning the basics of moral behavior in historical China was an integral part of a child's education, more important perhaps than learning how to read and write.
2. Please access *The Classic of Filial Piety* in parallel text at http://ctext.org/xiao-jing (accessed August 8, 2015). This quote from the opening paragraph/chapter introduces the theme and the goal of the work. James Legge (1815–1897), a most accomplished sinologist, is the translator. Hereafter cited as *The Classic of Filial Piety*.

调，孝的目的是塑造品格。开篇从《诗经》[3]中的"大雅"部分引述此行作为结束语："《大雅》云：'无念尔祖，聿修厥德'"。[4]

《孝经》用三分之一的篇幅解释了对生活在现实社会中的个人来说孝为何意。也就是说，一个人在担当各种不同社会和家庭职责时，怎样表现才算得上是孝。比如，如果一个人高居显赫官位，那么，对辖区内人民的体察尊重和尽忠职守就应该是这个人孝行的结晶和体现。

《孝经》的又一个三分之一解释了为什么孝是为人之根本。这部分强调了孝的自然属性："夫孝，天之经也，地之义也，民之行也"。[5] 换言之，孝是天经地义的，是人类最基本的行为准则。在父母之爱中长大的我们会有回报的意愿，这是人之常情，一个跟春播秋获一样的自然常态。在孔子看来，没有这样的意愿才是摒弃仁德，因为它有悖自然法则。《孝经》确实要求晚辈和处于从属地位的人多表达对长辈和上级的尊重，理由是：即使是天子，全天下的统治者，他也首先是他父母的儿子。恰恰是他对父母的尊重和侍奉培育了他治理天下的品德。

阅读以下的故事时，请不要忽略孝的本意和目的。《孝经》对父母之爱的阐述可能有些过于笼统，也许是把父母之爱的自然、无条件视为理所当然。但即便如此，这里所说的父母之爱也与从弱者手中攫取回报无关。相反，《孝经》强调了父母之爱是一种毫无杂念，只为孩子好的倾心之爱。这种爱是孩子对爱的最初体验，是孩子学习关爱他人的第一课。儒家的礼尚往来推崇由此爱而生的连锁效应，并把这样的反应——例如，一个孩子由爱产生的第一次美德之举——看做是孝的表现，因为孝是道德情感和美德的起源[6]。因此，从更广泛的意义上说，孝是指从家庭而生、由教化而成的爱人之心。

---

3. 《诗经》是中国第一部诗歌总集，由孔子编订。它的其它英译名还有：The Classic of Poetry, Book of Songs and Book of Odes等。《诗经》由公元前11世纪到公元前6世纪的诗歌作品组成，也是儒家经典之一。"大雅"是《诗经》的四个部分之一。
4. 此句引自《孝经》的第一个章节"开宗明义"。请去http://ctext.org/xiao-jing查看。
5. 请前往http://ctext.org/xiao-jing并参看《孝经》中题为"三才"的章节。
6. 网站同上。这段文字来自对《孝经》中题为"圣治"章节的思考。

"Great Refined Odes" of *The Book of Poetry*:³ "Do not just commemorate your ancestors; cultivate your virtue."⁴

About one-third of *The Classic of Filial Piety* is dedicated to what being "filial" means for individuals in society and details the varied duties of a person in different social and familial roles. For someone acting in the role of a high official, the act of *xiao* crystallizes in the respect for and good service to the governed.

Another third of the text explains why *xiao* is the most important of all human acts. That it is a natural attribute is emphasized: "Filial piety is the pattern of heaven, the standard of the earth, the norm of conduct for the people."⁵ The norm of our life—we grow up in our parents' love and have a desire to reciprocate that love—is as natural as sowing in spring and harvesting in fall. The absence of filial desire is, for Confucius, a rejection of virtue, because it violates the natural way. *The Classic of Filial Piety* does, in fact, require more displays of respect from children and those in subordinate positions, for even the Son of Heaven, the ruler of all under heaven, is first of all a son to his parents. And his respect and care for them in turn constitute his virtue to rule.

Please keep the goal of *xiao* in mind as you read the following stories. *The Classic of Filial Piety* may generalize parental love and take for granted its natural unconditional attributes, but the teaching is not at all about exacting returns from the less powerful. Instead, it emphasizes parental love as a child's first experience of love, the love of someone purely for his or her own self. It is a child's first lesson in what it means to care for another. Confucian reciprocity encourages like responses and regards such responses—for instance, a child's first ethical act—as an instance of *xiao*, or the very root of moral sensibility and virtue.⁶ So in a broader sense, *xiao* denotes the cultivated love of others that starts with family.

---

3. "Great Refined Odes" is one of the four parts of *The Book of Poetry*, which is also translated variously as *The Classic of Poetry*, *Book of Songs*, and *Book of Odes*. *The Book of Poetry* is one of the five Confucian classics composed of poems from the eleventh century to the sixth century BCE.
4. Please see the opening chapter, "The Scope and Meaning of the Treatise," in *The Classic of Filial Piety*. The sentence in Chinese is "無念爾祖，聿脩厥德."
5. Please see the "The Three Powers" in *The Classic of Filial Piety*.
6. Please see "The Government of the Sages" in *The Classic of Filial Piety* for the thought developed here.

本章的四个故事都是孝在生活中演绎的片段。它们强调了孝常常被忽略的两个方面：孝的相关属性及其培育爱心的积极功能。《灯祭》展示了由父亲的爱和孩子的忠相互作用而构成的孝的整体。这家人积极的生活方式，以及他们对死亡的回应等，也向我们展示了在儒家文化中，孝是由什么而"责成"的。《寄钱》中，当儿子对尽孝道的义务有误解时，母亲幸福的源泉就变成了她获取人生快乐的障碍。《孝经》中还谈到君子应该如何有爱心，亲民如父母[7]。选入《秀鸭婆》这个故事是因为主人公身上体现了孝的另一面——悌，以及孝悌和君子尊严的关系。今天的中国社会还存在着不尽人意的方方面面。在《过完夏天再去天堂》里，子女们对父爱的视而不见，尤其令人痛心。与其说孝是理性的产物，不如说孝更是基于生活的情感。孝常在意想不到之处给力，无论是我们年轻，老了，还是已经故去。

---

7. 网站同上。这个观点来自对《孝经》中题为"广至德"这一章节的思考。尤其"恺悌君子，民之父母"这句话是上述所言的依据。

The four stories here are snapshots of *xiao* in action, emphasizing two oft-neglected aspects of the concept—*xiao*'s relational nature and its agency in cultivating love. "Father Makes the Lantern" presents a parent's love and a child's devotion as constituting parts of a whole; their family's engaging way of life and reaction to death show what "obliges" *xiao* in Confucian culture. When filial obligation is misunderstood in "Money Order," the mother's very source of happiness becomes an obstacle to her joy in life. *The Classic of Filial Piety* also speaks of the man of honor as being "affectionate" like "the father and mother of the people."[7] "Little She" is included for its emphasis on the *ti* aspect of *xiao* and its depiction of the link between *xiao* and personal honor. China today can be disheartening, especially when we see a father's love going unnoticed in "Heaven-Bound, but After Summer." Yet more a matter of the heart than a product of reason, *xiao* empowers in unexpected ways, no matter whether one is young, old, or even no longer living.

---

7. Please see "Amplification of 'the Perfect Virtue' " in *The Classic of Filial Piety*. The sentence in Chinese is "愷悌君子，民之父母."

1
灯 祭

迟子建

父亲在世时,每逢过年我就会得到一盏灯。

那不是寻常的灯。从门外的雪地上捡回一个罐头瓶,然后将一瓢开水倒进瓶里,啪的一声,瓶底均匀地落下来,灯罩便诞生了,再用破棉絮将它擦得亮亮的。灯的底座是木制的,有花纹,底座中心钉透一根钉子,把半截红烛固定在上面,待到夜幕降临时,点燃蜡烛,再小心翼翼地落下灯罩。我提着这盏灯,觉得自己风光无限。

父亲给我做这样一盏灯总要花上很多工夫。就说做灯罩,总要捡回五六个瓶子才能做成一个。尽管如此,除夕夜父亲总能让我提上一盏称心如意的灯。没有月亮的除夕夜,这盏灯就是月亮了。我提着灯怀揣一盒火柴东家走西家串,每到一家都将灯吹灭,听人家夸几句这灯有多好,然后再心满意足地点燃蜡烛去另一家。每每回到家里时,蜡烛烧得只剩下一汪油了。那时父亲会笑吟吟地问:"把那些光全折腾没了吧?"

"全给丢在路上了。"我说,"剩下最亮的光赶紧提回家来了。"

"还真顾家啊。"父亲打趣着我,去看那汪蜡烛油上斜着的一束蓬勃芬芳的光。

父亲说过年要里里外外都是光明的,所以不仅我手中有灯,院子里也是有灯的。高高挂起的是红灯,灯笼穗长长的,风一吹刷刷响。低处的是冰

1

FATHER MAKES THE LANTERN

Chi Zijian

When Father was alive, I would get a lantern every New Year. This was no ordinary lantern. From outside, Father would retrieve a glass jar covered in snow then pour a dipperful of boiling water into it. When the bottom of the jar snapped off evenly—*pa!*—the lantern shade was born. Father would polish it to a shine with used cotton fiber. The lantern base was made of finely grained wood. Half of a red candle was fixed at its center on an upward-pointing nail. Father would wait until night fell to light the candle, then carefully drop the shade in its place. I was pleased beyond words when I carried such lanterns in my hand.

Every New Year Father spent a lot of time making the new lantern for me. Just the shade alone would take five or six jars to get one to snap off right. Be that as it may, Father always managed to make a lantern to my heart's content. On those moonless nights of New Year's Eve, Father's lantern became the moon. I would carry the lantern, along with a box of matches, and make the rounds from house to house, blowing out the candle at each stop and enjoying the compliments I received until, fully satisfied, I would light the candle again and depart for another house. By the time I returned home, all that remained of the candle was a puddle of wax. Father would then playfully inquire, "Did you squander all that light?"

"I left all that light on the road," I would reply, "but came rushing back with the brightest."

"How very thoughtful of you!" Father would joke as he looked at the vigorous and sweet-smelling light leaning from the puddle of wax.

Father said all must be lit up inside and outside on New Year's, so not only did I have a lantern in my hand, there were also lanterns in our courtyard. High up, red lanterns were hung, with long tassels that rustled in the wind;

灯，放在大门口的木墩上。无论是高出屋脊的红灯，还是安闲地坐在低处的冰灯，都让人觉得温暖。但不管它们多么动人，都不如父亲送给我的灯美丽。因为有了年，就觉得日子是有盼头的；因为有了父亲，年也就显得有声有色；而如果又有了父亲送我的灯，年则妖娆迷人了。

我一年年地长大了，后来，父亲不再送灯给我，我已经不是那个提着灯串来串去的小孩子了。我开始在灯下想心事。但每逢除夕，院子里照例要在高处挂起红灯，在低处摆上冰灯。

然而，父亲没能走到老年就去世了。父亲去世的当年我们没有点灯。别人家的院子里灯火辉煌，我们家却黑漆漆的。我坐在暗处发呆：点灯的时候父亲还不回来，看来他是迷路了。我多想提着父亲送我的灯到路上接他回来啊。爸爸，回家的路这么难找吗？从此之后，虽然照例要过年，但是我再也没有提着灯的福气了。

一进腊月，家里就开始忙年。姐姐会来信说年忙到什么地步了，比如说被子拆洗完了，各种吃食也谁备得差不多了，然后催我早点儿回家过年。所以，不管我身在哈尔滨，西安还是北京，总是干里迢迢地冒着严寒往家奔，当然今年也不例外。腊月廿六我赶回家中，母亲知道这个日子我会回去的，因为腊月廿七那天，我们姐弟要"请"父亲回家过年。

我们去看父亲了。给他献过烟和酒，又烧了些纸钱，已经成家立业的弟弟叩头对父亲说："爸爸，我有自己的家了，今年过年去儿子家吧，我家住在……"弟弟把他家的住址门牌号重复了几遍，怕父亲记不住。我又补充说："离综合商场很近。"父亲生前喜欢到综合商场去买皮蛋来下酒，那地方想必他是不会忘的。

ice lanterns sat low on the wooden blocks at the gate. Whether they were red lanterns above the roof or the low-lying icy ones sitting cozily on their blocks, the lanterns all made people feel warm. But however lovely they might have been, they were not as beautiful as the lanterns Father gave me. The New Year's celebration gave us something to look forward to as we went about our everyday lives. Because Father was a part of it, the New Year was colorful and full of life, and adding Father's lantern gave the occasion an enchanting charm.

Year by year, I grew up, and eventually Father stopped making lanterns for me. I was no longer the child making the rounds with a lantern in her hand but a young woman who found herself absorbed in her own thoughts under lantern light. Still, on every New Year's Eve, red lanterns would hang high and ice lanterns would lie low in our courtyard.

Then Father died before his time. We did not light any lanterns that year. Amid our neighbors' brightly lit courtyards, ours was pitch-black. I sat thinking in darkness: *It's time to light the lanterns, yet Father is still not home. He must have gotten lost. How I wish I could meet him on the road and lead him back with the lantern he gave me lighting the way! Father, is it really so hard to find the way home?* From that time on, the custom of the New Year's celebration has continued in our family, but I forever lost the good fortune of receiving a lantern from my father.

Still, once the twelfth lunar month rolled around, preparations for the New Year would start. My elder sister would write to tell me their progress, that they had, for example, picked out the stitches and washed all the cover sheets of quilts and that the many different dishes were almost ready. She would urge me to get home soon. It didn't matter if I was in Harbin, Xi'an, or Beijing, I would brave the freezing cold and rush the hundreds of miles toward home. This year was, of course, no exception. I got home on the twenty-sixth. Mother knew I would be back on that day, because on the twenty-seventh my younger brother and I would always go to "invite" Father home for the New Year.

We went to see Father. We offered him wine and cigarettes and burned some paper money. My brother, now married with a family, kowtowed to him and said, "Dad, I have a family of my own now. Please come home with me for the New Year this time. My home is at . . ." He repeated the address a number of times to make sure Father could remember it. I helped by adding, "It's very close to the department store," because Father used to frequent the store to get preserved eggs to go with his drink. He must still remember the place.

父亲的房子上落着雪，有时从树林深处传来几声鸟鸣。我们一边召唤着父亲回家过年，一边离开墓地。因为母亲住在姐姐家，所以我们都到那儿去了。姐姐的孩子小虎刚过周岁，已经会走路了。一进门母亲就抱着小虎从里屋出来了，我点着小虎的脑门说："把你姥爷领回来过年了。"小虎乐了，他一乐大家也乐了。

可是，当晚小虎哭个不休。该到睡觉的时辰了，他就是不睡。母亲关了灯，千般万般地哄，他却仍然嘹亮地哭。直到天亮时，他才稍稍老实起来。姐夫说："可能咱爸跟到这儿来了，夜里稀罕虎了。"说得跟真事儿似的，我们都信了。父亲生前没有见过他的外孙，而他又是极喜欢孩子的。我们从墓地回来，纷纷到了姐姐家，他怎么会路过女儿的家门而不入呢？而他一进门就看见了小虎，当然更舍不得离开了。

母亲决定把父亲"送"到弟弟家去。早饭后，母亲穿戴好，推着自行车，对父亲说："孩子也稀罕过了，跟我到儿子家去过年吧。"母亲哄孩子似的说："慢慢跟着走。街上热闹，可别东看西看的，把你丢了，我可就不管了。"

母亲把父亲"送"走的当夜小虎果然睡得很安稳。第二天早晨起来，他把屋子挨个走了个遍，一双黑莹莹的眼睛滴溜溜地转着，东看西看，仿佛在找什么。小虎是不是在想：姥爷到哪儿去了？

初三过后，父亲要被"送"回去了。我多希望永远也不"送"他回去。天那么冷，他又有风湿病，一个人往回走会是什么样的心情呢？

正月十五到了。多年前的这一天，在一个落雪的黄昏，我降临人世。那时天将要黑了，窗外还没有挂灯，父亲便送我一个乳名：迎灯。没想到我迎来了千盏万盏灯，却再也迎不来父亲送给我的那盏灯了。

Snow fell on Father's house; from deep in the woods came the sporadic twittering of birds. As we were leaving the graveyard, we called out over and over for Father to come home for the New Year.

Because Mother was staying at my sister's house, the family gathered there. Her son Xiaohu was only one year old and had just started to walk. As soon as we stepped in, Mother emerged from the back room holding Xiaohu in her arms. I tapped on his forehead and told him, "We've brought your grandpa home for the New Year." Xiaohu smiled—a smile that made everyone happy.

But that night, oddly, Xiaohu cried nonstop. He wouldn't go to sleep when it was his bedtime. Mother turned off the light and tried her best to calm him down, but Xiaohu kept wailing loudly. He didn't quiet down until dawn. My brother-in-law said, "It might be that Father followed you here. He must have been playing with Xiaohu last night." He spoke as if he were an eyewitness, and we all chose to believe him. Father died before he had a chance to meet his grandson, but he was a man extremely fond of children. How could Father have passed by his daughter's house when we came from the graveyard? He certainly couldn't have torn himself away when, once inside, he saw Xiaohu.

Mother decided to "take" Father to my brother's house. After breakfast, she dressed in clothes suitable for going out. As she walked her bike from the house, she said to Father, "You've played with your grandson, now it's time to come with me to your son's house for the New Year." As if talking to a child, Mother gently added, "Take it easy and follow me. The streets are crowded. You'll be on your own if you get distracted and lost."

As expected, Xiaohu slept soundly that night. When he got up the next morning, he went around the house from room to room, his black eyes darting here and there, as if searching for someone. Could he have been wondering: *Where is Grandpa?*

On the fourth day of the New Year, we "took" Father back. How I wished we had never needed to do that. It was cold, and he had rheumatism. How would he feel having to go back alone?

It was the fifteenth day of the first lunar month. On this day, many years ago, I was born at the snowy dusk. Darkness was falling and the lanterns outside were ready to go up. Father therefore nicknamed me "Yingdeng," which means "inviting the lanterns." I had "invited" tens of thousands of lanterns but had never anticipated that a time would come when I would no longer receive a lantern from Father.

走在冷寂的大街上，忽然发现一个苍老的卖灯人。那灯是六角形的，用玻璃做成的，玻璃上还贴着"福"字。我立刻想到了父亲，正月十五这一天父亲的院子该有一盏灯的。我买下了一盏灯，天将黑时，将它送到了父亲的墓地。"嚓"地划根火柴，周围的夜色就颤动了一下。父亲的房子在夜色中显得华丽醒目，凄切动人。

　　这是我送给父亲的第一盏灯。那灯守着他，虽灭犹燃。

(2012)

Walking along the cold, deserted street, I suddenly encountered an old peddler of lanterns. The lanterns were hexagonal in shape, made of glass, and with the character that means "blessing" on them. Father came to mind immediately—*There should be a lantern in Father's yard on this day!* I got a lantern and brought it to Father's grave at dusk. *Crash!* The air around Father's house shook at the strike of the match. It stood out with mournful splendor in the darkness of the night.

This was the first lantern I gave Father. It kept him company. The candle might have burned out, but the light shone on.

(2012)

VOCABULARY AND USAGE

破	pò	worn	你的棉衬衫都穿破了。
花纹	huāwén	natural pattern	这种木头的花纹很好看。
(钉)透	(dìng) tòu	penetrate	子弹穿透了我的手心。
(半)截	(bàn) jié	section; length	这根蜡烛太长了，做灯笼一小截就够了。
待(到)	dài (dào)	by the time when	待到明年金秋时我们再相会。
夜幕	yèmù	curtain of night	"夜幕降临"比"天黑了"更诗意一些。
降临	jiànglín	befall; descend	
小心翼翼	xiǎoxīnyìyì	with utmost care	老人睡着了，她小心翼翼地关上了门。
风光无限	fēngguāngwúxiàn	exultant	戴着金牌回国，她风光无限。
做成	zuò chéng	make (into)	这盏灯是用罐头瓶做成的。
落(下)	luò (xià)	drop; lower down	秋风落尽了园中的树叶。
称心如意	chènxīnrúyì	utmost satisfaction	这份工作称心如意！
怀揣	huáichuāi	carry	年轻人大都怀揣梦想。
人家	rénjiā	other people	她跟人家说要去美国。
串	chuàn	go from place to place; run about	在乡下，春节就是走村串寨、探亲访友的时间。
有多好	yǒu duō hǎo	how great it is	她见人就说回到家有多好。

心满意足	xīnmǎnyìzú	satisfied	他只要吃饱睡好就心满意足。
汪	wāng	a measure word for liquid	这么一大汪血，人一定伤得不轻。
折腾	zhēteng	do something repeatedly; mess around	她一会儿点灯，一会儿灭灯，很快把灯折腾坏了。
赶紧	gǎnjǐn	hurriedly	天黑了，你赶紧回家吧。
顾家	gùjiā	love and care for one's family	很多独生子女都很顾家。
打趣	dǎqù	banter; tease	这个演员很会打趣，所以有很多粉丝。
蓬勃	péngbó	full of vitality	这里的教育事业近几年蓬勃发展。
芬芳	fēnfāng	fragrant	春天的园子里花朵芬芳。
穗	suì	tassel	这灯笼穗儿是用丝线做的。
动人	dòngrén	moving; touching	她讲的故事很动人。
(有)盼头	(yǒu) pàntou	hope; good prospects	儿子是她的盼头。
有声有色	yǒushēngyǒusè	vivid	她故事讲得有声有色。
妖娆迷人	yāoráo mírén	enchanting and charming	最妖娆迷人的是江南的山水。
则	zé	be; then	不进则退。
发呆	fādāi	in a daze	他在一旁发呆老半天了。
走到(老年)	zǒudào (lǎonián)	live to; get to	他陪伴着她走到了生命的尽头。
灯火辉煌	dēnghuǒhuīhuáng	brightly lit	一到圣诞节这条街就灯火辉煌。
漆黑	qīhēi	pitch-black; pitch-dark	"黑漆漆"这用法来自"漆黑，"都是很黑的意思。
忙年	mángnián	prepare for the Spring Festival	腊月底了，家家都忙年呢。
地步	dìbù	extent	作为朋友，我只能做到这个地步了。
千里迢迢	qiānlǐtiáotiáo	far away; all the way	每年春节，他都千里迢迢赶回老家过年。
廿	niàn	twenty	农历还用廿表示日期。
献(烟, 酒)	xiàn (yān, jiǔ)	offer respectfully	她把此书献给已故的父亲。
成家立业	chéngjiālìyè	married and established	父母期待儿子早日成家立业。

FATHER MAKES THE LANTERN 49

想必	xiǎngbì	most probably	起飞十小时了，想必她已安全到达了。
不休	bùxiū	nonstop	那里总是战乱不休。
(时)辰	(shí) chén	traditional Chinese time unit(s)	时辰到了，该上路了。
千般万般	qiānbānwànbān	all the different kinds/ways	我就是千般万般努力，报不上名也没用。
哄(孩子)	hǒng (háizi)	lull	妈妈终于把孩子哄睡着了。
稀罕	xīhan	care about; love	这位老人一辈子稀罕字画。
纷纷	fēnfēn	one after another	记者们纷纷赶到现场。
挨个	āigè	one by one	桌上的菜她挨个尝了一遍。
滴溜溜	dīliūliū	going round and round	他不说话，两只眼睛却滴溜溜地转。
乳名	rǔmíng	infant name	乳名是婴儿时的小名。
冷寂	lěngjì	quiet and lonely	乡下的冷寂很难熬。
划(火柴)	huá (huǒchái)	strike	火柴湿了，划不着了。
凄切	qīqiè	mournful	看着她凄切的表情我很难过。
(虽灭)犹(燃)	(suīmiè) yōu (rán)	as if; still	文中的父亲虽死犹生。

QUESTIONS FOR DISCUSSION

1. How is this a story of *xiao*, with *xiao* meaning "cultivated love of others"?
2. How do you understand the title of the story? How is Father a lantern?
3. How does the story present *xiao*'s (natural) transmission in time?
4. Please retell the family's ritual of getting Father home for the New Year. How do you explain the existence of such a ritual/custom?
5. Could Xiaohu really be looking for Grandpa that morning? How does the juxtaposition of the "real" and the "imagined" work in the story?
6. How do the narrator and her family cope with the fact that Father has passed away? What have you learned from them about the local view of the dead and the living?
7. What positive functions of *xiao* tradition do you see from this story?

1. 这怎么会是一个关于"孝"的故事呢?"孝"在此意为教化养成的爱心。
2. 你对本篇的题目是怎样理解的?为什么说父亲是灯?
3. 在这个故事里,"孝"是怎样(自然)传承的?
4. 请用自己的话讲讲这家人请父亲回家过年的仪式过程。你怎么解释这样的仪式或习俗的存在?
5. 小虎那天早上真的是在找姥爷吗?真实与想象的迭用在本篇起到了什么作用?
6. 叙述者和家人是如何应对父亲离世这一事实的?通过这一家人你对当地的生死文化有了什么了解?
7. 这个故事让你看到了"孝"传统哪些积极正面的功能?

AUTHOR BIO

Born in 1964, Chi Zijian is arguably the most accomplished female writer in China today. She began writing in 1983 and has published a dozen full-length novels, including *Shuxia* (树下), *Chenzhong Xiangche Huanghun* (晨钟响彻黄昏), *Wei Manzhouguo* (伪满洲国), and *Chuanguo Yunceng de Qinglang* (越过云层的晴朗); many novellas; and short story and essay collections. Her work has been translated into French, Japanese, English, and Italian. This story was adapted from her semiautobiographical prose "Lantern Offering" (灯祭) in memory of her father. It first appeared in the second volume of her four-volume collection of prose *Chi Zijian Sanwen* (迟子建散文) in 2009. Two popular journals in China, *Selected Micro-fiction* (微型小说选刊) and *Love • Marriage • Family* (爱情婚姻家庭), reprinted it in 2013. In real life Chi Zijian's father was an elementary school principal who died in 1985. Her autobiographical novella on losing her husband after four years of marriage, *All the Nights in the World* (世界上所有的夜晚), won the Lu Xun Literature Prize in 2007; this was the third time she had won the award, and to this day she remains the only three-time winner. In recent years, Chi Zijian's work has dealt increasingly with everyday subjects and introspective themes. For some readers her writing is the lamp of beauty and dignity of human life in modern Chinese literature.

2
秀鸭婆[9]

韩少功

这个汉子绰号"秀鸭婆",眼下就坐在我面前,提到的一段婚礼胡闹,到让我略有印象。当时是婚后第二天吧,大家意犹未尽上门起哄。姚大甲用一个陪嫁的马桶罩住他脑袋,整的他两手困于糖果,腾不出手来摘马桶,只能瓮声瓮气地喊:"憋死我了,憋死我了……救命啊……"那样子实在好笑。

大甲乐颠颠地强令他交代洞房勾当,否则要脱掉他的裤子。他死死抓住裤头,一个劲地央求:"我讲,我讲。"

有人不耐烦:"那你就快讲!"

他左看看,右看看,发现自己无处可逃,才吞吞吐吐地说:"昨天晚上见她眼睛翻白,全身出汗,以为她会死了……后来才晓得,那是她喜欢……"

大家一片浪浪的大笑。

他趁机逃出魔掌,跳到远处,一脸涨红。"你们这些城里崽……好拐啊,好拐啊,好拐啊……"一时竟骂不出别的什么话。

---

9. "秀鸭婆" is a local colloquial expression. "秀" in Chinese denotes elegance and beauty, "鸭" means literally a duck, and "婆" an old woman. "Little She" is an instance of free translation based on our understanding of the text.

2
LITTLE SHE

Han Shaogong

The man nicknamed "Little She" now sat right in front of me. The mention of our naughty behavior at his wedding[8] helped refresh my memory of him. It must have been the day after the ceremony... Still hungover from the night before, we invited ourselves to his house for some more fun. Our friend Yao Dajia put a nightstool, a dowry gift from the bride's family, over Little She's head. He couldn't remove it because his hands were busy giving candies to us. He looked really funny, because all he could do was to moan pathetically from under the stool, "Help, help... you are suffocating me..."

The mirthful Dajia demanded an account of his consummation and threatened to pull off Little She's pants if he didn't comply. Holding onto his underwear, Little She pled for mercy. "Okay, okay... I'll tell you."

Someone got impatient: "Tell us now!"

He looked around—there was no way out—so he stammered, "Last night, when she rolled her eyes, drenched in sweat, I thought she was going to die... I didn't know she was having an orgasm..."

Everybody burst into salacious laughter

He took the opportunity to get free, leaping out of our devilish reach, his face all red. "You city folks,[9] you are bad, bad... bad..." He couldn't even come up with anything to call us other than "bad."

---

8. The details may vary depending on local customs, but the traditional practice of "teasing the newlyweds in the nuptial chamber" (闹洞房 *nào dòng fáng*) has been popular in China for a long time. Friends play jokes, mostly on the groom, to add to the celebration. Ang Lee's 1993 film *The Wedding Banquet* captured the complexity of the merrymaking.

9. The revelers were "sent-down youth" from cities. Chinese readers who know the history of this phenomenon and Han Shaogong's writing from the late 1960s and early 1970s would easily recognize them.

新娘子正巧挑水回家，见新郎叫骂不已，又听到众人大笑，猜出了什么，一张粉脸羞得通红，放下担子就跑，洒了好多水在青石板上。

这以后的故事是别人告诉我的，还有一些是经别人提示，我从遗忘中慢慢打捞出来的。是茶场里盖仓库还是盖宿舍？反正都差不多吧，这位队长去梁上钉稟条，一脚踩空，砸在一堆乱砖上，据说把男人的东西砸坏了。

坊间的传说是从此他很少回家去，有一天走进家门竟发现老婆抱着一个汉子在床上打滚，脱下的衣服丢得到处都是。狗叫声把床上人惊醒了。他当时进退两难，羞恼万分，竟把自己一张脸憋出了猪肝色。他后悔自己回家来取棉衣。

他老婆倒是大方，下床整理衣装和头发，把衣服递给野汉子，等对方穿戴好，还当着老公的面送野汉子出门。她回来后一声不吭，做好了饭菜，自己却不吃，收拾了几件衣物，抱孩子出门去了娘家。

村里几个后生劝他去把老婆接回来，他眼睛红红地说："没用，没用。她身子回来了，心还是在外边。"

有人怒气冲冲，鼓动他去把那个狗婆子打一顿。

他抹了把脸："这事怪不得她，只怪我。"

他变得沉默少言，只是一说到儿子就津津乐道，十分陶醉，眼中露出明亮的光辉。据他说，那个小崽子还不满两岁就能抓笔写字，虽然满纸都是天书，但一个格子里画几下，很有章法似的。

At that moment, the bride happened to enter, carrying the water she'd fetched. When she heard the groom's shouting of "bad" among our wild laughter, she sensed what had happened. Her pink face turned red with embarrassment. She dropped the buckets and ran out, spilling a lot of the water on the bluestone path.

What happened afterward, I learned partly from others. I salvaged the rest, with help, from the fragments of faded memory. Was it for a dorm or a warehouse at the tea farm? It doesn't really matter. Our man, a team leader by then,[10] slipped and fell when he went up the beam to build the herringbone structure. He crash-landed on a pile of bricks below; the fall, it is said, crushed his manhood.

As rumor on the street had it, he seldom went back home after that. One day when he did go home, he found his wife making passionate love to another man, their clothes flung all over. The dog barked and startled the two in bed. Uncertain whether he should stay or leave and choking with shame and anger, Little She's face turned the color of a pig's liver, and he instantly regretted his trip home for winter clothes.

His wife, however, appeared poised and dignified. She got out of bed, put on her clothes, and arranged her hair before she handed her fellow adulterer his clothes. After he was fully dressed, she saw him off at the gate, despite the presence of her husband. She didn't say a word to Little She when she came back in. She cooked a meal but didn't eat any of it herself. She packed some clothes and left for her mother's with their child in her arms.

A couple of guys in the village urged him to go get her back. He said, his eyes reddening, "It won't work, it won't work. She'll probably come back to me, but her heart won't."

Some, enraged, urged him to go beat the crap out of that bitch.

He ran his hand over his face: "It's not her fault. I'm the one to blame."

Afterward, he became a very quiet man, except when the subject of his son came up in conversation. He took great delight in talking about the boy, and a bright light shone from his eyes. He told people that his son could write with a pen before he was two and that although nothing was

---

10. A team was the administrative and production unit at the grass-roots level in China from 1958 to 1984. A team leader (队长) was the head of the unit.

他也惦记两个妹妹。大妹三岁那年,小妹出生,因为家里穷,又因为阴阳先生算出了两个命该过继的八字,被父母一起送给别人。父母去世以后,他常常买上几尺布和一包点心,翻过大王岭去看妹妹。两个妹妹一见他就哭,抱住他久久不放手。她们又黑又瘦的脸,结成麻绳一般的乱发,冻得满是血口子的手背,还有补丁叠补丁以至结成一大团的棉裤裆,让当哥的心痛如割。每次回家走到避人处,山坡上那两个小黑影不见了,融入天边晚霞里了,他就泪如泉涌。

三十岁那年,他去给父母上了坟,然后来到两个妹妹的继父继母跟前,扑通一声双膝跪地,前额砸在地上:"对不起,我要把她们带走。"

妹妹的继父母相互对视了一眼,不好说什么,只是请他起来。"也难得你当哥哥的有情有义,不过这七八年下来,不算我们两家说妥的三担谷,我们就算是养两只羊,也要吃掉成山的料吧?就算养两只鸡,也要吃掉一船的谷吧?"

"你们放心,我绝不让你们吃亏。你们说多少,就是多少。"

"这不是小数,你再想想。"

"不,今天你们不答应,我不会起来。"

双方后来商议的结果,是当哥的拆了两间屋,加上东讨西借,凑足了二十担谷的钱,总算把两个妹妹接回了家。

就凭这一条,不管他如何戴绿帽子,村里人说起他还是跷一根拇指;不管他婆娘如何浪,如何野,如何伤风败俗,村里人说起她也没太多恶语。

intelligible, with a few strokes in each grid, the page as a whole appeared to have some art of composition to it.

He couldn't get his mind off his two little sisters either. The younger one was born when the elder one was three. Too poor to raise the girls—whose lot, according to a fortune-teller, was to be adopted anyway because of the dates and times of their births—his parents gave them away together. After his parents died, he often climbed over the Dawang Ridge to visit them, bringing them pastries and a yard or two of material for making clothes. They'd cry the moment they saw him, holding his hands and not letting go. Their faces were dark and thin; their hair messy like knotted hemp; the backs of their hands covered with bleeding frostbites; and the stacked patches of their trousers bunched between their legs. The sight pierced their elder brother's heart. On his way home, when he had passed beyond their sight and the two little dots on the hillside vanished beyond the horizon with the sunset, he would burst into tears.

He turned thirty that year. After visiting his parents' grave, he went to his sisters' foster parents. He dropped to his knees and hit the ground with his forehead. "I'm sorry but I must take them with me," he said.

The foster parents looked at each other. It felt awkward to say anything, so they asked him to get to his feet. "You are a dear, good elder brother, but they have been with us for seven or eight years. Aside from the 300 *jin* of grain the two families agreed upon, had they been two sheep, a mountain of additional food would have been consumed . . . a boatful of grain would have been eaten, just to feed two chickens."

"Please be assured. I won't let you suffer any loss. It's how much you say it is."

"It's not a small amount. Please think it over."

"There is no need. I won't get up today until you agree."

As a result of their settlement, the elder brother tore down two rooms of his house and sold the building materials. He borrowed from here and there and got enough money for 2,000 *jin* of grain. Eventually, he succeeded in bringing his two little sisters home.

This deed alone got the villagers' thumbs-up when they talked about him, despite the fact that he'd been made a cuckold. Licentious, wild, and indecent she might have been, but the village gossip about his wife was rather forgiving because the husband and wife were determined to raise the two little sisters and they succeeded. They sent them to school for a

因为夫妻俩硬是把两个妹妹养大,让她们补读了几年书,还给小妹治好了癞子,把她送去省城治好了眼疾。待她们成人,哥嫂给她们各备一份嫁妆,一大柜,一中柜,两挑箱,四床绣花被,把她们打扮成镜子里的两朵花,风风光光嫁了出去。人们说,两个妹妹出嫁时都是哭得昏天黑地,哭得送行的女人们无不撩起袖口或衣角暗自拭泪。

秀鸭婆为此欠下了不少债,包括一位堂叔的钱,利滚利,三年间滚成了六百多元。这位堂叔几乎引起乡亲们的公愤,但秀鸭婆一直认账,坚持还完了最后一分钱。堂叔是一位孤老,死后还全靠这个侄子送终。他又出钱又出米,力排众议,到处张罗,坚持要为堂叔"做七",圆圆满满地完成了七天奠礼。"不是一家人,不进一个门——不管怎么样,他是我叔。"这是他事后对乡亲们的解释。

不久前遇到他时,他已经老了,还瘸了一条腿,已不能上房干活,只是帮儿子看守一个煤气站,卖罐装液化气的那种。遇到生意清冷,他就在屋后的湖边钓鱼。

他淡淡地说:"草木一秋,人生一世,这日子过得太快了。"

"梁队长,你这一辈子可不容易。"

"也没什么,大家都一样。"

"有些人不会这么想。"

"做好人,当然是要吃亏的。"

"是这话。"

"有时候会觉得很累,也没什么意思。"

"我相信。"

"一天天扛,总觉得自己扛不下去了。"

"人都没有铜头铁臂,都不是神仙,都有扛不下去的时候。"

"你会不会关虾子?"他突然换了个话题。

few years to make up for what they'd missed. They got the little one cured of a fungal infection and took her to the provincial capital for treatment of her eye disease. When the girls were old enough to marry, their brother and sister-in-law had prepared for each of them a dowry of a big wardrobe, a chest of drawers, two trunks, and four embroidered quilts. The husband and wife dressed them up so the two girls looked like flowers in the mirror and sent them off in style. Both sisters cried their hearts out as they were leaving and caused all the women seeing them off to wipe their tears silently with their sleeves or the hems of their garments.

Little She amassed a lot of debt in doing all this, including money he borrowed from an uncle, which with compound interest over three years became more than 600 yuan. A public outrage almost broke out against his uncle in the village, but Little She insisted on honoring the debt and paid it off to the last cent. Because the uncle was childless, it was Little She who took care of his burial when he died. Little She wouldn't hear that it wasn't his responsibility. He provided money and rice for the funeral, attending to every detail. He followed the ritual of "observing the seventh" and brought the seven-day service round to a perfect conclusion. "We are family living in the same compound and using the same gate. He was my uncle—that's what counts," he explained to the folks of the village afterward.

When I saw him again not long ago, he was old and crippled. No longer fit to work on roofs, he just watched a gas station for his son, the kind of store that sold liquid gas tanks. He would go fishing by the lake behind the store when business was slack.

"A year for plants, a life for humans, it is all too short," he said softly.

"Team Leader Liang, life surely hasn't been easy for you."

"I don't know about that. Life treats everybody the same."

"Not everybody thinks this way."

"A good man is bound to take a beating."

"Indeed."

"Sometimes being good wears me out and gets boring."

"I hear you."

"Under its weight every day, I have long felt that I can't carry on any more."

"It happens to everyone. Humans are not made of iron; we are not God." He suddenly changed the topic. "Do you know how to catch shrimp?"

"梁队长,我想起来了,当初就是你挑一担行李,送我到公路口……"

"白露一过,虾子就肥了,就呆了。"

他好像有点儿耳背,根本没看到我的惊讶和激动,只是冲着我笑了一下,再次把钓钩甩出去。我久久地凝视水面,凝望水里的青山倒影,水里的白云和蓝天,还有一只无声飞过的孤单白鹭。

(2013)

"Team Leader Liang, it came to me just now that you were the one who saw me off at the entrance to the highway, with my luggage on your shoulder pole..."

"Shrimp get fat and dumb soon after White Dew."[11]

He seemed a little hard of hearing. Totally oblivious to my realization and excitement, he simply smiled at me before he cast his line and hook again. I gazed at the surface of the lake for a long time, at the reflections of the green mountains, the white clouds, the blue sky in the water, and the lone egret flying silently across it.

(2013)

VOCABULARY AND USAGE

绰号	chuòhào	nickname	他来自东北，绰号"北大荒"。
眼下	yǎnxià	at the moment	你没看她眼下正忙着呢?
胡闹	húnào	mischief	婚礼"胡闹"是个习俗，为的是喜庆和热闹。
略	lüè	slightly	他的死因我略知一二。
意犹未尽	yìyóuwèijìn	not yet content; reluctant to leave	精彩的表演已结束，我却意犹未尽，不愿离开。
起哄	qǐhòng	jeer, boo and hoot	新娘子来了，闹婚的人开始起哄。
整	zhěng	make someone suffer; persecute	就是他妈妈做错了你也不能整孩子呀!
困(于)	kùn (yú)	be stranded	这只受伤的鸟被困于笼中。
腾出	téngchū	free oneself; make way	我今天太忙，腾不出空送你去打球。
摘	zhāi	take off	她只有晚上睡觉时才摘下假发。
好笑	hǎoxiào	laughable	他这是拿别人的痛苦开心，有什么好笑的?

---

11. White Dew is the fifteenth of the twenty-four seasons in the traditional Chinese calendar; it usually starts on September 7 or 8 and ends around September 22 or 23.

瓮声瓮气	wèngshēng wèngqì	growled; in a low, muffled voice	他说话瓮声瓮气的。
乐颠颠	lèdiāndiān	joyfully	听了我的解释他乐颠颠地回家了。
强令	qiánglìng	force	老板也不能强令员工周末加班。
勾当	gōudàng	dirty business	他的那些非法勾当跟我没关系！
死死	sǐsǐ	tightly	我死死抓住小偷不放。
一个劲	yīgèjìn	persistently	我已经道歉了，你为什么还一个劲哭呢？
央求	yāngqiú	beg	女儿再三央求，爸爸还是不同意。
吞吞吐吐	tūntūntǔtǔ	haltingly	你说话吞吞吐吐，心里一定有鬼。
晓得	xiǎodé	know	你哪里晓得这事儿的重要性呀！
浪	làng	dissolute	说女人"浪"也是说她放荡的意思。
涨红	zhànghóng	reddened	人害羞的时候脸会涨红。
崽	zǎi	young (of animals)	"城里崽"是指从城里来的年轻人。
拐	guǎi	crook	这里"拐"有"不厚道"和"骗人"的意思。
不已	bùyǐ	endlessly	这事我是做错了，已经后悔不已了。
羞	xiū	bashful	她羞得满脸通红。
经	jīng	through; after	这事儿经她一提醒我就想起来了。
遗忘	yíwàng	forget	他为人处事的真诚让人无法遗忘。
生产队长	shēngchǎn duìzhǎng	a production team leader	生产队长是一个生产队的负责人。
踩空	cǎi kōng	make a misstep	他一脚踩空掉到井里。
坊间	fāngjiān	in the streets	坊间传闻不可信。
打滚	dǎgǔn	roll	他肚子疼得直打滚。
丢	diū	mislay	他的房间很乱，丢满了脏衣服。
进退两难	jìntuìliǎngnán	in a dilemma	我对他又爱又恨，进退两难。

羞恼万分	xiūnǎowànfēn	extremely ashamed and angry	他虽然羞恼万分却没有责怪妻子。
憋	biē	suppress	他强憋着自己的怒火，脸都憋紫了。
野汉子	yěhànzi	male adulterer	"野汉子"跟"野小子"的意思不一样。
吭	kēng	utter a sound	我跟你说话呢，你为什么不吭声？
后生	hòushēng	young man	说这话的后生不太懂事。
怒气冲冲	nùqìchōngchōng	ablaze with anger	他怒气冲冲地问我，"你怎么能把孩子丢了？"
鼓动	gǔdòng	instigate; stir up	他一定是受人鼓动才动手打了妻子。
狗婆子/狗东西	gǒupózi/gǒudōngxi	bitch/son of a bitch	你说她是狗婆子，那你就是个狗东西。
(打一)顿	(dǎyī) dùn	a measure word	我玩游戏赢了十块钱，你为什么还打我一顿？
津津乐道	jīnjīnlèdào	take delight in talking about	如今喝茶时髦，很多人对茶文化津津乐道。
陶醉	táozuì	be infatuated with	他一说起儿子就一副陶醉的样子。
光辉	guānghuī	radiance	谁不喜欢太阳升起的光辉呢？
小崽子	xiǎozǎizi	a term of endearment, usually for small children	这小崽子眼睛里有故事。
满(纸)	mǎn (zhǐ)	full of; covered with	这满篇的废话是谁写的？
天书	tiānshū	abstruse writing	你在读天书吧，我怎么一句都听不懂。
章法	zhāngfǎ	orderly ways	他年纪不大，做事却很有章法。
惦记	diànjì	be concerned about	他惦记的不是妻子的过失，而是自己的过错。
阴阳先生	yīnyáng xiānsheng	geomancer	算命要请阴阳先生。
生辰八字	shēngchénbāzì	date and time of birth and their interpretation	我生辰八字不好，所以运气才这么差。
过继	guòjì	adopt	你们自己不能生，就过继一个孩子吧。

叠	dié	one on top of another	他说话的时候低着头，双手叠在胸前。
结(成)	jié (chéng)	form	天冷时水会结成冰。
裤裆	kùdāng	crotch (of trousers)	这种裤子的裤裆太短了。
心痛如割	xīn tòng rú gē	hurting badly	两个妹妹过得不好，哥哥心痛如割。
避人处	bì rén chù	a place where no one could see	楼梯拐角是个避人处，她常躲在那儿打电话。
融入	róngrù	integrate; merge into	你想融入主流社会吗？
泪如泉涌	lèirúquányǒng	tears gushing forth	"泪如泉涌"是说眼泪就像泉水一般流出。
上坟	shàngfén	visit someone's grave	清明节是给亲人上坟的日子。
扑通	pūtōng	sound of falling into water; plop; thump	他毫不犹豫，扑通一声跳进了湖里。
有情有义	yǒuqíngyǒuyì	kind and just	他是个有情有义的好大哥。
(说)妥	(shuō) tuǒ	ready; settled; finished	放心吧，你的事儿我已经都办妥了。
(东)讨(西)借	(dōng) tǎo (xījiè)	ask for; beg for	在这里，"讨"和"要"的意思差不多。
凑	còu	pool (money)	她夏天必须打很多工才能凑齐下一年的学费。
凭	píng	by reason of; rely on	他们凭自己的行动和业绩赢得尊敬。
戴绿帽子	dài lǜ nàozi	be a cuckold	在他的家乡，妻子给丈夫戴绿帽子就是伤风败俗。
伤风败俗	shāngfēngbàisú	immoral	
恶语	èyǔ	abusive expressions	乡亲们理解她，没有用恶语伤害她。
硬是	yìngshì	just; simply; obstinately	明明是他干的，可他硬是不承认。
昏天黑地	hūntiānhēidì	(feel) dizzy	这药劲儿很大，吃得我昏天黑地。
撩	liāo	lift up	看到地上有水，她撩起了裙子。
拭	shì	wipe (away)	"拭泪"就是"擦去眼泪"的意思。

张罗	zhāngluo	get busy about	每个周末回家，爸妈都为我张罗一桌好饭。
力排众议	lìpáizhòngyì	against all the odds	她有理有据，所以能力排众议，得到支持。
扛	káng	shoulder; endure	房租再涨我就扛不住了。
关	guān	shut; lock up; catch	我今天在树林里关了两只兔子。
耳背	ěrbèi	hard of hearing	他不想接我的话，所以就装耳背没听见。
甩	shuǎi	cast; swing	他大鞭子一甩，马就跑了起来。

QUESTIONS FOR DISCUSSION

1. Write a character sketch of Little She.
2. Why didn't his wife feel ashamed of her transgression?
3. Why didn't he divorce his wife? What sustains their marriage?
4. What signifies Little She's maturation at thirty?[12]
5. How is his expression of manhood an embodiment of *xiao*?[13]
6. Is there a "Big He" in Little She? How does the unity of the two fully flesh out the title character?
7. What do you think of the ending, especially as a comment on the status of *xiao* culture in contemporary China?

1. 请描述一下秀鸭婆这个人物。
2. 为什么他的妻子不对自己的出轨感到愧疚？
3. 为什么秀鸭婆不跟妻子离婚？是什么维系了他们的婚姻？
4. 什么证实了秀鸭婆的三十而立？
5. 从什么意义上说他成熟男人的标志也是对孝的一种表达？

---

12. "三十而立" (*sānshíérlì*) is among the most famous of Confucian sayings. James Legge's translation is: "At thirty, I stood firm." Among other translations are: "At thirty, I can be independent" and "At thirty, I establish myself."
13. "长兄如父" (*zhǎngxiōngrúfù*), translated literally as "elder brother like father," is another popular Chinese expression. Its origin has been attributed to Mencius (372–289 BCE), the most important interpreter of Confucianism and a sage second only to Confucius himself.

6. 秀鸭婆也是个铮铮男子汉吗？故事怎样用 "秀女人" 与 "铮男人" 的重合塑造了主人公丰满、有血有肉的形象？
7. 你对故事的结尾有何感想，尤其是把它看成中国孝文化现况的脚注时？

AUTHOR BIO

Born in 1953, Han Shaogong has published four full-length novels, eight collections of novellas and short stories, and seven volumes of prose and essays, some of which have been translated into Dutch, English, Italian, French, Korean, and Vietnamese. As a representative writer of the "roots-seeking" (寻根文学 *xúngēn wénxué*) school of the 1980s, Han Shaogong has written such major works as the novellas *Ba Ba Ba* (爸爸爸), *Nü Nü Nü* (女女女), and *Gui Qu Lai* (归去来). Other of his well-known works include *Yuelan* (月兰), *A Dictionary of Maqiao* (马桥词典 *mǎqiáo cídiǎn*), *Shannan Shuibei* (山南水北), *Riye Shu* (日夜书), and *Geming Houji* (革命后记).

The writer and his work have been the subject of many academic forum discussions and scholarly articles in China and abroad. Julia Lovell, the translator of *A Dictionary of Maqiao*, nominated Han for the 2011 Newman Prize for Chinese Literature, which he subsequently won. Her opening lines summarize Han's achievements and importance in contemporary Chinese literature: "[Han Shaogong is] a Chinese writer who intertwines, with exceptional artistry and originality, human perspectives of the local and the global, and whose career exemplifies the creative revolution that has taken place in Chinese writing since 1976."[14] Written from the perspective of a sent-down youth, many of the 115 entries in *A Dictionary of Maqiao* have their roots in the everyday life of people like Little She. Because of his depth of thought and uniqueness of expression, Han Shaogong is a phenomenon of contemporary Chinese literature.

---

14. For the full text of Julia Lovell's nomination, go to www.ou.edu/uschina/newman/HanShaogong.html (accessed August 8, 2015).

3
寄 钱

白旭初

回乡办完父亲的丧事,成刚要母亲随他去长沙生活。母亲执意不肯,说乡下清静,城里太吵住不惯。成刚明白,母亲是舍不得丢下长眠在地下的父亲。成刚临走时对母亲说:过去您总是不让我寄钱回来,今后我每个月给您寄200元生活费。母亲说乡下开销不大,寄100元就够用了。

母亲住的村子十分偏僻,乡邮员一个月才来一两次。如今村子里外出打工的人多了,留在家里的老人们时时盼望着远方的亲人的信息,因此乡邮员在村子里出现的日子是留守村民的节日。每回乡邮员一进村就被一群大妈、大婶和老奶奶围住了,争先恐后地问有没有自家的邮件。然后又三五人聚在一起或传递自己的喜悦或分享他人的快乐。

这天,乡邮员又来了,母亲正在屋后的菜园里割菜,邻居张大妈一连喊了几声,母亲才明白是叫自己,慌忙出门从乡邮员手里接过一张纸片,是汇款单。母亲脸上洋溢着喜悦,说是儿子成刚寄来的。邻居张大妈夺过母亲手里的汇款单看了又看,羡慕得不得了,说,乖乖,2400元哩!人们闻

3
MONEY ORDER

Bai Xuchu

After Father's burial in their hometown, Cheng Gang suggested that Mother go live with him in Changsha. Stubbornly, Mother turned down the offer, claiming that she liked the quiet of the countryside and would not be able to handle the noise of a city. But Cheng Gang knew the real reason. Mother couldn't bear to leave Father to sleep his eternal sleep alone in his grave. Before Cheng Gang left, he said to Mother that even though she hadn't let him send home money before, he would be sending her 200 yuan each month from now on. "It doesn't take much to live in the country," Mother responded. "One hundred yuan is plenty."

The village where Mother lived was a remote place where the postman called only once or twice a month. Since in those days a great many villagers had left to work elsewhere, the elderly family members who stayed behind were always yearning for news of loved ones from afar. The days when the postman visited had become occasions for celebration. Every time he arrived, a crowd of aunties and grannies would immediately surround him, rushing to ask whether their family members had sent mail. Moments after, they would gather in groups of threes or fives, sharing their joy or rejoicing in the happiness of others.

One day when the postman arrived, Mother was harvesting vegetables in the garden behind her house. She didn't hear Aunt Zhang, one of her neighbors, call for her until the woman had shouted several times. Mother rushed out and got a piece of paper from the postman—it was a money order. Beaming with joy, she announced it was from her son Cheng Gang. Aunt Zhang snatched the money order from Mother and checked it over many times, green with envy: "It's a whopping 2,400 yuan!" Her exclamation drew people over. The large money order passed from hand to hand

声都聚拢来,这张高额汇款单像稀罕宝贝似的在大妈大婶们手里传来传去的,每个人都是一脸的钦羡。

母亲第一次收到儿子这么多钱,高兴得睡不着觉,半夜爬起来给儿子写信。母亲虽没上过学堂,但当过村小教师的父亲教她识得些字写得些字。母亲的信只有几行字问成刚怎么寄这么多钱回来?说好一个月只寄100元。成刚回信说,乡邮员一个月才去村里一两次,怕母亲不能及时收到生活费着急。成刚还说他工资不低,说好每个月寄200元的,用不完娘放在手里也好应付急用呀。看完了成刚的信,母亲甜甜地笑了。

过了几个月,成刚收到了母亲的来信,信只短短几句,说成刚不该把一年的生活费一次寄回来,明年寄钱一定要按月寄,一个月寄一次。

转眼间一年就过去了。成刚因单位一项工程工期紧脱不开身,回老家看望母亲的想法不能实现了。他本想按照母亲的嘱咐每月给母亲寄一次生活费,又担心忙忘了误事,只好又到邮局一次给母亲汇去2400元。

二十多天后,成刚收到一张2200元的汇款单,是母亲汇来的。成刚先是十分吃惊,后百思不得其解,正要写信问问母亲,却收到了母亲的来信。母亲又一次在信上嘱咐说,要寄就按月给我寄,要不我一分也不要。

一天,成刚遇到了一个从家乡来长沙打工的老乡,成刚在招待老乡吃饭时,顺便问起了母亲的情况。老乡说,你母亲虽然孤单一人生活,但很快乐。尤其是乡邮员进村的日子,你母亲像过节一样欢天喜地。收到你的汇款,她要高兴好几天哩。

among the aunties as a rare treasure, and envious admiration was written all over their faces.

Having received so much money this first time from her son, Mother was so happy that she could not sleep. She got up in the middle of the night and wrote her son a letter. Although Mother had no formal education, Father, who had been the village elementary school teacher, had taught her to read and write simple characters. The letter was only a few lines long. It simply asked Cheng Gang why he had sent so much money when they had agreed to 100 yuan each month. Chang Gang replied, saying that since the postman went only once or twice a month, he couldn't bear the thought of Mother's money not arriving on time. Cheng Gang also added that he earned a good salary and that the agreement was 200 yuan every month. The extra, he explained, was because it might not be a bad idea for Mother to have money in hand for an emergency. After reading Cheng Gang's letter, Mother smiled happily.

A few months passed before Cheng Gang heard back from Mother. The letter was, again, only a few sentences long, admonishing Cheng Gang that he should not send the stipend for a whole year all at once, and that next year he must agree to do it monthly.

A year passed in the blink of an eye. Cheng Gang, caught up in a project with a hard deadline, could not go home to visit Mother as planned. He wanted to send her money every month as she requested, but he was afraid that he would inconvenience her if he forgot when work got busy. He decided to go to the post office and mail her the 2,400 yuan all at once again.

Twenty-odd days later, Cheng Gang got a money order for 2,200 yuan from Mother. After his initial surprise, Cheng Gang thought long and hard about the matter, but couldn't figure out why she had done this. Just as he was going to write to ask her about it, Mother's letter arrived. Once again, she instructed him that if he insisted on sending her money, he had to do it in once a month increments; otherwise she wouldn't accept a penny.

One day in Changsha, Cheng Gang ran into a migrant worker from his village. Cheng Gang treated him to a meal and took the opportunity to inquire about Mother. The fellow villager told Cheng Gang that although his mother lived alone, she was very happy, especially on the days when the postman came from town. "She is as joyous as if celebrating a holiday. A money order from you is enough to make her elated for days."

72　寄　钱

　　成刚听着听着已泪流满面，他明白了，母亲坚持要他每个月给她寄一次钱，是为了一年能享受12次快乐。母亲心不在钱上，而在儿子身上。

(2002)

Tears ran down Cheng Gang's face as he listened. He had come to realize that Mother insisted on a monthly schedule because she wanted to enjoy this happiness twelve times a year. Mother didn't care about the money; she missed hearing from her son.

(2002)

VOCABULARY AND USAGE

办丧事	bàn sāngshì	make funeral arrangement and conduct burial service	为父母办理好丧事是儿女的义务。
执意	zhíyì	insist on	下雨了，她却执意不打伞。
舍不得	shěbùdé	hate to part with	妈妈舍不得我去美国。
长眠	cháng mián	eternal sleep; die	昨天爷爷在医院阖眼长眠。
开销	kāixiāo	expenditure	城里的开销比乡下大。
偏僻	piānpì	out of the way	我的住地偏僻却很安静。
盼望	pànwàng	long for; hope for	儿子一结婚我就盼望着抱孙子。
留守	liúshǒu	stay behind	乡下的留守儿童很可怜。
争先恐后	zhēngxiānkǒnghòu	strive to be the first and fear to lag behind	在北京坐地铁，上车时一定要争先恐后。
传递	chuándì	pass on; hand around	他参加了奥运会火炬传递。
汇款单	huìkuǎndān	remittance order	汇款单也传递亲情。
稀罕	xīhan	rare	这物件稀罕，买不到的。
羡慕	xiànmù	admire and envy	我羡慕她的好成绩。
乖乖！	guāiguai	Good gracious!	乖乖！这雷声真响！
钦羡	qīnxiàn	respect and admire	我对他的能力钦羡无比。
脱身	tuōshēn	get away	我正在上课，没法脱身。

误事	wù shì	cause delay; hold things up	不用心学习会误大事的。
百思不得其解	bǎi sī bù dé qí jiě	have thought hard and still cannot make sense of it	让他百思不得其解的是母亲要避开简单找麻烦。
招待	zhāodài	entertain guest(s)	请好好招待来访的客人。
顺便	shùnbiàn	conveniently	我路过一个加油站，就顺便进去买了包烟。
老乡	lǎoxiāng	fellow villager; fellow townsman	我们是老乡，家住一个村。
孤单	gūdān	alone; lonely	我跟家人天天视频不孤单！

QUESTIONS FOR DISCUSSION

1. Describe in your own words this mother-son relationship. How is it different from your relationship with your parents?
2. Do you find Mother demanding or unreasonable?
3. What needs does Mother have beyond daily necessities?
4. Has Cheng Gang failed as a son in any way? What did he do wrong?
5. In what sphere of life does Mother's "authority" reside?
6. Why doesn't Mother simply tell her son the real reason for her demand?
7. What caused Cheng Gang's tears at the end?

1. 请用你自己的话描述一下这里的母子关系。你与父母的关系跟他们有什么不同？
2. 你会不会觉得母亲的要求有点儿过分或是不近情理？
3. 除了生存必需品外，母亲还有什么需求？
4. 成刚这个儿子是不是有不合格的地方？他哪儿做错了？
5. 故事中母亲的"权威"来自何方？
6. 母亲为什么不直截了当告诉儿子她所提要求的真正原因呢？
7. 结尾时成刚为何泪流满面？

AUTHOR BIO

Aili Mu interviewed Bai Xuchu (1941–) in 2008. When she asked him whether Mother's request wasn't a bit unreasonable, he was angered by the question but kept his cool. We often associate *xiao* with providing for our parents in their old age. Bai Xuchu disagrees. He stays faithful to the *Book of Rites* (礼记) and insists that *xiao* is making our best effort to understand our parents' hearts and minds and not to go against their wishes.[15] For Bai Xuchu, adhering to *xiao* qualifies one as a decent human being and grants one the opportunity to feel good in life.

Published in *Changde Evening News* (常德晚报) in June 2002, this story has been reprinted many times nationwide. By 2006 it had appeared in more than fifteen different anthologies. It has even been adapted into a picture book.

Born into a family of scholars, Bai Xuchu was only able to get a middle school education during the Cultural Revolution. He started his career doing chores in a pickle factory but retired as an accomplished journalist for the Changde television station and a freelance short-short story writer of national repute. He attributes his professional success and happy life to his passion for reading and writing. Bai Xuchu has written and edited a few collections of short-short stories; among them is the Ding Ling Literature Award (丁玲文学奖) winner *Dance Partners* (夫妻舞伴). Bai is known for his insightful details and for his concern with ordinary people, especially how changing values impact their daily life.

---

15. The line in Chinese, in the pre-Qin (475–221 BCE) Confucian classic *The Book of Rites*, goes like this: "孝子之养老也，乐其心不违其志." For more detail, see entry 48 "内则Nei Ze," http://ctext.org/liji/nei-ze (accessed August 8, 2015). This line has been a popular saying in the Chinese lexicon for a long time.

4
过完夏天再去天堂

墨中白

老人感觉到这个夏天在一天天变凉。

老人要走了。

老人不想走。老人舍不得居住的土屋，更舍不得他多年的老伴。老伴为他养育五儿三女，吃了一辈子苦。

老人和老伴儿孙满堂，可儿孙们却很少去他们住的土屋。每年麦收，五个儿子就会给他们送来食用的小麦，女儿们过节也会送来点酒和肉。

老人和老伴知足。

老人知道儿女们都有子女，要供他们读书，还要为他们结婚操心，就像当年他们为他们操心一样。

儿孙们活的幸福，老人就快乐。老人常把快乐说给老伴听，可老伴总唠叨着。怨他们多时不来土屋。

老人安慰老伴说，孩子们忙。你要是闷得慌，就陪我到北沟边放羊吧，和羊说话，也很快乐的。

老伴没有理他，却说，娃是嫌咱们老呢！

老人不再说话了，搂着羊儿问，我们老吗？

羊叫了两声。老人高兴地对老伴说，瞧，羊说咱们还年轻哩！

老伴就笑骂，老不正经的。

4

HEAVEN-BOUND, BUT AFTER SUMMER

Mo Zhongbai

The old man could feel summer getting cooler day by day.
He was dying.
The old man didn't want to die. He couldn't bear the thought of leaving his clay house. He especially hated leaving his wife behind. She had given birth to and raised five sons and three daughters for him and they had shared a life of hardship.

The old man and his wife had many children and grandchildren, but their family seldom came to visit them at their clay house. Every year after summer harvest, his five sons would bring them some wheat for food. His daughters would bring them some wine and meat during holidays.

The old man and his wife did not complain.

They understood that their children also had children of their own. They had to worry about tuition, wedding expenses, and so on, just as the old man and his wife had worried back in their day.

The old man was happy as long as his children and grandchildren were happy. He often communicated his happiness to his wife, who, unlike him, fretted when their children had not visited their clay house for a long time.

The old man would comfort her, saying, "Our children are busy. Come with me to herd sheep at the north grove if you are bored. It's fun to talk with sheep."

His wife would ignore him and say, "They are avoiding us because we are too old."

Falling silent, the old man would put his arm around a sheep and ask it, "Do you think we are old?"

The sheep would bleat twice, and the old man would grin and say to his wife, "See, the sheep says we are still young!"

"You old rascal," she'd retort, laughing.

老人喜欢老伴骂这句话。

老人不服老，直到那个夏日走回老屋，摔倒了，才发觉真的老了，想爬，手脚却不听使唤。

老人站不起来了，躺在床上。

老人不能动，可心像镜子一样明亮。

看着老伴弯着近九十度的腰忙着照顾自己，老人真想快一点走。

老人当过兵，打过鬼子，不相信有天堂。可老伴信奉神，说好人会升天堂。

老人真希望有天堂，早两年过去，把那边安排好，将来好接老伴在天堂一起生活。

老人躺在床上，想着天堂的事，可脑子清醒，清醒的老人想喝水，拿桌上的水杯，手碰杯时，人却滚掉下床来。望着不到半米高的床，却不能上去，老人的心好疼。

老伴回家，看到躺在地上的的老人，伸手拉。老人说，年轻时抱不动我，现在如何拉得起！

老伴去找儿子，五儿、四儿、三儿外出打工。二儿赶集没回家，大儿在北沟放羊。老伴只好叫来乡邻才把老人抬到床上。

晚上，老伴弯着腰，来到大儿家，让他去把老人家睡的床腿锯短点。

大儿子说，找老二吧，他家有锯。

老伴到二儿家，二儿子说，好好的床腿，锯掉干嘛？老大呢？

俺家的锯条断了。二儿媳妇不高兴地说。

老伴没有再说，弯腰，拄棍，蹒跚着，走回场上土屋。

He liked to be called that by his wife.

The old man had refused to give in to old age until the summer day he fell on his way back home. He began to realize how old he really was when he couldn't move his limbs to crawl.

He couldn't stand up anymore and became bedridden.

Although he was incapacitated, the old man's heart remained as lucid as a mirror.

As he watched his wife busily take care of him, her back hunched over at a right angle, the old man wanted to depart as fast as he could.

He had served in the military and fought the Japanese in the Second World War. He didn't believe in heaven, but his wife did, and she told him good people would go there.

The old man really wished there were a heaven. He would like to go there a couple of years ahead of his wife, to set things up, so he might receive her into their new life together.

Although he was hallucinating about heaven, the old man remained clear-minded. The clear-minded old man was thirsty, so he reached for the cup of water on the table. No sooner had his hand touched the cup than he fell off the bed. When he looked up at the bed, less than half a meter off the ground, and found that he could not get back into it, his heart ached.

His wife returned. She tried to help him up when she saw him lying on the ground. The old man said to her, "You couldn't do it when you were young, how do you expect to do it now?"

The old lady went to their sons for help, but the third, fourth, and fifth sons had left town for work, the second was at the market, and the eldest was herding sheep at the north grove. She had to ask villagers to come over to get the old man back into bed.

That night, the old lady walked with a stoop to her eldest son's house and asked him to go shorten the legs of the bed.

"Please go check with your second son. He has a saw," he told her.

The old lady went to her second son's house. He asked, "Why do you want to cut off the legs of a good bed? Can't my older brother do it?"

Their second daughter-in-law was annoyed. "Our saw is broken," she said.

The old lady said nothing. Bent over her cane, she stumbled back toward their clay house by the threshing ground.

来到床边，老伴拉着老人的手说，你还不如早一点走好呢。

老人握住老伴的手说，我也想，可这么热的天，儿孙们披麻戴孝，受不了，酒席上的菜也不能放……

你管那么多干嘛……

谁叫他们是咱的儿孙呢，我一天没走，心里还在装着他们。

要不，你过完夏天再去天堂吧。

老人说，我尽力撑吧。

老人的儿子还是找来锯把床腿锯短了。

老人能拿到桌上的水杯，可很少能喝尽杯里的水。

更多的时候，老人是在数着夏天的日子。看着床前的电风扇，老人想，自己同它一样，过完这个夏天，也该歇工了。可又一想，明年夏天，天热，电风扇还会不停地转，而那时的自己呢？也许真的有天堂，要不这活生生的灵魂到哪里去呢？

老人感觉自己离天堂越来越近，已经闻到天堂门外桂花树上飘来的香味了。

老人对老伴说，通知儿孙们回家吧。

老伴问，不能再过几天走？

老人说，夏天就该走的，天凉了，再冷，我怕去天堂的路滑！

老伴笑了，老不正经的，临走，也不改！

老伴一直陪着老人，直到老人微笑着离开。

老人的儿孙们回家，热闹风光地送走了老人。

五个儿子算账，扣除礼金，一家赔钱500元。

She came to the bedside, held the old man's hands in hers, and said, "You might as well leave early."

Taking her hands in his, the old man said, "I thought so, too. But it will be very hard for our children and grandchildren to endure this heat in mourning clothes, and the food for the funeral banquet will quickly go bad . . ."

"Why should you care so much?"

"They are our children and grandchildren, of course. I will care for them until I breathe my last breath."

"How about you hold on till the end of summer and then leave for heaven?"

"I'll try my best," the old man said.

Eventually, one of his sons found a saw and shortened the legs of the bed.

The old man was able to reach the cup now, but he hardly had the strength to finish the water in it.

The old man spent most of the time in bed counting the remaining days of summer. Looking at the electric fan at his bedside, the old man thought: *Like the fan, I will quit working at the end of summer, too.* And then he thought again: *When it gets hot next summer, the fan will begin turning again, but what will have become of me? Maybe there really is a heaven . . . Where else could my soul, still fully alive, go?*

The old man felt that he was getting closer to heaven—he could already smell the sweet scent of osmanthus from the trees outside heaven's gate.

He told his wife to call his children and grandchildren home.

His wife asked, "Can't you hold on for a few more days?"

The old man said, "I should have been gone in the summer. Now it's getting cold. I'm afraid that the road to heaven will become slippery when it gets colder!

His wife laughed, "You old rascal, true to yourself to the end!"

She stayed with him until, smiling, he departed.

The old man's children and grandchildren all came home and gave him a grand funeral.

His five sons calculated the expense: Each sustained a loss of 500 yuan after taking into account the cash gifts they had collected.

The daughters-in-law said, "The cool weather is a real blessing. The food won't go bad for another few days; some of the meat dishes can now

儿媳们说，天凉真好，菜能多放几天，有的肉还能回锅，要是碰上热天，这五十多桌酒席，可真赔大了。

老伴把保管一天的礼金包交出来后，分完钱，五个儿子互相望着；算好的帐，却多出2500元钱。

看着一家人又围着聚在一起核对着账款,老伴摇摇头，弯腰，拄棍，蹒跚着，走回场上的土屋。

(2007)

have a chance to be cooked twice. Had it been hot, we would have suffered a huge loss from this fifty-table banquet!"

The old lady handed them the cash gifts that had been under her care for the day. After dividing the money among them, the five sons looked at one another—there was 2,500 yuan more than they had calculated.

The old lady shook her head as the rest of her family gathered to double-check and recount the money. Bending over her cane, she stumbled back toward their clay house by the threshing ground.

(2007)

VOCABULARY AND USAGE

吃苦	chīkǔ	endure hardship	多吃苦才能成大事。
儿孙满堂	érsūnmǎntáng	have many children and grandchildren	儿孙满堂是大福气。
知足	zhīzú	content	知足者长乐。
供	gōng	pay for (education)	爸妈太穷，没钱供你上大学。
操心	cāoxīn	worry about; take pains	父母甘心为孩子操心一辈子。
唠叨	láodao	chatter	她一不高兴就唠叨起来没完。
怨	yuàn	complain	别怨孩子不懂事，是大人没有教育好。
安慰	ānwèi	console; comfort	两位老人相互安慰。
(得)慌	(de) huāng	awfully; unbearably	他一上课就困得慌。
老不正经	lǎo bu zhèngjīng	old but still licentious	文中老人的"老不正经"让老伴很开心。
(不)服老	(bù) fúlǎo	(do not) acquiesce to old age	他不服老，92岁了还天天上班。
摔倒	shuāidǎo	fall down	他摔倒了，再也站不起来了。
使唤	shǐhuàn	order about; use; handle	我想把话说清楚，可舌头不听使唤了。
信奉	xìnfèng	believe; believe in	基督教徒信奉上帝。
滚	gǔn	roll	那枚硬币滚进路边的草丛，不见了。

掉	diào	fall; drop	我睡觉不老实，从床上滚掉地上了。
老人家	lǎorénjiā	a respectful form of addressing a senior	这位老人家是新郎官儿的爷爷。
蹒跚	pánshān	stumble; hobble	他喝多了，蹒跚离去。
披麻戴孝	pīmádàixiào	be dressed in deep mourning	葬礼时，老人家的学生都为他披麻戴孝。
放	fàng	save; keep; preserve	天太热，这菜不冷藏的话，一天都放不了。
谁叫…	shuí jiào	…shouldn't have…	爸爸不该打你，可谁叫你不听话呢？
装	zhuāng	be concerned with	女儿的幸福，他时刻装在心上。
撑	chēng	hold out (until)	没有水，我们在沙漠里撑不了几天。
歇工	xiēgōng	stop working; knock off	你们工地一般几点歇工？
灵魂	línghún	soul; spirit	很多人相信灵魂不死。
飘(香)	piāo (xiāng)	(fragrance) floating/drifting	桂花一飘香秋季就到了。
(临)走	(lín) zǒu	(be about to) die; be gone	老人临走还为孩子们备好了办丧事的钱。
扣除	kòuchú	deduct	扣除饭费和房租哪里还有零花钱？
赔钱	péiqián	sustain economic losses	没人愿做赔钱的生意！
回锅	huíguō	twice-cooked	餐馆的回锅肉不好吃。

QUESTIONS FOR DISCUSSION

1. Write a character sketch of the old man, especially what makes him different from his wife.
2. Is the old man spoiling his children? Why isn't he mad when his love for his children goes unnoticed?
3. What is the essense of *xiao* for a parent? Does the old man exemplify it?
4. Do you feel sorry for the old couple?
5. How is the idea of "heaven" in this story different from the one with which you are familiar?

6. Where do you think the extra 2,500 yuan comes from? What do you think will happen when the five sons figure it out?
7. If the old man's heart is "as lucid as a mirror," what is being reflected?

1. 请给老人"画"张特写，尤其要展示他与老伴的不同。
2. 这位老人是不是太娇惯孩子了？他们对他的爱视而不见他怎么也不生气呢？
3. 对做父母的人来说，孝的真髓是什么呢？老人的言行是这一真髓的体现吗？
4. 你觉得这对老夫妻可怜吗？
5. 这个故事里天堂的概念跟你所熟悉的天堂概念有什么不一样？
6. 多出来的那2500元是哪儿来的？你觉得五个儿子明白以后会有什么反应？
7. 如果老人的心"像镜子一样明亮"，那它折射出了什么？

AUTHOR BIO

Aili Mu got to know Mo Zhongbai (1977–) through this award-winning story when serving as a judge for a 2007 national short-short competition in China. Talented, young, and handsome, Mo Zhongbai was full of energy; his writing career exploded thereafter. Now a member of the China Writers Association, Mo Zhongbai has published four volumes in diverse genres: the short-short collection *Heaven as in the Gate of Heaven and Peace* (天安门的天); two volumes of novellas and short stories, *Recollections of Northern Jiangsu* (苏北往事) and *The Eagle over Potala Palace* (布达拉宫天空的鹰); and a volume of prose essays, *Warmhearted Strangers* (温暖的陌生人). Many of these works first appeared in prestigious literary journals across China—Beijing, Anhui, Shandong, Gansu, Jiangsu, Tibet, and Wuhan. Mo Zhongbai has won two national awards: the Wu Cheng'en Literature Award (吴承恩文学) and the Pu Songling Literature Award (蒲松龄文学奖).

Born Cheng Liang (陈亮) in a village in Sihong, Jiangsu Province, Mo Zhongbai had never left the small town of Plum Blossom until October 2014. Before that, Mo had turned down an offer of a salaried editorial job with a metropolitan publisher. In 2013 he even gave up his comfortable newscaster job at the township and assumed the office of party secretary after winning a village election. His village work diary, which offers a window into his inner world, can be found at http://blog.sina.com.cn/s/articlelist_1296379313_0_1.html. The entry for August 24, 2014, for example, registered how he, then in his thirties, juggled many different roles—a son, a husband, a father, a village leader, and an emerging writer—and how he was learning to love it. http://blog.sina.com.cn/s/articlelist_1296379313_0_1.html.

Mo Zhongbai never attended college or received formal training in creative writing. Writing came along for him "like a sheep grazing along the country road it knows." He writes because his heart aches seeing the rural China he knew disappearing. Words "well up" with his nostalgic desire to retain it under the acacia tree at the end of his village, by the haystacks in the fields, and along the little streams of his hometown. The old man in the story was a real part of that vanishing life. The story was born of Mo Zhongbai's desire to honor him. Yet never for a moment does Mo Zhongbai regard himself as the voice of the marginalized: "Their pain and my ache are different. They experience the hurt; I not necessarily."

Mo Zhongbai left for Suqian in 2014 after all to join the literary academy in that city of 5.9 million people. The following description is a summary of the academy provided by Mo Zhongbai.

> Suqian Literary Academy (宿迁市文学院), a new section in Suqian Federation of Literary and Art Circles (宿迁市文联), was established on March 31, 2014, with six authorized staff members and full funding from the government. The Academy is tasked with representing the city's literary production, training literary talent, leading literary studies, and serving the public needs for art and literature.

A good knowledge of academies like this and people in them is beyond the scope of this book. Their large network in China starts with the China Federation of Literary and Art Circles on top, with provincial-level institutions in the middle, and the city-level organizations at the base. Getting to know these institutions, which have no counterpart in the West, may be a necessary step for readers wanting to understand China's cultural orientation.[1]

第三章

阴阳[1]

　　本章中的故事对非中华文化背景的学生来说也许在理解上尤其有难度。故事中根植于文化的潜台词和传统观念，以及所展示的复杂女性问题，都是这些学生所不熟悉的。他们对故事的乡村背景也有可能会感到很陌生。在今天，虽然那些关于中国女性由于各种原因不得不进入没有爱情的婚姻的故事已经过时了，但对中国女性概念化的看法，也就是把她们看成是柔弱、被边缘化、无话语权的弱势群体的偏见，还是常常误导读者对女性人物的行为和她们行为动机的认识过于简单化。比方说，有些对中国的习俗有一知半解的读者常会觉得《心事》中女主角的言行不可思议。相当一部分西方学生认为他们不能接受《翠兰的爱情》中翠兰争取爱的方式。而《糟糠》则常常被西方读者当作有情人终不能成眷属的悲剧来读。虽然这些解读都各有其道理，但它们或许也向我们揭示了一个长期存在的问题：阅读不同文化的作品时，人们不知不觉会戴上自己文化信仰和期待的有色眼镜。所以本章刻意选择了"阴阳"这个标题，目的就是要把阅读朝着注重中国的和作品产生当地的思想文化体系的方向调整。

　　阴阳是中国哲学的核心概念之一，一直是影响中华文化发展方向的至关重要的因素。阴阳代表对立且互利的力量处于相互依存的持久动态之中。在共同作用所形成的不断变化中，阴阳相互转化，互为彼此。当我们把阴阳解释成分开的两极，我们就会把这些不断发展、不可分割的力量简化为对立的双方，甚至敌手。其实，我们可以放心地推断：在这些故事里的中

---

1. 英文中也常把"阴阳"写成"yin and yang"或是"yin yang"。这里之所以用"yin-yang"的表达有两个原因：一是强调阴阳的不可分割性；二是想突出这样的观点：阴阳作为二元两极，与其说是客观存在，不如说是观念的产物。

CHAPTER 3

YIN-YANG[1]

The stories in this chapter may be particularly challenging for students of other cultures. In addition to relying on subtext and traditionally held beliefs, these stories also illustrate complicated gender issues and rural settings that may be unfamiliar to readers outside China. Although stories of Chinese women being forced to marry for reasons other than love are becoming dated, the conception of Chinese women as weak, marginalized, and voiceless still often results in an overly simplified understanding of the motivation and actions of female Chinese characters. For example, the heroine of "Two Minds" often confounds the expectations of readers who possess some prior knowledge of Chinese customs. Quite a few students have found Cuilan's behavior unacceptable. And "Forever by Your Side" is often read as a tragedy of loved ones obliged to part. Valid as these views are, they may also indicate an enduring problem: the tendency to read the works of another culture through the lens of one's own cultural beliefs and expectations. The title of this chapter is a deliberate attempt to reorient readers to a more local and Chinese frame of reference.

The concept of yin-yang lies at the heart of Chinese philosophy and has been essential to Chinese cultural orientation. Signifying opposite complementary forces, yin and yang are in an interdependent relationship and a continuous state of flux. They interact to form a dynamic process wherein they transform one another, including the metamorphosis into each other. When we interpret yin-yang as a binary, we reduce these ever-evolving

---

1. It is also written as "yin and yang" or "yin yang." Here the use of "yin-yang" is for two reasons: to emphasize yin and yang as an indivisible whole and to highlight their duality as more perceptual than real.

国农村，无论是生活在那儿的人还是发生在那儿的事儿，他／它们在人们的眼里都是兼具阴阳两面的。在那里，生活的悖论不过是自然存在；很少有谁会把女人的利益与男人的利益对立起来；想象他人时，更未必会把别人假设成没有尊严和体面的另类。

　　本章故事的作者们都不是专业作家，他们也没有刻意挑战现存的或是传统的观念等。对于他们来说，创作是一个愉快的、有理疗效果的生活经历；在创作中，他们努力发掘适当的形式，表达自己对日常生活事件的反响。因此，排除杂念和偏见的欣赏可能是走入本章故事阴阳动态的有效方法。在你阅读《心事》，经历故事的节奏重复和人物的情绪升级的时候，请停下来品味一下生活悖论的情趣，尤其是激情与理性在故事中的暧昧、你对这种暧昧的反应，以及它给你带来的思考。当你遇到翠兰的时候，请试看故事如何在这个人物的塑造上达到了筹划谋略和浪漫磊落的统一，而翠兰又是如何在当今的中国恪守着传统而创意地活着。读到《糟糠》时，你可能已经学会了用阴阳关系的视角去理解作品。那么你就会发现，在传统文化传承较好的中国农村，活在传统里的中国人是如何协调情（个人情感）和理（道德规范）的关系的，以及他们是如何对待生活中的牺牲和满足的；你也会看到故事是如何在表达勇敢放手之凄苦的同时，赞赏糙中之雅，悲中之美，坚持之勇气的。

and interrelated forces into opposites, even adversaries. In the rural China of these stories, it is safe to infer that people and things are viewed as having both yin-yang aspects and that the paradoxes of life are natural. Women's interests are not seen as opposed to the interests of men. To assume others are good and decent human beings is not uncommon.

None of the authors here are professional writers, nor are they much concerned about challenging accepted or traditional views. For them, creative writing is a pleasurable therapeutic experience, wherein they find appropriate formal expressions for their reactions to the events of everyday life. Disinterested appreciation is a valid approach to the yin-yang dynamics at work in the stories. As you experience the repetition of actions and the acceleration of emotions in "Two Minds," pause to reflect on how the enjoyment of life's paradoxes and the ambiguous roles of passion and reason have impacted you. When you encounter Cuilan, try to see how the story reconciles in her the contradictions of strategy and romantic spontaneity and of adhering to conventions while living creatively. You may have developed a yin-yang approach to reading by the time you get to "Forever by Your Side." If so, you will find how more traditional rural China negotiates *qing* (情 how people feel) and *li* (理 norms of ethical behavior). You may discover how rural China handles the relationship between life's sacrifice and satisfaction, how it appreciates grace in coarseness, the beautiful in what seems tragic, and the courage it takes to persist, as well as the bitterness of bravely letting go.

1
心事

王琼华

　　德牯到邻居家喝接亲酒。
　　平日，他就喜欢喝几杯，又看到桂花挑了一张凳子，与自己同桌坐着，心里美滋滋的，喝起酒来兴致十足。只是他的酒量不大，七八杯下肚，脸就红起来。同桌的人看到桂花与二德牯时不时眼对眼，说："二德牯也该敬桂花一杯吧。一桌子人，你二德牯谁都敬到了，唯独桂花这杯酒不敬说不过去吧。"
　　桂花说："谁敬我都不喝。我不会喝酒。"
　　"那我们敬二德牯，他喝双杯酒！"
　　二德牯站起身子，大声说："喝就喝！反正是寡妇的裤子不经劝！"一仰脖儿，把一杯酒倒入嘴里。屁股还没落下，坐在一侧的人扯了扯他的衣角。
　　"有事？"二德牯弯下身子，巴起眼问了一句。
　　邻座小声嗔怪："该掌嘴！你刚才怎么说？"
　　"我说什么？本来就这回事，寡妇的裤子……"
　　二德牯还没把话说完，自己先瞠目结舌了。过了好一阵儿，他才缓缓把眼睛望向桂花，发现桂花把头扭开了，好像不想理自己。
　　村里人早在咬耳朵，老单身公二德牯想娶桂花，桂花好像也有这么一点儿意思。

1
TWO MINDS

Wang Qionghua

Er Degu went to a neighbor's house for a wedding banquet. On ordinary days he liked to have a drink or two, but today he was really in the mood to indulge. His heart had melted with happiness to see Guihua choose a bench at his table and sit down. His capacity for liquor, however, was limited. His face turned red after seven or eight cups. Someone at the table, when he caught Er Degu and Guihai frequently exchanging looks, suggested, "Er Degu should propose a toast to Guihua, too. It wouldn't be right if you skipped Guihua after toasting everyone else at the table."

Guihua replied, "I'm not going to drink to anybody's toast. I don't drink."

"We'll toast to Er Degu, then. He'll drink double for both of you."

Er Degu rose to his feet and bellowed, "Not a problem! After all, does a widow need much persuasion to take off her pants?" Tilting his head, he emptied the cup into his mouth. Before he could sit down, the person next to him pulled at the hem of his shirt.

"What's the matter?" Er Degu bent down, raised an eyebrow, and asked impatiently.

"I could slap you right now. How could you say that?" the person next to him whispered reproachfully.

"What did I say? You know how it is, a widow doesn't need . . ."

Er Degu, wide-eyed and tongue-tied, couldn't finish his sentence. After a long pause, he moved his eyes slowly in Guihua's direction—only to find Guihua looking away, as if deliberately ignoring him.

Rumors had long been circulating in the village that the old bachelor Er Degu wanted to marry Guihua and that Guihua seemed to reciprocate his feelings a little.

桂花以前嫁过人，寡妇也当了一两年了。

可眼前，二德牯真想掌自己的嘴。

晚上，二德牯躺在床上，心里乱糟糟的。真是自己找背运来走！他不停埋怨自己。一定要找桂花说一说，这成了二德牯的一桩心事。

第二天早晨，他挑着水桶走到村口水井旁挑水，把两桶水吊上来，又撑着扁担站在井旁，不时往村口瞅瞅。

桂花每天早晨也是这个时候挑水，二德牯想借这个机会跟桂花说上几句话。没多久，桂花挑着水桶来了。

"对不起，桂花。"二德牯低下头，说，"那句话我不该说。"

"什么话？"

"就是寡妇裤子……"

桂花乜了他一眼，没吭声。

"我不是其他意思，只是说我喝酒直爽。"

"那就多喝一点儿。"

二德牯觉得桂花的话不冷不热，心里更着急——"我给你赔个不是。我不该说这种漏风漏气掉牙齿的话。"

桂花突然"哼"了一声，"哐当"、"哐当"把两桶水吊上来，没再答话，挑起水桶径直走了。二德牯咧开嘴巴，愣愣望着她顺着青石板路远去的背影。

但二德牯还不死心。他觉得桂花不是小心眼儿，这回肯定是一时赌气。

于是，二德牯过了两天又在巷子口拦住桂花，说："对不起，桂花，要不你掌我的嘴。"

"咦，你怎么变得像老太婆一样？"

"我……我真的错了。"

"错在哪里？"

"错就错在不该说。"

"不该说？看样子错在哪里你自己还稀里糊涂。好了好了，你最好跳进东江湖洗个冷水澡，别再昏头昏脑的。"

Guihua had been married before. She had been a widow for a year or two now.

At the moment, Er Degu really did want to slap himself in the face.

That night, while he was lying in bed, distracting thoughts filled his head. He kept blaming himself. *You're really bringing yourself bad luck! You must go talk to Guihua.* From then on, he was obsessed with this thought.

The next morning, he went to fetch water from the well at the village entrance. He hoisted the two buckets of water, then stood leaning on his shoulder pole by the well, casting his eyes toward the entrance constantly.

Every morning Guihua came to fetch water at this time, too. Er Degu wanted to take the opportunity to talk to her. Pretty soon Guihua appeared, two buckets on her shoulder pole.

"I'm sorry, Guihua," Er Degu lowered his head, then added, "I shouldn't have said that."

"Said what?"

"About a widow's pants . . ."

Guihua squinted at him but did not say a word.

"I didn't mean to offend you. When I drink, the words just shoot from my lips."

"In that case, you should drink more."

Guihua's response seemed lukewarm, which worried Er Degu even more. "Please accept my apology. I shouldn't have said those damned words."

Abruptly, Guihua let out a "humph." With a *cling-clang*, she drew up the two buckets of water. Shouldering them on her pole, she walked away without another word. With his mouth hanging open, a bewildered Er Degu watched her disappear up the bluestone path.

Er Degu would not accept defeat. He knew Guihua wasn't petty. *She really must be mad at me this time*, he thought.

Two days later, he again stopped Guihua as she came to the entrance of a lane. "I'm sorry, Guihua. Slap me, if it will make you feel better," he said.

"Huh? Why are you acting like an old granny?"

"I . . . I was truly wrong."

"For what?"

"For saying things I shouldn't have."

"Shouldn't have? It looks like you still don't get it. Well, so be it. You better go take a cold dip in Dongjiang Lake, so you won't be so muddleheaded."

二德牯犯愁了，这下真的得罪了桂花。还能找个什么法子补救呢？他思来想去，最后找到隔壁的婶子，求她出面去说情。没多久，婶子一脸怒气回来，进门就把脚一跺，说："二德牯，我不该帮你去说这个事，桂花那话怎么叫人听得下？她还说，她要嫁到隔壁那个村子里去。"二德牯往下一蹲，左手死死地拧着头发。

婶子看了看，又有点怜悯起来，叹道："你这剁脑壳的，这结人家都解不开，还是你自己去解吧。"

他觉得婶子说得有道理。

攥攥拳头，他蹬蹬地往桂花家走去。他感到困惑，平日在村里最好讲话的桂花怎么一下子变了，难道她真要嫁给人家？看来她是觉得自己的认错态度不好吧。

桂花瞪了他一眼，说："看样子，你还像个男人，也敢上门来。"

"我是来认错的。请你原谅我这个下九流。"

"是吧。"

"我会改的，桂花。"

"改什么？有什么好改的？"桂花没好气地说。

"我、我不是好男人。"二德牯结结巴巴的。

"当然不是好男人！连寡妇的裤子也要劝她脱掉？"桂花看了看他，腔调又怪怪的，"你怎么晓得寡妇的裤子不经劝？"

二德牯不晓得怎么答话。

"你劝过？"

二德牯摇摇头。

桂花那眼神突然变了，火辣辣的。"怎么，想不想劝一劝？"

二德牯身子哆嗦了一下，又是摇摇头。

"那你给我滚——"桂花突然吼道。

(2006)

Er Degu was stumped. *I really must have offended Guihua this time. What else can I do to make things right?* He thought and thought and eventually went to the auntie next door and asked her to talk to Guihua on his behalf. Pretty soon she came back, her face flushed with anger. Stamping her feet as soon as she walked in, she said, "Er Degu, I shouldn't have gone on your behalf. What Guihua said was not fit for anyone's ears!" She also said that Guihua planned on marrying someone from the neighboring village. Er Degu collapsed. Squatting, he wrung his hair tightly with his left hand.

The auntie next door looked at him. Feeling sorry for him, she suggested with a sigh, "You knucklehead! This is a knot no one can untie but you. So get at it."

Er Degu thought her suggestion made sense.

To gird himself, he clenched his fists a couple of times, then strode to Guihua's house. He was confused: *How come the most amenable person in the village has changed suddenly? Is she really going to marry someone else? It must be that she didn't find my apologies sincere enough.*

Guihua gave him a dirty look, "So you are man enough to come yourself."

"I'm here to apologize. Please forgive me for being such a jerk."

"Oh?"

"I'll change, Guihua."

"Change what? What's there to change?" Guihua said fretfully.

"I . . . I'm not a good man," Er Degu stammered.

"Of course, you aren't. You want to take off a widow's pants." Guihua looked at him, something was odd about her tone. "How do you know it doesn't need much to get a widow out of her pants?"

Er Degu didn't know what to say.

"Have you tried?"

Er Degu shook his head.

Suddenly the look in her eyes changed, gleaming with passion, "Well, do you want to?"

Trembling, Er Degu shook his head.

"Then, get out of here!" Guihua exploded.

(2006)

VOCABULARY AND USAGE

心事	Xīnshì	a load on one's mind	这么小的孩子哪会有心事？
接亲	Jiēqīn	receive the bride	儿子结婚，他摆酒席接亲。
挑	Tiāo	choose; select	她可是个百里挑一的好姑娘。
美滋滋	měizīzī	pleased with oneself	能用中文带着爸妈在中国旅游，大卫心里美滋滋的。
兴致十足	xìngzhì shízú	be in the best of spirits	说起足球，他兴致十足。
下肚	Xiàdù	gulp down	两杯酒下肚，她的话多起来。
唯独	Wéidú	only	别的事儿你可以自由决定，唯独这件事我不能依你。
说不过去	shuō bú guò qù	hardly justifiable	你连春节都不回家就说不过去了。
寡妇	Guǎfù	widow	"寡妇"是指丈夫去世了的女人。
不经劝	Bùjīnquàn	easy to persuade	他让你干你就干，这么不经劝？
仰	Yǎng	face upward	在这里，"仰脖"跟"仰头"差不多，都是脸朝上的意思。
脖	Bó	neck	
(一)侧	Cè	side	车左侧的后门刮坏了。
扯	chě	pull	他扯了一下我的胳膊叫醒了我。
巴(眼)	bā (yǎn)	open (eyes wide)	这孩子巴开两眼就哭，肯定是饿了。
嗔怪	chēnguài	blame; chide	她嗔怪我忘了她的生日。
掌嘴	zhǎngzuǐ	slap	你不乖乖听话，小心我掌你的嘴！
本来就这回事	běnlái jiù zhè huí shì	That's how it is.	解释什么？本来就这回事嘛！
瞠目结舌	chēngmùjiéshé	be struck dumb	眼前的奇迹惊得她瞠目结舌。
阵	zhèn	a measure word for a period of time	你好一阵子没来家里坐坐了。
缓缓	huǎnhuǎn	slowly	他缓缓抬起头，一脸歉意。

扭(头)	niǔ(tóu)	turn; twist	他一扭头，怒气冲冲地走了。
(搭)理	(dā)lǐ	acknowledge; respond	她一整天都没(搭)理我。
咬耳朵	yǎoěrduo	whisper	老师第一天上课就说："课上不许交头接耳咬耳朵。"
有意思	yǒuyìsi	falling for someone; checking someone out	你这么关心她，一定是对她有意思了。
乱糟糟	luànzāozāo	perturbed	他说错了话，心里乱糟糟的很着急。
(走)背运	(zǒu)bèiyùn	bad luck	你也会有走背运的时候。
埋怨	mányuàn	blame	出了问题不要总是埋怨别人。
桩	zhuāng	a measure word	他的那桩心事村里人都心知肚明。
挑水	tiāoshuǐ	carry (buckets of) water (on a shoulder pole)	她每天去河边挑活水吃。
吊	diào	lift	只有起重机才能吊起这么大的石块。
撑	chēng	support	他用四根扁担撑起了这个帐篷。
扁担	biǎndān	carrying pole	
瞅	chǒu	cast a glance	他吓得都不敢瞅桂花一眼。
乜	miē	squint; askew	她乜了一眼我做的手工，还是不满意。
不冷不热	bùlěngbúrè	neither hostile nor friendly	主人不冷不热的态度让我很不舒服。
赔不是	péibúshì	apologize	跟一个人说"对不起"就是给他赔不是。
漏	lòu	leak	这个气球漏气。
哐当	kuāngdāng	a clashing sound	大铁门哐当一声关上了。
径直	jìngzhí	straight	他转身径直往站台走去。
咧(嘴)	liě(zuǐ)	draw back the corners of one's mouth	那孩子咧嘴大哭的样子真难看。
愣	lèng	stare blankly	他愣在那里，半天无话。
背影	bèiyǐng	a view of someone's back	我看着她的背影消失在夜幕中。
不死心	bù sǐxīn	unwilling to give up	她已经走了，不死心也没用了。

小心眼儿	xiǎoxīnyǎner	petty	谁说女人小心眼儿？
赌气	dǔqì	feel wronged and act rashly out of spite	你不该跟父母赌气离家出走。
拦	lán	bar; block	他伸手拦住我，不让我通过。
稀里糊涂	xīlǐhútú	muddleheaded	他整天稀里糊涂的，哪天考试都不知道。
昏头昏脑	hūntóuhūnnǎo	muddleheaded	我昨晚没睡好，现在昏头昏脑的没法学习。
犯愁	fànchóu	worry	快开学了，他还在为学费犯愁呢。
这下(子)	zhèxià (zi)	thus; this time	这步棋你走错了，这下子是输定了。
得罪	dézuì	offend	他这话说得不合适，得罪了很多选民。
补救	bǔjiù	remedy	这个错误没法补救了。
思来想去	sī lái xiǎng qù	think back and forth	你这样思来想去睡不着觉，还不如早点儿下决心呢。
隔壁	gébì	next door	她住我隔壁。
出面	chūmiàn	act on behalf of	这事儿哪能让父母为我们出面解决？
说情	shuōqíng	intercede for someone	这事儿你请谁说情都没用。
跺(脚)	duò(jiǎo)	stamp (foot)	他一生气就跺脚吼叫。
拧	nǐng	wring; twist	要开门得先拧一下门把手。
剁	duò	chop	"你这剁脑壳的"是个方言表达，是说你脑子不开窍，真想帮你剁开，让你开窍。
脑壳	nǎoké	skull	
结	Jié	knot	很多产品用中国结做广告。
攥	zuàn	ball one's fist	你攥拳头干什么？想打人？
蹬蹬	dēngdēng	sound of thrusting against the ground	听到孩子的哭声，他快步蹬蹬往家跑。
困惑	kùnhuò	perplexed	桂花的态度也让读者很困惑。
好讲话	hǎojiǎnghuà	soft-hearted and easygoing	虽然那位老师很好讲话，上好他的课却不那么容易。
下九流	xiàjiǔliú	people of humble professions	"上九流"和"下九流"的不同仅仅是职业吗？
没好气	méihǎoqì	sulkily; snappily	她心情不好，对谁都没好气。

结巴	jiēba	stammer	学演讲治好了我的结巴。
腔调	qiāngdiào	tone of voice	你怎么这种腔调跟老人说话？
火辣辣	huǒlàlà	burning	她火辣辣的眼神把他惊住了。
哆嗦	duōsuo	shiver	他不是冷得哆嗦，是吓得哆嗦。

QUESTIONS FOR DISCUSSION

1. What is going on in this story? Does Guihua like Er Degu or not? Why is Guihua mad? What does she really want?
2. Does the ending surprise you? Did it make you laugh?
3. How is this courtship unique or not so unique?
4. Is this just a case of a misunderstanding? If not, what other obstacles do Er Degu and Guihua face? Who/what is their biggest obstacle?
5. What paradoxes of life does the story capture?
6. Is Er Degu's continuing to apologize a good or a bad thing? Will it help save this relationship?
7. Write in as few words as possible what happens next in the story.

1. 故事里到底发生了什么？桂花喜欢不喜欢二德牯？她气在哪儿？她到底想要什么？
2. 故事的结尾你料到了吗？让你笑出声了吗？
3. 二德牯的求爱方式很特殊还是很一般？为什么这么说？
4. 二德牯和桂花只是沟通理解有问题吗？如果不是，那他们之间还有什么障碍？谁／什么是他们最大的障碍？
5. 这个故事捕捉到了什么样的生活悖论？
6. 二德牯不停地道歉是个好事还是坏事？他这样做有助于他们关系的发展吗？
7. 给这个故事写个最简短的续——接下来发生了什么？

AUTHOR BIO

An amateur writer since the 1980s, Wang Qionghua (1971–) has published more than 800 short-shorts. More than 120 of them have been anthologized in annual collections or reprinted by such prestigious or popular journals as *Selected Fiction, Selected Short-Shorts, Selected Micro-fiction,* and *Readers*. In 2012 his story "The Last Bowl of Soya Beans" ("最后一碗黄豆") served as the reading comprehension text for the college entrance examination in Liaoning Province. "Two Minds," his representative work, was written in 2006 when he was heading the Organization Department of the Communist Party of China Linwu County Committee, Hunan Province. The department was the human resources engine for a county of about 400,000 people.

Wang Qionghua attributes his understanding of human predicaments and his ability to present complex moments of life to his rich and diverse experiences. From a pancake man to a warehouse keeper to a clerical staff member to deputy director of the Education Bureau of Chenzhou Municipality, the office he currently holds, Wang Qionghua has worked in more than a dozen professions. The one not included in this count is his role as volunteer promoter of the short-short genre. He has made use of his administrative power to facilitate educational-cum-promotional events for short-short fiction both locally and nationally. He is also a vice-chairperson of the Chenzhou Federation of Literature and Art and a vice-chairman of Chenzhou Writer's Association and does interior design for fun. He ranks among the top short-short writers in China.

2
翠兰的爱情

李伶伶

翠兰看上了村里的单身汉马成。
　　翠兰托媒人去马成家说媒，媒人回来说，马成不同意。翠兰问为啥？媒人吞吞吐吐不想说。翠兰直着急，让媒人尽管说，媒人才说，马成说你太厉害，不敢娶。翠兰一听，心说，你越不敢娶，我还越要嫁给你！

　　翠兰家的米快吃没了，地里的活太多，她没时间去买，就想让谁上集时帮她捎一袋回来。正在街上等着，马成过来了。翠兰叫住他，问他是不是上集去？马成说是。翠兰就说，那你帮我买一袋大米吧。马成因为拒绝了翠兰，再见到她，有点不好意思，正犹豫呢，翠兰说，咋，求你这点儿事都不行？马成忙说行。

　　翠兰去地里干活，把大门从里锁了，从后门出去。中午回来见大门被人动过，就知道是马成送米来过了。翠兰洗洗手，换件衣服，想去马成家取米。想了想，又没去。晚上，翠兰刚吃过饭，就听见有人敲大门，马成在外面喊，翠兰，翠兰。翠兰没做声，听了一会儿，没动静了，才睡下。

　　第二天一早，翠兰早早就去了马成家。到了他家，也不进院，隔着墙喊：马成，马成，你昨晚是不是去我家了？那声音，大得四邻八舍都能听

2
CUILAN'S LOVE

Li Lingling

Cuilan fell in love with Ma Cheng, a bachelor in her village. Cuilan sent a matchmaker on her behalf to Ma Cheng's house, but the woman returned with Ma's refusal. Cuilan asked why he had refused. The matchmaker, speaking one word but swallowing the next, was reluctant to say. More and more agitated, Cuilan hammered at her to tell no matter what, so the matchmaker said, "Ma Cheng says that you're too sharp to make a good wife." When Cuilan heard this, she said to herself, "The more afraid you are of me, the harder I'll work to be your wife!"

Cuilan was running out of rice, but she was too busy working in the fields to get more. She thought of asking someone to bring her a sack from the market. As she was in the street looking for someone to ask, she saw Ma Cheng walking in her direction. She stopped him and asked if he was on his way to the market. When he answered yes, she told him to get her a sack of rice. Ma, who felt a little awkward at seeing Cuilan after rejecting her, hesitated. Cuilan beat him to the punch, "What's the problem? You won't even help me with a trifle like this?" Ma quickly agreed to help her.

Cuilan latched the front door from inside her courtyard and left for work through the back door. When she came back at noon, she knew Ma Cheng had come by to deliver the rice, because the front door had been pushed slightly ajar. She washed her hands and changed into clean clothes. She intended to go to Ma Cheng's house to get the rice, then thought better of it and decided not to go. That evening, just after dinner, Cuilan heard a knock at her door. Outside, Ma Cheng called her, "Cuilan, Cuilan." She didn't respond. She listened; after a little while the calling stopped and she went to bed.

The next morning, Cuilan arrived at Ma Cheng's house very early, but she did not try to enter the courtyard. She yelled from outside, "Ma Cheng,

见。翠兰喊完了就在外面等。马成还没出来,马成的邻居桂芳先出来了,看见翠兰,脸一沉,转身回去了。

翠兰见桂芳这样,就知道媒人说的是真的。媒人说,马成之所以不同意和翠兰的亲事,还有一个原因,就是他心里惦着桂芳呢。

桂芳已经回自个儿屋去了,马成才出来。见是翠兰,就说,我昨天给你送了两趟米,你都没在家。翠兰说,我昨天在地里干了一天活,晚上吃完饭,到吴二婶家坐了一会儿。马成也没细究,就把大米送到翠兰家。

翠兰在地里碰见了吴二婶。吴二婶悄声问她,你跟马成啥时候到一起的?翠兰说,二婶你可别乱说。吴二婶说,我怎么是乱说呢,马成上你那去,谁不知道啊。翠兰笑着也不辩解。

没过多久,桂芳和马成闹僵了,桂芳说马成心不诚,和别的女人不清不白。翠兰心里喜,可表面上却显得很焦急,她去找马成,问他传言是不是真的,桂芳是不是在说她,她可以跟桂芳解释清楚。马成说,不用解释,越解释越不清。

夏天还没过完,桂芳就嫁人了。马成很失落,经常望着桂芳住过的院子发呆。翠兰见马成这样,也不去打扰他。

秋天来了,家家户户都忙了起来。翠兰也忙,她割完了豆子想割高粱时,镰刀坏了,就去马成家借。

翠兰一进院就听见一阵哭声,是马成的儿子小东。马成没在家。小东饿了,想自己泡方便面吃,结果把暖壶弄倒了,开水把小东的手烫伤了。

Ma Cheng, did you come to my house last night?" She was so loud that all the neighbors nearby could hear her. Once she was done shouting, she waited at Ma Cheng's courtyard door. Guifang, a neighbor of Ma Cheng's, came out before Ma Cheng did. Her face darkened when she saw Cuilan. She turned around and went back in immediately.

Guifang's reaction convinced Cuilan that the matchmaker's words had been true—the other reason for Ma Cheng's refusal of Cuilan was Guifang, to whom Ma Cheng had taken a fancy.

Ma Cheng did not show up until Guifang had disappeared into her own house. When he saw Cuilan, he said, "I tried to deliver the rice to your house twice yesterday, but you were not home." Cuilan replied, "I was working in the fields the whole day, then I paid Auntie Wu a short visit after dinner." Ma Cheng accepted her words without fuss and helped bring the rice to her home.

In the fields, Cuilan bumped into Auntie Wu, who asked in a whisper, "Since when have you been with Ma Cheng?" "What nonsense!" replied Cuilan. "I'm serious," Auntie Wu continued. "Ma Cheng visits you at your house. Everybody knows it." Cuilan smiled and made no attempt to debate or defend herself.

The trouble between Guifang and Ma Cheng came to a head soon after. Guifang accused Ma Cheng of being insincere and coveting other women. Cuilan was delighted, but pretended to be worried about Ma Cheng. She went to ask him if the rumor was true, if Guifang thought she was the other woman, and said she would be willing to go to Guifang and clear his name. Ma Cheng said there was no need and any attempt to clarify things would only complicate the situation.

Guifang got married before the summer was over. Ma Cheng, distraught, was often seen staring at Guifang's house in a daze. Seeing Ma Cheng in such a state, Cuilan left him alone.

Fall arrived. Every household began to bustle with activity, and so did Cuilan's. She finished harvesting beans. When she was moving on to sorghum, her sickle broke, so she went to Ma Cheng's to borrow one of his.

The moment she stepped into Ma Cheng's courtyard she heard someone crying. It was Xiaodong, Ma Cheng's son. Ma Cheng was not at home. Xiaodong was hungry and had tried to make instant noodles for himself. The hot water had scalded his hands when the thermos bottle toppled over.

翠兰抱起小东就往医院跑，医生把小东受伤的手包扎好了，马成才赶到。马成心疼地看着儿子，想抱抱他，被翠兰一把推开。翠兰说，有你这样的爹吗？把孩子的手烫成这样！

说完，抱起小东就走。马成在后面跟着，几次想接过小东，翠兰都不给。

翠兰把小东抱回了自己家，马成也要进来，被翠兰挡在了门外。晚上，马成来接小东，小东不回。小东说，翠兰婶做的饭比你做的好吃。马成想进屋坐会儿，被翠兰拦住了。翠兰说，太晚了，你就别进来了。

小东住在翠兰家不愿意走了，马成来接了好几次，小东都不回。马成说，这孩子，真不懂事。翠兰说，大人比孩子还不懂事。说完，又要关大门。马成说，等等，等等，你怎么总不让我进门呢？翠兰说，我的门，可不是随便进的。马成愣了愣，没说话，走了。

当天晚上，媒人就来了，来替马成说媒。

(2009)

Cuilan picked Xiaodong up and dashed toward the hospital. Ma Cheng didn't make it there until the doctor had already dressed Xiaodong's burns. Ma Cheng, hurting for his son, tried to hold him, but Cuilan pushed him away, "I've never seen a father like you! How could you allow this to happen?"

With these words, Cuilan picked up Xiaodong and walked out. Ma Cheng, trailing behind her, tried a few more times to take hold of his son, but to no avail.

Cuilan took Xiaodong to her own home. When Ma Cheng tried to get in, she stood in his way. That evening, Ma Cheng returned to fetch Xiaodong, but the boy refused to leave. He told his father, "Auntie Cuilan makes yummy dishes, tastier than yours." Ma Cheng wanted to come in and sit down, but was turned away once more. "It's getting late," Cuilan said, "and it would be inappropriate to let you in."

Xiaodong made Cuilan's house his own and didn't want to leave. Many times, Ma Cheng came to take him back home, but Xiaodong wouldn't leave. "This kid really doesn't know how to behave," Ma Cheng said. "I know an adult who's even worse," Cuilan responded. With these words, Cuilan began to close the door again. "Wait a minute, wait a minute!" Ma Cheng interrupted, "Why do you keep me out all the time?" "To get in my door," Cuilan responded, "one must perform the appropriate ritual." Ma Cheng's face went blank, then he left without a word.

That very evening, a matchmaker came on Ma Cheng's behalf to ask for Cuilan's hand in marriage.

(2009)

VOCABULARY AND USAGE

看上	kànshàng	take a fancy to; fall for	他看上了一位同班的女生。
托人	tuō rén	ask someone; entrust someone with something	她今天要加班，不得不托人把孩子从学校接回家。
说媒	shuōméi	act as matchmaker	他请邻居去女孩家说媒。
尽管(说)	jǐnguǎn(shuō)	feel free to (say)	这东西我有的是，你尽管拿。

上集	shàngjí	go to the market	你今儿上集去不？
捎	shāo	take along something to or for someone	你散步回来帮我捎份今天的晚报，好吗？
叫住	jiào zhù	stopped	她非要走，我没能叫住。
拒绝	jùjué	refuse; reject	我拒绝了她的无理要求。
犹豫	yóuyù	hesitate	他犹豫了一下才答应。
咋	ză	why	他叫了半天门，你咋不开呢？
四邻八舍	sìlínbāshè	one's near neighbors	她的哭声四邻八舍都听到了。
(脸一)沉	(liăn yī) chén	pull (a long face)	他脸一沉说："人早死了！"
细究	xì jiū	scrutinize; get to the bottom of something	问题出在哪儿，你们一定得细究。
辩解	biànjiě	defend; explain	这事儿越辩解越说不清。
闹僵	nào jiāng	come to a deadlock	他们俩闹僵了，分手了。
(心)诚	(xīn) chéng	sincere; sincerity	他以诚待人，有很多朋友。
不清不白	bùqīngbùbái	neither innocent nor clean; have an illicit relationship	女朋友不许他和别的女人不清不白。
泡	pào	soak	这锅要泡一会儿才好洗。
暖壶	nuǎnhú	thermos bottle	暖壶是很多中国人的生活必需品。
包扎	bāozhā	bind up a wound	我们用纱布包扎伤口。
赶到	gǎndào	rushed to	我们赶到机场时飞机已经起飞了。
挡	dǎng	block; keep off	一棵被风刮倒的树挡住了我的路。
替	tì	for	我替你把书拿来了。

QUESTIONS FOR DISCUSSION

1. Why doesn't Cuilan go get the rice from Ma Cheng at noon that day? Why doesn't she open the door when Ma Cheng brings the rice to her that evening? Why does she go to Ma Cheng's early next morning and make her visit known to all?
2. Does Cuilan cause the breakup between Ma Cheng and Guifang?
3. Does Cuilan love Ma Cheng? Is Cuilan trying to force love on Ma Cheng?
4. Why is Xiaodong necessary in this story? Will Cuilan and Ma Cheng be happy together?
5. What do you think of the way that Cuilan goes about getting her man? Are you delighted or dismayed by her behavior?
6. What does the story say about love and the little details of everyday life?
7. What does the image of Cuilan do to clichés about Chinese women?

1. 翠兰为什么不当天中午去马成家取米？那晚马成来送米她又为什么不开门？而她又为什么第二天一大早就去马成家门口大声吆喝？
2. 翠兰是马成和桂芳分手的罪魁祸首吗？
3. 翠兰爱马成吗？翠兰在逼马成爱她吗？
4. 这个故事里为什么要有小东？翠兰和马成的结合会幸福吗？
5. 你对翠兰搞定马成的方式有什么看法？她的言行让你高兴还是失望？
6. 关于爱和每日生活之琐碎，这个故事有着什么样的阐释？
7. 翠兰这一形象怎样冲击了关于中国女性的陈腐观念？

AUTHOR BIO

Li Lingling (1975-) grew up in North Willowton (北柳树屯), a division of Three Small Pieces of Stone Village (小三块石村) in west Liaoning Province. She had only been outside her town a couple of times before writing this story in 2009. When she was fifteen, she fell off her bike on her way to school and was subsequently diagnosed with progressive muscular atrophy. She started writing short-shorts twenty years ago. With only one limb—her right hand—still functional, she wrote herself to national fame.

Her speech at an award ceremony in Beijing in March 2015 characterizes her view of writing's role in her life.

"Although ill-fated, I've had great luck in life. *Selected Works of Fiction* (小说选刊) reprinted two of my stories; both have brought me joy and happiness beyond expectation."

The first story is "Cuilan's Love." In 2010 it caught the eye of Yu Shengli, a top-notch television producer. Under his encouragement, Lingling expanded the two-page story into thirty-four episodes of a television drama. The royalty for the screenplay enabled her to buy a home in the city of Huludao in 2014 and to move her parents from their ancestral home into a life to which they had long aspired. "I'm extremely happy for being able to reciprocate my parents' love this way."

Her second story that *Selected Works of Fiction* reprinted is "A Mathematician's Love" ("数学家的爱情") published in 2014. It brought her to Beijing for the first time one year later—the story was nominated for an award by the China Writer's Association. Three months after its appearance in *Selected Works of Fiction*, the story was adopted as part of the college entrance exam for Liaoning Province. "Because of my disability, I was not able to attend high school, let alone college. My work participating in the Exam like this instead made up for the loss."

Lingling's hard work is for a simple goal: "I don't want to be a dependent; I want to live with dignity." She is finishing up her second screenplay now and is busy putting together her first collection of short-shorts for publication. "I want to sustain this urban life with the fruit of my own labor." Lingling is thankful for life's cruel sweetness: it confines a youthful girl to a wheelchair and affords her, in the meantime, rich experience of love and beauty.

3
糟 糠

伍中正

糟糠是那年冬天没了男人的。
　　单着身的黑皮是糟糠的叔[2]。糟糠嫁过来的时候,黑皮还替老大心甘情愿的出了钱。

糟糠男人的丧事是黑皮过来细细地料理的。

料理完糟糠男人的丧事,单着身的黑皮就对糟糠说:嫂,娃还小,趁早嫁汉呢。

糟糠看了看还小的娃,又望望眼前的黑皮,没多说什么。

糟糠没有离开村庄,也就是没离开糟糠男人生活过的村庄。

春天来了,村里树上长满了春天的叶子。

糟糠就跟着春天进入了春天,村庄的燕子在天上飞,在画里飞。

糟糠带着娃车秧水。

糟糠就把娃放在田埂上,那娃不哭。

架好瘦瘦的水车,糟糠就车,车得满脸满头是汗。车一会,歇一会。

---

2. Here "叔" is a short term for "小叔子," i.e., her husband's younger brother.

3

FOREVER BY YOUR SIDE[2]

Wu Zhongzheng

That winter, Zaokang lost her husband.

Heipi was Zaokang's younger brother-in-law and a bachelor. When Zaokang married into the family, he volunteered money to help his elder brother with expenses.

It was Heipi who came over and, with great care, saw to his older brother's funeral.

After the funeral, Heipi advised Zaokang, "Elder Sister, your child is still young. The sooner you remarry, the better."

Zaokang looked at her small child and at her bachelor brother-in-law right in front of her. She didn't say anything, at least in words.

Zaokang didn't leave the village. That is, she didn't leave the village where her husband had lived.

Spring came. Trees in the village were covered with spring leaves.

Following in the season's footsteps, Zaokang entered spring the way swallows in the village fly to the sky, fly as if in a painting.

When she went to irrigate her rice field, Zaokang brought her child along. She sat the child on a ridge outlining her field. The child did not cry.

She set up the narrow waterwheel and started to work. Soon sweat was streaming down her face. She had to alternate work with rest.

---

2. "Zaokang" (糟糠) is a loaded name. Originally a term for the food of poor people, it takes on additional meaning in the phrase "糟糠之妻," which can be translated as "a wife who has shared her husband's hard lot." It is an allusion to the classic story from *The Book of the Later Han* that made the saying "糟糠之妻不下堂" ("a wife who has shared her husband's hard lot must never be cast aside") a byword in China. The line is part of the answer an official gave Emperor Guangwu (5 BCE–57 CE) when he tried to act as a go-between for his sister who wanted to marry the official. In 2013 a student from Taiwan, Liu Fangyin, first translated the title as "Always by Your Side." She argued for her translation with the help of the story from the Han dynasty. Her work inspires the current translation.

当那车盘上的水滑落下去后，糟糠就想起和男人一同车水的样。车水的手就慢慢地停下来。

糟糠竟忘了坐在田埂上的娃。

那娃掉在田里了，发出了哭声。糟糠才回过神来。

糟糠再不敢想那死去的男人，连忙抱起那娃。

黑皮过来，问：还车不车呃嫂？

糟糠看了看等水的绿绿的秧。

车呃！

糟糠站一边，黑皮站在一边，两人面对面地车水，车上的水在车盘上甩出的水花，一朵一朵的。

糟糠不歇，黑皮也不歇。

有人看见糟糠和黑皮车水，就说，糟糠怕是黑皮的了。

糟糠要打年糕了。糟糠对黑皮说，叔，接你过来做年糕。

黑皮就过来帮忙，打浆，烧火，担水，蒸熟了年糕又做。

做完，黑皮就说：嫂，再没事儿就走了。

糟糠也不留黑皮，拿出两块年糕递给黑皮，黑皮接了年糕就走。

年就在乡村欢快的气氛中走过。

过了年，黑皮要出去一趟，走之前，黑皮对糟糠说：那娃靠着你呢。

糟糠一听，眼泪断线般落下来，不是滋味。

黑皮是第二天中午回来的。黑皮满脸红晕，像喝了不少的酒。

黑皮回来的时候，带来一个人。那人牛高马大，稳稳地在糟糠面前一站，糟糠就知道是回什么事了。

糟糠对黑皮说：叔，下辈子还做你的嫂。

黑皮红红的脸上还漾开了浅浅的笑。

往后，糟糠车水是跟那男人一块车的。

As water passed through the wheel, it brought to Zaokang's mind the memory of when she turned the wheel with her husband. Her hands slowed down, and then stopped.

Zaokang forgot about her child sitting on the ridge of the field.

He fell into the water-covered field and cried, which brought Zaokang back to the present.

She did not dare to think about her deceased husband again. She rushed over and picked up her child.

Heipi came over and asked, "Elder Sister, do you want to go on?"

Zaokang looked at her parched seedlings.

"Of course!"

Face-to-face, they worked, with Zaokang on one side and Heipi on the other. The water the wheel brought up spun out a constant spray in the shape of one blossom after another.

Zaokang did not take a break; neither did Heipi.

Some people saw Zaokang and Heipi working together and said Zaokang would most likely become Heipi's woman.

It was time for Zaokang to make rice cakes. Zaokang asked Heipi, "Brother, can we get you to make rice cakes with us?"

Heipi went over to help. He mashed the rice, fetched water, and tended the fire. They steam-cooked a cake. When it was done, they made more.

Finished, Heipi said, "Elder Sister, if there is no more work, I'm leaving."

Zaokang didn't ask him to stay. She brought out two cakes and handed them to him. Taking the cakes, he left.

The Spring Festival came and went in the cheeriness of the countryside.

Heipi had to go out of town after the festival. Before he departed, he said to Zaokang, "That child depends on *your* care."

Hearing this, tears streamed down Zaokang's face; wrenching, inexpressible emotions surged up in her.

Heipi came back at noon the following day. His face was red—he must have had quite a bit to drink.

Heipi returned with someone tall and strong. When the man stood firm as a rock in front of Zaokang, she knew what this was about.

Zaokang said to Heipi, "Brother, I'll still be your sister-in-law in my next life."

A slight smile was barely discernible on Heipi's red face.

Zaokang started working on the waterwheel with the man.

往后,糟糠打年糕是跟那男人一起打的。

糟糠是那年冬天随牛高马大的男人往村庄外走的。糟糠的大衣是那男人替她裹紧的,雪在村庄不停地飘飞。

满身是雪的黑皮就远远地跟着。在出村口的路上,黑皮不想止步。

糟糠边走边对那男人说:带我走的,记得不记得黑皮的老大?

记得!

糟糠又说:带我走的,记得不记得黑皮?

记得!

糟糠还问:带我走的,往后还回来看不看黑皮?

看!

糟糠吼:那你就对后面满身是雪的黑皮说,让他回家。

男人领悟,使出浑身力气,喊:黑皮,不送了黑皮。

巨大的喊声让那大得无比的雪一层层湮没,显得憔悴。

糟糠在那一声里,流下了泪。

黑皮止步,倚着村头那树,任眼前的雪无序的飞……

(2005)

Zaokang began to make rice cakes with the man.

The following winter, Zaokang left with that tall, strong man. The man wrapped Zaokang tightly up in her overcoat. Snow was flying all around the village as they walked off.

Heipi, covered with snow, followed them at a distance. He didn't even stop when he had reached the edge of the village.

"Hey, will you always remember my first husband?" Zaokang asked the man who was taking her away.

"I will!"

"Will you forever remember Heipi?"

"I will!"

"Will you bring us back here to visit Heipi?"

"Of course!"

"Then tell the snow-covered Heipi behind us to go home!" Zaokang yelled.

The man understood. He shouted at the top of his voice, "Heipi, please go home."

Too weak to get through the terribly thick falling snow, the man's loud cry seemed desolate.

In the echo of the cry, Zaokang shed tears.

Heipi stopped, leaning against the tree at the end of the village, letting the snowflakes swirl aimlessly before his eyes...

(2005)

VOCABULARY AND USAGE

糟糠	zāokāng	poor men's foodstuffs	"糟糠之妻"指的是跟丈夫一起吃过苦的妻子。
心甘情愿	xīngānqíngyàn	with all one's heart	为孩子当牛做马我也心甘情愿。
料理	liàolǐ	arrange; manage	妈妈去世后，姐姐负责料理家务，呵护我们长大。
趁早	chènzǎo	before it is too late	暴风雨要来了，我们趁早回家吧。
车(秧)水	chē(yāng)shuǐ	draw water to irrigate a (rice) field using a waterwheel	他们一起给稻田车水。
回过神	huíguòshén	come to one's mind	她半天才从震惊中回过神来。

怕是	pàshì	I'm afraid; I suppose	你放到股市的钱怕是回不来了。
打(年糕)	dǎ(niángāo)	make (rice cakes)	妈妈用米打年糕；哥哥用铁打镰刀。
不是滋味	bú shì zīwèi	feel bad; upset	看着妈妈吃苦她心里不是滋味。
牛高马大	niúgāomǎdà	tall and strong	这孩子能吃，长得牛高马大。
漾(开)	yàng(kāi)	ripple; brim over	听到这个喜讯，他唇边漾出笑意。
浑身	húnshēn	from head to toe	"浑身"在这里跟"全身"的意思一样。"使出浑身力气"就是把全身的力气都用上了。
湮没	yānmò	annihilate	他的小书很快被铺天盖地的出版物湮没了。
憔悴	qiáocuì	haggard	虽然憔悴了许多，这位昔日的明星依旧充满活力。
倚	yǐ	lean on	她把头倚在我的肩上睡着了。
任(凭)	rèn(píng)	let; allow; at the mercy of	她不急也不躲，任(凭)雨点狂打在身上。
无序	wúxù	disorderly	自由竞争是混乱无序的竞争吗？

QUESTIONS FOR DISCUSSION

1. Why is the heroine named Zaokang?
2. Are Zaokang and Heipi in love? Do you see any expression of feelings between them?
3. Who/what is it that keeps Heipi and Zaokang apart?
4. Why is Zaokang grateful to Heipi for "imposing" a husband on her?
5. How does the change of seasons function in the story? What do you make of the last image?
6. Does love mean letting go?
7. Why isn't the story a tragedy for Chinese readers? Does the question-and-answer scene impact you? What other emotions are there besides the bitterness of parting?

1. 女主人公的名字为什么叫糟糠？
2. 糟糠和黑皮是不是相爱？你有没有看到他们之间的感情流露？
3. 是谁，是什么让有情人终不能成眷属？
4. 黑皮"强加"给糟糠一个丈夫，糟糠为什么反而会感激黑皮？
5. 季节的变化在故事中起了什么作用？你如何理解小说的最后一幕？
6. 爱意味着放手吗？
7. 为什么这个故事对中国读者来说不是个悲剧故事？那三问三答的高潮可曾对你有震撼？在他们的分别之苦里还能体味到人生的啥滋味？

AUTHOR BIO

Wu Zhongzheng (1968–) is a farmer. A native of Changde, Hunan Province, Wu started writing in the late 1980s. He paid out of his own pocket to study at Lu Xun Institute of Literature in 1990. His works have appeared in *Farmers' Daily* (农民日报), *Beijing Literature* (北京文学), *Tianjin Literature* (天津文学), *Yellow River Literature* (黄河文学), and many other established journals. He sold a silo of grain for his first computer. His published pieces now number over 1,500, mostly short-short stories. He composed many of his stories while working in his perfectly manicured fields—an idyllic scene with flowing water below and flying egrets above. One could say he dreams atop a bed of literature, since he keeps all the journals where his works have appeared in drawers beneath his mattress. A top short-short writer from rural China, the nationally known Wu Zhongzheng seems anomalous to many of his fellow villagers, because he is content with what his writing has brought him. The modest royalties from his stories are not enough to substantially change his life; they are but a token of the indispensable joy that the experience of writing has given him. In 2004 Wu Zhongzheng put out his first collection of short-shorts *Over That Mountain* (翻越那座山). He had published two more volumes, *Listening to Peach Flower Blossoming* (倾听桃花开放的声音) and *That Tree* (就要那棵树), by 2010. Wu represents many farmers in contemporary China who enjoy the aesthetic dimension of life and the satisfaction it brings.

第四章

统治[1]

《纽约时报》在2015年5月采访了斯坦福大学的弗朗西斯·福山教授。他在谈到中国治理的话题时，这样说道：

中国真的是在秦汉的时候就发明了现代官僚体制。这个体制在官僚选择和规范管理方面有着相对客观公正的程序。但是对我来说，还有一个很大的实实在在的问题没有解决：虽然我们可以看到这些古老的传统跟治理当今中国的体制之间有一定的相似性，但在实证层面上，我们对中国执政体系如何工作知之甚少。[2]

其实即便是土生土长的中国人，也很少有几个对当今中国的执政体系如何运作有准确、透彻的了解，更不用说对这一官僚体系两千多年来的演变有足够的认知。虽然关于当代中国的一般性书籍也常常试图纳入对中国执政体系的介绍，但那些介绍通常不全面，也缺乏福山教授号召大家去做的实证研究。这个体制内部不断的变化和不停的调整也进一步加大了了解它的困难。我们认为，那些构成中国官僚体系的官员们可以在这里帮把手——阅读他们基于工作经历所撰写的文学作品会为我们打开一个了解中

---

1. 英文的"govern"或是"governance"能否确切表达中文"统治"的意思，这在学术界还是一个悬而未决的问题。如果"治"的意思已经是"govern"，那么为什么中文的表达还需要另外一个字？本章的故事大概不能为你量化英文的"govern"或是"governance"在多大程度上传达了"统"字所包含的"聚集"、"一起"、"所有"和"团结统一"的意思，但希望这些故事能使读者对中文的表达为什么需要"统"字有进一步的了解。
2. 2015年五月，《纽约时报》记者就福山教授的两本新书，《政治秩序的起源》和《政治秩序和政治衰败》，对他进行了采访。请上《纽约时报》的Sinosphere网站查看采访的全文。(http://sinosphere.blogs.nytimes.com/2015/05/01/q-and-a-francis-fukuyama-on-chinas-political-development/ 最后一次查访在 04/25/16）。

CHAPTER 4

GOVERNANCE[1]

When the *New York Times* interviewed Francis Fukuyama of Stanford University in May 2015, he gave this response concerning the topic of China's governance:

China really invented modern bureaucracy at the time of the Qin and Han dynasties, with relatively impersonal forms of official selections and bureaucratic rules. But for me, there's a big empirical question: You can see certain similarities between those traditions in ancient China and the system that governs China today, but I think we know relatively little empirically about how the Chinese government works.[2]

In truth, few native Chinese have a thorough understanding of how, exactly, the Chinese government works or an awareness of how the bureaucratic system has evolved over two millennia. General introductory books about contemporary China often attempt to include the Chinese system of governance, but usually they are not comprehensive and lack the empirical study that Professor Fukuyama calls for. The constant changes and perpetual adjustments within the system itself make the

---

1. It is still an open issue whether the word "govern" or "governance" can convey the meaning of 统治 in Chinese. If 治 is "govern," why does the Chinese expression need another character in it? The stories in this chapter may not help you quantify how much the Chinese collocation to "gather," "together," "all," and "unite," carried by the other character, 统, is communicated by this translation, but they can, we hope, give you a better sense of why "统" is in the vocabulary.
2. For a full account of the interview on Professor Fukuyama's two recent books, *The Origin of Political Order* and *Political Order and Political Decay*, please go to the *New York Times* blog *Sinosphere*, accessed on October 23, 2015, http://sinosphere.blogs.nytimes.com/2015/05/01/q-and-a-francis-fukuyama-on-chinas-political-development.

国复杂治理体系的独特窗口。本章故事的作者都是中国的基层官僚，他们都在县一级的政府部门任职。

虽然中国的政治体制在不断变化，不同区域也存在着差异，现在的中国，在北京的中央政府之下大约有五层行之有效的地方政府：省，地/市，县，乡/镇，村。县级这个层次处于五层结构的中间。中国今天大约有2,860多个县，这其中包括县级市。每个县级政府都可以说是国家功能机构在当地的缩影。对在美国体制内长大的学生来说，县法院就是县级最高权力机构，这种中国式的县政府结构会使他们感觉摸不着头脑。

中国的县通常在规模上比美国县大，结构也更复杂。市，一般来说，不是地级就是县级；而市里的区通常都是县级。县级权力机构通常缺不了这样五个组成部分：县人民政府，其最高领导被称为县长；中共县委，其最高领导被称为县委书记；县纪律检查委员会，简称县纪检；县人民代表大会，简称县人大；还有县人民政治协商会议，简称县政协。

许多中国的官衔和职能在英文中找不到对应的翻译。这给来自其他国家和文化背景的学生带来了很大困惑。一个典型的例子就是，虽然县政府是负责制定计划和执行政策的行政部门，它的重大决策必须先经中共县委首肯。所以，中共县委的工作已与县政府的行政功能融合；而县委书记则有可能是县一级最具影响力的决策者。乡镇一级的权力机构在很大程度上重复了县级机构。这一点，读者可以在第二个故事《清潭》中看到。

一个县政府至少由40至50个不同部门构成，而在人口超过一百万以上的大县则有可能多达100至150个以上。一般来说，每个县都有十来个或是

task of understanding it even more difficult. Perhaps reading the literature by the officials who constitute the Chinese bureaucratic system and whose writings are based on their work experiences can offer a unique window into the complex systems of Chinese governance. The authors of the stories in this chapter all work at the county level of Chinese bureaucracy.

Although a system in flux and with regional variations, China's government currently has, below the central government in Beijing, roughly five practical levels of local government: the province, prefecture/municipality, county, township, and village. The county level is in the middle of the hierarchy. There are about 2,860 counties and cities with county status in China today. Each functions like a miniature state at the local level. For students in the United States, for whom county authority is represented by the courthouse, this can be an alien idea.

Chinese counties are generally larger in scale and more complicated in structure than their American counterparts. Cities are mostly at prefecture or county level. Districts in a city are usually at the county level. Among the organizational bodies that constitute county authorities these five are usually present: the People's Government of the county (县人民政府 *xiàn rénmín zhèngfǔ*) and its head, the county governor (县长 *xiàzhǎng*); the Communist Party of China (CPC) county committee (中共县委 *zhōnggòng xiànwěi*) and its head, the secretary (县委书记 *xiànwěi shūjì*); the county Party Disciplinary Inspection Committee (县纪律检查委员会 *xiàn jìlǜ jiǎnchá wěiyuánhuì*); the county People's Congress (县人民代表大会 *xiàn rénmín dàibiǎo dàhuì*); and the county People's Political Consultative Conference (县人民政治协商会议 *xiàn rénmín zhèngzhì xiéshāng huìyì*).

Many Chinese official titles and their functions, for which there are no English equivalents, have presented great challenges for students of other counties and cultures. For example, while the county People's Government is the executive branch charged with making plans and implementing policies, the CPC County Committee must first approve the government's major decisions. So the CPC County Committee has been integrated into the decision-making process and its secretary could possibly be the most influential decision maker at the county level. The county structure of power is to a large extent duplicated at the township level, as you can see in the second story, "The Clear Pond."

A county government is constituted of forty to fifty units at least, though there can be as many as one hundred to one hundred fifty or more

更多的下属乡镇。各级官员和公务员们要在不同级别和部门纵横交错的关系网中生存实属不易。县政府还负责一些服务性行业的运做，如学校，医院，图书馆等。县政府机构也有扶持像商店，工厂和公司等一些企事业单位的责任。例如在第三个故事《大红苕》中就有一个这样隶属县农业局的商店。这家商店在故事中还有点儿小功能。

让学生去想像一个中国县长的角色和职责很不容易；这对在美国中西部长大的学生尤其难。因为在那里，通常是几个人的监事委员会或是董事会管理着一个县相对简单的事务。还有，从古到今，中国的老百姓与他们政府的关系，跟大多数其他国家比，似乎更密切些。这也可能增加学生们想像中国的难度。

这里选择的三位作家，他们的首要职责是政府官员，文学创作不过是他们的业余爱好。然而，这三位官员都著作等身，也都是著名的中国作家协会会员。在中国，像这三位"身兼二职"的写作官员有很多，特别是在基层。这些现代文人对当代中国社会和文化有着不可忽略的影响。现在是对他们的作用和贡献做更全面的了解和评估的时候了。

for large counties with populations greater than one million. On average, a county has a dozen or more subordinate towns. To navigate the intragovernmental web of horizontal and vertical relationships is no small matter for civil servants and officials. The county government also runs service-oriented units such as schools, hospitals, and libraries and maintains enterprise units such as shops, factories, and other companies. One such shop has a role in the third story, "Big Sweet Potatoes."

It is also hard for students to imagine the role of a county governor in China, especially if they grow up in a place like the American Midwest, where a board of supervisors or commissioners often manages a county's relatively simple affairs. Additionally, it may be that, historically, Chinese people have been more involved with their government institutions than people of most other countries.

The three writers selected here are first and foremost government officials. Creative writing is but a sideline for them. Yet all three have earned prestigious membership in the China Writers Association with volumes of published work. "Moonlighting" bureaucrats like these three are common in China, especially at the grass-roots level. These modern literati have exerted tremendous influence on contemporary Chinese society and culture. A fuller understanding of their roles and contributions is overdue.

1
铺石板

周波

那天快下班了,有群众把东沙拦在了办公室里。
什么事?东沙问。
铺石板的事。群众说。
东沙哈哈大笑,说:我早就知道你们会来找我的。
镇长,听说古街里的水泥路要改成石板路?群众又问。
只是个想法,还不成熟。东沙说。
多可怕的想法哟,要是真铺下去的话,那可是劳民伤财的事。群众说。
镇长,群众对铺石板有意见?办公室主任后来问东沙。
是呀,没意见才是怪事呢。东沙说。
主任努努嘴,听不懂东沙讲的话。东沙则拍了拍他的肩膀,笑着说:策划一下,群众会赞成铺石板的。主任又努努嘴,显然,还是有点一知半解。
翌日,东沙就去了趟古街。其实即使群众不来反映,他心里也一直牵挂着那事儿。只是,这石板不是想铺就能铺的。东沙自己心里清楚,他在等一个合适的时间窗口。
东沙提着一根竹竿,像盲人似的边走边敲。好奇的群众不断地围过来:镇长,这好好的水泥路敲它干啥?是不是要铺石板啊?

1
THE STONE-PAVING PROJECT

Zhou Bo

One day, right before Dongsha got off work, some townspeople blocked him from leaving his office.

"What's the matter?" Dongsha asked.

"It's about the stone-paving project," the townspeople answered.

Dongsha burst out laughing. "I knew you would come to see me about that."

"Mr. Mayor, is it true that the cement roads of the Old Street area are going to be replaced by stone-paved roads?" the townspeople asked.

"It's just an idea, nothing is firm yet," Dongsha answered.

"What a lousy idea. It's going to be a real waste of money and manpower if it goes through," the townspeople said.

Later, the chief of the township general office asked, "Mr. Mayor, do the townspeople have misgivings about the stone-paving project?"

"Yes. It would be odd if they didn't," Dongsha replied.

The office chief pursed his lips. He was having a hard time understanding Dongsha. Patting him on the shoulder, Dongsha said with a smile, "We craft a plan, and then wait for them to come around." The office chief pouted his lips again. Obviously, he still had only a very superficial understanding of the matter.

Dongsha made a trip to the Old Street area the next day. The stone-paving project would have been on his mind even if the townspeople had not shown up to voice their opinion. In reality, the project would be easier said than done. Dongsha knew this very well. He was waiting for the right window of opportunity.

With a bamboo pole in his hand, Dongsha kept tapping the roads like a blind man as he walked along. Curious townspeople continuously came around: "Mr. Mayor, why are you tapping on the good cement roads? Are you checking things out for stone-paving?"

东沙抬起头说：不铺了，我看水泥路不错。

听镇长这么说，群众哄地一声笑开了，弄堂里还响起了欢呼的掌声。

可是，我发愁呢。东沙说。

东沙镇长，有什么愁呢？我们帮你解决。群众问。

我向上面承诺了要铺石板，现在没法去交代。东沙说。

这事简单，选条小弄堂随便铺一下去交差不就行了。有群众提议，我们也不能过于为难领导。提议马上得到大家的响应。

谢谢啦！东沙微笑着收起了竹竿。

回到办公室后的东沙紧急召集有关人员，交代铺石板的事。东沙说：我们现在要铺一条样板路，必须高标准去完成。

样板路完成后群众就不反对其他路铺石板了？主任说。

群众本来就没反对，反对的是不符合群众利益的事情。东沙说。

主任又努努嘴，这回他似乎听懂了些什么。

因为得到了群众的理解，样板路铺得相当顺利。不久，完工了。

那天快下班了，又有群众把东沙拦在了办公室里。

什么事？东沙问。

铺石板的事。群众说。

东沙哈哈大笑，说：我早知道你们回来找我的。

群众说，是哟，怪我们见识少，以前不知道石板路会这么好。

好在哪儿呢？东沙故意问。

"Nope." Dongsha raised his head and answered, "The cement roads look just fine."

These words from the mayor set off an outburst of laughter. There were even cheers and applause from the alleyways.

"But I have worries now," Dongsha said.

"Mayor Dongsha, what's bothering you?" the townspeople asked. "Let us help you."

"I have made the commitment to my superiors to pave the roads with stone. Now what do I tell them?" Dongsha asked.

"It's easy. Pick a small alleyway, pave it how you like, and then you'll have a report to give them," someone in the crowd suggested. "We shouldn't make things too difficult for Mayor Dongsha, right?" His proposal immediately got the approval of everyone present.

"Thanks!" Dongsha smiled and put away his bamboo pole.

Upon returning to his office, Dongsha took emergency action to gather the relevant personnel and delegated the task of stone-paving. "What we are paving will be the sample road," Dongsha said. "It must be of the highest quality."

"Will this sample road silence all objections to stone-paving other roads?" the office chief asked.

"Townspeople don't necessarily object to stone-paved roads. What they object to are projects that are not in their best interest," Dongsha said.

The office chief pouted his lips again, but this time he seemed to be able to make some sense of things.

With people's sympathy on their side, the township stone-paved the alleyway without a hitch, and the task was soon accomplished.

One day, right before Dongsha got off work, a group of townspeople blocked him from leaving his office.

"What's the matter?" Dongsha asked.

"It's about the stone-paving project," the townspeople answered.

Dongsha burst out laughing. "I knew you would come to see me about that."

"It was our fault for not knowing better before; we admit it," the townspeople said. "We never expected that a stone road could be this good."

"What's so good about it?" Dongsha asked purposefully.

"All the sewers are dredged; no one worries about floods anymore. The water pipes are upgraded; no one worries about water outages anymore.

阴沟全疏通了，再不怕洪涝了；自来水管重新装了，再不怕停水了；夏天走在石板路上也凉快了；古街的味道也浓了……群众说。

东沙接着问，那今天各位找我是……

我们来要求铺石板路的事，看镇长给不给面子。群众说。

不行，样板路完工后镇里不打算在古街铺石板了。东沙很冷静地说。

这……这……镇长，镇里当初可是想铺石板的呀。群众刚才的热情顿时像被浇了一盆凉水。

今天过来只代表你们几个人，还是古街所有老百姓？东沙问。

应该可以代表古街老百姓吧，如果有什么问题我们去做工作。群众说。

不行，不能铺。东沙说。

镇长，群众有要求了，应该可以铺了。主任贴着东沙的耳朵悄悄说。

你懂个屁！东沙把茶杯往桌子上一扔。在场的群众都被吓了一跳。

后来几天，不断有群众来找东沙。主任说镇长出差去了。群众不信，说镇长的车子还在呢。其实，那几天东沙的确在外面出差，只不过他本来没必要出这趟差。东沙向主任交代，有情况随时汇报。

那几天，主任一天一个电话，群众要求很强烈，可以行动了吗？东沙却说，最佳的时间窗口还没来临。

有一天，主任汇报说：古街上的横幅都打出来了。东沙问怎么回事。主任汇报说群众强烈要求古街铺上石板路。东沙终于爽朗地笑起来，开始吧！

那天，东沙出差回到家，老婆如晶指着他的鼻子出气，差点把我也当成石板铺下去了，你躲避啥呀？

In summer, it's cooler to walk on the stone. The Old Street area has an added charm because of it . . ." the townspeople said.

Dongsha asked another question: "So you've come to see me today because . . ."

"We've come to request more stone-paved roads. We hope, mayor, that you will respect our wishes," the townspeople asked.

"I can't," Dongsha said, keeping his cool. "The township has no plans for more stone roads in the Old Street area beyond the sample road."

"But . . . Mr. Mayor . . . It was the town's original idea to stone-pave the area." Dongsha's answer had doused the people's enthusiasm like a bucket of cold water.

"Are you speaking for those who are gathered here today or on behalf of all the folks in the Old Street area?" Dongsha asked.

"We should be able to represent everybody," the townspeople said. "If not, we will work it out among ourselves."

"Nope. Can't do it," Dongsha said.

The office chief whispered into Dongsha's ear, "Mr. Mayor, we ought to do it now—at the request of the townspeople."

"What do you know!" Dongsha banged his teacup on the table, an act that startled everyone present.

In the days that followed, the townspeople came and went constantly looking for Dongsha. The office chief told them that the mayor was away on business. They didn't believe him, saying that the mayor's car was still in the parking lot. Dongsha was indeed away on business those days, but he didn't really need to make the trip. Dongsha had instructed the office chief to keep him posted on any new development.

During that time, the office chief called Dongsha every day. "The townspeople's demand is getting intense. Shall we act now?" But Dongsha replied that the best window of opportunity was yet to come.

One day the office chief informed Dongsha that a big banner had appeared on the Old Street. Dongsha asked what it was for. The office chief reported that people were adamantly demanding stone roads in the Old Street area. Finally, Dongsha let out a hearty laugh. "Let's get to work."

That day, Dongsha returned home from his business trip. With her finger in his face, his wife Rujing vented her anger: "They would have used me as a slab of stone to pave the road if they could. Why are you hiding?"

东沙笑着说，女人家懂什么。不是我不相信群众，是群众有些事不明真相需要我们去引导。

如晶说，你在镇里群众工作都是这么做的？

东沙说，现在流行策划。如果当初脑门一热不顾群众所思所想就去铺石板，不知后果会如何。我也是没办法下的办法嘛。

如晶没好气地说，只此一回，重犯小心我去告你。

东沙捂着自己的嘴，一脸孩子气地说，知道了，夫人。

(2011)

Dongsha said with a smile: "What do you womenfolk know? It's not that I don't trust the townspeople. They need our guidance for things they don't know anything about."

"This is how you work with townspeople?" Rujing questioned.

"It's fashionable to strategize nowadays," Dongsha said. "If I had acted on impulse and stone-paved the roads at the outset, without taking into consideration people's views and opinions, who knows how it would've ended up? After all, I am just giving them a way out where none existed before."

"I'll let you off the hook this time," Rujing said curtly. "I may just have to report you if there's a repeat offense."

His hands over his mouth, Dongsha responded with the innocence of a child: "Yes, ma'am!"

(2011)

VOCABULARY AND USAGE

成熟	chéngshú	mature	时机还不成熟，我们再等等。
劳民伤财	láomínshāngcái	waste money and manpower	建造这么大的办公楼多劳民伤财啊！
努嘴	nǔ zuǐ	purse one's lips	他努着嘴想了半天，还是不懂。
策划	cèhuà	plot; plan	这场有趣的节目是他策划的。
一知半解	yīzhībànjiě	have a superficial knowledge of	他对中文只是一知半解，做不了这个项目的翻译。
翌日	yìrì	next day	翌日就是明天。
趟	tàng	a measure word	上周我出了趟差。
牵挂	qiānguà	concern; worry	你的身体，你的学习都是我每天的牵挂。
竹竿	zhúgān	bamboo pole/rod	现在还有盲人用竹竿探路。
像...似的	xiàng...sìde	it seems like...	儿子初次离家，妈妈像丢了魂似的。
围	wéi	surround; encircle	这位明星常被粉丝围起来请他签名。

哄	hōng	an onomatopoeia	树上的鸟哄地一下全飞了。
弄堂	nòngtáng	lane; alley	南方的弄堂跟北方人的胡同是一回事儿吗？
发愁	fāchóu	worry	他发愁考不上大学。
承诺	chéngnuò	commitment	你的签字就是你的承诺。
交代	jiāodài	(1) account for; (2) give order to	1) 出了问题我是要向上级交代的。 2) 镇长每天一上班先向下属交代工作。
怪	guài	blame	这事儿不怪他，怪我没交代清楚。
交差	jiāochāi	report to the leadership after finishing a task	我跟你出去玩，回来拿什么向老板交差？
不就行了	bújiùxíngle	Wouldn't ... be sufficient?	渴了，喝点儿水不就行了？
过于	guòyú	excessively	对我来说，明尼苏达的气候过于寒冷。
为难	wéinán	make it hard for	我不想让父母为难，所以自己打工赚学费。
召集	zhāojí	convene	院长每季召集一次全院师生大会。
符合	fúhé	meet; be in line with; accord	有市场需求不等于符合人民的利益。
见识	jiànshi	experience and insight	出国学习能长见识。
阴沟	yīngōu	sewer	雨水顺着阴沟流到河里。
疏通	shūtōng	dredge	这条河泥沙多，需要经常疏通。
洪涝	hónglào	flood	洪水造成的灾害是涝灾，因此有"洪涝"一说。
给面子	gěi miànzi	show respect	要想自己有面子就得时时想着给别人面子。
当初	dāngchū	at the beginning; in the first place	我们当初是没打算要二胎的，可现在政策变了。
顿时	dùnshí	immediately; suddenly	话一出口，他顿时就后悔了。
浇	jiāo	dash (water)	她拿起手边的一杯水浇灭了火苗。
在场	zàichǎng	be present	车祸发生时我不在场。

吓一跳	xià yí tiào	be surprised; freak out	这房子贵得吓了我一跳。
来临	láilín	approach; arrive	全家人都在为春节的来临忙活着。
横幅	héngfú	banner	道路的两旁有很多人打着横幅欢迎她。
爽朗	shuǎnglǎng	heartily	我请他喝茶聊天儿，他爽朗地答应了。
差点(儿)	chàdiǎn(er)	almost; nearly	我今天上班差点儿迟到了。
躲避	duǒbì	hide; dodge	他不敢回家是为了躲避上门要债的人。
不明真相	bùmíngzhēnxiàng	ignorant of the facts/truth	对不起，我不明真相错怪了你。
引导	yǐndǎo	guide	这么小的孩子还是需要大人引导的。
脑门一热	nǎomén yī rè	on impulse	我当初脑门一热就买下了这所老房子。
所思所想	suǒ sī suǒ xiǎng	thinking; thoughts	我知道你的所思所想都在这个孩子身上。
重犯	chóng fàn	repeat (a mistake)	我绝不会重犯同样的错误。
告	gào	sue; accuse	你这是漫天要价，我要去市场管理部门告你。
捂	wǔ	cover	我一发火吼叫她就捂起耳朵离开。
一脸…气	yīliǎn…qì	with … all over one's face	他乜了对手一眼，一脸傲气。

QUESTIONS FOR DISCUSSION

1. What is your impression of Dongsha as a grass-roots official?
2. Why is there an absence of personal identity in the representation of the townspeople?
3. Does the mayor have the townspeople's best interests at heart?
4. What is it in the mayor's behavior that bothers you?
5. Does the ending surprise you? Why does the story need to have Rujing in it?

6. Does the structure of repetition and reversal work for you?
7. Does this seem like an example of good governance? Why or why not?

1. 你对东沙这个基层官员印象如何?
2. 为什么镇上的乡亲们没有哪个人是有名有姓的?
3. 镇长是把镇上人的最大利益装在心里了吗?
4. 镇长的所作所为哪一点让你难以接受?
5. 结尾你料到了吗？为什么这个故事要有如晶这个人物？
6. 故事重复加反转的结构用得好吗?
7. 可以把故事里发生的视为良政典范吗？请说说为什么。

AUTHOR BIO

Zhou Bo (1968–) seems to be fortune's favorite both as an official and a writer. A charismatic man in his forties with a master's degree in Chinese, Zhou Bo is now deputy chief of the Bureau of Culture, Media, Press, and Publication in Zhoushan, a prefecture-level city of islands in eastern China with a population of 1,146,000. Zhou Bo also serves as a vice-chairperson of the Zhoushan Writer's Association and enjoys national popularity in short-short literary circles. His writings have been published in seven volumes. His "Headline News" ("头条新闻") and his collection of short-shorts with the same title are among his best-known works and have won him many awards.

Zhou Bo does not want to see what has happened to Chinese sports—which are very competitive but not a real cultural power—happen to Chinese literature. He takes the aesthetic dimensions of life very seriously and dreams of a literature of the people, by the people, and for the people. Critical self-reflection is an integral part of his official function, as is shown in this story based on his real-life experiences. For a more comprehensive look at Zhou Bo's life as an official and a writer, please go to his blog at http://blog.sina.com.cn/xingzoudeshali, especially the section entitled "Gnosis of Life in the Countryside" ("乡村感悟") to see how the two sides integrate.

Zhou Bo was assigned to serve in Dongsha Township from 2009 to 2013, before his promotion to chief of the Press, Media and Publication Bureau of

Daishan County. An ancient town with a four thousand-year history, Dongsha was home to a few hundred small businesses and cottage industries when Zhou Bo arrived. But the modern concrete roads were more than an eyesore—they sealed, in Zhou Bo's opinion, the town's history. He proposed a change after three weeks on the job. This story was written in 2011, after the stone-paving project had been completed and deemed a success.

2
清 潭

蔡楠

陈大臣

我的门是在清早被擂开的。我在睡懒觉。一天一夜的车轴雨把乡村公路浇得像面条,下不了地,出不去门,你说不睡懒觉干什么?可门被擂得山响,这懒觉就睡不成了。我打开门,就看见了那个胡子拉碴、一脸凶相、花格衬衣上沾满了泥水的人。还没等我说话,那人就嚷嚷,我姓冯。走啊,是人的就跟我走,救人去,救人去!

我就跟着他走了出来。邻居们也跟着他走出来。我们就看见一辆四个圈的奥迪像只蛤蟆一样扎在了村边的道沟里。车门被卡住了,司机卡在方向盘和驾驶座位之间动弹不得。我和邻居们走到近前,看清了牌照和人,我们转身便往自己家门口走。

别走啊!拉车拉车,不能眼睁睁见死不救!姓冯的蹚着齐脚踝的泥赶过来。

里面的人有钱,让他花钱找别人救吧!我说。

是啊,他马大能耐不是很能耐吗?怎么就能耐到沟里去了?邻居们说。

姓冯的张开双臂拦住我们,见死不救也判刑。不管里面的人是谁,今天一定要救。我是新来的乡长。谁走,看我以后怎么收拾他!

我们停下,互相望望又一起望着前面的汉子。

2
THE CLEAR POND

Cai Nan

CHEN DACHEN

Someone was hammering at my door. It was early in the morning, and I was still sleeping. It had rained all day and all night, and the country road had been soaked soft as a noodle. I couldn't go work in the fields; I couldn't go out for fun. What else could I do except sleep in? But the pounding on my door forced me out of bed. I opened the door and saw a man. His unshaven face gave him a menacing look, his plaid shirt was blotted with mud and rain. He yelled out before I could say a word, "I'm Feng. Come with me. Come, if you still have a heart, and help save a life!"

I followed him out, as did my neighbors. Soon we saw an Audi with its four-ringed logo lying like a toad in a ditch at the edge of the village. Its doors were stuck, as was the man who was trapped between the steering wheel and the driver's seat. Once my neighbors and I got closer, we recognized the license plate and the man, and we all turned around and headed for home.

"Hold it! Come get the car out. Please. You can't leave him there to die!" Feng rushed toward us through the ankle-deep mud.

"The man inside has money. Let him hire someone to rescue him," I said.

"Right. Isn't he Mighty Ma? How come Mighty Ma ended up in a ditch?" my neighbors echoed.

Mr. Feng blocked our way with extended arms. "It's a crime not to help in this life-or-death situation. We must rescue him, no matter who he is. I'm the new mayor in town. You'll have to answer to me later if you leave now!"

We stopped and looked at one another before our eyes settled on the man in front of us again.

望什么望？不像乡长？瞧，那是我的行李，我今天上班第一天就遇到了这个！

我顺着他的手指望去。我望见了奥迪后面戳着一辆破旧的摩托车，车上真的绑着被褥、脸盆什么的。不过，早就被泥浆糊住了。

我向大伙儿保证，我上任后要干的第一件事就是修好这条路！但这个人必须先救！冯乡长的眼睛瞪了起来。那件花格衬衣簌簌地往下掉着泥片子。

我们就把马大能耐救了上来。

冯乡长没说虚话，通往省国道的这条路他果然修好了。四米宽半尺厚，路面硬化得很好。最让人惊讶的是，修路没动乡里一分钱，是他找马大能耐赞助的。马大能耐是乡里一家造纸厂的老板。听说冯乡长找他拉赞助是走着去的，十几里地，只拎着一瓶衡水老白干。一瓶酒喝完，冯乡长晃晃悠悠回到了乡政府。第二天资金就打进了乡户头。

公路成了人们的眼珠子，冯乡长也成了乡里的心尖子。

宋希望

说实话，我很看不惯冯乡长的样子。粗粗拉拉，咋咋呼呼，不修边幅，似乎永远穿着他那件旧花格衬衣四处晃荡。可人家是领导，看不惯也得伺候人家。我在乡党政办工作，我的本职工作是写材料。可郑书记还让我负责给冯乡长打开水、拾掇卫生。在家里都是老公伺候我，在单位却伺候别人的老公。真是他奶奶个腿！

"What? You don't believe I am the mayor? Look, my luggage is over there. I didn't expect that you would welcome me this way on my first day of work!"

My eyes followed his finger—I saw a beaten-up motorbike parked behind the Audi. There was indeed a bedroll and a washbasin, among other such common items, tied to the motorbike. They were, however, already covered with mud.

"It's my promise to you all: the first thing I'm going to do after I take office is to fix this road! But right now we must rescue this man." Mayor Feng put on a stern face as mud clumps continued to roll off of his plaid shirt.

So we rescued Mighty Ma.

Mayor Feng kept his word and fixed the road to the interstate as promised. It was four meters wide and sixty centimeters thick with a well-hardened surface. Most surprising of all, the township did not spend a penny on it. Mayor Feng got Mighty Ma to sponsor the project. Ma was the owner of a paper mill in town. It is said that Mayor Feng went to solicit funding from Ma on foot, with only a bottle of Hengshui Laobaigan liquor in hand, and walked a distance of more than a dozen kilometers. After the liquor in the bottle was gone, Mayor Feng hobbled his way back to the township government, and the fund for the road was wired to the township account the next day.

The road became a community treasure, and Mayor Feng a beloved townsman.

SONG XIWANG

Frankly, I couldn't stand the sight of Mayor Feng. He was coarse, loud, unkempt, and forever sloshing around in the same worn-out plaid shirt. But he was the boss. I had to assist him no matter what I thought of him. I work in the Township General Office for both the Party and the government. My job is to write speeches and reports, but Secretary Zheng also charged me with fetching hot water for Mayor Feng and with cleaning his office. What a load of crap! Even at home, it's my husband who waits on me. But at work, I had to wait on someone else's husband!

那天，我赶写一篇关于建设文明生态平衡村的汇报闹了夜儿，起晚了。等到把孩子送幼儿园后，就迟到了。我赶紧先去乡长那里，办公桌上铺满了资料，他正一边翻阅书本，一边嚼着方便面吃。那吃相像个孩子。

我喏嚅着说，乡长对不起，我迟到了。你看，卫生没有整，开水也没有打！

冯乡长头也没抬，继续翻阅书本，呜呜噜噜地说，没事！

我赶紧拿起暖瓶想去锅炉房，冯乡长却把我叫住了，宋希望，以后你不用管我了，你好好写材料吧！我又不是小孩子，自己能照顾自己！

完了！乡长记仇了！我心一凉，空暖瓶掉在地上，碎了。

我等着乡长给我穿小鞋，等着乡长调我走。这一天终于来了。那是一个周末，我还在给书记写讲话稿，冯乡长把我叫到他屋里，摸着胡子拉碴的下巴对我说，你提前回家吧。

我小心地问，为什么？我可是很努力啊。书记周一的讲话稿还没写好，你怎么能让我回家呢？

冯乡长拽下来一根胡子，说，我做了一个调查，每天下午下班前是你们最紧张的时候，赶着回家，赶着挤车接孩子，你有好几次都因为晚接孩子被老师批评了。所以，从今天起，你们有孩子的女同志可以提前一小时下班！早早回家喂孩子、洗衣服做饭、孝敬爹娘、孝敬公婆。你去下个通知吧！

那材料呢？周一书记还要讲话呢！我说。

拿来，我写。冯乡长坐在了办公桌前。

那天晚上，我对老公说，我们冯乡长是最有派的男人，他的花格子衬衫是乡里的一道风景！

One day I got up late because I stayed up the night before writing a report on building sustainable villages of civility. After I dropped my child at the kindergarten, I arrived late for work. I rushed to Mayor Feng's office first thing. His desk was messy with documents, and he was flipping through the pages of a book and chewing on instant noodles like a kid.

"I'm sorry, Mr. Mayor, for being late," I muttered. "You must have noticed. I've yet to clean your office and fetch the hot water."

Mayor Feng didn't even look up. "No worries," he blurted out, as he continued to flip through the book.

I picked up the thermos quickly, but before I could head out to the boiler room, Mayor Feng stopped me: "Song Xiwang, please don't do this for me anymore, and concentrate on what you must write. I'm not a child. I can take care of myself."

Oh, no. It's all over! Mr. Mayor now holds a grudge against me. As my heart sank, the empty thermos dropped to the ground and broke into pieces.

I started waiting for the mayor to squeeze my shoes about it—for the day he would get rid of me. It finally came on a Friday, as I was writing a speech for Secretary Zheng. Mayor Feng brought me to his office. With his hand rubbing his scruffy chin, he said to me, "Please go home early."

"Why?" I asked, carefully. *I have been working hard*, I thought. *How could you send me home when I am not done with Secretary Zheng's speech for Monday?*

Mayor Feng plucked a hair from his beard and said: "I did some research. The most frantic time of the day for you folks is when you get off work in the afternoon. You want to get home quickly, and you have to catch the crowded bus to pick up your kid. The kindergarten teachers have reprimanded you several times for picking your child up late. So from now on, female employees with kids can get off work an hour early! Go and get home early to feed your kid, do your laundry, cook and care for your parents or in-laws. Please go notify everyone in writing of this."

"What about the speech?" I asked. "Secretary Zheng is to give the speech on Monday."

"Bring it to me. I'll finish it," Mayor Feng said, as he sat down at his desk.

I told my husband that evening that Mayor Feng was the classiest man around and his plaid shirt a pretty sight to see in town.

郑布林

我倒真小看了小冯。这家伙很有两下子。现在看来,我把他要来大湾乡当乡长是要对了,也是要错了。

我本来是想要个有能力的好帮手。可这家伙能力是有,却不能帮我忙,还净给我添乱。暂不说他修路和自己搞个人崇拜的事了,就说眼下马大能耐造纸厂的事情吧。虽说你救了人家的生命,可也让人家出资修路了啊。按说这关系应该越来越好,可他不,现在又要让人家停产改造。马大能耐不干了,他找到我这里来告状。他说,郑书记你看我可是给咱地方上做了贡献的人哪,税我一分也没少拿,修路捐款我可是哪回也不耍滑。你看冯乡长这人硬是和我过不去,他把我都整到县里了。环 保局来找我,让我停产整治废水排放系统,要整顿半年呢!要是这样,我干脆关张得了!

我急了。我把小冯找来。我问他,小冯,这么大的事你也不和我商量一下?

他在我的办公桌前一边挖着鼻孔,一边嘟哝着,刻不容缓啊郑书记,造纸厂污染严重,周围地里都不长庄稼,附近臭气熏天,老百姓喝的水都有怪味儿,再耽误下去会出人命的。所以,我就写了报告递给县里了。

你赶紧把报告给我要回来——我把心爱的紫砂茶杯都摔在了地上。

ZHENG BULIN

I have indeed underestimated Little Feng.[3] He is really something. It now appears that I was both right and wrong to choose him to be mayor of Dawan Township.

My original intention was to get a capable helping hand. This fellow is capable all right, but instead of being my helping hand, he has done nothing but rock my boat. Let's put aside his issue of using the road to build himself a cult of admirers and focus on the current problem at Mighty Ma's paper mill. It is true Feng saved Ma's life, but he also took his money to fix the road. Their relationship should be getting better, but Feng won't let it. Now, he is asking Ma to suspend production in order to fix his plant. Mighty Ma is fed up with this crap. He has come to me to complain. Ma said, "Look, Secretary Zheng, I have been a great contributor to our local community. I pay my taxes in full and I have never played fast and loose with the donations for road construction. But look at Mayor Feng, he is literally trying to undercut me. He's sicced the county authorities on me. The county Environmental Protection Bureau checked me out and ordered me to halt production until I fix the wastewater discharge system. This project will take half a year! If I do that, I might as well shut the mill down for good."

I was furious. I called Little Feng in and asked: "Why didn't you check with me before you made a big decision like this?"

He was standing in front of my desk. He grunted while picking his nose, "Secretary Zheng, we have no time to lose. The pollution by the paper mill is so serious that crops aren't growing around it; the stench nearby is overpowering; even the drinking water has an odd taste to it. Delaying further would have put people's lives in danger, so I wrote the report and sent it to county authorities."

"You go and get that report back right now!" I even hurled my favorite purple sand[4] teacup to the ground.

---

3. It is common for a senior superior to prefix his address of a younger colleague with "little" (小 *xiǎo*).
4. Purple sand ceramic products, made from the local clay of Yixing in Jiangsu Province, are usually handcrafted and valuable. The making of fine quality ceramic in Yixing goes as far back as Song dynasty (tenth century). Today an everyday utensil like a teapot or teacup is often used, as well as cherished, as a piece of artwork.

结语

  冯乡长就去了县里。可是他这一去就没有回来。返程途中,他的摩托车和一辆货车撞在了一起。就在他修好的那条路上。是陈大臣报的信。当宋希望领着乡政府的人赶到时,冯乡长躺在血泊里已经没有了气息。那件花格旧衬衣,沾满了比夏天黄昏还要红的鲜血。人们在他衬衣口袋里翻出了那份让造纸厂停产整顿的报告,还有5元8角钱。
  冯乡长死后,大湾乡的人在那个路口立了块碑,上面刻了两个大字:清潭。
  清潭是冯乡长的名字。

(2011)

EPILOGUE

So Mayor Feng went to the county seat, and it was a trip of no return. His motorbike crashed into a van on his way back home, on the very road that he had helped fix. Chen Dachen brought the news. By the time people from the township government arrived, led by Song Xiwang, Mayor Feng had lost all signs of life and was lying in a puddle of blood. That worn-out plaid shirt of his was soaked redder than the summer sunset. In its pocket, they found the report requesting that the paper mill halt production for renovation. Along with the report was a 5 yuan note and 80 cents in change.

Later, the people of Dawan Township erected a stone tablet at the crossroads where Mayor Feng died. Engraved on it were two large characters: 清潭.[5]

It was Mayor Feng's given name, Feng Qingtan. It means "clear pond."

(2011)

VOCABULARY AND USAGE

擂	léi	beat; pound	粉丝们摇旗擂鼓为他加油。
睡懒觉	shuìlǎnjiào	sleep in	他因为睡懒觉上课迟到了。
车轴	chēzhóu	axle	车轴是车的一个重要部件。
车轴雨	chēzhóuyǔ	nonstop rain	这车轴雨已经下了两天两夜。
浇	jiāo	drenched	大雨把这草坪浇软了，你还是等明天割草吧。
下地	xiàdì	go work in the field	我这几天不能下地了，要去北京录节目。
山响	shānxiǎng	thunderous	他要是睡着了，你就是把门擂得山响，他也听不见。

---

5. The play on words emerging from the similarities between 清潭 (qīngtán, clear pond) and 清官 (qīngguān, clean official) may be lost in translation. The name in Chinese, however, is indicative of a longing for the latter.

胡子拉碴	húzilāchā	a stubbly chin	你可不能这么胡子拉碴地去相亲。
相	xiàng	the look	我一定能赢,因为人人都说我有冠军相。
奥迪	àodí	a transliteration of Audi	她喜欢奥迪牌的车。
蛤蟆	háma	toad	你这是癞蛤蟆想吃天鹅肉——没门!
扎	zhā	plunge (headlong)	路上有冰,我急刹车时一头扎进了旁边的道沟。
动弹不得	dòngtan bù dé	cannot move	大石头压住了他的双臂,让他动弹不得。
眼睁睁	yǎnzhēngzhēng	unfeelingly	我不能眼睁睁地看着别人欺负我的孩子!
见死不救	jiànsǐbújiù	not to help a dying man	我是医生,不能见死不救。
蹚(水)	tāng	wade	这里的水已经齐腰深了,你蹚不过来,千万别冒险。
齐	qí	reach the height of	
脚踝	jiǎohuái	ankle	老年人做运动尤其要注意保护脚踝。
能耐	néngnài	ability	他没有什么真能耐。
判刑	pànxíng	sentence (to prison)	在我们这儿,打自己的孩子也是要判刑的。
收拾	shōushi	settle accounts with somebody	他做的坏事太多了,早就该收拾他了。
汉子	hànzi	man; fellow	你说话算数,是条汉子。
戳	chuō	stand	你别戳在那儿不动,帮着摆摆碗筷、端端菜。
摩托车	mótuóchē	motorbike	我们县里开电动摩托车的人还是比开小轿车的人多。
绑	bǎng	fasten	他把行李绑在摩托车的后座上。
被褥	bèirù	bedding	被褥都是床上用品;褥子铺在身下,被子盖在身上。
泥浆	níjiāng	mud	这里的土质好,稠泥浆可以用来糊墙。
糊	hú	paste	
上任	shàngrèn	take office	你是哪一年去山东上任的?

瞪眼睛	dèng yǎnjīng	stare; glare	他一瞪眼睛我们就知道他生气了。
簌簌	sùsù	an onomatopoeic term for rustling	小风吹来，树叶簌簌发响。
虚(话)	xū(huà)	empty; false (words)	他言行一致，从不说虚话。
眼珠子	yǎnzhūzi	eyeball	她爱护这部手机就像爱护自己的眼珠子。
拉(赞助)	lā(zànzhù)	draw; appeal (for support)	你是他的朋友，不该拉他赞助这个没有前途的项目。
赞助	zànzhù	sponsor	
拎	līn	carry	说一个人会给领导拎包是说他善于巴结讨好上级。
老白干	lǎobáigān	Laobaigan (a popular brand of liquor)	他跟女朋友表白前喝了一碗老白干壮胆。
晃悠/荡	huàngyou/dang	swinging	他喝醉了，走路直晃悠/荡。
(把钱)打进(账户)	(bǎqián) dǎjìn (zhànghù)	transfer (money into an account)	妈妈每个月都及时把生活费打进我的账户。
(心)尖子	(xīn)jiānzi	tip-top; the most important; the best of its kind	她的孩子是她的心尖子。
看不惯	kànbúguàn	detest; frown upon	我干活粗拉，丈夫看不惯，也常受婆婆指责。
粗拉	cūlā	coarse; crude	
咋呼	zāhu	loud; show off; bluster	妈妈常说女孩子要稳重，不能咋咋呼呼的。
不修边幅	bùxiūbiānfú	slovenly	不修边幅的男人才酷呢！
四处	sìchù	everywhere and all directions	你有空去中国四处看看。
伺候	cìhou	wait on; serve	孩子、病人、老人都需要我们耐心伺候。
本职(写)材料	běnzhí (xiě) cáiliào	one's job; one's duty prepare written material	给领导写材料是我的本职工作，给他们端茶倒水不是。
拾掇	shíduō	tidy up	你该拾掇一下自己的房间了。
生态平衡	shēngtài píng héng	ecological balance	向河里排放污水会破坏生态平衡。

汇报	huìbào	report	她为了赶写汇报昨夜睡得很晚。
赶写	gǎn xiě	dash off	
闹夜	nàoyè	a colloquial expression for "burning the midnight oil"	您都这么大年纪了，真不该闹夜了，身体吃不消的。
嚼	jiáo	chew	她老了，已经嚼不动花生米这样的食物了。
吃相	chīxiàng	manner of eating	你能从一个人的吃相看出他的教养？
嗫嚅	nièrú	mutter; speak haltingly	他嗫嚅着吐出几个字，我们都不明白什么意思。
打(水)	dǎ(shuǐ)	draw; fetch	打饭，打水，打酱油这些事儿如今已经不多见了。
呜呜噜噜	wūwulūlu	unclear sounds	你呜呜噜噜说什么呢？
记仇	jìchóu	bear a grudge	你太多心了，他不是那种一点儿小事就记仇的人。
(心)凉	(xīn)liáng	disappointed; disheartened	三年没有他的音讯，她的心彻底凉了。
穿小鞋	chuānxiǎoxié	make things harder for someone	他觉得自己很完美，老板对他不满是给他穿小鞋。
拽	zhuài	pull; drag	他拽了拽袖子说，"不长不短，正好！"
孝敬	xiàojìng	show filial respect for	对长辈的孝敬应该是发自内心的。
下通知	xià tōngzhī	make an announcement	明天有暴风雪，学校下通知停课。
有派	yǒu pài	charismatic	他是个又自信又谦虚、十分有派的好演员。
有两下子	yǒu liǎngxiàzǐ	have real ability and skills	没有两下子她能当镇长吗？
家伙	jiāhuo	guy; fellow	这家伙有前科，别相信他。
净	jìng	entirely; only	一夜大风，满地净是落叶。
添乱	tiānluàn	mess things up	孩子在这里只会给你添乱。
崇拜	chǒngbài	worship	很多读者崇拜莎士比亚。

按说	ànshuō	in the ordinary course of events	按说我们队实力很强不该输的。
耍滑	shuǎhuá	act in a slick way	他上学的时候就常耍滑，抄别人的作业。
硬是	yìngshì	obstinately	明明是他干的，可他硬是不承认。
和…过不去	hé…guòbúqù	find fault with someone	我喜欢的你一定说难看，你为什么总是和我过不去？
关张	guānzhāng	close down	在年头，商店开张关张是常有的事儿。
得了	déle	let it go at that; forget it	你在这儿没有身份，不能找工作，我看你还是离开得了。
挖(鼻孔)	wā(bíkǒng)	pick (one's nose)	在别人面前挖鼻孔不太雅观。
嘟哝	dūnong	mumble (complaints)	他不满意地嘟哝了几句。
刻不容缓	kèbùrónghuǎn	permit no delay	教育改革刻不容缓。
臭气熏天	chòuqìxūntiān	overwhelming stench	那个化工厂的周围臭气熏天。
老百姓	lǎobǎixìng	ordinary people	她事事处处为老百姓着想，是个好领导。
耽误	dānwù	delay	这事儿人命关天，一分钟也不能耽误！
出人命	chūrénmìng	cause death	开车不小心会出人命的。
递(给／到)	dì(gěi/dào)	hand over to; deliver	她把火炬递到我的手中。
返程	fǎnchéng	return (trip)	我去了就没打算回来，没想过要买返程票。
途中	túzhōng	during the journey	到芝加哥还有500多英里呢，途中必须停下来加油。
撞	zhuàng	hit; collide	她撞到了桌子角上，把头撞破了。
血泊	xuěpò	a pool of blood	他胸部中弹，倒在血泊中。
气息	qìxī	breath	医生到达时他已气息全无。
立	lì	erect	他们在那块田的中央为乡长立了块碑。
碑	bēi	upright stone tablet	

QUESTIONS FOR DISCUSSION

1. Who are Chen Dachen, Song Xiwang, Mighty Ma, Zheng Bulin, and Feng Qingtan? What demographic groups do they represent?
2. Whose narrative, in your opinion, identifies Mayor Feng most accurately? What does the narrative technique employed here say about human perception and identity?
3. How does Mayor Feng deal with Mighty Ma at first? Why is Feng's way effective? Is his way commendable in your opinion?
4. Do you like his executive order regarding female employees with children?
5. What is his leadership style, especially in contrast to that of Zheng Bulin?
6. What have you learned about the Party-State bureaucracy at work from this story?
7. Why did Mayor Feng get the report back? Is he a hero or a coward? Why do the local people commemorate Mayor Feng?

1. 谁是陈大臣、宋希望、马大能耐、郑布林和冯清潭？他们分别代表那些不同群体？
2. 你认为谁的描述说出了最真实的冯乡长？这里的叙述技巧在启发对认知和自我（identity）什么样的思考？
3. 冯乡长开始的时候是怎样跟马大能耐打交道的？他方式为什么很有效？你觉得他的做法值得赞赏吗？
4. 你喜欢冯乡长为有孩子的女性职工所下的行政通告吗？
5. 冯乡长的领导风格是什么样的？他与郑布林的风格有什么不同？
6. 关于中国党政官僚机构的运作，你从这个故事中都学到了什么？
7. 冯乡长为什么把报告要回来了？他是个英雄还是个胆小鬼？为什么当地的老百姓会纪念他？

AUTHOR BIO

Cai Nan (1965–) works with townships like this on a daily basis as chief of the General Office at Renqiu Local Tax Bureau in Hebei Province. A native of Renqiu County, Cai Nan proudly sees himself as an offspring of the Lotus Lake School, an influential contemporary school of literary thought and artistic expression from his native region. Cai Nan enjoys writing in his spare time and loves reading international writers and Nobel Prize winners in translation. He has published seven collections of stories and two volumes of prose and essays. Literary journals and magazines across China have carried his fictional works, among them prestigious venues like *People's Literature* (人民文学), *Beijing Literature* (北京文学), *Tianjin Literature* (天津文学), *Great Wall* (长城), and *Readers* (读者). Among his best-known works are "Fish Walking" ("行走在岸上的鱼"), "Looking Back at Life at the Moment of Death" ("生死回眸"), "August Mood" ("八月情绪"), and "Life CD" ("叙事光盘"). His blog profile emphasizes three things: his membership in China's Writers Association, his directorship on the short-short story committee at the Hebei Writers Association, and his position as vice-chairman of the Cangzhou Writers Association. A representative writer of the short-short genre in China, Cai Nan is best known for his experiments with the art form and innovative contribution to its success; his ability to present complexity in economic prose; and his sense of social responsibility, which he invests quite a bit in the character of Mayor Feng in "The Clear Pond."

3
大红苕

曾平

大河村的苏大个子,种红苕种出了名气。前两天,在省城举办的农展会上,他送展的大红苕,获了金奖。

县府办吴主任叫来了小刘,要他去一趟大河村,把情况弄清楚,立马拿出一个经验材料来。吴主任还特意给小刘派了一辆车。小刘进县政府办公室时间短,说什么也不该单独派车。以至于驾驶员小游,在车上,还一个劲地问小刘,吴主任是你亲戚?

小刘从吴主任办公室出来就直奔大河村。谈到工作,小刘浑身上下有使不完的劲。还有两个月,小刘公务员就转正了。他想干出成绩,给领导留个好印象,以后,有个好前途。

小刘在大河村蹲了一整天,回来,关在屋子里熬了一整夜。第二天,打着哈欠,揉着一双熊猫眼,把材料送到吴主任手里。

吴主任接过材料开始看。小刘忐忑不安地望着吴主任,以期从他脸上看出一些首肯和赞许来。小刘学的是文秘,大学里就开始在报刊上发表文

3
BIG SWEET POTATOES

Zeng Ping

Big Su of Dahe Village had made a name for himself growing sweet potatoes. Two days ago, his showpiece won the gold medal at the state fair in the provincial capital.

Afterward, Chief Wu from the General Office of County Government[6] summoned Little Liu. He asked Little Liu to make a trip to Dahe Village to check on everything and to report on Big Su's experience immediately. Chief Wu also arranged a car for Little Liu, specifically for the trip. A novice to the General Office, Little Liu shouldn't have been given such a privilege, so Little You, the driver, kept pressing him even when they were well on the road, "Is Chief Wu a relative of yours?"

Little Liu made straight for Dahe Village from Chief Wu's office. When it came to work, Little Liu exuded boundless enthusiasm from head to heel. In another two months, he would obtain his permanent civil servant status. He wanted to impress his superiors by doing great work and accumulating honors for the great future that lay in front of him.

Little Liu spent the whole day in Dahe Village and the whole night working on the report after he got back to his room. Yawning and rubbing his eyes, which now had dark circles under them, he handed the report to Chief Wu the next day.

Chief Wu took the report and began to read. Anxiously, Little Liu looked at him, hoping to find signs of approval and praise. He had majored in secretarial studies in college and had started to publish in newspapers and journals when he was still a student, so everyone called him a wit. County Governor Li's secretary had recently assumed the

---

6. This general office runs the county government's daily affairs. In his secretarial and coordinating functions, the office chief has close ties to the high-level county bureaucrats.

章,大家都叫他才子。最近,李县长的秘书到镇上做副书记去了。小刘浮想联翩,会不会是李县长和吴主任在考察自己呢?

吴主任很快把材料递过来,要小刘再看看。

小刘看不清吴主任的表情,一头雾水。小刘只得拿着材料看。其实,材料小刘都能背诵了。

小刘写了苏大个子如何起早贪黑,顶着炎炎暑日,冒着倾盆大雨精耕细作。他将苏大个子除草总结为"两早两利用",施肥总结为"三勤一减四注意",从育苗到栽插到收获总结为"两提前三到位"。他还把苏大个子的红苕和周边群众的红苕进行比较,按苏大个子的种植办法,一亩地,至少增产三四百斤。

他把这种栽种方法命名为"苏式栽种法",材料结尾,他满含深情地写道,苏式红苕栽种法,是红苕种植技术的创新,是农民增收的福音,完全应该在全县全市乃至全省推广。

小刘把材料盯着看了两遍,没有发现错别字病句,也没有发现和上级精神冲突之处,并且突出农民增收,建设社会主义新农村主题,说什么也该是一篇好材料啊!

吴主任笑笑,说,还没发现问题?

小刘使劲想了又想,始终想不出,只好说,没有。

吴主任开导说,小刘啊,得动脑筋啊!

小刘挺委屈,写这个材料,他算绞尽脑汁了。

吴主任看他不开窍,只好说,这材料,得重新写。

小刘急了,说,为什么?

吴主任拍拍他的肩膀,说,别急,慢慢来啊!

吴主任只好点拨他,说,你想想啊,苏大个子的新型红苕种哪里来的啊?

小刘说,乡农技站啊?

office of deputy party secretary in a nearby township government. Little Liu's imagination ran wild: *Could County Governor Li and Chief Wu be testing him, assessing him?*

Soon Chief Wu handed the report back to Little Liu and asked him to take another look at it.

Little Liu, unsure of what Chief Wu's facial expression meant, couldn't make heads or tails of what was going on. He felt obligated to check over the report in his hand, but truthfully, he had already committed the whole report to memory.

Little Liu wrote about how Big Su got up early and worked late, and how he farmed intensively and carefully whether under the scorching summer sun or in pouring rain. He summarized Big Su's weeding method into "two early starts and two good strategies," his fertilizing technique into "triple diligence plus one deduction and four cautions," and the process from seeding to planting to harvesting into "two in advance and three in place." He also compared Big Su's output with those around him. Big Su's way of farming yielded at least 300 to 400 *jin* more per *mu*.

Little Liu named Big Su's method "the Su farming style." At the end of the report he wrote with deep feeling that the Su style of growing sweet potatoes was a scientific innovation that meant good news for increased production. Absolutely, it merited promotion throughout the county, the municipality area, and even the province.

Twice, Little Liu closely checked the report. He didn't see any misuse of words or syntactical errors, nor could he find anything that contradicted the directives from the higher authorities. And with the prominence given to the themes of increasing farmers' output and of building a new socialist countryside, this should be a good report no matter how you read it.

Chief Wu smiled and asked, "Still don't see any problem?"

Little Liu thought long and hard, but couldn't come up with anything. Finally he had to say, "No."

Chief Wu urged him, "Rack your brain, Little Liu!"

Little Liu felt hurt. Writing this report, he had racked all the brain he had.

Seeing that Little Liu was stuck, Chief Wu told him: "You must rewrite this report."

Little Liu was upset, "Why?"

"Calm down and take it easy," Chief Wu said, patting him on the shoulder.

Chief Wu felt he ought to set things straight for Little Liu. "Think about it, where did Big Su get the new sweet potato seeding?"

吴主任继续点拨，说，给红苕施的化肥呢？

小刘说，也是乡农技站啊？

吴主任说，这就对了。农技站是从哪里来的呢？

小刘说，农业局啊？

吴主任说，这就对了。农业局谁领导啊？

小刘说，李县长啊！

小刘惊奇地说，主任的意思是写李县长？

吴主任说，这就对了。

小刘挺困惑挺迟疑，说，主任，这有些牵强附会吧？

吴主任语重心长地说，小刘啊，这叫牵强附会吗？不是！如果你硬要说是，我告诉你啊，我们这些文秘人员，还真要有点这样的基本功呢！

(2011)

"From the township agrotechnical station, of course," answered Little Liu.

"What about the fertilizer used?" Chief Wu continued.

"Also from the township agrotechnical station," Little Liu answered.

"That's right!" Chief Wu said, and then asked, "Who set up the station?"

"The Bureau of Agriculture, of course," Little Liu said.

"Right again!" Chief Wu continued, "Who leads the Bureau of Agriculture?"

"County Governor Li!" Little Liu said and was shocked by his own realization: "You mean I should write about County Governor Li?"

"Now you get it!" Chief Wu answered.

Little Liu, confused and reluctant, asked again, "Isn't this stretching things too far, Chief Wu?"

Chief Wu replied in all earnestness, "Little Liu, how could this be stretching things too far? No! If you say it is, I will tell you that we secretarial staff truly need the basic skill of being able to stretch things too far!"

(2011)

VOCABULARY AND USAGE

农展会	nóngzhǎnhuì	the agricultural fair	今年的农展会，他送展的产品是自己种的大白菜。
送展	sòng zhǎn	send to an exhibition for display	
派	pài	assign; send	县长派我去机场接客人。
转正	zhuǎnzhèng	become a regular employee	通过了这次考试，我就可以转正了。
蹲	dūn	stay	蹲点儿就是去一个基层单位工作、调研。
熬夜	áoyè	stay up late	他为按时写完报告熬了一整夜。
忐忑不安	tǎntèbùān	nervous; uneasy	我忐忑不安地等待着考试结果。
才子	cáizǐ	gifted scholar	据说唐伯虎是明朝江南第一才子。
浮想联翩	fúxiǎngliánpiān	thoughts filled one's mind	今天的电影让我浮想联翩。
一头雾水	yītóuwùshuǐ	cannot make heads or tails of something	这道题太难了！我到现在还是一头雾水，不知怎么做。

起早贪黑	qǐzǎotānhēi	work from dawn to dusk	为了能让我在美国读书，爸爸妈妈起早贪黑地工作。
倾盆大雨	qīngpéndàyǔ	torrential rain	这样的倾盆大雨下不长。
精耕细作	jīnggēngxì zuò	farm with meticulous care	精耕细作不如多用农药化肥省事儿省力。
增产	zēngchǎn	increase production	今年粮食增产了所以粮价下调了。
盯	dīng	fix one's eyes on	他盯着那张地图看了一上午。
突出	tūchū	give prominence to	这篇报告突出了农民的勤劳和智慧。
绞尽脑汁	jiǎojìnnǎozhī	rack one's brain	我绞尽脑汁也没想出什么好办法。
开窍	kāiqiào	begin to understand	这孩子心眼实，脑子常常不开窍，还麻烦您多费心点拨着点儿。
点拨	diǎnbō	give hints	
牵强附会	qiānqiángfùhuì	far-fetched	你的解释牵强附会，我不会相信的。
语重心长	yǔzhòngxīncháng	sincere and earnest	爸爸的话语重心长，我记在心上了。

QUESTIONS FOR DISCUSSION

1. Is this a story of a novice getting his first taste of workplace politics? How are the office politics different here?
2. Why is Little Liu so serious about the report?
3. Why does the driver keep asking Little Liu, "Is Chief Wu a relative of yours?"
4. "[W]e secretarial staff truly need the basic skill of being able to stretch things too far!" Does Chief Wu really believe in what he says? Why?
5. Although both may have selfish motivations, Little Liu is still different from Chief Wu. What sets them apart?
6. How does the "presence" of County Governor Li function in the story? What/who is the object of criticism here?
7. Zeng Ping, the author, wrote this story while serving in the same official capacity as County Governer Li. How does this fact affect your understanding of this story and Chinese bureaucratic institutions?

1. 这是一个关于新手初涉单位政治的故事吗？这里的办公室政治跟你所熟悉的有什么不同？
2. 小刘为什么把这个报告这么当回事儿？
3. 司机为什么会追问小刘，"吴主任是你亲戚？"
4. "我们这些文秘人员，还真要有点这样的基本功呢！"——吴主任真信他自己说的这些话吗？为什么？
5. 虽然小刘和吴主任可能都有自私的动机，但两人毕竟不是一回事儿。他们的不同在哪里？
6. 李县长不露面儿的存在在故事中起了什么作用？这篇故事批评锋芒的所指是谁／什么？
7. 作者曾平写这个故事时所任官职跟李县长类似。这一事实会怎样影响你对这个故事以及中国官僚体制的理解？

AUTHOR BIO

Zeng Ping (1970–) is a farmer's son. After graduating college, he taught at a rural school. His articles in the local newspaper caught the attention of county authorities, and his official career soon took off. Zeng Ping started from a position much like that of Little Liu's in the story and worked his way up through the ranks. In his thirties, he was head of the government of Longmatan District, part of the Luzhou Municipality in Sichuan Province, with a population of more than 340,000. Zeng Ping also has been on the fast track of advancement with his creative writing. His published works now number more than three hundred, more than one hundred of which have been reprinted by such prestigious journals as *Selected Fiction* (小说选刊), *Fiction Monthly* (小说月报), *Beijing Literature* (北京文学), *Selected Short-Shorts* (小小说选刊), *Selected Micro-fiction* (微型小说选刊), and *Writer's Digest* (作家文摘). The majority of Zeng Ping's fiction is novellas and short stories. Some of his short-shorts are also nationally known, for example, "The Eyes Behind" ("身后的眼睛") and "On That Rainy Night" ("雨夜"). Many of his short-short stories have been anthologized, including "Big Sweet Potatoes." Zeng Ping wrote this story when he was serving in a capacity equivalent to that of the County Governor Li in the story.

第五章

自我（特征、身份、认同）

关注当代中国文化的人可能会发现这样一个悖论：越来越多的人，包括那些个人意识空前高涨的年轻人，选择职业时是听从家人的意见的。虽然当今的环境比以往任何时候都更加鼓励自我发展，但它却没能有效地引起对独特自我更多的关注，也没能带来更强烈的实现一己之梦的愿望。相反，人们通常依旧将个人利益理解为与群体利益相辅相成，还是在不懈努力地把个人喜好跟家庭义务协调一致。如何理解这种与个人自我意识膨胀背道而驰的"反向"发展？以往公认的观点——中国人缺乏自我意识，以群体为重而牺牲个人——已不足以解释今日之现状。

Identity是一个复杂的概念，在中文里没有与之对应的表达。我们需要用"特征"、"身份"、"认同"三组六个字，才能粗略地表达identity的意思。这六个字反映了中国人对identity问题的复杂思考。慎思这其中的蕴意，尤其是当读者面对陌生的习俗和观念时，可能会成为进入本章故事的有效蹊径。

《兄弟们长大》让我们看到，为个人特质做标识、帖标签是徒劳的。故事里兄弟们的identity可能更像尼采《快乐的科学》中的灵魂，也是不断变化的力量之相互作用的结果。与此同时，每个兄弟那迷一般的独特魅力，又不受制于任何道德判断的羁绊，始终如一。兄弟们成长中的变化以及变化的结果让我们不禁要问，刻意打造与众不同的self-identity意味着什么？虽然self-identity建构着我们每时每刻的存在，也可能的确有一贯性，但谁能定义它、锁定它？与众不同的identity的形成大概不会终结，而是永远都在生活的探索、变化和整合中不断成形。

CHAPTER 5

IDENTITY

Observers of contemporary Chinese culture may discover a paradox: more people, many with an unprecedented sense of individuality, are following career paths chosen by their families. Today's milieu, more encouraging of self-development than ever, has not done much to develop more concern for the unique self or a stronger desire for the realization of personal dreams. Instead, individual interests are still often understood to be in agreement with those of the group; personal preferences are still in the process of aligning with family obligations. How do we understand this "inverse" movement to the development of individual identity? The accepted account of the dedication to the group over the individual in Chinese ideas of identity is no longer sufficient.

The fact that it takes six Chinese characters in three combinations to convey a rough idea of "identity" shows that "identity" is a complex concept and that the Chinese language does not have an established terminology for it. Reflection on the complexity of Chinese thought on this idea can be a productive approach to the stories in this chapter, especially as readers encounter what may be unfamiliar practices and perceptions.

"Brothers" shows the futility of trying to map or label idiosyncrasies. More like the Soul in Friedrich Nietzsche's *The Gay Science*, the personal identity of each brother is also an interaction of changing forces; yet their enigmatic uniqueness remains constant and defies judgment. How and what the brothers turn out to be makes us wonder what it means to construct a distinct self-identity. Although it forms who we are from moment to moment, and may prove consistent, it cannot be definite or certain. The formation of distinct personal identity is probably never finished but is continually processed through life's ongoing exploration, transformation, and integration.

《井不自知水多少》所讲的故事有说教性，但它用隐喻的方式，诠释了一个颇有新意的关于自我和identity形成的观点。这个观点深植于佛教的"缘起"之说和毛泽东思想的"群众路线"。请体会一下，用群体的力量来塑造个性化发展这样的悖论是否也有其深刻的道理。对故事的主人公耿自民——一个村官来说，答案是肯定的。他父亲传授的成长理论一方面有对个人identity并非孤立的理解，另一方面也包括了对人们可无限伸延之能力的信心。他这样的理解和信心皆因世间的一切都处于联动关系状态之中。当耿自民决定去直面未知的时候，他在展示对人类共有正能量信赖的同时也以实际行动表现了自己独特的个性。

我们惯于把identity与种族、性别、阶级、宗教、族裔、职业或性取向等挂钩。雅克·德里达是个出生于阿尔及利亚的法国人。他说自己的"出生决定了他既是这一个也是那一个。"[1] 他对民族国家identity的批评提请那些仰仗权利、制服机制和所谓主权意识建构起来的"主体"反思identity到底是什么，以及把它具象化的后果。《舅母》中的舅母有个神秘的抉择，它是对把identity具象化的彻底否决。对舅母此举的这般理解是读懂这篇揪心小说的关键，也是理解二十世纪六十年代一个中国乡村女子对生活深远影响的关键。

对德里达来说，国籍是个"不确定的、近来才有的、靠不住的、人为的"[2]东西。边界也是同样。舅母的蒙古村庄就座落在这样一条边界上；村民的生活方式也无时无刻不在经历变化。跟许多人一样，舅母愿以自己的劳动成果为豪，但她绝不允许任何人把她与某个东西、某种行为或某一结果划等号。这种不确切、不靠谱的等式是对她人格尊严的最大侵犯，她必须不惜一切代价予以回绝。只要是生活就会有意想不到的事情。舅母与他人和解的方式和效果也说明她存在的意义远远超越了她所做的食物。相对于

---

1. 雅克·德里达, *Monolingualism of the Other or The Prosthesis of Origin*, 译者 帕特里克·门萨（斯坦福大学出版社，1998）。第13页。
2. 同上，第15页。

By way of metaphor, the didactic storytelling of "Water in the Well" introduces a nuanced view of self and identity formation. The view is deeply rooted in the Buddhist principle of "dependent origination" and the Maoist notion of "mass line." Please see whether the paradox of individuation through collective strength here makes any sense to you. It does for the protagonist Geng Zimin, whose work identity is as a village official. His father's theory of individual development includes an understanding of individual identity as inseparable from others and a faith in endless human capacity because of the interconnectedness of all. When Geng Zimin decides to give the unknown a chance, he is entrusting himself to the power of shared humanity and also making a statement about individual uniqueness.

Too often we associate identity with race, gender, class, religion, ethnicity, occupation, or sexual orientation. A Frenchman born in Algeria, Jacques Derrida claimed that he was "at once one and the other by birth."[1] His critique of national identity invites the "I" associated with power, mastery, and sovereignty to reflect on what identity is and the consequences of objectifying it. To read the titular character's mysterious act in the story "Auntie" as an ultimate rejection of such objectification is key to understanding the intense drama and profound impact of a rural Chinese woman's life in the 1960s.

Citizenship for Derrida is "precarious, recent, threatened and artificial."[2] The same can be said of borders. Auntie's Mongolian village is located on such a border, and the villagers' ways of life are undergoing transitions. Auntie, like many laborers, is happy to be identified by the fruits of her labor, but she cannot tolerate being equated with any one thing, one action, or one result. Such an equation, precarious and artificial, is the worst violation of her human dignity, and she must reject it at all cost. What life is devoid of unpredictability? As Auntie's act of reconciliation shows, she represents much more than the food she makes. As no categorization sufficiently captures any individual experience, no identifier

---

1. Jacques Derrida, *Monolingualism of the Other; or, The Prosthesis of Origin*, trans. Patrick Mensah (Stanford, Calif.: Stanford University Press, 1998), 13.
2. Ibid., 15.

人的生活和经历，没有什么分类命名可以是完整无缺的，也没有哪个标识可以精准无误。舅母英勇地捍卫了她的自由和尊严。

《恋人》中寓言式的呈现把生活推至极致，让我们看到把想像中的identity 当了真的后果。阅读时也请注意死亡来临时那颇具喜剧色彩的一刻。在那一刻里，布欢儿或许是带着对爱的满足步入天堂。

can completely encapsulate an individual. Auntie has defended her freedom and dignity heroically.

The allegory in "The Love of Her Life" pushes things to extremes and shows what happens when an imagined identity is believed to be real. Please do not ignore the comic touch of this story at the moment of death. In it, you may find that Buhuaner does not die of a broken heart.

1
舅 母

俞胜利

姥家是蒙族人居住的庄子。蒙族人的庄子被一层厚实的庄稼围裹着。

在人们的印象中,蒙族人历来都以放牧为生,其实也不知从哪个朝代起,就有一些部族悄悄地改变了生存方式,变放牧为种粮。姥姥家就是个典型的例子。

姥姥、姥爷是几十年前撒手走的。如今,他们二老留下的院落里只剩下舅舅一家。

舅舅家我去的次数不少,给我留下印象最深的要数舅母。

舅母长得很平常,颧骨下的两块肉一年四季总是紫红的。

舅母说话声比蚊子声大不了多少,鸡们、猪们上了灶台、进了屋,这样的声音是吓不走它们的。于是舅母就把手脚一齐做出轰撵的架式。无奈,这动作也没有一点火爆凶狠的味道,尽管畜牲们走了,也都是昂首挺胸地走的。

那年疏散人口,我疏散到了奶奶家。记得端午节刚过,舅母来了。她来接我去住几日。

1
AUNTIE

Yu Shengli

My mother's family lived in a village inhabited by Mongolians. Fields of thick crops surrounded it.

In people's minds, Mongolians were nomads who had always made a living by grazing. As a matter of fact, some Mongolian tribes had been quietly changing their way of life, transitioning from grazing to farming, since before who knows which dynasty. Mother's family was a typical example of this.

My maternal grandma and grandpa had left us decades ago. Now only my uncle's family lived in the ancestral courtyard they had bequeathed. I'd been to Uncle's many times. His wife, Auntie, was the member of the family who impressed me the most.

Auntie was plain-looking with two chubby areas that were always purplish right under her cheekbones.

When she talked, she sounded like a mosquito, a little louder, but not much. She was too soft-spoken to scare away the chickens and pigs when they got into the house and onto the hearth. Auntie would then try to gesticulate threateningly to get them out. This gesture of hers, however, carried little temper and ferocity. The animals would get out all right, but they moved arrogantly, with their chins up and their chests puffed out.

That year, urban populations underwent dispersion, and I was evacuated to my paternal grandma's house. I remember that Auntie came right after the Dragon Boat Festival to take me to her place for a few days.

舅母坐在炕上，刚喝下一口水，就一眼瞥见炕上六婶刚纳完的一只鞋底儿，她顺手拿过来看了一眼，便微笑着对六婶说，弟媳是左手做活吧。六婶便连连点头。

奶奶过后对庄里人说：没见拿针线，只看了眼人家做完的活，就知道是左手右手做的活计，你们谁行？

舅母做起活来慢得让人着急。多急的事，在她脸上你也找不出半个急字来。手脚更是慢慢悠悠。灶下添一把火，灶上就贴饼子，嘴上跟你搭着话，还不时抓一把玉米粒扔给院里的鸡们。动作虽慢，流水作业似的。哪个先，哪个后，她心里有数。常常是转眼功夫就把一桌在乡下人看来很考究的饭菜做好，招待远方来客。

舅母最拿手的是做小米饭。出了锅的小米饭盛在碗里刷刷响，像是在盛一碗沙子，饭粒之间毫不粘连，做熟的饭与生小米一样，看不出丝毫膨胀和变化。嚼在嘴里就是硬，半碗饭吃下去，牙根就酸疼的不想再吃了。

有一年爷爷到姥姥家接我回去过年，临走时，舅母做了一次这样的饭为我们送行。吃完饭，爷爷就带我回来了。

第二天吃完早饭，后院贵头家的来串门。坐炕上没多久，奶奶就说：老爷子昨天去孩子姥姥家，孩子他舅母给做了顿小米干饭，老爷子回来一个劲儿说饭做得好吃。说咱庄里没他舅母那样的巧媳妇，他一辈子还没吃过这么好吃的小米饭呢！

Auntie sat down on the *kang* bed.[3] After her first sip of water, she spotted the shoe sole that my Sixth Auntie had just finished on the bed. She picked it up for a quick look, and then said to Sixth Auntie, smiling, "You must be left-handed." Sixth Auntie nodded repeatedly.

My paternal grandma challenged her villagers afterward: "Can any of you tell simply by looking at the finished product, without seeing the person with needle and thread in hand, whether the work was done left-handed or right-handed?"

Auntie's slow pace of work could wear out your patience. However pressing it was that the job be finished, you wouldn't see any trace of urgency on her face, to say nothing of her movements. She would add more wood to the fire before pasting pancakes to the wok, chatting with you all the while, and occasionally throwing handfuls of corn to the chickens outside. Slow as she was, Auntie operated like an assembly line. She knew well what came first and what came after. Often, in the blink of an eye, she'd have a meal, quite elaborate for country folks, ready to treat her guests from afar.

Auntie's specialty was boiled millet. The steaming-hot grains of millet sounded like sand when you put them in a bowl. They did not get sticky, and the cooked millet looked the same as the uncooked. They didn't swell or seem to change in any way. They were hard to chew. Halfway through a bowl, your jaws would get tired, and you would want to stop eating.

One year, my paternal grandpa came to take me to his house for the New Year. Before we departed, Auntie made her specialty to see us off. I left with Grandpa after the meal.

After breakfast the next day, Guitou's wife, from the courtyard behind ours, dropped in. My paternal grandma told her about the millet meal soon after she sat down on the *kang* bed. "When his grandpa went to fetch him yesterday, his Auntie treated them to a meal of millet. Since they got back, his grandpa has been saying over and over how great it was. He said no daughter-in-law in our village had such skill, and that it was the best boiled millet he'd ever had!"

---

3. A *kang* bed is a heated sleeping platform commonly used in villages of northern China. The heat comes from the kitchen stove linked to the bed by flues. The fire from cooking dinner warms up the bricks and clay, from which the bed is built, and provides enough warmth during the freezing winter nights.

我实在不明白，就问奶奶，那么硬，那么难嚼的小米饭爷爷怎么还说好吃呢？奶奶说，这样的饭是极难做的，啥时下米，煮米，捞饭的时间，焖饭的火候等等都是关节，马虎不得。你舅母做的这饭，硬，可不生，熟，又不烂，越嚼越香！能把小米饭做得这么地道的，十个巧媳妇里也难挑出来一个。

我后来知道，这小米饭是舅母为待客专做的。但这样的小米饭舅母不轻易做，也不是谁来都做。

有一年冬天，我又去住姥姥家。一天早晨，我刚起来，门外有人喊，原来是大表哥未来的丈人出外办事路过这里。那年大表哥十六岁。亲家登门，一家人自然热情接待。转眼，灶间就飘出了香味。不一会儿，饭桌摆到了炕中央，表妹端上一大碗白菜冻豆腐，一碟韭菜炒鸡蛋，两碟自家腌的咸菜。门帘一掀，表哥把饭盆端进来，是一盆油黄油黄的小米饭。

这会儿，舅舅正和亲家聊得满面红光，见大表哥把饭盛好了，就拿起了筷子客套地请亲家吃饭。亲家端起了碗，舅舅这才把第一口饭扒进嘴里。他嚼了一口，猛地停下来一怔，眼皮眨了几眨，又把嘴里的饭快速地嚼了几下，脸就刷地拉了下来，但又若无其事地忙给亲家夹菜去了。

我不明白原由，看了一眼大表哥，才发现大表哥也在偷偷地拿眼睛瞄舅舅。

这会儿，舅母进来了，一边在围裙上擦手一边和亲家客气着，眼神似乎没个着落，像在躲闪什么。

舅母刚拿起饭勺子准备盛饭，桌子那边的舅舅却把碗往桌上一放。舅舅这个微小的动作别人大概没注意到，我却听出这碗放得有些重，忙瞥了一眼舅母，舅母盛饭的手停了一下，两眼注视着窗外。停顿虽是极短，可那眼神却让我忘不了。那眼神很是空洞。

I simply couldn't understand and asked Grandma why Grandpa liked that hard-to-chew millet so much. "It's very difficult to make," Grandma said, "you must be very careful at every juncture—when to put millet in, how to boil it, strain it and steam it, in what temperatures and for how long, and so on. Your auntie's millet is hard to chew but it is not undercooked; it is well done but not overcooked. When it's boiled, the more you savor it, the tastier it becomes! We'd be lucky if we could find one among ten skilled housewives who could make millet that well."

I didn't know until later that this boiled millet was a special treat for guests. Auntie did not make it often; nor did every visitor get to taste it.

One winter I went to stay at Auntie's again. As soon as I got up one morning, I heard someone outside calling. It turned out be my eldest cousin's future father-in-law. He was just stopping by while running an errand. My cousin brother was sixteen at the time. When an in-law came to visit, the family naturally treated him warmly. Soon, that familiar aroma wafted in from the kitchen. In short order, the table was set up on the middle of the *kang* bed. A cousin sister set out a big bowl of cabbage stewed with frozen bean curd and a dish of stir-fried eggs with chives, along with two saucers of homemade pickles. Then with the lift of the door curtain, my cousin brother brought in the food basin—a basin of glistening golden millet.

Uncle was conversing animatedly with his in-law. He politely picked up his chopsticks and invited his in-law to start after my cousin brother filled the bowls. Uncle ate his first morsel only after his in-law had taken up his bowl. His jaw came to an abrupt stop mid-chew. He gave a start, blinked, quickly chewed some more, and then pulled a long face. Then, pretending nothing was amiss, he got busy serving his in-law.

Puzzled, I glanced at my cousin brother, only to find that he was also secretly looking at Uncle.

At that moment, Auntie came in. Wiping her hands on her apron, she politely acknowledged her in-law, but her eyes seemed unable to settle, as if they were trying to dodge something.

Just as she began to scoop some millet into her bowl with the ladle, Uncle laid his bowl down at the other end of the table. Though Uncle's slight movement probably drew no notice from others, it struck me as being oddly forceful. I shot a glance at Auntie—her hands froze, her eyes gazing out the window into the distance. The moment was brief; but the look in her eyes engraved itself on my mind. It was a look of total emptiness.

那次饭，虽然吃着还是硬，但多少软了点，我还能勉强接受。但我却不知道，就因为饭软了点，才发生了令我一直难以理解的事情。

吃完饭，我就和二表哥拿着冰车到河边去了。二表哥扛着冰车在田埂上跳来跳去地跑着，我走在后面，舅母那空洞的眼神老在我眼前闪动。

姥姥家那条河自西向东沿着庄子划了个曲里拐弯的弧，一年四季都在勾引人。夏天能光着腚游水。春秋天做个鱼叉叉鱼，顶不济也能打它半日水漂。冬天，用几根木棍钉成一个方板，底下平行着砸进两根铁丝，冰车就做成了。盘腿往上一坐，手里攥住两把冰锥往冰上一扎，双手往下往后一用力，冰车就歪歪斜斜地滑出去了。尽管这些无法与城里的冰车相比，但在乡下，便不再有更高的奢望。坐在简陋的冰车上，竟也玩得忘了姓什么。

人能忘了姓什么，却忘不了吃。我和二表哥玩得肚子叫了才收拾了冰车往家走。

在姥姥家，冬闲时吃两顿饭。我们回到家时饭桌已经摆好。舅舅见我们回来了就打了声招呼，然后一迈腿上了炕，盘腿坐在正首，拿起筷子说，吃吧！孩子们就狼似地吞了起来。

我吃下去半个玉米饼子时，才发现舅母不在桌边。又想起早饭时舅母那空洞的眼神，就朝灶间喊舅母来吃饭吧。舅母应了一声，还是没进来。我就发现大表哥也吃的不似往日狼乎，还不时偷偷瞄舅舅一眼。

我又喊了舅母两次，依旧没来吃，也就顾不了许多，自顾扫荡着桌上的饭菜。

吃差不多了，就陆续打着响嗝放下了筷子，表兄妹们忙着往下收拾着。

妥当了，舅舅下炕出了屋。

The boiled millet was still hard to chew, but a little softer than before. I could manage it fine with an effort and didn't realize that the slightly softer millet would be the cause of an event that would long baffle me.

After the meal, I went with my second cousin brother to ski at the bank of the river. He bore the skibob on his shoulder, running and jumping along the ridges of fields, while I followed, the vacant expression in Auntie's eyes flashing through my mind.

The river nestling up to Auntie's village zigzagged from west to east. It was a place of seductive charm all year round—great for skinny-dipping in summer and spear fishing in spring and fall with homemade spears. If nothing else, you could spend half a day there skipping stones. In winter, we'd make a square board with wooden sticks, run two wires horizontally through the bottom, and voila, a skibob was born! We'd sit cross-legged on it with two icepicks in hand. With a hard push down and backward, the skibob would waggle out onto the slippery ice. Although it was nothing like the skibobs in the city, we kids in the countryside had no desire for anything fancier. Sitting on our crude skibob, I enjoyed myself so much that I forgot who I was.

I could afford to forget myself, but not my next meal! My cousin and I only picked up our skibob to head home when our stomachs began growling.

During winter break, it was the local custom to have only two meals a day. Food was on the table when we got home. Uncle greeted us, and then raised his leg to get on the *kang* bed. He sat cross-legged at the head of the table and picked up his chopsticks. As soon as he said, "Go ahead," we kids gobbled away.

Half of a corn pancake later, I realized that Auntie was not there. The empty look in her eyes at breakfast flashed across my mind again. I called toward the kitchen for Auntie to come eat. She answered yes, but didn't come to join us. I noticed that my eldest cousin brother didn't seem to have his usual appetite either. He kept shooting secret glances at Uncle.

I called for Auntie a couple more times. When she still didn't come, I forgot my concern and turned my attention to the food on the table.

One after another, belching loudly, we laid down our chopsticks when the food was almost gone. My cousins got busy clearing the table.

When it was all cleared, Uncle got off the *kang* bed and left.

一会儿,舅母进来了,朝我笑了笑,眼却毫无笑意。然后就翻柜子,动动这,看看那,眼神不再无着落,把要看的东西看得很仔细,似乎要看进眼睛里去。又依次地把表哥表妹们叫到身边,小声地说了些什么。

　　我当时坐在炕里,靠着窗户往外胡乱地看着。舅母声音很小,我也听得真切,都听懂了,却又像是没听懂,都是些家常话没啥新鲜的。心想,有啥好说的?

　　舅母叫表妹把枕头拿过来,就躺在了炕头,不再说话。脸上少见的宁静,两只眼睛老望着窗外一个什么地方。大表哥两手揣在袖筒里、屁股靠在炕沿边,不像站也不像坐,看住一个地方也是不动。隔一小会儿,就突然看一眼舅母,再飞快地把眼神放回原处。坐在炕梢的小表妹纳着一只鞋底,哧啦、哧啦的拉线声拉得人心烦。

　　整个屋子似乎在憋着什么。有那么一霎间我觉得这间大屋子快要哭起来。

　　舅舅回来了,又靠着柜子站着。看着有些零乱的屋子,又看看躺着的舅母,又把眼眨了几眨后就朝灶间走去。

　　突然,舅舅喊了大表哥一声,大表哥急忙跑了出去,我一伸头,就见舅舅手里拿着一个小坛子,让大表哥看,又说了句什么,大表哥就"呜"地哭出了声,然后"咣当"一声开了门飞跑出去。

　　眨眼间,饲养员二表舅跑来了,满身还挂着草沫子。随后,忽啦啦又来了好些中年和上年纪的老人。一个梳着蒙族发型的老太太一进屋就噜噜一口蒙语,二表舅连连点头。忙跟表哥们说,快去轧绿豆!两个中年女人跟孩子们风一样刮出去了。

　　这时,人们就对舅舅指手划脚,指鼻子瞪眼,蒙汉两种语言与唾沫星子混杂在一起倒向蹲在地上的舅舅。舅舅那会儿只是低着头,一口接一口地抽烟,偶尔抬头说一句什么。

Auntie came in shortly after and gave me a smile that was not reflected at all in her eyes. She then searched through her drawer, touching one thing and looking at another. There was purpose in her eyes now—as if she were trying to imprint the objects on her memory. She looked at each piece with meticulous care. She then brought my cousins to her one by one and whispered in their ears.

I was sitting on the inside of the *kang* bed at the time, leaning against the window and looking out aimlessly. Auntie's voice was very low. I listened earnestly. I heard every word, yet I didn't understand what was going on. Nothing new was being said, just the trifles of everyday life. *What's the point?* I wondered.

Auntie had her daughter bring over a pillow. She lay down and stopped talking. Her face was oddly serene; her eyes fixed on a place outside. My eldest cousin brother, with his hands inside his sleeves and his butt against the bed, was half standing and half sitting. He was also staring and motionless. He would, however, dart his eyes toward Auntie occasionally, then quickly settle his gaze back where it had been. My youngest cousin sister was sitting at the edge of the *kang* bed, making the sole of a shoe. The sound of her pulling the thread through grew rather annoying.

The whole room seemed to be under enormous pressure. For a moment, I felt that this big room was going to burst out crying.

Uncle came back and stood against the drawer. He looked around the somewhat messy room, and then at Auntie lying there. His eyes blinked a few times before he headed for the kitchen.

Suddenly Uncle let out a cry for my eldest cousin brother. As he ran out quickly, I craned my neck and saw Uncle holding a little jar for my eldest brother to see. "Arghh," he cried, weeping as he heard what Uncle had to say. *Cling-clang!* He opened the door and dashed out.

In the blink of an eye, Second Uncle, the breeder, was there, grass clippings all over him. At his heel quite a few middle-aged and elderly folks swept in. An old lady with a Mongolian hairstyle entered, babbling instructions in Mongolian. As Second Uncle nodding repeatedly, he told my cousin brothers, "Run make some green bean milk!" My cousin brothers and two middle-aged women swished out like the wind.

People were now pointing fingers at Uncle. Switching between Chinese and Mongolian, they snorted and stared, sputtering as they dumped criticism upon him. Uncle squatted with his head down; all he

舅母这会儿脸上依然平静。两眼还是望着窗外那个老地方一动不动。谁跟她说什么，人们说舅舅什么，她都没有任何表情。可我还是发现有一行泪水顺着舅母的眼角悄悄往下走，走得那么静，静的我甚至有那么半分钟几乎听不到整个屋子里的乱哄哄。多少年后的一天，当我听到一只小提琴演奏出几个纤细哀婉的旋律时，我突然想到了舅母眼角那行悄悄走着的泪水……

绿豆碾成了面，早有人把水烧开，冲了一碗，半生半熟的端了进来。众人扶起舅母让她喝了，一连喝了两碗。

有人就开始揉着舅母肚子。没一会儿，舅母就下了炕，几个人就扶着舅母去了茅房。

一小会儿，又去了一次。一连几次。

没人告诉我究竟是怎么回事。

都很晚了，看看舅母没什么事了，人们才三三两两散去。一家人谁也没有说话，便匆忙收拾了，早早钻进被窝。

熄了灯，我睁大眼睛瞅着朦胧中的房梁，努力地琢磨着这一天发生的事。

早晨一睁眼，都起来了，被子叠得齐整，舅母半靠在叠好的被子上，众人都有事无事地找着事做，只是不见了大表哥，我问正做饭的表妹，她说大表哥找他丈人去了，我问找他干啥，表妹说，商量事儿吧。

果然，过了晌午，大表哥和他丈人来了。一进屋就问啥事呀？舅母说请他帮忙拉点木头，怕孩子说不清，所以请他来。又说了些无关紧要的事儿。一边坐着的舅舅只是哼哼哈哈。事儿说完了，亲家就要走，被大表哥

could do was puff away on one cigarette after another, only occasionally looking up to say something.

Auntie was as peaceful as before. Her eyes were still fixated on the place outside. She hadn't reacted at all to the words directed to her or against Uncle, but I was able to spot streams of tears silently escaping from the corners of her eyes—so silently that they momentarily took me away from the noisy disorder of the room. Years later, when I heard a lovely, sorrowful melody on a violin one day, Auntie's quiet streams of tears unexpectedly came to mind.

As soon as the green beans were crushed into a powder, someone already waiting there poured boiling water over it in a bowl. They brought this half-cooked green bean milk to Auntie. Many hands helped Auntie up to drink the liquid, two bowls in a row.

The next thing was to rub Auntie's stomach. Before long, Auntie got out of bed. Several people lent their arms to support her as they led her to the latrine.

She went a second time a short while later, then a third time, and then a few more times ...

No one told me just what was going on.

Late that night, once they'd made sure that Auntie was all right, people began to disperse in twos and threes. Not a word was exchanged in the house. We got ready and slipped into bed as fast as we could.

The lights were off. I opened my eyes wide and stared at the beam in the darkness above me, trying hard to make sense of what had happened that day.

Everybody was up when I woke the next day. The quilts were neatly folded, and Auntie, sitting, was leaning lightly against them. Everybody else was busy with something they either had or didn't have to do. Only my eldest cousin brother was missing. I asked my cousin sister, who was cooking, where he was, and was told he'd left to get his in-law. "Why?" I asked. "To talk about things, perhaps," she said.

As expected, my eldest cousin brother came back in the afternoon with his in-law, who asked, upon arrival, about the urgent business. Auntie then requested his help with moving some wood, and added that she'd wanted him to come because she'd feared a child might not say clearly what she needed him to do. They engaged in small talk for a while, with Uncle hemming and hawing on the sidelines. When the conversation was over and the in-law got up to leave, my cousin brother anxiously prevented him. Auntie said she

死活拽住。舅母说，到吃饭时候了，还能让你空肚子回去？亲家也就不再客气，坐炕头和舅舅对着抽烟。

转眼，灶间又烟雾缭绕，热气腾腾，见不到人上身，只看到舅母的两条腿在烟雾里蹚来蹚去。我偶尔路过灶间就被熏得鼻涕眼泪。舅母进屋时，我看见她的脸毫无血色，手上端的盆子也像是很沉的样子。

很快菜就上了桌子。主菜换了一样，其它依旧，依然两碟两碗。大表哥又把饭盆端了进来，竟又是一盆黄亮亮的小米饭！

吃饭时，舅母早早进来，亲家招呼她快来吃吧，她说不舒服，你们吃吧，吃饱了。她就坐在炕边纳着鞋底，尽管脸色依然苍白，但一针一线还很自如，表情比往常更加端庄。

大表哥依旧口嚼着饭，眼睛偷偷瞄几眼舅舅，但不再是怯怯的。

舅舅一边一板一眼地往嘴里扒着饭细细地嚼，一边不失礼数地照顾着身边的亲家。稳稳当当地透露着一家之主十足的自信。他不看舅母一眼，但我分明感到他在用眼睛的余光感觉着舅母。

饭是比昨天硬多了，我像嚼沙子般的艰难，半小碗不到，牙根就酸疼难耐，就搁下碗到一边去玩。

几天后爷爷来接我。舅舅一家人把爷爷和我送出庄子，大表哥又陪我们走了一段。我在前边跑着，往河里扔着石子。大表哥跟爷爷在后边说着什么。

回到奶奶家已经很晚，草草收拾后倒头就睡，一觉天亮。早饭后，我就把许多糊涂事问奶奶，奶奶说，你舅母喝了卤水！生绿豆又泻又解毒，亏

couldn't let him go at mealtime on an empty stomach. The in-law acquiesced and sat down opposite Uncle on the *kang* bed to enjoy a smoke with him.

The kitchen was instantly alive with steam and smoke, which completely enshrouded Auntie's upper body and knocked me flat with tears when I happened to pass by. All I could see were Auntie's feet running around. She looked pale, and the basin in her hands seemed heavy as she appeared at the doorway.

The dishes were on the table quickly, two main courses and two pickles, as before. One of the main courses was different from yesterday, but the rest of the meal was the same. When my cousin brought the food basin in, the boiled millet glistened inside!

Auntie came in earlier than usual that day. The in-law invited her to eat at the table, but she said she was a little under the weather. "You go ahead and eat," she urged us, "and eat well." She then sat at the edge of the *kang* bed and worked on a sole, one stitch at a time, poised and at ease. Still pale, she looked more dignified than ever.

My eldest cousin brother still kept glancing at Uncle as he chewed, but there was boldness in his eyes now.

As Uncle methodically attended to his food, chewing carefully, he took care of his in-law with due etiquette, with the air of a fully secure and confident patriarch. He never looked at Auntie, but I could certainly feel him watching her with his peripheral vision all the time.

The boiled millet was much harder to chew than yesterday. I felt like I was munching on sand. It wore on my teeth painfully after less than half a bowl, so I left the table to play.

A few days later, my paternal grandpa came to fetch me. Auntie's whole family went to see us off at the edge of the village. My eldest cousin brother accompanied us a little further. He talked with Grandpa as I ran ahead along the river, throwing stones in its waters.

It was late when we got home. I washed up hastily, hit the pillow, and slept soundly till the next day. After breakfast, I brought my many confusing questions to Grandma. "It was brine that your aunt took," Grandma told me.[4] "Raw green-bean milk cleanses and detoxifies. Luckily your uncle

---

4. A strong solution of salt and water, brine is used in Chinese cooking, especially in making tofu. The amount used is usually very small, as the idiomatic saying goes, "Drops of brine turn soymilk into bean curd—there is always one thing that subdues another（卤水点豆腐，一物降一物）. Brine overdose, however, can be dangerous and life threatening.

你大舅精明，发现得早，晚一会儿就没救了。我又问，舅母为什么要喝卤水呢？奶奶又叹了口气，把两手放在屁股底下坐着，两眼望着窗外远处山坡上的庄稼说：庄稼人哪！你不懂啊。之后，她把身子一前一后，轻轻地晃着。

(1992)

was quick-witted and realized it in time. Otherwise it would have been too late." "Why would Auntie drink brine?" I asked. Grandma sighed. Sitting on her two hands and looking through the window at the crops on the distant hillsides, she uttered these words: "We peasants, how could you understand us?" Then she gently rocked back and forth.

(1992)

VOCABULARY AND USAGE

撒手	sāshǒu	pass away	爷爷是去年撒手走的。
数	shǔ	be uppermost	咱村里数他名气大了。
架式	jiàshi	pose	他做出了要动手的架式。
轰撵	hōng niǎn	drive out	我把邻居的鸡轰撵出去。
纳(鞋底)	nà(xiédǐ)	sew/make (cloth soles of shoes)	手工纳鞋底很花时间，也很费劲。
活计	huóji	(handicraft) work	村里的媳妇，针线活计数她做得好。
搭话	dāhuà	get in a word; talk; answer	他走过去与她搭话之前已经观察她老半天了。
拿手	náshǒu	good at	她唱陕北民歌最拿手。
刷刷	shuāshuā	an onomatopoeia	风吹树叶刷刷响。
酸疼	suānténg	sore; painful	我第一次锻炼之后肌肉酸疼了好几天。
盛(饭)	chéng(fàn)	fill a bowl	我盛了满满一碗米饭。
贵头家的	guìtóujiāde	Guitou's wife	贵头家的喜欢跟奶奶聊天。
老爷子	lǎoyézi	father or grandfather	我们家老爷子的规矩可多了。
火候	huǒhou	duration and degree of heating	炒这个菜一定要讲究火候。
腌(咸菜)	yān (xiáncài)	preserve in salt; pickle	把鱼腌了留着冬天吃吧。
掀(门帘)	xiān (ménlián)	lift up (curtain)	她一掀门帘就进去了。
原由	yuányóu	reason	你生气总得有个原由吧。
弧	hú	a curve	彩虹是天上一道美丽的弧。
勾引	gōuyǐn	allure; seduce	你甭想用好吃的勾引我。

顶不济	dǐngbújì	at least	这瓜顶不济还能解解渴。
砸	zá	pound	他把钉子砸进了木板。
扎	zhā	prick	弟弟用铅笔头尖扎我。
冬闲	dōngxián	slack winter season	冬闲的时候地里没什么农活可做。
狼乎	lánghū	like a wolf	他饿极了，吃得狼乎，很快就扫荡了桌上的饭菜。
扫荡	sǎodàng	wipe out	
打嗝	dǎgé	issue a belch	你知道人为什么会打嗝吗？
着落	zháoluò	whereabouts	走丢的孩子有着落了！
揣	chuāi	tuck (into)	他把手揣在袖筒里取暖。
筒	tǒng	tube; cylinder	
隔	gé	after an interval of	校园的大钟隔一刻钟响一次。
(炕)沿	(kàng)yán	brim; bank	你不知道在井沿上玩很危险吗？
哧啦	chīlā	an onomatopoeia	纳鞋底抽麻线时会发出"哧啦"声。
忽啦啦	hūlālā	an onomatopoeia	忽啦啦从外面进来很多人。
轧	zhā	press hard to make powder	古人常用石磨轧谷米。
指手划脚	zhǐshǒuhuàjiǎo	gesticulate; find fault with	你不了解情况，不该对当事人指手划脚。
唾沫星子	tuòmò xīngzi	spittle	他激动时说起话来会唾沫星子乱飞。
乱哄哄	luànhōnghōng	in noisy disorder	别出去，街上乱哄哄的。
演奏	yǎnzòu	play a musical instrument	她在演奏一首优美的钢琴曲。
纤细	qiānxì	slim; fine	纤细的芦苇在风中摇弋。
哀婉	āiwǎn	sadly moving	戏的最后一幕哀婉动人。
碾	niǎn	grind	去用石碾把谷子碾成面！
朦胧	ménglóng	obscure	雨很大，窗外一片朦胧。
死活	sǐhuó	simply	他死活都不肯住院。
烟雾缭绕	yānwù liáorào	smoke curling up	现代化的厨房有抽油烟机，再不会烟雾缭绕了。
热气腾腾	rèqìténgténg	steaming hot	饺子刚出锅，热气腾腾。

熏	xūn	suffocate by smoke	大部分乘客是因为打不开门窗被烟熏死的。
瞄	miāo	throw a quick glance	我可以瞄一眼你的卧室吗？就一眼。
怯怯的	qièqiède	timid	小姑娘怯怯的样子很让人心疼。
一板一眼	yìbǎnyìyǎn	methodically	他做事一板一眼很有条理。
稳稳当当	wěnwěndāngdāng	safe and secure	他稳稳当当地当选为村长。
透露	tòulù	reveal	他的眼神透露着自信。
一家之主	yījiāzhīzhǔ	the head of a family	我家真正的一家之主是妈妈。
礼数	lǐshù	courtesy; right behavior	妈妈常说懂礼数比学算数更重要。
难耐	nánnài	intolerable	南方的夏天闷热难耐。
搁	gē	put down	他才坐下来三分钟就把书一搁，又出去玩了。
草草	cǎocǎo	rush through carelessly	他草草地看了一眼我的文章就说不行。
倒头	dǎotóu	lie down	他玩累了，倒头就睡了。
亏	kuī	thanks to	亏你记性好我们才没迷路。
没救	méijiù	no cure for; hopeless	他流血太多，怕是没救了。

QUESTIONS FOR DISCUSSION

1. Why would Auntie drink brine? Was it an attempt to save face, to regain power, or to defy her husband?
2. What role do the details of everyday life play in the story?
3. What is the relevance of the skibob episode to the rest of the story?
4. What does the making of millet have in common with farming? What values does such an agrarian society possess?
5. What identifies and defines Auntie?
   a. What is making food for her? What is a household chore?
   b. Is Auntie in a position of power? Where does power lie in this story?
   c. What is she to her family, extended family, and the community?

6. Could legal/equal rights for women be the solution to the problem Auntie encounters? How do you like Auntie's method of reconciliation?
7. How does the story highlight shared humanity beyond categorizations of race, gender, class, ethnicity, age, and so on?

1. 舅母为什么要喝卤水？她是企图挽回颜面吗？还是为了夺回权力？或是为了向丈夫示威？
2. 每日生活的细节在这个故事中起到了什么作用？
3. 去河边滑冰车的那一段跟整个故事有什么关联？
4. 做小米饭和种庄稼有什么相通之处？这样的农业社会有着什么样的价值体系？
5. 舅母的标识特征是什么？什么东西可以定义舅母？请想一想：
   a. 对舅母来说，做饭意味着什么？家务活意味着什么？
   b. 舅母有权力有地位吗？这个故事中，权力的源泉在哪儿？
   c. 舅母对她的家人意味着什么？对亲朋好友呢？对她所属的群体呢？
6. 赋予女性法律／平等权力能解决舅母所面临的问题吗？你对故事结尾处舅母与他人和解的方式怎么看？
7. 这个故事是如何突出超越种族、性别、阶级、族裔和年龄等类别区分的共有人性的？

AUTHOR BIO

Yu Shengli (1956–) is a native of Chengde, Hebei Province, and works at China Film and TV Production Ltd, a joint venture with China Central Television (CCTV) and China International Television Corporation. Yu Shengli graduated from the Beijing Broadcasting Institute, now the Communication University of China, in 1978. He worked for China National Radio until he joined CCTV in 1993 as a writer/director. Ten years later, in August 2003, he stepped into his current post as a producer/director at the Yu Shengli Studio.

Yu Shengli is also a writer, media critic, and master's (thesis) advisor. He published his first story in 1988. He wrote "Auntie" in 1992, and *People's Literature* (人民文学) published it. In 1997 his novella *Lao Liu* (老六) was named among the best five in China. He joined the China Writers

Association in 2001. His collection of fiction has been used for teaching at Beijing University, and his critical essays have been published in *Wenyi Bao* (文艺报) and *People's Daily* (人民日报). He started his academic service as an advisor of graduate studies for the Communication University of China in 2002.

A celebrity himself, Yu Shengli is better known for his keen eye for talent and for identifying successful scripts. He has participated in producing three of China's six most-watched TV series of the last decade, the groundbreaking *The Big Family* (大宅门) among them. Peers respect him for his gift and passion; we admire him for his reverence for the honest labor that sustains life and tradition and his appreciation for spiritual and ethical conduct rooted in everyday life in general and the agrarian tradition in particular. "Auntie" is considered one of the best short stories of Chinese literature from the 1990s.

2
兄弟们长大

周涛

十七八岁时，有个念头像谜一样困扰着我，那就是我们兄弟四个将来长大了究竟会干什么。当时，周二，周三，周四还在读初中或小学，每个生命都是一个谜，等待时间去揭破。时光过去三十年，谜底大致揭开了。

先说周二。

周二幼时模样周正，黑发乌睛，腼腆少语。入学读书，成绩时好时坏，落差极大。老实说，他很聪明，就是喜欢和坏孩子厮混，受影响。父亲的对策是，每当他的成绩糟糕到一定程度时，就给他转学。初到一校，人生地疏，学习成绩骤升，甚至还担任学习委员或班长职务。

好景不长，多则半年，少则两月，他便与班上最差劲的学生混在一起，最后达到私自把班费拿去与同伙大吃烤羊肉的地步，于是再转学。到了初三，周二弃文学武，抢军帽，养狼狗，舞枪弄刀，一落到底。众皆叹曰："唉，周二是一块好钢，可惜打了狗链子。"

上山下乡时，他去米泉县插队。米泉县近，每月可回一两次。当时正流行白回力鞋，周四买了一双，视如珍宝，唯恐周二抢走，每逢他回来，

2

BROTHERS

Zhou Tao

When I was about seventeen or eighteen years old, a thought obsessed me like a puzzle—what would we four brothers end up doing when we grew up? Zhou Second, Zhou Third, and Zhou Fourth were still in middle school or elementary school; every life was a mystery waiting to unfold through time.

Thirty years have now passed. The mystery is mostly revealed.

First, let's look at Zhou Second.

When he was young, Zhou Second was a handsome, shy boy with dark eyes and black hair, and few words. When he started school, his grades were unpredictable and fluctuated drastically. To put it bluntly, he was a very smart boy who loved to fool around with bad kids and who was too susceptible to their influence. Father's way of dealing with him was to get him transferred whenever his grades dropped below a certain level. When new to a school and a stranger to the place and people, Zhou Second's grades would skyrocket. He could even make it to the position of head boy or class leader.

But the good times never lasted. Whether it took as long as half a year or as short as two months, Zhou Second would get involved with the worst students in the class. When it eventually got so bad that he secretly used the class fund to treat his buddies to kebab, he would get transferred again. When he was a junior in middle school, he abandoned the pen for the sword, robbing people of their army caps, raising wolfhounds, and brandishing swords and spears. His grades hit the floor. Everyone sighed, "What a pity, Zhou Second, a great piece of steel has been made into a dog's chain."

When educated youth began being sent down to the countryside, Zhou Second went to live and work with a production team in Miquan County.

必不穿，精心藏匿。周二回家，绝口不问白回力，也不找寻，仿佛不感兴趣。待其返回米泉，周四放学回家，没进门，先问："周二走了吗？"母答："走了。"周四顾不得放书包，一头钻进鸡窝，翻找先前藏的回力鞋。结果，头还在鸡窝里，哭声已经闷闷地传了出来——鞋被周二偷走了！不久，周二回来，丢下一双脏鞋扬长而去。

周四精心刷洗、晾干、上粉、藏至父母卧室弹簧床最里处夹层。结果，周二返回米泉，周四的哭声又闷闷地从床底下传出来。

周二查找藏匿之物神出鬼没，不用东翻西找，每每手到擒来。后来到了公安局，他干过派出所，当过股长，破得几件案子，以查找赃物为能事。问他，笑答："我能猜着坏人的心思——和我原来的心思差不多。"

周三小周二两岁，从小眼睛近视，小小的鼻子上架着一副七百度的眼镜，身子细瘦，动作却较常人快半拍，吃饭如抢，常遭训斥。

小学四年级以后，周三喜欢读《参考消息》，每报必读，津津有味。小学六年级时，他对世界各国地理位置、首府总统或时事政治皆了如指掌。师范毕业后，周三在郊区一所职工学校教书。忽一日，他跑进城来告诉我，报上登出新疆电视台向社会公开招考编辑、记者，他去报了名。

Since the county was near us, he could come home a couple of times each month. White Warrior brand shoes were in style at the time, and Zhou Fourth got a pair. But he wouldn't wear them when Zhou Second came home. He treasured them so much that he hid them carefully, fearful that Zhou Second would snatch them away. Zhou Second never said a word about the shoes, nor did he go look for them when he was home. He acted as if he had no interest in them at all. The day Zhou Second left, the first thing Zhou Fourth asked after school, before he even entered the house, was, "Is he gone?" Mom answered, "Yes, he is." Before he could put down his backpack, Zhou Fourth dove headlong into the chicken coop to search for the shoes he'd hidden there. His head still in the coop, we heard his muffled crying— Zhou Second had taken the shoes. Soon after, when Zhou Second came back again, he left the pair of shoes, now filthy, as he walked off to Miquan.

Zhou Fourth painstakingly scrubbed, dried, and powdered the shoes before he hid them between the inner layers deep inside our parents' spring bed. But when Zhou Second left for Miquan after his next visit, we heard Zhou Fourth's muffled crying again from under the bed.

Zhou Second, talented at locating hidden things with great dexterity and preternatural swiftness, always found what he was looking for without really having to search for it. He ended up working for the Public Security Bureau. He served in local police stations and soon held the position of captain. He had cracked quite a few criminal cases and had proven himself particularly good at finding stolen goods. When asked how, he answered with a smile, "I know how a bad guy's mind works—not that different from mine a while back."

Zhou Third was two years younger than Zhou Second. Nearsighted since childhood, he had a thick pair of glasses that hung on his little nose. Skinny, he moved a half-beat faster than most people. He ate like there was no tomorrow, a behavior for which he was reprimanded frequently.

Since fifth grade, he had been in love with *Reference News*, and read the paper every day with great relish. By the time he was a sixth grader, he had learned the map of the world by heart and knew heads of state, capitals, and current affairs as well as the palms of his own hands. After graduating from a teachers college, he taught at a trade school in the suburbs. Suddenly one day, he came to town to tell me that Xingjiang TV station was advertising in the newspaper for editors and journalists and that he had signed up for the qualification exam.

据说当时报考者甚众,还有名牌大学新闻系毕业生,难度很大,周三自觉输人一筹。不料结果一公布,周三竟名列第一。如今,他在新疆电视台干编辑、记者,已有多年。

周四小眼睛,大鼻子,黄手。有人说他长得像南斯拉夫电影《桥》里的"猫头鹰",也有人说他像《瓦尔特保卫萨拉热窝》里的德军中尉,还有人说他的眼睛鼻子酷似成龙,总之一副武夫模样。

周四很少穿新衣裳,总是不断地钻进哥哥们穿旧变小的衣服里去,破衣旧衫,敞胸露怀,肚子从小就圆圆地鼓起,大冬天喝凉水,满不在乎。

当时有人建议周四长大后当举重运动员,我却觉得他是个入伍从军的材料,因为那时他就率领着差不多大的孩子,黑脸花脸,往来驰骋,俨然一个儿童领袖。

周四十五岁时,已经壮实有力。一次,我顺手想在他头上打一巴掌,不料他一低头,就势一个马步下蹲,右臂箍住我两条腿,一挺身,把我架在半空,仰着脸笑嘻嘻地说:"哥,还打不打了?"

我感受到了正在发育中的新生命强有力的提醒和挑战,从那以后,特别了解"后生可畏"这个词。

周四十五岁时就在心理上担负起保护我的职责。有一次在机关礼堂看电影,我坐前排,他坐在后面很远。因为替一位老人打抱不平,我与后排的一群二流子发生争执。话没说几句,为首的一个家伙从座位上一跃而起,准备动手。我还没反应过来,"啪"一声,一记响亮的耳光把那家伙又打回座椅里。我一看,是周四。他恶狠狠地指着那家伙说:"你再动动,我捏死你这个臭虫!"

They say that many people registered for the exam, among them journalist majors who had graduated from famous universities. In the face of such enormous obstacles, Zhou Third felt that he was at a disadvantage from the start. When the results were announced, who'd have thought, Zhou Third would place first? He has worked as an editor and a journalist for Xingjiang TV station to this very day.

Zhou Fourth had small eyes, a big nose, and yellowish hands as a boy. Some people said that he looked like "The Owl" in the Yugoslavian film *The Bridge*; others thought he resembled the German lieutenant in *Walter Defends Sarajevo*; still others believed that he had the eyes and the nose of Jackie Chan; anyway, he had the look of a man of prowess.

Zhou Fourth seldom wore new clothes, and always had to squeeze into the hand-me-downs that were too small for his brothers. Worn and tattered, the clothes left him bare-chested. He had a bulging round tummy as a child and drank unboiled water in the cold of winter—he didn't give a damn.

Someone suggested that Zhou Fourth should be a weightlifter when he grew up, but I thought he was made for the military, because he was already leading kids his age—with tanned and dirty faces—charging this way and that, as if he were their commander.

At fifteen Zhou Fourth was already strong and sturdy. Once I tried casually to tap him on the head. Unexpectedly, he ducked and, following the momentum, crouched in a horse-riding stance, his right arm looping around my legs. Suddenly he straightened up, lifting me halfway in the air. Smiling up at me, he asked, "Still want a fight, Bro?"

I felt then a powerful warning, and the challenge a growing and youthful life can present, and learned firsthand what the old expression "the young are to be regarded with awe" really meant.

At fifteen Zhou Fourth had already taken it upon himself to protect me. One day, we were watching a movie in the assembly hall. I was in the front row and he was sitting far in the back. I got into a quarrel with a bunch of punks behind me while trying to defend an elderly person. After a few words, the leader of the group leaped out of his seat, ready to strike. Before I could react, *smack*, a loud slap on his face returned him to his seat. I looked, and saw Zhou Fourth. He pointed at the guy with rage: "You move again, and I'll squish you like a gnat!"

周四做事就是这般干净利落,一看就是个冲锋陷阵的材料,谁知最后却当了中学教师。

兄弟们长大了,原来如此。

(2011)

Zhou Fourth handled everything crisply like this. At first glance, you could tell such a man was made to charge into enemy lines. Who would have thought he would end up becoming a middle school teacher?

And this is how we brothers have turned out...

(2011)

VOCABULARY AND USAGE

究竟	jiūjìng	in the end; actually	你究竟是爱她还是爱我？
谜底	mídǐ	answer to a riddle	他五秒钟就猜中了谜底。
模样周正	móyàng zhōuzhèng	good-looking; having good features	他的五个儿子，就老二的模样还算周正。
揭开	jiēkāi	uncover; reveal	怎样才能把谜底揭开？
腼腆	miǎntiǎn	shy	那小姑娘腼腆得可爱！
落差	luòchā	drop height	这里河水的落差是三米。
厮混	sīhùn	fool around	别和坏孩子厮混在一起！
对策	duìcè	countermeasure	你有解决问题的对策吗？
人生地疏	rénshēngdìshū	not familiar	这里人生地疏，你出去散步别走太远了。
骤(升/降)	zhòu(shēng/jiàng)	suddenly; swiftly (rise/fall)	今天气温骤降三十度。
学习委员	xuéxí wěiyuán	a class committee member with study-related duties	在班里当学习委员的同学学习成绩一定要好。
私自	sīzì	without permission	你是军人，没有命令不可私自行动！
班费	bānfèi	class fund	"班费"是一个班级的活动经费。
同伙	tónghuǒ	partner (in crime)	他抢银行的同伙被警察抓住了两个。
弃	qì	give up	他十八岁弃学从军，成了一名职业军人。
舞枪弄刀	wǔqiāngnòngdāo	brandish swords and spears	你是个女孩子，怎么也喜欢舞枪弄刀的？
众	zhòng	many people	春日到，众鸟欢叫。

皆	jiē	each; all	爱美之心，人皆有之。
叹	tàn	sigh	她叹了口气说，可惜了。
曰	yuē	say	"子曰"就是"孔子说"的意思。
打(铁/链子)	dǎ(tiě/liànzi)	forge (iron/chain)	谁会用最好的钢铁去打小钉子？
(下乡)插队	(xiàxiāng)chāduì	go live and work in a production team in the countryside	文革期间，很多中学毕业生都下乡插过队。
唯恐	wéikǒng	fear	他唯恐自己的藏匿处被警察发现。
藏匿	cángnì	conceal; hide	
晾干	liànggān	air-dry	这么潮湿的天气，洗好的衣服一天都晾不干。
上	shàng	apply	他用各色彩笔给画上色。
夹层	jiācéng	inner layer	这种冰砖有巧克力夹层！
神出鬼没	shénchūguǐmò	come and go like a shadow; elusive	那小偷神出鬼没，很难抓到。
东翻西找	dōngfānxīzhǎo	search everywhere	他东翻西找也没发现任何犯罪证据。
每每	měiměi	often	她每每独自饮酒到深夜。
手到擒来	shǒudàoqínlái	capture easily	我去抓他定会手到擒来。
破案	pò'àn	solve a case	这位警察是破案高手。
以…为能事	yǐ…wéinéngshì	be particularly good at something bad	他以陷害他人为能事。
赃物	zāngwù	stolen goods	他能猜到小偷匿藏赃物的地方。
遭	zāo	meet with	这几年他连遭不幸。
津津有味	jīnjīnyǒuwèi	be very fond of	这本书他读得津津有味。
了如指掌	liǎorúzhǐzhǎng	know…like the palm of one's own hand	妈妈对我的那点儿心事了如指掌。
甚众	shèn zhòng	quite a few	反对他的人不少，可拥护他的人也甚众。
输人一筹	shū rén yì chóu	be a leg down on someone	没上过名校的人常会在竞争时觉得输人一筹。
干(编辑)	gàn (biānji)	work (as an editor)	他一家三代都是干公安的。
中尉	zhōngwèi	lieutenant	上尉是中尉的上级吗？

酷似	kùsì	be exactly like	他长得酷似他的母亲。
一副…模样	yí fù…móyàng	wear an air of	你看那孩子,一副天真可爱的模样。
敞胸露怀	chǎngxiōnglùhuái	bare-chested	这么冷的天,你敞胸露怀的,要生病的!
满不在乎	mǎnbúzàihu	do not care at all	他很讲究穿,对吃却满不在乎。
入伍从军	rùwǔcóngjūn	join the military	他十八岁那年入伍从军,一辈子没离开部队。
率领	shuàilǐng	lead; command	他率领一个小分队去敌后寻找雷恩。
驰骋	chíchěng	gallop	在人生的旅途上自由驰骋是很多人的梦想。
俨然	yǎnrán	just like	你穿上这身西服,俨然是个大人了。
马步(下蹲)	mǎbù (xiàdūn)	straddle (squat) as though riding a horse	"马步"就是像骑着一匹马那样的步法。
箍	gū	hoop; bind	他用双臂紧紧箍住我,让我动弹不得。
后生可畏	hòushēngkěwèi	the young are to be respected	长江后浪推前浪,后生可畏啊!
担负	dānfù	shoulder	我是大哥,得担负关照弟、妹的责任。
打抱不平	dǎbàobùpíng	defend someone against an injustice	哥哥为人正直,总爱打抱不平。
二流子	èrliūzi	loafer; rascal	二流子好吃懒做。
争执	zhēngzhí	argue	他们常争执可从不动手。
为首的	wéishǒude	headed by; the head	在这个原始的部落,为首的是一位老妇人。
一跃而起	yí yuè ér qǐ	jump up	他听到枪声一跃而起。
一记耳光	yí jì ěrguāng	a slap in the face	弟弟恶狠狠地给了那小子一记响亮的耳光。
恶狠狠	èhěnhěn	ferociously	
捏	niē	nip; squeeze	她用手捏死了一只蚂蚁。
臭虫	chòuchóng	bugs	我被臭虫咬得睡不着。
干净利落	gānjìnglìluò	neat; neatly	她做事干净利落,从不拖泥带水。
冲锋陷阵	chōngfēngxiànzhèn	charge and shatter enemy positions	打仗时他冲锋陷阵不怕死,是个好战士!

QUESTIONS FOR DISCUSSION

1. How would you describe Zhou Second? What point does the story make with this criminal-minded public security officer?
2. How would you characterize the life trajectory of Zhou Third?
3. Do you think Zhou Fourth is in the wrong profession? Why?
4. What do the brothers' life trajectories say about identity?
5. What is the danger of making generalizations about a person or a people?
6. Why has this story also been a favorite of students from other cultures?
7. Does identity liberate as well as confine the individual?

1. 你怎么看周二这个人物？故事通过这个心思跟罪犯差不多的公安人员表达了什么？
2. 周三的生活轨迹有什么特色？
3. 你觉得周四是不是选错了职业？为什么？
4. 故事中几个兄弟的生活道路阐释了对自我（identity）这一问题什么样的看法？
5. 给一个人或是一类／族／国人做综述、下结论会有什么样的危险？
6. 来自不同文化的学生都很喜欢这个故事，为什么呢？
7. 自我（identity）的概念会不会既解放个人又限制个人？

AUTHOR BIO

Zhou Tao (1946–) defies any label of identification. A Han Chinese by birth, he spent the first few years of his life floundering in wartime China between Shanxi and Hebei. He settled down in Xinjiang at the age of nine with his parents. Now 70, Zhou Tao refers to himself as a "northwestern barbarian" (西北胡儿 *xīběi húer*), that is, a man of complex cultural existence who owes his very being to the interactions of his culture of origin with that of Uighurs, Kazakhs, Hui, Uzbeks, and Tajiks in Xinjiang for six decades. Zhou Tao also perceives himself as a Han Chinese whose ancestors, to use his own words, "have been a barbarian, a nomad, an assassin, and a savage beauty." He entered Xinjiang University in 1965 and majored in Uighur. An active Red Guard during the Cultural Revolution and a sent-down youth in 1971 to 1972, Zhou Tao had a chance to see China and learn the hardship of earning his own living by farming. When working for the City of Kashi in 1979, he made a name for himself with the publication of the long poem *August Orchard* (八月的果园). As a result, he was specially recruited by the military and became a salaried professional writer at the rank of company commander in the Culture Department of Urumqi Military Area Command.

Now a poet and essayist of national fame at the rank of a major general, Zhou Tao has become a literary phenomenon. In place of a long list of awards, we recall here some of the efforts made to describe him: "the representative of the New Frontier Poetry," "a Xinjiang literary giant," "one of the Three Musketeers of Military Literature," "the soul of the city," and "the reincarnation of a Himalaya eagle." People often present Zhou Tao's works, especially *Rare Bird* (稀世之鸟) and *Grazing Along the Great Wall* (游牧长城), to departing friends as a "precious Xinjiang local specialty." Zhou Tao credits his success to the advantages that "cultural hybridization" has brought him—the combined strength of Islamic civilization, the cultures of Central Asia, the unrestrained life on the prairie, and their enrichment of and impact on the culture of the Central Plains.

3
恋人

史铁生

八十岁,老吴住进了医院的病危室。"一步登天"的那间小屋里,一道屏风隔开两张病床,谁料那边床上躺的老太太竟是他的小学同桌。怎么知道的?护士叫到老吴时,就听那边有人一字一嚼地问道:"这老爷子,小时候可是上的幸福里三小吗?"老吴问,"您哪位?""我是布欢儿呀,不记得了?"若非这名字特别,谁还会记得?

"五年级时就听说你搬家到外地去了,到底是哪儿呀?"

"没有的事儿。"老吴说,"我们家一直都在北京。"

屏风那边沉寂半晌,而后一声长叹。

布欢儿只来得及跟老吴说了三件事。一是她从九岁就爱上老吴了。二是她命不好,一辈子连累得好多人都跟着她倒霉。布欢儿感叹说,没想到临了临了,还能亲自把这些事告诉老吴。

3
THE LOVE OF HER LIFE

Shi Tiesheng

At eighty, Lao Wu entered the room at the hospital for the critically ill. One step away from heaven, a screen separated the two beds in that small room. Who would have guessed that the old lady in the other bed would happen to be Lao Wu's elementary school desk-mate? How did he discover this? When a nurse called for Lao Wu, the woman on the other bed asked fastidiously, "May I ask, Mister, whether you attended the Third Elementary School at Happiness Lane when you were a kid?"

Lao Wu became curious, "May I ask who you are?"

"This is Buhuaner! Don't you remember me?"

If it hadn't been for the peculiarity of the name, who would have? Lao Wu wondered.

"I heard that your family moved to another city in fifth grade. Which city was it?"

"Nonsense," Lao Wu said, "My family has never left Beijing all these years."

There was an extended period of silence on the other side of the screen, and then a long sigh.

Buhuaner lived only long enough to tell Lao Wu three things. The first was that she fell in love with him when she was nine years old; the second that bad luck had feasted on her all her life, which got many people near her into trouble. Buhuaner cried out in astonishment at this unexpected opportunity before the end of her time to tell Lao Wu all these things in person.

All what things?

哪些事儿呢？小学毕业，布欢儿再没见到老吴，但她相信来日方长。中学毕业了，还是没有老吴的消息，不然的话，布欢儿是想跟老吴报考同一所大学的。直到大学毕业，到了谈婚论嫁的年纪，老吴仍如泥牛入海，布欢儿却是痴心未改，对老吴一往情深。一年年过去，一次次地错过婚姻，布欢儿到了三十岁。偏有个小伙跟她一样痴情，布欢儿等老吴一年，他就等布欢儿一年。谁料，三十七岁时布欢儿却嫁给了另一个人，只因那人长相酷似老吴——从少年时的照片上看。

"这人，还好吧？"

"他就不算个人！"

为啥不算个人布欢儿也没说，只是说，否则母亲也不会被气死。

那次婚姻让布坎儿心灰意冷，很快就跟第一时间向她求婚的人登了记。婚后才发现，这人还是长得很像老吴——从少年老吴的发展趋势看。

"怎么样，你们过得？"

"过是过了几年，可后来才知道，咱是二奶！"

"这怎么说的！"

怎么说？布欢儿一跺脚，离婚，出国，嫁个洋人，再把女儿接出去上学……一晃就是二十年。有一天接到个电话，是当年一直等着她的那个小伙子打来的。

"过的还好吗，你？"

"还是一个人，我。"

"咋不结婚呢，你？"

"第一回我被淘汰。第二回我晚了一步。第三回嘛，这不，刚打听到你住哪儿。"

"唉，你这个人哪！"

"我这个人性子慢。你呢，又太急。"

Buhuaner never saw Lao Wu again after graduating elementary school, but she put her faith in the fact that they had many years ahead of them. There was still no news of Lao Wu when she finished high school, otherwise she would have applied, together with Lao Wu, to the same university. Buhuaner's love for Lao Wu remained unaltered and as profound as ever all the way to her college graduation, when she reached the age of marriage. But Lao Wu was like clay oxen entering the sea—never to be heard from again. Year after year, time and again, Buhuaner missed opportunities to marry, and then she turned thirty. It just so happened that a young man was infatuated with her as much as she was with Lao Wu. Just as Buhuaner waited for Lao Wu year after year, this man waited for Buhuaner. To everybody's surprise, at the age of thirty-seven, Buhuaner married a different man, her only reason was that the guy looked much like Lao Wu—at least in his childhood photos.

"This man, was he okay?"

"He was not worthy of being called a man!"

Buhuaner didn't say why, just that her mother wouldn't have died because of the antipathy between them had he been a real man.

The experience depressed Buhuaner, so as soon as she could, she registered again to marry the first person that asked for her hand. She didn't realize until after the wedding that her new husband also looked much like Lao Wu—especially when she allowed for how each of them must have aged.

"How was your life with him?"

"We did have a life for a few years. But later I found out I was just his mistress!"

"How could he do that?"

How could he! Buhuaner stamped her foot, got divorced, left China, and married a foreigner. She then brought her daughter out to go to school abroad... In the blink of a eye, twenty years passed. One day, she got a call. It was from the man who had waited for her years ago.

"Is all well with you?"

"Still by myself am I."

"Why not get married, you?"

"Eliminated the first round; too late for the second; and the third, you see, I just found out where you live."

"Ai, what can I say!"

"I'm slow tempered, and you, too fast."

约好了来家见面，布欢儿自信已有充分的心理准备，可一开门她还是惊倒在沙发里：进来一个完全不认识的小老头儿……

　　老吴回普通病房之前，拄着拐棍儿到屏风那边去看了看他的同桌。

　　四目相对，布欢儿惊叫道："老天，他才真是像你呀！"

　　"你是说哪一个？"

　　"等了我一辈子的那个呀……"

　　这是布欢儿告诉老吴的第三件事儿。

(2012)

They set a time to meet at Buhuaner's home. She was confident she was psychologically prepared for the meeting; yet she was still knocked back down into her seat when the door opened and in walked a total stranger—a small old man . . .

Before he returned to the general ward, Lao Wu, leaning on his cane, walked to the other side of the screen to visit his desk-mate.

When they were face-to-face, Buhuaner yelled out in surprise, "Good heavens! He looks exactly like you!"

"Who are you talking about?"

"The one who waited for me his entire life . . ."

This was the third thing Buhuaner told Lao Wu.

(2012)

VOCABULARY AND USAGE

病危	bìngwēi	critically ill	得知父亲病危，他马上请假往家赶。
一步登天	yíbùdēngtiān	one step to heaven	住进"一步登天"这个病房的人都是病危快死了的人。
屏风	píngfēng	screen	屏风就是好看，挡挡眼，哪里能隔音呢？
同桌	tóngzhuō	desk-mate	你还记得我，你小学的同桌吗？
沉寂	chénjì	silence; stillness	她用歌声打破了沉寂。
半晌	bànshǎng	a long while	他想了半晌也没想起我是谁。
连累	liánlèi	involve; implicate	我好汉做事好汉当，绝不连累别人。
倒霉	dǎoméi	have bad luck	她觉得自己是命中注定一辈子要倒霉。
临了	línliǎo	at the end of one's life	他一辈子省吃俭用，临了还是欠了一屁股债。
来日方长	láirìfāngcháng	many a day is yet to come	虽说来日方长，我们也不能放松每日每时的努力。
谈婚论嫁	tánhūnlùnjià	plan to get married	你们俩到了谈婚论嫁那一步了吗？
泥牛入海	níniúrùhǎi	disappear	他这一走如泥牛入海，再无音讯。

痴心	chīxīn	infatuation	他痴心未改，对自己的初恋依旧一往情深。
一往情深	yìwǎngqíngshēn	deeply in love	
错过	cuòguò	miss; let slip	别为错过的机会后悔了，来日方长，再努力吧。
偏(偏)	piān(piān)	contrary to expectation	他终于来了，可我偏偏又不在家！
心灰意冷	xīnhuīyìlěng	disheartened	英语考试不及格让他对去美国上学的事儿心灰意冷。
登记(结婚)	dēngjì(jiéhūn)	register (for marriage)	我们今天登记了，下个月举行婚礼。
趋势	qūshì	tendency	你有发胖的趋势，要小心饮食多运动啦。
(一)晃	(yí) huàng	flash past	大学四年一晃就过去了。
淘汰	táotài	eliminate	这个方法太落后了，早就该淘汰了。
性子	xìngzi	temper	你性子急，应该找个慢性子的丈夫。
拐棍	guǎigùn	walking stick	不知不觉，我们就到了走路要拄拐棍的年纪。

QUESTIONS FOR DISCUSSION

1. What was Lao Wu to Buhuaner all her life? And Buhuaner to Lao Wu?
2. Was there a final revelation for Buhuaner? Would she die smiling? Why?
3. "Lǎo" in Chinese, besides "old," can also mean "always" and the pronunciation of "wú" can imply "nonexistent." Could this reading of "Lao Wu" add some allegorical significance to the story?
4. Breaking down "Buhuaner" into its separate syllables, we get "bù huān ér," which sounds exactly like "not happy child" in Chinese. Why is this significant?
5. How does the story play with/converge such concepts as "stranger" and "loved one"?
6. Discuss the tone of this story. As readers, with whom do your sympathies lie?
7. How does the story testify to the truth of Han Shaogong's eulogy of Shi Tiesheng (see "Author Bio" following this section)?

1. 在布欢儿的一生中，老吴意味着什么？而在老吴的一生中，布欢儿又意味着什么？
2. 布欢儿临终前顿悟了吗？她会不会带着微笑离开呢？为什么？
3. "老"在中文里，除了"年纪大了"，也有"总是"的意思，而"吴"跟"无"又是谐音。如果把"老吴"这个名字理解为"不曾存在，"这样的解读能否给故事添加些许寓意？
4. "布欢儿"听起来跟"不欢儿"一样。为什么对这个名字做这样的理解有意义？
5. 这个故事是怎样重叠把玩了像"陌生的人"和"所爱的人"这样的概念的？
6. 请讨论一下故事的语调／语气。作为读者，你更同情故事中的哪一位人物。
7. 下面的作者简介中引用了一些韩少功对史铁生的赞誉。这个故事从哪些方面印证了韩少功所言？

AUTHOR BIO

Shi Tiesheng (1951–2010) was a bright star in Chinese literature. Life was not easy for him. He graduated from the middle school attached to Tsinghua University in 1967. An educated youth who went down to the countryside in 1969, Shi Tiesheng farmed and raised cattle in a village in Yan'an in Shaanxi Province for three years until paralysis brought him back to Beijing in 1972. He found a job in a neighborhood factory and worked there, despite being confined to a wheelchair, from 1972 to 1974. In 1998 he was diagnosed with uremia and endured dialysis every other day for the last thirteen years of his life. He died of a sudden stroke four days before his sixtieth birthday on December 31, 2010.

Shi Tiesheng published his first short story "The Law Professor and His Wife" ("法学教授及其夫人") in 1979. Despite his illness, Shi Tiesheng produced a large quantity of quality work. His widely known short stories "My Distant Qingpingwan Village" ("我的遥远的清平湾") and "Grandma's Stars" ("奶奶的星星"), his novella *The Stories of Educated Youth in the Countryside* (插队的故事), his prose piece "The Temple of Earth and I" ("我与地坛"), his prose collection *Notes in Sickness* (病隙碎笔), and his unique full-length novel *Wo de Dingyizhilü* ("我的丁一之旅") are but a few of his better-known works. He also adapted his short story "Life as a String" ("命若琴弦") into a successful screenplay. He won many awards and has been translated into different languages.

In his essay "Believe in God by Day and Believe in Buddha at Night" ("昼信基督夜信佛"), published posthumously in the December issue of *Harvest* (收获) in 2012, Shi Tiesheng unveiled a discovery: "Death is impossible" (死是不可能的). The reason is that "death is but a state of living being" (死也就是生的一种形态)—a state that is beyond the vision of the observer "I." Shi Tiesheng's treatment of an individual as a limited being in "The Love of Her Life," published in the same issue of *Harvest*, brings us close to his reflections on love, the future, life, and death. Shi Tiesheng's special challenges in life obliged him to contemplate these issues; yet he emerged from suffering, celebrating love, wisdom, understanding, and the eternal journey of becoming a Buddha. He placed his hope in the continuous effort on the eternal journey: "I believe, the meaning of tomorrow lies precisely in the possibility of further perfecting one's own action" (我只相信，明天的意义，惟在进一步完美行动的可能).

His fellow writer Han Shaogong remembered him with these words: "a miracle of a life" (生命的奇迹), "a peak of literature" (文学的高峰), "most powerful and dignified" (至强至尊), and one who had reached "the spiritual heights of his time" (当代精神的高度). Our experience with this story has shown that Shi Tiesheng's work allows readers "to touch eternity in the twinkling of an eye" (在瞬息中触摸永恒), "to enter endless expanses of life from a particle" (在微粒中进入广远), and "to smile generously from the heart" (打心眼里宽厚地微笑).[5]

---

5. Please go to http://baike.baidu.com/view/39292.htm (accessed April 26, 2016) to read Han Shaogong's original words

4
井不自知水多少

高怀昌

大学生村官耿自民是杨树庄的村主任助理。助理嘛,说是个村官是个村官,说不是个村官也不是个村官,但时下对委派到村里的大学生就是这么个称呼,耿自民也就不在乎了。他在乎的是,他所在的这杨树庄,在乡里乃至县里,都是中等靠上的村,农业水平、经济状况、村容村貌、村民生活等方面,均属比上不足、比下有余,因而,村民们纵向比横向看,心理比较平衡。心理一平衡就矛盾少、问题少、事情少,工作就好开展,村民就好相处,成绩就好取得。

可是,就在耿自民干得顺风顺水、小有成就的时候,上级突然决定,要把他从现在的村改派到沙窑村。

沙窑村是个大村穷村落后村,人多地少村风差,土地承包这么多年,别的村都富了,改变模样了,沙窑村却依旧贫穷落后,发展缓慢,尤其是村里出了一起从未出过的凶杀案,使该村更是陷入一片混乱。为此,市里专门抽出一名干部担任该村党支部书记,并要求尽快调整村两委班子,稳定村民思想,扭转混乱局面,改变沙窑村的落后面貌。

4
WATER IN THE WELL

Gao Huaichang

The college graduate and village official, Geng Zimin, was an assistant to the director of Poplar Village. As to the status of such an assistant, if you say he is a village official, then he is, and if you say he is not, then he is not. Geng Zimin didn't really care about the title, since this was what college graduates sent down to work in villages were called nowadays. What he did care about was Poplar Village. It was an above-average village in the township, and even in the county. In areas such as agricultural output, economic development, village appearance, and standards of living, Poplar Village might not have been at the top, but it was better off than most. So the villagers developed a confident sense of themselves when they checked up and down and looked around. This state of mind resulted in fewer conflicts and problems and reduced workloads; it also facilitated work conditions, interactions among villagers, and the achievement of common goals.

However, just as Geng Zimin was sailing with the wind downstream and developing the sense of an achiever, higher authorities suddenly decided to transfer him from his current Poplar Village to Sand Kiln Village.

Sand Kiln Village was big, poor, and backward. It had more people per area of land and lax morals. The land contract system had been in place for many years. While other villages turned around and become rich, Sand Kiln Village had been slow to develop and remained as poor and as backward as before. The village was also in turmoil because of an unprecedented murder case. Because of this, the municipal authorities selected an official to be the secretary of the village branch of the Communist Party of China and requested expedited restructuring of the village Party branch and the village administrative committee. The goal was to reassure the villagers, turn the situation around, and start transforming Sand Kiln Village.

耿自民就是这个时候被改派到沙窑村的，于是就不愿意，就赌气，就谎称父亲病重，回了老家。

顶着火烧火燎的大太阳在地里浇地的老耿，见儿子哭丧着脸回来了，便知必是心里有了疙瘩，遇上难题了，于是边浇地边探听儿子的心事。待老耿弄清了儿子生气的原因，便对儿子说，村里的事，挺不好搞的。你住村一年多了，我想着，不容易。既然回来了，就跟我好好浇浇地，把心里的事静一静。　村里的事，是个操心累人的事。看你晒得跟我一个颜色，我就想着，挺苦的。

儿子说，吃苦受累我不怕，可是，眼看就要出成绩了，就要有选拨的机会了，却给我换了那么一个烂村子。还不是故意坏我机会、给我难堪吗？

老耿说，烂村子，才能显本事，说不定是哪个领导看上了你的啥本事哩。

儿子说，我有啥本事吗？在那个杨树庄，还是下苦劲跟别人学着干的呢，有啥本事？

老耿说，那……那你是不是在那个好村待久了，待得怕苦怕累了？

儿子说，从小到大，我啥时候怕苦怕累过？我是怕没那个本事，到那儿以后干不好，干砸了，给那个本来就乱的村子，乱上加乱。

老耿说，哦，是个理儿。那你就跟我浇地，咱边浇地边好好唠扯唠扯。

老耿说，我娶你娘的时候，你爷爷奶奶都有病，就不敢娶，怕多个负担，多些难处，可是，你娘来了，很能干，帮助我把啥事都扛过来了。你

Geng Zimin was reassigned to Sand Kiln Village at this time, and he felt wronged. Out of spite, he lied, saying that his father was terribly sick, and so was allowed to return to his home village for a visit.

Lao Geng was watering fields under the scorching sun when he saw his son come back wearing a mournful face. He knew immediately that he had a knot in his heart—that he must have encountered some kind of trouble. While watering the fields, he asked his son some questions. Once he had learned the reason for his son's anger, he said to him, "Village affairs are hard to handle. The way I see it, it must be tough to have lived there for over a year. Now you are back, come enjoy watering the fields with me and let your mind calm down. Village work is grueling. Seeing that you are as tanned as I am, I said to myself, 'It must have been tough there.'"

His son responded, "I don't mind the job being tough, but transferring me to a lousy village like that when success is within reach and the chances for promotion are close at hand . . . Isn't this a deliberate effort to ruin my opportunities, to embarrass me?"

Lao Geng said, "A lousy village is your chance to show your abilities. Possibly a superior of yours saw something in you."

"What abilities do I have?" his son said. "Even at Poplar Village, all I did was learn, painstakingly, from others. What abilities do I have?"

"Could . . ." Lao Geng said, "could it be just that you've stayed in an easy village for too long and become fearful of hardships?"

"From boy to man," his son asked, "have I ever cringed from hardships? What I'm afraid of is that I don't have what it takes and can't make things work once I'm there. When I screw up, I will be adding to the misfortunes the village is already going through."

"Yes, what you said makes sense," Lao Geng responded. "How about joining me, so that we can talk things out while watering the fields?"

Lao Geng said to his son, "When I married your mom, your grandparents were both sick. For a while, I dared not go through with the wedding because I was afraid that she would be one more burden to bear and we would have more difficulties. But when your mom came, a very capable woman, she improved things by helping me lift all our burdens. And when you were in high school, our family went through a tough time. I worried about you being too good a student, about my not being able to pay for your education once you got into college. I had wanted you to start

上到中学时，家里难，我只怕你学习好了，考上大学供不起，想让你早点帮我干活儿，谁知你偏偏就考上了……

老耿说，家里的事，你是知道的，房子翻盖了，你爷爷的后事料理了，拖拉机、收割机买了，你奶奶的身体也好些了，你也大学毕业了……这么多年，这么多作难事，一宗一宗都挺过去了。

老耿说，这人的心胸啊，是被一宗一宗的难事撑大的；这人的本事呀，也是被一宗一宗的难事难大的。我活到现在明白了，这人哪，谁也不知自己的能力有多大。我要是知道能把这么多的困难都扛好，你爷爷还能走那么早吗？塌窟窿欠账也得住院哪！

老耿说，你看这口井，是土地承包第二年打的，周遭三百多亩地，每年几遍水，都是它浇的。三十年出头了，抽出多少水呀。这井啊，不知自己的水有多少；要是知道了呀，一下子冒出来，别说这三百多亩地，就是咱们全村，也全都被它淹完了。

听了爹的话，耿自民跟爹浇完地，背上行囊，到沙窑村报到去了。

(2012)

working for me as soon as possible. But as chance would have it, you did get into college...

"You know how things have turned out with our family," Lao Geng reminded his son. "The house is renovated; we've paid our last duties to grandpa; we've purchased the tractor and the harvester; your grandma's health is improving; and you've graduated college... We have encountered many troubles over the years, now they have passed by, one by one."

Lao Geng continued, "The mind of a person is stretched broader by the difficulties he faces. The same is true of the abilities of a man. They increase with each difficulty overcome. At my age, I've come to see that nobody knows exactly how capable he is. Had I known I could survive all these troubles, your grandpa wouldn't have left so early! However big a hole of debt I dug, I should have paid for him to be hospitalized!"

"Look at this well," Lao Geng said. " We dug this well the year after we contracted the land. More than three hundred *mu* of land surrounds it. It waters the land several times a year. How much water must we have drawn from it over the past thirty-odd years! This well doesn't know how much water it has. If it did, and chose to gush out, our entire village, not just these three hundred *mu* of land, would have been submerged by it."

After he heard these words, Geng Zimin finished watering the fields with his father. Then he picked up his luggage and headed for Sand Kiln Village.

(2012)

VOCABULARY AND USAGE

村官	cūn guān	village official	你们这儿的大学生村官是正式公务员吗?
委派	wěipài	delegate	公司领导委派她去行业年会上发言。
称呼	chēnghū	address; appellation	请问怎么称呼您?
乃至	nǎizhì	and even	教室里乃至走廊上都挤满了听他演讲的人。
容貌	róngmào	appearance	在他的领导下，这个小山村的容貌焕然一新。
均	jūn	without exception	你交代的工作我均已按时完成。

比上不足，比下有余	bǐshàngbùzú, bǐxiàyǒuyú	better off than some, worse off than others; reasonably good	我们现在比上不足比下有余，可是如果不继续努力，我们很快就会落后的。
纵/横向	zòng/héngxiàng	vertical/horizontal	京广铁路不是横向的，它连接南北，是纵向的。
平衡	pínghéng	balance	她车骑得太快，急刹车时失去了平衡，摔了下来。
相处	xiāngchǔ	get along with	她脾气温和，很好相处。
村风	cūnfēng	village culture	老人们常说这里的村风已大不如从前了。
承包	chéngbāo	contract	我要进城打工，就把自己的地承包给邻居了。
缓慢	huǎnmàn	slow; slowly	这项工程进展缓慢，按时完工已经是不可能的了。
凶杀案	xiōngshā àn	homicide case	这里很安全，从未发生过凶杀案。
陷入	xiànrù	fall into	专家们突然离开，项目陷入困境。
抽	chōu	pick out; select	请抽三个最好的学生去巴黎参加比赛。
该	gāi	that (above-mentioned)	我最向往的学校是北大，但愿能早日成为该校的学生。
调整	tiáozhěng	adjust; arrange	董事会调整了公司的领导班子和中层管理人员。
两委班子	liǎng wěi bānzi	"两委" refers to the village Party branch (村党支部) and the village administrative committee (村委会); "班子" means "organizational body."	
稳定	wěndìng	stable; stabilize; stability	先给他打一针，把情绪稳定下来再说。
扭转局面	niǔzhuǎn júmiàn	turn around situation	队员们知道只有靠自己的努力才能扭转眼前0:2的被动局面。
面貌	miànmào	look; feature	生活好了，山里人的精神面貌也跟过去大不一样了。

谎称	huǎngchēng	lie; claim	他谎称回家去参加奶奶的葬礼一星期没来上课。
火烧火燎	huǒ shāo huǒ liǎo	feel terribly hot	在午后的大太阳下干活，他的肩膀和后背都火烧火燎地痛。
哭丧着脸	kū shàng zhe liǎn	pull a long face	他心里有个解不开的疙瘩，所以一天到晚都哭丧着脸。
疙瘩	gēda	knot	
探听	tàntīng	try to find out	父亲说话前用心地探听了解了儿子的情况。
累人	lèi rén	tiring	照顾老人和小孩儿都是既要操心又很累人的活儿。
吃苦受累	chīkǔ shòulèi	have a rough time	小时侯多吃苦受累长大才能经得住风雨。
眼看	yǎnkàn	very soon	河水还在涨，眼看着就要漫上堤岸了。
选拨	xuǎnbá	select	经过层层选拨，她终于走上了总经理的位子。
烂	làn	messy; awful	那家工厂是个烂摊子，你可千万不要去那里工作。
坏	huài	ruin	警察突然出现，坏了我马上就要做成的好买卖。
难堪	nánkān	embarrassed	你真不够朋友，让我在女朋友面前难堪。
下(苦劲)	xià(kǔjìn)	put in (great effort)	要学好中文必须下苦功夫多读书。
乱上加乱	luàn shàng jiā luàn	add to the chaos	妈已经住院了，你要是再病了，那真是乱上加乱了。
翻盖	fāngài	renovate; replace	每年夏天，四周都有邻居翻盖房顶。
宗	zōng	a measure word	此地不安全，一年内发生过多宗凶杀案件。
撑	chēng	expand	你装了太多的东西，口袋都快撑破了。
塌	tā	collapse; cave in	车库的屋顶被大雪压塌了。

窟窿	kūlong	hole; loophole; debt	你再办多少张信用卡也没用，借债还债是堵不上你的窟窿的。
塌窟窿	tākūlong	owe a debt	他为给儿子娶媳妇塌下了十万元的窟窿。
周遭	zhōuzāo	surrounding area; about	这个大学城的周遭都是玉米地。
抽(水)	chōu(shuǐ)	obtain by drawing from (as from a well)	每年常规的身体检查都是要抽血的。
行囊	xíngnáng	luggage	"囊"是"袋子"的意思，装行李的袋子就是行囊了。

QUESTIONS FOR DISCUSSION

1. Is this a story about realizing your potential?
2. Is this a story about confronting one's preconceptions?
3. How is the well metaphor used differently in this story?
4. What is Lao Geng's view of self and identity?
5. What properties of a well does the story use to reference identity?
6. Why is the son named "Zimin" (自民 zìmín), which could mean "from the people" in Chinese?
7. What is the role of the father in the story?

1. 这是一个关于实现自我能力和价值的故事吗？
2. 这是一个跟个人偏见做斗争的故事吗？
3. 这个故事对井之比喻的运用有什么新意？
4. 老耿怎么看自己和自我（identity）？
5. 这个故事用了井的哪些属性来参照自我（identity）？
6. 为什么故事中儿子的名字叫"自民"？之所以问这个问题是因为这两个字在中文里可以被理解为"来自人民。"
7. 父亲在故事中起了什么样的作用？

AUTHOR BIO

Gao Huaichang (1955–) often publishes under his pen name of Jin Chang (金昌). Born of illiterate parents in a village in Jiaohu Township, Hua County, Henan Province, Gao Huaichang spent the first twenty years of his life in his hometown and became a farmer after graduating high school in 1974. He enlisted in 1976 and fought in the the War of Defensive Counterattack (自卫反击战) in Vietnam in 1979. He returned to a civilian life in his hometown in 1988 and worked for a district government in the City of Xinxiang until his retirement. He enrolled in the Economic Management program at Zhengzhou University and was awarded a college degree in 1990 after he successfully completed his two-year study.

The hardship his parents had been through, partly due to the lack of education, motivated him in school, and he fell in love with literature and reading. He tried his hand at writing and published two pieces in 1980. He did not return to writing until the end of 1999. As he was replacing his old desk calendar with a new one, it suddenly occurred to him that it would soon be too late if he did not pick up his pen right away. He has made good on his New Year's resolution for 2000. Gao Huaichang appreciates these words from a fellow veteran: "If my job is to clean, give me a few years and I will be the best janitor in the profession," yet Gao Huaichang writes more from a passion beyond his control than from the desire to become the best. He nevertheless has participated in many general and themed competitions at the local and national levels. His short-short "The Driver and the Professor" ("司机与教授") won a major award in 2004, and his novella *Looking for the Thief* (寻贼) won a themed competition in Quanzhou in Fujian Province in 2015. Gao Huaichang feels most comfortable writing prose and has won many prizes in competitions in Hunan, Hubei, Guangdong, Tianjin, Henan, and Ningxia.

Gao Huaichang has published, to date, more than seventy short-shorts and a dozen short stories and novellas and has written [not published] two full-length novels. His education in Chinese tradition and the imprints of his military and government service are distinctly visible in "Water in the Well." Writing this story at the age of fifty-six, he aspired to deeper understanding of "our culture" and hoped to share his understanding with the young.

第六章

脸面

谁不看重脸面？爱面子是人之天性[1]。所谓看重"脸面"通常是指对个人尊严或荣誉的关注。西方有关"脸面"的说法往往侧重公共或自我形象——在解决矛盾冲突或是追求生意成功等实用目标时是丢面子了还是得面子了？在中国，"脸面"到底是什么？这个问题让中国人和西方人都十分困惑。过去近一百五十年的研究只是刚刚触及到了这一重要文化观念的复杂性。本章的故事提请大家注意脸面问题常被忽略的几个方面："脸"和"面"的不同，"给面子"的重要性，以及对脸面毫无功利之心的关注。

早在七十多年前Hu Hsien-chin就明确指出"脸面"有双重含义。它既是"脸"，即来自堂正品德的脸；又是"面"，即植根于成功和地位的面子[2]。一个人要得到他人的"尊重和/或敬畏"，必须两者兼而有之[3]。故事《脸面》，正如其标题所示，既说"脸"也讲"面"，还关心两者之间的关系。李老二对王小六所表达的等级需求观不屑一顾，把王小六伸出的橄榄枝当作财大气粗的显摆；而王小六想要赢回失去的东西，回避自己过去对社会道德准则的背叛是不可能的。李、王双方怎样做才能全面照顾到问题的方方面面？王小六怎样才能重新赢得家乡人的信任？David Ho的这句话或许为我们指点了迷津："人本就不该**争脸**，因为无论社会地位如何，恪守文化规范是一个人

---

1. 请参看David Yau-Fai Ho 1976年在《美国社会学杂志》上发表的"On the Concept of Face,"第81 (4)期，882页。
2. 请参看Hsien Chin Hu 1944年在《美国人类学家杂志》上发表的"The Chinese Concept of 'Face'," 第46(1)期，45–64页。
3. David Yau-Fai Ho这样定义"脸面"："'脸面'就是一个人的体面加上他可以从他人那里得到的敬畏，或者说赢得这样的敬畏就是有脸面。这里，体面／敬畏是来自一个人在社会关系网中相应的位置，以及他是否在哪个位置上发挥了应有的作用，还有人们对他平日言谈举止的认可度。请参看如上的同一篇文章，第883页。

CHAPTER 6

FACE

Concern for "face," generally understood to be synonymous with concern for dignity or prestige, is universal.[1] Western ideas about face usually stress public or self-image, or losing and saving face while resolving conflicts or pursuing such utilitarian goals as success in business. What face means in China, however, has perplexed both Chinese and Westerners. Studies over the past one hundred fifty years or so have only touched on the complexity of this important cultural concept. Stories in this chapter call attention to some of its often neglected aspects: the differentiation of *liǎn* (脸) and *miàn* (面); the importance of *giving* face (给面子 *gěi miànzi*); and the nonutilitarian dimension of "face work."

Three-quarters of a century ago Hsien Chin Hu made clear that face is both *liǎn*, face that comes from moral integrity, and *miàn*, face rooted in success and status.[2] To claim "respectability and/or deference" from others,[3] one must have both. The story "Face" ("脸面" "*liǎnmiàn*") is, as the title suggests, about both *liǎn* and *miàn* and their connections. Li Laoer debunks Wang Xiaoliu's hierarchy of needs and dismisses his olive branch as ostentatious. What Wang Xiaoliu has lost cannot be regained without addressing his infraction of the society's moral code. How should the two

---

1. David Yau-Fai Ho, "On the Concept of Face," *American Journal of Sociology* 81, no. 4 (1976): 867–84.
2. Hsien Chin Hu, "The Chinese Concept of "Face," *American Anthropologist* 46, no. 1 (1944): 45–64.
3. Ho gives this definition of "face" in "On the Concept of Face": "Face is the respectability and/or deference which a person can claim for himself from others, by virtue of the relative position he occupies in his social network and the degree to which he is judged to have functioned adequately in that position as well as acceptably in his general conduct" (883).

起码的责任……"⁴一个人在有脸面之前，他能够也必须先赢得人们对其刚正不阿之品德的信任。

虽然"Save face"一词是英文的创造；但关照顾及他人的脸面却是每个文化都认真遵循的行为，中国文化尤其如此。八十年前，林语堂曾这样表达过对中国人脸面观的无奈：它过于精巧不能洗，太难捕捉不能刮；却又是最足珍惜的实质，强大到人们愿为它捐躯。面对把脸面当作礼物"赐予"、"送给" 或是"呈上"所产生的巨大力量，林语堂有些迷茫⁵。虽然林语堂的思考更侧重于这些做法的负面影响，我们很幸运有吴念真的《重逢》来帮助了解它们的正能量。或许这些正能量更接近脸面观发展的初衷。《重逢》中两人在计程车中微妙、和善的互动是人性大度风雅的终极体现，用没用语言都已不重要。这里，脸面跟地位的高低无关，"呈上"的对象是一个既无权又无名的落魄之人；这里，对他人情感的尊重和竭尽全力避免他人尴尬的努力，让我们看到了生命之美如盛开的台湾栾树之花朵。比尔·德雷克的这些话精辟地阐述了为什么中国人会不辞辛劳地"给予"或"关照"脸面："……在全世界的中国社区都是这样，一个人要是有了脸面，这就意味着他最宝贵的财富——滋养、构成他全部身份和认同的纽带——的增值。而如果一个人因他人之举而有了脸面，那他就是收到了最美好、最丰厚的礼物。"⁶

《鸡怕鸽破脸》中的暗喻隐含了恶语伤人与实际暴力的一种关系。同时，叙述人的经历似乎还在暗示，精心培育的社会关系有着超越实现功利目标的审美功用。学习吉尔特·霍夫斯塔德在务实文化层面的研究有助于

---

4. 同上，第870页。
5. 请去这个网页 http://www.eduzx.net/philosophy/11982.html 阅读林语堂"中国人的面子"全文。最后查看在2016年4月25日。
6. 请去这个网页 http://www.internationalman.com/articles/what-is-face-in-asian-culture-and-why-should-we-care 阅读比尔·德瑞克"What Is 'Face' In Asian Culture and Why Should We Care?"一文。最后查看在2016年4月25日。

of them attend to each of these aspects of face? What does it take for Wang Xiaoliu to regain his community's trust? A line from David Ho may be great counsel to all: "One does not speak of gaining lien [liǎn] because, regardless of one's station in life, one is expected to behave in accordance with the precepts of the culture."[4] One can and must earn the confidence in his/her moral integrity before he or she can have face (脸面 liǎnmiàn).

The phrase "to save face" is an English-language idiom. To save someone else's face has, however, been a concern of every culture in general and of Chinese culture in particular. Eighty years ago, in his frustration over face—too delicate to wash and too elusive to shave, yet substantial enough to be treasured and so powerful that people willingly die for it—Lin Yutang wondered about the power to grant or give face, to present face as a gift.[5] While Lin Yutang focused more on the negative potentials of such practice, we are lucky to have Wu Nianzhen's "A Golden Rain" to facilitate an understanding of its positive energy, which may come closer to the original intent behind the development of the concept. The subtle and gentle interaction, with and without words, between the two characters in the cab, is an ultimate manifestation of human decency. Here face is not hierarchical; it is given to one with neither prestige nor power. In the respect for another's feelings, in the effort to avoid incurring the slightest embarrassment, we are invited to see life as being as beautiful as the blossom of the golden-rain flower. These lines from Bill Drake show best why the Chinese people would go to great lengths to give/save face: "Gaining Face in all Chinese communities worldwide enhances what is most precious, *the nurturing bonds which comprise one's whole identity.* When a person gains Face by the act of another, there is no gift more appreciated or significant."[6]

The metonymical implication of "Chickens Hate Pecked Faces" suggests a connection between calling forth unpleasant feelings with words and the actual inflicting of violence. Yet the experience of the narrator seems to also suggest that the careful construction of social relationships

---

4. Ibid., 870.
5. Lin Yutang's article is available at www.eduzx.net/philosophy/11982.html (accessed April 26, 2016).
6. Please see Bill Drake's article "What Is 'Face' in Asian Culture and Why Should We Care?," *International Man*, accessed April 26, 2016, www.internationalman.com/articles/what-is-face-in-asian-culture-and-why-should-we-care.

建立必要的人际关系和维护有效的人脉；而这个故事给我们呈现的则是对脸与面亲密共存的欣赏，以及敬畏他人给人生带来的那种精神和审美上的愉悦、美好和满足。

　　然而，为达到某种功利实际的目的而刻意追求所谓的精神与审美则可能导致负面的影响。过度看重面子，也就是全神贯注地盯着是谁让我丢了面子，而我又怎么才能扳回面子等等，也会害己害人的。发生在故事《茶楼》里的情形或许能帮我们记住这一点。

can do much more than fulfill utilitarian goals. While a study of Geert Hofstede's pragmatic cultural dimensions can help one maintain appropriate interpersonal relationships and effective networks, the story presents the appreciation of face's mutuality and deference to others as a joyful spiritual/aesthetic experience of life's beauty and satisfaction.

But deliberate pursuit of the spiritual/aesthetic with pragmatic intent can lead to harm; the excessive attention to face, that is, what another has done to make *me* lose it and what *I* can do to gain it back, can be detrimental. The images from "At the Teahouse" may help us remember this.

1
重逢

吴念真

  事业失败后才发现,除了开车自己好像连说得出口拿得出手的专长都没有,所以最后他选择了开计程车。
  只是没想到台北竟然这么小,计程车在市区里跑还是容易碰到以前商场上的客户或对手。熟人不收费,自己倒贴时间和油钱也不算什么,最怕遇到的是以前的对手,车资两百三给你三百块,奉送一句:不必找啦,留着用!外加一个奇怪的眼神和笑容,那种窝囊感让人觉得不如死了算了。
  所以后来他专跑机场,说可能不会遇到类似难堪的状况而且也不用整天在市区没目的地转,让自己老觉得像个已经被战场淘汰的残兵败将,或者像中年游民一般感到无望。
  不过,他也承认跑机场的另一个奢望是,如果前妻带着孩子们偷偷回台的话,说不定还有机会和孩子们见上一面。"离婚后就没见过……我只能凭空想象他们现在的样子。"
  孩子和前妻一直没碰上,没想到先碰到的反而是昔日的恋人。
  他说那天车子才靠近,他就认出她来了。曾经那么熟悉的脸孔和身体……而且除了发型,二十年她好像一点也没变。

1
A GOLDEN RAIN

Wu Nianzhen

He didn't realize, at least until after his business had failed, that driving was the only special skill he had worth mentioning. So he ended up a taxi driver.

It had never occurred to him that Taipei might be so small. Doing business in the city proper he could easily run into previous clients or his competitors as passengers. He refused to charge acquaintances—not a big deal for him to give up his own time or pay for the gas. The most difficult of all his encounters were when he had to serve his past competitors. They gave him 300 yuan when the fare was 230, and accompanied the payment with a throwaway comment, "Keep the change—you are going to need it!" He felt like a total loser; it was a living hell to be forced to suffer their odd looks and sniggers.

Because of all this, he decided to only work the airport route, in the hope that he could avoid any more embarrassing situations, as well as the aimless fare hunting that went with driving in the city. Both made him feel like the defeated remnant of a battlefield or a hopeless middle-aged vagrant.

He also admitted, however, that there was another hope he clung to in running the airport route: he might have the opportunity to see his kids, if his ex-wife happened to secretly come back to Taiwan with them. "I can only imagine what they look like now. I haven't seen them since the divorce..."

He had not yet gotten a chance to see his kids and ex-wife when, to his surprise, he ran into his ex-lover instead.

He said that he recognized her as soon as he pulled up, that face and that body once so familiar to him ... With the exception of her hairstyle, she didn't seem to have changed at all in twenty years.

上车后，她只说了一个医院的名字和"麻烦你"之后，就沉默地看着窗外，反而是他自己一直担心会不会因为车子里的工号牌而被她认出来。不过，她似乎没留意，视线从窗外的风景上收回来之后，便拿出电话打。

　　第一通电话听得出她是打回澳洲的家，听得出先生出差去了英国。她轮流跟两个孩子说话，要一个男孩子不要为了打球而找借口不去上中文课，还要一个女孩好好练钢琴，然后说见到外婆之后会替他们跟她说爱她等等。最后才听出是她母亲生病了，因为她说："我还没到医院，不过妈妈相信外婆一定会平安。"

　　他还记得她母亲的样子和声音以及她做的一手好菜，更记得两人分手后的某一天，她母亲到公司来，哽咽地问他："你怎么可以这样对待我女儿呢？"那种颤抖的语气和哀怨的眼神让人忘不了。

　　打完家里的电话，接着打给她的公司，利落的英文，明确的指令加上自然流露对同事的关心，一如既往。他们大学时候是朋友，毕业之后他去当兵，而她在外商公司做事；他退伍后，她把一些客户拉过来，两个人合伙做。三年后，公司从两个人增加到二十几个人，生意大有起色，而他却莫明其妙和一个客户的女儿发生了一夜情……

　　说莫明其妙其实是借口。他想，到现在也没什么好否认的……一来是陌生的身体总比熟悉的刺激，还有……这个客户公司的规模是我的几百倍，那时不是流行一句话，娶对一个老婆可以省掉几十年的奋斗！

　　最后车子经过敦化南路，经过昔日公司的办公室，两旁的台湾栾树正逢花季，灿烂的秋阳下一片亮眼的金黄。

Once inside, she told him only the name of the hospital, followed by an "if you don't mind . . ." before she looked out the window and fell into silence. He was the one who spent the ride wondering whether or not she would recognize him from his work ID inside the taxi. She, though, didn't seem to notice. Once she took her eyes off the scenery outside, she took out her phone and began to dial.

He could tell the first calls were made back home to Australia. Her husband was apparently in England on business. One after the other, she spoke with her two kids, telling the boy not to use ball games as an excuse to miss Chinese class and the girl to practice her piano well. She then assured them that she'd give their love to Grandma once she saw her. He didn't realize that her mother must be sick until she said, "I'm not at the hospital yet, but Mom is positive that Grandma will be fine."

He could still remember her mother's look, her voice, and her great cooking. And he would never forget that day after they broke up. Her mother came to the company and asked him, sobbing, "How could you treat my daughter like that?" Her trembling voice and her mournful eyes had engraved themselves on his memory.

When she was done with the calls back home, she went on to call her company. In her crisp English, she gave clear instructions, and he noticed that her spontaneous flow of genuine concern for her colleagues was still there, just as it had always been.

In college, the two of them had been friends. After graduation, he had gone on to serve his term in the military while she went to work for a foreign company. When he was discharged, she brought some clients over from her former company, and the two of them became business partners. Three years later, their company of two grew into one with two dozen employees. Just as their business was showing signs of great promise, he—for no reason anyone could fathom—had a one-night stand with the daughter of a client . . .

To say "no reason anyone could fathom" was a cop-out. *Well,* he thought, *with things as they stood now, there is no point in denying the real reason for what he had done . . . After all, a stranger's body is always more exciting than a familiar one, and also, her father's company had been hundreds of times bigger than mine . . . Wasn't it the saying of the time that the right wife could save you dozens of years of struggle?*

后座上当年的恋人正跟之前公司的某个同事话家常,说台北,说澳洲,说孩子,说女儿到了这个年龄阶段的感受,然后说停留的时间以及相约见面吃饭,说:"让我看看你们现在都变成什么模样。"

　　车子最后停在医院门口,他还在躲避,也犹豫着要不要跟她收费或者给她打个折,没想到后头的女人忽然出声,笑笑,用极其平静的语气说:"我都已经告诉你我所有近况,告诉你我现在的心情,告诉你我对一些人的思念……什么都告诉你了,而你……连一声Hello都不肯跟我说?"

(2012)

The taxi finally turned onto South Dunhua Road and soon passed the offices of their defunct company. The golden-rain trees of Taiwan flanking the road were in full bloom under the bright autumn sun, giving off a dazzling, gilded hue.

His former sweetheart in the backseat was now talking with a former colleague of theirs. They chatted about how they were feeling about Taipei, Australia, and their children, especially now that their daughters had reached a certain age. Then they talked about her stay and made plans to have a meal together. "It'll give me a chance to see what you look like now," she said.

Finally the taxi pulled over at the hospital entrance. Still trying to avoid her, he was also debating whether he should charge her at all or give her a discount when, to his surprise, the woman behind him spoke in a very calm voice, smiling, "I've updated you on everything about me, my state of mind, people I miss . . . everything that I could think of, and you . . . you don't even want to say hello to me?"

(2012)

VOCABULARY AND USAGE

说得出口拿得出手	shuōdéchūkǒu nádéchūshǒu	presentable; deserve to be seen	我们是去参加婚礼！就这么点儿东西？能说得出口拿得出手吗！
选择	xuǎnzé	select; selection	现在的孩子选择多了，可他们面对的竞争也更激烈了。
计程车	jìchéngchē	taxi; cab	开计程车是个很辛苦的职业。
倒贴	dàotiē	lose; subsidize	我心甘情愿倒贴钱支持儿子创业。
车资	chēzī	carfare; fare	在这里，"车资"就是打的费用，也可以说"车钱。"
奉送	fèngsòng	offer as a gift	有家电影院为了吸引早场观众免费奉送油条。
外加	wàijiā	in addition; plus	他一人要了三份套餐，还外加一份冰淇淋。

窝囊	wōnang	feel vexed and helpless	被机器人打败了,他也不觉得特别窝囊。
算了	suànle	let it be; let it pass; forget about it	反正这道题我不会做,随便写个答案算了。
类似	lèisì	similar; analogous	不稀奇,类似的垃圾文章报上网上每天都有。
残兵败将	cánbīngbài jiàng	remnants of a defeated army	我们都是残兵败将,没有能力再拼杀了。
奢望	shēwàng	extravagant hopes; wild wishes	爸爸,你不该奢望大学四年我门门功课都拿满分。
凭空	píngkōng	out of thin air; without foundation	关于他的这些说法并不都是凭空捏造的。
昔日	xīrì	formerly; in olden days	我十分想念昔日的同学和朋友。
沉默	chénmò	silent; silence	他装着不认识我,跟我擦肩而过,却沉默着不说话。
留意	liúyì	pay attention to; look at	你想做房地产生意就该留意股市楼市的行情。
视线	shìxiàn	sight; view	那座新起的高楼挡住了我家观海的视线。
通	tōng	a measure word	他先打了一通电话,然后又出去喝了一通酒。
轮流	lúnliú	take turns	学校没有专职清洁工,学生们轮流打扫卫生。
哽咽	gěngyè	choked (with sobs)	我哽咽着,说不出话来。
颤抖	chàndǒu	shudder; shiver	他气得胡子都颤抖起来。
哀怨	āiyuàn	sad	她没说什么,但眼神里的哀怨总让我心里有些不安。
眼神	yǎnshén	expression in one's eyes	
利落	lìluo	deft; agile; crispy	爸爸做起家务活来比妈妈还利落。
指令	zhǐlìng	order; command	我们团队的每个人都严格按照主管的指令行事。
流露	liúlù	reveal; betray	一听说要加班,他脸上立刻流露出不满。
一如既往	yīrújìwǎng	as always	她的美一如既往;二十年没有一点儿变化。

大有起色	dà yǒu qǐsè	improved significantly	自从你交了一个中国朋友，你的中文大有起色。
莫明其妙	mòmíngqímiào	inexplicable; baffling	他没病没灾的，死的是有些莫名其妙。
一夜情	yīyèqíng	one-night stand	她不能接受丈夫跟别的女人的"一夜情,"所以决定跟他离婚。
刺激	cìji	stimulating; exciting	这部电视剧有些场面太刺激，儿童不宜。
栾树	luánshù	golden-rain tree	台湾栾树多种多样；开出的红花黄花都很漂亮。
逢	féng	come upon	我们2008年夏天去北京的时候正逢奥运会开幕。
灿烂	cànlàn	splendid; glitter	你看，孩子们脸上的笑容多灿烂！
打折	dǎzhé	discount; on sale	你一直想要的那件衣服现在打折了。

QUESTIONS FOR DISCUSSION

1. When do you think the female passenger recognized her ex-boyfriend? Why didn't she say hello to him right away? What would you have done under similar circumstances?
2. Why was it necessary for her to make so many phone calls?
3. Do you remember the third paragraph from the end? Is it necessary? What does it add to your reading of the story?
4. Is her question at the end meant to humiliate the man or to rekindle an old flame?
5. Could her question in any way be a gesture of reconciliation, respect, closeness, and understanding?
6. Does her way of handling his problem of "face" resonate with you?
7. Which translation do you like better as the title of the story: "Meet Again," "Reunion," or "A Golden Rain"? Explain.

1. 你觉得那位女乘客什么时候认出了她的前男友？她为什么没有立马上前去打招呼？如果是你，你会怎样做？
2. 为什么女乘客有必要打这么多电话？
3. 你对故事的倒数第三段有印象吗？这段文字有必要吗？它对你的阅读 有什么进一步的帮助？
4. 女乘客最后的问题是为了羞辱前男友吗？或是为了重燃旧情？
5. 说她的问题表达的是一个和解、尊重、亲近加理解的姿态，你同意吗？
6. 女主角关照男主角"脸面"问题的方式能引起你的共鸣吗？
7. 这几个翻译中，你觉得哪一个做故事的标题更好一些："Meet Again," "Reunion," 还是 "A Golden Rain"？请说明。

AUTHOR BIO

Wu Nianzhen (1952–) was born in Ruifang, Taiwan. He went to college for an accounting degree after his service in the army. He started writing fiction in the mid-1970s and penned his first screenplay in 1978. Now Wu Nianzhen is better known as a scriptwriter, a director, and a leading artist of the visual media, having written more than sixty screenplays, many of which have been made into films and won such awards as Golden Horse Awards for Best Original Screenplay (金马奖最佳原著剧本) and the Hong Kong Film Award for Best Screenplay (第十届香港电影金像奖最佳编剧). Here we acknowledge him as "the best storyteller in Taiwan," who enjoys large readerships on both sides of the Taiwan Strait and beyond. Like many writers of short-shorts, Wu Nianzhen started creative writing to accommodate his own interests outside of work and study; yet unlike most writers of short-shorts, Wu Nianzhen landed a job writing screenplays for the Central Motion Picture Corporation before he finished business school. His most well-known works include *A Special Day* (特别的一天, 1988), *These People, Those Things* (这些人，那些事, 2010), and *Taiwan, Say the Truth* (台湾念真情, 2011).

You may already know that Wu Nianzhen is one of the screenwriters for Hou Xiaoxian's 1989 film *A City of Sadness*. Some of you may have seen him as the protagonist in Edward Young's award-winning 2000 film *Yi Yi*. Many of his works in different media represent the best of the Chinese cultural tradition and its contemporary manifestation.

2
脸　面

魏永贵

　　王小六回老家的时候开了一辆半旧的小货车。
　　本来王小六是可以开一辆更好的车回家的。王小六在外面挣了钱，开辆好车回家可以好好露露脸。问题是，回村的路坑坑洼洼，磕磕碰碰好车消受不起，而且最重要的是，小货车可以装东西。
　　眼下，车厢里就装着一件重要的东西。
　　王小六已经三年没回家了。三年前下学不久的王小六在路上"顺"了一辆破自行车，骑了不到五十米赶巧拉肚子，扔了自行车就钻进了路边的厕所。等他提着裤子出来的时候，丢自行车的李老二已经领着戴警帽的在外面等他了。后来王小六就在拘留所里蹲了七天。
　　本来王小六是可以不蹲号子的，可他必须交几百块钱的罚款。娘含着眼泪捏着才借的钱去看王小六的时候，王小六坚决不干。王小六说娘你一点也不会算账，我蹲了号子就不用交钱，就省钱了，就等于硬生生赚了几百块钱，就等于在号子里打工了。娘说你个挨刀子的到这个时候了是钱重要还是脸面重要啊。
　　王小六说在没有钱的时候脸面就不那么重要。
　　蹲了几天号子出来的时候王小六还是考虑到了脸面。他就直接去了外面。几年工夫终于混了个人模狗样，三年后的腊月底就开了车回了家。

2
FACE

Wei Yonggui

Wang Xiaoliu went back to his hometown in a used van. He could have gone in a better vehicle. He had made a lot of money. To go back in a nice car would be a good way to show off, but the problem was that the road to his village was bumpy with potholes. A nice car might not be able to withstand the jolts. Most importantly, the van had the space to hold stuff.

There was something important in the van now.

Wang Xiaoliu had been away from home for three years. One day three years ago, not long after he had dropped out of school, he "led away" an old bicycle in the street on the sly. As he was riding away, he had a sudden attack of diarrhea. He had to abandon the bicycle and rush to a roadside toilet fifty meters from the crime scene. When he got out of the toilet, still pulling up his pants, the bicycle's owner Li Laoer was already waiting for him with uniformed officers. Wang Xiaoliu ended up serving seven days in a detention center.

Wang Xiaoliu didn't actually have to be detained if he paid a fine of a few hundred yuan. When his mother came, weeping, with the money she had just borrowed to bail him out, Wang Xiaoliu resolutely turned her down. He said to his mother, "You don't know how to do the math at all. We don't need to pay as long as I stay in here. That's a money-saving deal, like I was working in jail and made a solid few hundred yuan."

"You disappointing dummy!" his mother replied. "What's more important now, money or the dignity of your face?"

"Face is not worth much when you don't have money," Wang Xiaoliu said.

However, when he got out a few days later, Wang Xiaoliu couldn't forget about face. He left town immediately. After a few years of hard work,

王小六加大油门把车开到坡上家门口的时候，正在喂猪食的娘叫了一声。接着眼泪鼻涕也下来了。娘说天啦你个挨刀子的你怎么又偷了人家的汽车回来呢。

王小六咧着大嘴就笑了。王小六说娘这车不是我偷的是我自己买的。王小六边说边掏出了一摞五颜六色的小本本。王小六说娘你看这些是我的证件证明车不是偷的是我自己买的又自己开回来的。

娘就是不信。王小六在家待了两天娘就抹了两天眼泪。

第三天王小六开着小货车去了镇上。转了小半天终于把小货车堵在了李老二的自行车前头。

李老二还是骑着那辆破自行车。李老二说小六子你出息了啊不做自行车生意改做汽车生意了。李老二说罢又补充了一句：只是别又赶上拉肚子了。

王小六笑着说你说话怎么有股厕所的味道，骂人不揭短打人不打脸，都是哪辈子的事了。

李老二就呵呵的笑。

王小六踢了李老二的自行车一脚，然后给李老二点了一颗烟。王小六说老二哥咱们商量个事，你的这辆旧车我收了，或者是算我买了，我也不会亏待你。瞧，我已经给你准备了一辆新车，还是市面上有牌子的。

王小六一边说一边就从小货车的后厢里搬出一辆还裹着包装纸的自行车。

这回轮着李老二笑了。李老二说小六子看来你是真出息了。人家都说为富不仁你却正好相反，你这是回家扶贫来了。宁愿做赔本的买卖呀，好人，你可真是个好人。

he was eventually able to establish himself. So now, three years later and before the Chinese New Year, he was driving home in his van.

Wang Xiaoliu stepped on the gas and drove the van up the slope to his house. As he was pulling up to the door, his mother, who at the moment happened to be tending the pigs, cried out in surprise and began weeping and sniffling. "Good grief!" she said. "You disappointing dummy! So you're in the business of stealing cars now!"

Hearing this, Wang Xiaoliu grinned from ear to ear. "Mother," he laughed, "I didn't steal this van; I bought it with my own money." As he was saying this, he produced a stack of certificates in various colors from his pocket. "Please take a look, Mother. They are my certificates. They are proof that the van is not stolen. I bought it and drove it home myself."

Wang Xiaoliu's mother did not believe him. She cried the whole two days he stayed with her.

On the third morning he was home, Xiaoliu drove to town in his van. He circled around for almost half a day before he was eventually able to park his van right in front of Li Laoer's bicycle.

Li Laoer was still riding the same old bike. "Well done, Little Xiaoliu," Li Laoer said. "You've traded your bicycle business for one in motor vehicles!" He then added, "This time, may God save you from attacks of diarrhea."

With a smile, Wang Xiaoliu said, "Why do I smell something rotten in your words? You shouldn't call people out like this or blindside them. After all, that mistake of mine was a long time ago."

Li Laoer chuckled.

Wang Xiaoliu kicked Li Laoer's bicycle tire and then lit a cigarette for him. "Brother Laoer," Wang Xiaoliu said, "I've got a proposal for you. I'd like to have your old bicycle. I want you to understand that I'm buying it from you. I won't shortchange you. Look, I've already got you a new one, a name-brand bicycle from the market."

As he spoke, Wang Xiaoliu brought out the bicycle, still in its cellophane, from the back of his van.

It was Li Laoer's turn to laugh. He said, "Little Xiaoliu, You've really made something of yourself! People say that a rich man can't be benevolent, and you've proven them wrong. So, you've come back home to help the poor. And you'd rather do it at your own expense! Nice. What a nice guy you are!"

王小六说哪里我们都是乡里乡亲。一边又递给李老二一颗烟。

这一次李老二没有接烟。

李老二说小六子你也太聪明大了。我知道你惦记我这辆破自行车是因为它让你产生了痛苦的回忆,这辆自行车一天不消失你就一天不安宁,是不是。你现在有钱了开始讲究脸面了,你想收回这个破自行车挽回你的脸面。可你光顾你王小六的脸面却忘了 我李老二。你也不想想,我用一辆破车换回一辆新嘎嘎的车,镇上的人岂不是骂我是占便宜的人,到时候我的脸面又往哪里搁。

王小六好半天说不出话来。

王小六最后说老二哥你把事情想复杂了,我们再商量商量。

王小六说话的时候几乎有些哀求了,把着李老二的自行车不松手。

李老二拍了一把没有垫子的自行车屁股,车弹簧哗啦直响。李老二说你打老远拉回来一辆新车却要跟我换旧车,你自己复杂还说我复杂。

李老二有些不耐烦了,推着车准备走。李老二口气很硬地说王小六你把手拿开,张老四还等着我去打麻将呢。

王小六就松了手。就看着李老二甩腿骑上了那辆破自行车东倒西歪走了。

自行车咔嚓咔嚓的声音像刀子一样一下下扎在王小六的心里。

(2010)

Wang Xiaoliu said, "Please don't say that. We are folks of the same town." Wang Xiaoliu offered Li Laoer a second cigarette as he spoke.

This time Li Laoer did not take it.

Li Laoer said, "Little Xiaoliu, you've been too clever for your own good. I know you can't let go of my broken bicycle because it reminds you of your painful past. You won't have peace of mind until the day it's gone, right? Now you have money, so you are particular about your face, too. You want this old bicycle to be the means of redeeming your face. But while you have been obsessed by thought of saving your own face, you forgot to consider mine. Just think about it. If I trade my old bicycle for a brand-new one from you, wouldn't the town call me a freeloader? How will I keep my face when the time comes?"

For a long while, Wang Xiaoliu could not think of a response. Finally he said, "Brother Laoer, you put too much thought into a simple matter. Let us reconsider it."

Wang Xiaoliu was almost begging when he said these words. His hands gripped Li Laoer's bicycle, unable to let go.

Laoer smacked the unpadded seat of the bicycle, causing the springs to rattle. He said to Wang Xiaoliu, "You came all the way back home with a new bicycle, to trade it for my old one. You are the one who has put too much thought into a simple matter, not me."

Li Laoer was getting impatient and began to push his bicycle away. He said in a firm voice, "Wang Xiaoliu, please get your hands off my bicycle. Zhang Laosi is waiting for me to play mah-jongg."

Wang Xiaoliu released his grip. He watched Li Laoer mount his bicycle with a swing of one leg and ride off, swerving left and right.

Like a knife, the clanging sound of the old bicycle pierced Wang Xiaoliu's heart repeatedly.

(2010)

VOCABULARY AND USAGE

露脸	lòuliǎn	look good	这年头，有大房子大车才露脸呢！
坑坑洼洼	kēngkēngwāwā	bumpy; potholes	这路坑坑洼洼的，车上人又多，有个磕磕碰碰也是难免的。
磕磕碰碰	kēkēpèngpèng	knock (against) and bump (into)	
消受不起	xiāoshòu bùqǐ	cannot enjoy/endure	爷爷年纪大了，长途飞行他的身体消受不起。
(车)厢	(chē) xiāng	cargo space; box; car	货车结实，车厢又大又，不怕磕碰还好装东西。
下学	xiàxué	leave/quit school	她十五岁就下学去城里打工了。
赶巧	gǎnqiǎo	happen to	赶巧她要进城，我就搭了个顺风车。
拉肚子	lādùzi	suffer from diarrhea	他食物中毒了，这几天一直在拉肚子。
戴警帽	dài jǐngmào	wear a police cap	这里，"戴警帽的"指的是地方治安警察。
拘留所	jūliúsuǒ	jail; detention center	他因为偷了一辆自行车被关进了拘留所。
蹲	dūn	squat	说一个人在"蹲号子"就是说他因为犯法被关进了拘留所或是监狱。
号子	hàozi	a prison cell	
含泪	hán lèi	with tears in one's eyes; tearfully	妈妈含泪看着女儿上了去美国的飞机。
捏	niē	hold between the fingers	他捏起一根蚯蚓，左看右看，一点儿也不怕。
硬生生	yìng shēng shēng	directly and forcibly	老师们用一个月的时间硬生生地把学生成绩提高了百分之二十。
你个挨刀子的	nǐ ge ái dāozi de	a local curse—"You deserve to be stabbed," meaning "You are such an unforgivable person."	我怎么生了你这么个挨刀子的，不好好学习，一天到晚只想着赚钱？

混	hùn	drift along; get by	这回开奔驰了，看样子你在外面混得还不错啊。
人模狗样	rénmúgǒu yàng	pretending to be what one is not	他就爱人模狗样地上电视，谈人生经验、理财诀窍什么的。
眼泪鼻涕	yǎnlèi bítì	tears and nasal mucus	浓烟熏得他眼泪鼻涕直流。
摞	luó	a measure word; pile	小心，别把那摞盘子碰倒了。
五颜六色	wǔyánliùsè	multicolored; colorful	园子里开着五颜六色的花。
抹眼泪	mǒ yǎnlèi	wipe one's eyes; weep	她输掉比赛以后一直在抹眼泪。
转	zhuàn	walk around	爸爸退休后常去附近的一个古董市场转转。
堵	dǔ	block up	前边有个车祸，堵住了两条车道。
有/没出息	yǒu/méi chūxi	promising/not promising	这孩子小时吃了不少苦，长大一定有出息。
罢	bà	end; finished	听罢奶奶的话，他啥也没说，起身走了出去。
骂人不揭短，打人不打脸	mà rén bù jiē duǎn, dǎ rén bù dǎ liǎn	not to catch people on the raw or hit them in the face	你做事别太绝了，骂人不揭短，打人不打脸，学学怎么给别人留面子！
颗	kē	a measure word	他用一颗糖换走了她一颗心。
哪辈子	nǎbèizi	a long time ago	那都是哪辈子的事儿了，你怎么还放在心上？
算	suàn	count; regard	好了好了，这话，就算我没说吧。
亏待	kuīdài	treat shabbily	你怎么可以这样亏待自己的身体？
扶贫	fúpín	alleviation of poverty	中央政府又公布了新的扶贫政策。
赔本	péiběn	sustain losses in business	没人愿做赔本的买卖。

聪明大了	cōngmíng dàle	too smart for one's own good	一个人聪明大了会自以为是,把好事办坏了。
光	guāng	only	别光顾着学习书本知识而忘了生活经验的重要。
嘎嘎	gāgā	an onomatopoeia	他崭新的自行车在石板路上嘎嘎作响。
岂不是	qǐbúshì	(an indicator of a rhetorical question) isn't it; wouldn't it be	你这样做岂不是让我丢人现眼?
占便宜	zhàn piányi	gain extra advantage by unfair means	我用新车换你的旧车,怎么是占你的便宜呢?
垫子	diànzi	cushion; pad	这车太旧了,车坐上的软垫子都磨坏了。
弹簧	tánhuáng	spring	这张弹簧床太硬了,弹性不够好。
哗啦	huālā	an onomatopoeia	一年四季房后的小河都在哗啦哗啦地流淌着。
直	zhí	continuously	把冷气关上吧,孩子冻得直哆嗦。
打(老远)	dǎ (lǎoyuǎn)	from (far away)	你这么多的摩托车都是打哪儿弄来的呀?
甩	shuǎi	swing; fling	老牛不停地甩动着尾巴。
东倒西歪	dōngdǎo xīwāi	reel right and left; lurch	小树被大风吹得东倒西歪。
咔嚓	kāchā	an onomatopoeia	"咔嚓"一声,护栏断了,很多人摔下山去。

QUESTIONS FOR DISCUSSION

1. What is wrong with Wang Xiaoliu's strategy?
2. What do you think of Li Laoer's reaction to Wang Xiaoliu's proposal?
3. Does the story help you to understand the Chinese saying that "among the most disgusting is a patronizing face"?

4. Does Abraham Maslow's hierarchy of needs[7] help you understand the difference between Wang and Li?
5. How does recognizing the simultaneous presence of many needs help reconcile the possible conflicts between *lian* (脸) and *mian* (面)?
6. Does the Confucian teaching "What you do not want done to yourself, do not do to others" seem helpful here?
7. Why does Wang Xiaoliu feel so hurt at the end? Should Li Laoer reconsider? Is it possible to resolve the problem so that both characters are content?

1. 王小六拿新车换旧车的这一招有什么不妥?
2. 你怎么看李老二对王小六提议的反应?
3. 有句中国俗话说"最可憎的是恩人的脸。"这个故事能帮助你理解它的意思吗?
4. 亚伯拉罕·马斯洛的层次需求理论能帮助你理解王小六和李老二之间的分歧吗?
5. 承认多种需求的同时存在如何能帮助消解"脸"和"面"可能发生的冲突?
6. 孔子"己所不欲,勿施于人"的教导在这里有帮助吗?
7. 结尾处,为什么王小六心里那么难受?李老二是不是应该重新考虑王小六的提议?有没有可能找一个让双方都满意的办法来解决这个问题?

AUTHOR BIO

Some of the best short-short writers I have met wear a uniform, the way Wei Yonggui (1961–) does when he is at work. They are public security professionals working for local government, bureaus of public security to be exact. When the Traffic Police Department of the Public Security Bureau

---

7. Abraham Maslow (1908–1970) was a psychologist best known for his concept of hierarchy of needs. Maslow argued that essential human needs and how these needs were fulfilled defined human experience. Please see if the delineation of the different levels of needs in Maslow's hierarchy helps you understand the conflict between the two characters and if the dynamic interaction of different levels of needs could help explain why the way(s) the needs are fulfilled are important. For a good understanding of Maslow's hierarchy of needs, please read the article "Abraham Maslow" at http://www.pursuit-of-happiness.org/history-of-happiness/abraham-maslow/, accessed February 18, 2017.

in the City of Weihai in Shandong Province advertised a reporter's position in 1989, Wei Yonggui, an editor for a local literary journal in Guangshui County in northeastern Hubei Province at the time, got the job. Instead of a résumé, he brought his published stories with him to the job interview. Known as "the writer from the police force" in the City of Weihai, Wei Yonggui is now responsible for educating the public with relevant knowledge and information at the Publicity Department of the Bureau. The character Wang Xiaoliu might very well be drawn from someone Wei Yonggui has worked with in real life.

A writer of philosophical reflections and romantic temperament, Wei Yonggui is among the most influential short-short writers in China today. He has published around five hundred stories, the best of which are collected in four volumes entitled *Forgetmenot* (空地的鲜花), *Snowwall* (雪墙), *Dance in the Snow* (雪上的舞蹈), and *Love Poison* (爱的毒药). He is the winner of many awards for short-shorts, including a gold medal for a national short-short story competition, the 2008 Bing Xin Book Award (冰心图书奖), and the Golden Sparrow Award (金麻雀奖) in 2009.

3
茶楼

陈勇

茶客们站在茶楼上,一边品茗,一边欣赏胭脂河的良辰美景。望穿水色,河水仿佛在熊熊燃烧。极目远眺,河水弯弯,湖水漪漪,平如明镜,静如处女,纤尘不染。 茶主人触情生情,举杯道:"有情待客何须酒?促膝谈心好品茶。"

茶客立即回应:"美酒千杯难成知己?清茶一盏也能醉人。"众茶客齐声叫好。须臾,茶客起身,沉吟片刻道:"小天地,大场合,让我一席。"

半天,无人应对。刹时,茶楼里悄悄的,听得见人心脏跳动的声音,尴尬时分,一少年终于接过话头:"论英雄,谈古今,喝它几杯。"

众人抚掌叫绝。兴头上,一只黑狗窜上茶楼。文弱书生们见了庞然大物,吓得退避三舍,几个胆小的还尖叫着跑出茶楼。

茶主人见状,怒火中烧,操起一根扁担砍下去。一声惨叫,黑狗倒在血泊之中。

一袋烟工夫,狗主人气势汹汹上门来,兴师问罪。茶主人刚开始鸭子死了,嘴还在那里硬着。狗主人拿起茶杯,用手轻轻一摆, 茶杯立即捏成碎片!好汉不吃眼前亏,茶主人只得低头认罪。

3
AT THE TEAHOUSE

Chen Yong

Upstairs in the teahouse, patrons were standing and sipping tea, enjoying one of the great moments in the beauty of the Rouge River. Straining their eyes expectantly, they saw the river ablaze in raging fire. Staring as far as their eyes could reach, they beheld the river curve and bend, and the lake ripple and sparkle. The surfaces of the water were as smooth as a mirror, as serene as a maiden, and perfectly clean. Touched by the sight, the proprietor of the teahouse raised his cup and chanted, "A heart-to-heart over tea, better than wine for hospitality."

Straightaway, one of the patrons responded with a couplet of his own: "Many cups of great wine may still divide; a simple mug of green tea can also delight." All cheered in unison. After a short pause, the man rose and, muttering a bit at first, gave the first half of another couplet: "A small place, for big occasions, where all share the same space."

For quite a while, no one was able to provide a fitting second half. The teahouse went quiet—so quiet that one could hear the beat of one's own heart. Eventually, amid the embarrassing silence, a young man took up the task: "Size up heroes, ancient or modern, when all enjoy a few cups."

Just as all were clapping, right at the height of their amazement, a black dog came charging in out of nowhere. Terrified by the huge monster, the frail versifiers retreated out of sight, and the most frightened patrons ran shrieking for the door.

Enraged by the scene, the proprietor picked up a bamboo pole and hacked at the dog. The dog uttered a heart-rending cry and then dropped dead in a pool of its own blood.

In the time it would take to smoke a pipe, the owner of the dog came for revenge, rushing in furiously with his men. At first, the proprietor tried to

赔钱了事。哪知,狗主人依然不依不饶。茶主人有几分不满,小声嘀咕道:还要怎么样?

狗主人跷起二郎腿,一定一顿地说:上门道歉!

办不到!茶主人不知吃了什么壮胆药,竟然吼了起来。那好,咱们骑驴看唱本——走着瞧,狗主人一挥手,手下喽罗扬长而去。

狗主人一伙走远了,茶客们才伸着脑袋走出来,安慰茶主人一番。一茶客苦中作乐,又吟起对联来:"山好好,水好好,开门一笑无烦恼。"

茶主人心情坏到极点,仍不忘附庸风雅,打肿脸充胖子,接下联:"来匆匆,去匆匆,饮茶几杯各西东。"

(2006)

bluff his way out of the situation by acting tough. The dog owner picked up a teacup and, with a slight twist of his fingers, crushed it to pieces instantly. Only a fool goes looking for trouble when the odds are against him. The proprietor had to submit and accept his responsibility.

The proprietor thought that he could settle the matter by offering some money, but to his surprise, the dog owner refused to let the dead dog lie. The proprietor was quite unhappy. In a low voice, he asked, plaintively, "What else do you want?"

Crossing his legs, the dog owner spit out his demand one word at a time: "An apology at my house!"

"Over my dead body!" the proprietor shouted, with a courage that he didn't know he had.

"We'll see about that!" replied the dog owner. With a wave of his hand, he swaggered out with his minions.

After the thugs were long gone, the patrons poked out their heads and reemerged. They tried to comfort the proprietor. One of them, in an effort to make the best of a bad situation, uttered the first half of a couplet: "Beautiful waters caress gorgeous mounts, a greeting with smiles dismisses all worries."

The proprietor, though terribly upset, did not forget the poise of a man of letters. To keep up appearances, he finished off the couplet: "Hurried departures follow hasty arrivals; a scattering after tea leaves nothing behind."

(2006)

VOCABULARY AND USAGE

茶客	chákè	customer at a teahouse	茶客们会觉得来茶楼品茗比去酒吧喝酒更典雅时尚一些。
品茗	pǐnmíng	sip and taste tea	
欣赏	xīnshǎng	appreciate; admire	这座茶楼也是欣赏美景的好地方。
胭脂	yānzhī	rouge	女人出门是要搽点胭脂涂点口红的。
良辰美景	liáng chén měi jǐng	a beautiful moment amid beautiful scenery	那天花好月圆的良辰美景至今仍历历在目。

望穿水色/ 望穿秋水	wàngchuān shuǐsè/ wàngchuān qiūshuǐ	gaze through and beyond the water/ gaze with eager expectation (of someone's return)	"望穿水色"来自成语"望穿秋水,"但比后者少了些等待的意味。
极目远眺	jímùyuǎntiào	gaze into the distance; as far as one can see	他登上山顶极目远眺,"江山如此多娇"的诗句蓦上心头。
漪漪	yīyī	ripples	"湖水漪漪"是说湖面上布满细小的波纹。
处女	chǔnǚ	virgin; maiden	过去处女是指未婚未嫁的女子。
纤尘不染	Xiānchén bùrǎn	untainted by even a speck of dust	邻居家总是窗明几亮,纤尘不染。
触情生情	chùjǐngshēngqíng	be moved by one's surroundings	故地重游使我触景生情,回想起很多儿时的往事。
何须	hé xū	what is the need; there is no need	她都跟你分手了,你何须再为她操心?
促膝谈心	cùxītánxīn	sit side by side and talk heart-to-heart	我常跟好友促膝谈心。
知己	zhījǐ	a confidant	我的丈夫也是我一生难得的知己。
盏	zhǎn	a measure word for a lamp, cup, or bowl	每天晚上先生都为我斟上一盏红酒。
须臾	xūyú	a moment; an instant	出门在外须臾不可离的应该是朋友呢还是防人之心呢?
沉吟	chényín	mutter to oneself; ponder	她拿起笔,低头沉吟良久,写下了这幅对联。
片刻	piànkè	a moment; a short time	请稍候片刻,我去去就来。
天地	tiāndì	universe; world	他一天到晚喝茶看书,活在自己的小天地里。
一席	yīxí	a space; a place	中国文坛上有他一席之地。
刹时	shàshí	in a flash; suddenly	听到儿子出车祸了的消息,她的脸刹时没了血色。

话头	huàtóu	thread of a conversation	我刚开始讲他就打断了我的话头。
抚掌叫绝	fǔzhǎngjiào jué	applaud	所有的观众都为刚才的表演抚掌叫绝。
兴头上	xìngtóushàng	at the height of one's enthusiasm	她现在不在花钱的兴头上，是不会买这辆车的。
窜	cuàn	scurry	草地里突然窜出来了一条蛇。
文弱书生	wénruòshū shēng	frail men of letters	他瘦瘦的身材带个眼镜，活生生一个文弱书生。
庞然大物	pángrándàwù	colossus	鲸鱼应该算是动物界里的庞然大物了。
退避三舍	tuìbìsānshě	retreat to avoid a conflict	国君不想跟邻国交战，已经命令他的军队退避三舍。
怒火中烧	nùhuǒzhōngshāo	furious; simmering with rage	他傲慢的举止令她怒火中烧。
气势汹汹	qìshìxiōngxiōng	aggressive; fierce	老板气势汹汹的样子吓坏了新来的员工。
兴师问罪	xīngshīwèn zuì	mobilize troops for a punitive expedition	茶楼老板是错了，但狗的主人就应该这样向他兴师问罪吗？
鸭子死了嘴还硬	yāzi sǐle zuǐ hái yìng	refuse to admit defeat/a mistake	你真是鸭子死了嘴还硬，明明做错了，还死不承认。
不依不饶	bùyībùráo	unwilling to forgive; relentless	这件事儿他一定会不依不饶追到底。
跷二郎腿	qiāo èrlángtuǐ	lift up (a leg) (sit) cross-legged	你不该跟父母说话的时候还跷着二郎腿。
骑驴看唱本——走着瞧	qí lǘ kàn hàngběn—zǒu zhe qiáo	reading a book while riding a donkey—wait and see (who is right)	谁对谁错，咱们骑驴看唱本——走着瞧！
喽啰	lóuluo	underling; minions	他不是主犯，不过是个帮着行凶的小喽啰。
苦中作乐	kǔzhōngzuòlè	find joy in hardship, suffering, adversity, etc.	做什么工作能一点儿不辛苦？你要自己学会苦中作乐才是。

附庸风雅	fùyōngfēngyǎ	mingle with men of letters and pose as a lover of culture; arty-crafty	有钱的人附庸风雅是为了赢得地位和尊敬。
打肿脸充胖子	dǎ zhǒng liǎn chōng pàngzi	seek to impress by feigning to be more than what one is	公司都快破产了，你怎么还打肿脸充胖子，花那么多钱请客！

QUESTIONS FOR DISCUSSION

1. What kind of establishment does the owner want the teahouse to be?
2. What other needs must he juggle to meet besides serving tea?
3. Does he have what it takes to make his business succeed?
4. Why was the proprietor so mad at the dog? Did he kill it by accident?
5. Why does he react so strongly to the demand that he must apologize at the house of the dog owner?
6. Pay attention to the characters used to describe the patrons and the dog owner's men. What do you think is the nature of the conflict in the story?
7. With whom do you sympathize in the story?

1. 老板想把茶楼做成一个（有）什么样（特色）的生意？
2. 也就是说，除了给顾客沏茶倒水之外，茶楼老板还要兼顾什么其他的需求？
3. 茶楼老板有能力做好这样的生意吗？
4. 那条狗为什么会使茶楼老板火冒三丈？他是失手把狗打死了吗？
5. 对狗主人上门道歉的要求，茶楼老板的反应为什么会那么强烈？
6. 请留意故事中描述茶客和狗主人随从的用词。你怎么给故事中的冲突定性？
7. 在故事的各类人物中你同情谁？

AUTHOR BIO

Chen Yong (1963—) is an enigmatic writer. Literature seems a commodity for him, because he wants to produce more and more and has even set one hundred volumes as a goal for himself. Yet he considers literature is far too sacred for it to be just a commodity. He has subsidized the publication of many of his more than twenty collections of short-shorts and essays.

A native of Jianli in Hubei, Chen Yong obtained a college degree in Chinese in 1985 while working at his county's fertilizer plant. He joined the Bureau of Justice of Jianli County in 1992. At heart, Chen Yong is obsessed with literature and writing. He is especially crazy about the short-short genre. He started writing in the genre in 1995, and in 2008 he was granted membership to the China Writers Association. This is a distinct honor for Chen Yong, as he was the first in his county to gain entrance into the association. Some of his better-known collections are *At the Water Side* (在水一方), *A Bouquet of Carnations for You* (送你一束康乃馨), *Red Maple Leaves* (枫叶红了), and *A River for Lovers* (情人河). In 2015 Chen Yong also became a member of the China Literary and Art Critics Association, in part because of his two collections of critical essays: *On One Hundred Chinese Short-Short Writers in the World* (世界华文微型小说百家论) and *On One Hundred Contemporary Short-Short Writers in China* (中国当代微型小说百家论). He has published five other works of literary criticism.

Chen Yong is phenomenal not only because he is one of a few who straddle the roles of writer and critic of short-shorts in contemporary China; Chen Yong's infatuation with literature in general and for the short-short genre in particular is infectious. He enjoys the role of activist as much as that of writer and critic, encouraging fellow writers to join the Hubei Writers Association and introducing their works to publishers. As part of the "Chen Yong phenomenon," he also participated in the orchestration of a study forum on his own work in 2009. Few people are expecting him to produce one hundred volumes; yet many are genuinely touched by his single-minded dedication.

4
鸡怕鸽破脸

刘心武

  如今京郊农村嫁闺女，出阁头天还是要在自家宴请宾客。六叔家聘闺女，他去随份子。那第二天就要被婆家迎娶的堂妹，比他小两轮。

  因为天冷了，六叔家没在院子里搭棚子，亲友们全挤在几间北房里，围着大桌子吃喝。

  他进房，先跟六叔六婶堂妹贺喜，一眼瞥见六奶奶，少不得趋前特别致意。那六奶奶是家族里最能争风拔尖的女人，有着许多的故事。六奶奶见他来了，高兴得合不拢嘴，抓过他的手，握住不放，罩着蛛网般皱纹的脸上，漾出真诚的笑容，高声让六叔六婶来给他夹鱼肉，又让堂妹给他剥喜糖递香蕉。听起来六奶奶的声音还跟敲空缸似的，洪亮不减当年。

  但是，这位六奶奶，多年前，那时他还是个半大孩子，跟他娘可没少磕碰。有一次，在村口，不知怎么起的头，六奶奶扬声晃臂，斥责他娘。娘不示弱，伶俐还嘴。两个人越吵越厉害，最后连脏话也冒出来了，围一群人在那儿。有真是劝架的，有阴阳怪气，明为劝解实际是火上浇油的。直到六叔跟他爹闻声赶来，两头说好话，才算将二人分别劝回家去。从那以后，他娘跟六奶奶虽说迎头遇上避不过时，也还能勉强含混招呼一下，但两人基本上断绝来往，互相的恶感，直到他娘患病去世，也未见消失。

4
CHICKENS HATE PECKED FACES

Liu Xinwu

Translated by Meng Jiangnan

Even today, people on the rural outskirts of Beijing still host celebrations at home the day before their daughters marry...

The daughter of his Sixth Uncle was getting married, so he went to the party with a gift. The cousin sister to be married the next day was twenty-four years his junior.

Due to the cold weather, his Sixth Uncle didn't erect tents in the yard—all the family and friends were packed into the few rooms on the north side of the house, feasting around big tables.

He stepped in and congratulated the bride-to-be and her parents first. When he spotted Sixth Grandma, he felt obliged to go over and give her a special greeting as well. That Sixth Grandma, known in the clan as a woman who always tried to come out on top, was a legend and the subject of many stories. She was ecstatic when she saw him. She grabbed his hands and refused to let them go, her face, a spiderweb of wrinkles, lit up with a genuine smile. In a loud voice, she told Sixth Uncle and Auntie to scoop him food from the fish and meat dishes and told the bride-to-be to unwrap some wedding candies and bring over some bananas for him. Sixth Grandma's voice still sounded like someone knocking on an empty earthenware vat; it was as loud and resounding as ever.

However, years ago, when he was still a growing boy, this Sixth Grandma had had many a quarrel with his mother. One day, for no particular reason anyone could remember, Sixth Grandma began scolding his mother at the village entrance, her voice raised and her arms waving excitedly. Mother had refused to back down and retorted sharply. The fight gradually got out of hand; soon, curses were spilling from their lips and a crowd of people surrounded them. Some were really trying to calm them down, but some were just there to meddle, muttering sarcastic comments and pouring oil on the fire under the pretense of mediating. It finally ended when Father

村口六奶奶对他娘不善，给他很强的刺激。娘被爹劝回家后，他听爹说："六奶奶是老辈儿，她再横也得让她几分才是。鸡怕鹐破脸，人怕扯断皮……"

他只记住了"鸡怕鹐破脸"。忽然想起，六奶奶最疼她家的鸡。她家的母鸡跟公鸡是按八配一放养的。两只公鸡一只雪花毛，一只红金尾，鸡冠窜得好高。小二十只母鸡一半纯白一半芦花毛。听说那群母鸡天天下蛋，临年关孵出的小鸡崽出壳都比别家的活泛。

第二天，他上学心不在焉，放了学就往六奶奶家奔，临近了，跟电影上的侦察兵似的，躲榆树后四面张望，没见人影，他就从兜里掏出准备好的大玉米粒，先往六奶奶家篱墙外的白公鸡身前扔去。白公鸡发现了好生高兴，立刻啄进一粒。听见动静，那只红金尾跑过来。他就故意把一个玉米粒抛到两只公鸡之间，两只公鸡就抢起来，几只母鸡也往这边凑。

他发现，抢到玉米粒的红金尾自己并不吞掉那玉米粒，而是衔到一只母鸡身旁，吐在地上，却又不马上让母鸡啄到，自己啄起吐出反复两三次，再让那母鸡啄进口。母鸡快乐地吞玉米粒，红金尾就趁机趴到母鸡身上扇翅膀。他等红金尾从母鸡身上下来，就故意再次往两只公鸡之间丢玉米粒。这次雪花毛抢得快，眼看要衔进喙里，那红金尾便耸起金身彩毛，跳起来跟雪花毛争夺，两只公鸡就那么恶斗起来，眼看着这只破了那只的鸡冠，那只破了这只的眼皮，还掉许多鸡毛，母鸡们吓得各自躲得远远的……

and Sixth Uncle, hearing what was going on, rushed over. Soothing both with apologies, they managed to get Mother and Sixth Grandma back to their separate homes. After that, the two women could still manage a forced greeting when it was impossible for them to avoid one another, but they basically cut all contacts with each other. The feeling of animosity between them did not disappear, not even when Mother grew sick and died.

Sixth Grandma's poor treatment of Mother that day had upset him immensely. After Father brought Mother home, he heard Father saying to her, "Sixth Grandma is an elder; no matter how difficult she is being, you have to humor her a little. As chickens hate pecked faces, people abhor torn skin..."

All he could remember of what his father had said were the words "chicken" and "pecked faces." It suddenly struck him that Sixth Grandma cherished her chickens more than anything. Her hens and her roosters were raised in an eight-to-one ratio. The two roosters, one with snowy white feathers, the other with a reddish-gold tail, had cockscombs that reached proudly to the sky. In total, the chickens numbered just short of twenty. Half were pure white and half had speckled feathers. He'd heard that the hens laid eggs every day. When the Spring Festival approached, even their chicks broke out of their shells livelier than those from other families.

The day after the argument, he was absentminded and hurried to Sixth Grandma's house as soon as school let out. When he got close, he hid behind an elm tree and surveyed the area like a scout in the movies. Seeing that no one was around, he got the big corn kernels he'd prepared out of his pockets and threw them first to the white rooster outside of Sixth Grandma's wattle wall. Thrilled at the sight of the kernels, the white rooster immediately gobbled one up. Hearing the commotion, the reddish gold-tailed rooster ran over. He purposely threw a kernel between the two, instigating a fight, as a few hens also edged their way toward the scene.

He noticed that the winner, the reddish gold-tailed rooster, didn't swallow his prize; instead, he walked over and spit it on the ground beside a hen. However, he did not let her snatch it up right away. The rooster did not let the hen have the prize until after he repeatedly spat it out and pecked at it a couple more times. Then, as the hen munched happily on the kernel, the reddish gold-tailed rooster took advantage of the opportunity to leap onto her back and flap his wings. He waited until the rooster landed back on the ground before tossing another kernel between the rivals again. This time the white rooster reached for the kernel more quickly. Just as he was about

忽听院子里有人声，想是六奶奶家的人觉得窗外的鸡叫声不对头，就要出屋观望，他忙一溜烟跑回家了。那晚吃饭，他问："鸡怕破脸，是说它们脸上出了血就活不成了吗？"爹娘先都望着他，又互望一眼，娘就说："咱们家哪只鸡破脸啦？刚才我拾蛋时还好好的。"爹就说："这小子心思不用在功课上，瞎积攒些个杂碎。"他就在心里反驳："这杂碎不正是您说的吗？"

再一天放学，他故意路过六奶奶家，发现六奶奶家篱内西边猪圈起出的粪堆上，有两堆还在冒热气的鸡毛，一堆是白的，一堆是彩色的。他就想，就怕破脸是真的啊？现在离过年还早得很呢，关于腊月的歌谣里有一句："二十七，杀公鸡。"村里各家都是临近那时候才会把公鸡先关在笼子里几天，叫"蹲鸡"，到二十七才割喉烫身褪毛，煮来当做年下一道佳肴。六奶奶家这么早就把公鸡杀了，既破财也不吉利啊！那天夜里，他想到自己为向着娘，报复六奶奶，竟把两只公鸡给害了，小小的心，阵阵发紧。

多年来，害死六奶奶家大公鸡的事，他一直没有对任何人讲起过，自己也终于淡忘。但是，在家族为送堂妹出嫁的聚会上，他意外地被六奶奶紧紧地握住手，六奶奶眼里的慈祥，是无论如何也假装不出来的。蓦地忆

to pick it up, the reddish gold–tailed rooster jumped to fight him for it, his colorful feathers all puffed out. A ferocious battle commenced. He looked on as the feathers went flying, one rooster broke the other's cockscomb and the other tore his opponent's eyelids. Scared hens fled far from the scene...

Suddenly, he heard a noise in Sixth Grandma's yard and figured that the family must have noticed that the clucks of the chickens were sounding peculiar. He dashed off for home, vanishing like vapor before they hustled out to check on the chickens. At dinner that night, he asked, "You said chickens hate broken faces, does that mean they will die when their faces bleed?" His parents looked at him, then at each other. Mother asked, "Which one of our chickens has a broken face? They were all fine when I went to get the eggs just now." Father simply said, "This child's mind is not on his schoolwork. He is wasting his time collecting useless nonsense." In his mind, the boy thought, "Weren't you the one who brought up this nonsense?"

After school the next day, he deliberately passed by Sixth Grandma's house. At the pigsty at the west end of her yard, just inside the wattle wall, he found two piles of steaming hot chicken feathers on top of the dung heap. One pile was white, the other multicolored. He thought, *What they say about broken faces is true!* The Spring Festival was still far away. In a folk song about the last month of the lunar year, there was a line that went like this: "On the twenty-seventh, slaughter the roosters." In the village, every family would cage their roosters for a few days when the date drew near. They called it "squatting the rooster." When the twenty-seventh arrived, they cut the roosters' throats, poured hot water on them, plucked their feathers, and cooked them into a delicious dish for the New Year's celebration. But Sixth Grandma's family had killed their roosters too early. It was bad luck and bad business too! That night, when he thought that he had taken Mother's side, getting revenge on Sixth Grandma and inadvertently murdering her two roosters, a thickness pressed in spasms upon his young heart.

Many years passed. He never told anyone of this incident that caused the death of Sixth Grandma's roosters, and he himself eventually began to forget about it, too. But he was caught by surprise by Sixth Grandma who held him tightly by the hands at this family reunion in honor of his bride-to-be cousin. No one could fake the genuine kindness in her eyes, no matter how hard they tried. All of sudden the second half of what Father said to Mother came into his mind: "People abhor torn skin." *Among ordinary folks like us,* he thought, *and all the more among kin and kinfolk, how could there*

起，爹说过的那话，后一句是"人怕扯断皮"。普通人之间，特别是有血缘关系的族人之间，哪来那么多深仇大恨？破脸不好，扯断皮不好。忘却前嫌，真诚和解，人生此刻，在被什么样的吉光照亮？

(2012)

be so much bitterness and deep-seated hostility? A pecked face hurts, as does torn skin. Forgetting the grudges of the past and reconciling sincerely will shine what indescribable, auspicious light on this moment of life!

(2012)

VOCABULARY AND USAGE

鹐	qiān	peck	小鸡把地上的谷子一个个鹐起来吃了。
嫁	jià	marry off a daughter; marry (a husband)	妈妈想把她嫁给一个有钱的商人，而她却想嫁新来的小学老师。
出阁	chūgé	(a woman) to get married	在古代，"阁"是未婚女子的住处，"出阁"就意味着出嫁。
聘	pìn	marry a daughter off	在河北的一些地方，女儿出阁也叫聘闺女，聘礼、聘金是少不了的。
随份子	suífènzi	chip in (for a group gift); present a red envelope with money in it as a wedding gift	朋友结婚，我们都去喝喜酒随份子了。
迎娶	yíngqǔ	(a man) marry; send a party to escort the bride to the groom's house	迎娶新娘子的队伍一早就出发了。
轮	lún	a round of twelve years	我大哥比我大一轮呢。
少不得	shǎobùdé	have to; cannot be avoided	这孩子太年轻，以后少不得常向您请教。
趋前	qūqián	step forward; hasten forward	我趋前跟他打招呼，他却扭头躲开了。
争风拔尖	zhēngfēng bájiān	strive to be top-notch	她个性很强不让人，事事都喜欢争风拔尖。
合不拢	hé bù lǒng	cannot close; cannot shut	他把孙子抱在怀里，笑得合不拢嘴。
罩	zhào	cover; being covered	奶奶满脸都是皱纹，笑起来的时候像是罩上了一张蜘蛛网。
(蜘)蛛网	(zhī)zhū wǎng	spiderweb; cobweb	
皱纹	zhòuwén	wrinkles	
漾出	yàng chū	brim over	看到妈妈，小宝贝的脸上漾出了幸福的微笑。

不减当年	bù jiǎn dāngnián	as in the old days	爷爷八十岁了，可他的精神头却丝毫不减当年。
磕碰	kēpèng	clash; have a disagreement	你不要总是和别人磕碰，尤其要尊重年长的乡亲。
起头	qǐtóu	start, begin (a topic, conversation etc.)	这场争吵是我起的头，应该由我来承担责任。
扬声	yángshēng	raise one's voice	能把声音放大的仪器叫扬声器。
晃	huàng	wave; shake	他晃了晃手说，"算了。"
斥责	chìzé	denounce	是你做了错事，凭什么斥责我？
示弱	shìruò	show the white feather; draw back	由于文化不同，有时候我们的礼让会被看成是示弱。
伶俐	línglì	quick-witted	她可是个十分伶俐的姑娘。
还嘴	huánzuǐ	retort	他心里不满，却很懂事地没有还嘴。
阴阳怪气	yīnyáng guàiqì	(of words or voice) dripping acid	你有话直说，别这么阴阳怪气的，让人不舒服。
刺激	cìji	irritate; upset	朋友自杀的事儿让他受了很大刺激。
横	hèng	unruly; peremptory	缺少家教的孩子有时会很横，不讲理也不懂得尊重别人。
让	ràng	make way; fall back; give ground; yield	你是哥哥，就该让着妹妹。
扯	chě	tear	这个信封太结实，我怎么扯都扯不开。
配	pèi	match	养动物应该一公配一母，这样他们才不孤独。
放养	fàngyǎng	breeding outside cages	我们这里民风好，放养在户外的羊从来没丢过。
(鸡)冠子	(jī) guānzi	crown; hat; comb	那只冠子高高的大公鸡最漂亮！
蹿	cuān	soar	这爆竹一点火儿就蹿上天。

临	lín	just before	每天临出门时妈妈都会嘱咐我开车小心。
年关	niánguān	the end of the year	年关就是年底，对欠账要还的人来说过年也是过关。
孵	fú	hatch	你见过母鸡孵小鸡吗？
心不在焉	xīnbú zàiyān	be preoccupied with something else	演出时他心不在焉，唱着唱着竟忘了歌词。
好生	hǎoshēng	quite; exceedingly	见到这位久仰的学者我好生激动。
啄	zhuó	pick; peck	人吃饭，鸡啄食。
抛	pāo	toss; cast	他临出界的刹那间把球抛给了队友。
凑	còu	move close to	事故现场很危险，你怎么还往前凑！
衔	xián	hold in the mouth	那只鸟妈妈把衔着的小虫子送到鸟宝宝的嘴里。
趴	pā	lie on one's stomach	我特别喜欢趴在沙滩上晒太阳。
耸	sǒng	rise straight up	七星岩很美，一座座青绿小山从镜子般的水面耸起。
不对头	búduìtóu	go wrong	有点儿不对头了，他去买瓶水怎么会这么老半天？
瞎	xiā	thoughtlessly	你又不了解情况，别瞎管。
积攒	jīzǎn	scrape up; accumulate	我积攒的这些俗语都是有大智慧的。
杂碎	zásuì	trivial matters	多关心点儿大事，别老盯着网上这些没用的杂碎。
反驳	fǎnbó	refute	他的话句句在理，让我无法反驳。
佳肴	jiāyáo	fine food	他喜欢用美味佳肴招待亲朋好友和客人。
破财	pòcái	suffer financial loss	他相信本命年容易破财，所以花钱格外小心。

向着	xiàngzhe	favor; side with	因为你最小，所以爸妈老是向着你，处处护着你。
发紧	fājǐn	(a) tightening (sensation)	附近幼儿园枪击惨案的消息让我心里阵阵发紧。
血缘	xuěyuán	ties of blood	这对兄妹没有血缘关系，却比亲兄妹更亲。
淡忘	dànwàng	fade from memory	年轻时的往事早已淡忘了，你就不要再提了。
蓦(地)	mò (di)	suddenly; unexpectedly	我蓦地回过神来，立刻跑着去追她。
忘却前嫌	wàngquè qiánxián	forget/bury the hatchet	让我们忘却前嫌，从头开始吧。

QUESTIONS FOR DISCUSSION

1. How would you describe the protagonist's experience at the party?
2. How does the flashback to his childhood, especially what happens to the chicken, fit in the story?
3. How did the child react to the death of the roosters? Why?
4. What does the story say about taking sides and seeking revenge?
5. Do we have the right to inflict pain on others for a "worthy" cause? Why?
6. Had the mother lived longer, do you think she and Sixth Grandma would have reconciled?
7. What does the moment in the "auspicious light" say about the nature of giving, presenting, or granting face?

1. 你怎么看主人翁在这个家宴上的经历？
2. 童年倒叙那部分，尤其是那段关于鸡的描写，跟故事怎样契合？
3. 看到两只大公鸡死了，孩子有什么反应？他为什么会有那样的反应？
4. 这个故事对偏袒和报复的行为说了些什么？
5. 我们可以为"正当"的理由加害他人吗？为什么？
6. 如果母亲不是那么早过世，你觉得她会跟六奶奶和好如初吗？
7. 故事中那个"吉光照亮"的时刻揭示了"给面子"的什么真谛？

AUTHOR BIO

Liu Xinwu (1942–) is a well-known name in China. Born in Chendu, Sichuan, he settled down in Beijing in 1950. He discovered he loved literature when he was a middle school student and started to publish literary works in 1958. After he graduated from college in 1961, he taught middle school for fifteen years. He became an editor for Beijing Publishing House in 1976 and the editor-in-chief for *People's Literature* (人民文学) in 1979. His short story "Head Teacher" (" 班主任"), published in 1977, marked the beginning of the "scar literature"[8] (伤痕文学) phenomenon. Liu Xinwu is a prolific writer; his full-length novel *Bell and Drum Tower* (钟鼓楼) was a winner of Mao Dun Literature Awards (茅盾文学奖) in 1992. In recent years, Liu Xinwu has become known as an accomplished redologist, that is, a scholar of the *Dream of the Red Chamber* (红楼梦).[9]

Liu Xinwu was invited to the United States twice, in 1987 and 2006. During his first trip, he spoke on the development of contemporary Chinese literature at Columbia University in New York and at twelve other colleges and universities. The focus of his talks on his second trip was his research on the *Dream of the Red Chamber*. Unique among Chinese writers of fiction, in 2007 he was invited by CCTV's famous *Lecture Room* (百家讲坛) program to share his research on *Dream of the Red Chamber*. His series of lectures generated great interest and quite a bit of controversy. Liu Xinwu's works have been translated into more than ten languages. Internationally known contemporary writers like Liu Xiuwu have been an inspiration to amateur short-short writers. In China, they help set the bar high and draw more critical attention to the genre.

---

8. "Scar literature" came into being in late 1970s after the Cultural Revolution ended. The often difficult and traumatic experience of the time, especially the sufferings that individuals had gone through, as well as the enduring love and humanity in the face of adversity, were usually the subject matter of scar literature.

9. *Dream of the Red Chamber*, one of China's Four Great Classical Novels (四大名著), is commonly accepted as the pinnacle of Chinese fiction. Redology, or the study of the novel, became a distinct discipline of study in the twentieth century. Liu Xinwu's sharing of his research on CCTV's *Lecture Room* (百家讲坛) program in 2007 rejuvenated the interests in the novel by bringing redology to the grassroots, making it accessible to the public and the people.

第七章

情爱／爱情

爱 不需要文字引介。真是这样吗？本章中有两个故事，《小忧伤》和《伪造的情书》，它们似乎轻而易举地就能跨越语言和文化的疆界；但另外两个故事，《古典爱情》和《如果你爱他，就让他心静》就非如此了。爱要在情境中理解；可又有谁能亲身经历人间所有的爱之情境呢？

《小忧伤》用七百二十一个汉字捕捉到了四个或许可以称之为情窦初开的瞬间，其中的两、三个都很像是爱情失败的尝试。故事用情境分段的形式使阅读轻松易懂，它的视角还让读者有机会去体味小男孩稚嫩的情感，他的困惑、孤独和沮丧等。然而，这个看起来单薄的故事会不会有更深的含义呢？故事为什么要突出爱的愚钝？又为什么把失败，尤其是最初的懵懂之爱的失败，写得那么可爱？小男孩的沮丧是否源于俗世的污浊？故事中，小男孩能捕捉到的和捕捉不到的，他能理解的和不理解的等，有着积极的互动。这样的互动反映了认知和知识的什么样的本质？人怎样才算有智慧？当我们思考这些问题的时候，当我们扪心自问为什么孩子的纯真如此诱人的时候，我们可能会窥见到那个在很多道家信徒看来是爱之源的东西。

《伪造的情书》是篇好作品，但它入选本集有一个非常实际的原因：作者邹静之文革期间是个"知青"，在乡下待了八年。他那一代人怎样看那一段经历？这篇小小说提供了一个感知的窗口。自我反思是这个故事的基调，而不是常见的那种对"上山下乡"运动的否定态度。说来也巧，他们那

CHAPTER 7

(ROMANTIC) LOVE

Love needs no introduction. Or does it? Two stories in this chapter, "Little Heartaches" and "Fake Love Letter," seem to cross cultural and linguistic boundaries quite easily; the other two, "A Gentleman's Love" and "Give Him Peace," do not. Love must be understood in context, yet it is impossible for anyone to share in the entire range of experiences of human love.

"Little Heartaches" captures, in 721 Chinese characters, four potentially romantic encounters, a couple of which perhaps resemble failed attempts at love. Not only does the episodic form make reading easy, the perspective allows readers to empathize with the boy's tender emotions, bewilderment, loneliness, and frustration. But is there more to this deceptively sparse story? Why does the story highlight love's folly? Why does it make failures, especially the early ones, endearing? Is there a connection between the boy's frustration and the contaminated world? What does the dynamic between what he captures (or fails to capture) and what he understands (or fails to understand) say about the nature of knowing and knowledge? What makes a person wise? When we think about these questions, when we look inside to understand why a child's innocence is so appealing, we may find what many Taoists believe to be the origin of love.

"Fake Love Letter," for all its literary merits, was chosen for a practical reason. The author, Zou Jingzhi, was a "sent-down youth" for eight years during the Cultural Revolution. This short-short story by him provides a window onto the way his generation felt about that time and experience. Self-reflection, rather than the familiar negative attitudes about the Down to the Countryside movement, predominates in the story. As it happens, the youth of this generation have been behind China's miraculous rise in

代人的身影一直活跃在中国过去三十多年神奇崛起过程中的。如今，很多中国党、政要职也是由这一代下过乡的知青在担任。

过去我们阅读《古典爱情》的时候，曾有美国学生谴责主人公鼓励学生跟他谈情说爱，觉得他是个没有职业道德的老师。而很多来自中国的留学生则认为这是一个关于陈规陋习，即迫使有过任何身体接触的男女结婚的故事。请努力跳出这样的阅读套路。对以下问题的思考可能对理解故事会有帮助：故事的历史背景是怎样的？为什么故事会把拯救生命写得比拯救面子容易？在中华文化传统里，怎样做人才能赢得为人师长的资格？老式君子们那永无休止的担心——自己待人处事是否做到了仁至义尽，怎样才能不辱儒家君子的体面风范等，希望这些观念会在反复的阅读中逐渐成为读者关注的重点。

最后一个故事，如果你期待的是一出道德剧，或是你想用恋母情结的框架去套它，或是你坚信夫妻感情必须绝对忠诚，那《如果你爱他，就让他心静》会让你失望。已经有不少读者认为男主人公所谓的脆弱几近荒唐，认为他拿职业生涯开玩笑的举止不可思议。但这或许还真的就是一个关于真爱的故事。请看如意。她在努力忠实于自己感情的同时，不辜负、不伤害任何一个自己所爱的人。她的爱或许不从一；但这种不排他的爱以其独特的方式给了她力量，并把她从一切戒律中解放出来，不管这戒律是来自神还是来自人。

爱情是个永恒的话题。本篇在爱情的大框架之下，不厌其烦地问着两个问题：第一，对他人的生活、命运等，我们有什么发言权？这里的"他人"泛指所有人，也特指生活在不同的时间、空间，有着自己历史使命、信仰、价值体系和生活方式的人。第二，我们能够用爱心为增进跨文化理解和交流积极地做些什么？

the past thirty some years. Those sent-down youths now hold many key positions in the Communist Party of China and within state authority.

In the past, the protagonist of "A Gentleman's Love" has been accused of being an unethical high school teacher encouraging a student's romantic advances. Many international students from China have read it as a story about the dated tradition that obliges marriage between a man and a woman who have engaged in any kind of physical contact. Please try to go further than these readings. Asking these questions may help: What is the historical context of the story? Why does the story make it easier to save someone's life than to save his or her face? What qualifies someone to be a teacher in Chinese cultural tradition? A gentleman's old-fashioned yet constant worry of not being able to do right by others, of failing to live up to the Confucian standards of human decency, may become a prominent concern as you read and reread the story.

Reading "Give Him Peace," you will be disappointed if you are expecting a morality tale, or if you attempt to locate the story within the framework of the Oedipus complex, or if fidelity is, for you, an absolute value in marriage. Quite a few readers have found the male protagonist almost ridiculous in his vulnerability and his courting of professional disaster. But perhaps this story is about true love nonetheless. Take Ruyi for example. She tries to stay true to her emotions and to remain loyal to all her loved ones at the same time. Her love may not be exclusive; yet that love does empower her in unique ways and sets her free, beyond the precepts set by men or God.

Love is a universal topic. Within its broad perimeter, the stories in this chapter constantly ask two questions: What qualifies us to say things about other people in general and about people of different time, space, and agency who have their own belief systems, values, and ways of life in particular? What can we do, with and through love, to proactively facilitate cross-cultural understanding?

1
小忧伤

赵瑜

一

我先喜欢上班里的一个女孩的，我暂时管她叫苏小小。

我给她画了一只可爱的小猪。尽管我画得不太像，但我把我的彩色蜡笔都用上了。

她看着我画的小猪哈哈笑，我以为她喜欢呢，就高兴地在一旁给她比划我昨天晚上看的电视剧，我说，陈真是这样和别人打的，这样这样子。

但她并没有继续笑，她把我的画随手扔到地上去了。

等到放学，我才知道，班里的另一个男生书包里藏着一大包饼干，苏小小一放学就和他一起回家了。

我拾起我画的那张小猪，很难过。

我并不气馁。

我把妈妈给我买铅笔的钱省了下来，买了一袋饼干。

我把那袋饼干，偷偷地放在苏小小的课桌里。

那天，苏小小没有来上课。

她转学走了。

我放学的时候，一个人吃完了那袋饼干。

二

被我们气哭的女孩子叫今英，个子很高，长得也漂亮。

我们跟在她身后喊她的名字。她不让我们喊，我们就喊她妹妹的名字。

1
LITTLE HEARTACHES

Zhao Yu

1

I was the first to fall for the girl in my class. I'll call her Su Xiaoxiao for my purposes here.

I drew a cute little pig for her. It didn't exactly look like a pig, but it used up every colored crayon I had.

She looked at the pig I drew and laughed. I thought she liked it. Excited, I began acting out scenes from the TV show I'd seen the night before, gesticulating wildly: "Chen Zhen punched like this, and this, and this . . ."

But her laughter didn't last. Carelessly, she threw my painting on the floor.

(I didn't realize until school ended that another boy in my class had brought a large bag of crackers in his backpack. Su Xiaoxiao went home with him as soon as school was out.)

Heartbroken, I picked up my painting.

But I remained undeterred.

Saving the money Mom had given me for pencils, I bought a bag of crackers with it instead.

Secretly, I placed the crackers in Su Xiaoxiao's desk.

But Su Xiaoxiao did not show up that day.

She had transferred to another school.

After school, I finished the bag of crackers, alone.

2

The girl we made cry was Jin Ying. She was tall and pretty.

We followed her one day, yelling out her name. When she told us to stop, we yelled out her little sister's name instead.

她还不让我们喊,我们想了想,只好喊和她坐在一起的男生的名字。
我们并没有发觉她和那个男生有什么亲密的举止,只是无聊地喊两句。
谁知道,今英却一下子坐在地上哭了,哭得相当伤心。
我和赵四儿吓得跑远了。

三

我喜欢上班里的一个女孩子,就和她一起玩丢沙包。
她把沙包丢给我,我往兜里一装就跑了。
第二天仍是这样,只要她丢沙包给我,我就往兜里一装就跑。
结果,她并不追着我要,却不再和我玩了。
有一天,我看着她和其他男孩子在一起玩得很开心,突然觉得伤心,把兜里装的沙包都扔到了墙角。

四

坐在我前排的女孩叫苹果,她的头发很长。
我喜欢一边听课一边看她的头发。
有一次,我看到她的头发上绑了一根红绳子和我家的酒瓶上的一样,就把我家酒瓶上的红绳子偷偷拿出来,悄悄地送给了她,她一下子脸红了。
第二天,她就换成了一个浅蓝色的束发绳子。我在我家的酒瓶子上到处找,也没有找到这种颜色的绳子。
我问她,她不理我,气呼呼地走开了。
我很纳闷儿。

(2010)

She didn't want us to do that, either. We thought about it, and began yelling the name of the boy with whom she shared a desk.

We really hadn't seen anything intimate between them; we were just bored.

Suddenly, she collapsed to the floor and began to cry as if her heart had been broken.

Frightened, Zhao Si'er and I ran off.

3

I became fond of a girl in my class, so I started playing beanbags with her.

When she tossed me the beanbag, I put it in my pocket and ran away.

The next day I did the same thing. The moment I got the beanbag from her, I pocketed it and ran away.

This time, she did not chase after me as I'd hoped. She just stopped playing with me altogether.

One day, as I watched her having lots of fun playing with other boys, I suddenly felt very sad. Taking all the beanbags out of my pocket, I threw them into the corner.

4

The girl seated in the row in front of me was named Apple. Her hair was very long.

I liked looking at her hair while listening to the teacher during class.

One day, I noticed that her red hair ribbon looked the same as the kind on a bottle of wine at home. I took the red ribbon off the bottle and sneaked it out of my house. I gave it to her in private, and her face instantly turned red.

The next day, she wore a light blue ribbon. I searched all the wine bottles in my house, but couldn't find a ribbon of the same color.

I went to ask her why she had changed colors, but she ignored me and angrily walked away.

I was bewildered.

(2010)

VOCABULARY AND USAGE

忧伤	yōushāng	sorrow; grief	他的忧伤无法用语言表达。
暂时	zànshí	temporarily	这消息暂时还不能告诉他。
管...叫...	guǎn... jiào...	call someone ...	我管这只狗叫旺财。
蜡笔	làbǐ	crayon	小孩子都喜欢用蜡笔给画上色。
比划	bǐhua	gesticulate; gesture	他一边说一边比划给我看。
随手	suíshǒu	readily; conveniently	我们应该养成出门前随手关灯的好习惯。
气馁	qìněi	lose heart	你别有点儿挫折就气馁，失败是成功之母。
省	shěng	save; economize	为了省钱，我们三人合租了一个单元。
相当	xiāngdāng	quite; fairly	她中文歌唱得相当好。
丢	diū	throw; toss	回到家我把书包一丢就出去跟小朋友玩"丢手绢"的游戏了。
兜	dōu	pocket; bag	我的裤子根本没有兜，怎么能把你的东西装进我的裤兜里呢？
装	zhuāng	load; pack	
束	shù	bundle; bind; tie	今天她过生日，妈妈给她束上了她最喜欢的发带。
到处	dàochù	everywhere	春节前商场里到处都是办年货的人。
纳闷(儿)	nàmèn(r)	feel puzzled; wonder	我很纳闷他去哪儿了。

QUESTIONS FOR DISCUSSION

1. How are the four anecdotes related? Are they all expressions of the little boy's psychology and puppy love?
2. Can you infer the author's attitude toward these events and the feeling invested in writing the story?
3. Is it meaningful for you to use language like this to "capture" such glimpses of life? Why?
4. Do any of these episodes remind you of your own childhood?

5. Does the boy do anything wrong in these incidents? Do these girls, especially the one in the fourth story, have a reason to be angry with the boy?
6. Do you see in the boy's perspective any reflection of the adult world of relationships?
7. Did you get a feel for contemporary China from these four pieces? Do you perceive anything unique about Chinese culture?

1. 这四小段轶事有什么联系？它们都是在写小男孩情窦初开的心理表现吗？
2. 你能推断出作者对这些轶事的看法吗？他在故事中注入了什么样的情感？
3. 对你来说，如此这般地用文字捕获这样的生活瞬间有意义吗？为什么？
4. 有没有哪一段故事让你回想起自己的童年？
5. 在这四段故事中，小男孩做错过什么吗？这些小女孩，尤其是第四段中的那个，她们有理由跟小男孩生气吗？
6. 你有没有从小男孩的视角看到什么大人关系世界的折射？
7. 你有没有从这四个小片段中感受到当代中国？你有没有从中发现中国文化的什么独特？

AUTHOR BIO

Zhao Yu (1976–), a native son of Lankao County, Henan Province, has earned two degrees in Chinese, one from Kaifeng Normal College and the other from Henan University. To further prepare for a career in Chinese literature, he participated in a class for authors at the Lu Xun Institute for Literature after his college education. He worked for the evening news of Zhongmu County and the youth magazine run by the Henan Provincial Communist Youth League and as an editorial director of a journal and a lecturer for a school of journalism before he took up the job as an editor for *Frontier* (天涯), a literary journal of national reputation. He is now a professional writer at the Henan Institute for Literature, a social organization that is part of the official state institution. He has published *Sixty-Seven Words* (六十七个词), *Female Tour Guide* (女导游), and four other full-length novels. Prominent among his six published collections of essays is *Little Heartaches* (小忧伤), from which our story comes.

Published in 2007, *Little Heartaches* is composed of twenty-three prose pieces encompassing 285 episodes. Zhao Yu prefaced it with the essay "I'm Boiling the Moon, What Do You Want to Add?" Inspired by *The Pillow Book* (枕草子) by the Japanese writer Sei Shōnagon (清少纳言), Zhao Yu fondly recalls his childhood in the 1980s before anime and home video games arrived. The perspective of a ten-year-old boy helps register a poor yet complete and rich rural life that he misses. Zhao Yu has a profound concern for children of today, for whom that slow-paced and pollution-free rural China, the seat of culture and tradition that nurtures the self-nature of all children, is no longer available. He credits his rural upbringing for his gift for detail and his ability to find profound meaning in daily life. His singularly innocent characters and his tribute to a disappearing way of life have won high praise from his fellow writers.

2
伪造的情书

邹静之

平生伪造的文字，有一封情书。

北大荒，一年的日子有半年与白雪相对。雪之单纯单调、之无奈，让人觉出无聊。打发日子最好的办法是打赌，其次是恶作剧。

壶盖是我一校友的外号，缘自何典已记不起来。壶盖比我们年长一两岁，以脏、懒、馋而遭人厌。壶盖身上养了不少虫，以虱子为多（地面部队），臭虫次之（坦克部队），跳蚤又次（空降兵）。壶盖因虫累赘，而面色苍白。终日坐在那儿，将手探入衣服内，清点、整编他的"三军"。时有自语似的演说嗫嚅而出。壶盖大多数精力都用来对付那些虫子，生活消沉、落寞。

想伪造一封情书给他，是我另一位校友"烧鸡"的主意。主意出了，由我来写。

当年并没有见过《情书大全》、《席慕蓉诗集》之类的书，只有凭空造句。为生动起见借用了一些当地的俗语和语气词。还记得其中的一些文字："XXX：你这小伙儿真不错！俗话说，浇花要浇根，浇（交）人要交心……你如想与我相识、相知、相爱的话，咱们某日中午在供销社门口相会……"署名用了当时很流行的"知名不具"，全文广用感叹号。

烧鸡读完后很觉不错，为表示对我文字的钦敬，买了一瓶劣质草籽酒奖赏我（追溯起来，那该算我挣的第一笔稿酬）。

2
FAKE LOVE LETTER

Zou Jingzhi

Among my fictional writings is a love letter. In the Great Northern Wilderness, we faced snow six months of the year. The indifference, monotony, and inevitability of snow generated a sense of boredom. The best way to kill time was to gamble and the second-best way was to play pranks on one another.

"Lid" was a schoolmate. The origin of his nickname is now beyond recall. A year or two older, Lid was despised by the rest of us for being filthy, lazy, and gluttonous. He fed quite a few insects with his own body, mostly lice (the marines), scabies (tanks), and, finally fleas (airmen). Because all of these bugs sucked his blood, Lid looked very pale. He'd sit there all day, his hands stuffed into his clothes, assessing and reorganizing his "army." Often, he would stammer out speeches to himself. Lid led a dejected and desolate life, spending most of his energy dealing with his insects.

Crafting a love letter to Lid was "Roast Chicken's" idea. He was another schoolmate of mine. Once he thought it up, I was responsible for writing it.

At the time, I hadn't seen books like *The Encyclopedia of Love Letters* or *The Collection of Xi Murong's Poetry*; I had to fabricate everything out of thin air, throwing in some local slang and idiomatic phrases for color. I can still remember parts of the letter verbatim: "Dear XXX, You are such a nice guy! As the proverb says, *when watering plants you must water the roots*, so when starting a relationship you must do it from the heart . . . If you want to meet me so we can get to know each other and fall in love, please come to the department store gate at noon on . . ." The letter, peppered with lots of exclamation marks, was signed, in the fashion of the day, "You-Know-Who."

Roast Chicken read it and thought it was good. To show his appreciation, he bought a cheap bottle of grass-seed liquor as my reward. (Looking back, I think that ought to count as the first royalty I ever earned!)

情书放在了壶盖脏而乱的铺上。大家边打扑克边留意他的种种举动。他被我们所见的大致过程如下：进屋，爬到上铺，发现情书，惊讶，坐读一遍，躺读一遍。呆想呆看再一遍，收起情书，此时有光彩从脸上溢出。

接下来的几天，壶盖大烧热水，洗煮自己的被褥和衣裤。因不同颜色相互濡染，宿舍中晾满了色彩可疑的裤褂。此间他去外连筹　借到了一件呢子外衣，一双懒汉鞋和一副皮手套。大家知道他在为那个虚假的相约而狂热地准备着。转眼全连三百多名知青都知道了，独瞒着他一人。这真有点残酷，我曾试着点了他两次，没用。他很兴奋，这戏必须演完了才能收场。

那是个壮烈的场面，壶盖在漫天大雪中，穿着单薄的不太合身的衣服站到了供销社门口，全连的男女知青，都在自己宿舍的窗户后看着他。雪落在他头上，雪落在他的睫毛上，雪落在他身上的雪上。壶盖平静而坚定地站着。

专心地等着那个时刻到来，甚至从头上掸去雪花的空暇都没有。他被单纯的雪染白着……

羞辱开始从我们的心里生出来，壶盖的坚定坦白，让人惭愧。烧鸡打开后窗喊他。大家都喊他。直至两个人跳出去，把那个不情愿的他架了回来。

以后的几天，他一言不发地穿着那套衣服沉默地出入。大家有点担心。有天晚上，我拿出那瓶草籽酒来，要求与他共享。他喝到中间时说并没有因为这事而恨我们。至今他也不相信那封信是假的，他知道有一个女孩会为他写这样炽烈的信。而那天是我们过早的出现，吓得她没出来，她总有一天会再与他相约。

……没什么可劝慰的了，他活得很坚定，同时心里有了期待。我们非常无聊。酒喝完了，他全无醉意，我不行了。

(2007)

We placed the letter on Lid's dirty bed. While playing poker, we watched his every move. Here is what we saw: Lid entered the room, climbed to the upper berth of the bunk bed, and found the letter. Looking surprised, he sat down and read it, then lay down and read it once more. Dazed, he stared at the letter and read it a third time. Then he put away the letter, a radiant glow washing over his face.

In the days that followed, Lid heated large quantities of water to wash and boil his bedding and clothes. Different colors bled into one another; laundry of dubious shades hung all over our dorm. He also made a trip to another company and managed to get hold of a woolen overcoat, a pair of loafers, and a pair of leather gloves. We all knew he was preparing frantically for that fake date. In the blink of an eye, all the three hundred-plus educated youth of the company knew the truth and they kept it from Lid. This was a bit too heartless. A couple of times, I tried to throw hints his way, but without success. He was elated; the drama had to play out in full before it could end.

It was a heroic scene. Snow was falling thick and fast when Lid went in a thin outfit that barely fit him to stand by the gate to the department store. All the educated youth of the company were watching him from the windows of their dorm. Snow was falling on his head, his eyelashes, and the rest of him as Lid calmly and resolutely stood there.

He was waiting so single-mindedly that he didn't bother to brush the snow off his head. The innocent snow was turning him white...

A sense of shame rose in our hearts; Lid's firmness and candor made us feel terrible. Roast Chicken opened the back window to call him in and everybody joined in the effort. Eventually, two of us had to jump out and bring the reluctant Lid back inside.

In the days that followed, Lid didn't speak a word, just walked in and out of the dorm clad in the same outfit. We were all worried. One evening, I took out my bottle of grass-seed liquor and asked him to have some with me. Halfway through the bottle, he told me that he didn't hate us for what had happened because he didn't think the letter was a fake. He really believed that there was a girl who would actually write him a letter of such burning passion. She had just been scared away because we showed up too early that day, but she would arrange to meet him again.

I couldn't console him or make amends. He lived with a firm sense of purpose, and now his heart was set in expectation. We were the pathetic ones. When the liquor was gone, I passed out, but he stayed completely sober.

(2007)

VOCABULARY AND USAGE

平生	píngshēng	in one's life	他平生从没离开过美国。
北大荒	běidàhuāng	the Great Northern Wilderness	北大荒位于中国东北部，那里气候寒冷，土地肥沃。
无聊	wúliáo	bored; boring	这部电视剧的情节很无聊。
打发	dǎfa	pass (time)	暑假期间，我常常出去逛街买衣服打发时间。
打赌	dǎdǔ	bet; make a bet	你敢就今年的总统选举跟我打个赌吗？
恶作剧	èzuòjù	mischief; practical joke; monkey business	四月的愚人节是恶作剧的好机会。
缘自	yuánzì	originate from; stem from	这个成语缘自司马迁的《史记》。
典	diǎn	classical texts	《史记》和《汉书》都是中文典籍。
(年)长	(nián) zhǎng	be senior to; older	姐姐长我八岁；哥哥长我四岁。
懒	lǎn	lazy	谁说天下人都好吃懒做？
馋	chán	be fond of (food); covetous	眼不馋，心不贪。
虱子	shīzi	lice	中国有句歇后语：秃子头上的虱子——明摆着的。
次之	cì zhī	followed by; second to	文中"臭虫次之"是说臭虫的数量只比虱子少。
跳蚤	tiàozǎo	flee	跳蚤会咬人的，会让你睡不着觉！
累赘	léizhuì	encumbrance; burdensome	出去野营带着高跟鞋只会是累赘。
终日	zhōngrì	all day long	加州是个好地方，终日阳光灿烂。
探入	tàn rù	stretch into	我把手探入水中，试试温度。
清点	qīngdiǎn	check and count	老师每天早上都会清点学生出勤人数。
整编	zhěngbiān	regroup	军队需要经常整编才能保持战斗力。
消沉	xiāochén	dejected; low-spirited; depressed	离婚以后，他一直很消沉，终日闷闷不乐。

落寞	luòmò	lonely	谢谢你在我落寞时给予的关照！
为…起见	wèi…qǐjiàn	for the purpose of; in order to	为公平起见，每个人的回答都必须在三十秒以内。
交心	jiāoxīn	open hearts to each other	他们俩是能交心的好朋友。
署名	shǔmíng	sign; signature	这封信的署名是知名不具。
知名不具	zhīmíng bújù	anonymously	
广	guǎng	extensively	这款手机在中国和印度都广受欢迎。
钦敬	qīn jìng	admire and respect	我对父辈充满了钦敬。
劣质	lièzhì	of poor quality; inferior	这条劣质的裤子只穿了两次就开线了。
奖赏	jiǎngshǎng	reward; prize	奖学金应该是对学习的奖赏吧。
追溯	zhuīsù	trace back	中国的历史可以追溯到几千年以前。
稿酬	gǎochóu	money paid for a piece of writing	我用这本书的稿酬带妈妈去欧洲转了转。
濡染	rúrǎn	dip (in ink); imbue; immerse; influence	他从小就上国际学校，受到了东西方文化的交叉濡染。
筹借	chóujiè	raise and borrow	你为什么不向朋友和家人筹借创业资金呢？
懒汉鞋	lǎnhànxié	Chinese cloth shoes with elastic gussets	那时懒汉鞋流行是因为它穿起来方便，又很舒服。
独	dú	only	开会时间到了，独她还缺席。
瞒	mán	conceal from	他瞒着妈妈玩游戏。
点	diǎn	offer hints; give tips	这题对他来说太难了，你点他也没用。
残酷	cánkù	cruel	你不能没收我的手机，这对我太残酷了！
收场	shōuchǎng	end	自己闹的笑话只能自己出来收场。
掸	dǎn	brush lightly; whisk	她轻轻地掸去了身上的灰尘。
空暇	kòngxiá	free time; leisure	我忙得没有空暇陪家人出去吃饭。
睫毛	jiémáo	eyelashes	他站在那里一动不动，连睫毛都不眨。

染	rǎn	dye	你的红围巾掉色，染花了我的白衬衫。
羞辱	xiūrǔ	shame; dishonor	最让他难过的是自己的错误使父母蒙受羞辱。
共享	gòngxiǎng	share; shared	地球是大家共享的家园。
炽烈	chìliè	burning fiercely	他炽烈的爱融化了我的心。
劝慰	quànwèi	console	这时候他是听不进别人的劝慰的。

QUESTIONS FOR DISCUSSION

1. What does the first line of the story tell you about the narrator? Why is this important?
2. "Weisheng Holding the Column" (尾生抱柱 wěishēngbàozhù) is an idiom from *Zhuangzi*:[1] "Floods came while Weisheng waited beneath a bridge for his beloved. He stands his ground even though the flood takes his life." Is this story simply a re-envisioning of the Weisheng idiom?
3. Please draw a character sketch of Lid. How is Lid different from and similar to the narrator?
4. Do you think Lid's action was heroic? Why did the narrator and his friends start to feel ashamed?
5. How does your own culture of origin treat this sense of shame?
6. Confucian culture places much emphasis on this sense of shame. "Propriety, righteousness, honesty, and the sense of shame (礼义廉耻 lǐ yì lián chǐ)" are the four virtues of behavior. Does this story help you understand why this is the case?
7. What does "sober" mean in this context?

---

1. The most succinct introduction of Zhuangzi and *Zhuangzi* goes like this: "Zhuangzi (Chuang-tzu 庄子 "Master Zhuang" late fourth century BC) is the pivotal figure in Classical Philosophical Daoism. The *Zhuangzi* is a compilation of his and others' writings at the pinnacle of the philosophically subtle Classical period in China (fifth to third century BC)." For a more comprehensive understanding of Zhuangzi and *Zhuangzi*, please visit https://plato.stanford.edu/entries/zhuangzi/, accessed on February 18, 2017, and read the entry "Zhuangzi."

1. 本篇的开场白让你对叙述人有了什么样的了解？为什么这样的开场很重要？
2. "尾生抱柱"是"庄子"里的一个典故。尾生在桥下等待自己的恋人时，洪水来了。尾生没有离开，结果，洪水夺走了他的性命。"伪造的情书"仅仅是这一典故的当代翻版吗？
3. 请描述一下壶盖这个人物。请说说壶盖与叙述人的不同和相同。
4. 你觉得壶盖的行为有什么壮烈之处吗？为什么叙述人，以及跟他一起恶作剧的朋友们，会对自己的所作所为感到羞耻？
5. 你的母语文化怎样对待这样的羞耻感？
6. 儒家文化很重视这样的自我羞耻感。礼义廉耻是儒家文化的四个行为美德。这篇故事帮助你理解为什么会是这样了吗？
7. 在本文的情境中，"清醒"是什么意思？

AUTHOR BIO

Zou Jingzhi (1952–) is a prolific writer known mostly for his works for the stage and screen. Born in 1952 in Nanchang, Zou moved with his family a year later to Beijing, a city with which he identified because of his love for the Beijing dialect. Sent down to the northeast in 1969, he spent eight years farming and acting. In jest, he said that he was a tough seedling from the field who had also been tempered by the hard work of a bricklayer and the technical challenges of a carpenter after he returned to Beijing in 1977. He valued every job he had, though they fell far short of his original dream of becoming an animal keeper. He eventually decided to pursue becoming an opera singer and trained for many years. After he published his first short-short story and poem, his infatuation with language took over.

His writing covers a wide range of genres: poetry, prose, fiction, drama, librettos for operas, and screenplays for film and television. Royalty-rich himself, he has also been a moneymaker for the television industry. His series *Kang Xi Incognito Travel* (康熙微服私访记), *The Eloquent Ji Xiaolan* (铁齿铜牙纪晓岚), and *The Sweet Fragrance of Huaihua in May* (五月槐花香) entertained the Chinese people for years. His most recent award-winning screen adaptation is Zhang Yimou's film *Coming Home* (归来, 2015). In 2014, together with Xu Haofeng and Wong Kar Wai, he won best screenplay at the Thirty-Third Hong Kong Film Awards (第三十三届香港电影金像奖).

Known as the leading playwright of China, Zou Jingzhi has also written librettos for two Western-style operas: *Xi Shi* (西施) and *The Chinese Orphan* (赵氏孤儿). Coming of age amid the Cultural Revolution, Zou and his generation have a special attachment to that time, which may be felt in the story's embrace of innocence, love, and hope.

3
古典爱情

王奎山

我年轻的时候在一所乡下中学教书。那所学校的布局大体上是这样子的： 学校的大门朝南。进了大门是一条大路，把学校分成两半。东边是教师办公室、教室、学生宿舍。西边是一个大操场。大操场的北头一眼水井，水井再往北就是学生食堂。

一个星期天的下午，我因为实在没事可干（我那时还没结婚），就在大操场的北头篮球架下练投篮。正玩得投入的时候，忽然听到一个女同学在水井那里叫喊，快来呀，有人掉井里啦！我听到喊声，不敢怠慢，立即跑到水井那里"扑通"一下就跳了下去。等我跳进去以后才发现，落水的是一个女同学。女同学抓到我如同抓到了一根救命的稻草，双手紧紧地搂住我的脖子，再也不肯丢开。我一手抠着井壁上的砖缝，一手搂着女同学的腰，把她托出水面，才对她喊道，别搂我的脖子，别搂我的脖子！女同学这时已经清醒过来了，遂松开了她的双手。我用手搂着她的腰，她的丰满的乳房则紧紧地贴在我的脸上，让我想躲都无法躲开。

这时，食堂里做饭的大师傅赶了过来。他们放下来一个淘米用的竹篓，先是把女同学拉上去，然后又把我也拉了上去。原来，女同学和同伴一起到井边打水（那时候学校里还没有自来水），不小心掉到了井里。

当天晚上，我奋不顾身救女同学的事就传遍了整个校园。

被救的女同学叫蔡琴，是高二（3）班的学生。那时候学生年龄都比较大，听她的班主任说，蔡琴已经19岁了。

3

A GENTLEMAN'S LOVE

Wang Kuishan

I taught at a rural middle school as a youth. Here was, roughly, the layout of the school. The front gate faced south. From the gate, a road divided the school into two halves. Faculty offices, classrooms, and student dormitories were in the eastern part; in the western part there was a large area for sports with a well at the north end. Farther north from the well was the school cafeteria.

One Sunday afternoon I was so bored (and at the time still single) that I went to shoot hoops at the goal on the north end of the sports area. As I was practicing, I heard a girl shouting by the well: "Help! Someone's fallen in the well!" I heard the cry and knew it was serious, so I ran over immediately and with a splash jumped in the well. I didn't know the person drowning was another girl student until I was in the well. She grabbed me as if I were her only hope. Her hands, clamped tightly around my neck, refused to let go. With one hand holding onto the brick ridge on the wall and the other securing her around her waist, I brought her above the surface of the water. It was only then that I yelled, "Let go of my neck! Let go of my neck!" She had come to her senses by then and released her grip. With my hand still around her waist, I couldn't avoid her voluptuous breasts jammed in my face, even if I'd tried.

Just then, a cook from the cafeteria arrived. He lowered down a large basket for washing rice and brought up first the student, then me. It seemed that she had gone to the well to fetch water with her friends (the school didn't have running water then) and had accidentally fallen in.

That evening, the tale of my bravery was all over campus.

The female student was Cai Qin, a junior in class three. Students were older back then. Cai Qin's headmaster told me that she was already nineteen.

我以为这事就这样子结束了，谁知道这才仅仅是个开始。

过了十几天，蔡琴一个人来到我的宿舍，红着脸对我说，她大（父亲）让我到她家去一趟。我以为是要感谢我，说，那不算个啥事，很平常的。蔡琴的脸更红了，说，俺大让你一定去一趟。既然她这样说，那就去一趟吧。我这时才有些认真地看了蔡琴一下。她个子高高的，皮肤很白，比较胖，发育很好的样子。

到了星期天，蔡琴早早地在学校大门口等我。我骑了学校的一辆公用的自行车，带上蔡琴，朝她家赶去。路过一个乡村小店的时候，蔡琴跳下了车子。我见状也忙下车。这时蔡琴对我说，你买点东西吧。买东西？买什么东西？我有些莫名其妙。蔡琴笑笑，说，烟啊酒啊什么的。反正不兴空着手的。我虽然心中有些不悦，但尽量掩饰着不让蔡琴看出来，毕竟我是她的老师啊。

我随着蔡琴进了小店。店主一看我和蔡琴进去，连问也不问，自作主张地拿了两瓶林河大曲、两条黄金叶香烟给我，我只好乖乖地掏钱。

当时，我们这里正流行喝"张宝林"，即张弓大曲、宝丰大曲、林河大曲。黄金叶烟是公社书记一级的干部才吸的，我当时吸的是两角钱一包的淮河烟。我那时一个月的工资才42.5元，这下子花去了我月工资的三分之一。

午饭及其隆重，鸡鸭鱼肉全上。蔡琴的爸爸之外，还有蔡琴的大伯和舅舅，还有生产队的队长、会计。蔡琴红着脸跑前跑后，脸上洋溢着幸福的红晕。

回到学校，我把这事跟家在本地的位老师说了，老兄劈胸给我一拳头，说，你小子，走了桃花运了！原来，蔡琴家如此接待我，是把我当成她家的女婿了。我说，不会吧？老兄说，怎么不会？你把人家的黄花大闺女都搂了，你不当女婿谁当！

I thought that was the end of the story. Who could have guessed that it was just the beginning?

Two weeks later, Cai Qin came to my room, alone. Blushing, she told me that her father had requested a visit from me. I thought he wanted to thank me, so dismissed the request by saying, "There's no need for all that. It was no big deal, nothing out of the ordinary." Cai Qin's face grew even redder than before. "My father insists that you pay him a visit," she said. Since she put it like that, I felt I had to go. It was then that I got my first serious look at her. She was tall with light, soft skin, a little on the heavy side, but with a well-developed figure.

Sunday arrived. Cai Qin came for me early in the morning and waited at the gate. I borrowed a school bike and rode to Cai Qin's home with her sitting on the rear luggage rack. As we were passing by a small country store, Cai Qin jumped off the bike. I had to pull over and get off as well. "Please buy something," Cai Qin said. I was puzzled. "Buy something? Buy what?" With a smile, Cai Qin made some suggestions: "Things like cigarettes, alcohol, or similar. At any rate, you can't show up empty-handed." Although I was somewhat annoyed, I tried to hide my reluctance—I was, after all, her teacher.

Following Cai Qin, I entered the store. The moment the storekeeper saw us come in, without even bothering to ask what we wanted, he took the liberty of pulling two bottles of Linhe Daqu and two cartons of Gold Leaf cigarettes from the shelves. I had no choice but to pay.

At the time, Zhang Bao Lin, that is, Zhanggong Daqu, Baofeng Daqu, and Linhe Daqu, were popular brands here. But Gold Leaf brand cigarettes were mostly for top-ranking commune officials. Huai River, the brand I smoked, was only 20 cents a pack. My monthly salary was 42.50 yuan at the time. Those gifts now had cost me a third of it!

The lunch was grand, with all kinds of meat dishes. Along with Cai Qin's father, her great-uncle from her father's side and uncles from her mother's side were present. The production team leader and the accountant were also in attendance. Cai Qin busied herself with serving, her face flushed with happiness.

Upon returning to school, I told a local teacher what had happened. This fellow thumped me on the chest, "You lucky dog, you've made quite a catch!" It turned out that Cai Qin's family had received me as their future son-in-law. I didn't believe him, "No, it can't be . . ."

我这才认识到问题的严重，但是事情已经晚了。按照当地风俗，我等于已经和蔡琴订过婚了。两年以后，我和蔡琴正式办理了结婚手续。

补记：

前不久我应邀参加了一个子侄辈的婚礼。新郎因为知道我是个文化人，非要我讲几句。我却之不恭，就讲了上面的故事。谁知道，效果出奇的好，赢得一阵热烈的掌声。不仅如此，新郎新娘还一起跑上来，一边一个，搂着我的脖子亲。新郎说，叔，我真羡慕你！新娘说，叔，你太可爱了，我爱你！

(2012)

"Of course it can!" he said. "You've held their daughter, a budding virgin flower, in your arms. If you're not the candidate for son-in-law, who is?"

I suddenly realized how serious the situation was, but it was too late. According to local custom, Cai Qin and I were as good as engaged. Two years later, I went through with it and got married to Cai Qin.

Epilogue...

Not long ago, I was invited to the wedding of a young relative. Since the groom knew I was a man of letters, he insisted that I say a few words. It would have been presumptuous of me to refuse, so I told the story above. To my surprise, it was a hit and was given a hearty round of applause. Not only that, the bride and groom both ran over to me. They flanked my sides, threw their arms around me, and gave me kisses. The groom cried out, "Uncle, how I envy you!" and the bride yelled, "Uncle, you are so cute! I love you!"

(2012)

VOCABULARY AND USAGE

布局	bùjú	layout; composition	这个小区的规划和布局都很合理。
眼	yǎn	a measure word for a well	村口的那眼井虽说远些，可水比家门口这眼甜些。
实在	shízài	really	大雪封山出不了门，待在家里实在是太没意思了！
投入	tóurù	dedicated; absorbed; engrossed	她学中文特别投入，为练口语交了很多中国朋友。
怠慢	dàimàn	slight; trifle with	消防队员的工作是灭火救灾，容不得一刻的怠慢松懈！
落水	luòshuǐ	fall into water	他来了，我们这些落水的人就有了那根救命的稻草。
救命稻草	jiùmìng dàocǎo	a life-saving straw	
抠	kōu	dig; delve into; grasp	我抠紧岩石的缝隙，一步步往上爬。
井壁	jǐng bì	wall of a well	这眼井的井壁是用青砖砌成的。
砖缝	zhuān fèng	brickwork joint	没想到砖缝里还能长出小草！
托	tuō	support from underneath	餐馆的服务员一般都是托着盘子上菜。

遂	suì	then; thereupon	星期六早上突降大雨，周末出游的计划遂落空。
贴	tiē	rub against	他们长久相拥，脸贴脸，像小时一样亲密。
奋不顾身	fènbùgùshēn	be daring, regardless of personal danger	消防队员们奋不顾身地冲进火海，寻找被困人员。
班主任	bānzhǔrèn	a teacher in charge of a class	从小学到大学，每个班都有一位班主任老师负责。
公用	gōngyòng	public; for public use	公园的椅子是公用的，为什么不让我在这儿睡觉？
带	dài	take along	在有些城市，骑车带人是违法的。
(见)状	(jiàn) zhuàng	(see) this state; this situation	一位老人晕倒了，我见状立刻打了急救电话。
不兴	bùxīng	impermissible; not allowed	我们这里不兴在戏院里大声说话或是嗑瓜子的。
不悦	bú yuè	unhappy; unhappiness	当老师的要学会掩饰不悦，不能跟学生发火。
掩饰	yǎnshì	hide; conceal	
自作主张	zìzuò zhǔzhāng	act on one's own; self-assertive	你有事要跟大伙商量，不可自作主张。
大曲	dàqū	hard liquor	大曲酒的酒精浓度很高。
乖乖	guāiguāi	obediently	他手里有枪，所以我只好乖乖地举起双手。
掏钱	tāo qián	pay	我请你出来吃饭，怎么能让你掏钱？
隆重	lóngzhòng	ceremonious; grand	双方家长为他们举办了隆重的婚礼。
跑前跑后	pǎo qián pǎo hòu	running back and forth	他为筹借项目的启动资金跑前跑后地忙了一年。
洋溢	yángyì	be permeated with	大伯脸上洋溢着丰收的喜悦。
红晕	hóngyùn	blush; flush	她就喝了一口酒，脸上便泛起了红晕。
劈	pī	right in/against; straight on	想着在海里游泳浪涛劈面的自在，我溜出了校门，不料却劈头撞上了班主任。
走运	zǒuyùn	have good luck; be in luck	你所谓的成功不过是走运罢了。
桃花运	táohuāyùn	great luck with the opposite sex	好几个女孩同时喜欢你？你真是走了桃花运了！

黄花大闺女	huáng huā dà guīnǚ	(virgin) maiden	民间把未婚、未曾有过性生活的少女称为黄花大闺女。
女婿	nǚxù	son-in-law	女子之夫为婿，所以女儿的丈夫就是女婿。
子侄辈	zǐzhíbèi	the younger generation of (sons and nephews)	你既是父亲又是叔叔，为子侄辈做个好榜样是你的责任。
非(要)	fēi(yào)	insist on	这是你的工作，你干嘛非要把不相干的人扯进来？
却之不恭	quèzhī bùgōng	(it would be) impolite to decline	您热情邀请，我却之不恭，那就从命了。
效果	xiàoguǒ	effect; result	这种药效果特别好，药到病除。
出奇	chūqí	surprisingly; unusually	这个中国小男孩拉丁舞跳得出奇好。
赢得	yíngdé	gain; win	他最大的愿望是赢得当地老百姓的尊敬和爱戴。

QUESTIONS FOR DISCUSSION

1. Which of these two alternative translations of the title is more appropriate: "A Classic Love" or "The Love Trap"?
2. Is this a story of a teacher encouraging a lovestruck student? Why do the townspeople and the girl's family welcome the relationship?
3. The protagonist seems more resigned to the situation than happy about it, yet he enters the "trap" willingly. Why?
4. Why does the teacher seem to have little say about his own marriage here?
5. What do you think of the teacher's compliance with local custom? He seems to have doubts about it, but chooses not to challenge it.
6. In the culture where a teacher is revered as much as heaven, earth, rulers, and ancestors (天地君亲师), how might a teacher live up to society's expectations? Does the story give us any idea?
7. The narrator has been twice a savior—first of the girl's life, then of the family's face. Do you think the newlyweds in the epilogue get that?

1. 本篇英文标题的另外两个版本，"A Classic Love" 和 "The Love Trap," 哪一个对故事更合适些呢？
2. 这篇故事是写老师纵容爱上了他的女学生吗？为什么当地人和女方家人都希望成全这段关系呢？
3. 与其说故事的男主角是为这层关系高兴不如说他好像无可奈何；然而，他还是心甘情愿地步入"陷阱。"这是为什么呢？
4. 为什么这位老师似乎对自己的这场婚姻不持太多的发言权？
5. 这位老师似乎对当地的习俗有质疑，但决定不去挑战它。你对他这入乡随俗的做法怎么看？
6. 在"天地君亲师"的文化中，为人师者怎样才能不负众望，赢得跟"天、""地、""君、""亲"同样的尊敬呢？这个故事给了你什么启发？
7. 故事的男主角曾两度出手相救——先是救女孩的性命，后是"救"她和她家人的面子，你觉得补记中的那对新婚夫妇看明白这一层了吗？

AUTHOR BIO

Born in Queshan, Wang Kuishan (1946–2012) was among the most dedicated and the most admired short-short writers in China. Although it was unusual for a rural young man at that time, he graduated from Kaifeng Normal College when he was only twenty-two. He was also sent to the countryside to be tempered through manual labor for four years before he became a high school teacher of Chinese in 1972. He joined the Queshan Federation of Literature and Art in 1985. Writing, short-shorts especially, was a major part of his job until his retirement. His published works include fictional stories, prose pieces, and informal essays, many of which appear in the two collections *Calcutta Straw Hats* (加尔各答草帽) and *Short-Short Stories by Wang Kuishan* (王奎山小小说).

Wang Kuishan kept writing until the day he died in Zhumadian of Henan Province in May 2012. This story is among the last he wrote. A Confucian gentleman with the wisdom of a Taoist sage, Wang Kuishan was at peace with himself and the world. Although he had kept a low profile, he was still recognized nationally as one of the "spark plugs" for the genre's comeback in the 1980s and a most accomplished writer in the short-short genre. His stories "Red Embroidered Shoes" ("红绣鞋"), "Parting" ("别情"), and "Chasing the Wild Boar" ("打野猪"), among others, have enjoyed great popularity. In 2011 Wang Kuishan won the Lifetime Achievement Award (小小说创作终身成就奖) for the short-short genre. He represents the best of "common-people writers" (平民作家 *píngmín zuòjiā*).

Deeply concerned with the changing ways of life in China, Wang Kuishan often looked back affectionately to his rural roots as his way of staying connected to what was important. In life, he was a quiet, smiling man who always listened attentively and spoke little; in death, he is a revered master whose enigmatic power continues to inspire later writers.

4
如果爱他,就让他心静

安石榴

他和她是同事。

他们相识的时候,各自都结了婚,可他还是对她一见倾心。

他是那种浑身透明的人,心和脸完全朝向阳光,所以他的心事路人皆知。她却很内向,平静得湖水似的,哦,不是"似的",就是平静的湖水。

他在公司里是个大拿,当他经过千辛万苦拿下一个称心的大项目,呼啸着凯旋时,必定大喊大叫:"如意呢?如意呢?"他要把好消息第一个告诉她。接下来庆功宴的时候,他会因了她一句很平常的祝贺之词高兴得手舞足蹈,完全地沉醉,是的,完全地沉醉。他会更加地张扬自己个性中最为优秀的因子,在整个晚上出尽风头,吸足眼球,赚足面子。

然后,深夜散去时,他会细心地安排人送她回家。回过头来,再约上三五铁子找一个地方继续狂饮。酒至酣处,他便无语,无语并陷入痴想。铁子们发现了,问他,老大,怎么了?他便陡然从梦中醒来似的,偏着头,扬着眼,发出清晰的呓语:如意怎么那么瘦呢?

铁子们第一次听到这句话时异常兴奋:瘦?多瘦啊?这么说你到底把她拿下了?

他会突然垂下头,无比痛苦。

铁子们终于知道,没有进展,他只是细致地关心到她的一点一滴,怜惜她到心底罢了。

相同相似的情景反复多次之后,铁子们愤愤然抱怨:老大,你也太痴情了,这么心疼她,怎么就拿不下她呢?

是的,拿不下。

一个狂风暴雨的加班之夜,几个一同加班的同事不约而同地给他们创造条件,加紧手中的工作,然后巧妙地,不动声色地,一个一个隐退。当她发现这个状况的时候,办公室里只有她和他了。雷电和暴雨中节能灯营造出清冷孤寂的气氛,办公室空旷而暧昧,她已经感觉到了一种际遇的迫近。她转身亦要离去,他却一把抓住了她的胳膊,他看着她,没有说话,

4
GIVE HIM PEACE

An Shiliu

Translated by Chen Qiao

He and she were colleagues. Both were married to others before they met; yet he'd fallen helplessly in love with her at first sight.

He was the type of man who is transparent from head to toe—his heart and its expressions completely open to the sun. His feelings were no secret to anyone. She, on the other hand, was introverted and as calm as a lake. Well, not just like one—she *was* a calm lake.

He was a star at the firm. Each time he won a big contract, after having gone through all kinds of difficulties, and returned in triumph, he would shout "Ruyi, Ruyi, where are you?" He always wanted her to be the first to know. At the celebration party that followed, he would dance with joy at the smallest word of congratulations from her, intoxicated with happiness. Yes, absolutely intoxicated! Throughout the party, he would be his liveliest, most charming self, drawing the utmost acclaim, attention, and respect.

When the party dispersed late at night, he would carefully arrange for her ride home, then come back to find a few close friends to go out drinking somewhere. When he had a bit too much, he would become silent, then lapse into a reverie of love. Seeing his odd behavior, his friends would ask, "Hey man, what's wrong?" Suddenly, as if waking from a dream, he would squint and tilt his head, blurting out a bizarre but simple question: "How come Ruyi is so thin?"

The first time they heard this, his friends got really excited "Thin? You sure? So you finally succeeded!"

Instantly, he hung his head in agony.

His friends then knew there had been no progress. He was just truly concerned about her, every little bit of her, and treasured her deep in his heart.

泪水却突然汹涌而来，是的呀，汹涌而来。他是坐在椅子里的，他其实很高大，她是站在椅子旁边的，她小巧玲珑的身材轻易地就被他拉到了他的身边。她看着他，看着他狂放不羁的泪水，张开襟怀拥抱了他。她把他的头拢在自己的肩上，轻轻地。当他试图站起来的时候，她用了力，把他安定在椅子上，断绝了他寻找她嘴唇的情爱之旅；他接着企图滑落自己的身段，她又用了力，阻止了他向柔软的欲望激情探索。女人啊，谁说她们没有力量呢？她把他牢牢地安置在她的肩上，一分钟过去了，五分钟过去了……泪水停止了。

他的嗅觉得到了修缮，随后判断力重新找到归属，他闻到了她的体香，不是香水打造的各种女人的味道，是一种本色的、传统的、唤起幼年依恋的、淡淡的需要用心才能感受到的味道，像蔓延的绿色的旷野；无际的黄色的麦田；悠长的温馨的记忆……博大，温暖，包容……哦，妈妈的味道！

于是，他的心静下来，沉入安宁……

十年后，她从公司辞职去开一个画廊，这时候他已经是公司总经理，他们一直保持着纯粹的友情。他的女秘书像他当年追求她那时一样，追到路人皆知。女秘书帮助她处理交接事务，两个女人相处整整一个上午，除了工作，没有闲话。最后，女秘书叹口气，说：如意姐，你难道不想给我一

Many similar scenes later, his indignant friends could no longer hold back their disdain, "Man, what a lovesick brother! How come, caring and loving as you are, you haven't gotten with her yet?"

Well, he couldn't.

One stormy night, his colleagues who were working overtime in the office tried to create an opportunity for him to be with Ruyi. As if by unspoken agreement, they raced through their work and quietly, conveniently, vanished one at a time. By the time Ruyi realized what had happened, only the two of them were left. Amid thunder and lightning, the energy-saving lights created an uneasy, secluded atmosphere; a seductive ambience circulated through the spacious office. She could feel that something was about to happen. She turned around to leave, but suddenly he grabbed her by the arms. Silently, he stared at her, tears pouring down his cheeks—yes, pouring, like torrential rain. Sitting in the chair next to her, he, a strong, tall man, brought her exquisite body close to his with a light tug. Looking at the uncontrollable tears streaming down his face, she embraced him with open arms, softly resting his head on her shoulder. When he tried to stand up, she gently pushed him back down in the chair, thwarting his amorous attempt for her lips. He then tried to slip downward. Again, gently, she stopped him from seeking her tender body. Women! Who said they aren't powerful? She kept his head locked on her shoulder. One minute passed, five minutes passed ... Eventually, his tears stopped.

His sense of smell returned with his presence of mind. *He could smell her—a scent different from the manufactured fragrances of other women. She smelled natural, traditional. The scent was so faint only his heart could detect it, yet so strong it evoked the bonds of childhood. It called to mind the sprawling green wilderness and the golden expanse of wheat fields, lingering loving memories ... broad and profound, warm and kind, magnanimous ... Oh, it was the smell of Mother!*

He calmed down then, falling into a state of peace ...

Ten years later, she resigned from the firm to open a gallery. He had already been made CEO by then, and they had kept up their genuine friendship all those years.

It was known to all at the time that his female secretary was chasing after him, just as he had chased Ruyi before. The two women spent a whole morning together as the secretary was helping relieve Ruyi of her shift. It was all work, not a word of small talk. At the end of the morning, the

点忠告吗？她拍了拍女秘书的肩膀温和地笑了，摇了摇头。她不是那种好为人师的女人，不过她的确有话，只是那句话深埋在她的心底、永远不会示人。

那句话是：如果爱他，就让他心静。

(2012)

secretary let out a sigh, "Ruyi, don't you want to give me some advice?" With a modest smile, Ruyi patted the secretary on the shoulder and shook her head. Not the type to dish out advice, she did have something to say—something that dwelled so deep in her heart she would never share it with anyone.

"If you love him, give him peace."

(2012)

VOCABULARY AND USAGE

一见倾心	yíjiànqīngxīn	love at first sight	他们一见倾心，很快就结了婚。
路人皆知	lùrénjiēzhī	known by everyone	他的音乐天赋是路人皆知的事实。
大拿	dàná	a person with power and/or great skills	他是我们公司开发新产品的大拿。
称心	chènxīn	gratifying; gratified	他找到了一个称心如意的工作。
呼啸	hūxiào	whiz; scream	空中一架飞机呼啸而过。
凯旋	kǎixuán	triumphant return	拿破仑修了凯旋门迎接胜利归来的将士。
手舞足蹈	shǒuwǔzúdǎo	dance with joy	拿到了耶鲁大学的奖学金，她高兴得手舞足蹈。
张扬（个性）	zhāngyáng (gèxìng)	bring (individuality) into full play; publicize; display	其实说话做事不张扬也是她张扬自己独特个性的方式。
因子	yīnzǐ	factor; gene; trait	小王的大脑里有最优秀的数学因子。
出风头	chūfēngtou	show off; be in the limelight	他是不会放过任何一个出风头的机会的。
尽	jìn	to the greatest extent	你们想尽一切办法救他了吗？
吸眼球	xī yǎnqiú	catch someone's eye; eye-catching	媒体的很多做法是为了吸住观众的眼球。
足	zú	ample; enough; as much as	我真的是酒足饭饱了，我们喝了足有一斤大曲。

铁子	tiězi	sworn friend; buddy	东北话的"铁子"就是咱们北京人所说的 铁哥们。
酒至酣处	jiǔzhìhānchù	near-drunkenness	俗话说的好，酒至酣处吐真言。
陡然	dǒurán	unexpectedly; abruptly	最近，这家网站用户数量陡然上升。
呓语	yìyǔ	crazy talk; talk in one's sleep	他因高烧呓语不断，可没人知道他到底在说什么。
垂	chuí	hang down	她害羞得脑袋垂到了胸前。
怜惜	liánxī	care about dearly; take pity on	小女孩娇小无助的样子令人怜惜。
罢了	bàle	a particle indicating "that's all"	别跟我说要洗头，你就是不想与我约会罢了。
愤愤然	fènfènrán	indignantly	眼看着得不到多数人的支持，他只好愤愤然地退出了选举。
不约而同	bùyuē'értóng	happen to coincide	来年的这一天，他们又不约而同地来到这里。
加紧	jiājǐn	speed up; hurry up	客人明天要来提货，请加点儿紧吧。
巧妙	qiǎomiào	clever; ingeniously	发言人巧妙地回答了这些敏感问题。
不动声色	búdòngshēngsè	maintain one's composure	对方在激化矛盾，他却不动声色，保持淡定。
隐退	yǐntuì	retreat; disappear (from society, politics)	这位主持人在事业高峰时隐退了，回到家乡小镇当起了一名小学老师。
营造	yíngzào	construct; build	美好的人生是要靠自己的努力精心营造的。
清冷孤寂	qīnglěng gūjì	chilly and lonely	你有这么多儿孙辈的孩子，老年怎么会清冷孤寂呢？
空旷	kōngkuàng	open; spacious	如今离了婚的她在这空旷的大房子里形单影孤。
而	ér	and; as well as	这里的百姓勇敢而善良。
暧昧	àimèi	ambiguous; vague	如果他和你玩暧昧，那就说明他还是不够喜欢你。

际遇	jìyù	fate; chance	到目前为止，我生活中最美好的际遇就是在庐山碰到了你。
迫近	pòjìn	approach; close in on; imminent	枪声告诉我们敌军在一步步迫近。
亦	yì	also; too	中文有个说法叫 盗亦有道。
小巧玲珑	xiǎoqiǎo línglóng	little and dainty; small and delicate	圣诞树上挂满了小巧玲珑的饰品。
狂放不羁	kuángfàng bùjī	unrestrained; uninhibited	我很佩服他那狂放不羁的精神。
襟怀	jīnhuái	bosom; breadth of mind	她有着一个负责任女性博大而坦荡的襟怀。
拢	lǒng	hold; draw (near) to; gather up	妈妈把孩子拢在怀里，轻声唱起了一支摇篮曲。
安定	āndìng	settle; stabilize	有了冰淇淋，那孩子就能在椅子上安定一小会儿了。
断绝	duànjué	sever; break off	我早已和那个犯罪团伙断绝了一切关系。
情爱之旅	qíng'àizhīlǚ	journey of love	这对恋人说他们的情爱之旅没有终点。
滑落	huáluò	slide; slip off	肥皂一次又一次从她手中滑落。
身段	shēnduàn	figure	她身段柔软，跳起舞来很好看。
柔软	róuruǎn	soft; lithe	
欲望	yùwàng	desire/lust; craving	欲望和爱分得开吗？欲望是成功之母吗？
牢牢地	láoláodi	firmly	小时候看的童话故事我都牢牢地记在心里了。
安置	ānzhì	arrange for; find a place for	我得先安置好了孩子和老人再回公司上班。
修缮	xiūshàn	repair; renovate;	房子可以修缮，那人的感情呢？
判断力	pànduànlì	ability to judge; judgment	只有头脑冷静才能保持清晰的判断力。
归属	guīshǔ	a place where one feels that one belongs	对很多人来说，家是归属；可对我来说，信仰是归属。

本色	běnsè	true; inherent quality	本色的东西一定是天然的吗？英雄的本色是什么？
蔓延	mànyán	spread; extend	我家园子里的野草四处蔓延，邻居们都有意见了。
旷野	kuàngyě	open field	这空阔平坦的旷野很适合养马放牧。
悠长	yōucháng	long-drawn-out	自从有了高铁就听不到火车悠长的汽笛声了。
温馨	wēnxīn	softly fragrant; warm	杭州给我的感觉是舒适而温馨。
依恋	yīliàn	be attached to; be reluctant to leave	小孩子对父母会有强烈的依恋。
交接	jiāojiē	hand over; take over	这项工作的交接进行得很顺利。
闲话	xiánhuà	chat; digression	上班还是不聊天为好，闲话太多会影响工作的。
忠告	zhōnggào	sincere advice; counsel	您临别的忠告我都牢记在心了。
好为人师	hàowéi rénshī	like to lecture others	"好为人师"跟"助人为乐"不一样，区别在于动机和目的。
埋	mái	bury	她把心里话埋在了心底，永远地留给了自己。
示人	shì rén	show or reveal to others	谁的心中没有点儿不愿示人的秘密呢？

QUESTIONS FOR DISCUSSION

1. How does this story complicate usual notions of romantic love?
2. Do you empathize with the main character's emotional struggle?
3. At what point in the story do you realize that Ruyi is resistant to the idea of becoming involved with the man?
4. What do you think of the paean to motherhood in the story? What in the story do you see as expressions of motherhood?
5. Are Ruyi and the man faithful to their respective spouses? How does the story approach the concepts of love and fidelity? How does the yin-yang dynamic work in the story's handling of the emotional and the ethical?

6. Does Ruyi love him? Should Ruyi love him? Is Ruyi denying herself happiness? Why can't she say what's in her heart? Please comment on the possible stances that this story takes toward the four questions.
7. Do you agree with the following observation about An Shiliu's work?[2]

When An Shiliu dramatizes intense and delicate emotions, she does not flatten her characters with moral judgment or puncture their flaws with righteousness. Instead, she treats them with respect, as intriguing, self-reflective human beings capable of navigating their own weaknesses and constraints.

1. 这个故事怎样把通常的浪漫爱情复杂化了?
2. 你理解、同情男主人公的情感挣扎吗?
3. 你读到什么地方的时候意识到了如意是不会跟男主人公有任何瓜葛的?
4. 这篇小说盛赞母性,你对此做何感想? 小说中的哪些东西在你看来是母性的表达?
5. 男女主人公对他们各自的妻子、丈夫忠不忠? 故事是如何探讨爱情和忠贞问题的? 阴阳的互动是如何体现在故事对情感与伦理的处理之中的?
6. 如意爱他吗? 如意应该爱他吗? 如意是在自虐摒弃幸福吗? 如意为什么不能把心里的话说出来? 请说说本篇小说对上述四个问题所持的立场。
7. 你同意如下对安石榴作品所做的评价吗?

安石榴的小说戏剧化地呈现了强烈细腻的情感。她不用道德判断把人物压扁; 也不自诩正义化身去痛揭他人之短。相反,她尊重她这些奇妙的、具有自我反思能力的人物; 相信他们能够克服自己的短处,超越自己的局限。

---

2. Aili Mu came to know An Shiliu's work relatively late. She wrote down these lines after she read a number of An Shiliu's works in the summer of 2014 and was deeply impressed.

AUTHOR BIO

An Shiliu (1964–) was born in a dragon year, on the day when "the dragon raised its head" (龙抬头), that is, the second day of the second month by the Chinese lunar calendar, when frozen earth and all the lives in it awakened. The youngest of a family of ten in which everybody loved to read, An Shiliu grew up imbued with a respect for literature. The image of her father reading with a pair of glasses on his nose and a magnifying glass in his hand and her mother's enthusiastic participation motivated her to read everything her family possessed and her elder siblings brought home. The first foreign book of fiction she read was *David Copperfield*; at the time, it cost her eldest sister most of her monthly pay.

Her real name is Shao Meiying (邵玫英). An Shiliu is the name of the youngest fairy in a story by Feng Menglong (冯梦龙, 1574–1646, a Ming dynasty writer), whose cool personality she loved when she was a little girl. But An Shiliu did not emerge as her pen name until she was forty-four years old. A daughter of a forestry engineer in Hailin, Heilongjiang Province, she went to teach in a vocational school of forestry after her education in a teachers college. She then married, became a mother, and settled into an ordinary life as a civil servant in the city of Mudanjiang. Her first try at writing literature was her participation in the 2008 national short-short competition for rookie writers organized by the *Journal of Garden of Flower* (百花园), a major publisher of the short-short genre in China, and she emerged as the second-place winner after four rounds.

In the short span of eight years, this rookie has become a recognized authority and a teacher of the genre. Admiring strangers go to visit her to relate the joy of reading her and to learn from her. An Shiliu also shares her thoughts and experiences through correspondence and online discussion forums. She has added five volumes of short-short collections to her 2008 award-winning piece "Mr. Guan" ("关先生"); among them are *Big Fish* (大鱼), *Vegetarian* (全素人), and *Elegance and Embarrassments* (优雅与尴尬). Some of the stories in her collections have been reprinted by such popular journals as *Youth Literary Digest* (青年文摘) and *Readers* (读者). For An Shiliu, writing brings her peace of mind on her continuous journey of self-cultivation. She also believes that the short-short genre has endless possibilities.

Among her many fans is Chen Qiao, a student from China majoring in math at Iowa State University. He admired the universal relevance of this story, yet was torn by the protagonist's struggle. He translated the story with utmost sincerity in the hope of bringing the story's broad implications of human life and love to people of different cultures.

第八章

婚姻

无论来自何种文化背景，人们都深谙寻觅真爱的不易，维持婚姻的艰辛，以及永葆爱情之树常青的困难。本章故事的特别之处在于它们各自应对这些难题的方式。从每个人物特有的挫折、挣扎和解决问题的办法中，想必读者能感受到当代中国有追求的青年所面临的挑战。

在世界的每个角落都能找到年近三十，或三十出头，甚至年龄更大些的未婚女性。这个现象在张玛丽这样的职业女性群体中可能会更突出。《张玛丽》是第一个故事的标题，但这个故事绝非仅仅停留在叙述寻找那个特殊的另一半有多难。当今中国的所谓"剩女"现象已经成为一个社会问题。所谓"剩女"，一个既暴露出偏见又反映了焦虑的称谓，通常是指单身、受过教育、生活独立，年龄在二十七岁以上的女性。"剩女"现象出现在女少男多，比例为100：115的中国[1]尤其令人难以置信。希望兴华写这样一位剩女的故事能开启你对一个古老文化如何面对这一新挑战的探索。

本章的四个故事都涉及中国的快速发展对婚姻制度的影响，其中最令人心悸的可能要数《怀念张美丽》。根据世界银行的统计数据，中国城市人口在2011年超过了农村人口。这一变化带来的不幸后果在故事中显而易

---

1. 信息来自中央情报局图书馆网站：https://www.cia.gov/library/publications/the-world-factbook/fields/2018.html. 最后一次浏览在 03/16/16.

CHAPTER 8

MARRIAGE

People of all cultures know the struggle of finding true love, the trials of managing relationships, and the difficulties in keeping love fresh. What makes the stories in this chapter special is the way each one deals with these problems. From the uniqueness of their frustration, struggle, and resolution, you may get a feel for the challenges that aspiring young people face in contemporary China.

It is common to see unmarried women in their late twenties, early thirties, and even older, everywhere in the world. It is probably more common with career women like Mary Zhang, the titular character in our first story. But the story "Mary Zhang" introduces much more than the problem of finding that special someone. In China today, "leftover girls" or "shelved ladies" (剩女 shèngnü) have become a social phenomenon. Usually referring to single, educated women with money who are over twenty-seven years old, these terms betray both biases and anxieties. The issue is all the more mind-boggling when we take into consideration that for every one hundred women in China there are one hundred fifteen men.[1] This story by Xing Hua depicting a female professional thus categorized can be your gateway to exploring how an ancient culture confronts this new challenge.

Although all four stories show the impact of China's rapid development on the institution of marriage, the most disturbing among them may be "Missing Zhang Meili." According to World Bank statistics, China's urban population surpassed its rural population in 2011. The unfortunate

---

1. Data from the Library of the Central Intelligence Agency, accessed March 16, 2016, www.cia.gov/library/publications/the-world-factbook/fields/2018.html.

见。这样的后果通常也是阅读关注的焦点。然而，当读者的阅读理解更深入一些，超越了爱情消失却拒绝接受的表象，他们可能就会开始理解中国人的日常生活为现代化的进程付出了何等的代价。从故事向更本真的生活方式"回归"的愿望中，读者或许也能感受到当代中国面向昔日之美好所做的再定位。

有读者建议张美丽的丈夫离婚算了。对这些读者来说，《结婚成本》中的和尚必须为新娘再买个更大的公寓这件事很不可思议："结婚不就是两个人快乐地在一起吗？"关于这个问题，故事没有给出一个明确的答案，相反却是呈现了情感生活与社会经济层面生活的不可分割。买房子难，用房子为爱遮风挡雨更难，但最难的是永不放弃对爱的希望和信念。我们的心为和尚和婷婷悬着。

当我们用心去创造，而不是用严格的数字去比量夫妻间的平等时，我们就会感受到《薄荷的邀请》中的阳光缕缕。谁说一个人只能在工作岗位或公共场合施展权职？"解"个人生活之"冻"，有什么能比用自己的双手来的更有效？故事对日常生活审美向度——对柴、米、油、盐中诗意——的赞美尤为可贵。这种在平凡中发现非凡的活法为我们指明了另一条可行的生活之路，以及在这条路上人们不同的价值和欣赏标准。女主角在婚姻螺旋式下滑时反思自我，她的应对方式是不是更负责任、更有担当的活法？也许我们早该接受薄荷的邀请，好好想想到底怎样才能成就更有意义，更美好的生活。

consequences of this transition evident in the story are usually the focus when reading. But if you read more deeply than the obsession with fading love and its denial, you may begin to understand the price people are paying for modernization in everyday life. In the desire to "return" to what seems like a more original and authentic way of life, you may also sense contemporary China's (re)orientation toward the good things of its past.

For those who advised Zhang Meili's husband to get a divorce, it is puzzling why Monk in "The Cost of Marriage" absolutely *had* to buy a second and larger apartment for his bride-to-be. Shouldn't marriage be just about being happy together? Instead of clear answers, the story presents matters of the heart as inseparable from the socioeconomic aspects of life. It is difficult to buy a home; it is even more difficult to shelter love within a home; and most difficult of all is to not give up on love and trust. Monk and Tingting leave us unsettled.

There seem to be a ray of sunshine in "The Mint's Invitation" when we measure equality with empathy rather than with strict numbers. Who says that positions of power can only be located in the workplace or in the public sphere? What could thaw what is "frozen" in your life better than your own hands? The story's celebration of the aesthetic dimensions of everyday life—the poetry in firewood, rice, oils, and salt (柴米油盐 *chái mǐ yóu yán*)—is especially endearing, because the discovery of the extraordinary in the ordinary points toward an alternative way of life and its different appreciation. Might the protagonist's self-reflective way of dealing with the downward spiral of her marriage be a more responsible way of being? Perhaps it is time to accept the mint's invitation and think about what constitutes a more meaningful and beautiful human existence.

1
张玛丽

兴华

  其实，张玛丽大名不叫张玛丽。白领嘛，总会有个英文名字。CBD 里做着一份外表光鲜、冷暖自知的工作，她也还算满足。站在茶水间的大玻璃窗前，看天桥上的一对情侣在吵架，张玛丽听不清楚他们在说些什么，却在心里编造着那些对话的内容，乐此不疲。女的跑开了，男的去追，慢慢脱离了视线，张玛丽的导演加编剧的职务也就自动瓦解了。她转身放咖啡杯的时候，忽然冒出一个念头：自己好久没和人吵架了，好想找个人吵吵架。

  张玛丽是个低调平和的人，依旧会有男同事对她说些模棱两可的话，约她去郊游、看电影之类的。她知道，男同事的夸奖是香水，只能闻，不能尝。张玛丽也会在周末的下午躺在沙发上看杂志时，对自己说，其实一个人挺好的。有时，她甚至会说出声来。现在"挺好"确实不能算是什么褒义词了，她也知道。

  张玛丽有时候也会想刺激一把，和闺蜜约好周末去酒吧，她也会在里面换上黑色的内衣。可是，张玛丽终归是个保守的人，她知道如果爱情是饭，她不愿意饥一顿饱一顿的。就像大多数人会遇到的情况一样，不知道怎么的，张玛丽这个说起来还不错的"畅销品"，就走上了相亲的路。 不那

1
MARY ZHANG

Xing Hua

Actually, her given name wasn't Mary Zhang. A sophisticate, she felt she had to have an English name. She worked for CBD, a job that from the outside looked wonderful; only she knew its thorns. Still, she had little to complain about. At the moment, she was standing in front of a large window in the tearoom, watching a pair of lovers argue on the skywalk. She couldn't tell what they were saying, but she imagined the content of their exchange and silently reveled in it. When the girl ran away, the boy ran after her, and gradually they moved out of her sight. Mary Zhang's role of director-cum-playwright thus came to an end. As she turned to put down her coffee cup, it suddenly occurred to her—she hadn't been in an argument with someone for a long time. How she wished she had someone with whom she could pick a fight!

Mary Zhang was an even-tempered person who kept a low profile. There were still male colleagues who would talk to her in that there-is-more-going-on-here-than-meets-the-ears kind of way, asking her out for a day trip or a movie or something. She knew that their compliments were just like perfume—nice to smell but not to swallow. On weekends, lying on her sofa reading magazines in the afternoon, Mary Zhang would tell herself that it was actually quite nice being single. Sometimes, she would even say it out loud. Nowadays, "quite nice" wouldn't really be thought of as an affirmation, and she knew it.

Every now and then, Mary Zhang would crave some excitement. She would put on her black lingerie when she went out with her girlfriends to a bar, but Mary Zhang was a conservative woman after all. If love were food, she wouldn't want to gorge herself one day and starve the next. Perhaps predictably, Mary Zhang, a pretty good catch as she was, somehow found herself navigating the treacherous terrain of blind dating. She was

么物质，也不那么理想；没太多要求，可也有些讲究。大多数的相亲，都像看张飞表演昆曲或者朗诵《声声慢》一样，完全不是那么一回事。

老妈给她介绍的"金主"，第一次见面就带她去吃辽参，不停的重复："我要的女人不用出去工作的，在家待着就行，做饭都不用。"张玛丽听得盆股吱吱作响，觉得自己就是个生育机器。

大学同学给她介绍的活泼可爱的音乐青年，边对她秀自己腰上纹的五线谱，边栩栩如生地讲在草原音乐节上与新结识的姑娘一起看着星星多么浪漫。张玛丽不用问他年龄，已经觉得自己"嗖"一下就老了，不敢想。

可是，无论如何，张玛丽还是没办法拒绝那些相亲的邀请，并且觉得别人介绍的时候越来越注意对她的措辞，仿佛是对一个弱者进行施舍的时候还要注意她的尊严，尽量地小心谨慎。自己真的就老成这个样子了吗？张玛丽对着镜子抹眼霜的时候想。

自己买菜，自己做饭，自己刷碗，自己看电视，自己睡觉，自己定闹表，自己提垃圾袋。不都说要相信在不远的一个地方正有一个人在慢慢地慢慢地爱上你吗？可他妈的那个人在哪儿呢？！当然了，张玛丽只在自己心里才说脏话。梨不熟不香，张玛丽吃梨的时候对自己说。张玛丽累了，对自己说，总会好的。她有点怕过年回家了。

(2011)

neither very materialistic nor idealistic. She didn't ask for much, but she was particular about certain things. Most of her blind dates were surreal, like watching Zhang Fei, a military general, perform Kun operas or recite romantic poems.

Her mom introduced her to a "gold bachelor," who took her to a fancy restaurant for *liao shen* on their first date. He kept repeating, "My woman doesn't need to go out to work. She will just hang around the house. She doesn't even need to cook." As she listened, Mary Zhang could hear her hip bones squeak. He made her feel she was nothing more than a child-bearing robot.

Her friends from college introduced her to an energetic and handsome young lover of music. He told her vividly how romantic it was to stargaze with girls he'd just met at the Grasslands Musical Festival, as he showed her the bars of music tattooed on his waist. There was no need to ask him how old he was, because Mary Zhang felt she had become old in a flash. Unbelievable.

No matter what, though, Mary Zhang did not decline an invitation to a date. And she started to notice that, when introducing her, people chose their words more and more carefully. It was as if they were giving alms to someone destitute while trying to remain sensitive to her sense of dignity. "Have I really grown so old?" Mary Zhang asked herself as she applied her eye cream in front of her mirror.

She bought groceries by herself, cooked by herself, did the dishes by herself, watched TV by herself, slept by herself, set the alarm clock by herself, and took the trash out by herself. *Don't they say that there's always someone close by who is slowly and gradually falling in love with you? But where the hell is he?!* Of course, Mary Zhang would only use such language in her mind. "An unripe pear is not sweet," she murmured to herself while eating one. Mary Zhang was tired, and so said to herself, "It will be fine."

All the same, she was a little apprehensive about going home for the New Year.

(2012)

VOCABULARY AND USAGE

大名	dàmíng	one's formal personal name; given name	我姓王，大名叫中兴，小名是中中。
外表	wàibiǎo	outward appearance	她找男朋友只有两个标准，一是外表光鲜，二是会赚钱。
光鲜	guāngxiān	shiny; fresh and bright	
冷暖	lěngnuǎn	cold or warm; happy or sad	"如人饮水，冷暖自知"的意思是亲身经历了才知道其中的感受。
乐此不疲	lècǐbùpí	enjoy a thing and never get tired of it	每天去学校接送孙子是他的大事，他乐此不疲。
脱离	tuōlí	break away from	警察及时赶到，被困的人们才脱离了危险。
瓦解	wǎjiě	collapse; dissolve	他在公司的地位没人能够动摇瓦解。
冒出	mào chū	burst out; emerge	他一着急，说话时就会冒出家乡的方言。
念头	niàntou	thought; idea	你这实体和网店结合的念头太有创意了。
低调	dīdiào	low key; low profile	为什么父母总是跟我说做人要低调呢？
依旧	yījiù	still	毕业十年了，他依旧暗恋着当年同桌的她。
模棱两可	móléng liǎngkě	vague; ambiguous	你的话模棱两可，我还是不知道该怎么办。
郊游	jiāoyóu	outing; go on an outing	北大每年都组织留学生出去郊游看长城。
夸奖	kuājiǎng	praise	你可别把男人的夸奖太当真，小心上当受伤害。
(刺激一)把	(cìjī yī) bǎ	a measure word	您请再加把劲儿，早点儿做完大家都能松口气！
闺蜜	guīmì	a woman's best girlfriend	我们闺蜜之间无话不说。

终归	zhōngguī	after all	他终归是个孩子，犯错儿是难免的。
饥	jī	hungry	长身体的孩子不能这样饥一顿饱一顿的。
不知道怎么的	bù zhīdào zěnme de	inexplicably	小区里不知道怎么的突然停电了，一片黑暗。
畅销品	chàngxiāo pǐn	best seller	这个品牌的咖啡最近一直是我们网站的畅销品。
张飞	Zhāng Fēi	a military general (168 – 221 c.e.)	张飞是三国时期的蜀汉名将，既勇敢又鲁莽。
昆曲	kūnqǔ	Kun opera; Kunqu opera	昆曲是中国传统戏曲中最古老的剧种之一。
朗诵	lǎngsòng	read/recite with cadence	他才三岁，就能背诵很多首古诗词了。
"声声慢"	shēngshēngmàn	a tune name in Chinese poetry	"声声慢"是宋词的一个词牌名。
辽参	liáo shēn	an expensive dish with sea cucumber	辽参价格很高，所以有些人就把它当作身份象征了。
盆骨	péngǔ	pelvic bone	有人把女人的盆骨比作孩子最初的摇篮。
吱吱作响	zhīzhī zuò xiǎng	creaking	我听到门吱吱作响，会不会是有小偷进来了？
秀	xiù	show; show off	她特别喜欢在网络上秀她做的菜。
纹	wén	tattoo	她在背上纹了一朵玫瑰。
五线谱	wǔxiànpǔ	staff; stave	你想学弹钢琴就得先学识五线谱。
栩栩如生	xǔxǔrúshēng	lifelike	徐悲鸿画的马栩栩如生，比真的还好看。
措辞	cuòcí	wording; diction	我们说话应该时刻注意措辞，千万不能伤害他人的自尊。

弱者	ruòzhě	the weak	你可别因为他年龄小、身体弱就称他为弱者。
施舍	shīshě	give alms; handout	一个正常人不应该靠别人的施舍生活，自食其力才会有尊严。
小心谨慎	xiǎoxīnjǐnshèn	careful and cautious	带小孩过马路一定要小心谨慎。
尊严	zūnyán	dignity	一个人的尊严不能靠别人给，要自己赢得。
抹	mǒ	daub; smear	我用餐刀在面包片上抹了一层黄油。
眼霜	yǎnshuāng	eye cream	这种眼霜特有效，一定能抚平你眼角的皱纹。
不都说…	bùdōushuō	Isn't it true that…; Everyone says…	不都说农村很脏很穷吗？怎么此地既干净又富有？
脏话	zānghuà	bad language; profanity	有小孩子在场，你注意不要说脏话！

QUESTIONS FOR DISCUSSION

1. Why doesn't the story provide Mary Zhang's given name?
2. Why does Mary Zhang enjoy imagining the words to the argument she witnesses?
3. How is Mary Zhang "conservative"? What are the things that Mary Zhang is particular about as far as dating and marriage are concerned?
4. Why doesn't Mary Zhang turn down those blind dates? And why is Mary Zhang apprehensive about going home for the New Year?
5. What in Mary Zhang's mind-set, lifestyle, self-perception, and expectation surprises you? Why?
6. What did you learn about the "leftover girls" or "shelved ladies" phenomenon in China from this story?
7. What do you think of Mary Zhang's use of the aphorism "An unripe pear is not sweet" in this context?

1. 为什么故事没有给出张玛丽的大名，也就是她的真名字？
2. 张玛丽为什么很乐意去想象窗外争吵的那对年轻人在说什么？
3. 为什么说张玛丽"保守"？在交男朋友和婚姻问题上，她很在意哪些事情？
4. 张玛丽为什么不拒绝别人介绍的相亲？她为什么有些害怕回家过年？
5. 张玛丽的心态、生活方式、自我想象和对未来的期待等，有什么让你感到吃惊的吗？为什么？
6. 这个故事让你对中国所谓的"剩女"现象有了什么样的了解？
7. 张玛丽在文中用了"梨不熟不香"这个格言。你怎么看张玛丽对这个格言的使用？

AUTHOR BIO

In lieu of an author bio, we register here our failed attempt to find Xing Hua. This story has been a favorite of many readers; its subject matter and narrative perspective offer unique ways to approach an important phenomenon in contemporary China. We hope Xing Hua is happy to see that his/her story is included here. It has struck resonant chords among readers of diverse cultures and backgrounds.

To find Xing Hua, we first contacted the publisher of the anthology where we found this story. The publisher of the anthology then reached out to *Sanlian Life Weekly* (三联生活周刊), the journal that first carried the story, for information on Xing Hua. What we have been able to find so far is as follows: (1) Xing Hua used to work for ABB or Asea Brown Boveri Ltd.; (2) the ABB address Xing Hua left with *Sanlian Life Weekly* is outdated; (3) ABB has informed the publisher of the anthology that Xing Hua has left the company; and (4) *Sanlian Life Weekly* confirms that it owns the copyright to this story. We have paid *Sanlian Life Weekly* for the right to publish this story here.

Although it is rare that we cannot locate the writer of a story, the mobility of these short-short writers who are not professionals and the unpredictability that comes with this mobility are commonplace. These writers have to prioritize in life; they may stop publishing and disappear for some time; and they will, we hope, reemerge with renewed energy as well as enriched experiences.

2
结婚成本

赵瑜

我的朋友和尚是个出色的单身青年。他有车有房有理想，每每被身边的女人迷恋。然而一旦谈及结婚，和尚总是像触电一样陷入恐惧。是婚姻的成本让他感到不安。他的理想就是自由的活着。然而，婚姻总是意味着要牺牲掉这些，要陷入日常生活的琐碎中，挣扎在物质的斤斤计较中，让他厌倦。

现实是，他终究会遇到一个能融化自己的女人，她有湿润的眼睛，可以依靠的微笑，以及完全温暖的内心。和尚被一个叫婷婷的女人打动，第一次想牵着一个女人的手，走得远一些，更远一些。

那么，只好付出婚姻，约束自己的同时，也完整地拥有对方的爱恋。

和尚现在的房子是五十平方米的一居，婚姻要求他必须另购一套婚房。和婷婷商议完之后，两个人将各自所有的积蓄都拿了出来，可以贷款买一套大房子。然而，让他们感到难过的是，房贷政策出现了新变化，这变化稍显恶意，对购买第二套房子的人几乎仇视。

如果和尚和婷婷结婚以后再买房，那么，因为和尚已经有了一套房子，哪怕和尚将这套房子卖掉，他们再购房也算是第二套房。第二套房子，不仅首付要提高，而且房子银行贷款的利息也提高了很多。和尚和婷婷计算了

2
THE COST OF MARRIAGE

Zhao Yu

My friend Monk was an attractive young bachelor. He had a car, a home, and ambitions, so women often went crazy for him. But whenever the topic of marriage was brought up, Monk would recoil as if from an electric shock. It was the cost of marriage that panicked him. His dream was simply to live free, and marriage would necessarily mean giving up that freedom for a mundane, everyday existence. To be caught up in a life of having to pinch pennies for material things would tick him off.

But the reality was that Monk had been destined to meet a girl who would touch his heart and dissolve his resolve. She had dewy eyes, a winning smile of dependability, and a thoroughly warm heart. A girl named Tingting had captivated Monk. For the first time, he wanted to take a girl's hand and walk farther, and even farther, with her.

Since this was how things were, marriage was the price he had to pay. By restricting himself in this way, he also gained full possession of her love for him.

Monk's home was a one-bedroom apartment of fifty square meters. As was customary, he would have to buy another place for the marriage. After talking it over, he and Tingting both took out all the money they had saved—enough to get a loan for a big home. But to their dismay, there had been a change in the mortgage policy. The change was inconvenient to everyone, but to those who wanted to purchase a second home, it was downright punitive.

If Monk and Tingting were to buy the home after they got married, it would then be counted as their second property, because Monk already owned a home. This would not change even if Monk sold his current apartment before they got a new one. The second property not only required a

一下，如果婚后购房，那么，一套百十平方米的房子，他们生生要多付出近三十万元。

经过温暖而彼此信任的协商，两个人决定先不领取结婚证，推迟婚期，然后共同出资将房子买下来。显然，这个时候，两个人只能以婷婷的名义来购买婚房，因为和尚的名字已经用过一次了，感情的温度远远超过了日常生活的琐碎，一点点利益算得了什么呢？

和尚忙碌着去银行申请贷款，然而，在银行里，他遇到了爱情的另外走向。一些和他有着共同愿望的人是如何降低成本的呢？假离婚。一些需要购买第二套房子的夫妻，为了少付首付和贷款利息，等房子贷款批下来之后，再复婚。然而，有一些人，不留神就弄假成真了。感情被一套房子拆得七零八落。

和尚反复被银行的职员提醒，没有结婚，就将房产办到恋人的名下，对方如果变心，财产无法分割。

和尚一开始不予理会，认为别人恶俗，拿他们热烈而诚挚的爱情和金钱相比较，实在荒诞。然而，到了房地产公司才发现，那些亲密的恋人竟然拿着公证书前来购房，他们用现实主义的态度对待彼此，理智得残酷，公证书上写得明晰，如果分手，房产应该如何分配，等等。

也有一个做律师的朋友，在吃饭的时候，反复劝和尚说最好还是签个简单的协议，要不然，就让婷婷打个借条，证明这套房子一大半的费用是和尚付的。和尚是个多么理想主义的人啊，他自然不予理会。

然而，不知怎么的，在和婷婷的相处中，和尚的内心仿佛多了一点点灰尘，那是这套房子里的灰尘，无论如何也打扫不干净。

higher down payment, it also attached a much higher interest rate to their mortgage. They did the math: if they waited to buy after they got married, they would have to pay almost 300,000 yuan more for a home of one hundred square meters.

After some frank and honest talk, Monk and Tingting decided they should postpone getting their marriage certificate and push back their wedding so they could put their money together and purchase a property first. It was obvious to them now that they could only make the purchase in Tingting's name, for Monk's was already on record as a property owner. The warmth of their love had far transcended such trivialities of daily life—a small disadvantage like this wasn't really anything.

Monk got busy applying for a loan. There, however, he encountered the other turns love often takes. How did married people in similar circumstances bring down the cost of buying a second property? They faked a divorce, of course. Those couples would secure a loan to reduce the down payment and the interest rate before resuming the marriage. Some of them, however, only came to realize too late that the deceit had become a reality. Love was shattered into pieces by a piece of property.

The bank clerks repeatedly reminded Monk that since he was not married, once he put the property under his beloved's name, its value would not be split between them if she had a change of heart.

At first, Monk turned a deaf ear to them. He thought they were vulgar, and certainly it was absurd to measure his passionate and genuine love for Tingting in terms of money. But when he arrived at the real estate company, he was surprised to see that intimate lovers were purchasing a home together with a notarization. They treated each other realistically and were being cruelly logical. The notarization clearly stated how the property would be distributed if they broke up or in the case of other eventualities.

While having a meal with him, Monk's lawyer friend also advised him, repeatedly, that it would be best if he signed a simple agreement with Tingting or at least got her to write an IOU as proof that Monk had paid for most of the home. Monk, idealist that he was, unsurprisingly chose to ignore this advice.

However, for no reason he could fathom, Monk felt that in his subsequent dealing with Tingting his heart seemed to have acquired a little layer of dust, dust gathered from the cost of the home. No matter how hard he tried, he couldn't seem to wipe it off.

婷婷仿佛也变得敏感起来，一说到婚姻，说到房子贷款办下来以后，婷婷便觉得自己的尊严受到了伤害。两个无话不说的亲密恋人，就这样，被一套房子硌痛了。

原本对婚姻有无限期待的和尚，这次终于又遇到了婚姻成本的问题。他开始发现婷婷的缺陷；对自己无限温暖的身体正在被她自己的敏感遮蔽。两个人有时候不约而同地心情不好，像两只小刺猬，想要相互取暖，却被对方的刺扎到。

一开始，和尚所预算的婚姻成本不过是要付出时间，牺牲自己的小部分理想，甚至是将自己变成爱情中的平庸者，以融化另外一个身体。现在，他才发现，原来婚姻的成本更多的是物质的层面，是房子，是生存的宽度，是彼此互相打开心灵所要承担的金钱数额。

和尚有一天喝醉了酒，哭了，说，他和婷婷的房子贷款批下来了，但是婚姻却无限期延长了。婷婷将钱还给了他，说，他有些犹豫，这伤害了她。

我们看着和尚，无法安慰他，只是觉得，婚姻的成本，原来总比当事人所预料的要多一些。

(2012)

Tingting seemed to have gotten touchier than before. She felt insulted when the topic of the wedding was brought up in the same breath as the loan approval. The pebble of a piece of property was now hurting the two intimate lovers who used to share every thought.

Monk, who initially had such high expectations for his marriage, now was confronted with the price of it. He started to notice Tingting's flaws. The body that had been a source of endless warmth to him was now veiled by her touchy susceptibility. Sometimes the two of them got into a bad mood at the same time. Like two little hedgehogs, they wanted to draw close for warmth, but ended up being poked by each other's bristles.

In the beginning, Monk had thought the only cost of marriage was no more than his time and giving up some small part of his dreams. It was even okay for him to become ordinary if his ardor could meld his lover's body to his. Now, finally, he had figured out that the cost of marriage was mostly material—it was a piece of real estate, the viable breadth of living space, the amount of money that one was asked to risk to open another's heart.

One day, Monk got drunk and wept. He said that the bank had approved their loan, but the wedding had been postponed indefinitely. Tingting had returned all his money to him, and told him that his hesitation hurt her.

We looked at Monk, unable to console him. All we could think of was that the price of marriage, it turned out, is always more than what you expect.

(2012)

VOCABULARY AND USAGE

触电	chùdiàn	get an electric shock	这里的电路系统很安全，从未发生过触电事故。
恐惧	kǒngjù	fear; terrified	一提结婚他就恐惧，成本太高了。
琐碎	suǒsuì	trivia; trifling	没有生活的琐碎会有生活的精美吗？
斤斤计较	jīnjīnjìjiào	haggle over every ounce; fuss about tiny details	你为什么要跟自己的亲人斤斤计较家务活谁做了多少？

厌倦	yànjuàn	be tired of	我厌倦了这种每天上班下班没有变化的生活。
终究	zhōngjiū	after all; eventually	她终究是会了解你的用心的。
融化	rónghuà	melt; thaw	高冷的她被他的真情融化了。
湿润	shīrùn	moist	看到姐姐眼眶湿润起来，他后悔话说重了。
打动	dǎdòng	touch; move	我被他的演讲打动了。
牵(手)	qiān (shǒu)	lead along (by holding the hand)	他们能牵手共度一生吗？
积蓄	jīxù	save; savings	一般人都会把积蓄存入银行。
贷款	dàikuǎn	loan; provide a loan	如今大部分人买房、买车是需要贷款的。
稍	shāo	somewhat; a little	这条裙子的质量看上去比那条稍好点。
仇视	chóushì	be hostile to	你为什么这么仇视有钱人啊？
哪怕	nǎpà	even though	他太胆小了，哪怕外面有一点儿动静，他都会紧张害怕。
提高	tígāo	increase; raise	在中国学习半年，我的中文水平提高了不少。
利息	lìxī	interest (on a loan)	银行下调了存款利息。
生生	shēngshēng	compulsory; forcibly	好好一对恋人却生生被房子的难题拆散了。
近	jìn	close to; about	爸妈每年要为我付近五十万人民币的学费。
领取	lǐngqǔ	go and get	你来邮局领取邮件是要拿领取通知的。
协商	xiéshāng	talk things over	你们先好好协商一下再做决定。
推迟	tuīchí	put off; postpone	这事儿我们推迟到下次会议再讨论吧。
出资	chūzī	provide the fund	中国政府出资在全球办了很多孔子学院。
…算得了什么？	suàndéliǎo shénme	(shucks) it wasn't anything	为自己的女儿花这点儿学费算得了什么？
忙碌	mánglù	busy; bustle about	妈妈为我们、为这个家忙碌了一辈子。

走向	zǒuxiàng	direction; orientation	一看地图就知道这条山脉的走向了。
降低	jiàngdī	lower	你们必须降低成本，可我不能降低要求。
批	pī	pass; approve	银行很快就批了他们的贷款申请。
留神	liúshén	look out; take care	在大城市里开车一定要多留神。
弄假成真	nòngjiǎ chéngzhēn	pretense turns into reality	他们先是闹着玩，可后来弄假成真，打了起来。
拆	chāi	tear apart (down)	他把电脑拆了，装不回去了。
七零八落	qīlíngbāluò	pieces in disorder	园子里的花被大雨打得七零八落。
不予理会	bù yǔ lǐhuì	ignore; dismiss	他对我的建议不予理会。
恶俗	èsú	nasty and vulgar	我不喜欢这种恶俗搞笑没有品味的段子。
诚挚	chéngzhì	sincere	他们不能像以前那样诚挚相待了。
荒诞	huāngdàn	absurd	生长在乡土中国的人还常会感到现代逻辑的荒诞。
明晰	míngxī	clear	戴上新眼镜，所有东西都变得明晰鲜亮了。
要不然	yàoburán	otherwise; or else	走快点吧，要不然就迟到了。
打(借条)	dǎ (jiètiáo)	write (an IOU)	你要跟我借钱得先打张借条。
内心	nèixīn	innermost being; inward	房子的事儿给他的内心造成很大痛苦。
仿佛	fǎngfú	as if; seem	她的工作热情真高，仿佛不知道累似的。
敏感	mǐngǎn	sensitive; vulnerable	她刚离婚，对这样的话题很敏感。
无话不说	wúhuà bùshuō	tell one another everything	她俩一直是无话不说的好朋友。
硌痛	gè tòng	hurt by grit (in the shoe)	鞋里有颗小沙粒，把我的脚硌痛了。
缺陷	quēxiàn	defect; flaw	谁能十全十美没有一点儿缺陷呢？
遮蔽	zhēbì	shroud; cover; hide from view	今年的八月十五阴天，乌云遮蔽了月亮。

刺猬	cìwei	hedgehog	刺猬是身上长有很多刺的小动物。
取暖	qǔnuǎn	warm oneself (by a fire)	冬天的时候，我喜欢坐在火炉边取暖。
不过是	búguòshì	only; merely	你现在面临的不过是个小小的挑战，不要害怕。
平庸	píngyōng	mediocre	过普通人的日子就是平庸吗？
心灵	xīnlíng	heart and soul; internal spirit;	都说孩子的心灵比大人的纯洁，你同意吗？
承担	chéngdān	undertake; bear	是你签的字，你就得承担所有责任。
延长	yáncháng	extend; delay	他不知这样的等待会延长到哪一天。

QUESTIONS FOR DISCUSSION

1. What does the story tell you about China's push to modernize and urbanize?
2. Is the new mortgage policy responsible for Monk's dilemma?
3. Is Tingting's sense of dignity old-fashioned?
4. How do laws and regulations affect love and our ability to love?
5. Why is the male protagonist named Monk?
6. Was Tingting being reasonable/unreasonable when she returned Monk's money? Were Monk's previous misgivings about her misplaced after all?
7. Would their marriage have been a happy one? Why or why not?

1. 这个故事让你对中国现代化、城市化的推进有了什么样的了解？
2. 那个新按揭政策是"和尚"困境的罪魁祸首吗？
3. 婷婷的尊严意识是不是太老套了？
4. 法律和规章制度怎样影响爱和对爱的付出？
5. 男主人公的名字为什么会是"和尚"？
6. 婷婷把钱还给了"和尚。"婷婷的这个做法合不合情理？"和尚"先前对婷婷的疑虑是不是真的没有必要？
7. 如果婷婷和"和尚"结婚了，他们会幸福吗？请说说你的看法。

AUTHOR BIO

This is the same Zhao Yu who wrote "Little Heartaches" in 2007. As the innocence of rural China in the earlier story is disappearing, the frustration of living in urban China in this story is mounting. Zhao Yu wrote "The Cost of Marriage" for his column in a metropolitan daily. This, for him, is a case of circumstance swaying genuine human emotions; and the circumstance is China's rapid economic development. The crumbling of the space for true love is an issue the young in contemporary China face; it is also, in Zhao Yu's opinion, a challenge for humanity. In early 2016 Zhao Yu provided a more recent view of his concerns:[2]

> Writing slowed down in 2015. I've begun to see that many of my views now are a betrayal of my former self. I've also begun to feel that there isn't that much to writing after all. To put things down in words is no longer the most important thing; more valuable are all the activities of mind before writing, the collisions, negotiations, and impacts of thoughts. To publish no longer matters so much when publishers do not share my views of beauty. Reviews of my work do not carry much weight when their goals are either to categorize me or see their own work in print. I've come to realize that writing is but a thought process, a soliloquy. Nothing more.

---

2. Please find this paragraph in Chinese at http://blog.sina.com.cn/s/blog_6a25a9b50102 w3ov.html, accessed on February 18, 2017. Although there are only a few new entries to this personal blog each month, the site provides abundant intimate information about Zhao Yu's views and his state of mind. The passage used in the bio is the opening paragraph of his entry on January 9, 2016, when he was reflecting on the events of the previous year.

3
怀念张美丽

叶仲健

我越来越怀念张美丽了。怀念她的一颦一笑,一举手一投足……

应该悼念她,而不是怀念她。

初夏。夜晚八点钟。出租房。昏黄的灯光下,米兰正准备去上班。工作之前,她必定要花上半个多小时化妆。或者说,化妆也是她工作的一部分。

此时,米兰正在拔眉毛。拔得极细致,一根一根。她的眉毛几乎被她拔光。她还说有了钱要去做激光褪毛,把眉毛全部褪掉,只留下眉痕,然后再用眉笔画上假眉毛。

我不懂把眉毛全部褪掉有什么好看,更不懂为什么褪掉了以后还要画上去。米兰的心思我永远不懂。

可是,我说,张美丽永远烙在我的记忆里,我经常梦见她的样子:梳着两条粗粗的辫子,辫子落落大方地搭在胸前。夏天的时候,她喜欢穿着有大朵大朵花的的确良上衣,下身是一条深蓝色的直筒裤,脚上是一双平底凉鞋。夏天是她一年四季中最美的时候。她皮肤有点儿黑,但看起来很健康。她有着爽朗的笑声,一笑起来就露出洁白的牙齿。每当听到那句"村里有个姑娘叫小芳",我的脑海里总是闪现出她的样子。

我说着,望了一眼米兰。她正将乳白色的洗面奶点在脸上,分成四点:额头、下巴、两颊,然后均匀地抹开。我闭着眼都可以想象出她一系列的

3

MISSING ZHANG MEILI

Ye Zhongjian

I miss Zhang Meili more and more. I miss her frown, her smile, her every gesture and movement...

I should say I mourn her rather than miss her.

Early summer. Eight o'clock in the evening. In a rented room. Under a dim light, Milan is getting ready for work. Every day, before she leaves, she spends more than half an hour making herself up. You might say that putting on makeup is also part of her job.

At this moment, Milan is fixing her eyebrows. She is plucking, meticulously, one hair after another. Her eyebrows are almost gone now. She has said that she'll go get her eyebrows removed by laser when she has the money. She intends to get rid of them completely, leaving only the outlines. She'll then apply false eyebrows to the outlines with a pencil.

I don't see how it would look nice to have one's eyebrows all plucked out, and I understand even less why one would remove them in the first place just to paint them back on again. I have never figured Milan out.

"But," I say, "Zhang Meili has left her permanent mark on my memory. I see her often in my dreams, wearing two thick braids which rested gracefully on her chest. In summer, she liked wearing Dacron shirts with big floral patterns, dark blue, boot-cut pants, and a pair of flat sandals. Of the four seasons, she looked most beautiful in summer. Her skin was a little dark, but she looked very healthy. Her laughs were cheerful, and her spotless white teeth showed when she laughed. Whenever I heard the song, 'A Girl Named Xiao Fang in Our Village,' Zhang Meili's face came to my mind."

As I am talking, I shoot a glance at Milan. She is now dabbing milk-white face wash on her face. She applies it to four areas: her forehead, jaw, and both cheeks, then evens it out. By now, I can see her routine with my eyes

动作：先用洗面奶清洁面部，然后拍上爽肤水，然后涂上润肤露，再然后打上粉底。

我说，张美丽是一个害羞的女孩。我的家离她家挺近，经常在路上碰个正着。每次碰到她，她总不敢跟我打招呼，总抿着嘴跑开。其实我当时也是一个很害羞的人，我喜欢她，可是我不敢向她表白。

在乡下，晚上是宁静的，可是我们这群年轻人不甘寂寞。每当夜晚，只要天气不坏，我们就结伴在乡村的土路上闲逛，一边逛一边聊天，任家乡的灰尘沾满双脚。

她也喜欢跟她的女伴在乡村的土路上闲逛，远远地，没见到她们的身影，就听到她们叽叽喳喳的像麻雀一样的声音。走近了，我们中间的几个男孩就跟她们开玩笑。她们中的几个也会俏皮地顶上几句。但我从没听到张美丽出声顶过我们。她只是笑，黑夜里，在人群中发出银铃般的笑声。

我想，要不是媒人的撮合，我和张美丽可能永远都走不到一块儿，即便我们彼此喜欢着对方。巧的是，那天，媒婆向我和她娘说，他们看起来那么般配，干吗不就近结个亲？也许我娘和她娘以前也这么想过，经媒人这么一提，都说好。我乐坏了。

米兰似乎没在听我讲话，她撅着嘴描口红。昏黄的灯光下，米兰的嘴唇开始泛起暗紫色。她瞄了一眼台上的表，时间已经过去半个小时，她要赶时间去上班。我想我也必须剪短我回忆的内容。

我说，她表面上看起来羞怯柔弱，做起事儿来可是个好把式。洗衣做饭、挑水砍柴、耕田插秧，都不在话下。农忙时节，她喜欢戴一顶草帽，脖子上搭一条湿毛巾，流汗时，用湿毛巾抹一下脸。其实我更喜欢她不戴

closed—first, clean her face, then pat on toner, apply lotion, and finally smear on foundation.

I continue. "Zhang Meili was a shy girl. Since my home was not far from hers, I ran into her often. Every time we met, she would run away from me grinning a toothless smile, too afraid to say hello. I was, to be honest, also quite shy at the time. I had a crush on her but dared not confess it to her.

"In the countryside, it was peaceful and quiet at night. But we young folk didn't want to keep quiet. Every day at nightfall, weather permitting, we hung out on the country dirt road and talked as we walked, allowing the dust of our hometown to cover our feet.

"Zhang Meili liked hanging out with her girlfriends on the country road. Far in the distance, before I could see them, I could hear their chattering like sparrows. As they got closer, some of the boys among us would crack jokes with them and some of them would come back at us with jokes of their own. I never heard Zhang Meili answer back, though. She just laughed, and so, drifting from the crowd into the darkness, her laughs rang like silver bells.

"I believe that if it hadn't been for the efforts of the matchmaker, Zhang Meili and I probably wouldn't have been able to tie the knot, even though we both were in love with each other. It was a lucky coincidence. The day the matchmaker said to my mother and hers that Zhang Meili and I looked like a great match, she asked, 'Why don't your families take advantage of how near you are to one another and become one through marriage?' It was possible that both mothers had already had the same thought, because they went along immediately with the matchmaker's proposal. 'Terrific,' they said. I was elated."

Milan doesn't seem to be listening to me. She pouts her lips to apply her lipstick. Her lips begin to turn dark purple in the dim light. She glances at the clock on the desk. Half an hour has passed. She is in a hurry to get to work. I know I have to cut short my reminiscence.

I go on. "Zhang Meili might have looked shy and vulnerable, but she was actually very good with both domestic chores and farmwork. Washing and cooking, fetching water and gathering firewood, plowing and planting—everything was a cinch for her. During busy farm seasons, she would wear a straw hat and put a wet towel around her neck. When sweat ran down her face, she used the towel to wipe it off. I actually preferred to see her without the hat. When sweat dampened her bangs, she gathered them neatly

草帽的样子,汗水打湿她的刘海儿,她用手一拢,刘海儿就服服帖帖地绕到耳际后,脸上因为汗水的滋润,显得更加圆润。

米兰完成了最后一道工序,缩在沙发里,从烟盒里抽出一支烟,点燃,吸一口,然后将打火机甩在茶几上。她再深吸一口,吐出一道浓浓的烟。烟升腾起来,绕在灯下,许久也不散去。

我说,我见到你抽烟,就想起她对我说的话。她说她不喜欢年轻人抽烟,不喜欢年轻人的嘴里散发出烟臭味。她说只有像她爹一样上了年纪的人才抽烟。她说年轻人就该有年轻人的样子,要健康,要有朝气。她说吸烟有害健康不说,还费钱。所以直到现在,我也不会抽烟,一口也不抽。

米兰有点不耐烦地抽完一支烟,将烟蒂摁熄在烟灰缸里,开始换衣服。她脱掉睡衣,换上了一套紧身的吊带连衣裙。穿好了,她又拿起香水瓶,往腋下喷了几下。其实我很早就跟她说过,她没有狐臭,一点也没有,根本不需要喷香水。

在她做这些的时候,我依旧没有停止对张美丽的想念。我说,其实在乡下挺好的,每天都过得开开心心的。要不是她听了同学的话,执意要去城里工作,我才不会带她到城里。我不觉得城里有多好。人多不说,工作还难找, 东西又贵,出门就要花钱。城里人彼此之间很生分,不像我们乡下人那样亲……时针即将指向九点,米兰穿好衣服,挎上挎包,准备出门。

我朝她的背影喊,张美丽!

米兰很生气地回过头,我跟你说过多少次了,我现在叫米兰,不叫张美丽!你在这里叫叫也就算了,在人多的地方千万别叫我张美丽。

我说咱们就不能回乡下生活吗?

我以前的张美丽,现在的米兰,没回答我,只乜了我一眼,然后重重地甩上了那扇门。

(2012)

behind her ear with a brush of her hand. Her face, damp with perspiration, appeared even more radiant."

Milan completes the final step of her routine. She curls up on the sofa, removes a cigarette from her case, lights it, takes a puff, and then throws the lighter onto the coffee table. She takes another deep drag and lets out a cloud of smoke. The smoke rises, lingers under the lamp, and hangs there.

I say to Milan, "When I see you smoke, I think of what Zhang Meili once said to me. She said she detested the smell of tobacco from the mouths of young people. She said that only people of her father's age smoked, that a young person should look like a young person, healthy and full of vigor. She said smoking was bad for your health, and costly. So to this day, I have not learned how to smoke. I don't smoke, period."

Milan finishes her cigarette impatiently and, quite impatiently, grinds the butt out in the ashtray. Then she starts to change clothes. She takes off her pajamas and gets into a tight-fitting dress with straps. Done dressing, she picks up a bottle of perfume and sprays under her armpits. I had actually told her long ago she didn't need perfume; she never had any body odor.

While she is doing all this, I keep thinking about Zhang Meili. I say, "It was actually really nice living in the countryside. We spent every day happy and content. I wouldn't have brought her to town if she hadn't insisted on coming and working here after her classmate advised it. I didn't think it was all that great in town. The crowds aside, it was hard to find a job here. Things were expensive. You had to spend money the second you stepped out your door. Unlike we country folks, who treat one another like family, the people in town were all strangers..."

The hour hand is pointing at nine o'clock. Milan puts on her jacket, ready to step out with her handbag.

I call after her, "Zhang Meili!"

Milan turns her head angrily. "I've told you over and over: I am Milan now, not Zhang Meili! I'll let you off the hook this time, but make sure you don't call me Zhang Meili in front of people!"

I plead, "Can't we just go back to the country?"

My Zhang Meili before, my Milan now, glares at me. Without a word, she slams the door.

(2012)

VOCABULARY AND USAGE

颦	pín	knit the brows	她的一颦一笑中流露着万般风韵。
举手投足	jǔshǒutóuzú	every move and act; gesture	她举手投足大方自然,很讨人喜欢。
悼念	dàoniàn	mourn	我们怀念的人可能在远方,但我们悼念的人一定已经逝去。
褪(毛)	tuì (máo)	shed (hair on the body)	在乡下过年,各家各户都是自己杀鸡褪毛。
痕	hén	trace	洪水留在墙上的水痕有一人高。
烙	lào	burn (into memory)	烙在心底的伤痛是忘不了的。
梳(辫子)	shū (biànzi)	wear (ponytail)	为什么清朝的男子都梳一根长辫子?
落落大方	luòluòdàfāng	natural and graceful	她举手投足落落大方。
搭	dā	hang (over)	他把一只手搭在我的肩上说:"有我在别担心。"
脑海	nǎohǎi	head; brain	往日的她又常常在我脑海里闪现。
闪现	shǎnxiàn	flash before one	
颊	jiá	cheeks	一看她红红的脸颊就知道是个健康的孩子。
一系列	yīxiliè	a series of	这一系列的问题都是你一时粗心造成的。
拍(爽肤水)涂	pāi (shuǎng fūshuǐ)	pat; apply (toner)	妈妈每天就涂点儿润肤露,从来不往脸上拍什么爽肤水。
(润肤露)	tú (rùnfūlù)	apply (lotion); daub	
打(粉底)	dǎ (fěndǐ)	apply; put on	你粉底打得太厚,把脸上的灵气都遮没了。
碰个正着	pèng ge zhèngzháo	happen upon each other	他转身要逃,结果与对面来的警察碰个正着。

抿(嘴)	mǐn (zuǐ)	close (mouth) lightly	读到有趣的地方，她就抿嘴笑笑。
表白	biǎobái	confess one's love	你这么爱她，为什么不向她表白？
不甘寂寞	bù gān jìmò	unwilling to be out of the limelight	不甘寂寞的人会不会更有创造性？
结伴	jié bàn	form companionships; go in company with	他喜欢与朋友结伴旅游。
闲逛	xián guàng	stroll; lounge	我喜欢一个人到处闲逛。
沾满	zhān mǎn	be stained (covered) with	从林子里回来，他靴子上沾满了泥巴。
叽叽喳喳	jījizhāzhā	chirp; chatter continuously	三个女孩儿在一起叽叽喳喳了一个晚上。
俏皮	qiàopí	wittily; lively and delightful	这个聪明的小姑娘很会说俏皮话。
顶	dǐng	retort; answer back; go against	有些十几岁的孩子很喜欢跟父母顶着干。
彼此	bǐcǐ	both parties; one another	婚姻中彼此的尊重和关照很重要。
般配	bānpèi	be well matched	这对夫妻一个爱说话、一个很会听，特别般配。
就近	jiùjìn	(do or get something) nearby	我们小时候都是就近上学。
结亲	jiéqīn	become related by marriage	孩子们领了结婚证，咱们两家就正式结亲了。
经…这么一提	jīng… zhème yītí	after such a reminder…	经朋友这么一提，她突然记起了那个老孟。
…坏了	…huàile	extremely…	看到他主动联系我，我高兴坏了。
撅	juē	protrude; stick up	她一不开心就撅嘴。
描	miáo	trace (the outline of)	你把眉毛描的太黑了，有点儿假了。
泛起	fànqǐ	appear; emerge	月光下，湖面泛起点点银光。
回忆	huíyì	recollection	四年的大学生活给我留下美好的回忆。

好把式	hǎobǎshì	highly skilled at	做农活，他可是个好把式。
不在话下	bùzàihuàxià	nothing difficult	他是长跑运动员，走两公里的路对他来说不在话下。
打湿	dǎshī	wet; damp	我的衣服被雨水打湿了。
服帖	fútiē	obedient; well arranged	你用点儿发乳，卷起的头发就会服帖了。
耳际	ěrjì	ears; around the ears	耳际的头发还是太长，你再帮我修一下吧。
圆润	yuánrùn	smooth and round; mellow	她圆润的脸庞散发着青春的气息。
工序	gōngxù	(a) procedure	这个零件的制作工序复杂。
缩	suō	huddle; cower	她缩在沙发的一角看书。
甩	shuǎi	toss; throw; fling	他一回家就把手机甩在了沙发上。
浓烟	nóng yān	dense smoke	电厂烟筒冒出的浓烟说明他们还在用煤发电。
许久	xǔjiǔ	for a long time	我们坐在餐厅里聊了许久。
摁	èn	press (with hand or finger)	后面的车一直在摁喇叭，是不是我们开得太慢了？
熄	xī	extinguish; put out	消防员用灭火器熄灭了大火。
吊带	diàodài	sling; strap	妹妹喜欢穿吊带衫。
喷	pēn	spray	她出门前必得喷香水。
狐臭	húchòu	body odor	有狐臭的人要多洗澡。
…不说，…还…	…bù shuō,…hái…	not to mention; leave aside	城里这么挤不说，很多地段还不安全。
生分	shēngfen	distant; aloof	多年不见，儿时的玩伴长大了，也都变得生分了。
挎	kuà	carry on the arm	她胳膊上挎着一个篮子，里面放满了鲜花。

QUESTIONS FOR DISCUSSION

1. Is this story about the mutability of supposedly immutable things, like love?
2. Why doesn't the husband like the changes in his life? Use the story to support your view.
3. Why doesn't he get a divorce and be done with it?
4. Can you pinpoint where you realized, in reading the story, that Zhang Meili and Milan were one and the same?
5. Why does the story pay such close attention to the ritual of Milan getting ready for the night?
6. What aspect(s) of rural life in this story strikes you as refreshing?
7. Does this story help you understand the struggles of everyday people due to contemporary China's steep increase in urbanization?

1. 这个故事是在写本应一成不变的东西的易变性吗？比方说像爱这种东西？
2. 故事中的丈夫为什么不喜欢他生活中的变化？请用文中的具体例子说明你的观点。
3. 这位丈夫为什么不离婚，一了百了呢？
4. 你能说出你是在阅读中的哪一刻意识到张美丽就是米兰的吗？
5. 为什么这个故事对米兰晚间上班前收拾打扮的程序进行了如此细致的描写？
6. 故事中的乡下生活有哪些方面让你感觉清新愉悦？
7. 这个故事能帮助你理解在中国城市化飙进的过程中平民老百姓每日的挣扎吗？

AUTHOR BIO

A native of Lianjiang County, Fujian Province, Ye Zhongjian (1982–), following his family, started his migration toward the city at the age of twenty-three. He could not help reminiscing about the small village life he had left behind as they were getting closer to the urban life to which they had aspired. Being who he is, he says, he has abided by the doctrine of means

(中庸之道 *zhōngyōng zhī dào*) faithfully since childhood. He is therefore happy being a man of more thoughts than he expresses.

After graduating from a special college training program in 2001, he worked for the local radio and TV bureau, a subsidiary of China Mobile Communications Corporation, and the local branch of the State Administration of Taxations before he founded a finance and tax consulting firm. A conscientious person, Ye Zhongjian gives his best at work, and that makes his days go by faster.

Writing short-shorts is but a spare-time hobby. Yet Ye Zhongjian has managed to become a nationally acknowledged "emerging writer" (明日之星 *míng rì zhī xīng*) after winning third place in a national competition for novices in 2008. Such prestigious journals as *Selected Fiction* (小说选刊), *Readers* (读者), and *Yilin Magazine* (意林), as well as *Selected Short-Shorts* (小小说选刊) and *Selected Micro-fiction* (微型小说选刊), have published his works. Many of them have been included in annually compiled anthologies; among them "Missing Zhang Meili," "Looking for Liang Shanbo" ("寻找梁山伯"), and "Tuberose in May" ("五月夜来香"). Ye Zhongjian has just returned to writing in 2016 after a few years' silence.

4
薄荷的邀请

田双伶

时令过了谷雨,她家门前的小园子,仍是空空的、黄黄的一片,好像一个心情不好的妇人,板着一张蜡黄的素脸。

她的心情就很不好。怎么可能好呢?从那场婚姻中流落出来,她就病了,整日昏沉沉的,头痛、恶心、烦躁、失眠,黑苦的中药汤汁喝了一碗碗,也没减轻多少。

而邻家和她一样大的园子,此时已热闹喧腾腾一片了。春韭已割了好几茬儿,垄间的油菜日渐稠密,薄荷的嫩芽从惊蛰到现在都没停止过往外拱,一芽芽一丛丛地四处蔓延。她每次都心悸地看上一眼,等它越过边界的时候,就毫不犹豫地将它拔掉。

她端着一杯红茶站在园子里,晒着上午十点钟的太阳,看胖胖的邻家女人蹲在地里割韭菜,看她腰间露出一道让人心惊的赘肉。她想,可惜了这么好的园子,怎么能种这些俗气的蔬菜呢?应该栽上蔷薇或是紫藤,让它

4

THE MINT'S INVITATION

Tian Shuangling

Translated by Zhang Shuhan

Grain Rain[3] had already passed, but the small garden in front of her house was still barren and sallow, like a woman in a bad mood pulling a sickly straight face.

She happened to be in a bad mood. How could she be in a good one? Ever since she wandered into exile from that marriage, she'd been sick, stricken with drowsiness, headaches, nausea, irritation, and insomnia. Bowl after bowl of dark and bitter traditional Chinese medicine hadn't helped her feel much better.

Her neighbor's garden, the same size as hers, was already teeming with thriving greens at this time. The spring chives had been harvested several times already. The canola was becoming denser between the ridges, day by day. Ever since the Awakening of Insects,[4] the young mint leaves had been inching out in all directions, one sprout and shrub at a time. When she looked at them, she shuddered. Once they crossed the border, she'd pull them out without a second thought.

She was standing in her garden with a cup of black tea in her hand, basking under the 10 a.m. sun, and watching the stout woman next door squatting in her garden, harvesting chives. She eyed the regrettable fold in her neighbor's waist, then thought what a shame it was for such a beautiful garden. How could she use it to grow such lowly vegetables? There should have been roses or wisterias planted there to climb up the window bars,

---

3. Grain Rain (谷雨 *gǔyǔ*) is the sixth solar term in the traditional East Asian calendar. It usually falls between April 19 and 21, when an increase in the amount of rain greatly benefits the crops.
4. Awakening of Insects (惊蛰 *jīngzhé*) is the third of twenty-four solar terms. It is when the sun is at the celestial longitude of 345 degrees and thunderstorms wake up the hibernating insects.

们顺着窗栏往上攀，藤蔓垂下一簇簇小花，坐在花香里读书喝茶，多好。可是，从初冬搬倒这里，她还不知道该怎么去栽种花木，园里自然是空空的春风不度。

邻家女人吃力地站起身，看见她，隔着低矮的栅栏递过一把韭菜，说，前天下了场雨，就蹿着长起来了，你也尝尝鲜。

她的笑容掩起了不屑，说，谢了，我不习惯那味道。

邻家女人笑呵呵地说，我家那口子呀，特爱吃韭菜馅饺子，每次包饺子他都能吃好多。

她听了，无力地垂下眼皮摇摇头说，我头痛。转身要回屋。

女人看她摇头闭眼痛苦的样子，说，你等等。说完弯腰掐了几片薄荷叶，在指间揉碎，朝她伸过手说，来。

她怯怯地将头低垂着伸过去，听话地让女人把那一团青绿涂在太阳穴上。瞬间，一丝清凉从太阳穴沁入鬓角，将她从混沌中缓缓唤醒。

真是奇了，她向邻家女人道谢。女人乐呵呵地指着地上的薄荷说，管用你就随便掐，掐了还会发的。

天依然晴好。隔着栅栏，她细细看邻家的园子，西墙角扯的晾衣绳上，五彩斑斓地挂满了衣物：孩子的小衣裤、男女皱巴巴的衣裤，女人的花上衣，褪了色的床单被罩，一看就是含棉量不高爱起球的化纤织物。

邻家女人身上穿件松松垮垮的睡衣，端着红色塑料盆给菜浇水。屋里传出孩子的哭闹声，女人一边吆喝男人去哄孩子，一边叨叨着菜叶上怎么长了虫子。

她与邻家，只隔着一道木栅栏，却仿佛隔了世间的一层烟火。这样的俗日子，在她眼前，生动着，美好着。

clusters of florets hanging down from their vines. How pleasant it would be, she thought, to read books and drink tea in the fragrance of flowers! But she had just moved there last winter. She hadn't learned how to grow a flower garden yet, so naturally spring had yet to visit her barren garden.

The woman next door lumbered to her feet, saw her, and offered some chives over the low garden fence, "The chives shot up after it rained the day before yesterday. Please have a fresh taste of the season."

A smile hid her disdain, "Thanks, but the odor doesn't agree with me."

The neighbor responded merrily, "My husband loves dumplings with chives in the filling. He stuffs himself every time I make them."

The woman listened, and then with an effort, lowered her eyelids, shook her head, and said, "I have a headache." She turned to go back inside.

Her neighbor, seeing her painful look as she shook her head with her eyes closed, asked her to wait. She then bent down, nipped a few mint leaves, crumbled them into pieces with her fingers, and extended her hand in invitation, "Come over."

The woman leaned over diffidently, her head obediently lowered, and let her neighbor rub the gobbet of green onto her temples. A refreshing feeling instantly spread over her scalp, gradually awakening her from her disordered state of mind.

It was really amazing! She thanked her neighbor. The woman pointed cheerfully to the mint on the ground and said, "Feel free to take them if it helps. They'll grow back."

. . . It was another nice day. The woman discreetly looked across the fence at her neighbor's garden. The clothing line in the west corner was hung full of colorful clothes: small items for children, wrinkled clothes for men and women, a woman's floral top, a faded cheap bedsheet and a duvet cover. From one look, you could tell they were made of blended fabric with low cotton content, prone to pill formation.

The neighbor was in her loose sleepwear, watering vegetables with a red plastic basin in her hand. A baby's cry came from the house. She called for her husband to go comfort the baby while wondering out loud why there were insects on the vegetable leaves.

The two houses had only a wooden fence between them; but it seemed as if a screen separated her from a living world of smoke and fire. Her neighbor's mundane life, now shimmering in front of her eyes, had become marvelous!

邻家女人指着地上那丛青绿的薄荷，唤她，过来摘呀。

她一次次走进邻家的园子。三片两片薄荷叶就那么一掐一揉一抹，一丝清凉，竟然让她的头痛一天天好起来。

每到中午时分，隔壁的厨房里便传出有节奏的叮当声，继而爆油锅的刺啦声，葱花的香气飘过来。她贪婪地嗅着那香，觉得自己像个窥视的小鬼，在吸纳人间的烟火。

屋里只她一人，静得很。她越来越怕这种静了。静，如一个无声无形的鬼，悄然藏在身旁，一丝丝吸纳她的元气。

她将冰冷的咖啡壶，面包机，料理机，都收到柜子里，又去超市买了花围裙，在菜场买了韭菜、鲜肉和面粉，备全了调料，她想包回饺子，做个勤快妇人。

往日冷清的厨房热闹起来。她笨拙地调馅、和面、擀皮儿，不一会儿，鼻尖上手臂上全是面粉，照镜子一看，自己都笑得不行。饺子煮熟了，她盛了一个尝，一下子烫了舌头嘴唇，泪都出来了。抹泪的那一瞬间她怆然失神：从前的婚姻，独独缺了这烟火气呀。自己做给那人吃的，什么鲜花沙拉、海鲜料理，对脾胃都没有亲和力；即使那人爱吃的饺子、汤圆，也煮的都是速冻食品，难怪那人苦笑着说吃得胃寒，都成了速冻人了。

婚姻就是这样冷下来得。原来想把恋爱时的浪漫情调带到婚姻里，如同把黄山的云雾装入坛子里一样不现实。

她将饺子煮好，晾凉，小心地盛进保温盒，拎着出门，坐上工交车转过大半个城市。她要去送给那个人吃。

Pointing at that green mint shrub on the ground, the neighbor beckoned her, "Come pick some!"

She walked into the neighbor's garden many times after that, plucking a couple of mint leaves each time, crushing them and rubbing them to get that refreshing feeling—and surprisingly, just like that, her headaches were eventually cured.

Every noon, a noisy, clattering rhythm would come from her neighbor's kitchen, followed by the popping sound of chopped green onion in heated oil, and its delicious smell. She sniffed greedily, felt like a spying elf inhaling the essence of the human world next door.

She was alone in her house, and it was very quiet. More and more, she grew afraid of this silence. Like an apparition without sound or form, it hid by her side, furtively draining her vitality, bit by bit.

She put away the cold coffeemaker, bread maker, and food processor in the cupboard. Then she went to the supermarket and bought an apron with a flowery pattern. She got chives, ground pork, and flour from the food market, and all the seasonings she needed. For once, she wanted to make dumplings and be a busy housewife.

The deserted kitchen bustled with life. Clumsily, she made the filling, the dough, and the dumpling skins. In a short while, the tip of her nose and her arms were covered with flour. She looked at herself in the mirror and couldn't help giggling. When the dumplings were cooked, she scooped one up and tasted it, only to burn her tongue and lips, and draw tears to her eyes. As she was wiping her tears, it suddenly dawned on her—what her marriage lacked was exactly this kind of smoke and fire! The food she made for her man, flower salad and seafood sushi and so on, did not appeal to his stomach nor did it agree with his kidneys. Even the dumplings and the glutinous rice balls he liked, he only got flash-frozen, not freshly cooked. No wonder he said with a wry smile that the food made him cold from the inside out and was turning him into a frozen man.

That was how their marriage had cooled off. It turned out that her wish to keep the romance of their courtship during marriage was as unpractical as trying to bottle the clouds and fogs of Mount Huangshan.

She boiled some dumplings, cooled them, then carefully put them into a thermal box and went out. She rode the bus all the way across the city. She did this to bring the dumplings to him.

当她把饭盒端给那人，掀开盖子，她看到了一双黑眸闪出的惊喜，顷刻化为湿润。

她的日子开始活色生香。每天清晨，她步履轻盈地拎着篮子去菜场，回来后篮子里装满了新鲜的菜蔬、鱼和豆腐，米粮菜蔬在她的手中如花落花开。饭食做好装好，而后，拎着保温盒，坐上公交车绕过一条条街道，送到那人面前。洗手坐羹汤，原来也是如此的幸福。她明白了以往朋友说的那句话：再精美的瓷器，能有粗瓷大碗端在手里实在吗？

立夏过了五六天，那人和她一起回到家里。她牵着那人的手去看邻家的园子，欢欣地指给他看，却惊奇地发现：邻家的薄荷，竟然不管不顾地，已经在她家的园子里恣意丛生，串了一大片。

以前她曾经想，等它越过边界的时候，就毫不犹豫地将它拔除，可是，这绿叶舒展的薄荷，谁能拒绝得了它呢？

她说，我们采些做薄荷茶，邀请我们的邻居来品尝吧。

那人说，好啊。

初夏的空气中，清凉的薄荷香气从她的园子里弥漫开来。

(2012)

When she brought the thermal box to him and opened the lid, she saw his dark eyes light up, then quickly grow wet.

Her life regained its color. Every morning at dusk, she would go to the market with a basket in her hand and a spring in her step. When she came back, her basket would be full of fresh vegetables, fish, tofu, and so on. Food came to life and blossomed in her hands. When the meal was cooked and packed, she'd take the bus across many streets to bring it to her man. Who'd have thought that the simple acts of washing hands and making soup could also bring her so much happiness! She finally understood what a friend once said, "However fine a porcelain utensil, it can't be as dependable as a coarse, sturdy bowl!"

Five or six days after the Start of Summer,[5] he came back home to her. She led her man by the hand to the neighbor's garden. As she was happily showing him the garden, she found to her surprise that her neighbor's mints had taken the liberty of crossing over. They had taken root in her garden and were spreading generously over a large area.

She had once thought she would pull them out without hesitation. Well, this mint with green, spreading leaves, who had the power to resist it?

"Let's pick some mint to make tea and invite our neighbor over," she suggested.

"Sure," the man said.

The refreshing fragrance of mint spread from her garden into the early summer air.

(2012)

---

5. Start of Summer (立夏 *lìxià*) is the seventh solar term; it begins around May 5 and ends around May 21.

VOCABULARY AND USAGE

时令	shílìng	seasons	羊肉热量很高，夏天吃不合时令。
板脸	bǎnliǎn	have a taut face	你不高兴也不能在顾客面前板着脸。
蜡黄	làhuáng	sallow	她病得不轻，脸色蜡黄。
素脸	sùliǎn	face without makeup	你是大明星，哪能素脸出门？
流落	liúluò	drift out	你怎么会一个人流落到这里？家人都哪儿去了？
减轻	jiǎnqīng	ease; alleviate	这药治不好你的病，但能减轻你的痛苦。
汤汁	tāngzhī	soup; broth	这样煲汤，肉没什么味道了，汤汁却格外鲜美。
热闹喧腾一片	rènào xuānténg yīpiàn	lively and noisy a scene of ...	除夕的家乡，到处都是一片热闹喧腾的景象。
好	hǎo	an adverb to emphasize	这首歌我今天又听了好几遍。
茬	chá	a measure word (for a crop); batch	这里气候温暖，一年至少可以种两茬庄稼。
渐	jiàn	gradually; by degrees	天气渐冷，出门要多穿点儿衣服。
拱	gǒng	sprout up through the earth	小苗已经拱出土了，春天真的是来到了。
晒	shài	bask in (sunshine)	他的皮肤一晒就黑。
赘肉	zhuìròu	unwanted fat; bulge	真想把腰上的赘肉减掉！
攀	pān	climb; clamber	常春藤顺着墙一直攀到了房顶。
簇	cù	a measure word; pile; bunch	窗边开着一簇小紫花。
春风不度	chūnfēngbú dù	no sign of spring	为什么邻家园子春意盎然，我家的却春风不度？
蹿	cuān	shoot up; leap up	雨后竹节上蹿的可快了。

尝鲜	cháng xiān	have a taste of seasonal delicacy	这是今年的第一茬韭菜，你尝尝鲜吧。
掐	qiā	pinch; nip	她掐了一下他的胳膊，把他弄醒了。
丝	sī	a measure word	从门缝透进来一丝凉气。
清凉	qīngliáng	cool and refreshing	夏天大家都爱喝茶和酸梅汁等清凉饮料。
沁入	qìn rù	soak into; permeate	这花香从鼻孔沁入肺腑。
鬓角	bìnjiǎo	temple	爸爸的头发已从鬓角处开始变白。
道谢	dàoxiè	express one's thanks	他拿到大奖时首先向他小学的语文老师道谢。
管用	guǎnyòng	effective	这药真管用，药到病除。
晾	liàng	air; dry in the sun	在这两棵树之间扯根绳子可以晾衣服。
斑斓	bānlán	bright/multicolored	新英格兰的十月，红枫争妍，秋色斑斓。
皱巴巴	zhòubābā	wrinkled; crumpled	衣着简朴不丢人，但皱巴巴的不整洁很丢人。
含	hán	contain	这些饮料都放了很多糖，也就是说含糖量都很高。
爱	ài	tend to; be apt to	她就是爱计较小事的那种人，别跟她一般见识。
起球	qǐ qiú	piling; balling up	材质好的衣服是不会起球的。
吆喝	yāohe	cry out; shout; yell	有人敲门，妈妈吆喝我去开门。
叨叨	dāodao	chatter away	这点儿小事她叨叨了好几天了。
长	zhǎng	there exist; have	菜叶上长虫子是正常的。
继而	jì'ér	then; afterward	他说出了问题所在，继而又提出一系列解决办法。

爆锅	bàoguō	quick stir-fry in hot oil	中国人做很多菜的第一步都是用葱花儿爆锅。
刺啦	cīlā	an onomatopoeia	油锅热了，下菜时就会发出刺啦的声响。
调(馅儿)	tiáo (xiàn'er)	make, season, and mix (filling)	很多在北方长大的女孩子都会调馅儿、擀皮、包饺子。
擀	gǎn	roll (out a dumpling wrapper)	
瞬间	shùnjiān	(a) moment; (in an) instant	看到妈妈躺在病榻上的那一瞬间，我泪流满面。
怆然	chuàngrán	sad; mournfully	她意识到了问题的严重性，怆然失神。
失神	shīshén	out of sorts	
亲和力	qīnhélì	affable; friendly; approachable	他这个人很有亲和力，身边总是围着很多朋友。
坛子	tánzi	jar; earthen jar	这个坛子可以用来做泡菜。
拎	līn	lift; carry	他从地上拎起箱子走了。
眸	móu	pupil of eye; eye	他双眸明亮，神气十足。
闪	shǎn	spark; flash	一个念头闪过我的脑海。
顷刻	qǐngkè	instantly; in no time	他的一句"对不起"使多年的恩怨顷刻消解。
活色生香	huósèshēngxiāng	lively and colorful	日子要过的活色生香就得在柴米油盐上下功夫。
步履轻盈	bùlǚqīngyíng	light-footed; breeze along	心情愉快就会步履轻盈。
羹汤	gēngtāng	broth	在外她是女主管，回家她洗手做羹汤。
瓷器	cíqì	porcelain; chinaware	轻薄精美的瓷器往往中看不中用。
恣意	zìyì	willful; recklessly	六月的野草恣意丛生，怎么拔都拔不尽。
丛生	cóngshēng	overgrown	
串	chuàn	string together; cluster together	我用一根线串起十颗珠子。

舒展	shūzhǎn	stretching; unfolding; extending	经济舱的座位太挤，没有舒展手脚的空间。
采	cǎi	pluck; gather	她从花园里采回些鲜花。
品尝	pǐncháng	taste; sample	在中国，每到一地，我都会去品尝特色的美食。
弥漫	mímàn	pervade; diffuse	屋里弥漫着咖啡的浓香。

QUESTIONS FOR DISCUSSION

1. Can you describe the main character? Can you guess her background? Age? Values? Economic status?
2. Can you describe the woman next door? Why did the main character look down upon her in the beginning?
3. Who would want to "bottle the clouds and fogs of Mount Huangshan"? Why is the story critical of such a view of life?
4. What does mint represent in this story? How does this story connect this plant's life with human life?
5. Discuss the use of some of the twenty-four solar terms, especially why it is important to use them in this story.
6. Do you believe the way to a man's heart is through his stomach? What is cooking to the woman when food blossoms in her hands as she cooks?
7. Is this story antifeminist? Or is it that it has a different view of gender equality and of what constitutes positions of power?

1. 你能描述一下女主人公吗？能猜一下她的背景，包括年龄、三观、经济状况等吗？
2. 你能描述一下邻家女人吗？故事一开始，女主人公为什么瞧不起她？
3. 什么样的人想 "把黄山的云雾装入坛子"？故事为什么对这样的生活观持批评态度？
4. 薄荷在故事中意指什么？这个故事怎样把薄荷的属性和生活的道理联系起来？
5. 请讨论一下故事对时令节气的运用，尤其是这样的运用为什么在故事中很重要。

6. 你相信让男人吃好他才会爱你吗？如果 "粮米菜蔬" 在做饭女人的手中 "花落花开，"那做饭对她来说是一种什么样的经历？
7. 这是一个反女性主义的故事吗？还是故事对什么是性别平等、权利地位由什么组成等有着不同的见解？

AUTHOR BIO

If there is such a thing as a representative image of Chinese women, Tian Shuangling (1976–) might be it. She is traditional and modern, belongs to the small town and the big city at the same time, loves everyday life and enjoys the metaphysical. Born into a family of educators in Xinxiang County, Henan Province, Shuangling graduated from the Chinese Department of Henan University. She worked as a teacher, a news reporter, and an editor before she joined the staff of *Selected Short-Shorts* (小小说选刊), arguably the best journal of the short-short genre in China, in 2006.

Thanks to her mother, she was exposed to fairy tales, poetry, and traditional Chinese culture from childhood. She began to publish poetry and prose essays in newspapers when touched by people and things around her in high school. Her experience as a news reporter and her involvement in psychological counseling later on brought her into contact with women of different social classes. When she learned about the vicissitudes of their fates and their complex states of mind, her writing focused on the contemplation of their issues—the value of their existence and the nature of their emotional problems. Since she made the transition in 2004 from prose to short-short stories, she has become increasingly concerned with female psychology and sentiments. Taking material from real life, often a snapshot of the everyday, Tian Shuangling approaches her female subjects with maturity, understanding, and empathy, and she articulates their unique feelings and views of life, love, and marriage from their perspectives. Among her recent works are "The Mint's Invitation" ("薄荷的邀请"), "No Spring Here" ("春天别来"), "Colorado Moonlight" ("科罗拉多的月光"), and "Scissors' Matchmaking for the Needle" ("剪刀替针做媒人").

Tian Shuangling's works have appeared in many publications; her stories have also been selected for publication in many anthologies and annual collections. When writing, she takes advantage of the ideas/moods/ beauty of traditional Chinese poetry in depicting the subtle psychology of her female characters, which, she believes, can be felt but not fully spoken. She does not write to register experiences or emotions; she aspires for the poetic beauty of language, which makes reading a pleasurable experience. For Tian Shuangling, her female characters—their experiences, attitudes, understanding of love, empathy, and self-reflective behavior—are sources of wisdom and expressions of beauty.

第九章

易

矛盾文学奖是中国最高的文学奖项之一。该奖每四年颁发一次，奖励最佳长篇小说的作家。五位作家在2015年获此殊荣。本章的两位作者，王蒙和格非，便是这五人中的两位。在结尾的一章中选用他们的故事，意在为读者提供一个机会，了解一下当代中国最有影响力的作家和思想家是怎样看待变化和预示未来的。

小小说《未来》取自王蒙的《尴尬风流》（2005）一书。那是一本打破了线性外壳的非常规小说。它由三百多个跟《未来》类似的小故事组成，勇于自嘲的老王是这些故事的中心人物——一个既乐观明智又忧心忡忡，还时不常就会出点儿错的老人。《尴尬风流》的新颖结构体现了作者对现实世界非线性的认知，同时也表达了他回追中国传统想象的愿望。对生活的悖论没有答案，很尴尬；但能为生活操心、能质疑现实、能选择或放弃不同的可能等，也是蛮"风流"的。《未来》这个小故事，它内省和反思的基调，再加上王蒙乐观的态度，折射出了当代中国面向未来的态度——一个一如既往根植于传统的态度。

CHAPTER 9

CHANGES

One of the highest awards for literature in China is the Mao Dun Literary Award (矛盾文学奖). It is awarded every four years to writers of full-length novels. Five authors received this honor in 2015. The authors included in this chapter, Wang Meng and Ge Fei, are two of the top five. Ending this volume with their stories is meant to provide readers an opportunity to see how some of the most influential writers and critical thinkers in contemporary China perceive changes and envision the future.

The short-short "Future" is taken from Wang Meng's *Embarrassing and Enchanting* (尴尬风流, *Gāngà fēngliú*, 2005), an unconventional book of fiction that cracks its linear shell into over three hundred pieces similar in style to the titular story. The self-deprecating Lao Wang is at the center of all the stories. Although optimistic and wise, he constantly worries and is all too prone to making mistakes. *Embarrassing and Enchanting*'s innovative structure results from its writer's view of reality as nonlinear, as well as from his desire to recover a traditional Chinese imagination. Embarrassing as it may be not to have any answers for life's paradoxes, it's enchanting to be able to worry and question reality, as well as to let go and accept life's possibilities. The introspective and reflective tone combined with Wang Meng's optimistic attitude makes this story an important reflection of contemporary China's stance toward the future, a stance that, as always, is rooted in the past.

《易经》（约公元前12世纪）是中华文明的基石之著。《易经》的"易"字强调现实不可分割的三个方面："简单"、"变"和"不变"[1]。宇宙的运动之所以"简单"是因为它们"自然"（自己使然）。虽然"变"是所有物象的本质，而变化的状态，或者说"变"作为抽象的宇宙规律，是不变的；同时，每个"变"的现象，它内在的规律，如太阳东升西落等，也是不变的。只有当我们从这几方面综合理解老王对当代中国变化的担忧时，我们才有可能开始体会理解他的感受。在他眼前发生的变化到底是什么？过度的欲望和人为的操作给"自然"的宇宙规律带来了什么？在追求以生理快感和金钱利润为主导的时代，不变的生活之常到哪里去了？《未来》这个故事提请读者思考中国社会的现状以及它的走向。

道德判断不会对理解《不可知的偶然》中的人物有太多帮助。毕竟，绝对真理，以及得到它的途径，这些东西在中国文化传统中的地位甚微。给一个孩子贴上一个"说谎者"的标签有什么好处呢？它不过是给不可能也不应该类化的人戴上了一个类别的帽子，再次见证了两极观的幼稚罢了。阅读这个故事的时候，铭记中国人由"易"而来的宇宙观会帮助读者的理解。如果我们视天下生命为息息相关，并同处于变化的过程之中，那很有可能故事中的那一男一女也会把孩子成长变化的潜力看得比什么都重要，也希望为实现这一潜力尽绵薄之力。这样的对众生命脉相连的确认也揭示了儒家和道家的一个基本信仰——人类对善和美的自然向往。

《不可知的偶然》是最好不过的收卷篇，因为它涉及到许多此书所收故事的主题。其中尤其值得一提的是依礼而行的重要性；人类相互依赖关系的根本性；阴阳的运作和功用；人类和自然界的活力及不确定性；形而上的奥妙及其形而下的体现；真挚无私的爱；identity作为各种力量相互作用的动态存在；对他人尊严的敬重；向善的本能；德行的愉悦；还有在赏识

---

1. 请参阅钱钟书的《管锥篇》（香港：中华书局，1979）1：6-7和孙筑瑾的《中英文抒情诗中的重复诗学》（芝加哥大学出版社，2011年）一书的第8页。以上对"易"的理解受益于他们的著作。东汉的郑玄（25-220 AC）对"易"的阐述也很有帮助。下面这个网页有对郑玄见解的介绍：http://baike.baidu.com/subview/2693/5404041.htm?fromtitle=易经&fromid=153636&type=syn。

The Book of Changes (易经 *Yijing*, ca. twelfth-century B.C.E.) is a foundational work of Chinese civilization. An accepted understanding of the *yi* of *Yijing* emphasizes three indivisible aspects of reality: "simple," "change," and "no change."[1] Cosmic movements are simple, because they are *ziran* (self-thus). Although change is the nature of all physical phenomena, the state of change, or change as the abstract law of the cosmos, stays constant, and the internal pattern for each phenomenon, such as the sun's rising in the east and setting in the west, reflects no change. When we understand Lao Wang's concerns about the changes in contemporary China in these combined senses, we may begin to feel what he feels. What are the changes happening in front of his eyes? What have excessive desires and human manipulation done to *ziran*, the self-thus of cosmic patterns? What happens to the constant of life when subjugation to physical pleasure and financial profit dominate? This story invites contemplations about where Chinese society is now and where it is going.

Moral judgment does not help much in understanding the characters in "Unknowable Possibilities." After all, Chinese cultural traditions place little value on absolute truth or access to it. What good does it do to label the boy a "liar" besides categorizing what cannot be categorized and reconfirming a simplistic binary view? The Chinese cosmic visions from *yi* may be helpful to remember while reading. When everyone is regarded as connected and thus equally affected by the process of transformation, it becomes possible that the man and woman in the story value the boy's potential for growth more than anything else and want to help realize it. Such acknowledgment of the interconnectedness of all beings also suggests a fundamental Confucian and Taoist belief in the simple human inclination toward the good and the beautiful.

"Unknowable Possibilities" is a fitting story with which to close the volume, because it touches on many of the themes present in the stories collected here, especially the value of respectful actions appropriate to their contexts, the fundamental sense of the reciprocity of human relationships,

---

1. Please see Qian Zhongshu's *Guanzhui bian* (Hong Kong: Zhonghua, 1979, 1: 6–7); and Cecilia Chu-chin Sun's *The Poetics of Repetition in English and Chinese Lyric Poetry* (Chicago: Chicago University Press, 2011, 8). Reading them inspires an understanding of *yi*. The elaboration of Zheng Xuan (郑玄) of the Eastern Han dynasty (25–220 CE) at http://baike.baidu.com/subview/2693/5404041.htm?fromtitle=易经&fromid=153636&type=syn also helped.

世间一切内在联系的同时，关注眼下和现实的必要。毋庸赘言，帮助学生提高语言能力是本书的重要目的，倘若这里所选的小小说同时还能像其它文学作品一样，通过阅读的愉悦引发学生对上述主题的进一步思考，那么为他们创造跨文化学习机会的真正有价值的目的也就达到了。

the working of yin and yang, the unpredictability and vitality of nature and the human world, the metaphysical and its physical expressions, love for a person for his or her own sake, identity as the interaction of forces forever changing, the respect for human dignity, the innate inclination in all to do good and the pleasure that comes from virtuous behavior, and the necessity of attention to the present moment and real life while recognizing the inner connectedness of the universe. Like all works of literature, the short-shorts collected here will have served a real purpose if, along with improving language abilities, they function as a delightful tool for further reflections on these issues and opportunities for cross-cultural learning.

1
未来

王蒙

老王家的对过儿,出现了一批高级铺面房。老王无端地相信,这里边应该有一家邮局,一家工商银行,一家医疗诊所,也许还有一家中药铺。他们家离这一类店铺太远了,随着年纪日大,他太希望能就近解决各种需要了。

过了几天,传出消息,说是这一片房屋将提供给福利彩票机构。老王有些失望,但一想,有限地搞那么一点福利彩票,也不一定是坏事,可以推行某些福利事业,可以满足游戏心理,哪怕是侥幸心理,可以让一些人就业,可以逗你玩与逗自己玩……万一要中一回特等奖呢?就让大家同时做着这样的梦过日子吧。

过了几个月,挂出了牌子,有一个大门脸儿的铺房将作为棋牌室使用。不久又出现了说法,说是有些棋牌室可能会搞变相赌博,当然,你看不出来,客人们只玩筹码,玩完了再用现钱结算。

老王有点忧心忡忡,安慰自己说,管那么多干啥?社会在前进,人们的生活空间与活动内容正在延伸,旧的不得温饱的矛盾解决了,必然会出现新的矛盾,再过许多年还不是一样?美国或者欧洲还不是一样?

1
FUTURE

Wang Meng

Across the street from Lao Wang's home, a cluster of high-end storefronts had appeared. Lao Wang supposed, for no particular reason, that a post office, an ICBC bank branch, a clinic, and possibly a traditional Chinese drugstore should fill the space. Presently, these facilities were very far from his home. As he got older, he wished more and more that his various needs could be met closer to home.

A few days later, there was news: welfare lotteries would soon move into the cluster of storefronts. Lao Wang was disappointed until, on second thought, he began to see that small-scale, limited welfare lotteries might not be a bad thing at all. Some social programs might be started because of the lotteries, and they would also satisfy the desire for recreation, even the mind's continued hope for good luck. The lotteries might even create some employment opportunities. Plus, they could prove entertaining for everyone, including himself... *Oooh what if I drew a winning number and collected a special prize? So, let people live the way they want. Let them keep dreaming their common dream...*

A few months later, a shop with a large front put up its plate. It was going to be a venue for playing chess and cards. Soon a new cause for concern was bandied about. It was said secret gambling might be going on in some of the rooms. Not that anyone would be able to tell—clients dealt only in chips. Cash was used only to settle up at the end.

Lao Wang began to worry a little about the place, but he comforted himself by saying, "Why should I care? Society's moving forward; people's living spaces and the stuff of life are both expanding. When the old problem of getting food and clothing is solved, new difficulties are bound to emerge. Isn't this the case with the United States and Europe? This situation isn't going anywhere!"

又过了两个月，棋牌室的字样不见了，变成了什么咨询公司。老王更糊涂了，咨询个啥？公司个啥？其他更多的房子呢？世界日新月异，老王只见老来不见长进，一边待着去吧。

后来咨询公司的字样也不见了，又说是要变成函授学校了……到底这一片房子会派上些什么样的用场呢？

又有人说，其实还没有装修好呢，根本就没定下来到底怎么使用。修好了，再招商，然后才知道。

老王想起了年轻时候看过的苏联导演导的契科夫的话剧《万尼亚舅舅》，那里面有句台词："我真想知道呀，我真想知道呀！"

知道就知道，不知道就不知道。未来在前边闪耀着，像灯光，像皮影，像水面的涟漪。我们等待你，未来！

(2010)

Two months passed. The signboard for the chess and card store disappeared. The place became a consulting firm. Lao Wang was even more puzzled. *What firm? Consulting for what? What are the other rooms going to be used for?* The world was changing with each passing day. Lao Wang felt that he was getting old and left behind the times. *Out of the way, old man!*

Later on, the plate for the consulting firm disappeared too. Rumor had it that it was going to become a correspondence school. *What on earth will this cluster of properties be for?*

Then people were saying that, actually, the space still needed to be furnished and decorated. It wasn't decided at all how it would be used. First fix it, and then invite businesses to fight for it, then we'd know.

Lao Wang remembered Chekhov's *Uncle Vanya*, a play he once saw when he was young, which had been put on by a director from the Soviet Union. He still recalled a line from the play, "I really want to know, I really want to know!"

Well, it's fine to know and it's fine not to know. The future flashes ahead, like the light from a lamp, a shadow play, or the ripples on the surface of the water. We are waiting for you, future!

(2010)

VOCABULARY AND USAGE

对过	duìguò	across; opposite	我家对过是家书店。
铺面	pùmiàn	store; storefront	这些铺面地段好，所以租金很贵。
无端	wúduān	for no reason at all	你怎么无端就生气呀？
侥幸	jiǎoxìng	luckily; by a fluke	那场车祸中只有他侥幸生还。
就业	jiùyè	(obtain) employment	你运气真好，大学一毕业就能顺利就业。
逗	dòu	play with; amuse	这个喜剧小品真逗人。
中奖	zhòngjiǎng	win a prize in a lottery	他昨天买的彩票中了一个大奖。

门脸儿	ménliǎner	shop front; facade	门脸儿大有气派，容易吸引顾客。
变相	biànxiàng	in disguised form	包装变小就是变相涨价。
赌博	dǔbó	gamble	他赌博成瘾，最终输光了家产。
筹码	chóumǎ	gaming chip; bargaining chip	赌场里面只用筹码不用现金。
结算	jiésuàn	settle accounts	公司每个月底都要结算一次账目。
忧心忡忡	yōuxīnchōngchōng	deeply worried	公司效益不好，他对自己的前途忧心忡忡。
延伸	yánshēn	extend; spread	这条小路一直延伸到海边。
咨询	zīxún	consult	我有问题想找专家咨询一下。
日新月异	rìxīnyuèyì	change with each passing day; rapid progress	科技的进步日新月异。
老来	lǎolái	old age	叔叔老来得子，欢喜无比。
长进	zhǎngjìn	progress	只要坚持学习就一定会有长进。
函授	hánshòu	correspondence course	他是通过函授学的会计，已经拿到执照了。
派用场	pài yòngchǎng	put to use	他当兵时的经验在办案中派上了用场。

QUESTIONS FOR DISCUSSION

1. What about contemporary life disappoints Lao Wang?
2. What is Lao Wang's thought process about welfare lotteries?
3. What does China have in common with the United States and Europe, according to Lao Wang?
4. The use of the storefront space keeps changing. How does Lao Wang feel about the changes?

5. Do you think it is a good idea to fix the space first and then invite competition for it? Why or why not?
6. Please share your thoughts on this line: "Well, it's fine to know and it's fine not to know."
7. Discuss the different ways that the three images in the last paragraph invite us to think about changes and the future.

1. 当代生活的哪些方面让老王失望了？
2. 老王关于福利彩票的思考过程是怎样的？
3. 在老王眼里，中国跟美国和欧洲有什么相同之处？
4. 那些铺面房的用场不停在变，老王对这样的变化有何感想？
5. 先把铺面房装修好然后再招商，你觉得这是个好主意吗？为什么？
6. 请谈谈你对文中这句话的看法："知道就知道，不知道就不知道。"
7. 请说说最后一段中的那三个比喻怎样从不同的角度启发我们思考变化和未来。

AUTHOR BIO

Born in Beijing, Wang Meng (1934–) came of age with the founding of the People's Republic of China (PRC). He joined the Communist Party of China (CPC) in 1948 and wrote his first full-length novel *Qingchun Wansui* (青春万岁, 1953) at the age of 19. He was designated a "rightist" for the critical stance of his short story "A Newcomer to the Organizational Department" ("组织部来了个年轻人," 1956). He labored for the next twenty-some years, sixteen of which were among the Uighurs in Xingjiang. He returned to Beijing and to writing in 1978 after the Cultural Revolution. He is now an active and most respected figure in the field of Chinese literature. It is difficult to list his major works because there are too many of them. In addition to ten full-length works of fiction, Wang Meng has published over thirty volumes of novellas and short stories, two volumes of poetry, seven volumes of prose essays, and five volumes of autobiography. His many collections of essays also cover a wide range, from literary criticism to talks on creative writing, to a research monograph on the *Dream of the Red Chamber* (红楼梦) and philosophical reflections.

Wang Meng can be a great entry point to a comprehensive understanding of China today. Wang Meng became a member of the CCP's Central Committee in 1986 and held the office of Minister of Culture of the PRC until 1989. Now in retirement, Wang Meng holds honorary professorships at many universities, yet he identifies himself as a lifetime student. His fellow writer Tie Ning attributes Wang Meng's comprehensive influence on contemporary Chinese literature to this attitude toward learning and admires his inexhaustible passion, vigor, empathy, and wisdom. Wang Meng enjoys large readerships both within and outside China. He was nominated for a Nobel Prize in 2000. Wang Meng is also recognized in China as one of the most significant contributors to the development of the short-short genre.

2
不可知的偶然

格非

1980年夏天，我参加了第一次高考，毫无意外地，我落榜了——化学和物理都没有超过40分。母亲决意让我去当木匠。

当时木匠还是个很让人羡慕的职业。我们当地有很多有名的木匠，但我母亲请不到，她请了家里的一个亲戚。这个木匠因自己是有手艺的，觉得自己特别牛，很是凶悍。他对我母亲说，这个孩子笨手笨脚的，不严厉是学不出来的，我要是打他你会舍得吗？母亲只得说，你打吧。我很不喜欢这个翘着腿坐在木椅上的人——我和他无冤无仇，他为什么要打我？我就对母亲说，我要考大学，而且要考重点大学。母亲睁大了眼睛说，孩子，你怎么能说这样的话呢？你连门都没有摸到呢。你要是考上大学，我们都要笑死了。

就在我灰了心，要去当木匠的时候，一位镇上姓翟的小学老师，敲开了我家的门。他与我非亲非故，素不相识。我至今仍然不知他是如何寻访到我们村的。我依然清晰地记得，夜已经很深，大家都睡了，他戴着草帽，站在门外，把我母亲吓了一跳。他见了我劈头就说，你想不想读谏壁中学？——那是我们当地最好的中学。我当然是很愿意的。他说他可以把我引荐给那里的他的一位朋友。

当我拿着翟老师的亲笔信到了谏壁中学，他的那位朋友却告诉我，语文、数学必须拿到60分，不然无法进入补习班。他说，让我看看你的高考成绩单。

2
UNKNOWABLE POSSIBILITIES

Ge Fei

In the summer of 1980, I took the National College Entrance Exam for the first time. It was no surprise that I failed—my grades for chemistry and physics were less than 40 percent. Mother decided that I should become a carpenter.

At the time, carpentry was still a very desirable profession. There were many famous carpenters in our area, but they were beyond Mother's means. So she asked a relative to be my master. This carpenter saw himself as a craftsman, so when he showed up, he was cocky and rude. He said to my mother, "This youngster is clumsy. It will take strict discipline to make him learn this trade. Will you be able to stand it if I beat him?" "You have my permission," my mother was forced to reply. I disliked this man immediately, who sat in our wooden chair with his legs crossed. *Why would he want to beat me up? I hadn't offended him in any way.*

So I told Mother that I was going to retake the College Entrance Exam, and I was going to enter a major university. Mother's eyes popped open; she said, "My child, stop talking this way! You don't even know how to find the *actual* entrance to a college. If you got into college, we'd all die laughing."

Just as I was about to take up carpentry in despair, an elementary school teacher, with the last name of Zhai, came from town and knocked on our door. He was neither kith nor kin; I had never met him before. To this day, I don't know how he got to my village and found me. But I do remember clearly that it was late into the night and people were already sleeping. Standing at the door and wearing a straw hat, he gave Mother a start. The moment he saw me he asked, "Do you want to go to Jianbi High School to prepare for next year's College Entrance Exam?" I wanted to very much, of course. Jianbi was the best high school in my area. He told me that he could provide me with a letter of recommendation to a friend he had there.

在决定命运的时候,我的脑子还算比较清醒。我知道我的成绩根本不能进入这个补习班,我也知道无论如何不能够把口袋里的成绩单给他看,于是我说,我把成绩单丢了。

"你可以去丹徒县文教局查一查,把分数抄来。"他说完,给了我一个地址。

县文教局在镇江,青云门六号。在马路边上,我只要随便跳上一辆公共汽车,就可以回家,永远做一个木匠的学徒。可是如果我去镇江的文教局呢?事情结果是一样的,我还是会得到一张一摸一样的成绩单,还是无法进入谏壁中学,还是要返回家乡,做一个学徒,为我的师傅递上热毛巾,听任他打骂。

我徘徊了两个小时。镇江对我而言,是一座陌生的大城市,它实在太远了,我从来没有去过那里。我其实是一个很保守的人,不会轻易冒险,不会去做我觉得非分的事情。我觉得我是有百分之九十的可能是要回家的。我根本没有去过镇江,而且去了也不知道县文教局在哪里。这些都是我无法逾越的困难。但那一次,不知道是什么原因,我鬼使神差地登上了前去镇江的过路车子。

到了县文教局,正好是下班时间,传达室老头儿冷冷地说,现在下班了,你不能进去。

我想也罢,我进去又有什么用呢?在我打算掉头离开的时候,有人叫住了我:小鬼,你有什么事?

我看见两个人,一男一女,往外面走。我说我的高考成绩单丢了,能不能帮我补一下?

男的说,下班了,明天吧。

女的则说,我们还是帮他补办一下吧,反正也不耽误时间。

他们把我带回办公室,帮我查找档案,又问我办这样的成绩单,有什么用处。

When I arrived at Jianbi High School with teacher Zhai's handwritten letter, that friend of his told me that to get into the study class, my scores for Chinese and mathematics on the entrance exam I failed must be 60 or higher. "Show me your grade book," he said.

My head was fairly straight at this fateful moment. I knew the scores I got were nowhere near high enough to get into the class. I also knew that I mustn't show him the grade book in my pocket, no matter what. "I lost it," I replied.

"You can go to the Bureau of Culture and Education of Dantu County to get your score sheet. Bring me a copy." After saying this, he handed me the address.

The county's Bureau of Culture and Education was located at Six Qingyun Gate Road in Zhenjiang. Standing on the curb, I knew I could easily jump on a bus, go home, and be a carpenter for the rest of my life. Even if I did make the trip to the Bureau of Culture and Education in Zhenjiang, the result would be the same. I would get a copy of the same grade report, which would still keep me out of Jianbi High School. I would have to go back home and be an apprentice to my master, handing him hot towels while being at his mercy for beatings and scolding.

For two hours, I hesitated. For me, Zhenjiang was an unfamiliar big city, too far away. I'd never been there before. I was actually a cautious type who did not venture out easily or just act on impulse. I knew the chance that I would head home was 90 percent. I wouldn't know how to get to the Bureau of Culture and Education even if I went to Zhenjiang. These were all insurmountable obstacles. But that day, for reasons beyond my understanding, I got on a passing bus to Zhenjiang, as if led by ghosts and gods.

I arrived at the Bureau of Culture and Education at exactly closing time. The old man at the reception desk said in a cold voice, "Take off. I can't let you in."

"Fine," I thought. "What's the use, anyway?" Just as I was turning around to leave, someone stopped me, "What's up, kid?"

I saw two people, a man and woman, walking out. I said that I had lost my grade report and asked, "Could you help me get a replacement copy?"

The man said, "Too late today. How about tomorrow?"

But the woman said, "Let's help him with a replacement. It doesn't take much time."

我沉默了一下，突然说："我的成绩单没丢。"
"那你来这里干什么？"他们显然有些生气了。
我于是讲了高考的落榜，讲了自己很想去谏壁中学补习，但是没有达到他们要求的分数线。我说我一定要读这个补习班，去考大学。
那个女的说，这怎么行？男的不吭声，他抽着烟，盘算了好一会儿。他让我出去等回话。十分钟后，他说，唉，帮你办了。
我那时很小，十五岁，穿的衣服很破旧。大概他是因此萌发了帮助之心。
他们问我需要多少分，我说语文70分，数学80分。说完了很后悔，因为这个分数已经可以考上大学了。我又把分数改过来了，语文68分，数学70分。写完了之后要盖章，但是在这节骨眼上，公章突然找不到了。
他们翻遍了抽屉，打开又合上。这对于一个小孩子来说，可能是最紧张的时候。没有章不就完了吗？事实上公章就在手边，大概是当时大家都太紧张了吧。
女的盖完了章，轻轻说了一句："苟富贵，莫相忘。"[2] 我的眼泪一下子就流出来了。那是我迄今为止见过的最美丽的女性。我的感激出于如下理由：她竟然还会假设我将来会有出息。
我似乎没有说什么感激的话，拿着成绩单，飞跑着离开了。等回到家的时候，我一天都没有吃饭，整个人都要虚脱了。
第二年，我再次参加高考，开始了在大学的求学之路。
对我而言，生活实在是太奥妙了，它是由无数的偶然构成的。你永远无法想象，会有什么人出现，前来帮助你。我这样一个人，怎么可能相信生

---

2. The historical allusion to this popular saying is in *Records of the Historian* by Sima Qian (ca. 145 or 135-86 BC); or in volume 48 on Chen Sheng (陈胜 ?-208 BC), to be exact. Before Chen Sheng led the peasant uprising that rocked the foundation of Qin dynasty, he worked as a hired farm hand. One day working in the fields, Chen Sheng articulated "苟富贵，无相忘" to let his fellow farmers know that he would not forget them when he became successful one day. His fellow workers laughed at him. Please also see the vocabulary list for this entry.

They went back into their office with me. As they were looking for my file they asked why I needed this grade report.

I was silent for a moment before I blurted out, "I didn't lose my grade report."

"Then what are you here for?" Obviously, they were a little upset.

I then told them of my failed attempt at getting into college, my frantic hope to attend Jianbi High School, and the fact that I didn't have the grades required to get into the study class. I said that I must get into this class, so I could get ready for the College Entrance Exam next year.

"This won't do," the woman said, hesitating, but the man didn't say anything. He smoked a cigarette and thought for a long time. Then he told me to wait outside. Ten minutes later, he emerged. "Okay, we're going to help you out," he said.

I was fifteen at the time, small and in shabby clothes. Perhaps this was why the desire to help me took root in them.

They asked me what grades I needed. I said 70 for Chinese and 80 for mathematics. I regretted it the moment I said this, because with these scores I would have been in college already. Quickly, I changed the grades to a 68 in Chinese and a 70 in mathematics. After entering the grades, they needed to stamp the document with a seal. But the seal, at this crucial moment, was suddenly nowhere to be found.

The man and woman searched everywhere, opening and closing all the drawers. For a kid of my age, this was a most nerve-wracking moment. *I'd be done without the seal!* Turns out, the seal was actually right at the tips of their fingers. (It's possible that everyone was a little nervous that evening.)

After she stamped the document, the woman said to me softly, "Remember this moment when you are successful." Instantly, my eyes filled with tears. To this day, she is the most beautiful woman I have ever met. This is why I was grateful to her: she went so far as to assume that I would one day be successful!

I don't think I said anything to show my gratitude. I took the grade report and ran. When I got home, I felt I might pass out—I'd had nothing to eat all day.

The next year I took the College Entrance Exam for the second time and continued my journey of learning at college.

Life, for me, is just miraculous. Formed by an endless number of fortuitous possibilities, it is forever beyond me to predict who will appear with

活是一成不变的呢？为什么我会那么喜欢博尔赫斯，喜欢休谟，喜欢不可知论？因为我觉得生命是如此脆弱，而生活很神秘。我觉得这跟我后来的写作，也有相关之处。

(2012)

a helping hand. How could a person like me believe life is static? Why do I love Borges and Hume and embrace the unknown so much? It is because I feel that human life is so vulnerable, yet life is so magical. Later on, it was this feeling, I believe, that effected my engagement with writing.

(2012)

VOCABULARY AND USAGE

不可知	bùkězhī	unknowable; unknown	投资风险是不可知的。
偶然	ǒurán	fortuitous; chance	他的成功并非偶然，除了自己的努力还有贵人相助。
高考	gāokǎo	College Entrance Examination	每逢全国高考，县城都实行交通管制，不许摁喇叭。
落榜	luòbǎng	flunk a competitive exam	他想上北大，结果落榜了，心里十分难过。
超过	chāoguò	exceed	你有三门课没有超过最低分数线，只能留级了。
决意	juéyì	be determined	正在医学院就读的他决意弃医从文。
请(不到)	qǐng (búdào)	cannot afford	你快想法凑钱吧，钱少是请不到好律师的。
手艺	shǒuyì	skill; craftsmanship	过去，一门精湛的手艺是生存的保障，现在呢？
牛	niú	awesome	你也太牛了，同时被斯坦福和普林斯顿录取！
凶悍	xiōnghàn	fierce and tough	他摆出一副凶悍的样子要来打我。
笨手笨脚	bènshǒubènjiǎo	clumsy	我这孩子笨手笨脚的不适合学跳舞。
翘(腿)	qiào (tuǐ)	legs crossed	你在课堂上这样翘腿坐着不礼貌。
无冤无仇	wúyuānwúchóu	without any ill feeling	原本无冤无仇的两家人从此不说话了。
重点大学	zhòngdiǎn dàxué	key universities	清华、北大、浙大、南大等都是全国最好的重点大学。

素不相识	sùbùxiāngshí	not acquainted with each other before	他奋不顾身跳入水中，去救一个素不相识的小孩。
寻访	xún fǎng	inquire after; look for	他去台湾寻访早年去了那里的父亲。
引荐	yǐnjiàn	recommend; give a referral	你能把我引荐给你的导师吗？
听任	tīngrèn	allow; let be	他从不主动接近女生，总是说要听任上天安排。
徘徊	páihuái	hesitate; linger	他来晚了，在会议室外面徘徊，不知该不该进来。
非分	fēifèn	presumptuous	第一次见面，不要提什么买房子买车的非分要求。
逾越	yúyuè	pass; go beyond	他们之间不可逾越的障碍是价值观的不同。
鬼使神差	guǐshǐ shénchāi	doings of ghosts and gods; unexpectedly	他竟相信了她的话，鬼使神差地交出了手中的武器。
也罢	yě bà	all right (when making a concession)	也罢，既然我的计划花钱太多，就按你说的做吧。
小鬼	xiǎoguǐ	kid (a term of endearment)	小鬼，你可要珍惜这个的机会！
盘算	pánsuàn	deliberate; calculate	他细心盘算着该怎么用这笔钱。
节骨眼	jiēgǔyǎn	crucial moment	事情已经到了节骨眼上，你怎么能放弃呢？
翻遍	fān biàn	rummage through	她翻遍了衣柜也没找到那条裙子。
苟	gǒu	if	"苟富贵，莫相忘"在这里的意思是"如果有一天你富贵了，请不要忘记这一刻"。
莫	mò	do not	
假设	jiǎshè	presume; suppose	我只是个弱小的穷孩子，她却假设我会有美好的未来。
虚脱	xūtuō	collapse; pass out	我没吃饭就跑步，十公里下来都快虚脱了。
奥妙	àomiào	profound and marvelous	大自然和生活都是如此之奥妙！

一成不变	yīchéngbúbiàn	unchanging	世上哪有一成不变的东西？人的感情也不例外。
脆弱	cuìruò	delicate; fragile	这个孩子的感情有点儿脆弱，请你多关照她。

QUESTIONS FOR DISCUSSION

1. What does Zhai, the elementary school teacher, do in the story? Should this have been his responsibility? Why does he go out of his way to do it?
2. Does Mother care less about her son than a stranger does because she does not encourage him to retake the College Entrance Exam? Do you understand why she agrees that the master carpenter can beat her son?
3. Should the man and the woman from the Bureau of Culture and Education have helped the boy? What makes them so nervous that they cannot find the seal? What motivates them to break the rules for the boy?
4. Why does the woman think this is a moment to remember? What does the story say about right and wrong?
5. What perception of human nature does the story show?
6. What is the story's attitude toward the unknown/unknowable?
7. How should we anticipate changes in life? What is this story's revelation?

1. 故事中小学的翟老师做了件什么事儿？那是他该管的事儿吗？他为什么不怕麻烦一定要做这件事儿？
2. 我们能因为孩子的妈妈没有鼓励他再次参加高考就说她还不如一个陌生人关心她的孩子吗？你理解妈妈为什么同意木匠师傅可以打她的孩子吗？
3. 文教局的那一男一女该不该帮这个孩子？是什么让他们紧张得找不到公章了？他们为这个孩子违章违法的动机是什么？
4. 为什么那个女的觉得那是一个应该铭记的时刻？这个故事的是非观是怎样的？
5. 关于人的本性，这个故事表达了什么样的看法？
6. 这个故事对未知／不可知持什么样的态度？
7. 我们应该怎样预见／迎接生活中的变化？这个故事给了你什么样的启示？

AUTHOR BIO

Ge Fei (格非, 1964–) is the pen name of Liu Yong (刘勇). Like the boy in the story, he was a native of Dantu County of Zhenjiang Municipality. Born in 1964, he got into a major university—Eastern China Normal University—in Shanghai in 1981. He became an assistant professor at his alma mater in 1985. After he received his Ph.D. in literature in 2000, he joined the Chinese Department of Tsinghua University in Beijing. Ge Fei has been teaching, doing research, and publishing since 1986. Better known in the West as an experimental writer of the late 1980s and early 1990s, Ge Fei remains indifferent to such designations. He has been an avid student of traditional Chinese literature and narrative since the mid-1990s. A writer and a scholar well-versed in the literatures of East and West, Ge Fei places high value on innovation.

Many of Ge Fei's "avant-garde" fictions have been translated into English. Among them are the short stories "Remembering Mr. Wu You" ("追忆乌攸先生," 1986), "Green Yellow" ("青黄," 2001), "Mona Lisa's Smile" ("蒙娜丽莎的微笑," 2010), and "Song of Liangzhou" ("凉州词," 2010), and the novellas *Lost Boat* (迷舟, 1987), *A Flock of Birds* (褐色鸟群, 1989), and *Banner of Desire* (欲望的旗帜, 1996). His first novel, *The Invisibility Cloak* (隐身衣, 2012), will appear in an English translation in 2016. His works have also been translated into French, Japanese, and Italian.

Ge Fei has won many awards. The most recent, the Mao Dun Literary Award (矛盾文学奖), was awarded to him in 2015 for his *Jiangnan Trilogy* (江南三部曲), which includes three novels: *Renmian Taohua* (人面桃花, 2004), *Shanhe Rumeng* (山河入梦, 2007), and *Chun Jin Jiangnan* (春尽江南, 2011). Ge Fei represents the cutting edge of Chinese intellectual learning and thinking. We hope that the story reprinted here opens the door for you to many more of Ge Fei's writings as well as his reflections on human existence and the nature of writing.

拼音索引
PINYIN VOCABULARY INDEX

A

矮	ǎi	short	S2C1
爱	ài	tend to; be apt to	S4C8
挨个	āigè	one by one	S1C2
暧昧	àimèi	ambiguous; vague	S4C7
哀婉	āiwǎn	sadly moving	S1C5
哀怨	āiyuàn	sad	S1C6
安定	āndìng	settle; stabilize	S4C7
安慰	ānwèi	console; comfort	S4C2
安置	ānzhì	arrange for; find a place for	S4C7
按说	ànshuō	in the ordinary course of events	S2C4
熬(日子)	áo (rìzi)	get through; survive	S3C1
熬夜	áoyè	stay up late	S3C4
奥迪	àodí	a transliteration of Audi	S2C4
奥妙	àomiào	profound; marvelous	S2C9

B

罢	bà	end; finished	S2C6
罢了	bàle	a particle indicating "that's all"	S4C7
巴(眼)	bā	open (eyes wide)	S1C3
(把钱)打进(账户)	(bǎqián) dǎ jìn (zhànghù)	transfer (money into an account)	S2C4
百思不得其解	bǎi sī bù dé qí jiě	have thought hard and still cannot make sense of it	S3C2
办丧事	bàn sāngshì	conduct funeral and burial services	S3C2
(半)截	(bàn) jié	section; length	S1C2

班费	bānfèi	class fund	S2C5
斑斓	bānlán	bright/multicolored	S4C8
板脸	bǎn liǎn	have a taut face	S4C8
般配	bānpèi	be well matched	S3C8
半晌	bànshǎng	a long while	S3C5
班主任	bānzhǔrèn	a teacher in charge of a class	S3C7
绑	bǎng	fasten	S2C4
饱	bǎo	full	S1C8
爆锅	bàoguō	quick stir-fry in hot oil	S4C8
包扎	bāozhā	bind up a wound	S2C3
碑	bēi	upright stone tablet	S2C4
北大荒	běidàhuāng	the Great Northern Wilderness	S2C7
被褥	bèirù	bedding	S2C4
背影	bèiyǐng	a view of someone's back	S1C3
笨	bèn	slow-witted	S2C1
本来就这回事	běnlái jiù zhè huí shì	That's how it is.	S1C3
本色	běnsè	true; inherent quality	S4C7
本职	běnzhí	one's job; one's duty	S2C4
笨手笨脚	bènshǒubènjiǎo	clumsy	S2C9
避人处	bì rén chù	a place where no one could see	S2C2
彼此	bǐcǐ	both parties; one another	S3C8
毕恭毕敬	bìgōngbìjìng	extremely deferential	S3C1
比划	bǐhua	gesticulate; gesture	S1C7
比上不足，比下有余	bǐshàngbùzú, bǐxiàyǒuyú	better off than some, worse off than others; reasonably good	S4C5
扁担	biǎndān	carrying pole	S1C3
辩解	biànjiě	defend; explain	S2C3
变相	biànxiàng	in disguised form	S1C9
表白	biǎobái	confess one's love	S3C8
憋	biē	suppress	S2C2
鬓角	bìnjiǎo	temple	S4C8
病危	bìngwēi	critically ill	S3C5
脖	bó	neck	S1C3
(不)服老	(bù) fúlǎo	(do not) acquiesce to old age	S4C2
不甘寂寞	bù gān jìmò	unwilling to be out of the limelight	S3C8
不减当年	bù jiǎn dāngnián	as in the old days	S4C6

不是滋味	bú shì zīwèi	feel bad; upset	S3C3
...不说,... 还...	...bù shuō,... hái...	not to mention; leave aside	S3C8
不死心	bù sǐxīn	unwilling to give up	S1C3
不予理会	bù yǔ lǐhuì	ignore; dismiss	S2C8
不悦	bú yuè	unhappy; unhappiness	S3C7
不知道怎么的	bù zhīdào zěnme de	inexplicably	S1C8
不动声色	búdòngshēngsè	maintain one's composure	S4C7
不都说...	bùdōushuō	Isn't it true that...; Everyone says...	S1C8
不对头	búduìtóu	go wrong	S4C6
不过是	búguòshì	only; merely	S2C8
不经劝	bùjīnquàn	easy to persuade	S1C3
不可知	bùkězhī	unknowable; unknown	S2C9
不就行了	bújiùxíngle	Wouldn't...be sufficient?	S1C4
不冷不热	bùlěngbúrè	neither hostile nor friendly	S1C3
不明真相	bùmíngzhēnxiàng	ignorant of the facts/truth	S1C4
不清不白	bùqīngbùbái	neither innocent nor clean; have an illicit relationship	S2C3
不兴	bùxīng	impermissible; not allowed	S3C7
不休	bùxiū	nonstop	S1C2
不修边幅	bùxiūbiānfú	slovenly	S2C4
不已	bùyǐ	endlessly	S2C2
不依不饶	bùyībùráo	unwilling to forgive; relentlessly	S3C6
不约而同	bùyuē'értóng	happen to coincide	S4C7
不在话下	bùzàihuàxià	nothing difficult	S3C8
补救	bǔjiù	remedy	S1C3
布局	bùjú	layout; composition	S3C7
步履跟跄	bùlǚliàngqiàng	falter	S3C1
步履轻盈	bùlǚqīngyíng	light-footed; breeze along	S4C8

C

采	cǎi	pluck; gather	S4C8
踩空	cǎi kōng	make a misstep	S2C2
才子	cáizǐ	gifted scholar	S3C4
残兵败将	cánbīngbàijiàng	remnants of a defeated army	S1C6

藏匿	cángnì	conceal; hide	S2C5
残酷	cánkù	cruel	S2C7
灿烂	cànlàn	splendid; glitter	S1C6
草草	cǎocǎo	rush through carelessly	S1C5
操心	cāoxīn	worry about; take pains	S4C2
(一)侧	cè	side	S1C3
策划	cèhuà	plot; plan	S1C4
噌	cēng	whoosh!	S2C1
茬	chá	a measure word (for a crop); batch	S4C8
差点(儿)	chàdiǎn(er)	almost; nearly	S1C4
拆	chāi	tear apart (down)	S2C8
茶客	chákè	customer at a teahouse	S3C6
馋	chán	be fond of (food); covetous	S2C7
颤抖	chàndǒu	shudder; shiver	S1C6
长眠	cháng mián	eternal sleep; die	S3C2
尝鲜	cháng xiān	have a taste of seasonal delicacy	S4C8
畅销品	chàngxiāo pǐn	best seller	S1C8
敞胸露怀	chǎngxiōnglùhuái	bare-chested	S2C5
超过	chāoguò	exceed	S2C9
扯	chě	pull	S1C3
扯	chě	tear	S4C6
车(秧)水	chē (yāng) shuǐ	draw water to irrigate a (rice) field using a waterwheel	S3C3
(车)厢	(chē) xiāng	cargo space; box; car	S2C6
车轴	chēzhóu	axle	S2C4
车轴雨	chēzhóuyǔ	nonstop rain	S2C4
车资	chēzī	carfare; fare	S1C6
趁(热)	chèn (rè)	take the chance; seize the advantage	S3C1
嗔怪	chēnguài	blame; chide	S1C3
沉寂	chénjì	silence; stillness	S3C5
沉默	chénmò	silent; silence	S1C6
沉吟	chényín	mutter to oneself; ponder	S3C6
称心	chènxīn	gratifying; gratified	S4C7
称心如意	chènxīnrúyì	utmost satisfaction	S1C2
趁早	chènzǎo	before it is too late	S3C3
撑	chēng	hold out (until)	S4C2

拼音索引 PINYIN VOCABULARY INDEX

撑	chēng	support	S1C3
撑	chēng	expand	S4C5
盛(饭)	chéng (fàn)	fill a bowl	S1C5
承包	chéngbāo	contract	S4C5
承担	chéngdān	undertake; bear	S2C8
承诺	chéngnuò	commitment	S1C4
称呼	chēnghū	address; appellation	S4C5
成家立业	chéngjiālìyè	married and established	S1C2
成熟	chéngshú	mature	S1C4
瞠目结舌	chēngmùjiéshé	be struck dumb	S1C3
诚挚	chéngzhì	sincere	S2C8
驰骋	chíchěng	gallop	S2C5
吃苦	chīkǔ	endure hardship	S4C2
吃苦受累	chīkǔ shòulèi	have a rough time	S4C5
哧啦	chīlā	an onomatopoeia	S1C5
炽烈	chìliè	burning fiercely	S2C7
吃相	chīxiàng	manner of eating	S2C4
痴心	chīxīn	infatuation	S3C5
斥责	chìzé	denounce	S4C6
重犯	chóng fàn	repeat (a mistake)	S1C4
崇拜	chǒngbài	worship	S2C4
冲锋陷阵	chōngfēngxiànzhèn	charge and shatter enemy positions	S2C5
臭	chòu	disgusting	S3C1
瞅	chǒu	cast a glance	S1C3
抽	chōu	pick out; select	S4C5
抽(水)	chōu (shuǐ)	obtain by drawing from (as from a well)	S4C5
抽搐	chōuchù	twitch	S3C1
抽身	chōushēn	get away	S3C1
惆怅	chóuchàng	sad; melancholy	S3C1
臭虫	chòuchóng	bugs	S2C5
筹借	chóujiè	raise and borrow	S2C7
筹码	chóumǎ	gaming chip; bargaining chip	S1C9
臭气熏天	chòuqìxūntiān	overwhelming stench	S2C4
仇视	chóushì	be hostile to	S2C8
出风头	chūfēngtou	show off; be in the limelight	S4C7

出阁	chūgé	(a woman) get married	S4C6
出面	chūmiàn	act on behalf of	S1C3
出奇	chūqí	surprisingly; unusually	S3C7
出人命	chūrénmìng	cause death	S2C4
出头	chūtóu	a little over	S3C1
出众	chūzhòng	outstanding	S2C1
出资	chūzī	provide the fund	S2C8
触电	chùdiàn	get an electric shock	S2C8
触情生情	chùjǐngshēngqíng	be moved by one's surroundings	S3C6
处女	chùnǚ	virgin; maiden	S3C6
揣	chuāi	tuck (into)	S1C5
串	chuàn	go from place to place; run about	S1C2
串	chuàn	string together; cluster together	S4C8
传递	chuándì	pass on; hand around	S3C2
穿小鞋	chuānxiǎoxié	make things harder for someone	S2C4
怆然	chuàngrán	sad; mournfully	S4C8
垂	chuí	hang down	S4C7
春风不度	chūnfēngbúdù	no sign of spring	S4C8
戳	chuō	stand	S2C4
绰号	chuòhào	nickname	S2C2
次之	cì zhī	followed by; second to	S2C7
伺候	cìhou	wait on; serve	S2C4
刺激	cìji	irritate; upset	S4C6
刺激	cìji	stimulating; exciting	S1C6
(刺激一)把	(cìjī yī) bǎ	a measure word	S1C8
刺啦	cīlā	an onomatopoeia	S4C8
瓷器	cíqì	porcelain; chinaware	S4C8
刺猬	cìwei	hedgehog	S2C8
聪明大了	cōngmíng dàle	too smart for one's own good	S2C6
从容	cōngróng	calm and unhurried	S3C1
丛生	cóngshēng	overgrown	S4C8
凑	còu	pool (money)	S2C2
凑	còu	move close to	S4C6
簇	cù	a measure word; pile; bunch	S4C8
粗拉	cūlā	coarse; crude	S2C4
促膝谈心	cùxītánxīn	sit side by side and talk heart-to-heart	S3C6

拼音索引 PINYIN VOCABULARY INDEX

窜	cuàn	scurry	S3C6
窜	cuān	soar	S4C6
蹿	cuān	shoot up; leap up	S4C8
脆弱	cuìruò	delicate; fragile	S2C9
村官	cūn guān	village official	S4C5
村风	cūn fēng	village culture	S4C5
措辞	cuòcí	wording; diction	S1C8
错过	cuòguò	miss; let slip	S3C5

D

打 (粉底)	dǎ (fěndǐ)	apply; put on	S3C8
打 (老远)	dǎ (lǎoyuǎn)	from (far away)	S2C6
打肿脸充胖子	dǎ zhǒng liǎn chōng pàngzi	seek to impress by feigning more than what one is	S3C6
打 (借条)	dǎ(jiètiáo)	write (an IOU)	S2C8
打(年糕)	dǎ(niángāo)	make (rice cakes)	S3C3
打(水)	dǎ(shuǐ)	draw; fetch	S2C4
打(铁/链子)	dǎ(tiě/liànzi)	forge (iron/chain)	S2C5
打抱不平	dǎbàobùpíng	defend someone against an injustice	S2C5
打动	dǎdòng	touch; move	S2C8
打赌	dǎdǔ	bet; make a bet	S2C7
打发	dǎfa	pass (time)	S2C7
打嗝	dǎgé	issue a belch	S1C5
打滚	dǎgǔn	roll	S2C2
打量	dǎliang	look up and down	S3C1
打趣	dǎqù	banter; tease	S1C2
打湿	dǎshī	wet; damp	S3C8
(打一)顿	(dǎyī) dùn	a measure word	S2C2
打折	dǎzhé	discount; on sale	S1C6
大有起色	dà yǒu qǐsè	improved significantly	S1C6
大名	dàmíng	one's formal personal name; given name	S1C8
大拿	dàná	a person with power and/or great skills	S4C7
大曲	dàqū	hard liquor	S3C7

大肉	dàròu	pork	S3C1
搭	dā	hang (over)	S3C8
(搭)理	(dā)lǐ	acknowledge; respond	S1C3
搭话	dāhuà	accost	S3C1
搭话	dāhuà	get in a word; talk; answer	S1C5
带	dài	take along	S3C7
带拢(门)	dài long (mén)	close (door)	S3C1
待(到)	dài (dào)	by the time when	S1C2
戴	dài	wear	S2C6
戴绿帽子	dài lǜ nàozi	be a cuckold	S2C2
贷款	dàikuǎn	loan; provide a loan	S2C8
怠慢	dàimàn	slight; trifle with	S3C7
掸	dǎn	brush lightly; whisk	S2C7
担负	dānfù	shoulder	S2C5
淡忘	dànwàng	fade from memory	S4C6
耽误	dānwù	delay	S2C4
挡	dǎng	block; keep off	S2C3
当(问)	dāng	ought; should	S3C1
当初	dāngchū	at the beginning; in the first place	S1C4
到处	dàochù	everywhere	S1C7
叨叨	dāodao	chatter away	S4C8
悼念	dàoniàn	mourn	S3C8
刀刃	dāorèn	blade	S1C1
倒霉	dǎoméi	have bad luck	S3C5
倒贴	dàotiē	lose; subsidize	S1C6
倒头	dǎotóu	lie down	S1C5
道谢	dàoxiè	express one's thanks	S4C8
(得)慌	(de) huāng	awfully; unbearably	S4C2
得了	déle	let it go at that; forget it	S2C4
得罪	dézuì	offend	S1C3
瞪眼睛	dèng yǎnjing	stare; glare	S2C4
蹬蹬	dēngdēng	sound of thrusting against the ground	S1C3
灯火辉煌	dēnghuǒhuīhuáng	brightly lit	S1C2
登记(结婚)	dēngjì(jiéhūn)	register (for marriage)	S3C5
递(给/到)	dì (gěi/dào)	hand over to; deliver	S2C4
地步	dìbù	extent	S1C2

低调	dīdiào	low key; low profile	S1C8
滴溜溜	dīliūliū	going round and round	S1C2
典	diǎn	classical texts	S2C7
点	diǎn	offer hints; give tips	S2C7
点拨	diǎnbō	give hints	S3C4
惦记	diànjì	be concerned about	S2C2
垫子	diànzi	cushion; pad	S2C6
吊	diào	lift	S1C3
吊带	diàodài	sling; strap	S3C8
掉	diào	fall; drop	S4C2
叠	dié	one on top of another	S2C2
盯	dīng	fix one's eyes on	S3C4
顶	dǐng	retort; answer back; go against	S3C8
顶不济	dǐngbújì	at least	S1C5
(钉)透	(dìng) tòu	penetrate	S1C2
丢	diū	mislay	S2C2
丢	diū	throw; toss	S1C7
(东)讨(西借)	(dōng)tǎo(xījiè)	ask for; beg for	S2C2
东倒西歪	dōngdǎoxīwāi	reel right and left; lurch	S2C6
东翻西找	dōngfānxīzhǎo	search everywhere	S2C5
动人	dòngrén	moving; touching	S1C2
动弹不得	dòngtan bù dé	cannot move	S2C4
冬闲	dōngxián	slack winter season	S1C5
逗	dòu	play with; amuse	S1C9
兜	dōu	pocket; bag	S1C7
陡然	dǒurán	unexpectedly; abruptly	S4C7
独	dú	only	S2C7
堵	dǔ	block up	S2C6
赌博	dǔbó	gamble	S1C9
赌气	dǔqì	feel wronged and act rashly out of spite	S1C3
嘟哝	dūnong	mumble (complaints)	S2C4
断绝	duànjué	sever; break off	S4C7
对策	duìcè	countermeasure	S2C5
对过	duìguò	across; opposite	S1C9
蹲	dūn	stay	S3C4
蹲	dūn	squat	S2C6

顿时	dùnshí	immediately; suddenly	S1C4
剁	duò	chop	S1C3
跺(脚)	duò(jiǎo)	stamp (foot)	S1C3
躲避	duǒbì	hide; dodge	S1C4
躲避	duǒbì	evade; elude	S1C6
哆嗦	duōsuo	shiver	S1C3

E

恶狠狠	èhěnhěn	ferociously	S2C5
恶俗	èsú	nasty and vulgar	S2C8
恶语	èyǔ	abusive expressions	S2C2
恶作剧	èzuòjù	mischief; practical joke; monkey business	S2C7
摁	èn	press (with hand or finger)	S3C8
而	ér	and; as well as	S4C7
耳背	ěrbèi	hard of hearing	S2C2
耳际	ěrjì	ears; around the ears	S3C8
二郎腿	èrlángtuǐ	(sit) cross-legged	S3C6
二流子	èrliūzi	loafer; rascal	S2C5
儿孙满堂	érsūnmǎntáng	have many children and grandchildren	S4C2

F

发愁	fāchóu	worry	S1C4
发呆	fādāi	in a daze	S1C2
发紧	fājǐn	(a) tightening (sensation)	S4C6
翻遍	fān biàn	rummage through	S2C9
翻盖	fāngài	renovate; replace	S4C5
(反)倒	(fǎn)dào	yet; on the contrary	S3C1
反驳	fǎnbó	refute	S4C6
返程	fǎnchéng	return (trip)	S2C4
犯愁	fànchóu	worry	S1C3
泛起	fànqǐ	appear; emerge	S3C8
放	fàng	save; keep; preserve	S4C2
放(电影)	fàng	project on the screen	S2C1
放养	fàngyǎng	breeding outside cages	S4C6

仿佛	fǎngfú	as if; seem	S2C8
坊间	fǎngjiān	in the streets	S2C2
方圆	fāngyuán	surrounding area;	S2C1
非(要)	fēi(yào)	insist on	S3C7
非分	fēifèn	presumptuous	S2C9
分	fēn	a fen (1/10 of a mu)	S2C1
奋不顾身	fènbùgùshēn	be daring, regardless of personal danger	S3C7
芬芳	fēnfāng	fragrant	S1C2
纷纷	fēnfēn	one after another	S1C2
愤愤然	fènfènrán	indignantly	S4C7
逢	féng	come upon	S1C6
风光无限	fēngguāngwúxiàn	exultant	S1C2
奉送	fèngsòng	offer as a gift	S1C6
孵	fū	hatch	S4C6
符合	fúhé	meet; be in line with; accord	S1C4
扶贫	fúpín	alleviation of poverty	S2C6
服帖	fútiē	obedient; well arranged	S3C8
浮想联翩	fúxiǎngliánpiān	thoughts filled one's mind	S3C4
附庸风雅	fùyōngfēngyǎ	mingle with men of letters and pose as a lover of culture; arty-crafty	S3C6
抚掌叫绝	fǔzhǎngjiào jué	applaud	S3C6

G

嘎嘎	gāgā	an onomatopoeia	S2C6
该	gāi	that (above-mentioned)	S4C5
擀	gǎn	roll (out a dumpling wrapper)	S4C8
干净利落	gānjìnglìluò	neat; neatly	S2C5
干(编辑)	gàn (biānji)	work (as an editor)	S2C5
干儿子	gān érzi	godson; honorary son	S2C1
赶写	gǎn xiě	dash off	S2C4
赶到	gǎndào	rushed to	S2C3
赶集	gǎnjí	go to a market/fair	S2C1
赶紧	gǎnjǐn	hurriedly	S1C2
赶巧	gǎnqiǎo	happen to	S2C6
告	gào	sue; accuse	S1C4

搞(革命)	gǎo (gémìng)	start; make; carry on	S2C1
稿酬	gǎochóu	money paid for a piece of writing	S2C7
高考	gāokǎo	National College Entrance Examination	S2C9
隔	gé	after an interval of	S1C5
隔壁	gébì	next door	S1C3
搁	gē	put down	S1C5
硌痛	gè tòng	hurt by grit (in the shoe)	S2C8
疙瘩	gēda	knot	S4C5
给面子	gěi miànzi	show respect	S1C4
跟前	gēnqián	in front of; close to	S1C1
羹汤	gēngtāng	broth	S4C8
哽咽	gěngyè	choked (with sobs)	S1C6
拱	gǒng	sprout up through the earth	S4C8
供	gōng	pay for (education)	S4C2
共享	gòngxiǎng	share; shared	S2C7
工序	gōngxù	(a) procedure	S3C8
公用	gōngyòng	public; for public use	S3C7
勾当	gōudàng	dirty business	S2C2
勾引	gōuyǐn	allure; seduce	S1C5
苟富贵，莫相忘。	gǒufùguì, mòxiāngwàng	"苟"是"如果"的意思；"莫"是"不要"的意思。"如果有一天你富贵了，请不要忘记这一刻。" (Please remember this moment when you are successful.)	S2C9
狗婆子/狗东西	gǒupózi/gǒudōngxi	bitch/son of a bitch	S2C2
箍	gū	hoop; bind	S2C5
孤单	gūdān	alone; lonely	S3C2
鼓动	gǔdòng	instigate; stir up	S2C2
顾家	gùjiā	love and care for one's family	S1C2
刮	guā	scrape	S1C1
寡妇	guǎfù	widow	S1C3
怪	guài	blame	S1C4
拐	guǎi	crook	S2C2
乖乖	guāiguāi	obediently	S3C7
乖乖！	guàiguai	Good gracious!	S3C2
拐棍	guǎigùn	walking stick	S3C5

拐杖	guǎizhàng	walking stick	S2C1
关	guān	shut; lockup; catch	S2C2
关张	guānzhāng	close down	S2C4
管…叫…	guǎn…jiào…	call someone …	S1C7
管用	guǎnyòng	effective	S4C8
光	guāng	only	S2C6
广	guǎng	extensively	S2C7
光辉	guānghuī	radiance	S2C2
光鲜	guāngxiān	shiny; fresh and bright	S1C8
贵(校)	guì (xiào)	(respectfully) your (school)	S3C1
闺蜜	guīmì	a woman's best girlfriend	S1C8
鬼使神差	guǐshǐshénchāi	doings of ghosts and gods; unexpectedly	S2C9
归属	guīshǔ	a place where one feels that one belongs	S4C7
贵头家的	guìtóujiāde	Guitou's wife	S1C5
滚	gǔn	roll	S4C2
过继	guòjì	adopt	S2C2
过于	guòyú	excessively	S1C4

H

蛤蟆	háma	toad	S2C4
喊	hǎn	call; address a person as	S2C1
含	hán	contain	S4C8
含泪	hán lèi	with tears in one's eyes; tearfully	S2C6
函授	hánshòu	correspondence course	S1C9
汉子	hànzi	man; fellow	S2C4
好	hǎo	an adverb to emphasize	S4C8
好把式	hǎobǎshì	highly skilled at	S3C8
好多	hǎoduō	a good many	S3C1
好讲话	hǎojiǎnghuà	soft-hearted and easygoing	S1C3
好容易	hǎoróngyì	with great difficulty	S3C1
好生	hǎoshēng	quite; exceedingly	S4C6
好为人师	hàowéi…	like to lecture others	S4C7
好笑	hǎoxiào	laughable	S2C2
号子	hàozi	a prison cell	S2C6
和…过不去	hé…guòbúqù	find fault with someone	S2C4

合不拢	hé bù lǒng	cannot close; cannot shut	S4C6
何须	hé xū	what is the need; there is no need	S3C6
痕	hén	trace	S3C8
横	hèng	unruly; peremptory	S4C6
横幅	héngfú	banner	S1C4
哄(孩子)	hǒng	lull	S1C2
哄	hōng	an onomatopoeia	S1C4
洪涝	hónglào	flood	S1C4
轰撵	hōng niǎn	drive out	S1C5
红晕	hóngyùn	blush; flush	S3C7
后生	hòusheng	young man	S2C2
后生可畏	hòushēngkěwèi	the young are to be respected	S2C5
弧	hú	a curve	S1C5
糊	hú	paste	S2C4
划	huà	assign; allot	S2C1
划(火柴)	huá (huǒchái)	strike	S1C2
哗啦	huālā	an onomatopoeia	S2C6
滑落	huáluò	slide; slip off	S4C7
话头	huàtóu	thread of a conversation	S3C6
坏	huài	ruin	S4C5
…坏了	huàile	extremely…	S3C8
怀揣	huáichuāi	carry	S1C2
槐树	huáishù	locust tree	S1C1
缓缓	huǎnhuǎn	slowly	S1C3
缓慢	huǎnmàn	slow; slowly	S4C5
还嘴	huánzuǐ	retort	S4C6
晃	huàng	wave; shake	S4C6
晃悠/荡	huàngyou/dang	swinging	S2C4
黄花大闺女	huáng huā dà guīnǚ	(virgin) maiden	S3C7
谎称	huǎngchēng	lie; claim	S4C5
荒诞	huāngdàn	absurd	S2C8
慌忙	huāngmáng	hurried	S3C1
狐臭	húchòu	body odor	S3C8
胡来	húlái	fool with something; make trouble	S3C1
胡闹	húnào	mischief	S2C2
胡子拉碴	húzilāchā	a stubbly chin	S2C4
忽啦啦	hūlālā	an onomatopoeia	S1C5

糊弄	hùnong	fool; deceive; tongue in cheek	S1C1
呼啸	hūxiào	whiz; scream	S4C7
汇报	huìbào	report	S2C4
回锅	huíguō	twice-cook	S4C2
回过神	huíguòshén	come to one's mind	S3C3
回忆	huíyì	recollection	S3C8
汇款单	huìkuǎndān	remittance order	S3C2
混	hùn	drift along; get by	S2C6
浑身	húnshēn	from head to toe	S3C3
昏天黑地	hūntiānhēidì	(feel) dizzy	S2C2
昏头昏脑	hūntóuhūnnǎo	muddleheaded	S1C3
火候	huǒhou	duration and degree of heating	S1C5
火辣辣	huǒlàlà	burning	S1C3
火烧火燎	huǒshāohuǒliáo	feel terribly hot	S4C5
活计	huójì	(handicraft) work	S1C5
活色生香	huósèshēngxiāng	lively and colorful	S4C8

J

饥	jī	hungry	S1C8
继而	jì'ér	then; afterward	S4C8
计程车	jìchéngchē	taxi; cab	S1C6
记仇	jìchóu	bear a grudge	S2C4
叽叽喳喳	jījīzhāzhā	chirp; chatter continuously	S3C8
极目远眺	jímùyuǎntiào	gaze into the distance; as far as one can see	S3C6
积蓄	jīxù	save; savings	S2C8
积攒	jīzǎn	scrape up; accumulate	S4C6
际遇	jìyù	fate; chance	S4C7
(鸡)冠子	(jī) guānzi	crown; hat; comb	S4C6
颊	jiá	cheeks	S3C8
嫁	jià	marry off a daughter; marry (a husband)	S4C6
夹层	jiācéng	inner layer	S2C5
家伙	jiāhuo	guy; fellow	S2C4
加紧	jiājǐn	speed up; hurry up	S4C7
假设	jiǎshè	presume; suppose	S2C9
架式	jiàshi	pose	S1C5

佳肴	jiāyáo	fine food	S4C6
渐	jiàn	gradually; by degrees	S4C8
(见)状	(jiàn) zhuàng	(see) this state; this situation	S3C7
见识	jiànshi	experience and insight	S1C4
见死不救	jiànsǐbújiù	not to help a dying man	S2C4
减轻	jiǎnqīng	ease; alleviate	S4C8
降低	jiàngdī	lower	S2C8
讲究	jiǎngjiu	pay great attention to; be particular about	S3C1
降临	jiànglín	befall; descend	S1C2
奖赏	jiǎngshǎng	reward; prize	S2C7
嚼	jiáo	chew	S2C4
浇	jiāo	dash (water)	S1C4
浇	jiāo	drenched	S2C4
脚踝	jiǎo huái	ankle	S2C4
叫住	jiào zhù	stopped	S2C3
交差	jiāochāi	report to the leadership after finishing a task	S1C4
交代	jiāodài	(1) account for; (2) give order to	S1C4
交接	jiāojiē	hand over; take over	S4C7
交心	jiāoxīn	open hearts to each other	S2C7
绞尽脑汁	jiǎojìnnǎozhī	rack one's brain	S3C4
侥幸	jiǎoxìng	luckily; by a fluke	S1C9
郊游	jiāoyóu	outing; go on an outing	S1C8
皆	jiē	each; all	S2C5
结巴	Jiēba	stammer	S1C3
结	jié	knot	S1C3
结(成)	Jié (chéng)	form	S2C2
结亲	jiéqīn	become related by marriage	S3C8
结伴	jié bàn	form companionships; go in company with	S3C8
结算	jiésuàn	settle accounts	S1C9
节骨眼	jiēgǔyǎn	crucial moment	S2C9
揭开	jiēkāi	uncover; reveal	S2C5
睫毛	jiémáo	eyelashes	S2C7
接亲	jiēqīn	receive the bride	S1C3
尽	jìn	finish; all gone	S3C1
尽	jìn	to the greatest extent	S4C7

尽管(说)	jǐnguǎn(shuō)	feel free to (say)	S2C3
近	jìn	close to; about	S2C8
紧(敲轻捶)	jǐn (qiāo qīng chuí)	urgent(ly); tense(ly); quick(ly)	S3C1
襟怀	jīnhuái	bosom; breadth of mind	S4C7
斤斤计较	jīnjīnjìjiào	haggle over every ounce; fuss about tiny details	S2C8
津津乐道	jīnjīnlèdào	take delight in talking about	S2C2
津津有味	jīnjīnyǒuwèi	be very fond of	S2C5
进退两难	jìntuìliǎngnán	in a dilemma	S2C2
净	jìng	entirely; only	S2C4
井壁	jǐng bì	wall of a well	S3C7
经	jīng	through; after	S2C2
经…这么一提	jīng…zhème yītí	after such a reminder…	S3C8
精耕细作	jīnggēngxìzuò	farm with meticulous care	S3C4
精光	jīngguāng	with nothing left	S1C1
精确	jīngquè	precise; accurate	S2C1
警帽	jǐngmào	a police cap	S2C6
惊天动地	jīngtiāndòngdì	shock heaven and shake earth	S3C1
径直	jìngzhí	straight	S1C3
就近	jiùjìn	(do or get something) nearby	S3C8
就业	jiùyè	(obtain) employment	S1C9
究竟	jiūjìng	in the end; actually	S2C5
救命稻草	jiùmìngdàocǎo	a life-saving straw	S3C7
酒至酣处	jiǔzhìhānchù	near-drunkenness	S4C7
拒绝	jùjué	refuse; reject	S2C3
拘留所	jūliúsuǒ	jail; detention center	S2C6
局面	júmiàn	situation	S4C5
举手投足	jǔshǒutóuzú	every move and act; gesture	S3C8
撅	juē	protrude; stick up	S3C8
决意	juéyì	be determined	S2C9
均	jūn	without exception	S4C5

K

咔嚓	kāchā	an onomatopoeia	S2C6
揩(干)	kāi (gān)	wipe (clean)	S3C1
开窍	kāiqiào	begin to understand	S3C4
开销	kāixiāo	expenditure	S3C2

凯旋	kǎixuán	triumphant return	S4C7
看不惯	kànbúguàn	detest; frown upon	S2C4
看上	kànshàng	take a fancy to; fall for	S2C3
扛	káng	shoulder; endure	S2C2
扛长活	kángchánghuó	work as a farm laborer on yearly basis	S2C1
(炕)沿	(kàng)yán	brim; bank	S1C5
颗	kē	a measure word	S2C6
刻不容缓	kèbùrónghuǎn	permit no delay	S2C4
磕磕碰碰	kēkēpèng pèng	knock (against) and bump (into)	S2C6
磕碰	kēpèng	clash; have a disagreement	S4C6
吭	kēng	utter a sound	S2C2
坑坑洼洼	kēngkēngwāwā	bumpy; potholes	S2C6
恐惧	kǒngjù	fear; terrified	S2C8
空旷	kōngkuàng	open; spacious	S4C7
空暇	kòngxiá	free time; leisure	S2C7
抠	kōu	dig; delve into; grasp	S3C7
扣除	kòuchú	deduct	S4C2
哭丧着脸	kū shàng zhe liǎn	pull a long face	S4C5
裤裆	kùdāng	crotch (of trousers)	S2C2
窟窿	kūlong	hole; loophole; debt	S4C5
酷似	kùsì	be exactly like	S2C5
苦中作乐	kǔzhōngzuòlè	find joy in hardship, suffering, adversity, etc.	S3C6
挎	kuà	carry on the arm	S3C8
夸奖	kuājiǎng	praise	S1C8
哐当	kuāngdāng	a clashing sound	S1C3
狂放不羁	kuángfàngbùjī	unrestrained; uninhibited	S4C7
旷野	kuàngyě	open field	S4C7
亏	kuī	thanks to	S1C5
亏待	kuīdài	treat shabbily	S2C6
魁梧	kuíwǔ	big and tall; burly	S1C1
困(于)	kùn (yú)	be stranded	S2C2
困惑	kùnhuò	perplexed	S1C3
昆曲	kūnqǔ	Kun opera; Kunqu opera	S1C8

L

拉(赞助)	lā(zhànzhù)	draw; appeal (for support)	S2C4

拉肚子	lādùzi	suffer from diarrhea	S2C6
蜡笔	làbǐ	crayon	S1C7
蜡黄	làhuáng	sallow	S4C8
来临	láilín	approach; arrive	S1C4
来日方长	láirìfāngcháng	many a day is yet to come	S3C5
拦	lán	bar; block	S1C3
烂	làn	messy; awful	S4C5
懒	lǎn	lazy	S2C7
懒汉鞋	lǎnhànxié	Chinese cloth shoes with elastic gussets	S2C7
浪	làng	dissolute	S2C2
狼乎	lánghū	like a wolf	S1C5
朗诵	lǎngsòng	read/recite with cadence	S1C8
烙	lào	burn (into memory)	S3C8
老不正经	lǎo bu zhèngjīng	old but still licentious	S4C2
老白干	lǎobáigān	Laobaigan (a popular brand liquor)	S2C4
老百姓	lǎobǎixìng	ordinary people	S2C4
老来	lǎolái	old age	S1C9
老人家	lǎorénjiā	a respectful form of addressing a senior	S4C2
老乡	lǎoxiāng	fellow villager; fellow townsman	S3C2
老爷子	lǎoyézi	father or grandfather	S1C5
唠叨	láodao	chatter	S4C2
牢牢地	láoláodi	firmly	S4C7
劳民伤财	láomínshāngcái	waste money and manpower	S1C4
乐此不疲	lècǐbùpí	enjoy a thing and never get tired of it	S1C8
乐颠颠	lèdiāndiān	joyfully	S2C2
擂	léi	beat; pound	S2C4
泪如泉涌	lèirúquányǒng	tears gushing forth	S2C2
类似	lèisì	similar; analogous	S1C6
累人	lèi rén	tiring	S4C5
累赘	léizhuì	encumbrance; burdensome	S2C7
愣	lèng	be taken aback	S2C1
愣	lèng	stare blankly	S1C3
冷寂	lěngjì	quiet and lonely	S1C2
冷暖	lěngnuǎn	cold or warm; happy or sad	S1C8
立	lì	erect	S2C4
利落	lìluo	deft; agile; crisp	S1C6

利息	lìxī	interest (on a loan)	S2C8
力排众议	lìpáizhòngyì	against all the odds	S2C2
礼数	lǐshù	courtesy; right behavior	S1C5
(脸一)沉	(liǎn yī) chén	pull (a long face)	S2C3
连累	liánlèi	implicate	S3C1
怜惜	liánxī	care about dearly; take pity on	S4C7
晾	liàng	air; dry in the sun	S4C8
良辰美景	liáng chén měi jǐng	a beautiful moment amid beautiful scenery	S3C6
两委班子	liǎng wěi bānzi	"Two committees" (两委) refer to the village Party branch (村党支部) and the village administrative committee (村委会); "organizational body" conveys the meaning of "班子."	S4C5
晾干	liànggān	air-dry	S2C5
撩	liāo	lift up	S2C2
辽参	liáo shēn	an expensive dish with sea cucumber	S1C8
料理	liàolǐ	arrange; manage	S3C3
了如指掌	liǎorúzhǐzhǎng	know . . . like the palm of one's own hand	S2C5
咧(嘴)	liě(zuǐ)	draw back the corners of one's mouth	S1C3
劣质	lièzhì	of poor quality; inferior	S2C7
拎	līn	carry	S2C4
临	lín	just before	S4C6
(临)走	(lín) zǒu	(be about to) die; be gone	S4C2
临了	línliǎo	at the end of one's life	S3C5
灵魂	línghún	soul; spirit	S4C2
伶俐	línglì	quick-witted	S4C6
领取	lǐngqǔ	go and get	S2C8
流露	liúlù	reveal; betray	S1C6
流落	liúluò	drift out	S4C8
留神	liúshén	look out; take care	S2C8
留守	liúshǒu	stay behind	S3C2
留意	liúyì	pay attention to; look at	S1C6
拢	lǒng	hold; draw (near) to; gather up	S4C7
隆重	lóngzhòng	ceremonious; grand	S3C7

漏	lòu	leak	S1C3
露脸	lòuliǎn	look good	S2C6
喽罗	lóuluo	underling; minions	S3C6
路人皆知	lùrénjiēzhī	known by everyone	S4C7
乱上加乱	luàn shàng jiā luàn	add to the chaos	S4C5
乱哄哄	luànhōnghōng	in noisy disorder	S1C5
乱糟糟	luànzāozāo	perturbed	S1C3
栾树	luánshù	golden-rain tree	S1C6
略	lüè	slightly	S2C2
轮	lún	a round of twelve years	S4C6
轮流	lúnliú	take turns	S1C6
摞	luó	a measure word; pile	S2C6
落(下)	luò (xià)	drop; lower down	S1C2
落榜	luòbǎng	flunk a competitive exam	S2C9
落差	luòchā	drop height	S2C5
落落大方	luòluòdàfāng	natural and graceful	S3C8
落寞	luòmò	lonely	S2C7
落水	luòshuǐ	fall into water	S3C7

M

骂人不揭短,打人不打脸	mà rén bù jiē duǎn, dǎ rén bù dǎ liǎn	not to catch people on the raw or hit them in the face	S2C6
马步(下蹲)	mǎbù (xiàdūn)	straddle (squat) as though riding a horse	S2C5
埋	mái	bury	S4C7
麦趟子	mài tàngzi	rows of wheat	S2C1
瞒	mán	conceal from	S2C7
满(纸)	mǎn(zhǐ)	full of; covered with	S2C2
满不在乎	mǎnbúzàihu	do not care at all	S2C5
蔓延	mànyán	spread; extend	S4C7
埋怨	mányuàn	blame	S1C3
忙碌	mánglù	busy; bustle about	S2C8
忙年	mángnián	prepare for the Spring Festival	S1C2
冒出	mào chū	burst out; emerge	S1C8
冒昧	màomèi	make bold	S3C1
没好气	méihǎoqì	sulkily; snappily	S1C3
没救	méijiù	no cure for; hopeless	S1C5

每每	měiměi	often	S2C5
美滋滋	měizīzī	pleased with oneself	S1C3
门脸儿	ménliǎner	shop front; facade	S1C9
朦胧	ménglóng	obscure	S1C5
弥漫	mímàn	pervade; diffuse	S4C8
谜底	mídǐ	answer to a riddle	S2C5
面黄肌瘦	miànhuángjīshòu	emaciated	S3C1
面貌	miànmào	look; feature	S4C5
腼腆	miǎntiǎn	shy	S2C5
瞄	miáo	throw a quick glance	S1C5
描	miáo	trace (the outline of)	S3C8
乜	miē	askew	S1C3
抿(嘴)	mǐn (zuǐ)	close (mouth) lightly	S3C8
敏感	mǐngǎn	sensitive; vulnerable	S2C8
明晰	míngxī	clear	S2C8
蓦(地)	mò (di)	suddenly; unexpectedly	S4C6
抹	mǒ	daub; smear	S1C8
抹眼泪	mǒ yǎnlèi	wipe one's eyes; weep	S2C6
模棱两可	móléngliǎngkě	vague; ambiguous	S1C8
莫明其妙	mòmíngqímiào	inexplicable; baffling	S1C6
磨损	mósǔn	wear and tear	S3C1
摩托车	mótuōchē	motorbike	S2C4
模样周正	móyàng zhōu zhèng	good-looking; having good features	S2C5
眸	móu	pupil of eye; eye	S4C8
亩	mǔ	a unit of area (= 0.0667 hectares)	S2C1
(木)花纹	(mù) huāwén	natural pattern	S1C2

N

纳(鞋底)	nà(xiédǐ)	sew/make (cloth sole of shoes)	S1C5
哪辈子	nǎbèizi	a long time ago	S2C6
哪怕	nǎpà	even though	S2C8
纳闷(儿)	nàmèn(r)	feel puzzled; wonder	S1C7
拿手	náshǒu	good at	S1C5
乃至	nǎizhì	and even	S4C5
难堪	nánkān	embarrassed	S4C5

难耐	nánnài	intolerable	S1C5
闹僵	nào jiāng	come to a deadlock	S2C3
闹夜	nàoyè	a colloquial expression for "burning the midnight oil"	S2C4
脑袋	nǎodai	head; skull; brain	S1C1
脑海	nǎohǎi	head; brain	S3C8
脑壳	nǎoké	skull	S1C3
脑门一热	nǎomén yī rè	on impulse	S1C4
内心	nèixīn	innermost being; inward	S2C8
能耐	néngnài	ability	S2C4
你个挨刀子的	nǐ ge ái dāozi de	a local curse—"You deserve to be stabbed," meaning "You are such an unforgivable person."	S2C6
泥浆	níjiāng	mud	S2C4
泥牛入海	níniúrùhǎi	disappear	S3C5
廿	niàn	twenty	S1C2
碾	niǎn	grind	S1C5
(年)长	(nián) zhǎng	be senior to; older	S2C7
年关	niánguān	the end of the year	S4C6
念头	niàntou	thought; idea	S1C8
捏	niē	nip; squeeze	S2C5
捏	niē	hold between the fingers	S2C6
嗫嚅	nièrú	mutter; speak haltingly	S2C4
拧	nǐng	wring; twist	S1C3
牛	niú	awesome	S2C9
牛高马大	niúgāomǎdà	tall and strong	S3C3
扭(头)	niǔ(tóu)	turn; twist	S1C3
扭转	niǔzhuǎn	turn aound	S4C5
浓烟	nóng yān	dense smoke	S3C8
弄假成真	nòngjiǎchéngzhēn	pretense turns into reality	S2C8
弄堂	nòngtáng	lane; alley	S1C4
农展会	nóngzhǎnhuì	the agricultural fair	S3C4
努嘴	nǔ zuǐ	purse one's lips	S1C4
怒火中烧	nùhuǒzhōngshāo	furious; simmer with rage	S3C6
怒气冲冲	nùqìchōngchōng	ablaze with anger	S2C2
暖壶	nuǎnhú	thermos bottle	S2C3
女婿	nǚxù	son-in-law	S3C7

O

偶然	ǒurán	fortuitous; chance	S2C9

P

怕(是)	pà	I'm afraid; perhaps	S2C1
趴	pā	lie on one's stomach	S4C6
爬 (起来)	pá (qǐlái)	get up; climb	S3C1
派	pài	assign; send	S3C4
派用场	pài yòngchǎng	put to use	S1C9
拍 (爽肤水)	pāi(shuǎngfūshuǐ)	pat; apply (toner)	S3C8
徘徊	páihuái	hesitate; linger	S2C9
牌子	páizi	brand	S1C1
攀	pān	climb; clamber	S4C8
判断力	pànduànlì	ability to judge; judgment	S4C7
蹒跚	pánshān	stumble; hobble	S4C2
盘算	pánsuàn	deliberate; calculate	S2C9
盼望	pànwàng	long for; hope for	S3C2
判刑	pànxíng	sentence (to prison)	S2C4
庞然大物	pángrándàwù	colossus	S3C6
泡	pào	soak	S2C3
抛	pāo	toss; cast	S4C6
跑前跑后	pǎoqiánpǎohòu	running back and forth	S3C7
配	pèi	match	S4C6
配/不配	pèi/búpèi	be worthy/unworthy of	S3C1
赔本	péiběn	sustain losses in business	S2C6
赔不是	péibúshì	apologize	S1C3
赔钱	péiqián	sustain economic losses	S4C2
喷	pēn	spray	S3C8
盆骨	péngǔ	pelvic bone	S1C8
蓬勃	péngbó	full of vitality	S1C2
碰个正着	pèng ge zhèngzháo	happen upon each other	S3C8
批	pī	pass; approve	S2C8
披	pī	put on (over); cover	S3C1
劈	pī	right in/against; straight on	S3C7
披麻戴孝	pīmádàixiào	be dressed in deep mourning	S4C2
偏(偏)	piān(piān)	contrary to expectation	S3C5

偏僻	piānpì	out of the way	S3C2
片刻	piànkè	a moment; a short time	S3C6
瓢	piáo	gourd ladle; wooden dipper	S1C1
飘(香)	piāo(xiāng)	(fragrance) floating/drifting	S4C2
颦	pín	knit the brows	S3C8
聘	pìn	marry a daughter off	S4C6
品尝	pǐncháng	taste; sample	S4C8
品茗	pǐnmíng	sip and taste tea	S3C6
凭	píng	by reason of; rely on	S2C2
屏风	píngfēng	screen	S3C5
凭空	píngkōng	out of thin air; without foundation	S1C6
平衡	pínghéng	balance	S4C5
平生	píngshēng	in one's life	S2C7
平庸	píngyōng	mediocre	S2C8
破	pò	worn	S1C2
破案	pò'àn	solve a case	S2C5
破财	pòcái	suffer financial loss	S4C6
迫近	pòjìn	approach; close in on; imminent	S4C7
铺面	pùmiàn	store; storefront	S1C9
扑通	pūtōng	sound of falling into water; plop; thump	S2C2

Q

齐	qí	reach the height of	S2C4
弃	qì	give up	S2C5
骑驴看唱本—走着瞧	qí lǘ kàn chàngběn—zǒu zhe qiáo	reading a book while riding a donkey—wait and see (who is right)	S3C6
起球	qǐ qiú	piling; balling up	S4C8
起头	qǐtóu	start (a topic, conversation, etc.)	S4C6
起早贪黑	qǐzǎotānhēi	work from dawn to dusk	S3C4
岂不是	qǐbúshì	(an indicator of a rhetorical question) isn't it; wouldn't it be	S2C6
沏茶	qīchá	make tea	S3C1
气喘吁吁	qìchuǎnxūxū	gasp; be out of breath	S1C1
气馁	qìněi	lose heart	S1C7
气势汹汹	qìshìxiōng xiōng	aggressive; fierce	S3C6

气息	qìxī	breath	S2C4
漆黑	qīhēi	pitch-black; pitch-dark	S1C2
起哄	qǐhòng	jeer, boo, and hoot	S2C2
七零八落	qīlíngbāluò	pieces in disorder	S2C8
凄切	qīqiè	mournful	S1C2
掐	qiā	pinch; nip	S4C8
鹐	qiān	peck	S4C6
千般万般	qiānbānwànbān	all the different kinds/ways	S1C2
千里迢迢	qiānlǐtiáotiáo	far away; all the way	S1C2
牵(手)	qiān (shǒu)	lead along (by holding the hand)	S2C8
牵挂	qiānguà	concern; worry	S1C4
牵强附会	qiānqiángfù huì	farfetched	S3C4
纤细	qiānxì	slim; fine	S1C5
签约	qiānyuē	sign a contract	S2C1
腔调	qiāngdiào	tone of voice	S1C3
强令	qiánglìng	force	S2C2
跷	qiào	lift up (a leg)	S3C6
翘(腿)	qiào (tuǐ)	legs crossed	S2C9
憔悴	qiáocuì	haggard	S3C3
巧妙	qiǎomiào	clever; ingeniously	S4C7
俏皮	qiàopí	wittily; lively and delightful	S3C8
怯	qiè	timid; cowardly	S1C1
钦敬	qīn jìng	admire and respect	S2C7
钦羡	qīnxiàn	respect and admire	S3C2
沁入	qìn rù	soak into; permeate	S4C8
亲和力	qīnhélì	affable; friendly; approachable	S4C8
情爱之旅	qíng'àizhīlǚ	journey of love	S4C7
请(不到)	qǐng(búdào)	cannot afford	S2C9
清点	qīngdiǎn	check and count	S2C7
清冷孤寂	qīnglěng gūjì	chilly and lonely	S4C7
清凉	qīngliáng	cool and refreshing	S4C8
清秀	qīngxiù	handsome; pretty	S1C1
顷刻	qǐngkè	instantly; in no time	S4C8
倾盆大雨	qīngpéndàyǔ	torrential rain	S3C4
取暖	qǔnuǎn	warm oneself (by a fire)	S2C8
趋前	qūqián	step forward; hasten forward	S4C6
趋势	qūshì	tendency	S3C5

劝慰	quànwèi	console	S2C7
缺陷	quēxiàn	defect; flaw	S2C8
却之不恭	quèzhībùgōng	(it would be) impolite to decline	S3C7

R

染	rǎn	dye	S2C7
让	ràng	make way; fall back; give ground; yield	S4C6
绕(开)	rào (kāi)	bypass; detour	S3C1
热闹喧腾	rènào xuānténg	lively and noisy	S4C8
热气腾腾	rèqìténgténg	steaming hot	S1C5
认	rèn	enter into a certain relationship; adopt	S2C1
任(凭)	rèn(píng)	let; allow; at the mercy of	S3C3
人家	rénjiā	other people	S1C2
人模狗样	rénmúgǒu yàng	pretending to be what one is not	S2C6
人生地疏	rénshēngdìshū	not familiar	S2C5
日新月异	rìxīnyuèyì	change with each passing day; rapid progress	S1C9
容貌	róngmào	appearance	S4C5
融入	róngrù	integrate; merge into	S2C2
融化	rónghuà	melt; thaw	S2C8
柔软	róuruǎn	soft; lithe	S4C7
乳名	rǔmíng	infant name	S1C2
濡染	rúrǎn	dip (in ink); imbue; immerse; influence	S2C7
入伍从军	rùwǔ cóngjūn	join the military	S2C5
弱者	ruòzhě	the weak	S1C8

S

撒手	sāshǒu	pass away	S1C5
散乱	sǎnluàn	scattered	S3C1
扫荡	sǎodàng	wipe out	S1C5
扫视	sǎoshì	glance; run down	S3C1
刹时	shàshí	in a flash; suddenly	S3C6
晒	shài	bask in (sunshine)	S4C8

闪	shǎn	spark; flash	S4C8
闪现	shǎnxiàn	flash before one	S3C8
山响	shānxiǎng	thunderous	S2C4
上	shàng	apply	S2C5
上坟	shàngfén	visit someone's grave	S2C2
上火	shànghuǒ	get angry	S1C1
上集	shàngjí	go to the market	S2C3
上任	shàngrèn	take office	S2C4
伤风败俗	shāngfēngbàisú	immoral	S2C2
捎	shāo	take along something to or for someone	S2C3
稍	shāo	somewhat; a little	S2C8
少不得	shǎobùdé	have to; cannot be avoided	S4C6
舍不得	shěbùdé	hate to part with	S3C2
奢望	shēwàng	extravagant hopes; wild wishes	S1C6
甚众	shèn zhòng	quite a few	S2C5
神出鬼没	shénchūguǐmò	come and go like a shadow; elusive	S2C5
身段	shēnduàn	figure	S4C7
省	shěng	save; economize	S1C7
生产队长	shēngchǎn duìzhǎng	a production team leader	S2C2
生辰八字	shēngchénbāzì	date and time of birth and its interpretation	S2C2
生分	shēngfen	distant; aloof	S3C8
生生	shēngshēng	compulsory; forcibly	S2C8
生态平衡	shēngtài pínghéng	ecological balance	S2C4
《声声慢》	shēngshēngmàn	a tune name in Chinese poetry	S1C8
拭	shì	wipe (away)	S2C2
(时)辰	(shí)chén	traditional Chinese time unit(s)	S1C2
时令	shílìng	seasons	S4C8
示人	shì rén	show or reveal to others	S4C7
示弱	shìruò	show the white feather; draw back	S4C6
使	shǐ	use	S1C1
使(力气)	shǐ(lìqi)	use; apply	S3C3
使唤	shǐhuàn	order about; use; handle	S4C2
拾掇	shíduō	tidy up	S2C4
施礼	shīlǐ	salute; show courtesy	S1C1
施舍	shīshě	give alms; handout	S1C8

湿润	shīrùn	moist	S2C8
失神	shīshén	out of sorts	S4C8
视线	shìxiàn	sight; view	S1C6
实在	shízài	really	S3C7
虱子	shīzi	lice	S2C7
收	shōu	bring to an end; stop	S3C1
收场	shōuchǎng	end	S2C7
收拾	shōushi	settle accounts with somebody	S2C4
受累	shòulèi	be put to much trouble	S2C1
手到擒来	shǒudàoqínlái	capture easily	S2C5
手舞足蹈	shǒuwǔzúdǎo	dance with joy	S4C7
手艺	shǒuyì	skill; craftsmanship	S2C9
束	shù	bundle; bind; tie	S1C7
数	shǔ	be uppermost	S1C5
梳 (辫子)	shū (biànzi)	wear (ponytail)	S3C8
输人一筹	shū rén yì chóu	be a leg down on someone	S2C5
耍滑	shuǎhuá	act in a slick way	S2C4
刷刷	shuāshuā	an onomatopoeia	S1C5
甩	shuǎi	cast	S2C2
甩	shuǎi	toss; throw	S3C8
甩	shuǎi	swing; fling	S2C6
摔倒	shuāidǎo	fall down	S4C2
率领	shuàilǐng	lead; command	S2C5
爽朗	shuǎnglǎng	heartily	S1C4
爽朗	shuǎnglǎng	frank and outgoing	S3C8
谁叫…	shuí jiào	…shouldn't have…	S4C2
睡懒觉	shuìlǎnjiào	sleep in	S2C4
舒展	shūzhǎn	stretching; unfolding; extending	S4C8
疏通	shūtōng	dredge	S1C4
署名	shǔmíng	sign; signature	S2C7
顺便	shùnbiàn	conveniently	S3C2
顺手	shùnshǒu	do as a natural sequence	S3C1
瞬间	shùnjiān	(a) moment; (in an) instant	S4C8
说不过去	shuō bú guò qù	hardly justifiable	S1C3
(说)妥	(shuō) tuǒ	ready; settled; finished	S2C2
说得出口拿得出手	shuō de chū kǒu ná de chū shǒu	presentable; deserve to be seen	S1C6
说媒	shuōméi	act as matchmaker	S2C3

说情	shuōqíng	intercede for someone	S1C3
丝	sī	a measure word	S4C8
思来想去	sī lái xiǎng qù	think back and forth	S1C3
厮混	sīhùn	fool around	S2C5
死死	sǐsǐ	tightly	S2C2
死活	sǐhuó	simply	S1C5
四处	sìchù	everywhere and all directions	S2C4
四邻八舍	sìlínbāshè	one's near neighbors	S2C3
私自	sīzì	without permission	S2C5
耸	sǒng	rise straight up	S4C6
送展	sòng zhǎn	send to an exhibition for display	S3C4
素不相识	sùbùxiāngshí	not acquainted with each other before	S2C9
素脸	sùliǎn	face without makeup	S4C8
簌簌	sùsù	an onomatopoeic term for rustling	S2C4
算	suàn	count; regard	S2C6
…算得了什么?	…suàndéliǎo shénme	(shucks) it wasn't anything	S2C8
算了	suànle	let it be; let it pass; forget about it	S1C6
酸疼	suānténg	sore; painful	S1C5
穗	suì	tassel	S1C2
遂	suì	then; thereupon	S3C7
随份子	suífènzi	chip in (for a group gift); present a red envelope with money in it as a wedding gift	S4C6
随手	suíshǒu	readily; conveniently	S1C7
(虽灭)犹(燃)	(suīmiè) yōu (rán)	as if; still	S1C2
缩	suō	huddle; cower	S3C8
所思所想	suǒ sī suǒ xiǎng	thinking; thoughts	S1C4
琐碎	suǒsuì	trivia; trifling	S2C8

T

塌	tā	collapse; cave in	S4C5
塌窟窿	tākūlong	owe a debt	S4C5
抬举	táijü	show favor/respect	S1C1
叹	tàn	sigh	S2C5
探入	tàn rù	stretch into	S2C7

探听	tàntīng	try to find out	S4C5
弹簧	tánhuáng	spring	S2C6
谈婚论嫁	tánhūnlùnjià	plan to get married	S3C5
忐忑不安	tǎntèbùān	nervous; uneasy	S3C4
坛子	tánzi	jar; earthen jar	S4C8
趟	tàng	a measure word	S1C4
蹚(水)	tāng	wade	S2C4
汤汁	tāngzhī	soup; broth	S4C8
掏钱	tāo qián	pay	S3C7
桃花运	táohuāyùn	great luck with the opposite sex	S3C7
淘汰	táotài	eliminate	S3C5
陶醉	táozuì	be infatuated with	S2C2
腾出	téngchū	free oneself; make way	S2C2
替	tì	for	S2C3
提高	tígāo	increase; raise	S2C8
天地	tiāndì	universe; world	S3C6
天书	tiānshū	abstruse writing	S2C2
添乱	tiānluàn	mess things up	S2C4
挑	tiāo	choose; select	S1C3
挑水	tiāoshuǐ	carry (buckets of) water (on a shoulder pole)	S1C3
调(馅儿)	tiáo (xiàn'er)	make, season, and mix (filling)	S4C8
调整	tiáozhěng	adjust; arrange	S4C5
跳蚤	tiàozǎo	flee	S2C7
贴	tiē	rub against	S3C7
铁定	tiědìng	definite(ly)	S3C1
铁子	tiězi	sworn friend; buddies	S4C7
挺(住)	tǐng(zhù)	hold out	S3C1
听任	tīngrèn	allow; let be	S2C9
筒	tǒng	tube; cylinder	S1C5
通	tōng	know well	S2C1
通	tōng	a measure word	S1C6
同伙	tónghuǒ	partner (in crime)	S2C5
同桌	tóngzhuō	desk-mate	S3C5
透露	tòulù	reveal	S1C5
投入	tóurù	dedicated; absorbed; engrossed	S3C7
涂(润肤露)	tú (rùnfūlù)	apply (skin lotion); daub	S3C8

突出	tūchū	give prominence to	S3C4
途中	túzhōng	during the journey	S2C4
褪(毛)	tuì (máo)	shed (hair on the body)	S3C8
退避三舍	tuìbìsānshě	retreat to avoid a conflict	S3C6
推迟	tuīchí	put off; postpone	S2C8
推拿按摩	tuīná ànmó	massage	S3C1
吞吞吐吐	tūntūntǔtǔ	haltingly	S2C2
托	tuō	support from underneath	S3C7
托人	tuō rén	ask someone; entrust someone with something	S2C3
脱离	tuōlí	break away from	S1C8
唾沫星子	tuòmò xīngzi	spittle	S1C5
脱身	tuōshēn	get away	S3C2

W

挖(鼻孔)	wā(bíkǒng)	pick (one's nose)	S2C4
瓦解	wǎjiě	collapse; dissolve	S1C8
外表	wàibiǎo	outward appearance	S1C8
外加	wàijiā	in addition; plus	S1C6
往	wǎng	go (in a direction)	S1C1
汪	wāng	a measure word for liquid	S1C2
望穿水色/望穿秋水	wàngchuān shuǐsè/ wàngchuān qiūshuǐ	gaze through and beyond the water/gaze with eager expectation (of someone's return)	S3C6
忘却前嫌	wàngquè qiánxián	forget/bury the hatchet	S4C6
围	wéi	surround; encircle	S1C4
威风凛凛	wēifēnglǐnlǐn	with great dignity	S1C1
唯独	wéidú	only	S1C3
唯恐	wéikǒng	fear	S2C5
为难	wéinán	make it hard for	S1C4
为首的	wéishǒude	headed by; the head	S2C5
为…起见	wèi…qǐjiàn	for the purpose of; in order to	S2C7
委派	wěipài	delegate	S4C5
纹	wén	tattoo	S1C8
温馨	wēnxīn	softly fragrant; warm	S4C7
稳定	wěndìng	stable; stabilize; stability	S4C5

拼音索引 PINYIN VOCABULARY INDEX

稳稳当当	wěnwěndāngdāng	safe and secure	S1C5
文弱书生	wénruòshūshēng	frail men of letters	S3C6
瓮声瓮气	wèngshēngwèngqì	growled; in a low, muffled voice	S2C2
窝囊	wōnang	feel vexed and helpless	S1C6
捂	wǔ	cover	S1C4
无端	wúduān	for no reason at all	S1C9
无非	wúfēi	simply; only	S2C1
无话不说	wúhuàbùshuō	tell one another everything	S2C8
无聊	wúliáo	bored; boring	S2C7
无序	wúxù	disorderly	S3C3
无冤无仇	wúyuānwúchóu	without any ill feeling	S2C9
舞枪弄刀	wǔqiāngnòngdāo	brandish swords and spears	S2C5
呜呜噜噜	wūwulūlu	unclear sounds	S2C4
五线谱	wǔxiànpǔ	staff; stave	S1C8
五颜六色	wǔyánliùsè	multicolored; colorful	S2C6
误事	wù shì	cause delay; hold things up	S3C2

X

熄	xī	extinguish; put out	S3C8
细究	xì jiū	scrutinize; get to the bottom of something	S2C3
吸眼球	xī yǎnqiú	catch someone's eye; eye-catching	S4C7
洗尘	xǐchén	welcome (a traveler); help wash off the dust	S3C1
洗礼	xǐlǐ	baptism; severe tests	S3C1
稀罕	xīhan	care about; love	S1C2
稀罕	xīhan	rare	S3C2
稀里糊涂	xīlǐhútú	muddleheaded	S1C3
细节	xìjié	detail	S2C1
昔日	xīrì	formerly; in olden days	S1C6
瞎	xiā	thoughtlessly	S4C6
下通知	xià tōngzhī	make an announcement	S2C4
下(苦劲)	xià(kǔjìn)	put in (great effort)	S4C5
下地	xiàdì	go work in the field	S2C4
下肚	xiàdù	gulp down	S1C3
下九流	xiàjiǔliú	people of humble professions	S1C3

下手	xiàshǒu	put one's hand to; start	S1C1
(下乡)插队	(xiàxiāng)chāduì	go live and work in a production team in the countryside	S2C5
下学	xiàxué	leave/quit school	S2C6
吓一跳	xiàyítiào	be surprised; freak out	S1C4
衔	xián	hold in the mouth	S4C6
掀(门帘)	xiān (ménlián)	lift up (curtain)	S1C5
显(手艺)	xiǎn (shǒuyì)	display (skills)	S3C1
献(烟, 酒)	xiàn (yān, jiǔ)	offer respectfully	S1C2
闲逛	xián guàng	stroll; lounge	S3C8
闲话	xiánhuà	chat; digression	S4C7
羡慕	xiànmù	admire and envy	S3C2
陷入	xiànrù	fall into	S4C5
纤尘不染	xiānchénbùrǎn	untainted by even a speck of dust	S3C6
像...似的	xiàng...sìde	it seems like...	S1C4
想必	xiǎngbì	most probably	S1C2
相处	xiāngchǔ	get along with	S4C5
相当	xiāngdāng	quite; fairly	S1C7
相	xiàng	the look	S2C4
向着	xiàngzhe	favor; side with	S4C6
消受不起	xiāoshòu bùqǐ	cannot enjoy/endure	S2C6
消沉	xiāochén	dejected; low-spirited; depressed	S2C7
晓得	xiǎodé	know	S2C2
效果	xiàoguǒ	effect; result	S3C7
孝敬	xiàojìng	show filial respect for	S2C4
小崽子	xiǎo zǎizi	a term of endearment for small kids	S2C2
小鬼	xiǎoguǐ	kid (a term of endearment)	S2C9
小巧玲珑	xiǎoqiǎolínglóng	little and dainty; small and delicate	S4C7
小心谨慎	xiǎoxīnjǐnshèn	careful and cautious	S1C8
小心眼儿	xiǎoxīnyǎner	petty	S1C3
小心翼翼	xiǎoxīnyìyì	with utmost care	S1C2
(写)材料	(xiě) cáiliào	prepare written material	S2C4
歇工	xiēgōng	stop working; knock off	S4C2
歇晌	xiēshǎng	take a noon break	S1C1
协商	xiéshāng	talk things over	S2C8

心痛如割	xīn tòng rú gē	hurting badly	S2C2
(心)诚	(xīn) chéng	sincere; sincerity	S2C3
(心)尖子	(xīn)jiānzi	tip-top; the most important; the best of its kind	S2C4
(心)凉	(xīn) liáng	disappointed; disheartened	S2C4
心不在焉	xīnbúzàiyān	be preoccupied with something else	S4C6
心甘情愿	xīngānqíngyàn	with all one's heart	S3C3
心灰意冷	xīnhuīyìlěng	disheartened	S3C5
心灵	xīnlíng	heart and soul; internal spirit;	S2C8
心满意足	xīnmǎnyìzú	satisfied	S1C2
心事	xīnshì	a load on one's mind	S1C3
信奉	xìnfèng	believe; believe in	S4C2
欣赏	xīnshǎng	appreciate; admire	S3C6
行囊	xíngnáng	luggage	S4C5
兴师问罪	xīngshīwènzuì	mobilize troops for a punitive expedition	S3C6
兴头上	xìngtóushàng	at the height of one's enthusiasm	S3C6
兴致十足	xìngzhì shízú	be in the best of spirits	S1C3
性子	xìngzi	temper	S3C5
凶悍	xiōnghàn	fierce and tough	S2C9
凶杀案	xiōngshā àn	homicide case	S4C5
秀	xiù	show; show off	S1C8
羞	xiū	bashful	S2C2
羞恼万分	xiūnǎowànfēn	extremely ashamed and angry	S2C2
羞辱	xiūrǔ	shame; dishonor	S2C7
修缮	xiūshàn	repair; renovate;	S4C7
虚(话)	xū(huà)	empty; false (words)	S2C4
许久	xǔjiǔ	for a long time	S3C8
虚脱	xūtuō	collapse; pass out	S2C9
栩栩如生	xǔxǔrúshēng	lifelike	S1C8
须臾	xūyú	a moment; an instant	S3C6
选拔	xuǎnbá	select	S4C5
选择	xuǎnzé	select; selection	S1C6
血泊	xuèpò	a pool of blood	S2C4
学习委员	xuéxí wěiyuán	a class committee member with study-related duties	S2C5

血缘	xuěyuán	ties of blood	S4C6
熏	xūn	suffocate by smoke	S1C5
寻访	xún fǎng	inquire after; look for	S2C9

Y

雅(间)	yǎ(jiān)	elegant; stylish	S3C1
压抑	yāyì	hold back; constrain	S3C1
鸭子死了嘴还硬	yāzi sǐle zuǐ hái yìng	refuse to admit defeat/a mistake	S3C6
眼	yǎn	a measure word for a well	S3C7
眼看	yǎnkàn	very soon	S4C5
眼看着	yǎnkànzhe	in a moment; look on passively	S4C6
眼泪鼻涕	yǎnlèi bítì	tears and nasal mucus	S2C6
眼神	yǎnshén	expression in one's eyes	S1C6
眼霜	yǎnshuāng	eye cream	S1C8
眼下/前	yǎnxià/qián	at the moment	S2C2
眼睁睁	yǎnzhēngzhēng	unfeelingly	S2C4
眼珠子	yǎnzhūzi	eyeball	S2C4
腌(咸菜)	yān (xiáncài)	preserve in salt; pickle	S1C5
延长	yáncháng	extend; delay	S2C8
延伸	yánshēn	extend; spread	S1C9
厌倦	yànjuàn	be tired of	S2C8
湮没	yānmò	annihilate	S3C3
俨然	yǎnrán	just like	S2C5
掩饰	yǎnshì	hide; conceal	S3C7
烟雾缭绕	yānwù liáorào	smoke curling up	S1C5
胭脂	yānzhi	rouge	S3C6
演奏	yǎnzòu	play a musical instrument	S1C5
仰	yǎng	face upward	S1C3
漾出	yàng chū	brim over	S4C6
漾(开)	yàng(kāi)	ripple; brim over	S3C3
扬长而去	yángchángérqù	swagger off	S1C1
扬声	yángshēng	raise one's voice	S4C6
央求	yāngqiú	beg	S2C2
洋溢	yángyì	be permeated with	S3C7
舀	yǎo	scoop up/out	S1C1

咬耳朵	yǎoěrduo	whisper	S1C3
(咬)紧	(yǎo) jǐn	tight(ly)	S3C1
咬牙	yǎoyá	grit one's teeth	S3C1
要不然	yàoburán	otherwise; or else	S2C8
吆喝	yāohe	cry out; shout; yell	S4C8
妖娆迷人	yāoráo mírén	enchanting and charming	S1C2
也罢	yě bà	all right (when making a concession)	S2C9
野汉子	yěhànzǐ	male adulterer	S2C2
夜幕	yèmù	curtain of night	S1C2
亦	yì	also; too	S4C7
倚	yǐ	lean on	S3C3
以...为能事	yǐ...wéinéngshì	be particularly good at something bad	S2C5
一副...模样	yí fù...móyàng	wear an air of	S2C5
一记耳光	yí jì ěrguāng	a slap in the face	S2C5
一跃而起	yí yuè ér qǐ	jump up	S2C5
(一)晃	(yí) huàng	flash past	S3C5
一般见识	yībānjiàn shi	lower oneself to the same level as someone	S1C1
一板一眼	yìbǎnyìyǎn	methodically	S1C5
一步登天	yíbùdēngtiān	one step to heaven	S3C5
一成不变	yīchéngbúbiàn	unchanging	S2C9
一番	yīfān	bout	S3C1
一个劲地	yīgèjìn di	persistently	S2C2
一见倾心	yījiànqīngxīn	love at first sight	S4C7
一家之主	yījiāzhīzhǔ	the head of a family	S1C5
一脸(凶相)	yīliǎn (xiōng xiàng)	entire face (a fierce look)	S2C4
一脸...气	yīliǎn...qì	with...all over one's face	S1C4
一溜烟	yīliùyān	flee like a wisp of vapor; swiftly	S4C6
一溜烟	yīliūyān	(dash off) swiftly	S3C1
一律	yílǜ	all; without exception	S1C1
一片	yīpiàn	a scene of...	S4C8
一如既往	yīrújìwǎng	as always	S1C6
一头雾水	yītóuwùshuǐ	cannot make heads or tails of something	S3C4
一往情深	yìwǎngqíngshēn	deeply in love	S3C5

一席	yīxí	a space; a place	S3C6
一系列	yīxìliè	a series of	S3C8
一夜情	yīyèqíng	one-night stand	S1C6
一知半解	yīzhībànjiě	have a superficial knowledge of	S1C4
遗产	yíchǎn	legacy	S2C1
遗忘	yíwàng	forget	S2C2
依旧	yījiù	still	S1C8
依恋	yīliàn	be attached to; be reluctant to leave	S4C7
翌日	yìrì	next day	S1C4
漪漪	yīyī	ripples	S3C6
意犹未尽	yìyóuwèijìn	not yet content; reluctant to leave	S2C2
呓语	yìyǔ	crazy talk; talk in one's sleep	S4C7
引导	yǐndǎo	guide	S1C4
引荐	yǐnjiàn	recommend; give a referral	S2C9
阴沟	yīngōu	sewer	S1C4
阴阳怪气	yīnyángguàiqì	(of words or voice) dripping acid	S4C6
阴阳先生	yīnyáng xiānsheng	geomancer	S2C2
隐退	yǐntuì	retreat; to disappear (from society, politics)	S4C7
因子	yīnzǐ	factor; gene; trait	S4C7
硬生生	yìngshēngshēng	directly and forcibly	S2C6
硬是	yìngshì	just; simply; obstinately	S2C2
赢得	yíngdé	gain; win	S3C7
迎娶	yíngqǔ	(a man) marry; send a party to escort the bride to the groom's house	S4C6
营造	yíngzào	construct; build	S4C7
用心	yòngxīn	motive; intention	S1C1
有多好	yǒu duō hǎo	how great it is	S1C2
有两下子	yǒu liǎngxiàzǐ	have real ability and skills	S2C4
有派	yǒu pài	charismatic	S2C4
(有)盼头	(yǒu) pàntou	hope; good prospects	S1C2
有/没出息	yǒu/méichūxi	promising/not promising	S2C6
有情有义	yǒuqíngyǒuyì	kind and just	S2C2
有声有色	yǒushēngyǒusè	full of sound and colors; impressive	S1C2

有意思	yǒuyìsi	falling for someone; checking someone out	S1C3
悠长	yōucháng	long-drawn-out	S4C7
幽默	yōumò	humorous	S2C1
忧伤	yōushāng	sorrow; grief	S1C7
忧心忡忡	yōuxīnchōngchōng	deeply worried	S1C9
犹豫	yóuyù	hesitate	S2C3
欲望	yùwàng	desire/lust; craving	S4C7
逾越	yúyuè	pass; go beyond	S2C9
语重心长	yǔzhòngxīncháng	sincere and earnest	S3C4
怨	yuàn	complain	S4C2
圆满	yuánmǎn	perfect; satisfactory	S2C1
圆润	yuánrùn	smooth and round; mellow	S3C8
原由	yuányóu	reason	S1C5
缘由	yuányóu	reason	S1C1
缘自	yuánzì	originate from; stem from	S2C7
曰	yuē	say	S2C5
约摸	yuēmō	about; roughly	S3C1

Z

砸	zá	smash; mess up; ruin	S1C1
砸	zá	pound	S1C5
咋	zǎ	why	S2C3
咋呼	zāhu	loud; show off; bluster	S2C4
杂碎	zásuì	trivial matters	S4C6
崽	zǎi	young (of animals)	S2C2
在场	zàichǎng	be present	S1C4
暂时	zànshí	temporarily	S1C7
赞助	zànzhù	sponsor	S2C4
脏话	zānghuà	bad language; profanity	S1C8
赃物	zāngwù	stolen goods	S2C5
遭	zāo	meet with	S2C5
遭	zāo	encounter; suffer	S2C7
糟糠	zāokāng	poor men's foodstuffs	S3C3
则	zé	be; then	S1C2
增产	zēngchǎn	increase production	S3C4

扎	zhā	plunge (headlong)	S2C4
扎	zhā	prick	S1C5
轧	zhā	press hard to make powder	S1C5
摘	zhāi	take off	S2C2
盏	zhǎn	a measure word for a lamp, cup, or bowl	S3C6
沾满	zhān mǎn	be stained (covered) with	S3C8
占便宜	zhàn piányi	gain extra advantage by unfair means	S2C6
长	zhǎng	there exist . . . ; have	S4C8
长进	zhǎngjìn	progress	S1C9
掌嘴	zhǎngzuǐ	slap	S1C3
章法	zhāngfǎ	orderly ways	S2C2
涨红	zhànghóng	reddened	S2C2
张飞	Zhāng Fēi	a military general (168–221 CE)	S1C8
张罗	zhāngluo	get busy about	S2C2
张扬(个性)	zhāngyáng (gèxìng)	bring (individuality) into full play; publicize; display	S4C7
罩	zhào	cover; being covered	S4C6
招待	zhāodài	entertain guest(s)	S3C2
召集	zhāojí	convene	S1C4
着落	zháoluò	whereabouts	S1C5
这下(子)	zhèxià(zi)	thus; this time	S1C3
遮蔽	zhēbì	shroud; cover; hide from view	S2C8
折腾	zhēteng	do something repeatedly; mess around	S1C2
阵	zhèn	a measure word for a period of time	S1C3
整	zhěng	make someone suffer; persecute	S2C2
整编	zhěngbiān	regroup	S2C7
争风拔尖	zhēngfēngbájiān	strive to be top-notch	S4C6
争先恐后	zhēngxiānkǒnghòu	strive to be the first and fear to lag behind	S3C2
争执	zhēngzhí	argue	S2C5
挣扎	zhēngzhā	struggle	S3C1
直	zhí	continuously	S2C6
(蜘)蛛网	(zhī)zhūwǎng	spiderweb; cobweb	S4C6
知己	zhījǐ	a confidant	S3C6

知名不具	zhīmíng bújù	anonymously	S2C7
知足	zhīzú	content	S4C2
指令	zhǐlìng	order; command	S1C6
指手划脚	zhǐshǒuhuàjiǎo	gesticulate; find fault with	S1C5
执意	zhíyì	insist on	S3C2
吱吱作响	zhīzhī zuò xiǎng	creaking	S1C8
众	zhòng	many people	S2C5
重点大学	zhòngdiǎn dàxué	key universities	S2C9
忠告	zhōnggào	sincere advice; counsel	S4C7
终归	zhōngguī	after all	S1C8
终究	zhōngjiū	after all; eventually	S2C8
终日	zhōngrì	all day long	S2C7
中奖	zhòngjiǎng	win a prize in a lottery	S1C9
中尉	zhōngwèi	lieutenant	S2C5
骤(升/降)	zhòu(shēng/jiàng)	suddenly; swiftly (rise/fall)	S2C5
皱巴巴	zhòubābā	wrinkled; crumpled	S4C8
皱纹	zhòuwén	wrinkles	S4C6
周遭	zhōuzāo	surrounding area; about	S4C5
住	zhù	fixed; not moving	S3C1
拄	zhǔ	lean on; support oneself with a stick	S2C1
竹竿	zhúgān	bamboo pole/rod	S1C4
拽	zhuài	pull; drag	S2C4
转	zhuàn	walk around	S2C6
转正	zhuǎnzhèng	become a regular employee	S3C4
砖缝	zhuān fèng	brickwork joint	S3C7
桩	zhuāng	a measure word	S1C3
撞	zhuàng	hit; collide	S2C4
装	zhuāng	load; pack	S1C7
装	zhuāng	be concerned with	S4C2
壮胆	zhuàngdǎn	embolden	S1C1
庄稼人	zhuāngjiārén	peasant; farmer	S1C1
赘肉	zhuìròu	unwanted fat; bulge	S4C8
追溯	zhuīsù	trace back	S2C7
啄	zhuó	pick; peck	S4C6
咨询	zīxún	consult	S1C9
恣意	zìyì	willful; recklessly	S4C8

子侄辈	zǐzhíbèi	the younger generation of (sons and nephews)	S3C7
自作主张	zìzuòzhǔzhāng	act on one's own; self-assertive	S3C7
宗	zōng	a measure word	S4C5
纵/横向	zòng/héngxiàng	vertical/horizontal	S4C5
(走)背运	(zǒu) bèiyùn	bad luck	S1C3
走到(老年)	zǒudào (lǎonián)	live to; get to	S1C2
走向	zǒuxiàng	direction; orientation	S2C8
走运	zǒuyùn	have good luck; be in luck	S3C7
足	zú	ample; enough; as much as	S4C7
攥	zuàn	ball one's fist	S1C3
钻心	zuānxīn	pierce to the heart	S1C1
尊严	zūnyán	dignity	S1C8
做成	zuò chéng	make (into)	S1C2

英文索引

ENGLISH VOCABULARY INDEX

A

a beautiful moment amid beautiful scenery	良辰美景	liáng chén měi jǐng	S3C6
a clashing sound	哐当	kuāngdāng	S1C3
a class committee member with study-related duties	学习委员	xuéxí wěiyuán	S2C5
a colloquial expression for "burning the midnight oil"	闹夜	nàoyè	S2C4
a confidant	知己	zhījǐ	S3C6
account for; give order to	交代	jiāodài	S1C4
a curve	弧	hú	S1C5
a *fen* (1/10 of a *mu*)	分	fēn	S2C1
a good many	好多	hǎoduō	S3C1
a life-saving straw	救命稻草	jiùmìngdàocǎo	S3C7
a little over	出头	chūtóu	S3C1
a load on one's mind	心事	xīnshì	S1C3
a local curse—"You deserve to be stabbed," meaning "You are such an unforgivable person."	你个挨刀子的	nǐ ge ái dāozi de	S2C6
a long time ago	哪辈子	nǎbèizi	S2C6
a long while	半晌	bànshǎng	S3C5
(a man) marry; send a party to escort the bride to the groom's house	迎娶	yíngqǔ	S4C6
a measure word	(打一)顿	(dǎyī) dùn	S2C2
a measure word	颗	kē	S2C6
a measure word	趟	tàng	S1C4
a measure word	通	tōng	S1C6
a measure word	(一)桩(心事)	(yī) zhuāng (xīnshì)	S1C3

English	Chinese	Pinyin	Ref
a measure word	宗	zōng	S4C5
a measure word	(刺激一)把	(cìjī yī) bǎ	S1C8
a measure word	丝	sī	S4C8
a measure word (for crop); batch	茬	chá	S4C8
a measure word for a lamp, cup, or bowl	盏	zhǎn	S3C6
a measure word for a period of time	(好一)阵(儿)	(hǎo yī) zhèn (er)	S1C3
a measure word; pile; bunch	簇	cù	S4C8
a measure word for a well	眼	yǎn	S3C7
a measure word for liquid	汪	wāng	S1C2
a measure word; pile	摞	luò	S2C6
a military general (168–221 CE)	张飞	Zhāng Fēi	S1C8
a moment; a short time	片刻	piànkè	S3C6
a moment; an instant	须臾	xūyú	S3C6
a particle indicating "that's all"	罢了	bàle	S4C7
a person with power and/or great skills	大拿	dàná	S4C7
a place where no one could see	避人处	bì rén chù	S2C2
a place where one feels that one belongs	归属	guīshǔ	S4C7
a police cap	警帽	jǐngmào	S2C6
a pool of blood	血泊	xuèpò	S2C4
a prison cell	号子	hàozi	S2C6
a production team leader	生产队长	shēngchǎn duìzhǎng	S2C2
a respectful form of addressing a senior	老人家	lǎorénjiā	S4C2
a round of twelve years	轮	lún	S4C6
a scene of...	一片	yīpiàn	S4C8
a series of	一系列	yīxìliè	S3C8
a slap in the face	一记耳光	yí jì ěrguāng	S2C5
a space; a place	一席	yīxí	S3C6
a stubbly chin	胡子拉碴	húzilāchā	S2C4
a teacher in charge of a class	班主任	bānzhǔrèn	S3C7
a term of endearment for small kids	小崽子	xiǎo zǎizi	S2C2
a transliteration of Audi	奥迪	àodí	S2C4

英文索引 ENGLISH VOCABULARY INDEX

a tune name in Chinese poetry	《声声慢》	shēngshēngmàn	S1C8
a unit of area (= 0.0667 hectares)	亩	mǔ	S2C1
a view of someone's back	背影	bèiyǐng	S1C3
a woman's best girlfriend	闺蜜	guīmì	S1C8
(a woman) get married	出阁	chūgé	S4C6
(a) moment; (in an) instant	瞬间	shùnjiān	S4C8
(a) procedure	工序	gōngxù	S3C8
(a) tightening (sensation)	发紧	fājǐn	S4C6
ability	能耐	néngnài	S2C4
ability to judge; judgment	判断力	pànduànlì	S4C7
ablaze with anger	怒气冲冲	nùqìchōngchōng	S2C2
about; roughly	约摸	yuēmō	S3C1
abstruse writing	天书	tiānshū	S2C2
absurd	荒诞	huāngdàn	S2C8
abusive expressions	恶语	èyǔ	S2C2
accost	搭话	dāhuà	S3C1
acknowledge; respond	(搭)理	(dā)lǐ	S1C3
across; opposite	对过	duìguò	S1C9
act as matchmaker	说媒	shuōméi	S2C3
act in a slick way	耍滑	shuǎhuá	S2C4
act on behalf of	出面	chūmiàn	S1C3
act on one's own; self-assertive	自作主张	zìzuòzhǔzhāng	S3C7
add to the chaos	乱上加乱	luàn shàng jiā luàn	S4C5
address; appellation	称呼	chēnghū	S4C5
adjust; arrange	调整	tiáozhěng	S4C5
admire and envy	羡慕	xiànmù	S3C2
admire and respect	钦敬	qīn jìng	S2C7
adopt	过继	guòjì	S2C2
affable; friendly; approachable	亲和力	qīnhélì	S4C8
after all	终归	zhōngguī	S1C8
after all; eventually	终究	zhōngjiū	S2C8
after an interval of	隔	gé	S1C5
after such a reminder …	经…这么一提	jīng…zhème yītí	S3C8
against all the odds	力排众议	lìpáizhòngyì	S2C2
aggressive; fierce	气势汹汹	qìshìxiōng xiōng	S3C6
air-dry	晾干	liànggān	S2C5
air; dry in the sun	晾	liàng	S4C8

all day long	终日	zhōngrì	S2C7
all right (when making a concession)	也罢	yě bà	S2C9
all the different kinds/ways	千般万般	qiānbānwànbān	S1C2
all; without exception	一律	yílǜ	S1C1
alleviation of poverty	扶贫	fúpín	S2C6
allow; let be	听任	tīngrèn	S2C9
allure; seduce	勾引	gōuyǐn	S1C5
almost; nearly	差点(儿)	chàdiǎn(er)	S1C4
alone; lonely	孤单	gūdān	S3C2
also; too	亦	yì	S4C7
ambiguous; vague	暧昧	àimèi	S4C7
ample; enough; as much as	足	zú	S4C7
an adverb to emphasize	好	hǎo	S4C8
an expensive dish with sea cucumber	辽参	liáo shēn	S1C8
(an indicator of a rhetorical question) isn't it; wouldn't it be	岂不是	qǐbúshì	S2C6
an onomatopoeia	哧啦	chīlā	S1C5
an onomatopoeia	嘎嘎	gāgā	S2C6
an onomatopoeia	哗啦	huālā	S2C6
an onomatopoeia	忽啦啦	hūlālā	S1C5
an onomatopoeia	刷刷	shuāshuā	S1C5
an onomatopoeia	刺啦	cīlā	S4C8
an onomatopoeia	咔嚓	kāchā	S2C6
an onomatopoeia	哄	hōng	S1C4
an onomatopoeic term for rustling	簌簌	sùsù	S2C4
and even	乃至	nǎizhì	S4C5
and; as well as	而	ér	S4C7
ankle	脚踝	jiǎo huái	S2C4
annihilate	湮没	yānmò	S3C3
anonymously	知名不具	zhīmíng bújù	S2C7
answer to a riddle	谜底	mídǐ	S2C5
apologize	赔不是	péibúshì	S1C3
appear; emerge	泛起	fànqǐ	S3C8
appearance	容貌	róngmào	S4C5
applaud	抚掌叫绝	fǔzhǎngjiào jué	S3C6

英文索引 | ENGLISH VOCABULARY INDEX 433

apply	上	shàng	S2C5
apply (skin lotion); daub	涂 (润肤露)	tú (rùnfūlù)	S3C8
apply; put on	打 (粉底)	dǎ (fěndǐ)	S3C8
appreciate; admire	欣赏	xīnshǎng	S3C6
approach; arrive	来临	láilín	S1C4
approach; close in on; imminent	迫近	pòjìn	S4C7
argue	争执	zhēngzhí	S2C5
arrange for; find a place for	安置	ānzhì	S4C7
arrange; manage	料理	liàolǐ	S3C3
as always	一如既往	yīrújìwǎng	S1C6
as if; seem	仿佛	fǎngfú	S2C8
as if; still	(虽灭)犹(燃)	(suīmiè) yóu (rán)	S1C2
as in the old days	不减当年	bù jiǎn dāngnián	S4C6
ask for; beg for	(东)讨(西借)	(dōng)tǎo(xījiè)	S2C2
ask someone; entrust someone with something	托人	tuō rén	S2C3
askew	乜	miē	S1C3
assign; allot	划	huà	S2C1
assign; send	派	pài	S3C4
at least	顶不济	dǐngbújì	S1C5
at the beginning; in the first place	当初	dāngchū	S1C4
at the end of one's life	临了	línliǎo	S3C5
at the height of one's enthusiasm	兴头上	xìngtóushàng	S3C6
at the moment	眼下/前	yǎnxià/qián	S2C2
awesome	牛	niú	S2C9
awfully; unbearably	(得)慌	(de) huāng	S4C2
axle	车轴	chēzhóu	S2C4

B

bad language; profanity	脏话	zānghuà	S1C8
bad luck	(走)背运	(zǒu) bèiyùn	S1C3
balance	平衡	pínghéng	S4C5
ball one's fist	攥	zuàn	S1C3
bamboo pole/rod	竹竿	zhúgān	S1C4

English	Chinese	Pinyin	Ref
banner	横幅	héngfú	S1C4
banter; tease	打趣	dǎqù	S1C2
baptism; severe tests	洗礼	xǐlǐ	S3C1
bar; block	拦	lán	S1C3
bare-chested	敞胸露怀	chǎngxiōnglùhuái	S2C5
bashful	羞	xiū	S2C2
bask in (sunshine)	晒	shài	S4C8
be a cuckold	戴绿帽子	dài lǜ nàozi	S2C2
(be about to) die; be gone	(临)走	(lín) zǒu	S4C2
be attached to; be reluctant to leave	依恋	yīliàn	S4C7
be concerned about	惦记	diànji	S2C2
be concerned with	装	zhuāng	S4C2
be daring, regardless of personal danger	奋不顾身	fènbugùshēn	S3C7
be determined	决意	juéyì	S2C9
be dressed in deep mourning	披麻戴孝	pīmádàixiào	S4C2
be exactly like	酷似	kùsì	S2C5
be fond of (food); covetous	馋	chán	S2C7
be hostile to	仇视	chóushì	S2C8
be in the best of spirits	兴致十足	xìngzhì shízú	S1C3
be infatuated with	陶醉	táozuì	S2C2
be moved by one's surroundings	触情生情	chùjǐngshēngqíng	S3C6
be a leg down on someone	输人一筹	shū rén yì chóu	S2C5
be particularly good at something bad	以...为能事	yǐ...wéinéngshì	S2C5
be permeated with	洋溢	yángyì	S3C7
be preoccupied with something else	心不在焉	xīnbúzàiyān	S4C6
be present	在场	zàichǎng	S1C4
be put to much trouble	受累	shòulèi	S2C1
be senior to; older	(年)长	(nián) zhǎng	S2C7
be stained (covered) with	沾满	zhān mǎn	S3C8
be stranded	困(于)	kùn (yú)	S2C2
be struck dumb	瞠目结舌	chēngmùjiéshé	S1C3
be surprised; freak out	吓一跳	xiàyítiào	S1C4
be taken aback	愣	lèng	S2C1
be tired of	厌倦	yànjuàn	S2C8

be uppermost	数	shǔ	S1C5
be very fond of	津津有味	jīnjīnyǒuwèi	S2C5
be well matched	般配	bānpèi	S3C8
be worthy/unworthy of	配/不配	pèi/búpèi	S3C1
be; then	则	zé	S1C2
bear a grudge	记仇	jìchóu	S2C4
beat; pound	擂	léi	S2C4
become a regular employee	转正	zhuǎnzhèng	S3C4
become related by marriage	结亲	jiéqīn	S3C8
bedding	被褥	bèirù	S2C4
befall; descend	降临	jiànglín	S1C2
before it is too late	趁早	chènzǎo	S3C3
beg	央求	yāngqiú	S2C2
begin to understand	开窍	kāiqiào	S3C4
believe; believe in	信奉	xìnfèng	S4C2
best seller	畅销品	chàngxiāo pǐn	S1C8
bet; make a bet	打赌	dǎdǔ	S2C7
better off than some, worse off than others; reasonably good	比上不足，比下有余	bǐshàngbùzú, bǐxiàyǒuyú	S4C5
big and tall; burly	魁梧	kuíwǔ	S1C1
bind up a wound	包扎	bāozhā	S2C3
bitch/son of a bitch	狗婆子/狗东西	gǒupózi/gǒudōngxi	S2C2
blade	刀刃	dāorèn	S1C1
blame	怪	guài	S1C4
blame	埋怨	mányuàn	S1C3
blame; chide	嗔怪	chēnguài	S1C3
block up	堵	dǔ	S2C6
block; keep off	挡	dǎng	S2C3
blush; flush	红晕	hóngyùn	S3C7
body odor	狐臭	húchòu	S3C8
bored; boring	无聊	wúliáo	S2C7
bosom; breadth of mind	襟怀	jīnhuái	S4C7
both parties; one another	彼此	bǐcǐ	S3C8
bout	一番	yīfān	S3C1
brand	牌子	páizi	S1C1
brandish swords and spears	舞枪弄刀	wǔqiāngnòngdāo	S2C5

English	Chinese	Pinyin	Ref
break away from	脱离	tuōlí	S1C8
breath	气息	qìxī	S2C4
breeding outside cages	放养	fàngyǎng	S4C6
brickwork joint	砖缝	zhuān fèng	S3C7
bright/multicolored	斑斓	bānlán	S4C8
brightly lit	灯火辉煌	dēnghuǒhuīhuáng	S1C2
brim over	漾出	yàng chū	S4C6
brim; bank	(炕)沿	(kàng)yán	S1C5
bring (individuality) into full play; publicize; display	张扬 (个性)	zhāngyáng (gèxìng)	S4C7
bring to an end; stop	收	shōu	S3C1
broth	羹汤	gēngtāng	S4C8
brush lightly; whisk	掸	dǎn	S2C7
bugs	臭虫	chòuchóng	S2C5
bumpy; potholes	坑坑洼洼	kēngkēngwāwā	S2C6
bundle; bind; tie	束	shù	S1C7
burn (into memory)	烙	lào	S3C8
burning	火辣辣	huǒlàlà	S1C3
burning fiercely	炽烈	chìliè	S2C7
burst out; emerge	冒出	mào chū	S1C8
bury	埋	mái	S4C7
busy; bustle about	忙碌	mánglù	S2C8
by reason of; rely on	凭	píng	S2C2
by the time when	待(到)	dài (dào)	S1C2
bypass; detour	绕(开)	rào (kāi)	S3C1

C

English	Chinese	Pinyin	Ref
call someone …	管 … 叫 …	guǎn … jiào …	S1C7
call; address a person as	喊	hǎn	S2C1
calm and unhurried	从容	cōngróng	S3C1
cannot make heads or tails of something	一头雾水	yītóuwùshuǐ	S3C4
cannot afford	请(不到)	qǐng(búdào)	S2C9
cannot close; cannot shut	合不拢	hé bù lǒng	S4C6
cannot enjoy/endure	消受不起	xiāo shòu bù qǐ	S2C6
cannot move	动弹不得	dòngtan bù dé	S2C4

英文索引 ENGLISH VOCABULARY INDEX

capture easily	手到擒来	shǒudàoqínlái	S2C5
care about dearly; take pity on	怜惜	liánxī	S4C7
care about; love	稀罕	xīhan	S1C2
careful and cautious	小心谨慎	xiǎoxīnjǐnshèn	S1C8
carfare; fare	车资	chēzī	S1C6
cargo space; box; car	(车)厢	(chē) xiāng	S2C6
carry	怀揣	huáichuāi	S1C2
carry	拎	līn	S2C4
carry (buckets of) water (on a shoulder pole)	挑水	tiāoshuǐ	S1C3
carry on the arm	挎	kuà	S3C8
carrying pole	扁担	biǎndān	S1C3
cast	甩	shuǎi	S2C2
cast a glance	瞅	chǒu	S1C3
catch someone's eye; eye-catching	吸眼球	xī yǎnqiú	S4C7
cause death	出人命	chūrénmìng	S2C4
cause delay; hold things up	误事	wù shì	S3C2
ceremonious; grand	隆重	lóngzhòng	S3C7
change with each passing day; rapid progress	日新月异	rìxīnyuèyì	S1C9
charge and shatter enemy positions	冲锋陷阵	chōngfēngxiànzhèn	S2C5
charismatic	有派	yǒu pài	S2C4
chat; digression	闲话	xiánhuà	S4C7
chatter	唠叨	láodao	S4C2
chatter away	叨叨	dāodao	S4C8
check and count	清点	qīngdiǎn	S2C7
cheeks	颊	jiá	S3C8
chew	嚼	jiáo	S2C4
chilly and lonely	清冷孤寂	qīnglěng gūjì	S4C7
Chinese cloth shoes with elastic gussets	懒汉鞋	lǎnhànxié	S2C7
chip in (for a group gift); present a red envelope with money in it as a wedding gift	随份子	suífènzi	S4C6
chirp; chatter continuously	叽叽喳喳	jījīzhāzhā	S3C8
choked (with sobs)	哽咽	gěngyè	S1C6

English	Chinese	Pinyin	Ref
choose; select	挑	tiāo	S1C3
chop	剁	duò	S1C3
clash; have a disagreement	磕碰	kēpèng	S4C6
class fund	班费	bānfèi	S2C5
classical texts	典	diǎn	S2C7
clear	明晰	míngxī	S2C8
clever; ingeniously	巧妙	qiǎomiào	S4C7
climb; clamber	攀	pān	S4C8
close (door)	带拢(门)	dài long (mén)	S3C1
close (mouth) lightly	抿(嘴)	mǐn (zuǐ)	S3C8
close down	关张	guānzhāng	S2C4
close to; about	近	jìn	S2C8
clumsy	笨手笨脚	bènshǒubènjiǎo	S2C9
coarse; crude	粗拉	cūlā	S2C4
cold or warm; happy or sad	冷暖	lěngnuǎn	S1C8
collapse; cave in	塌	tā	S4C5
collapse; dissolve	瓦解	wǎjiě	S1C8
collapse; pass out	虚脱	xūtuō	S2C9
National College Entrance Examination	高考	gāokǎo	S2C9
colossus	庞然大物	pángrándàwù	S3C6
come and go like a shadow; elusive	神出鬼没	shénchūguǐmò	S2C5
come to a deadlock	闹僵	nào jiāng	S2C3
come to one's mind	回过神	huíguòshén	S3C3
come upon	逢	féng	S1C6
commitment	承诺	chéngnuò	S1C4
complain	怨	yuàn	S4C2
compulsory; forcibly	生生	shēngshēng	S2C8
conceal from	瞒	mán	S2C7
conceal; hide	藏匿	cángnì	S2C5
concern; worry	牵挂	qiānguà	S1C4
conduct funeral and burial services	办丧事	bàn sāngshì	S3C2
confess one's love	表白	biǎobái	S3C8
console	劝慰	quànwèi	S2C7
console; comfort	安慰	ānwèi	S4C2
construct; build	营造	yíngzào	S4C7

consult	咨询	zīxún	S1C9
contain	含	hán	S4C8
content	知足	zhīzú	S4C2
continuously	直	zhí	S2C6
contract	承包	chéngbāo	S4C5
contrary to expectation	偏(偏)	piān(piān)	S3C5
convene	召集	zhāojí	S1C4
conveniently	顺便	shùnbiàn	S3C2
cool and refreshing	清凉	qīngliáng	S4C8
correspondence course	函授	hánshòu	S1C9
count; regard	算	suàn	S2C6
countermeasure	对策	duìcè	S2C5
courtesy; right behavior	礼数	lǐshù	S1C5
cover	捂	wǔ	S1C4
cover; being covered	罩	zhào	S4C6
crayon	蜡笔	làbǐ	S1C7
crazy talk; talk in one's sleep	呓语	yìyǔ	S4C7
creaking	吱吱作响	zhīzhī zuò xiǎng	S1C8
critically ill	病危	bìngwēi	S3C5
crook	拐	guǎi	S2C2
crotch (of trousers)	裤裆	kùdāng	S2C2
crown; hat; comb	(鸡)冠子	(jī) guānzi	S4C6
crucial moment	节骨眼	jiēgǔyǎn	S2C9
cruel	残酷	cánkù	S2C7
cry out; shout; yell	吆喝	yāohe	S4C8
curtain of night	夜幕	yèmù	S1C2
cushion; pad	垫子	diànzi	S2C6
customer at a teahouse	茶客	chákè	S3C6

D

dance with joy	手舞足蹈	shǒuwǔzúdǎo	S4C7
dash (water)	浇	jiāo	S1C4
dash off	赶写	gǎn xiě	S2C4
(dash off) swiftly	一溜烟	yīliūyān	S3C1
date and time of birth and its interpretation	生辰八字	shēngchénbāzì	S2C2
daub; smear	抹	mǒ	S1C8

English	Chinese	Pinyin	Ref
dedicated; absorbed; engrossed	投入	tóurù	S3C7
deduct	扣除	kòuchú	S4C2
deeply in love	一往情深	yìwǎngqíngshēn	S3C5
deeply worried	忧心忡忡	yōuxīnchōngchōng	S1C9
defect; flaw	缺陷	quēxiàn	S2C8
defend; explain	辩解	biànjiě	S2C3
defend someone against an injustice	打抱不平	dǎbàobùpíng	S2C5
deft; agile; crisp	利落	lìluo	S1C6
definite(ly)	铁定	tiědìng	S3C1
dejected; low-spirited; depressed	消沉	xiāochén	S2C7
delay	耽误	dānwù	S2C4
delegate	委派	wěipài	S4C5
deliberate; calculate	盘算	pánsuàn	S2C9
delicate; fragile	脆弱	cuìruò	S2C9
denounce	斥责	chìzé	S4C6
dense smoke	浓烟	nóng yān	S3C8
desire/lust; craving	欲望	yùwàng	S4C7
desk-mate	同桌	tóngzhuō	S3C5
detail	细节	xìjié	S2C1
detest; frown upon	看不惯	kànbúguàn	S2C4
dig; delve into; grasp	抠	kōu	S3C7
dignity	尊严	zūnyán	S1C8
dip (in ink); imbue; immerse; influence	濡染	rúrǎn	S2C7
direction; orientation	走向	zǒuxiàng	S2C8
directly and forcibly	硬生生	yìngshēngshēng	S2C6
dirty business	勾当	gōudàng	S2C2
disappear	泥牛入海	níniúrùhǎi	S3C5
disappointed; disheartened	(心)凉	(xīn) liáng	S2C4
discount; on sale	打折	dǎzhé	S1C6
disgusting	臭	chòu	S3C1
disheartened	心灰意冷	xīnhuīyìlěng	S3C5
disorderly	无序	wúxù	S3C3
display (skills)	显(手艺)	xiǎn (shǒuyì)	S3C1
dissolute	浪	làng	S2C2

English	Chinese	Pinyin	Ref
distant; aloof	生分	shēngfen	S3C8
do as a natural sequence	顺手	shùnshǒu	S3C1
doings of ghosts and gods; unexpectedly	鬼使神差	guǐshǐshénchāi	S2C9
do not care at all	满不在乎	mǎnbúzàihu	S2C5
(do not) acquiesce to old age	(不)服老	(bù) fúlǎo	S4C2
(do or get something) nearby	就近	jiùjìn	S3C8
do something repeatedly; mess around	折腾	zhēteng	S1C2
draw back the corners of one's mouth	咧(嘴)	liě(zuǐ)	S1C3
draw water to irrigate a (rice) field using a waterwheel	车(秧)水	chē (yāng) shuǐ	S3C3
draw; appeal (for support)	拉(赞助)	lā(zhànzhù)	S2C4
draw; fetch	打(水)	dǎ(shuǐ)	S2C4
dredge	疏通	shūtōng	S1C4
drenched	浇	jiāo	S2C4
drift along; get by	混	hùn	S2C6
drift out	流落	liúluò	S4C8
drive out	轰撵	hōng niǎn	S1C5
drop; lower down	落(下)	luò (xià)	S1C2
drop height	落差	luòchā	S2C5
duration and degree of heating	火候	huǒhou	S1C5
during the journey	途中	túzhōng	S2C4
dye	染	rǎn	S2C7

E

English	Chinese	Pinyin	Ref
each; all	皆	jiē	S2C5
ears; around the ears	耳际	ěrjì	S3C8
ease; alleviate	减轻	jiǎnqīng	S4C8
easy to persuade	不经劝	bùjīnquàn	S1C3
manner of eating	吃相	chīxiàng	S2C4
ecological balance	生态平衡	shēngtài pínghéng	S2C4
effect; result	效果	xiàoguǒ	S3C7
effective	管用	guǎnyòng	S4C8
elegant; stylish	雅(间)	yǎ(jiān)	S3C1

English	Chinese	Pinyin	Ref
eliminate	淘汰	táotài	S3C5
emaciated	面黄肌瘦	miànhuángjīshòu	S3C1
embarrassed	难堪	nánkān	S4C5
embolden	壮胆	zhuàngdǎn	S1C1
empty; false (words)	虚(话)	xū(huà)	S2C4
enchanting and charming	妖娆迷人	yāoráo mírén	S1C2
encounter; suffer	遭	zāo	S2C7
encumbrance; burdensome	累赘	léizhuì	S2C7
end	收场	shōuchǎng	S2C7
end; finished	罢	bà	S2C6
endlessly	不已	bùyǐ	S2C2
endure hardship	吃苦	chīkǔ	S4C2
enjoy a thing and never get tired of it	乐此不疲	lècǐbùpí	S1C8
enter into a certain relationship; adopt	认	rèn	S2C1
entertain guest(s)	招待	zhāodài	S3C2
entire face (a fierce look)	一脸(凶相)	yīliǎn (xiōng xiàng)	S2C4
entirely; only	净	jìng	S2C4
erect	立	lì	S2C4
eternal sleep; die	长眠	cháng mián	S3C2
evade; elude	躲避	duǒbì	S1C6
even though	哪怕	nǎpà	S2C8
every move and act; gesture	举手投足	jǔshǒutóuzú	S3C8
everywhere	到处	dàochù	S1C7
everywhere and all directions	四处	sìchù	S2C4
exceed	超过	chāoguò	S2C9
excessively	过于	guòyú	S1C4
expand	撑	chēng	S4C5
expenditure	开销	kāixiāo	S3C2
experience and insight	见识	jiànshi	S1C4
express one's thanks	道谢	dàoxiè	S4C8
expression in one's eyes	眼神	yǎnshén	S1C6
extend; delay	延长	yáncháng	S2C8
extend; spread	延伸	yánshēn	S1C9
extensively	广	guǎng	S2C7
extent	地步	dìbù	S1C2
extinguish; put out	熄	xī	S3C8

extravagant hopes; wild wishes	奢望	shēwàng	S1C6
extremely...	...坏了	huàile	S3C8
extremely ashamed and angry	羞恼万分	xiūnǎowànfēn	S2C2
exultant	风光无限	fēngguāngwúxiàn	S1C2
eyeball	眼珠子	yǎnzhūzi	S2C4
eye cream	眼霜	yǎnshuāng	S1C8
eyelashes	睫毛	jiémáo	S2C7

F

face upward	仰	yǎng	S1C3
face without makeup	素脸	sùliǎn	S4C8
factor; gene; trait	因子	yīnzǐ	S4C7
fade from memory	淡忘	dànwàng	S4C6
fall; drop	掉	diào	S4C2
fall down	摔倒	shuāidǎo	S4C2
fall into	陷入	xiànrù	S4C5
fall into water	落水	luòshuǐ	S3C7
falling for someone; checking someone out	有意思	yǒuyìsi	S1C3
falter	步履踉跄	bùlǚliàngqiàng	S3C1
far away; all the way	千里迢迢	qiānlǐtiáotiáo	S1C2
farfetched	牵强附会	qiānqiángfùhuì	S3C4
farm with meticulous care	精耕细作	jīnggēngxìzuò	S3C4
fasten	绑	bǎng	S2C4
fate; chance	际遇	jìyù	S4C7
father or grandfather	老爷子	lǎoyézi	S1C5
favor; side with	向着	xiàngzhe	S4C6
fear	唯恐	wéikǒng	S2C5
fear; terrified	恐惧	kǒngjù	S2C8
feel bad; upset	不是滋味	bú shì zīwèi	S3C3
(feel) dizzy	昏天黑地	hūntiānhēidì	S2C2
feel free to (say)	尽管(说)	jǐnguǎn(shuō)	S2C3
feel puzzled; wonder	纳闷(儿)	nàmèn(r)	S1C7
feel terribly hot	火烧火燎	huǒshāohuǒliǎo	S4C5
feel vexed and helpless	窝囊	wōnang	S1C6
feel wronged and act rashly; out of spite	赌气	dǔqì	S1C3

English	Chinese	Pinyin	Ref
fellow villager; fellow townsman	老乡	lǎoxiāng	S3C2
ferociously	恶狠狠	èhěnhěn	S2C5
fierce and tough	凶悍	xiōnghàn	S2C9
figure	身段	shēnduàn	S4C7
fill a bowl	盛(饭)	chéng (fàn)	S1C5
find fault with someone	和…过不去	hé…guòbúqù	S2C4
find joy in hardship, suffering, adversity etc.	苦中作乐	kǔzhōngzuòlè	S3C6
fine food	佳肴	jiāyáo	S4C6
finish; all gone	尽	jìn	S3C1
firmly	牢牢地	láoláodi	S4C7
fix one's eyes on	盯	dīng	S3C4
fixed; not moving	住	zhù	S3C1
flash before one	闪现	shǎnxiàn	S3C8
flash past	(一)晃	(yí) huàng	S3C5
flee	跳蚤	tiàozǎo	S2C7
flee like a wisp of vapor; swiftly	一溜烟	yīliùyān	S4C6
flood	洪涝	hónglào	S1C4
flunk a competitive exam	落榜	luòbǎng	S2C9
followed by; second to	次之	cì zhī	S2C7
fool; deceive; tongue in cheek	糊弄	hùnong	S1C1
fool around	厮混	sīhùn	S2C5
fool with something; make trouble	胡来	húlái	S3C1
for	替	tì	S2C3
for a long time	许久	xǔjiǔ	S3C8
for no reason at all	无端	wúduān	S1C9
for the purpose of; in order to	为…起见	wèi…qǐjiàn	S2C7
force	强令	qiánglìng	S2C2
forge (iron/chain)	打(铁/链子)	dǎ(tiě/liànzi)	S2C5
forget	遗忘	yíwàng	S2C2
forget/bury the hatchet	忘却前嫌	wàngquè qiánxián	S4C6
form	结(成)	Jié (chéng)	S2C2
form companionships; go in company with	结伴	jié bàn	S3C8
formerly; in olden days	昔日	xīrì	S1C6
fortuitous; chance	偶然	ǒurán	S2C9

… ENGLISH VOCABULARY INDEX 445

(fragrance) floating/drifting	飘(香)	piāo(xiāng)	S4C2
fragrant	芬芳	fēnfāng	S1C2
frail men of letters	文弱书生	wénruòshūshēng	S3C6
frank and outgoing	爽朗	shuǎnglǎng	S3C8
free (oneself)	腾(出)	téng (chū)	S2C2
free time; leisure	空暇	kòngxiá	S2C7
from (far away)	打(老远)	dǎ (lǎoyuǎn)	S2C6
from head to toe	浑身	húnshēn	S3C3
full	饱	bǎo	S1C8
full of sound and colors; impressive	有声有色	yǒushēngyǒusè	S1C2
full of vitality	蓬勃	péngbó	S1C2
full of; covered with	满(纸)	mǎn(zhǐ)	S2C2
furious; simmering with rage	怒火中烧	nùhuǒzhōngshāo	S3C6

G

gain extra advantage by unfair means	占便宜	zhàn piányi	S2C6
gain; win	赢得	yíngdé	S3C7
gallop	驰骋	chíchěng	S2C5
gamble	赌博	dǔbó	S1C9
gaming chip; bargaining chip	筹码	chóumǎ	S1C9
gasp; be out of breath	气喘吁吁	qìchuǎnxūxū	S1C1
gaze into the distance; as far as one can see	极目远眺	jímùyuǎntiào	S3C6
gaze through and beyond the water/gaze with eager expectation (of someone's return)	望穿水色/望穿秋水	wàngchuān shuǐsè/ wàngchuān qiūshuǐ	S3C6
geomancer	阴阳先生	yīnyáng xiānsheng	S2C2
gesticulate; find fault with	指手划脚	zhǐshǒuhuàjiǎo	S1C5
gesticulate; gesture	比划	bǐhua	S1C7
get along with	相处	xiāngchǔ	S4C5
get an electric shock	触电	chùdiàn	S2C8
get angry	上火	shànghuǒ	S1C1
get away	抽身	chōushēn	S3C1
get away	脱身	tuōshēn	S3C2
get busy about	张罗	zhāngluo	S2C2

English	Chinese	Pinyin	Ref
get in a word; talk; answer	搭话	dāhuà	S1C5
get through; survive	熬(日子)	áo (rìzi)	S3C1
get up; climb	爬 (起来)	pá (qǐlái)	S3C1
gifted scholar	才子	cáizǐ	S3C4
give alms; handout	施舍	shīshě	S1C8
give hints	点拨	diǎnbō	S3C4
give prominence to	突出	tūchū	S3C4
give up	弃	qì	S2C5
glance; run down	扫视	sǎoshì	S3C1
go (in a direction)	往	wǎng	S1C1
go and get	领取	lǐngqǔ	S2C8
go from place to place; run about	串	chuàn	S1C2
go live and work in a production team in the countryside	(下乡)插队	(xiàxiāng)chāduì	S2C5
go to a market/fair	赶集	gǎnjí	S2C1
go to the market	上集	shàngjí	S2C3
go work in the field	下地	xiàdì	S2C4
go wrong	不对头	búduìtóu	S4C6
godson; honorary son	干儿子	gān érzi	S2C1
going round and round	滴溜溜	dīliūliū	S1C2
golden-rain tree	栾树	luánshù	S1C6
good at	拿手	náshǒu	S1C5
Good gracious!	乖乖!	guāiguai	S3C2
good-looking; having good features	模样周正	móyàng zhōu zhèng	S2C5
gourd ladle; wooden dipper	瓢	piáo	S1C1
gradually; by degrees	渐	jiàn	S4C8
gratifying; gratified	称心	chènxīn	S4C7
great luck with the opposite sex	桃花运	táohuāyùn	S3C7
grind	碾	niǎn	S1C5
grit one's teeth	咬牙	yǎoyá	S3C1
growled; in a low, muffled voice	瓮声瓮气	wèngshēngwèngqì	S2C2
guide	引导	yǐndǎo	S1C4
Guitou's wife	贵头家的	guìtóujiāde	S1C5
gulp down	下肚	xiàdù	S1C3
guy; fellow	家伙	jiāhuo	S2C4

H

haggard	憔悴	qiáocuì	S3C3
haggle over every ounce; fuss about tiny details	斤斤计较	jīnjīnjìjiào	S2C8
haltingly	吞吞吐吐	tūntūntǔtǔ	S2C2
hand over to; deliver	递(给/到)	dì (gěi/dào)	S2C4
hand over; take over	交接	jiāojiē	S4C7
(handicraft) work	活计	huóji	S1C5
handsome; pretty	清秀	qīngxiù	S1C1
hang (over)	搭	dā	S3C8
hang down	垂	chuí	S4C7
happen to	赶巧	gǎnqiǎo	S2C6
happen to coincide	不约而同	bùyuē'értóng	S4C7
happen upon each other	碰个正着	pèng ge zhèngzháo	S3C8
hard liquor	大曲	dàqū	S3C7
hard of hearing	耳背	ěrbèi	S2C2
hardly justifiable	说不过去	shuō bú guò qù	S1C3
hatch	孵	fú	S4C6
hate to part with	舍不得	shěbùdé	S3C2
have a rough time	吃苦受累	chīkǔ shòulèi	S4C5
have a superficial knowledge of	一知半解	yīzhībànjiě	S1C4
have a taste of seasonal delicacy	尝鲜	cháng xiān	S4C8
have a taut face;	板脸	bǎn liǎn	S4C8
have bad luck	倒霉	dǎoméi	S3C5
have good luck; be in luck	走运	zǒuyùn	S3C7
have many children and grandchildren	儿孙满堂	érsūnmǎntáng	S4C2
have real ability and skills	有两下子	yǒu liǎngxiàzǐ	S2C4
have thought hard and still cannot make sense of it	百思不得其解	bǎi sī bù dé qí jiě	S3C2
have to; cannot be avoided	少不得	shǎobùdé	S4C6
head; brain	脑海	nǎohǎi	S3C8
head; skull; brain	脑袋	nǎodai	S1C1
headed by; head	为首的	wéishǒude	S2C5
heart and soul; internal spirit;	心灵	xīnlíng	S2C8
heartily	爽朗	shuǎnglǎng	S1C4

English	Chinese	Pinyin	Ref
hedgehog	刺猬	cìwei	S2C8
hesitate	犹豫	yóuyù	S2C3
hesitate; linger	徘徊	páihuái	S2C9
hide; conceal	掩饰	yǎnshì	S3C7
hide; dodge	躲避	duǒbì	S1C4
highly skilled at	好把式	hǎobǎshì	S3C8
hit; collide	撞	zhuàng	S2C4
hold; draw (near) to; gather up	拢	lǒng	S4C7
hold back; constrain	压抑	yāyì	S3C1
hold between the fingers	捏	niē	S2C6
hold in the mouth	衔	xián	S4C6
hold out	挺(住)	tǐng(zhù)	S3C1
hold out (until)	撑	chēng	S4C2
hole; loophole; debt	窟窿	kūlong	S4C5
homicide case	凶杀案	xiōngshā àn	S4C5
hoop; bind	箍	gū	S2C5
hope; good prospects	(有)盼头	(yǒu) pàntou	S1C2
how great it is	有多好	yǒu duō hǎo	S1C2
huddle; cower	缩	suō	S3C8
humorous	幽默	yōumò	S2C1
hungry	饥	jī	S1C8
hurried	慌忙	huāngmāng	S3C1
hurriedly	赶紧	gǎnjǐn	S1C2
hurt by grit (in the shoe)	硌痛	gè tòng	S2C8
hurting badly	心痛如割	xīn tòng rú gē	S2C2

I

English	Chinese	Pinyin	Ref
I'm afraid; perhaps	怕(是)	pà	S2C1
ignorant of the facts/truth	不明真相	bùmíngzhēnxiàng	S1C4
ignore; dismiss	不予理会	bù yǔ lǐhuì	S2C8
immediately; suddenly	顿时	dùnshí	S1C4
immoral	伤风败俗	shāngfēngbàisú	S2C2
impermissible; not allowed	不兴	bùxīng	S3C7
implicate	连累	liánlèi	S3C1
improved significantly	大有起色	dà yǒu qǐsè	S1C6

in a daze	发呆	fādāi	S1C2
in a dilemma	进退两难	jìntuìliǎngnán	S2C2
in a flash; suddenly	刹时	shàshí	S3C6
in a moment; look on passively	眼看着	yǎnkànzhe	S4C6
in addition; plus	外加	wàijiā	S1C6
in disguised form	变相	biànxiàng	S1C9
in front of; close to	跟前	gēnqián	S1C1
in noisy disorder	乱哄哄	luànhōnghōng	S1C5
in one's life	平生	píngshēng	S2C7
in the end; actually	究竟	jiūjìng	S2C5
in the ordinary course of events	按说	ànshuō	S2C4
in the streets	坊间	fāngjiān	S2C2
increase; raise	提高	tígāo	S2C8
increase production	增产	zēngchǎn	S3C4
indignantly	愤愤然	fènfènrán	S4C7
inexplicable; baffling	莫明其妙	mòmíngqímiào	S1C6
inexplicably	不知道怎么的	bù zhīdào zěnme de	S1C8
infant name	乳名	rǔmíng	S1C2
infatuation	痴心	chīxīn	S3C5
innermost being; inward	内心	nèixīn	S2C8
inquire after; look for	寻访	xún fǎng	S2C9
insist on	非(要)	fēi(yào)	S3C7
insist on	执意	zhíyì	S3C2
instantly; in no time	顷刻	qǐngkè	S4C8
instigate; stir up	鼓动	gǔdòng	S2C2
integrate; merge into	融入	róngrù	S2C2
intercede for someone	说情	shuōqíng	S1C3
interest (on a loan)	利息	lìxī	S2C8
inner layer	夹层	jiācéng	S2C5
intolerable	难耐	nánnài	S1C5
irritate; upset	刺激	cìjī	S4C6
Isn't it true that . . . ; Everyone says . . .	不都说 . . .	bùdōushuō	S1C8
issue a belch	打嗝	dǎgé	S1C5
it seems like . . .	像 . . . 似的	xiàng . . . sìde	S1C4
(it would be) impolite to decline	却之不恭	quèzhībùgōng	S3C7

J

jail; detention center	拘留所	jūliúsuǒ	S2C6
jar; earthen jar	坛子	tánzi	S4C8
jeer, boo and hoot	起哄	qǐhòng	S2C2
join the military	入伍从军	rùwǔ cóngjūn	S2C5
journey of love	情爱之旅	qíng'àizhīlǚ	S4C7
joyfully	乐颠颠	lèdiāndiān	S2C2
jump up	一跃而起	yí yuè ér qǐ	S2C5
just before	临	lín	S4C6
just like	俨然	yǎnrán	S2C5
just; simply; obstinately	硬是	yìngshì	S2C2

K

key universities	重点大学	zhòngdiǎn dàxué	S2C9
kid (a term of endearment)	小鬼	xiǎoguǐ	S2C9
kind and just	有情有义	yǒuqíngyǒuyì	S2C2
knit the brows	颦	pín	S3C8
knock (against) and bump (into)	磕磕碰碰	kēkēpèng pèng	S2C6
knot	疙瘩	gēda	S4C5
knot	结	jié	S1C3
know	晓得	xiǎodé	S2C2
know . . . like the palm of one's own hand	了如指掌	liǎorúzhǐzhǎng	S2C5
know well	通	tōng	S2C1
known by everyone	路人皆知	lùrénjiēzhī	S4C7
Kun opera; Kunqu opera	昆曲	kūnqǔ	S1C8

L

lane; alley	弄堂	nòngtáng	S1C4
Laobaigan (a popular brand liquor)	老白干	lǎobáigān	S2C4
laughable	好笑	hǎoxiào	S2C2
layout; composition	布局	bùjú	S3C7
lazy	懒	lǎn	S2C7
lead along (by holding the hand)	牵(手)	qiān (shǒu)	S2C8
lead; command	率领	shuàilǐng	S2C5

leak	漏	lòu	S1C3
lean on	倚	yǐ	S3C3
lean on; support oneself with a stick	拄	zhǔ	S2C1
leave/quit school	下学	xiàxué	S2C6
legacy	遗产	yíchǎn	S2C1
legs crossed	翘(腿)	qiào (tuǐ)	S2C9
let; allow; at the mercy of	任(凭)	rèn(píng)	S3C3
let it be; let it pass; forget about it	算了	suànle	S1C6
let it go at that; forget it	得了	déle	S2C4
lice	虱子	shīzi	S2C7
lie; claim	谎称	huǎngchēng	S4C5
lie down	倒头	dǎotóu	S1C5
lie on one's stomach	趴	pā	S4C6
lieutenant	中尉	zhōngwèi	S2C5
lifelike	栩栩如生	xǔxǔrúshēng	S1C8
lift	吊	diào	S1C3
lift up	撩	liāo	S2C2
lift up (a leg)	跷	qiào	S3C6
lift up (curtain)	掀(门帘)	xiān (ménlián)	S1C5
light-footed; breeze along	步履轻盈	bùlǚqīngyíng	S4C8
like a wolf	狼乎	lánghū	S1C5
like to lecture others	好为人师	hàowéi	S4C7
little and dainty; small and delicate	小巧玲珑	xiǎoqiǎolínglóng	S4C7
live to; get to	走到(老年)	zǒudào (lǎonián)	S1C2
lively and colorful	活色生香	huósèshēngxiāng	S4C8
lively and noisy	热闹喧腾	rènào xuānténg	S4C8
load; pack	装	zhuāng	S1C7
loafer; rascal	二流子	èrliúzi	S2C5
loan; provide a loan	贷款	dàikuǎn	S2C8
locust tree	槐树	huáishù	S1C1
lonely	落寞	luòmò	S2C7
long for; hope for	盼望	pànwàng	S3C2
long-drawn-out	悠长	yōucháng	S4C7
look; feature	面貌	miànmào	S4C5
look good	露脸	lòuliǎn	S2C6

look out; take care	留神	liúshén	S2C8
look up and down	打量	dǎliang	S3C1
lose; subsidize	倒贴	dàotiē	S1C6
lose heart	气馁	qìněi	S1C7
loud; show off; bluster	咋呼	zāhu	S2C4
love and care for one's family	顾家	gùjiā	S1C2
love at first sight	一见倾心	yījiànqīngxīn	S4C7
low-keyed; low profile	低调	dīdiào	S1C8
lower	降低	jiàngdī	S2C8
lower oneself to the same level as someone	一般见识	yībānjiàn shi	S1C1
luckily; by a fluke	侥幸	jiǎoxìng	S1C9
luggage	行囊	xíngnáng	S4C5
lull	哄(孩子)	hǒng	S1C2

M

maintain one's composure	不动声色	búdòngshēngsè	S4C7
make (into)	做成	zuò chéng	S1C2
make (rice cakes)	打(年糕)	dǎ(niángāo)	S3C3
make a misstep	踩空	cǎi kōng	S2C2
make an announcement	下通知	xià tōngzhī	S2C4
make bold	冒昧	màomèi	S3C1
make it hard for	为难	wéinán	S1C4
make someone suffer; persecute	整	zhěng	S2C2
make tea	沏茶	qīchá	S3C1
make things harder for someone	穿小鞋	chuānxiǎoxié	S2C4
make way; fall back; give ground; yield	让	ràng	S4C6
make, season, and mix (filling)	调(馅儿)	tiáo (xiàn'er)	S4C8
male adulterer	野汉子	yěhànzǐ	S2C2
man; fellow	汉子	hànzi	S2C4
many a day is yet to come	来日方长	láirìfāngcháng	S3C5
many people	众	zhòng	S2C5
married and established	成家立业	chéngjiālìyè	S1C2
marry a daughter off	聘	pìn	S4C6
marry off a daughter; marry (a husband)	嫁	jià	S4C6

massage	推拿按摩	tuīná ànmó	S3C1
match	配	pèi	S4C6
mature	成熟	chéngshú	S1C4
mediocre	平庸	píngyōng	S2C8
meet; be in line with; accord	符合	fúhé	S1C4
meet with	遭	zāo	S2C5
melt; thaw	融化	rónghuà	S2C8
mess things up	添乱	tiānluàn	S2C4
messy; awful	烂	làn	S4C5
methodically	一板一眼	yìbǎnyìyǎn	S1C5
mingle with men of letters and pose as a lover of culture; arty-crafty	附庸风雅	fùyōngfēngyǎ	S3C6
mischief	胡闹	húnào	S2C2
mischief; practical joke; monkey business	恶作剧	èzuòjù	S2C7
mislay	丢	diū	S2C2
miss; let slip	错过	cuòguò	S3C5
mobilize troops for a punitive expedition	兴师问罪	xīngshīwènzuì	S3C6
moist	湿润	shīrùn	S2C8
money paid for a piece of writing	稿酬	gǎochóu	S2C7
most probably	想必	xiǎngbì	S1C2
motive; intention	用心	yòngxīn	S1C1
motorbike	摩托车	mótuóchē	S2C4
mourn	悼念	dàoniàn	S3C8
mournful	凄切	qīqiè	S1C2
move close to	凑	còu	S4C6
moving; touching	动人	dòngrén	S1C2
mud	泥浆	níjiāng	S2C4
muddleheaded	昏头昏脑	hūntóuhūnnǎo	S1C3
muddleheaded	稀里糊涂	xīlǐhútú	S1C3
multicolored; colorful	五颜六色	wǔyánliùsè	S2C6
mumble (complaints)	嘟哝	dūnong	S2C4
mumble; speak haltingly	嗫嚅	nièrú	S2C7
mutter; speak haltingly	嗫嚅	nièrú	S2C4
mutter to oneself; ponder	沉吟	chényín	S3C6

N

nasty and vulgar	恶俗	èsú	S2C8
natural and graceful	落落大方	luòluòdàfāng	S3C8
natural pattern	(木)花纹	(mù) huāwén	S1C2
near-drunkenness	酒至酣处	jiǔzhìhānchù	S4C7
neat; neatly	干净利落	gānjìnglìluò	S2C5
neck	脖	bó	S1C3
neither hostile nor friendly	不冷不热	bùlěngbúrè	S1C3
neither innocent nor clean; have an illicit relationship	不清不白	bùqīngbùbái	S2C3
nervous; uneasy	忐忑不安	tǎntèbùān	S3C4
next day	翌日	yìrì	S1C4
next door	隔壁	gébì	S1C3
nickname	绰号	chuòhào	S2C2
nip; squeeze	捏	niē	S2C5
no cure for; hopeless	没救	méijiù	S1C5
no sign of spring	春风不度	chūnfēngbúdù	S4C8
nonstop	不休	bùxiū	S1C2
nonstop rain	车轴雨	chēzhóuyǔ	S2C4
not acquainted with each other before	素不相识	sùbùxiāngshí	S2C9
not familiar	人生地疏	rénshēngdìshū	S2C5
not to catch people on the raw or hit them in the face	骂人不揭短, 打人不打脸	mà rén bù jiē duǎn, dǎ rén bù dǎ liǎn	S2C6
not to help a dying man	见死不救	jiànsǐbújiù	S2C4
not to mention; leave aside	…不说,…还…	…bù shuō,…hái…	S3C8
not yet content; reluctant to leave	意犹未尽	yìyóuwèijìn	S2C2
nothing difficult	不在话下	bùzàihuàxià	S3C8

O

obedient; well arranged	服帖	fútiē	S3C8
obediently	乖乖	guāiguāi	S3C7
obscure	朦胧	ménglóng	S1C5
obtain by drawing	抽(水)	chōu(shuǐ)	S4C5
(obtain) employment	就业	jiùyè	S1C9

English	Chinese	Pinyin	Ref
of poor quality; inferior	劣质	lièzhì	S2C7
(of words or voice) dripping acid	阴阳怪气	yīnyángguàiqì	S4C6
offend	得罪	dézuì	S1C3
offer as a gift	奉送	fèngsòng	S1C6
offer hints; give tips	点	diǎn	S2C7
offer respectfully	献(烟, 酒)	xiàn (yān, jiǔ)	S1C2
often	每每	měiměi	S2C5
old age	老来	lǎolái	S1C9
old but still licentious	老不正经	lǎo bu zhèngjīng	S4C2
on impulse	脑门一热	nǎomén yī rè	S1C4
one after another	纷纷	fēnfēn	S1C2
one by one	挨个	āigè	S1C2
one-night stand	一夜情	yīyèqíng	S1C6
one on top of another	叠	dié	S2C2
one step to heaven	一步登天	yíbùdēngtiān	S3C5
one's formal personal name; given name	大名	dàmíng	S1C8
one's job; one's duty	本职	běnzhí	S2C4
one's near neighbors	四邻八舍	sìlínbāshè	S2C3
only	独	dú	S2C7
only	光	guāng	S2C6
only	唯独	wéidú	S1C3
only; merely	不过是	búguòshì	S2C8
open; spacious	空旷	kōngkuàng	S4C7
open (eyes wide)	巴(眼)	bā	S1C3
open field	旷野	kuàngyě	S4C7
open hearts to each other	交心	jiāoxīn	S2C7
order; command	指令	zhǐlìng	S1C6
order about; use; handle	使唤	shǐhuàn	S4C2
orderly ways	章法	zhāngfǎ	S2C2
ordinary people	老百姓	lǎobǎixìng	S2C4
originate from; stem from	缘自	yuánzì	S2C7
other people	人家	rénjiā	S1C2
otherwise; or else	要不然	yàoburán	S2C8
ought; should	当(问)	dāng	S3C1
out of sorts	失神	shīshén	S4C8

out of thin air; without foundation	凭空	píngkōng	S1C6
out of the way	偏僻	piānpì	S3C2
outing; go on an outing	郊游	jiāoyóu	S1C8
outstanding	出众	chūzhòng	S2C1
outward appearance	外表	wàibiǎo	S1C8
overgrown	丛生	cóngshēng	S4C8
overwhelming stench	臭气熏天	chòuqìxūntiān	S2C4
owe a debt	塌窟窿	tākūlong	S4C5

P

partner (in crime)	同伙	tónghuǒ	S2C5
pass (time)	打发	dǎfa	S2C7
pass away	撒手	sāshǒu	S1C5
pass on; hand around	传递	chuándì	S3C2
pass; approve	批	pī	S2C8
pass; go beyond	逾越	yúyuè	S2C9
paste	糊	hú	S2C4
pat; apply (toner)	拍(爽肤水)	pāi(shuǎngfūshuǐ)	S3C8
pay	掏钱	tāo qián	S3C7
pay attention to; look at	留意	liúyì	S1C6
pay for (education)	供	gōng	S4C2
pay great attention to; be particular about	讲究	jiǎngjiu	S3C1
peasant; farmer	庄稼人	zhuāngjiarén	S1C1
peck	鹐	qiān	S4C6
pelvic bone	盆骨	péngǔ	S1C8
penetrate	(钉)透	(dìng) tòu	S1C2
people of humble professions	下九流	xiàjiǔliú	S1C3
perfect; satisfactory	圆满	yuánmǎn	S2C1
permit no delay	刻不容缓	kèbùrónghuǎn	S2C4
perplexed	困惑	kùnhuò	S1C3
persecute	整	zhěng	S2C4
persistently	一个劲地	yīgèjìn di	S2C2
perturbed	乱糟糟	luànzāozāo	S1C3
pervade; diffuse	弥漫	mímàn	S4C8

英文索引 ENGLISH VOCABULARY INDEX

English	Chinese	Pinyin	Code
petty	小心眼儿	xiǎoxīnyǎner	S1C3
pick (one's nose)	挖(鼻孔)	wā(bíkǒng)	S2C4
pick out; select	抽	chōu	S4C5
pick; peck	啄	zhuó	S4C6
pieces in disorder	七零八落	qīlíngbāluò	S2C8
pierce to the heart	钻心	zuānxīn	S1C1
piling; balling up	起球	qǐ qiú	S4C8
pinch; nip	掐	qiā	S4C8
pitch-black; pitch-dark	漆黑	qīhēi	S1C2
plan to get married	谈婚论嫁	tánhūnlùnjià	S3C5
play a musical instrument	演奏	yǎnzòu	S1C5
play with; amuse	逗	dòu	S1C9
pleased with oneself	美滋滋	měizīzī	S1C3
plot; plan	策划	cèhuà	S1C4
pluck; gather	采	cǎi	S4C8
plunge (headlong)	扎	zhā	S2C4
pocket; bag	兜	dōu	S1C7
pool (money)	凑	còu	S2C2
poor men's foodstuffs	糟糠	zāokāng	S3C3
porcelain; chinaware	瓷器	cíqì	S4C8
pork	大肉	dàròu	S3C1
pose	架式	jiàshi	S1C5
pound	砸	zá	S1C5
purse one's lips	努嘴	nǔ zuǐ	S1C4
praise	夸奖	kuājiǎng	S1C8
precise; accurate	精确	jīngquè	S2C1
prepare for the Spring Festival	忙年	mángnián	S1C2
prepare written material	(写)材料	(xiě) cáiliào	S2C4
presentable; deserve to be seen	说得出口拿得出手	shuō de chū kǒu ná de chū shǒu	S1C6
preserve in salt; pickle	腌(咸菜)	yān (xiáncài)	S1C5
press (with hand or finger)	摁	èn	S3C8
press hard to make powder	轧	zhá	S1C5
presume; suppose	假设	jiǎshè	S2C9
presumptuous	非分	fēifèn	S2C9
pretending to be what one is not	人模狗样	rénmúgǒu yàng	S2C6
pretense turns into reality	弄假成真	nòngjiǎchéngzhēn	S2C8

English	Chinese	Pinyin	Ref
prick	扎	zhā	S1C5
profound; marvelous	奥妙	àomiào	S2C9
progress	长进	zhǎngjìn	S1C9
project on the screen	放(电影)	fàng	S2C1
promising/not promising	有/没出息	yǒu/méichūxi	S2C6
protrude; stick up	撅	juē	S3C8
provide the fund	出资	chūzī	S2C8
public; for public use	公用	gōngyòng	S3C7
pull	扯	chě	S1C3
pull; drag	拽	zhuài	S2C4
pull (a long face)	(脸一)沉	(liǎn yī) chén	S2C3
pull a long face	哭丧着脸	kū shàng zhe liǎn	S4C5
pupil of eye; eye	眸	móu	S4C8
put down	搁	gē	S1C5
put in (great effort)	下(苦劲)	xià(kǔjìn)	S4C5
put off; postpone	推迟	tuīchí	S2C8
put on (over); cover	披	pī	S3C1
put one's hand to; start	下手	xiàshǒu	S1C1
put to use	派用场	pài yòngchǎng	S1C9

Q

English	Chinese	Pinyin	Ref
quick stir-fry in hot oil	爆锅	bàoguō	S4C8
quick-witted	伶俐	línglì	S4C6
quiet and lonely	冷寂	lěngjì	S1C2
quite; exceedingly	好生	hǎoshēng	S4C6
quite; fairly	相当	xiāngdāng	S1C7
quite a few	甚众	shèn zhòng	S2C5

R

English	Chinese	Pinyin	Ref
rack one's brain	绞尽脑汁	jiǎojìnnǎozhī	S3C4
radiance	光辉	guānghuī	S2C2
raise and borrow	筹借	chóujiè	S2C7
raise one's voice	扬声	yángshēng	S4C6
rare	稀罕	xīhan	S3C2
reach the height of	齐	qí	S2C4

English	Chinese	Pinyin	Ref
read/recite with cadence	朗诵	lǎngsòng	S1C8
readily; conveniently	随手	suíshǒu	S1C7
reading a book while riding a donkey—wait and see (who is right)	骑驴看唱本—走着瞧	qí lǘ kàn chàngběn—zǒu zhe qiáo	S3C6
ready; settled; finished	(说)妥	(shuō) tuǒ	S2C2
really	实在	shízài	S3C7
reason	原由	yuányóu	S1C5
reason	缘由	yuányóu	S1C1
receive the bride	接亲	jiēqīn	S1C3
recollection	回忆	huíyì	S3C8
recommend; give a referral	引荐	yǐnjiàn	S2C9
reddened	涨红	zhànghóng	S2C2
reel right and left; lurch	东倒西歪	dōngdǎoxīwāi	S2C6
refuse; reject	拒绝	jùjué	S2C3
refuse to admit defeat/a mistake	鸭子死了嘴还硬	yāzi sǐle zuǐ hái yìng	S3C6
refute	反驳	fǎnbó	S4C6
register (for marriage)	登记(结婚)	dēngjì(jiéhūn)	S3C5
regroup	整编	zhěngbiān	S2C7
remedy	补救	bǔjiù	S1C3
remittance order	汇款单	huìkuǎndān	S3C2
remnants of a defeated army	残兵败将	cánbīngbàijiàng	S1C6
renovate; replace	翻盖	fāngài	S4C5
repair; renovate;	修缮	xiūshàn	S4C7
repeat (a mistake)	重犯	chóng fàn	S1C4
report	汇报	huìbào	S2C4
report to the leadership after finishing a task	交差	jiāochāi	S1C4
respect and admire	钦羡	qīnxiàn	S3C2
(respectfully) your (school)	贵(校)	guì (xiào)	S3C1
retort	还嘴	huánzuǐ	S4C6
retort; answer back; go against	顶	dǐng	S3C8
retreat; to disappear (from society, politics)	隐退	yǐntuì	S4C7
retreat to avoid a conflict	退避三舍	tuìbìsānshě	S3C6
return (trip)	返程	fǎnchéng	S2C4
reveal	透露	tòulù	S1C5

reveal; betray	流露	liúlù	S1C6
reward; prize	奖赏	jiǎngshǎng	S2C7
right in/against; straight on	劈	pī	S3C7
ripple; brim over	漾(开)	yàng(kāi)	S3C3
ripples	漪漪	yīyī	S3C6
rise straight up	耸	sǒng	S4C6
roll	打滚	dǎgǔn	S2C2
roll	滚	gǔn	S4C2
roll (out dumpling wrapper)	擀	gǎn	S4C8
rouge	胭脂	yānzhi	S3C6
rows of wheat	麦趟子	mài tàngzi	S2C1
rub against	贴	tiē	S3C7
ruin	坏	huài	S4C5
rummage through	翻遍	fān biàn	S2C9
running back and forth	跑前跑后	pǎoqiánpǎohòu	S3C7
rush through carelessly	草草	cǎocǎo	S1C5
rushed to	赶到	gǎndào	S2C3

S

sad	哀怨	āiyuàn	S1C6
sad; melancholy	惆怅	chóuchàng	S3C1
sad; mournfully	怆然	chuàngrán	S4C8
sadly moving	哀婉	āiwǎn	S1C5
safe and secure	稳稳当当	wěnwěndāngdāng	S1C5
sallow	蜡黄	làhuáng	S4C8
salute; show courtesy	施礼	shīlǐ	S1C1
satisfied	心满意足	xīnmǎnyìzú	S1C2
save; economize	省	shěng	S1C7
save; keep; preserve	放	fàng	S4C2
save; savings	积蓄	jīxù	S2C8
say	曰	yuē	S2C5
scattered	散乱	sǎnluàn	S3C1
scoop up/out	舀	yǎo	S1C1
scrape	刮	guā	S1C1
scrape up; accumulate	积攒	jīzǎn	S4C6
screen	屏风	píngfēng	S3C5

English	Chinese	Pinyin	Ref
scrutinize; get to the bottom of something	细究	xì jiū	S2C3
scurry	窜	cuàn	S3C6
search everywhere	东翻西找	dōngfānxīzhǎo	S2C5
seasons	时令	shílìng	S4C8
section; length	(半)截	(bàn) jié	S1C2
(see) this state; this situation	(见)状	(jiàn) zhuàng	S3C7
seek to impress by feigning more than what one is	打肿脸充胖子	dǎ zhǒng liǎn chōng pàngzi	S3C6
select	选拔	xuǎnbá	S4C5
select; selection	选择	xuǎnzé	S1C6
send to an exhibition for display	送展	sòng zhǎn	S3C4
sensitive; vulnerable	敏感	mǐngǎn	S2C8
sentence (to prison)	判刑	pànxíng	S2C4
settle; stabilize	安定	āndìng	S4C7
settle accounts	结算	jiésuàn	S1C9
settle accounts with somebody	收拾	shōushi	S2C4
sever; break off	断绝	duànjué	S4C7
sew/make (cloth sole of shoes)	纳(鞋底)	nà(xiédǐ)	S1C5
sewer	阴沟	yīngōu	S1C4
shame; dishonor	羞辱	xiūrǔ	S2C7
share; shared	共享	gòngxiǎng	S2C7
shed (hair on the body)	褪(毛)	tuì (máo)	S3C8
shiny; fresh and bright	光鲜	guāngxiān	S1C8
shiver	哆嗦	duōsuo	S1C3
shock heaven and shake earth	惊天动地	jīngtiāndòngdì	S3C1
shoot up; leap up	蹿	cuān	S4C8
shop front; facade	门脸儿	ménliǎner	S1C9
short	矮	ǎi	S2C1
shoulder	担负	dānfù	S2C5
shoulder; endure	扛	káng	S2C2
shouldn't have ...	谁叫...	shuí jiào	S4C2
show; show off	秀	xiù	S1C8
show favor/respect	抬举	táijǔ	S1C1
show filial respect for	孝敬	xiàojìng	S2C4
show off; be in the limelight	出风头	chūfēngtou	S4C7
show or reveal to others	示人	shì rén	S4C7

show respect	给面子	gěi miànzi	S1C4
show the white feather; draw back	示弱	shìruò	S4C6
shroud; cover; hide from view	遮蔽	zhēbì	S2C8
(shucks) it wasn't anything	…算得了什么?	…suàndéliǎo	S2C8
shudder; shiver	颤抖	chàndǒu	S1C6
shut; lockup; catch	关	guān	S2C2
shy	腼腆	miǎntiǎn	S2C5
side	(一)侧	cè	S1C3
sigh	叹	tàn	S2C5
sight; view	视线	shìxiàn	S1C6
sign; signature	署名	shǔmíng	S2C7
sign a contract	签约	qiānyuē	S2C1
silence; stillness	沉寂	chénjì	S3C5
silent; silence	沉默	chénmò	S1C6
similar; analogous	类似	lèisì	S1C6
simply	死活	sǐhuó	S1C5
simply; only	无非	wúfēi	S2C1
sincere	诚挚	chéngzhì	S2C8
sincere; sincerity	(心)诚	(xīn) chéng	S2C3
sincere advice; counsel	忠告	zhōnggào	S4C7
sincere and earnest	语重心长	yǔzhòngxīncháng	S3C4
sip and taste tea	品茗	pǐnmíng	S3C6
sit side by side and talk heart-to-heart	促膝谈心	cùxītánxīn	S3C6
(sit) cross-legged	二郎腿	èrlángtuǐ	S3C6
situation	局面	júmiàn	S4C5
skill; craftsmanship	手艺	shǒuyì	S2C9
skull	脑壳	nǎoké	S1C3
slack winter season	冬闲	dōngxián	S1C5
slap	掌嘴	zhǎng zuǐ	S1C3
sleep in	睡懒觉	shuìlǎnjiào	S2C4
slide; slip off	滑落	huáluò	S4C7
slight; trifle with	怠慢	dàimàn	S3C7
slightly	略	lüè	S2C2
slim; fine	纤细	qiānxì	S1C5
sling; strap	吊带	diàodài	S3C8

slovenly	不修边幅	bùxiūbiānfú	S2C4
slow; slowly	缓慢	huǎnmàn	S4C5
slowly	缓缓	huǎnhuǎn	S1C3
slow-witted	笨	bèn	S2C1
smash; mess up; ruin	砸	zá	S1C1
smoke curling up	烟雾缭绕	yānwù liáorào	S1C5
smooth and round; mellow	圆润	yuánrùn	S3C8
soak	泡	pào	S2C3
soak into; permeate	沁入	qìn rù	S4C8
soar	窜	cuàn	S4C6
soft-hearted and easygoing	好讲话	hǎojiǎnghuà	S1C3
soft; lithe	柔软	róuruǎn	S4C7
softly fragrant; warm	温馨	wēnxīn	S4C7
solve a case	破案	pò'àn	S2C5
somewhat; a little	稍	shāo	S2C8
son-in-law	女婿	nǚxù	S3C7
sore; painful	酸疼	suānténg	S1C5
sorrow; grief	忧伤	yōushāng	S1C7
soul; spirit	灵魂	línghún	S4C2
sound of falling into water; plop; thump	扑通	pūtōng	S2C2
sound of thrusting against the ground	蹬蹬	dēngdēng	S1C3
soup; broth	汤汁	tāngzhī	S4C8
spark; flash	闪	shǎn	S4C8
speed up; hurry up	加紧	jiājǐn	S4C7
spiderweb; cobweb	(蜘)蛛网	(zhī)zhūwǎng	S4C6
spittle	唾沫星子	tuòmò xīngzi	S1C5
splendid; glitter	灿烂	cànlàn	S1C6
sponsor	赞助	zànzhù	S2C4
spray	喷	pēn	S3C8
spread; extend	蔓延	mànyán	S4C7
spring	弹簧	tánhuáng	S2C6
sprout up through the earth	拱	gǒng	S4C8
squat	蹲	dūn	S2C6
stable; stabilize; stability	稳定	wěndìng	S4C5
staff; stave	五线谱	wǔxiànpǔ	S1C8

English	Chinese	Pinyin	Ref
stamp (foot)	跺(脚)	duò(jiǎo)	S1C3
stand	戳	chuō	S2C4
stare blankly	愣	lèng	S1C3
stare; glare	瞪眼睛	dèng yǎnjīng	S2C4
start (a topic, conversation, etc.)	起头	qǐtóu	S4C6
start; make; carry on	搞(革命)	gǎo (gémìng)	S2C1
stay	蹲	dūn	S3C4
stay behind	留守	liúshǒu	S3C2
stay up late	熬夜	áoyè	S3C4
steaming hot	热气腾腾	rèqìténgténg	S1C5
stammer	结巴	Jiēba	S1C3
step forward; hasten forward	趋前	qūqián	S4C6
still	依旧	yījiù	S1C8
stimulating; exciting	刺激	cìji	S1C6
stolen goods	赃物	zāngwù	S2C5
stop working; knock off	歇工	xiēgōng	S4C2
stopped	叫住	jiào zhù	S2C3
store; storefront	铺面	pùmiàn	S1C9
straddle (squat) as though riding a horse	马步(下蹲)	mǎbù (xiàdūn)	S2C5
straight	径直	jìngzhí	S1C3
stretch into	探入	tàn rù	S2C7
stretching; unfolding; extending	舒展	shūzhǎn	S4C8
strike	划(火柴)	huá (huǒchái)	S1C2
string together; cluster together	串	chuàn	S4C8
strive to be the first and fear to lag behind	争先恐后	zhēngxiānkǒnghòu	S3C2
strive to be top-notch	争风拔尖	zhēngfēngbájiān	S4C6
stroll; lounge	闲逛	xián guàng	S3C8
struggle	挣扎	zhēngzhā	S3C1
stumble; hobble	蹒跚	pánshān	S4C2
suddenly; swiftly (rise/fall)	骤(升/降)	zhòu(shēng/jiàng)	S2C5
suddenly; unexpectedly	蓦(地)	mò (di)	S4C6
sue; accuse	告	gào	S1C4
suffer financial loss	破财	pòcái	S4C6
suffer from diarrhea	拉肚子	lādùzi	S2C6

ENGLISH VOCABULARY INDEX

English	Chinese	Pinyin	Ref
suffocate by smoke	熏	xūn	S1C5
sulkily; snappily	没好气	méihǎoqì	S1C3
support	撑	chēng	S1C3
support from underneath	托	tuō	S3C7
suppress	憋	biē	S2C2
surprisingly; unusually	出奇	chūqí	S3C7
surround; encircle	围	wéi	S1C4
surrounding area;	方圆	fāngyuán	S2C1
surrounding area; about	周遭	zhōuzāo	S4C5
sustain economic losses	赔钱	péiqián	S4C2
sustain losses in business	赔本	péiběn	S2C6
swagger off	扬长而去	yángchángérqù	S1C1
swing; fling	甩	shuǎi	S2C6
swinging	晃悠/荡	huàngyou/dang	S2C4
sworn friend; buddies	铁子	tiězi	S4C7

T

English	Chinese	Pinyin	Ref
take a fancy to	看上	kànshàng	S2C3
take a noon break	歇晌	xiēshǎng	S1C1
take along	带	dài	S3C7
take along something to or for someone	捎	shāo	S2C3
take delight in talking about	津津乐道	jīnjīnlèdào	S2C2
take off	摘	zhāi	S2C2
take office	上任	shàngrèn	S2C4
take the chance; seize the advantage	趁 (热)	chèn (rè)	S3C1
take turns	轮流	lúnliú	S1C6
talk things over	协商	xiéshāng	S2C8
tall and strong	牛高马大	niúgāomǎdà	S3C3
tassel	穗	suì	S1C2
taste; sample	品尝	pǐncháng	S4C8
tattoo	纹	wén	S1C8
taxi; cab	计程车	jìchéngchē	S1C6
tear	扯	chě	S4C6
tear apart (down)	拆	chāi	S2C8

English	Chinese	Pinyin	Ref
tears and nasal mucus	眼泪鼻涕	yǎnlèi bítì	S2C6
tears gushing forth	泪如泉涌	lèirúquányǒng	S2C2
tell one another everything	无话不说	wúhuàbùshuō	S2C8
temper	性子	xìngzi	S3C5
temple	鬓角	bìnjiǎo	S4C8
temporarily	暂时	zànshí	S1C7
tend to; be apt to	爱	ài	S4C8
tendency	趋势	qūshì	S3C5
thanks to	亏	kuī	S1C5
that (above-mentioned)	该	gāi	S4C5
That's how it is.	本来就这回事	běnlái jiù zhè huí shì	S1C3
the agricultural fair	农展会	nóngzhǎnhuì	S3C4
the end of the year	年关	niánguān	S4C6
the Great Northern Wilderness	北大荒	běidàhuāng	S2C7
the head of a family	一家之主	yījiāzhīzhǔ	S1C5
the look	相	xiàng	S2C4
the weak	弱者	ruòzhě	S1C8
the young are to be respected	后生可畏	hòushēngkěwèi	S2C5
the younger generation of (sons and nephews)	子侄辈	zǐzhíbèi	S3C7
then; afterward	继而	jì'ér	S4C8
then; thereupon	遂	suì	S3C7
there exist...; have	长	zhǎng	S4C8
thermos bottle	暖壶	nuǎnhú	S2C3
think back and forth	思来想去	sī lái xiǎng qù	S1C3
thinking; thoughts	所思所想	suǒ sī suǒ xiǎng	S1C4
thought; idea	念头	niàntou	S1C8
thoughtlessly	瞎	xiā	S4C6
thoughts filled one's mind	浮想联翩	fúxiǎngliánpiān	S3C4
thread of a conversation	话头	huàtóu	S3C6
through; after	经	jīng	S2C2
throw; toss	丢	diū	S1C7
throw a quick glance	瞄	miáo	S1C5
thunderous	山响	shānxiǎng	S2C4
thus; this time	这下(子)	zhèxià(zi)	S1C3

tidy up	拾掇	shíduō	S2C4
ties of blood	血缘	xuěyuán	S4C6
tight(ly)	(咬)紧	(yǎo) jǐn	S3C1
tightly	死死	sǐsǐ	S2C2
timid; cowardly	怯	qiè	S1C1
tip-top; the most important; the best of its kind	(心)尖子	(xīn)jiānzi	S2C4
tiring	累人	lèi rén	S4C5
to the greatest extent	尽	jìn	S4C7
toad	蛤蟆	háma	S2C4
tone of voice	腔调	qiāngdiào	S1C3
too smart for one's own good	聪明大了	cōngmíng dàle	S2C6
torrential rain	倾盆大雨	qīngpéndàyǔ	S3C4
toss; cast	抛	pāo	S4C6
toss; throw	甩	shuǎi	S3C8
touch; move	打动	dǎdòng	S2C8
trace	痕	hén	S3C8
trace (the outline of)	描	miáo	S3C8
trace back	追溯	zhuīsù	S2C7
traditional Chinese time unit(s)	(时)辰	(shí)chén	S1C2
transfer (money into an account)	(把钱)打进(账户)	(bǎqián)dǎ jìn (zhànghù)	S2C4
treat shabbily	亏待	kuīdài	S2C6
triumphant return	凯旋	kǎixuán	S4C7
trivia; trifling	琐碎	suǒsuì	S2C8
trivial matters	杂碎	zásuì	S4C6
true; inherent quality	本色	běnsè	S4C7
try to find out	探听	tàntīng	S4C5
tube; cylinder	筒	tǒng	S1C5
tuck (into)	揣	chuāi	S1C5
turn aound	扭转	niǔzhuǎn	S4C5
turn; twist	扭(头)	niǔ(tóu)	S1C3
twenty	廿	niàn	S1C2
twice-cook	回锅	huíguō	S4C2
twitch	抽搐	chōuchù	S3C1

U

English	Chinese	Pinyin	Ref
unchanging	一成不变	yīchéngbúbiàn	S2C9
unclear sounds	呜呜噜噜	wūwulūlu	S2C4
uncover; reveal	揭开	jiēkāi	S2C5
underling; minions	喽罗	lóuluo	S3C6
undertake; bear	承担	chéngdān	S2C8
unexpectedly; abruptly	陡然	dǒurán	S4C7
unfeelingly	眼睁睁	yǎnzhēngzhēng	S2C4
unhappy; unhappiness	不悦	bú yuè	S3C7
universe; world	天地	tiāndì	S3C6
unknowable; unknown	不可知	bùkězhī	S2C9
unrestrained; uninhibited	狂放不羁	kuángfàngbùjī	S4C7
unruly; peremptory	横	hèng	S4C6
untainted by even a speck of dust	纤尘不染	xiānchénbùrǎn	S3C6
unwanted fat; bulge	赘肉	zhuìròu	S4C8
unwilling to be out of the limelight	不甘寂寞	bù gān jìmò	S3C8
unwilling to forgive; relentlessly	不依不饶	bùyībùráo	S3C6
unwilling to give up	不死心	bù sǐxīn	S1C3
upright stone tablet	碑	bēi	S2C4
urgent(ly); tense(ly); quick(ly)	紧(敲轻捶)	jǐn (qiāo qīng chuí)	S3C1
use	使	shǐ	S1C1
use; apply	使(力气)	shǐ(lìqì)	S3C3
utmost satisfaction	称心如意	chènxīnrúyì	S1C2
utter a sound	吭	kēng	S2C2

V

English	Chinese	Pinyin	Ref
vague; ambiguous	模棱两可	móléngliǎngkě	S1C8
vertical/horizontal	纵/横向	zòng/héngxiàng	S4C5
very soon	眼看	yǎnkàn	S4C5
village culture	村风	cūn fēng	S4C5
village official	村官	cūn guān	S4C5
virgin; maiden	处女	chùnǚ	S3C6
(virgin) maiden	黄花大闺女	huáng huā dà guīnǚ	S3C7
visit someone's grave	上坟	shàngfén	S2C2

W

英文索引 ENGLISH VOCABULARY INDEX

wade	蹚(水)	tāng	S2C4
wait on; serve	伺候	cìhou	S2C4
walk around	转	zhuàn	S2C6
walking stick	拐棍	guǎigùn	S3C5
walking stick	拐杖	guǎizhàng	S2C1
wall of a well	井壁	jǐng bì	S3C7
warm oneself (by a fire)	取暖	qǔnuǎn	S2C8
waste money and manpower	劳民伤财	láomínshāngcái	S1C4
wave; shake	晃	huàng	S4C6
wear	戴	dài	S2C6
wear (ponytail)	梳(辫子)	shū (biànzi)	S3C8
wear an air of	一副…模样	yí fù…móyàng	S2C5
wear and tear	磨损	mósǔn	S3C1
welcome (a traveler); help wash off the dust	洗尘	xǐchén	S3C1
wet; damp	打湿	dǎshī	S3C8
what is the need; there is no need	何须	hé xū	S3C6
whereabouts	着落	zháoluò	S1C5
whisper	咬耳朵	yǎoěrduo	S1C3
whiz; scream	呼啸	hūxiào	S4C7
whoosh!	噌	cēng	S2C1
why	咋	ză	S2C3
widow	寡妇	guǎfù	S1C3
willful; recklessly	恣意	zìyì	S4C8
win a prize in a lottery	中奖	zhòngjiǎng	S1C9
wipe (away)	拭	shì	S2C2
wipe (clean)	揩(干)	kǎi (gān)	S3C1
wipe one's eyes; weep	抹眼泪	mǒ yǎnlèi	S2C6
wipe out	扫荡	sǎodàng	S1C5
with…all over one's face	一脸…气	yīliǎn…qì	S1C4
with all one's heart	心甘情愿	xīngānqíngyàn	S3C3
with great difficulty	好容易	hǎoróngyì	S3C1
with great dignity	威风凛凛	wēifēnglǐnlǐn	S1C1
with nothing left	精光	jīngguāng	S1C1
with tears in one's eyes; tearfully	含泪	hán lèi	S2C6
with utmost care	小心翼翼	xiǎoxīnyìyì	S1C2

without any ill feeling	无冤无仇	wúyuānwúchóu	S2C9
without exception	均	jūn	S4C5
without permission	私自	sīzì	S2C5
wittily; lively and delightful	俏皮	qiàopí	S3C8
wording; diction	措辞	cuòcí	S1C8
work (as an editor)	干(编辑)	gàn (biānji)	S2C5
work as a farm laborer on yearly basis	扛长活	kángchánghuó	S2C1
work from dawn to dusk	起早贪黑	qǐzǎotānhēi	S3C4
worn	破	pò	S1C2
worry	发愁	fāchóu	S1C4
worry	犯愁	fànchóu	S1C3
worry about; take pains	操心	cāoxīn	S4C2
worship	崇拜	chóngbài	S2C4
Wouldn't . . . be sufficient?	不就行了	bújiùxíngle	S1C4
wring; twist	拧	nǐng	S1C3
wrinkled; crumpled	皱巴巴	zhòubābā	S4C8
wrinkles	皱纹	zhòuwén	S4C6
write (an IOU)	打(借条)	dǎ(jiètiáo)	S2C8

Y

yet; on the contrary	(反)倒	(fǎn)dào	S3C1
young (of animals)	崽	zǎi	S2C2
young man	后生	hòusheng	S2C2

原文出处

BIBLIOGRAPHY

An Shiliu (安石榴), "Ruguo Ni Ai Ta, Jiu Rang Ta Anjing" ("如果你爱他，就让他心静") ["Give Him Peace"], in *Journal of Garden of Flower* 5 (2012): 33–34. Print.

Bai Xuchu (白旭初), "Ji Qian" ("寄钱") ["Money Order"], in *True Feelings* 8 (2002): 58. Print.

Cai Nan (蔡楠), "Qing Tan" ("清潭") ["The Clear Pond"], in *Mangzhong Literature* 3 (2011): 70–72. Print.

Chen Yong (陈勇), "Chalou" ("茶楼") ["At the Teahouse"], in *Jinshan Literature* 2 (2006): 37. Print.

Chi Zijian (迟子建), "Deng Ji" ("灯祭") ["Father Makes the Lantern"], in *2012 Annual Anthology of Short-Shorts*, ed. Xiaoming Yang, Yong Qin, and Jianyu Zhao. Guilin: Lijiang Publishing House, 2012, 26–28. Print.

Gao Huaichang (高怀昌), "Jing Bu Zi Zhi Shui Duoshao" ("井不自知水多少") ["Water in the Well"], in *Journal of Garden of Flower* 5 (2012): 4–5. Print.

Ge Fei (格非), "Bu Kezhi de Ouran" ("不可知的偶然") ["Unknowable Possibilities"], in *Wenyuan* 7.2 (2013): 62. Print.

Han Shaogong (韩少功), "Xiu Ya Po" ("秀鸭婆") ["Little She"], *Hainan Ribao* (海南日报) [*Hainan Daily*], April 14, 2013. Print.

Li Lingling (李伶伶), "Cuilan de Aiqing" ("翠兰的爱情") ["Cuilan's Love"], in *Journal of Tianchi Short-Short Stories* 10 (2010): 3. Print.

Liu Xinwu (刘心武), "Ji Pa Qian Po Lian" ("鸡怕鸽破脸") ["Chickens Hate Pecked Faces"], in *2012 Annual Anthology of Short-Shorts*, ed. Xiaoming Yang, Yong Qin, and Jianyu Zhao. Guilin: Lijiang Publishing House, 2012. 39–41. Print.

Liu Zhenyun (刘震云), 'Mingxing' Wai Zumu ("'明星'外祖母") ['Star' Grandma], in *Journal of Selected Short-Shorts* 11 (2011): 8–9. Print.

Mo Zhongbai (墨中白), "Guo Wan Xiatian Zai Qu Tiantang" ("过完夏天再去天堂") ["Heaven-Bound, but After Summer"], in *Journal of Selected Short-Shorts* 18 (2010): 49–50. Print.

Nie Xinsen (聂鑫森), "Xili" ("洗礼") ["Catharsis"], in *2012 Annual Anthology of Short-horts*, ed. Xiaoming Yang, Yong Qin, and Jianyu Zhao. Guilin: Lijiang Publishing House, 2012:35–38. Print.

Shi Tiesheng (史铁生), "Lian Ren" ("恋人") ["The Love of Her Life"], in *Harvest* 1 (2012): http://chuansong.me/n/394580.

Tian Shuangling (田双伶), "Bohe de Yaoqing" ("薄荷的邀请") ["The Mint's Invitation"], in *Fiction Monthly* 12 (2011): http://xxs.d0088.cn/archives/7848.html.

Wang Kuishan (王奎山), "Gudian Aiqing" ("古典爱情") ["A Gentleman's Love"], in *Fiction Monthly* 5 (2012): http://xxs.d0088.cn/archives/7016.html.

Wang Meng (王蒙), "Weilai" ("未来") ["Future"], *Wenhui Bao* (文汇报) [*Wenhui Daily*], January 6, 2010. Print.

Wang Qionghua (王琼华), "Xinshi" ("心事") ["Two Minds"], in *Journal of Selected Short-Shorts* 15 (2005): 45–7. Print.

Wei Yonggui (魏永贵), "Lianmian" ("脸面") ["Face"], in *2010 Annual Anthology of Micro-Fiction*, ed. Feng Bing and Yamei Chen. Guilin: Lijiang Publishing House, 2010. 140–2. Print.

Wu Nianzhen (吴念真), "Chongfeng" ("重逢") ["A Golden Rain"], in *Zhexie Ren, Naxie Shi* (《这些人, 那些事》). Nanjing: Yilin Press, January 2009. http://www.yooread.com/14/3367/149463.html.

Wu Zhongzheng (伍中正), "Zaokaong" (糟糠) ["Forever by Your Side"], *Changde Ribao* (常德日报) [*Changde Daily*], March 10, 2004. Print.

Xing Hua (兴华), "Zhang Mali" ("张玛丽") ["Mary Zhang"], *Sanlian Shehghuo Zhoukan* (三联生活周刊) [*Life Week*], October 4, 2010. Print.

Ye Zhongjian (叶仲健), "Huainian Zhang Meili" ("怀念张美丽") ["Missing Zhang Meili"], in *Tianchi Short-Short Stories* 2 (2012): 2. Print.

Yu Shengli (俞胜利), "Jiumu" ("舅母") ["Auntie"], *Liangyan* (《亮眼》). Beijing: China Writers Publishing House, 2000, 23–32. Print.

Zeng Ping (曾平), "Da Hong Shao" ("大红苕") ["Big Sweet Potatoes"], in *2011 Annual Anthology of Short-Shorts*, ed. Xiaoming Yang, Xin Guo, and Yunfeng Kou. Guilin: Lijiang Publishing House, 2011, 316–17. Print.

Zhao Xin (赵新), "Ti Naodai" ("剃脑袋") ["Skull Shave"], *Cangzhou Ribao* (沧州日报) [*Cangzhou Daily*], May 15, 2011. Print.

Zhao Yu (赵瑜), "Xiao Youshang" ("小忧伤") ["Little Heartaches"], *Short-Short Stories: Poetic Beauty* (《小小说•诗韵》). Shijiazhuang: Huashan Literary Publishing House, 2014, 7–9. Print.

——, "Jiehun Chenben" (结婚成本) ["The Cost of Marriage"], in *2012 Annual Anthology of Short-Shorts*, ed. Xiaoming Yang, Yong Qin, and Jianyu Zhao. Guilin: Lijiang Publishing House, 2012, 186–88. Print.

Zhou Bo (周波), "Pu Shiban" ("铺石板") ["The Stone-Paving Project"], in *Journal of Selected Short-Shorts* 22 (2011): 63–65. Print.

Zhou Tao (周涛), "Xiongdimen Zhangda" ("兄弟们长大") ["Brothers"], in *2011 Annual Anthology of Short-Shorts*, ed. Xiaoming Yang, Xin Guo, and Yunfeng Kou. Guilin: Lijiang Publishing House, 2011, 1–2. Print.

Zou Jingzhi (邹静之), "Weizao de Qingshu" ("伪造的情书") ["Fake Love Letter"], in *Journal of Selected Short-Shorts* 17 (2007): 10–11. Print.

语言文化的互动与融通——如何使用这本汉英对照教材
(HOW TO USE THIS PARALLEL TEXT TO TEACH CHINESE LANGUAGE AND CULTURE)

本书来自教学实践，其中大部分内容我曾用做高年级中文课的主教材。有些内容我也在用英文讲授的《当代中国》课中使用过。选修《当代中国》的很多学生是因为学中文而对了解中国社会和文化产生了兴趣，因此本卷中的双语文本也成为这门课一箭双雕、不可或缺的教材之一。近几年来，这些文本也已成为水平日渐提高的学生选修翻译课时，在比较与反思中学习语言和文化得心应手的材料。虽然用法各异，但越来越多的学生也将这些文本用作方便有效的自学工具。

本文主要从教学目标、对象、方式、进度和评估等方面介绍一下这本教材在高年级中文课上的使用。在进入细节之前，请允许我先对绪论中介绍过的教材构架再做一详尽说明。为了您的使用方便，也请允许我对主题短文，以及其它学习辅助工具的选择和功能，再做些进一步解释。

全书共分九章。每一章主要包括两个内容：章节主题短文和三到四篇汉英对照的小小说文本。每篇小说后附有三项辅助阅读工具：生词用法表、参考讨论题和作者简介。

每章开头的主题短文介绍涵盖该章所有故事的主题，而该主题的特殊文化含义和多元复杂性则由故事的中文原文和英文翻译文本体现。短文也采用汉英对照形式，以对跨语言、文化阅读有所帮助和指引。小小说原文及其英文翻译是这本教材语言文化学习和同步互动演练的主阵地。生词用法着重于发音有难度，中英文难以直接对应的生词和用法，多义字词在文本语境中的特定用法，以及成语、俗语、方言和特殊用语等。每个故事后的七个参考讨论题大都基于以往学生的学习难点而提出。这些问题试图将学生阅读注意力导往文本本身和关键细节，并以不同形式呼应章节主题，诱发其对中国的传统、观念、制度和文化等方面的深度思考。

作者简介部分的加入是采纳了审稿人的建议。教学实践已证明，它们对理解小说原文有巨大帮助。这些简介的珍贵之处还在于，本卷所选作者，除史铁生、王奎山已过世以外，仍都活跃于当代中国的各行各业。这些简介的写作，基于本人对作者的采访和平日与他们的交流。他们的成长道路、本职工作和创作经历等也都是了解当代中国和中国文化的独特窗口。

将阅读和学习用主题"框架"起来的理由有三：第一，追求理想的开放式阅读的有效方式之一，可能需要对不同文化理念、价值体系、思维框架等有见闻、有认知、有感受、有理解。在去年的一节课上，有位同学这样对我说，"我学中文这么久，还在中国住了一年，今天在这里第一次听说'礼'。"另一位学生则说，"我听说过'阴阳'，可是不知道到它在中国文化里的意思。"他们的话更坚定了我要为弥补当今文化教育之欠缺尽微薄之力的决心。

第二个理由听起来有点儿"悖论"：完全摆脱"束缚"自己的框架是不可能的，也没必要；多与其它的认知、价值体系接触交流才有可能做到身处"架"中而不被"框"住。也就是说，能"框"住一个人的大概会是那个他所不愿走出的、自己的生活和认知之"架"。当然，很少有人会承认这一点；然而，想挣脱束缚的愿望并不等于对束缚的自然摆脱，积极主动的努力是必不可少的。我在爱荷华州立大学的很多学生们已然意识到了这一点。他们的真诚令人感动："我是西方人，我所想的跟别的地方的人所想的不一样。我想知道别的地方的人都是怎么想问题的。"当我拿着"主题框架"这个想法征求他们的意见时，有一个回答是这样的："我现在的水平是，我对中国文化天真无知。我需要有一个参照系帮助我理解。"

第三个理由则更实际些。对于像我一样半生在中国文化中浸泡濡染的那些任课老师来说，这些短文或可帮助他们调动自己的生活阅历，使之与故事反映的内容以及篇章的主题融合起来，备课时事半功倍。主题框架的存在对于学生掌握内容和形式也皆有帮助。一位学生曾说，"我觉得批判性思考应该发生在看懂、理解之后。主题短文前置的结构帮助了我对原文的基本理解。"另一位则认为，主题短文可以一石二鸟："如果没有主题短文，一个没有生词的故事，我读完了可能还是不知道它的意思。有了主题短文，我还有陌生词汇的时候就差不多已经知道故事的意思。之后再学生词时则能记住。"希望学生们的这些话能够增强老师对这些短文教学合理性的认可。

下面再对什么样的字词和表达能进入生词用法表做些说明。先以"瓢"字为例。"瓢"字入选有两个原因：一是其发音对学生有挑战，拿不准是从"票"部还是从"瓜"部入手；二是即便提供了英文翻译（"dipper"），学生仍有可能不了解其确切意思。所以生词用法表中将其选入，并用"爷爷把葫芦切开做了两个瓢"的例句解决学生的疑惑。再比如"撑"字，它在若干个故事中出现，意思都不同。因为对词义多元和细微差别的掌握是这个阶段学习的重点，所以"撑"字多次入选于几个不同的生词用法表，以便学生掌握它在"多撑几天"，"快撑破了"和"撑个帐篷"等不同情形中的使用。有些常用的、学生已经认识了的字词,生词表也选了,原因是它们在相关小小说作品中的意思很特别。比如,"怨"的入选是因为它在上下文中被译成了特定的"fret";"乖乖,2400元哩!"中的"乖乖",在课文的英文翻译中是通过""whopping"一词体现的。生词表中对"怨"和"乖乖"在文中的特定用法都做了交代。

生词用法表中最后一栏是例句,它们均由短小简易的日常语言构成,其功能是进一步帮助学生理解掌握该字、词在小小说中的用法。比如,"这药吃得我昏天黑地"一句旨在帮助学生明白"昏天黑地"在那篇课文中的特定意思。大多数学生喜爱这种例句不配英文翻译的安排方式,他们希望自己有机会用中文学中文。此外,书中把"一脸……气"一类的表达称作用法,生词用法表中有简单的解释和例句。因为这本书中很少有学生完全没有接触过的语法点,加上对照阅读也能帮助学生记起和重温学过的知识,本教材就舍去了对语法用法的阐释。学生们也说不需要,这已不是他们学习和关注的重点。语言方面的大部分问题学生们都能自己解决;还有个别疑难点的话,课上问一下,讨论讨论也就解决了。一般来说,在使用此课本一个月之后,很多学生不用课本之外的任何参考资源即可自行解决有关字词的问题。

教学目标:

在爱荷华州立大学,高年级语言教学使用这些文本的整体目标是学生在语言文化学习的互动与融通中全面成长。近几年教学较为注重的几个具体方面则是词汇量的扩大和掌握,原文阅读理解能力的提高,口头成段表达能力的加强,以及对中国文化基本理念/概念的认知和开放性思考等。自然,教学目标设置应基于本校的特点有所侧重,也应根据当期学生的具体情况有所调整。

教材的构架服务于教学目的。每章的主题短文旨在提供语言学习必不可少的相关的文化知识,帮助学生在阅读之前对所读内容的文明、文化大背景有所了解,从而尽可能使阅读活动在原文语境中展开,从而在相关的上下文中准确地学习语言、掌握用法;同时对文化内容做有针对性的理解和有实际意义的思考。

汉英对照的主课文部分则通过两种语言的互助互补,帮助学生走心走情地进入活的语言文化的学习。学习过程中,艺术的愉悦和震撼带动语言能力的演练和提高;同时语言的学习和运用也引发对不同文化的自觉反思、分析、对比和探讨。这些双语文本既是学生温故知新、巩固拓展的主阵地,也是学生不断提高学习动力和自学信心的加油站。总之,这些小小说的中英文双语表达以其独特的方式和途径培养学生对语言文化不可分割的认知,以及驾驭中国语言和文化的能力。

生词用法表、参考讨论题和作者简介这三个辅助工具也忠实地服务于语言文化学习相辅相成、齐头并进的目的。这里主要关注后两者的设计目的。七个参考讨论题给学生提供一个契机，使其练习使用由三五句组成的小段话来表达一个思想或是回答一个问题。除了双语课文本身，对这些问题的回答还可以从作者简介中受到启发、找到参考。这是因为简介的撰写特地用心纳入了与故事相关的内容，努力呈现了每位作者的与众不同之处，以帮助学生理解原文。作者简介没有中文版，也是希望给学生提供一个创造性地使用中文的机会。当他们参考这里的内容回答问题时，他们就有了一个机会将自己的想法和体会转换成中文，并将其融入对问题的理解、分析和回答。

教学对象：

本书已在绪论中对各类可能的教学对象做过说明，这里只对主体对象，即学中文的高年级同学，再做些具体说明。

中文高年级这一群体人员构成复杂，水平参差，但注册上课的学生也应该都已经学过了一般的语音（拼音）、语法和用法知识，认识（不一定会写）最基本的1400-1800个汉字。当然，认识后又遗忘的情况时常发生，尤其是在那些想认真学，工作也需要他们学，而又最没有时间学的成年学生身上。我校学生的主体是一般的在校大学生，但我们的班上也经常会出现现役或退伍军人，接受培训的老师，公司职员等。工作和家庭常常会分散掉这些人的很多精力。用这一课本的一般在校生也都基本处于毕业前的超级繁忙期。对于这样一个学生水平差距大而时间、精力投入都有限的学生群体来说，这本教材的双语对照形式给了他们比一般教材更大更灵活的学习、使用和发挥空间。对于那些乐意又善于学习的学生来说，这本书也是快速有效地温习、重拾、巩固和自学的恰当工具。换句话说，使用这本教材会增大高年级教学对象的伸缩性。它能让那些忘了很多的学生放下包袱轻松回归；它能使白天时间和精力都有限的人在夜晚的静谧中自学；它在允许差距存在的同时能让不同水平的学生各自得到最大收益。

在爱荷华州立大学，用起这本教材最得心应手的学生群体是从中国回来的留学生。他们去中国之前一般已经上过150-300个小时的中文课。在中国的留学时间通常是一年左右，大部分人在中国是全职学中文。这个群体的学生近年来迅速增长；在我们这里，过去的两年成倍增长。这些学生回来后唯恐远离中文环境会使他们忘了所学的东西，但他们又不喜欢一般教材为他们条分缕析语言的每个部件和功能；他们有学习兴趣和动力，可又不愿死记硬背，受不了为灌输知识点而编出来的情境。这本教材迎合了他们的需求——大量接触原文，即应用中的活语言，并在阅读和使用中巩固已学知识，接纳有文化内涵的新东西，达到文化理解、语言技巧和交际水平等相关能力的同步提升。本教材在给这个特定学生群体提供了趣味深度阅读机会的同时，也给了他们发挥主观能动性、突破学习瓶颈的平台。

教学方式建议：

本书内容足够一门课一学期使用，但任课教师可根据需要灵活安排，两个学期内学完也可。前五章文化基础知识更集中一些；后四章用所学知识交叉解读的余地则更大。本书作为教材使用的方式和进度也都可以酌情调整。比如，每章的故事可分派不同用场：一篇做精读，一篇做泛读（每章都配有一篇篇幅较短，文字也相对容易的小小说，适合用于泛读），一篇留给学生做改写、续写、重译、改编成表演剧本等活动用。

使用这本教材对预习的要求较高。幸运的是喜欢这本教材的大部分学生不缺少学习动力和自学能力。这里，我以第一章为例，把在教学中积累的预习要求和实践分享一下。

学习每一个章节之前，学生首先要阅读章首介绍主题的短文。一般来说，只要求学生读英文版就够了，只要达到对主题观念的基本理解即可。短文的中文翻译主要供教师参考。当然，喜欢挑战的学生也可进一步对照英汉版本，在探索中收获额外的学习乐趣。

第一章的学习以一篇课文为精读，一篇课文为泛读，为期一周半。在课堂学习、讨论精读课文（第一个故事）之前，应要求学生务必做预习阅读，大致搞清楚故事内容。具体就是要达到以下三点：(1) 基本解决字、词和句子层面的问题；2）对故事的人物、情节和重要细节有大概了解；3）针对有待解决的问题做好课上提问准备。从过去几年学生的反映来看，达到上述目的较为有效的学习方法是"三遍递进阅读法"。下面做一简单介绍。

第一遍，以课后生词用法表为辅助工具，只读中文。可建议学生用不同颜色的笔标出1）疑惑点，其中很多可能会是人名、地名、特殊的表达和成语、典故等；2）看着眼熟却已经忘了发音和意思的字、词和表达；3）课后生词表里给出了解释的字、词和用法；以及4）没学过而且生词表里也找不到的字、词和表达。

第二遍，汉英对照阅读。学生要争取全部解决第一遍阅读时1），2），3）中的问题，同时部分解决4）中的问题。前三个问题的解决相对简单。比如，刚看到"文化大革命"这个中文表达时，学生们会猜测这大概是个专有名词。虽然iPad或是其它学习工具能帮着他们记起"革命"的发音和意思，他们却猜不到这五个字儿如此排列在一起的意思。这个问题只需看一下英文就能解决。因为学中文的一般美国或西方其他国家的学生早已多次在英文语境中读到、听到和学过"The Great Cultural Revolution"这个说法。解决

4）中的问题，英汉对照能帮助学习词义，但学生还是需要花时间查字典来确认读音。比如"黄昏"这个词，虽然在汉英对比过程中，英文的"dusk"会给学生在上下文中理解词义的足够信息，但"昏"的读法，学生还是要主动自行解决。

第三遍，带着问题读。阅读之前，要求学生先看一下故事后面的七个思考问题。如果有时间，也可以请他们重温一下章头短文。阅读时写下仍未解决的文字问题和理解问题，做好把这些问题带到小组和全班讨论的准备。大多数学生会建立自己的有效的预习阅读机制。对于那些过于相信程序的学生，任课老师可能需要提醒他们一下分析自己、认识自己的重要性，以利于他们根据自己的水平自行找到最合适的预习程序。

即便有双语对照，生词表里也已做解释，像"小心眼儿"和"下九流"这样的组合，学生还是有可能不明白，会把它们带到课堂上来。当他们认出了"眼睛"的"眼"，却还未曾接触过"眼儿"意为"孔"、"洞"的用法，他们会纳闷"眼"为什么会跟"小"配在一起，会觉得用"眼睛"表达"narrow-minded"的意思不合适。这都是很好的问题，因为在这一阶段，比认字更重要的可能是学习字／词的起源、来源、背景、变化、多种功能、灵活性和无限可能性。在"下九流"这样的词后面有大量的历史、社会、文化信息，语言的文化承载和意义也在解决这类词语所带来的问题中得到最佳呈现。

下表所列是学习一个章节的时程安排建议，由语言入手，由文化深入，经应用检验。

[表一] 一个章节教学实施进度表

课程设置：

1. 三学分课程；学生约10人；授课和演练百分之百用中文。
2. 一学期十七周；授课时间约十五周；每周两次课，各80分钟。
3. 对应每小时授课时间，学生课前课后需用三小时自学。

章节时程安排

日期/目的	学生课前要做的功课	课上活动
第一周星期二 1) 搞懂情节和内容	阅读本章开篇主题短文，对本章主旨有所了解。 阅读S1C1*若干遍，利用英汉对照的便利，生词用法表和课后的思考问题等了解清楚故事的内容。 做好如下准备：	从生活和文化传统入手，弄懂本章主题"礼"和"仁"。 做小考一，检查预习情况。** 以班／组为单位讨论解决每个同学带来的问题。

语言文化的互动与融通——如何使用这本汉英对照教材　479

	1）基本解决字词和句子层面问题。 2）对故事整体内容有大概了解。 3）准备好上课要问的文字和理解方面的问题。	以合适方式讲故事，复述课文。 课后作业： 每人／小组从课后七个问题中选一个，负责下节课对这一问题的讨论和解答。
第一周星期四 2）领会深层文化内涵	学生思考自己所负责的讨论题和带领讨论的方法。写出简单讨论提纲和要点。 阅读作者简介，思考作者的经历与作品的关系，将思考融入对讨论题的回答。 关注和思考其它六个讨论题。	用5－10分钟重温故事、通过问答使学生准确了解特定上下文中所发生的事。 做小考二，检测对课文和主题的理解。** 从拓展对小考二问题的讨论开始，进入对七个问题的讨论。 总结讨论：给出一套相关的词汇，让学生从中选出最能表达本章主题的一两个并说明理由。***
第二周星期二 3）学用结合的总结和检查	阅读弄懂泛读课文。 第一位同学准备报告（8－10分钟）。**** 可从两个规定题目中选择一个： 1）"我的故事"：讲一个自己生活经历中的故事并说明故事与本章主题关系。 2）"我的讲评"：基于中文原文，对本篇英文译文做出批评／讲评，给出改进建议。 第一组准备一个三分钟的小表演。表演题材必须来自本课精／泛读故事。***** 写完500字左右书面作业。******	理解泛读课文互动答疑。 比较泛读与精读课文。 讨论两篇作品对本章主题的反映。 第一个学生做报告："我的故事"或"我的讲评" 第一组同学的会话小表演。 交书面作业。
第二周星期四	第二章开始；模式相同；三节课一章。	

表中星号的六处内容说明如下：

*S1C1：意为"Story 1 in Chapter 1"，书中拼音和英文索引也以同样方式标示。此处，S1C1就是第一章中《剃脑袋》这篇小小说。

**小考一和小考二：小考是一箭双雕的工具。它既能保证出勤又为学生自己的课上表现和全班的课堂讨论做准备。这个好用的督促机制所需课堂时间很有限。第一个小考检查学生否认真完成预习阅读；第二个，则是测试学生对课文的基本理解和思考。下面两个例子，一方面就小考具体内容和操作给老师们提供个参考，一方面说明在后边的"教学评估"部分里，小考何以占了相当大的比重。

S1C1小考一: 判断对错

1) (　　) 二小这孩子要上小学了。
2) (　　) 故事中的这个小孩子什么都不怕。
3) (　　) 村里人都觉得剃阴阳头很好看。
4) (　　) 故事里的大人都不尊重这个孩子。

小考一是闭卷考试。它以几个相关的判断对错的问题检查课前预习,虽简单,但可给学生足够的压力认真预习。

S1C1小考二: 请回答下面三个问题中的一个

1) 小说里为什么有关于杀猪刮毛的描写?
2) 清水大叔真的用错剃刀了吗? 你为什么这样认为?
3) 爸爸在故事里起了什么作用?

以上小考为开卷。小说本身在如上三个问题的处理上都故意制造了模糊。对任何一个问题的回答都要求学生对故事有通篇的理解和思考。同时,虽然对任何一个问题的认真思考都会对理解全文有醍醐灌顶之效用,回答问题本身并不需要太复杂的文字。学生掌握的词汇和用法足以让他们用三两句话给出一个我们能看懂的回答。这里的问题跟学生已做准备的七个讨论题中的几个很相似,所以这个小考也为下一步的讨论环节做了准备。

***总结讨论: 这是一个全班一起对精读课文进行大讨论的环节,从形式到内容都应该是对课文的一个总结。我也是从多次失败中找到了推动讨论的方法: 给学生出一套近义或是反义的相关的词汇／词组,让他们从对每个词汇／词组的理解和辨析中寻找最贴切地表达了主题的那一个／组。继续以《剃脑袋》为例,我们的总结讨论可以给学生这样一套词: "尊重"、"得体"、"宽宏"、"委婉"、"赞誉"、"隐忍"、"关照"、"和事佬"、"给面子"、"以礼相待"、"真实"与"模糊"、"求真"与"情理"等。把这套词语写在黑板上或是投到屏幕上都可。我通常的做法是把这套词有选择地做成一张学生可以填写的简单卷子。如果学生有生词,做些热身活动熟悉一下这些词语是必要的。给他们点儿时间查手机,做笔记,交头接耳交换意见或是独立思考等也都是有利于讨论的准备工作。虽然这些词汇所涵盖主题的侧面和广度有所不同,但无论学生选择哪一个都不会错。所以每一个发言者都会是对理解小说的贡献。而当学生们从语言的层面学会了这套词汇的差异,找到了含义最广的表达时,他们对主题的理解也就更加深入了。

****个人报告: 这一环节有侧重不同的两个规定题目,供学生选择。"我的故事",可以讲述亲身经历,听来的、读到的也都无妨。这是一个跨文化、通过联系自己的生活和经历体味异同、展示理解的机会,颇受喜爱。但学生们往往容易走过头,沉浸在自己的文化里,"反客为主"地忘了我们的目的是跨越和超越。为了避免学生被所熟悉的东西左右,因表面的"异"而忽略了深层的"同",我一般在评估标准里写上: "报告人必须说明所讲故事与本章主题的联系。"这样的练习,可以培养对不同文化尊重; 大概也是超越依赖记忆掌握的所谓"规范",从而达到自然得体交流的较佳路径。

如个人报告的第一个规定题目是希望学生们能把自己的文化带进来反思,在存异求同中成长,那么第二个规定题目的重点则是在语言文字上。选择"我的讲评"这个题目的同学,他们的母语一般来说得是英文,因为这个题目的基本要求是对本篇英文译文做出批评并提出改进建议。直到今天,我用这些英汉对照文本做教材的时候还有学生提出非常好的修改意见。要有理有据地说清楚英文翻译为什么不够好并不容易。没有对中文故事的文字、文化、内容和主题的深刻理解,单凭对英文的母语感受难以作出适当批评并提出有说服力的修改建议。批评和改进翻译，对中英文两种语言的要求都很高，是检验学生的语言功力、开放思维和创新能力的好机会。即使他们评的改的不完美，也应该鼓励他们的勇敢、努力和思考。我真心希望这样的报告能培养学生"青出于蓝胜于蓝"的信心。一般来说，报告的PPT有三五个讲评点就能讲十分钟了。

*****小组表演既放松和活跃课堂气氛，也锻炼学生提纲挈领，展示对小说内涵的理解。大多数小小说都有几幕场景，拎出一两个编成对话演出来并不难。学生们的创造力无限，他们可以尽情施展。此活动可以不计成绩，算是为期中和期末的大表演做热身准备。

******书面作业：我尝试过这样几种形式：1）写命题短文；2）笔头回答课后的七个问题之一；3）写一篇批评修改英译文的随笔；4）续写故事。仍以S1C1《剃脑袋》为例，它的命题短文可以是："《剃脑袋》讲了个什么道理？"，"我们应该如何以'礼'教'礼'？"，"《剃脑袋》中的'真实'"等等。我对命题短文的尝试不太成功，障碍可能是题目的不易和抽象。学生除了复述情节以外，很少能够就题目写出500字。让学生把负责讨论过的问题写成短文也很少出彩，炒冷饭可能不是很有意思。我曾要求学生用一段话续写《心事》这个故事，想像描写中国农村的恋情，效果也不太理想，不是太短、太空就是显得不着边际。

同时，批改书面作业需要花很多时间，但学生到底会对作文中被纠正过的错误给予多大关注则很难判断。近两年我发现在他们写作文的时候为他们提供帮助似乎比在他们写完了之后给他们改对他们的学习更有益。所以，我正在试着给写这项作业的同学配上一个来自中国的留学生助教。写作业时让他们商量着来，由美国同学执笔，把想要表达的内容用相对正确的中文写／打出来。学生们目前的反应是在写作过程中可以学到很多东西。

教学评估：

因为是高年级课程，使用本教材评估方式基本是开放型的。评估涵盖全方位的听说读写，侧重词汇量和成段表达。具体操作中，既要关照各项语言技能的提高，又要考虑是否给创造性留足了空间。提升学习主动性，培养敬畏的态度，增强比较的能力、批判的眼光、以及反思自省的能力等等，这些都是评估所关注的方方面面。下表列出了各项评估方式的目的和所占比重，仅供参考。

[表二] 教学评估参照表

方式	目的	百分比
小考一：检查课前预习 (5分钟)	检查是否认真预习了课文	20% (2 X 10)
小考二：检查课文理解（10分钟）	检查对课文的理解程度	20% (2 X 10)
书面作业：每章一次 (500字左右)	检查整章学习效果	20% (2 X 10)
个人报告 (8-10分钟，用中文)	检查理解表达能力	10%
期中考试 (8-10分钟)	理解、表达、应用的全方位检测	10%
期末考试: 8-10分钟	理解、表达、应用的全方位检测	10%
动态评估	鼓励进步	5%
出勤参与	保障学习	5%

还需对期中和期末考试,以及倒数第二项的动态评估做些说明。

期中期末考试都是以小组为单位做表演。内容要基于教材中的一个故事（精读、泛读或没学过的都可）。这样安排是因为,改编、排练、表演等都是全方位的语言文化能力测验,而且改编本身需要进入当代中国普通人的角色,是展示对原文的理解和发挥创意的好平台。因学校不专门为期中考试留时间,对每一项必要准备活动的安排就显得十分重要。下面所列的每一项准备工作,最好都规定一个完成日期和评分值。

期中和期末考试需要以小组为单位按时完成的各项工作:

1）选好故事：至少两人一组作出决定
2）改编剧本：小品、对话、相声等形式均可
3）编排练：达到正常说话的熟练程度
4）小组表演：给全班表演,不看稿

因为说话是表演最重要的成分,剧本一定要达到所需长度,用于排练之前应经过老师检查。期末考试与期中基本一致,只是我会要求学生将表演拍成录像放到网上,考试时大家吃爆米花看录像即可。当然,更重要的是拍录像有助于反复练习,使口语表达达到精准。我曾尝试过邀请中国留学生来观看表演,并让他们根据自己听懂的程度给每个表演打个分。这些不熟悉美国学生发音的中国观众往往会是看懂了表演却没有听懂内容。我想说的是,这门课还没找到更好地改进学生语音语调的方式。

动态评估的目的是对学生的明显进步予以及时鼓励。记录学生的表现很麻烦,也会很有意思。如果一个学生开始时一问就红脸,什么都说不出,但一个月后当你问道,"读完《心事》有什么反应？",他的一声大喊"让我大笑！"会让人欣喜无比。类似这样的进步值得鼓励。

上好这门课,前两周很重要,需多费心费神。一开学就征求学生意见——他们想用那些故事做每章的精读和泛读课文,每个人自己想选用哪一篇来做学期报告——会对整个学期产生良好影响。让学生参与故事选择不仅能增强其学习动力,也可督促他们阅读学习,大致熟悉学期内容。一旦所学课文、个人报告、小组表演和期中考试定下来,一个学期的学习进度安排表就有了,学生也清楚知道报告和小组表演的时间,可及早准备。表演质量与人员搭配关系很大,并且期中和期末考试也以小组为单位进行,因此根据学生情况帮他们合理结组也是在开学初的重要工作。

· · ·

如何为学生搭建一个课前课后主动自学的平台是本教材十分关注的问题。小小说文体提供的适合学生思考、摸索、徜徉的多种多样的时间和空间，其多元、灵活、多变与学生已经习惯、为他们设计好了每一步骤的课本不太一样。这里每一篇课文都在逼使他们思考、寻找、筛选、处置、温故、纳新。常有学生说生词是在上下文中揣摩一段话的时候学的，这样了解的词意忘不了。学生还以《剃脑袋》一文中的"挖"字的使用为例告诉我，是小小说这样的课文让她意识到了作者遣词用句的原因。虽然她早就知道"挖"的意思，小小说鲜活的语言和内容让她感悟到了语言无穷的张力。

英语和西方文化都是学习中文和中国文化的好朋友、好帮手。在我为迟子建的故事《灯祭》的英文标题纠结很久之后，Michael Smith 提出了"Father Makes the Lantern"这个建议。我连连拍案叫绝。他通过"makes"一词的多重蕴意，给出了一个理解文中孝文化和家文化既形象直接又便捷易通的途径。学生已有的西方的文化和知识框架也会提供很多绝好的教学机会。他们认真的态度可能会使他们对于剃头刀是不是真用错了打破砂锅问到底。这就提供了思考《剃脑袋》对关键情节和内容"模糊"处理原因，以及阐释礼文化中"情"与"真"关系的好机会。

以学生的母语和文化为资源的做法也与本教材注意发挥任课老师优势的理念有关。很多高年级老师生长在中国，对中国文化有着与生俱来的感知和习惯，再加上后来的跨文化教育和生活经历，让你们对两种语言和文化都有较深刻的体会和驾驭能力。这可能是学生说在美国上高年级中文课效果有时会比在中国上更好的原因之一。老师对原文的理解有着学生难以企及的角度和深度；而当学生用西方的观念解读一篇作品时，老师又能以学生的认知框架和知识储备为出发点，用他们熟悉的语言和观念阐释异同。

高年级中文课老师也常常是用英文教授与中国相关课程的主力。这本教材也因此可以一箭双雕。以爱荷华州立大学的《当代中国》课为例。当学习与中国政治有关的话题时，此书的"(统)治"一章大受欢迎；讲到中国妇女问题，很多篇章中的故事可以信手拈来。经济发展、社会习俗、家庭观念等，也都能轻松地从书中找到适合的阅读内容。最激烈的讨论、最有见地的理解常常出现在《当代中国》这样的"内容"课上。学生说这本书里的故事是让其它介绍中国的教科书"骨架"丰满起来的"血肉"不无道理。用此书做教材，对那些正在学中文、学过中文或是想学中文的学生来说都是有百利而无一害的。

总之，我们已经培养了不少能去中国短期旅游或居住的人，未来世界需要更多对中国有深层了解、能用中文工作、能促进不同文明的沟通、共建世界和平的人。为了这一目的，本书力图使学生在经历语言文化互动、互助、互益、互补的感知中,体味异中之同、同中之异,达到对不同文化的深层了解,并通过审美体验养成跨文化的视野和能力。希望本教材能为学生在未来的中文或双语环境中享受生活并事业有成尽绵薄之力。

穆爱莉 2016年秋
爱荷华州立大学
世界语言文学系

CPSIA information can be obtained
at www.ICGtesting.com
Printed in the USA
FSHW011249030521
81082FS